Contents

COMPLETE SHORT STORIES

Elizabeth Taylor

virago

VIRAGO

This collection first published in Great Britain in 2012 by Virago Press
Reprinted 2012 (three times)

A CIP catalogue record for this book
is available from the British Library.

ISBN 978-1-84408-840-9

Typeset in Goudy by M Rules
Printed and bound in Great Britain by
Clays Ltd, St Ives plc

Papers used by Virago are from well-managed forests
and other responsible sources.

MIX
Paper from
responsible sources
FSC® C104740

Virago Press
An imprint of
Little, Brown Book Group
100 Victoria Embankment
London EC4Y 0DY

An Hachette UK Company
www.hachette.co.uk

www.virago.co.uk

Introduction

Most of the stories in this book were originally published in four volumes – *Hester Lily* (1954); *The Blush* (1958); *The Dedicated Man* (1965); and *The Devastating Boys* (1972) – but this edition includes several that have previously appeared only in magazines. Much of my mother's work was printed in the *New Yorker*, and I can remember the copies, with a deep crease down the centre, regularly arriving at our house. The crease was so that the parcel would qualify for printed-paper-rate postage, and it was only when I went to America in my teens that I saw for the first time flat copies on the bookstalls – they seemed strangely unfamiliar. My brother and I enjoyed the cartoons and later the articles and short stories, including our mother's own. We also enjoyed the *New Yorker's* generous gifts of a large ham at Christmas-time, a great treat when such things were scarce here. The literary editors Catherine White and William Maxwell became my mother's good friends, and she dedicated *The Blush* to Maxwell.

Before writing this introduction I had been reading the collections, smiling at forgotten memories and wishing I could ask my mother about several of the details and incidents and what had prompted her to include them. Many of the stories have an autobiographical streak, though sometimes no more than a thread; but throughout there are phrases and characters recognisable to those of us lucky enough to have known her. Two such tales are 'Plenty Good Fiesta' and 'The Devastating Boys'. The little Spanish boy she wrote about in 'Plenty Good Fiesta' eventually returned to his family in Spain, while 'Sep' and 'Benny' of 'The Devastating Boys' were frequent visitors at my parents' house. It is nearly fifty years since they first came, but they kept in touch with my father until his death a few years ago. My mother's fears about how she would manage to look after the children she reflected on as she wrote about Laura's doubts, but in fact my mother had an intuitive understanding of children and invariably elicited their love and respect. It has always struck me how shrewdly they are portrayed in her fiction. Once, in a letter to her agent, she reported that she was having difficulty in finding new ideas for her work, but had been delighted when my small daughter had told her not to worry as it would 'soon come down from your head' – a sage coun-sel which much cheered her grandmother.

Readers frequently ask about a writer's technique – how they develop their characters, use dialogue and so on. In an article, my mother once described how she set the scenes for her stories: 'The thing that I do, I have found, is to fasten to some detail, and then let the mind wander down any corridor it fancies, opening doors or ignoring them. There was once a blind man I saw on a bus. From that, watching him, wondering about him, I built up a whole story.' This was the 'Spry Old Character'. The man she described lived in a home for the blind on the edge of our village, and each afternoon was picked up by the same bus that I caught home from prep school. While the bus waited at the terminus on the common he would chat cheerily to the driver and conductor before being delivered safely back to his usual stop. Meanwhile, I would make my way to our house and, tucking into my tea, would listen to my mother read aloud to me – usually from E. Nesbitt or Noel Streatfeild. She was a good reader, and listening to her encouraged me to follow the practice with my own children – and grandchildren.

The title 'You'll Enjoy It when You Get There' came from a much-used family expression and an assurance frequently delivered to me when, after dressing for a party or the Pony Club dance (which naturally recalls another story, 'The Rose, the Mauve and the White'), I would start to say that I couldn't face it. My parents were wrong in their assertion, as I rarely did enjoy those occasions. What inspired the story, though, was what hap-pened to my mother at a rather stiff trade function with my father. Like me, she didn't enjoy it when she got there, and then humiliated herself by making the mistake of telling one poor bored man all about the adventures of her Burmese cat ... twice. Such was her ennui that she had never noticed his face, only the glittering chain of office resplendent on his chest. This little social gaffe distressed her, but I am ashamed to say that we, unsympathetically, delighted in the story.

There was a lot of laughter and leg-pulling in the family and my parents were very funny. I will always remember our joy at my father's indignant reaction when the publishers had advised my mother to change the name of Muriel in 'Hester Lily'. 'You can tell them from me that before I met you I very nearly married a girl called Muriel,' he said, and after a pause added: 'and I'll have you know that she was a very good swimmer.'

On one occasion when we were making the beds and listening to the morning story on the radio, my mother stopped what she was doing and said, 'This is strange, I know this story.' She then realised that it was one of her own. We heard later that a man had been submitting stories from the *New Yorker* to the BBC as his work, never imagining anyone in Britain would recognise them. That was not the only unwelcome surprise my mother was to have from the morning story programme. In 1959, 'Swan-moving' was scheduled to be broadcast, and when it was over, she wrote to a friend: 'After about a minute of rather stilted reading and slurred words, he suddenly stopped and began to mutter to himself about cuts he should have made – a silence – almost endless to me – and then he asked someone if he should start again. Another pause, and then an announcer said there seemed to be some trouble with the cuts that should have been made, and then played some gramophone records instead. Perhaps the poor man was taken ill. A woman on the bus wondered if I had written something rude, and, coming upon it for the first time, he had thought it better not to read it.'

The collection *The Dedicated Man* was inscribed to the writer Robert Liddell, with whom my mother maintained a friendship that began with a long correspondence. As he lived and worked in Athens, it was some time before they actually met. We had visited Greece in the 1950s, but it was not until later when my mother was in Athens alone that she finally met him. And although she was certainly nervous, their first meeting was unlike the one between Edmund and Emily that she portrays in 'The Letter-writers'. Robert, however, makes reference to it in his book *Elizabeth and Ivy*, which is about their shared friendship with Ivy Compton Burnett. After the colonels took over the government, my mother declined to go to Greece again; instead, she and my father would visit the area on cruises, and Robert would come aboard at various ports to see them.

Some reviewers criticised my mother for writing about only those places and people she knew. It was, I think, a misplaced judgement, as several stories were set well outside of her comfort zone and she was not wedded to the familiar. Writing to her agent Patience Ross, she alluded to a current project as being 'rather horrible', adding, 'and I dare say no one will like it'. This was 'The Fly-paper', and indeed the *New Yorker* didn't like it; William Maxwell asked her to consider altering the ending. However, I wonder whether readers of the tale will agree with me that without that ending there is no story. It later became a very chilling television film.

One of the many things that I recall about my mother was her deep love for art and the great pleasure she took in visiting galleries and exhibitions. This pleasure is captured in another of her letters, written in 1965: 'I nipped up to London yesterday, and bought the most beautiful picture at the Leicester Galleries. It is by Elinor Bellingham Smith – a dead still, frozen world. I long for the exhibition to be over so that I can have it home to stare at. I was frightened at spending so much money, but didn't take a taxi afterwards. Then this morning the cheque came for

"Tall Boy", and I thought, "This is marvellous, I am turning stories into pictures."'

As I write this, I pause and look up at the painting, which now hangs on my study wall, and I think to myself, her stories *are* pictures.

Joanna Kingham
2012

Hester Lilly

Muriel's first sensation was one of derisive relief. The name – Hester Lilly – had suggested to her a goitrous, pre-Raphaelite frailty. That, allied with youth, can in its touchingness mean danger to any wife, demanding protectiveness and chivalry, those least combatable adversaries, against which admiration simply is nothing. 'For if she is to fling herself on his compassion,' she had thought, 'at that age, and orphaned, then any remonstrance from me will seem doubly callous.'

As soon as she saw the girl an injudicious confidence stilled her doubts. Her husband's letters from and to this young cousin seemed now fairly guiltless and untormenting; avuncular, but not in a threatening way.

Hester, in clothes which astonished by their improvisation – the wedding of out-grown school uniform with the adult, gloomy wardrobe of her dead mother – looked jaunty, defiant and absurd. Every garment was grown out of or not grown into.

I will take her under my wing, Muriel promised herself. The idea of an unformed personality to be moulded and high-lighted invigorated her, and the desire to tamper with – as in those fashion magazines in which ugly duckling is so disastrously changed to swan before our wistful eyes – made her impulsive and welcoming. She came quickly across the hall and laid her cheek against the girl's, murmuring affectionately. Deception enveloped them.

Robert was not deceived. He understood his wife's relief, and, understanding that, could realise the wary distress she must for some time have suffered. Now she was in command again and her misgivings were gone. He also sensed that if, at this point, she was ceasing to suspect him, perhaps his own guilt was only just beginning. He hated the transparency of Muriel's sudden relaxation and forbearance. Until now she had contested his decision to bring Hester into their home, incredulous that she could not have her own way. She had laid about him with every weapon she could find – cool scorn, sweet reasonableness, little girl tears.

'You are making a bugbear of her,' he had said.

'*You* have made *her* that, to *me*. For months, all these letters going to and fro, sometimes three a week from her. And I always excluded.'

She had tried not to watch him reading them, had poured out more coffee, re-examined her own letters. He opened Hester's last of all and as if he would rather have read them privately. Then he would fold them and slip them back inside the envelope, to protect them from her eyes. All round his plate, on the floor, were other screwed up envelopes which had contained his less secret letters. Once – to break a silence – he had lied, said, 'Hester sends love to you.' In fact, Hester had never written or spoken Muriel's name. They had not been family letters, to be passed from one to the other, not cousinly letters, with banal enquiries and remembrances. The envelopes had been stuffed with adolescent despair, cries of true lone-liness, the letters were repellent with egotism and affected bitterness, appealing with naivety. Hester had been making, in this year since her father's death, a great hollow nest in preparation for love, and Robert had watched her going round and round it, brooding over it, covering it. Now it was ready and was empty.

Unknowingly, but with so many phrases in her letters, she had acquainted him with this preparation, which must be hidden from her mother and from Muriel. She had not imagined the letters being read by anyone but Robert, and he would not betray her.

'You are old enough to be her father,' Muriel had once said; but those scornful, recriminating, wife's words never sear and wither as they are meant to. They presented him instead with his first surprised elation. After that he looked forward to the letters and was disappointed on mornings when there was none.

If there were any guilty love, he was the only guilty one. Hester pro-ceeded in innocence; wrote the letters blindly as if to herself or as in a diary and loved only men in books, or older women. She felt melancholy yearn-ings in cinemas and, at the time of leaving home, had become obsessed by a young pianist who played tea-time music in a café.

Now, at last, at the end of her journey, she felt terror, and as the first ingratiating smile faded from her face she looked sulky and wary. Following Muriel upstairs and followed by Robert carrying some of her luggage, she was overcome by the reality of the house, which she had imagined wrong. It was her first visit, and she had from Robert's letters constructed a com-pletely different setting. Stairs led up from the side of the hall instead of from the end facing the door. 'I must finish this letter and go up to bed,' Robert had sometimes written. So he had gone up *these* stairs, she thought in bewilderment as she climbed them now.

The building might not have been a school. The mullioned windows had views of shaved lawns – deserted – and cedar trees.

'I thought there would be goal-posts everywhere,' she said, stopping at a landing window.

'In summer-time?' Muriel asked in a voice of sweet amusement.

They turned into a corridor and Robert showed Hester from another window the scene she had imagined. Below a terrace, a cinder-track encircled a cricket field where boys were playing. A white-painted pavilion and sight-screens completed the setting. The drowsy afternoon quiet was broken abruptly by a bell ringing, and at once voices were raised all over the building and doors were slammed.

When Muriel had left her – with many kind reminders and assurances – Hester was glad to be still for a moment and let the school sounds become familiar. She was pleased to hear them; for it was because of the school that she had come. She was not to share Muriel's life, whatever that may be, but Robert's. The social-family existence the three of them must lead would have appalled her, if she had not known that after most meal-times, however tricky, she and Robert would leave Muriel. They would go to his study, where she would prove – *must* prove – her efficiency, had indeed knelt down for nights to pray that her shorthand would keep up with his dictation.

From the secretarial school where, aged eighteen, she had vaguely gone, she had often played truant. She had sat in the public gardens, rather than face those fifteen-year-olds with their sharp ways, their suspicion of her, that she might, from reasons of age or education, think herself their superior. Her aloofness had been humble and painful, which they were not to know.

When Robert's offer had arrived, she had regretted her time wasted. At her mother's death she was seen clearly to be the kind of girl whom relatives must help, take under their roof as governess or companion, or to do, as in Hester's case, some kind of secretarial work.

In spite of resentment, Muriel had given her a pleasant room – nicely anonymous, ready to receive the imprint of a long stay – no books, one picture and a goblet of moss-roses.

Outside, a gardener was mowing the lawn. There, at the back of the house, the lawns sloped up to the foot of a tree-covered hillside, scarred by ravines. Foliage was dense and lush, banking up so that no sky was seen. Leaves were large enough to seem sinister, and all of this landscape with its tortured-looking ash trees, its too-prolific vegetation, had a brooding, an evil aspect; might have been a Victorian engraving – the end-piece to an idyllic chapter, hitting inadvertently, because of medium, quite the wrong note.

At the foot of the hillside, with lawns up to its porch, was a little church, which Hester knew from Robert's letters to be Saxon. Since the eighteenth century it had been used as a private chapel by the successive owners of the house – the last of these now impoverished and departed. The family graves lay under the wall. Once, Robert had written that he had discovered an adder's nest there. His letters often – too often for Hester – consisted of nature notes, meticulously detailed.

Hester found this view from her window much more pre-envisaged than the rest. It had a strength and interest which her cousin's letters had managed to impart.

From the church – now used as school chapel – a wheezy, elephantine voluntary began and a procession of choir-boys, their royal-blue skirts trailing the grass or hitched up unevenly above their boots, came out of the house and paced, with a pace so slow they rocked and swayed, towards the church door. The chaplain followed, head bent, sleeves flung back on his folded arms. He was, as Hester already knew, a thorn in Robert's flesh.

In the drawing-room, Muriel was pouring out tea. Robert always stood up to drink his. It was a woman's hour, he felt, and his dropping in on it was fleeting and accidental. Hugh Baseden stood up as well – though wondering why – until Muriel said: 'Won't you sit down, Mr Baseden?'

At once, he searched for reproof in her tone, and thought that perhaps he had been imitating a piece of headmasterliness – not for him. Holding his cup unsteadily in one hand, he jerked up the knees of his trousers with the other and lowered himself on to the too-deep sofa, perched there on the edge staring at the tea in his saucer.

Muriel had little patience with gaucherie, though inspiring it. She pushed aside Hester's clean cup and clasped her hands in her lap.

'What can she be doing?' she asked.

'Perhaps afraid to come down,' Robert said.

Hugh looked with embarrassment at the half-open door where Hester hesitated, peering in, clearly wondering if this were the right room and the right people in it. To give warning to the others, he stood up quickly and slopped some more tea into his saucer. Robert and Muriel turned their heads.

'We were thinking you must be lost,' Muriel said, unsure of how much Hester might have heard.

Robert went forward and led her into the room. 'This is Hugh Baseden. My cousin, Hester Lilly, Hugh. You are newcomers together, Hester, for this is Hugh's first term with us.'

Hester sank down on the sofa, her knees an inelegant angle. When asked if she would have sugar she said 'yes' in error, and knew at once that however long her stay might be she was condemned to sweet tea throughout it, for she would never find the courage to explain.

'Mr Baseden is one of those ghoulish schoolmasters who cuts up dead

frogs and puts pieces of bad meat under glass to watch what happens,'
Muriel said. 'I am sure it teaches the boys something enormously important, although it sounds so unenticing.'

'Do girls not learn biology then?' Hugh asked, looking from one to the
other.

Muriel said 'no' and Hester said 'yes': and they spoke together.

'Then that is how much it has all changed,' Muriel added lightly. 'That
marks the great difference in our ages' – she smiled at Hester – 'as so much
else does, alas! But I am glad I was spared the experience. The smell!' She
put her hand delicately to her face and closed her eyes. Hester felt that the
lessons she had learnt had made her repulsive herself. 'Oh, do you remember, Robert,' Muriel went on, 'last Parents' Day? The rabbit? I walked into
the Science Room with Mrs Carmichael and there it was, opened out,
pinned to a board and all its inside labelled. How we scurried off. All the
mammas looking at their sons with awe and anxiety and fanning themselves with their handkerchiefs, wondering if their darlings would not pick
up some plague. We must not have that this year, Mr Baseden. You must
promise me not. A thundery day ... oh, by four o'clock! Could we have
things in jars instead, sealed up? Or skeletons? I like it best when the little
ones just collect fossils or flint arrow-heads.'

'Flint arrow-heads are not in Hugh's department,' Robert said, although
Muriel knew that as well as he, was merely going through her scatter-brain
performance – the all-feminine, inaccurate, negligent act by which she dis-
sociated herself from the school.

'They are out of chapel,' Hugh said. The noise outside was his signal to
go. 'No rabbits, then,' he promised Muriel and turning to Hester, said:
'Don't be too bewildered. I haven't had much start on you, but I begin to
feel at home.' Then, sensing some rudeness to Muriel in what he had said,
he added: 'So many boys must be a great strain to you at first. You will get
used to them in time.'

'I never have,' Muriel murmured, when he had gone. 'Such dull young
men we get here always. I am sorry, Hester, there is no brighter company
for you. Of course, there is Rex Wigmore, ex-RAF, with moustache, slang,
silk mufflers, undimmed gaiety; but I should be wary of him, if I were you.
You think I am being indiscreet, Robert; but I am sure Hester will know
without being told how important it is in a school for us to be able to speak
frankly – even scandalously – when we are en famille. It would be impossible to laugh if, outside, our lips were not sealed tight ...'

'If everything is to be said for me,' Hester thought, 'and understood for
me, how am I ever to take part in a conversation again?'

From that time, Muriel spoke on her behalf, interpreted for her, as if she
were a savage or a mute, until the moment not many days later, when

she said in an amused, but matter-of-fact voice: 'Of course, you are in love with Robert.'

Muriel saved Hester the pains of groping towards this fact. She presented it promptly, fresh, illicit and out-of-the-question; faced and decided once for all. The girl's heart swerved in horrified recognition. From her sensations of love for and dependence upon this older man, her cousin, she had separated the trembling ardour of her youth and unconsciously had directed it towards the less forbidden – the pianist in the café for instance. Now, she saw that her feelings about that young man were just the measure of her guilt about Robert.

Muriel insinuated the idea into the girl's head, thinking that such an idea would come sooner or later and came better from her, inseparable from the very beginning with shame and confusion. She struck, with that stunning remark, at the right time. For the first week or so Hester was tense with desire to please, anxiety that she might not earn her keep. Robert would often find her bowed in misery over indecipherable shorthand, or would hear her rip pages out of the typewriter and begin again. The waste-paper basket was usually crammed full of spoilt stationery. Once, he discovered her in tears and, half-way across the room to comfort her, wariness overtook him. He walked instead to the window and spoke with his back to her, which seemed to him the only alternative to embracing her.

Twice before he had taken her in his arms, on two of the three times they had been together. He had met her when she came home from Singapore where her father had died, and she had begun to cry in the station refreshment-room while they were having a cup of tea. His earlier meeting was at her christening when he had dutifully, as godfather, nursed her for a moment. The third encounter she had inveigled him into. He had met her in London secretly to discuss an important matter. They had had luncheon at his Club and the important matter turned out to be the story of her misery at living with her mother – the moods, scenes, words, tears. He could see that she found telling him more difficult than she had planned, found it in fact almost impossible. Rehearsing her speeches alone, she had reckoned without his presence, his looks of embarrassment, the sound of her own voice complaining, her fear of his impatience. She had spoken in a high, affected, hurried voice, smiling too much and at the wrong moments, with a mixture of defiance and ingratiation he found irritating, but pathetic. He had had so little solace to offer, except that he was sure the trouble would pass, that perhaps her mother suffered, too, at the crisis of middle-age. At that, Hester had been overcome by a great, glowering blush, as if he had said something unforgivable. He did not know if it were some adolescent prudery in her, or the outrage of having excuses made for her enemy-mother. (For whom excuses might have been made, for she died not long after, of cancer.)

Now, as he stood at the window listening to her tears, he knew that she was collapsed, abandoned, in readiness for his embrace of consolation, and he would not turn round, although his instinct was to go to her.

He said, absurdly: 'I hope you are happy here,' and received of course only tears in answer.

Without physical contact he could not see how to bring the scene to an end. Bored, he surveyed the garden and thought that the box-hedge needed trimming. Beyond this hedge, hanging from the branches of fruit trees were old potatoes stuck with goose-feathers. He watched them twirling gaily above the currant bushes, not frightening the birds, but exciting or bemusing them.

She realised that he would not come to her, and her weeping sank into muffled apologies, over which Robert could feel more authoritative, with something reassuring to say in return and something to do. (He fetched a decanter of sherry.) His reassurances were grave, not brusque. He put the reasons for her distress sensibly back upon legitimate causes, where perhaps they belonged – the death of her mother, shock, strain, fatigue.

He sat by his desk and put on his half-moon reading-glasses, peered over them, swung about in his swivel-chair, protecting himself by his best old-fogey act.

'Muriel and I only want to make you happy.'

Hester flinched.

'You must never let this work worry you, you know.' He almost offered to get someone else to do it for her, his sense of pity was so great.

His reading-glasses were wasted on her. She would not look at him with her swollen eyes, but pointed her hands together over her forehead, making an eave to hide her face.

'But does Muriel *want* me here?' she cried at last.

'Could you be here, if she did not?'

'But do you?'

In her desperation, she felt that she could ask any questions. The only advice he ever wanted to give young people was not to press desperation too far, uncreative as it is; *not* to admit recklessness. Muriel had once made similar mistakes. It seemed to him a great fault in women.

'I shall only mind having you here if you cry any more. Or grow any thinner.'

He glanced down at his feet. She was not really any thinner, but Muriel had begun her work on her clothes, which now fitted her and showed her small waist and long narrow back.

'You are bound to feel awkward at first with one another,' Robert said. 'It is a strange situation for you both, and Muriel is rather shy.'

Hester thought that she was uncouth and sarcastic; but not shy, not for one moment shy.

'I think she is trying so hard to be kind and sympathetic,' he continued, 'but she must make her own place in your life. She would not be so impertinent as to try to be a mother to you, as many less sensitive women might. There is no precedent to help her – having no children herself, being much older. She has her own friends, her own life, and she would like to make a place for you, too. I think she would have loved to have had a daughter ... I can imagine that from the interest she takes in your clothes, for instance.' This was true, had puzzled Hester and now was made to shame her.

Muriel opened the door suddenly upon this scene of tears and sherry. Hester, to hide her face, turned aside and put up her hand to smooth her hair.

'Miss Graveney's address,' Muriel said. She stood stiffly in front of Robert's desk while he searched through a file. She did not glance at Hester and held her hand out to take the address from Robert before he could bring it from the drawer.

'Thank you, dear!' She spoke in her delicately amused voice, nodded slightly and left the room.

Outside, she began to tremble violently. Misery split her in two – one Muriel going upstairs in fear and anger, and another Muriel going beside her, whispering: 'Quiet! Be calm. Think later.'

Hester, with her new trimness, was less touching. She lost part of the appeal of youth – the advantage Muriel could not challenge – and won instead an uncertain sophistication – an unstable elegance, which only underlined how much cleverer Muriel was at the same game.

Muriel's cleverness, however, could not overcome the pain she felt. She held the reins, but could barely keep her hands from trembling. Her patience was formidable. Robert had always remarked upon it since the day he had watched her at work upon her own wedding cake. There were many things in her life which no one could do as well as she, and her wedding cake was one of them. She had spent hours at the icing – at hair-fine lattice-work, at roses and rosettes, swags and garlands, conch-shells and cornucopias. She had made of it a great work of art, and with a similar industry, which Robert only half-discerned and Hester did not discern at all, she now worked at what seemed to her the battle for her marriage.

Conceived at the moment of meeting Hester, the strategy was based on implanting in the girl her own – Muriel's – standards, so that every success that Hester had would seem one in the image of the older woman, and every action bring Muriel herself to mind. Patience, tolerance, coolness, amusement were parts of the plan, and when she had suddenly said: 'Of course you are in love with Robert,' she had waited to say it for days. It was no abrupt cry of exasperation, but a piece of the design she had worked out.

Before Hester could reply, Muriel stressed the triviality of such a love by going on at once to other things. 'If I were a young girl again I should have a dark dress made, like a Bluecoat Boy's – a high neck and buttoned front, leather belt, huge, boyish pockets hidden somewhere in the skirt. How nice if one could wear yellow stockings too!'

She rested her hand on her tapestry-frame and forced herself to meet Hester's eyes, her own eyes veiled and narrowed, as if she were considering how the girl would look in such a dress.

Hester's glance, as so often in the innocent party, wavered first. She had no occupation to help her and stared down at her clasped hands.

Muriel began once more to pass the needle through the canvas. Diligently, week by week, the tapestry roses blossomed in grey and white and blood-colour.

'Don't you think?' she asked.

She swung the frame round and examined the back of the canvas. It was perfectly neat. She sat sideways in her chair, with the frame-stand drawn up at one angle. Her full skirt touched the carpet – pink on crimson.

'Why do you say that?' Hester asked. 'What makes you say it?' She sounded as if she might faint.

'Say what?'

'About Robert.' Her lips moved clumsily over the name as if they were stung by it, and swollen.

'Robert? Oh, yes! Don't fuss, dear girl. At your age one has to be in love with someone, and Robert does very well for the time being. Perhaps at *every* age one has to be in love with someone, but when one is young it is difficult to decide whom. Later one becomes more stable. I fell in love with all sorts of unsuitable people – very worrying for one's mother. But by the time I met Robert I was old enough to be sure that *that* would last. As it has,' she added quietly; and she chose a strand of white silk and began to work on the high-lights of a rose petal.

'I once fell in love with a young man who drank like a fish,' she continued, for Hester seemed stunned into silence. 'He was really an evil influence. Very flashy. You remember how I warned you about Rex Wigmore your first day here?' She began to shake with mirth. 'Trying to be my own anxious mamma all over again. And all the time it was Robert! How lucky! For Robert is so gentle, so kind. He would never harm you. Nothing but good could come of a girl loving *him*. Yes, I can see Robert doing very well indeed, until the real one comes along. How furious he would be to hear us discussing him like this – men take themselves so seriously.'

'I am not discussing him,' Hester said, an ugly stubbornness in her manner. She snatched a handkerchief from her pocket and began to fidget with it, crushing it and smoothing it and staring at it in a bewildered defiance.

Muriel's white hand smoothed a woollen rose. 'I always leave the background till last.' She sighed. 'So dull, going on and on with the same colour.'

'It isn't true. He's my cousin, much older ... your husband ... I ... does he know?'

'Well, I haven't asked him. Men are too vain. I dare say he knows all right, though. It's very good for them, at his age ... makes them feel young.'

So Hester saw herself thrust into the service of nature, a coarse instrument, as good as anonymous. Muriel, spared such humiliation, could well smile, and congratulate herself. 'Don't fuss,' she said again in her most laughing voice. 'If I had known you *would*, I wouldn't have said it.'

'I wish I could go away.' Hester wrung her hands and looked towards the windows as if she might escape through them. 'You hate me being here. And now ...'

'Now?'

'Now you believe this about me, how can you bear me to be here? No wife could.'

At this, a stern, fastidious look came upon Muriel's face. She was silent for a moment, then said in a quiet and serious voice: 'I ... as a wife; Robert ... as a husband; our private life together I must leave out of this. It is between us only, and I never discuss my marriage.'

'There is no need to be rude to me,' Hester shouted, so great her frustration, so helplessly she felt herself up against Muriel's smooth contempt. She was forced into childishness.

At her outburst – for all of today was working for Muriel, she thought – the door opened.

'But surely there is nothing sinister in that?' Beatrice Carpenter asked. She was Muriel's closest friend and they were walking in the park before dinner. 'Young girls often cry. You rather surprise me, Muriel. You sound hysterical yourself.'

'It was the atmosphere of the room. It trembled with apprehension, and when I opened the door Robert looked at me with a dumbfounded expression, his eyes opened wide over those awful half-moon glasses he *will* wear, they – his eyes – looked so *blue* – a little boy's look, little boy in mischief.

"Don't spank me, Nanny." I hated him for a moment. Oh, I felt murderous. No, but I truly itched to hurt him physically, by some violent and abusive act, to hit him across the mouth, to ... ' She broke off in astonishment and looked about her, as if fearful of being overheard.

'You *are* in a bad way,' Beatrice said. 'The girl will have to go.'

'I know. But how? I have to be clever, not insistent. I can't be put into the position of getting my own way, for it would never be forgotten. It would last all our lives, such a capitulation, you know.'

Other married women *always* know; so Beatrice only murmured cosily.

Muriel said: 'The self-consciousness is so deadly. When I go back, he will look at me to see how I am likely to behave. Every time I go into a room, he glances at my face, so that I can no longer meet his eyes.'

'I never think embarrassment is a trivial emotion,' Beatrice said.

'It has altered everything, having her here; for we were just at an age of being able, perhaps, to relax, to take one another for granted, to let ourselves slip a little. It is a compensation for growing old, and one must find a compensation for that, if one can.'

'I cannot,' Beatrice said.

'For a day or two I tried to compete, but I will not be forced into the sort of competition I am bound to lose.' Muriel frowned and with a weary gesture unclipped her gold ear-rings as if she suddenly found their weight intolerable. She walked on with them clutched, warm and heavy, in her hand. Beatrice could not bear the sight of her fiery ear-lobes. She was upset, as when people who always wear glasses take them off for polishing and expose their wounded-looking and naked eyes. Muriel was never without ear-rings and might have caused only slightly less concern by suddenly unpinning her hair.

Beatrice said: 'An experienced woman is always held to be a match for a young girl, but I shouldn't like to have to try it. Not that I *am* very experienced.'

They sat down on a seat under a rhododendron bush, for now they were in the avenue leading to the house and their conversation had not neared its end, as their walk had.

By 'experience' both meant love affairs. Beatrice thought of the engagement she had broken in girlhood, and Muriel thought of Hugh Baseden's predecessor and his admiration for her, which she had rather too easily kept within bounds. It was, as Beatrice had said, very little experience and had served no useful purpose and taught them nothing.

'And then,' Muriel said, 'there is the question of the marriage-bed.' She was dropping the ear-rings from one hand to the other in her agitation. Far from never discussing her marriage, as she had assured Hester, she was not averse to going over it in every detail, and Beatrice was already initiated into its secrets to an extent which would have dismayed Robert had he known. 'There were always so many wonderful excuses, or if none came to mind one could fall inextricably into a deep sleep. He has really been fairly mild and undemanding.'

'Unlike Bertie,' Beatrice said, and her sigh was genuinely regretful.

'Now I am afraid to make excuses or fall asleep. I scent danger, and give in. That may seem obvious, too. It is very humiliating. And certainly a bore.'

'I sometimes pretend it is someone else,' Beatrice said. 'That makes it more amusing.' She covered her face with her hands, bowed down, rocking with laughter at some incongruous recollection. 'The most improbable men ... if they could know!'

'But you might laugh at the time,' Muriel said, in an interested voice.

'I do ... oh, I do.'

'Robert would be angry.'

'Perhaps husbands sometimes do the same.'

Muriel clipped her ear-rings back on. She was herself again. 'Oh, no!' she said briskly. 'It would be outrageous.'

'Marriage-bed' was only one of her many formal phrases. She also thought and talked of 'bestowing favours' and 'renewed ardours'. 'To no one else,' she told herself firmly. 'To no one else.' They walked on up the avenue in silence, Beatrice still trembling, dishevelled with laughter. 'To no one else?' Muriel thought, in another of those waves of nausea she had felt of late.

As they went upstairs before dinner, she felt an appalling heaviness. She clung to the banisters and Beatrice's voice came to her from afar. Clouded, remote and very cold, she sat down at her dressing-table. Beatrice took up the glass paper-weight, as she always did, and said, as she always said: 'These forever fascinate me.' She tipped it upside-down and snow began to drift, then whirl, about the little central figure. Muriel watched, the comb too heavy to lift. She watched the figure – a skating lady with raised muff and Regency bonnet – solitary, like herself, blurred, frozen, imprisoned.

'Will she be at dinner?' Beatrice was asking. She flopped down on the marriage-bed itself, still playing with the paper-weight.

Hester, at dinner, did not appear to Beatrice to be a worthy adversary to a woman of Muriel's elegance. She said nothing, except when coaxed by Muriel herself into brief replies; for Muriel had acquired courage and was fluent and vivacious, making such a social occasion of the conversation that they seemed to be characters in a play. 'This is how experienced people behave,' she seemed to imply. 'We never embarrass by breaking down. In society, we are impervious.'

Robert patronised their conversation in the way of husbands towards wives' women-friends – a rather elaborate but absent-minded show of courtesy. When Hester spilt some wine, he dipped his napkin into the water-jug and sponged the table-cloth without allowing an interruption of what he was saying. He covered her confusion by a rather long speech, and, at its end, Hugh Baseden was ready to take over with an even longer speech of his own. This protectiveness on their part only exposed Hester the more, for Beatrice took the opportunity of not having to listen to observe the girl more closely. She also observed that clumsiness can have a kind of appeal she had never suspected.

She observed technically at first – the fair thick hair which needed drastic shaping: it was bunched up with combs which looked more entangled than controlling. The face was set in an expression which was sulky yet capable of breaking into swift alarm – even terror – as when her hand had knocked against the wine-glass. The hands themselves were huge and helpless, rough, reddened, the nails cropped down. A piece of dirty sticking-plaster covered one knuckle. A thin silver bracelet hung over each wrist.

Then Beatrice next observed that Hugh Baseden's protectiveness was ignored, but that Robert's brought forth a flush and tremor. While he was sponging the table-cloth, the girl watched his hand intently, as if it had a miraculous or terrifying power of its own. Not once did she look at his face.

Beatrice thought that an ominous chivalry hung in the air, and she could see that every victory Muriel had, contributed subtly to her defeat. 'She should try less,' she decided. She was the only one who enjoyed her dinner.

The boys were all in from the fields and gardens before Robert and Muriel dined, but throughout the meal those in the dining-room were conscious of the school-life continuing behind the baize-covered doors. The sounds of footsteps in the tiled passages and voices calling went on for a long time, and while coffee was being served the first few bars of 'Marche Militaire' could be heard again and again – the same brisk beginning, and always the same tripping into chaos. Start afresh. Robert beat time with his foot. Muriel sighed. Soon she accompanied Beatrice out to her car, and at once Hester, rather than stay in the room with Robert (for Hugh Baseden had gone off to some duty), went up to her room.

Now, a curious stillness had fallen over the school, a silence drawn down almost by force. The 'Marche Militaire' was given up and other sounds could be heard – Muriel saying good-bye to Beatrice out on the drive, and an owl crying; for the light was going.

Hester knelt by her window with her elbows on the sill. Evening after evening she thought thunder threatened, and because it did not come she had begun to wonder if the strange atmosphere was a permanent feature of this landscape, and intensified by her own sense of foreboding. The black hillside trees, the grape-coloured light over the church and the bilious green lawns were the after-dinner scene, and she longed for darkness to cover it.

Beatrice's car went down the long drive. A door banged. So Muriel had come in, had returned to the drawing-room to be surprised at Hester's absence. That averted look, which she assumed when she entered rooms where Robert and Hester were alone, would have been wasted.

Hester leant far out of the window. Only the poplars made any sound – a deep sigh and then a shivering and clattering of their leaves. The other trees held out their branches mutely, and she imagined them crowded with sleeping birds, and bright-eyed creatures around their holes, arching their backs, baring their teeth, and swaying their noses to and fro for the first scents of the night's hunting. Her suburban background with its tennis-courts, laburnum trees, golden privet had not taught her how to be brave about the country; she saw only its vice and frightfulness, and remembered the adders in the churchyard and the lizards and grass-snakes which the boys collected. Fear met her at every turn – in her dealings with people, her terror of Muriel, her shrinking from nature, her anxiety about her future – ('You are scrupulously untidy,' Robert had said. Only a relative would employ her, and she had none but him.)

She made spasmodic efforts to come to terms with these fears; but in trying to face Muriel she fell, she knew, into sullenness. Nature she had not yet braved, had not penetrated the dense woods or the lush meadows by the lake where the frogs were. This evening – as a beginning and because nature was the least of her new terrors, and from loneliness, panic, despair – she moved away from the window, stumbling on her cramped legs, and then went as quietly as she could downstairs and out of doors.

In the garden, at each rustle in the undergrowth, her ankles weakened, but she walked on, treading carefully on the dew-soaked grass. A hedgehog zig-zagged swiftly across her path and checked her. She persisted, hoping thus to restore a little of her self-respect. She was conscious that each pace was taking her from her safe room, where nothing made her recoil but that phrase of Muriel's that she carried everywhere – 'Of course you are in love with Robert.' 'It was better when we wrote the letters,' she thought. 'I was happy then. I believe.'

As the severest test, she set herself the task of walking through the churchyard where a mist hung over gravestones and nettles. The sound of metal striking flint checked her, and more normal fears than fears of nature came to her almost as a relief; as even burglars might be welcomed in an

excessively haunted house. The dusk made it difficult for her to discern
what kind of figure it was kneeling beside a headstone under the church
walls; but as she stepped softly forwards across the turf she could see it was
an old lady, in black flowing clothes and a straw garden-hat swathed with
black ribbon. She wore gardening gloves and was planting out salvias and
marguerites.

Hester tripped and grazed her arm against some granite. At her cry of
pain, the old lady looked up.

'Oh, mercy!' she exclaimed, holding the trowel to her heart. 'For pity's
sake, girl, what are you doing?'

Her white face was violin-shaped, narrowing under her cheek-bones and
then widening again, but less, on the level of her wide, thin, lavender-
coloured lips. The sagging cords of her throat were drawn in by a black
velvet ribbon.

'I was only going for a walk,' said Hester.

'I should call it prowling about. Have you an assignation here? With one
of those schoolmasters from the house?'

'No.'

The old lady drove the trowel into the earth, threw out stones, then,
shaking another plant from a pot, wedged it into the hole. The grave
resembled a bed in a Public Garden, with a neat pattern of annuals. The
salvias bled hideously over a border of lobelias and alyssum. Their red was
especially menacing in the dusky light.

'I think a grave should have *formality*,' the old lady said, as if she knew
Hester's thoughts and was correcting them. '"Keep it neat, and leave it at
that," I warned myself when my father died. I longed to express myself in
rather unusual ways; my imagination ran riot with azaleas. A grave is no
place for self-expression, though; no place for the indulgence of one's own
likings. These flowers are not to my taste at all; they are in *no* taste.'

'Is this your father's grave, then?' Hester asked.

'Yes.' The old lady pointed with her trowel. 'The one you are lolling
against is Grandfather's. Mother chained off over there with my sister,
Linda. She did not want to go in with Father. I can never remember them
sharing a bed, even.'

Hester, removing her elbow from the headstone, peered at the name.
'Then you lived in the house?' she asked. 'This name is carved over the
stables.'

'Our home since the Dark Ages. Three houses, at least, on this site and
brasses in the church going back to the Crusades. Now there are only the
graves left. The name going too. For there were only Linda and I. Families
decline more suddenly than they can rise. Extraordinarily interesting. The
collapse of a family is most dramatic ... I saw it all happen ... the money

goes, no sons are born – just daughters and sometimes they are not quite the thing . . . my sister Linda was weak in the head. We did have to pinch and scrape, and aunts fastened to us, like barnacles on a wreck. Some of them drank and the servants followed their example. Then trades-people become insolent, although the *nouveaux riches* still fawn.' She turned up a green penny with her trowel, rubbed dirt from it and put it in her pocket. 'Our disintegration was fairly rapid,' she said. 'I *can* remember a time before it all overtook us – the scandals and gossip, threadbare carpets, dented silver, *sold* silver, darned linen. Oh, it usually goes the same way for everyone, once it begins. And very fascinating it can be. Dry rot, wood-worm, the walls subsiding. Cracks in plaster and in character. Even the stone-work in the house has some sort of insect in it.' She nodded proudly at the school. 'Unless they have done something about it.'

'Do you come here often?'

'Yes. Yes, I do. I tend the graves. It makes an outing. I once went to the school to have tea with Mrs Thingummy. A nice little woman.' This, Hester supposed, was Muriel. 'Interesting to see what they made of it. I liked the school part very much. I went all over, opened every door. I thought the chance might not come again. Into the servants' wing where I had never been before – very nice dormitories and bathrooms. The bathrooms were splendid . . . little pink, naked boys splashing under showers . . . a very gay and charming sight . . . I could hardly drag myself away. They scuttled off as shy as crabs. I expect the look of me startled them. What I did *not* admire was the way she had managed the private part of the house where we had tea . . . loose-covers, which I abhor . . . I thought it all showed a cool disregard for the painted ceiling. Never mind, I satisfied my curiosity and no need to be bothered with her again.'

Hester, though feeling that Muriel might in fairness be allowed to furnish her drawing-room as she pleased, was none the less delighted to hear this censure, especially over matters of taste. She longed to talk more of Muriel, for she had no other confidante, and this old lady, though strange, was vigorous in her scorn and might, if she were encouraged, say very much more.

'I live there now,' she began.

In the darkness, which she had hardly noticed, the old lady had begun to stack up her empty flower-pots.

'Then you will be able to do me a small favour,' she said. 'In connection with the graves. If it fails to rain tonight I should be obliged if you would water these plants for me in the morning. A good sousing. Before the sun gets strong.'

She pulled herself to a standing position with one hand on the gravestone. Her joints snapped with a frail and brittle sound as she moved.

Hester faced her across the grave and faced, too, the winey, camphorous smell of her breath and her clothes.

'Only Father's grave. I shall plant Mother's and Linda's tomorrow evening.'

She swayed, steadying herself against the stone, and then, with a swinging movement, as if on deck in wild weather, made off through the churchyard, lurching from one gravestone to another, her hands out to balance her, her basket hanging from her arm. She was soon lost to Hester's sight, but the sound of her unsteady progress, as she brushed through branches of yew and scuffled the gravel, continued longer. When she could hear no more, the girl walked back to the house. She had forgotten the snakes and the bats and all the terrors of nature; and she found that for a little while she had forgotten Robert, and Muriel, too; and the sorrows and shame of love.

As she crossed the lawn, Hugh Baseden and Rex Wigmore came round the house from the garages. Stepping out of the darkness into the light shed from upstairs windows, she looked pale-skinned and mysterious, and both men were arrested by a change in her. The breeze blew strands of hair forwards across her face and she turned her head impatiently, so that the hair was whipped back again, lifting up from her ears, around which it hung so untidily by day.

'I thought you were a ghost coming from the churchyard,' Hugh said. 'Weren't you nervous out there by yourself?'

'No.'

But her teeth began to chatter and she drew her elbows tight to her waist to stop herself shivering.

'What *have* you been up to?' Rex asked.

'I went for a walk.'

'Alone? How absurd! How wasteful! How unsafe! You never know what might happen to you. If you want to go for a walk, you could always ask me. I like being out with young girls in the dark. I make it even unsafer. And, at least, you could be quite sure what would happen to you then.'

'You are cold,' Hugh said. He opened the door and, as she stepped past him into the hall, brushed his hand down her bare arm. 'You *are* cold.'

Rex's remarks, which he deplored, had excited him. He imagined himself – not Rex – walking in the dark with her. He had had so few encounters with women, so few confidings, explorings, and longed to take on some hazards and excitements.

Rex, whose life was full enough of all those things, was bored and wandered off. He found her less attractive – hardly attractive at all – indoors and in the bright light of the hall.

*

Hester rarely spoke at meal-times, but next morning at breakfast she mentioned the old lady.

'Miss Despenser.' Muriel put her hand to her face as she had when speaking of the dead rabbit in the laboratory. She breathed as if she felt faint. 'She came to tea once. Once only. I wondered if I should pour whisky in her tea. She is the village drunk. I believe her sister was the village idiot. But now dead.'

'You shouldn't go out late at night on your own,' Robert said. 'You might catch cold,' he added, for he could really think of no reason why she should not go – only the vague unease we feel when people venture out late, alone – a guilty sense of having driven them out, or of having proved inadequate to keep them, or still their restlessness, or win their confidence.

'It is a wonder she could spare time from the Hand and Flowers,' Muriel said. 'I am surprised to hear of her tidying the graves in licensed hours.'

'And shall you water the plants?' Robert asked in amusement.

'I have done. She said, before the sun got too strong.'

'What impertinence!' Muriel said, and every lash at Miss Despenser was really one at Hester. She felt even more agitated and confused this morning, for Rex's words with their innuendo and suggestion had been spoken beneath her bedroom window the previous night and she, lying in bed, half-reading, had heard him.

Until that moment, she had seen the threat in Hester's youth, defencelessness and pathos; but she had not thought of her as being desirable in any more obvious way. Rex's words – automatic as they were, almost meaningless as they must be from him – proved that the girl might also be desirable in the most obvious way of all. Muriel's distaste and hostility were strengthened by what she had overheard. Still more, a confusion in herself, which she was honest enough to ponder, disquieted her. To be jealous of Hester where Robert was concerned was legitimate and fitting, she thought; but to be jealous of the girl's least success with other men revealed a harshness from which she turned sickly away. There was nothing now which she could allow Hester, no generosity or praise: grudged words of courtesy which convention forced her to speak seemed to wither on her lips with the enormity of their untruthfulness.

Her jealousy had grown from a fitful nagging to a chronic indisposition, an unreasonableness beyond her control.

She went, after breakfast, to her bedroom without waiting to see Hester follow Robert to his study. The days had often seemed too long for her and now pain had its own way of spinning them out. To go to her kitchen and begin some healing job like baking bread would have appeared to her cook as a derangement and a nuisance. She was childless, kitchenless; without remedy or relief.

Robert, she thought, had not so much become a stranger as revealed himself as the stranger he had for a long time been. The manifestation of this both alarmed her and stirred her conscience. Impossible longings, which had sometimes unsettled her – especially in the half-seasons and at that hour when the light beginning to fade invests garden or darkening room with a romantic languor – had seemed a part of her femininity. The idea that men – or men like Robert – should be beset by the same dangerous sensations would have astonished her by its vulgarity. Their marriage had continued its discreet way. Now, she could see how it had changed its course from those first years, with their anniversaries, secrets, discussions; his hidden disappointment over her abortive pregnancies; the consolation and the bitter tears – all embarrassing now in her memory, but shouldering their way up through layers of discretion to wound and worry her. She had allowed herself to change; but she could tolerate no change in Robert, except for the decline in his ardour, which she had felt herself reasonable in expecting.

In rather the same spirit as Hester's when she had faced the terrors of the churchyard the night before, Muriel now went into Robert's dressing-room and shut the door. She knelt down before a chest, and, pulling out the bottom drawer, found, where she knew she would find them, among his old school photographs, the bundle of letters she had written to him when they were betrothed.

She felt nausea, but a morbid impatience, as if she were about to read letters from his mistress. The first of the pile began: 'Dear Mr Evans . . .' It was a cool, but artful, invitation. She remembered writing it after their first meeting, thinking he had gone for ever and wanting to draw him back to her. 'I am writing for my mother, as she is busy.' Not only had he been drawn back, but he had kept the letter. Perhaps he had had his own plans for their meeting again. She might well have let things be and sat at home and waited – so difficult a thing for a young girl to do.

That first letter was the only time he was 'Mr Evans'. After that, he progressed from 'Dear Robert', through 'My Dear Robert', 'Dearest Robert', 'Robert Dearest', to 'Darling'. In the middle period of the letters – for he had preserved them chronologically – the style was comradely, witty, undemanding. ('Intolerably affected,' Muriel now thought, her neck reddening with indignation. 'Arch! Oh, yes!' Did Hester write so to him and could he, at his age, feel no distaste?) The letters, patently snobbish, shallow, worked up, had taken hours to write, she remembered. Everything that happened during the day was embroidered for Robert at night – the books she read were only used as a bridge between their two minds. The style was parenthetic, for she could not take leave even of a sentence. So many brackets scattered about gave the look of her eyelashes having been shed upon the pages. When she had written 'Yours, Muriel' or, later, 'Your Muriel', there was always more to come, many postscripts to stave off saying good-night. Loneliness, longing broke through again and again despite the overlying insincerity. She had – writing in her room at night – so wanted Robert. Like a miracle, or as a result of intense concentration, she had got what she wanted. Kneeling before the drawer, with the letters in her hand, she was caught up once more in amazement at this fact. 'I got what I wanted,' she thought over and over again.

His letters to her had often disappointed, especially in the later phase when possessiveness and passion coloured her own. Writing so late at night, she had sometimes given relief to her loneliness. Those were momentary sensations, but his mistake had lain in taking them as such; in writing, in his reply, of quite other things. 'But did you get my letter?' Muriel now read – the beginning of a long complaint, which she was never to finish reading; for the door opened and Robert was staring at her with an expression of aloof non-comprehension, as if he had suddenly been forced to close his mind at this intimation of her character.

Muriel said shakily: 'I came across our old letters to one another – or rather mine to you ... I could not resist them.'

He still stared, but she would not look at him. Then he blinked, seemed to cast away some unpleasant thoughts, and said coldly, holding up a letter which she still would not glance at: 'Lady Bewick is running this dance after the garden party. I came up to ask how many tickets we shall want.'

'I thought you were taking Latin,' Muriel said naively.

'They are having Break now.' And, indeed, if she had had ears to hear it, she would have known by the shouting outside.

'I should let her know today,' Robert said. 'Whom shall we take?'

Muriel was very still. Warily, she envisaged the prospects – Hester going along, too. Hester's brown, smooth shoulders dramatised by her chalk-white frock. Robert's glance at them. Muriel's pale veined arms incompletely hidden by her lace stole. Perhaps Hester was a good dancer. Muriel herself was too stiff and rather inclined, from panic, to lead her partner.

'Why could we not go alone?' she asked.

'We could; but I thought we should be expected to take a party.'

'Whom do you think?'

'I had no thoughts. I came to ask you.'

'I see.' 'He wants it every way,' she thought. 'For her to go, and for me to suggest it.' She tied up the letters and put them away.

'You should take Hester,' she said suddenly. She began to tremble with anger and unhappiness. 'I can stay at home.'

'I had no intention of taking Hester.'

'I suppose you are angry with me for reading those letters. I know it was wrong of me to open your drawer. I have never done such a thing in my life before.' She still sat on the floor and seemed exhausted, keeping her head bent as she spoke.

'I can believe that. Why did you now?' he asked.

For a moment, gentleness, the possibility of understanding, enveloped them; but she let it go, could think only of her suspicions, her wounded pride.

The tears almost fell, but she breathed steadily and they receded. 'I was bored. Not easy not to be. I remembered something ... I was talking to Beatrice about it yesterday ... I knew I should have written it somewhere in my letters to you. I was sure you wouldn't mind my looking.' Her excuses broke off and at last she dared to look at him. She smiled defiantly. 'I wrote them, you know. You seem as cross as if they were written by another woman.'

'They were,' he said.

She was stunned. She slammed the drawer shut and stood up. She thought: 'Those are the worst words he ever spoke to me.'

'I shall have to go,' he said. 'I suppose I can leave this till this afternoon.' He held up the letter in his hand. 'I didn't want to discuss it at lunch, that was all. The point is that Lady Bewick hoped we could take a partner for her niece who is staying there – she thought we could ask one of the staff. I wonder if Hugh ... '

'But he's so boring.'

'We need not stay together.'

'Take Rex.'

'Rex?'

'Why not? He dances well.'

'But he's so impossible. You have never disguised your scorn for him.'

'He would be better than Hugh – not so achingly tedious.' Irritability, the wish to sting, underlined her words. 'You are achingly tedious, too,' she seemed to imply. Her voice was higher pitched than usual, her cheeks flushed. He looked at her in concern, then said: 'All right. Three tickets, then.' He put the letter in his pocket and turned away.

As soon as he had gone, but too late, she broke into weeping.

They dined at home before the dance. Muriel was intimidating, but uncertain, in too many diamonds. When she brought out her mother's jewels, Robert always felt put in his place, though never before had they all come out at once. Her careless entrance into the drawing-room had astonished him. She was shrugged up in a pink woollen shawl, through which came a frosty glitter. Rex's look of startled admiration confirmed her fear that she was overdressed. 'She has never erred in that way before,' Robert thought: but she had shown several new faults of late; flaws had appeared which once he could not have suspected. There was, too, something slyly affected about the cosy shawl and the stir and flash of diamonds beneath it.

'It is only a countrified sort of dance,' Robert told Rex. His words were chiefly for Muriel, who should have known. 'Nothing very exciting. Good of you to turn out.'

He hoped that Hester would now feel that she would miss nothing by staying at home, that he could not have gone himself, except as a duty; or asked anyone else to go, except as a favour. His stone, which should have killed two birds, missed both.

Hester, wearing a day-frock and trying to look unconcerned, managed only a stubborn sullenness – a Cinderella performance Muriel thought wrongly, underlined by Rex's greeting to her – 'But you are coming with us, surely?' – when her clothes made it quite obvious that she was not.

Robert's shame, Muriel's guilt, Hester's embarrassment, seemed not to reach Rex, although for the other three the air shivered, the wine-glasses trembled, at his tactlessness.

'Too bad,' he said easily. 'Well, there is no doubt that you are coming.' He turned to Muriel, his eyes resting once more upon all her shimmering glitter. ('Ice', he called it, and – later, to Hugh Baseden – 'rocks the size of conkers. Crown jewels. The family coffers scraped to the bottom.')

The glances, which he had meant to appear gallant and flattering, looked so predatory that Muriel put her hand to her necklace in a gesture of protection, and a bracelet fell into the soup. She laughed as Rex leant forward and fished it out with a spoon and fork and dropped it into the napkin she held out. Her laughter was that simulated kind which is difficult to end naturally and her eyes added to all the tremulous glint and shimmer of her. Hester, coldly regarding her, thought that she would cry. A Muriel in tears was a novel, horrifying idea.

The bracelet lay on the stained napkin. 'The catch must be loose. I shan't wear it,' Muriel said, and pushed it aside.

'That will be one less,' Robert thought.

After dinner he had a moment alone with Hester.

'All rather awkward about this dance. I hope you don't mind, my dear. Don't like leaving you – like Cinderella.'

Hester could see Muriel, re-powdered, cocooned in tulle, coming downstairs and laughed at this illusion, remembering who did go to the ball in the fairy-tale. 'We must go to a real dance another time,' Robert said. 'Not a country hop, but a proper dance, with buckets of champagne.' But Muriel, rustling across the hall, finished this vision for them. 'I should sit with Matron,' he added.

'Oh, it is quite all right,' Hester said, with a brightness covering her extreme woundedness. 'I could not have gone with you tonight, or sit with Matron either; because I have another engagement, and now I must hurry.' With a glance at their halted expressions she ran upstairs, leaving behind an uneasiness and raised eyebrows.

The cistern in the downstairs cloakroom made a clanking sound and there was a dreadful rush of water. This always embarrassed Muriel, and she turned aside as Rex appeared.

Hester, at the bend of the stairs, called out in a ringing, careless voice: 'Oh, do have a lovely time.'

In this exhortation she managed to speak to them both in different ways – a difficult thing to do. Muriel felt herself condescended to and dismissed, unenvied, like a child going to a treat. But Robert's guilt was not one scrap appeased, and Hester did not mean it to be. He perceived both her pathos and her gallantry, as she desired. Her apparent lack of interest in their outing and her sudden look of excitement worried him. Even Rex was puzzled by her performance. 'Now what's she up to?' he wondered, as they went out to the car.

Yet, when she was in her own room Hester could not imagine where she might go. Recklessness would have led her almost anywhere, but in the end she could only think of the churchyard. As Miss Despenser had said, 'to water the graves makes an outing', and perhaps she could borrow a grave – Miss Linda's, for instance – and cherish it in such dull times as these.

When she arrived in the churchyard, she found that Miss Despenser had finished planting and was vigorously scrubbing the headstones. Dirty water ran down over an inscription. 'That's better,' were her first words to Hester as she came near.

'I watered the plants.'

'Yes, I noticed that.'

'Can I help you?'

Miss Despenser threw the filthy water out in a great arc over some other graves – not her own family ones, Hester was sure – and handed her the bucket. 'Clean water from the tap by the wall.'

'Is that where the adders were?'

'Adders?'

'There were some once. I thought they might have come again.'

'This is a fine thing – a stranger telling me about my own churchyard. I know nothing of adders. Are you a naturalist?'

'Oh, no! I am really rather afraid of nature.'

Miss Despenser threw out her arms and laughed theatrically. 'You're a damn witty girl, I know that. When I first met you I thought you were a bit of a nincompoop. You improve on acquaintance.' She turned to examine the lettering on the grave, and Hester went to fetch the water.

'Afraid of nature!' Miss Despenser said, when she returned. 'I appreciate that.'

The water, swinging in the pail, had slopped over into Hester's sandals and her feet moved greasily in them.

'So you're afraid of nature!' Miss Despenser said, and she grasped the bucket and threw the water over the headstones. Some went over her and more into Hester's sandals. 'She is drunk,' Hester thought, remembering Muriel's words and feeling annoyance that there should be any truth in them.

'The bucket goes back into the shed and the scrubbing-brush into the basket.' Miss Despenser shook drops of water off her skirt. 'And we will go down to call on Mrs Brimmer.'

'Mrs Brimmer?'

'A friend of mine. You are quite welcome. I will look in at the house first and leave the scrubbing-brush. Mrs Brimmer would think me rather eccentric if I went to see her with a scrubbing-brush in my basket.'

'Any adders?' she asked, when Hester came back from the tool-shed. The piquancy of her own humour delighted her and she returned to the allusion again and again, puzzling Hester – who expected drunkenness to affect the limbs, but not the wits, and was exasperated as the young so often are at failing to read an extra meaning into the remarks of their elders.

Through a kissing-gate they came into a wood of fir trees. Miss Despenser slid and scuffled down the sloping track which was slippery with pine-needles. Jagged white flints had surfaced the path like the fins of sharks, so that Miss Despenser tripped and stumbled until Hester took her arm. She thought that they must look a strange pair and – such was the creaking darkness and mysterious resinous smell of the wood – half-feared that as the path curved they might see themselves coming towards them through the trees, like a picture of Rossetti's she remembered called *How They Met Themselves*. 'I shouldn't care to meet myself,' she said aloud, 'in this dark place.'

'You wouldn't recognise yourself. You are much too young. When at long last you really learn what to look for, you will be too old to be alarmed.'

'I didn't mean that I should, or could; just that I'd hate it.'

'I meet myself every so often. "You hideous old baggage," I say, and I nod. For years I thought it was someone else.'

'This wood goes on and on,' Hester said nervously.

'Ah, you are frightened of adders.' When she had finished laughing, Miss Despenser said: 'When I go into the town to get the cat's meat, the chances are that as I go round by the boot shop I see myself walking towards me – in a long panel of mirror at the side of the shop. "Horrid old character," I used to think. "I must change my shopping morning." So I changed to Fridays, but there she was on Fridays just the same. "I can't seem to avoid her," I told myself. And no one can. Go on your holidays. You take yourself along too. Go to the ends of the earth. No escape. And one gets so bored, bored. I've had nearly seventy years of it now. And I wonder if I'd been beautiful or clever I might have been less irritated. Perhaps I am difficult to please. My mother didn't care for *herself*, either. When she died, the Vicar said: "It is only another life she has gone to, an *everlasting* life." An extraordinarily trite little man. He hadn't got much up here.' She tapped her forehead and stumbled badly. 'I said to him: "Oh dear, oh dear, for pity's sake, hasn't she had enough of herself?" I asked. He couldn't answer that one. He just stared at the glass of sherry I was drinking, as if he were taking comfort in the idea of my being drunk. "I believe in personality," I said. "You believe in souls." That's the difference between us. Souls are flattened out and one might very well spend an eternity with one's own – though goodness knows what it would be like – as interesting as a great bowl of nourishing soup. I always think of souls as saucers, full of some tepid, transparent liquid. Couldn't haunt anyone. Personalities do the haunting – Papa's for instance. Tiresome, dreadful things. Can't shake them off. Unless under the influence, of course.'

'Of drink, I suppose,' Hester thought.

'Of drink,' the old lady added.

'It *is* a gruesome place. I like trees which shed their leaves.'

The bark of the trees was blood-red in the dying light and there were no sounds of birds or of anything but branches creaking and tapping together. Then the pink light thinned, the trees opened out and blueness broke through, and in this new light was a view of a tilted hillside with houses, and a train buffeting along between cornfields.

'And there is my home,' Miss Despenser said. She scrambled down the bank into a lane and, as she brushed dust and twigs from her skirt, she crossed the lane and opened a gate.

Laurels almost barred the way to the little house, which was of such dark grey and patchy stucco that it looked sopping wet. The untidy curtains seemed to have rooms of blank darkness behind them. Shepherd's-purse grew round the mossy doorstep where a milk-bottle dribbling curdled milk had been knocked over.

'Welcome!' said Miss Despenser, throwing open the door upon such a smell of dampness and decay, such a chaotic litter, that Hester stepped aside to take a last full breath before going in.

*

'You were right. He *is* behaving abominably,' Muriel said to Robert as they danced.

Rex had reconnoitred, got his bearings, soon left Lady Bewick's niece and now was slipping out through the flap of the marquee with a girl in a green frock. Muriel saw his hand pass down the back of his gleaming hair in an anticipatory gesture as he went.

'He's lost no time in finding the most common-looking little minx in the room,' she told Robert. She was unsteady and almost breathless with frustration, not getting her own way. So far she had danced once with the doctor and the rest of the time with Robert.

'It's his duty, if nothing else,' she thought. But Rex and his duty made a casual relationship. 'Am I so faded, that he would rather be rude?' But Rex was firstly doing what he wanted to do. If rudeness was involved, it was only as a side-issue. 'It is because he knows I am inaccessible,' she told herself.

They continued to catch brief glimpses of Rex during the evening; at the bar, at the buffet. Someone else took Lady Bewick's niece to supper. As it grew later, the sky deepened its blue behind the black shapes of the garden trees – the monkey-puzzles darkly barbed; the cedars; and the yews clipped into pagodas and peacocks. Voices floated across the lawns; long skirts brushed the grass.

In twos, the dancers strolled in the enclosed warmth of the walled garden, sat on the terrace among the chipped statues, or gazed down at the silvered lily-leaves in the pool.

'A good thing we *didn't* bring Hester,' Muriel said. 'Rex would have left her stranded.'

'Sorry!' said Robert, as they fell out of step. They had never danced well together, yet they went on dancing. There was nothing to walk in the garden *for*, among all that pulsating romance. At their age.

In the end, Muriel's dance with Rex was accidental, during a Paul Jones. Hearing the first romping bars of this, she was all for going to the bar, but Lady Bewick hustled her into the dance – 'Now, *everyone*! You must' – and took her by the hand and led her to the circle. They revolved, with absurd smiles, feeling looked-over by the encircling men. Robert's expression was one of sudden gaiety, as if he were let off the leash for a moment. 'How many years has he had that suit?' Muriel wondered. 'Since he was at school, I should think. The sleeves are too short. He looks buttoned-up, spry, like a cock-sparrow. What can a young girl see in him, unless a father?' Yet could not that be a danger, especially if Robert were at the same time look- ing for a daughter? Rex bowed mockingly as he passed her; but his eyes were instantly elsewhere.

'An absurd game, like a child's,' Muriel thought, feeling outraged and also secretly dismayed at the thought of the music stopping as she faced blankness; then to trail disconsolately to a chair, watched by Robert, and by Rex. She had not learnt how to mind less than as a little girl at parties – the panic of not being chosen, the first seeds of self-mistrust.

But when the music stopped she was at once in the doctor's arms again. He came straight forward with his hands outstretched; easy to dance with, he waltzed away with her, bouncy, soft-treading, his rounded paunch doing the guiding. By fate or by manoeuvre, Rex had the green girl. Muriel could not see Robert and was inattentive to the dance as she tried to search him out. Then she saw him at the edge of the room. He had been left without a partner and now was going forward to claim a very plain woman in a pink frock and tortoiseshell-rimmed glasses. Muriel was at peace, until the next round. It was then that she found herself between Rex and another man when the music stopped. Both hesitated; then Rex seemed to master his unwillingness, smiled and stepped forward. Authoritatively he took her over; automatically pressed her to him. She made some remark, and, while his eyes still roved round the room, he smiled again and laid his cheek to her hair. 'What did you say?'

'I am his headmaster's wife!' Muriel thought indignantly; but her heart had cantered away.

'She *will* be angry,' Robert thought, as he caught sight of her. But it was she who had suggested bringing him. Robert – blame-evading – had known that Rex would behave like a bounder. Then, to his amazement, he saw that Muriel was smiling. She looked up at Rex, who shook his head teasingly, and then sank deftly back to his nestling embrace.

His eyes stopped following the girl in the green dress, for there was fun closer at hand.

'We shouldn't keep Mrs Brimmer waiting too long,' Miss Despenser said. She put the scrubbing-brush down on the hall-table. 'I must give the cat his supper before we go. Wander about. Make yourself at home.'

A great, gooseberry-eyed, striped cat walked stiffly out of the darkness, stretched, hooped up its back. 'Naughty cat, doesn't deserve supper. What is this? Another mess on the Soumak rug?' She took some newspaper from the clutter on the table and bent down to wipe at the clotted fringe. The cat leant against her legs as she did so, staring up at Hester, callously detached.

'Well, that's that!'

But it wasn't and, to escape the smell, Hester followed her to the kitchen, thinking: 'Only the graves can she keep clean.'

In the kitchen, the richness of litter was as if a great cornucopia of dirty dishes and decaying food had been unloaded over tables, chairs, shelves and stove. Flies had stopped their circling and eating and excreting for the day and now slept on the walls and ceiling. Miss Despenser tipped a cod's head out of a saucepan on to a dish on the floor, and Hester half-faintly wished she had stayed in the hall. The cat sniffed at the boiled, clouded eyes and walked away.

'Have you no help?' Hester asked.

'Not now. Gone are the days, alas! when there was a maid to do my hair. But if a woman of my age cannot dress her own hair she should be quite ashamed.'

'But not your hair. I meant all the dishes.'

'I have all day.'

She picked up a sticky-looking wine-glass and drank something from it. 'That was careless of me,' she said. 'I hate waste. And now for Mrs Brimmer!'

'How sweet the outside air,' Hester thought. As they walked down the lane to the village, warmth flowed between the hedges and she felt a great lassitude and unhappiness.

Miss Despenser struck along beside her, seemed conscious of her mood, and kept glancing up. 'Like some nauseating little dog asking for attention,' Hester thought, and looked at the hedgerow, ignoring her.

'If they're not good to you at that school, I am not surprised,' Miss Despenser said at last. 'I didn't like the wife. And he's as poor a nincompoop as ever there was, I think. Nimminy pimminy; but *she's* a thundering dunderhead, as my father used to call the Vicar. There was a beautiful panel in the drawing-room, and she has moved it away and put shelves up for her collection of mediocre china. It was a clever painting with a great deal of work in it. Detail. Rich in detail. Neptune, d'you know, simply smothered in barnacles and sea-weed; sea-serpents; tritons; dolphins. A great painstaking monsterpiece. I suppose she thought it indecent. The boys would've liked it, I am sure. If ever things get too much for you, you know, you must come and tuck in with me – at any time of the day or night. I have a spare room . . . Linda's room.'

Hester tried not to imagine poor Miss Linda's room (herself tucking into it), where she had lived, 'not quite all there' – and probably died.

'They are good to me,' she said.

'I thought you seemed rather on the mopy side.'

'No.'

'Perhaps in love?'

'Not in love. No.'

'Linda and I once were. With the same man fortunately. That was nice. We could discuss him at night. We always shared everything. Oh, we used to laugh, comparing notes, d'you know. If we met him . . . he used to ride a grey mare called Mirabella – you see, I remember the name even – he always raised his hat. Once I was hurrying to the post with a letter in my hand and he stopped and offered to take it for me.' She paused, reflecting on this long-ago kindness, then said: 'Well, you *ought* to be in love, I should say. Now is the time for it. Ah, there is Mrs Brimmer on the look-out for me.'

In the lighted bar-window of the pub a huge, cardiganed woman appeared. She raised her arms and laid a cloth over a bird-cage, then receded. She did not seem to see Miss Despenser.

Over the pub doorway, Hester saw the notice – 'Melanie Brimmer, licensed to sell Beer, Wines and Spirits.'

'Here I am at last, Mrs Brimmer,' Miss Despenser said, stepping into the flagged passage-way.

Mrs Brimmer, behind the bar, nodded vaguely at them. She then opened a bottle of Guinness, which seemed to flop into the glass in an exhausted way, and beside this she placed a glass of Madeira.

'Will you have the same?' Miss Despenser asked Hester.

'The same as which?'

'I like to sip at both.'

Miss Despenser began to pull at her skirts and pat herself and at last brought out a purse.

'Oh, I should like ... if I could have a sherry ...' ('Oh, God! I didn't know it would be a pub!' she thought. 'I have no money – nothing.') Again, she felt like running.

The sherry was handed to her by the silent Mrs Brimmer.

'And you, yourself, Mrs Brimmer?'

At last Mrs Brimmer spoke: 'No, I won't touch anything tonight if it's the same to you. I had one of my turns after tea.' She began to tap her fingers rhythmically between her lower ribs. 'Heart-burn. Stew keeps repeating.' She belched softly and gravely.

Hester sipped, then moved her eyes slowly round the room. Two old men played dominoes at a trestle-table. By the empty fireplace, Hugh Baseden had risen from his chair and stood waiting awkwardly to be recognised.

After the next absurd circling in the dance, Muriel faced a blank – the chain of men had thinned, broken, just in front of her as the music stopped. Robert, not far away, knowing how she hated to feel conspicuous or unclaimed even in the smallest ways, made a little gesture of frustration to her, as if to say he would have helped her if he could. She smiled and put on an exaggeratedly woebegone expression and moved aside.

'Time to knock-off for the old noggin,' Rex said, putting his arm through hers. He had been a fighter-pilot in the war and in certain situations tended

to resuscitate the curious *mélange* of archaisms and slang which once had
been his everyday language.

'So you were left, too?'

'I didn't go in. I was stooging round the perim as it were, on the look-
out.'

'Oh, I see.'

'I hope you have no objection, ma'am.'

'None.'

After two whiskies, they went into the garden. The music came to an
end with a jarring clash of cymbals, then clapping; but Rex and Muriel
walked on down the terrace.

'The landed gentry don't do themselves half badly,' Rex said, slapping
a statue across the buttocks as they passed it. 'Hardly a hot-bed of
Bolshevism.'

Inside the marquee a man's voice rose above the confusion of sound
which then gradually sank. 'Forty-nine!' was shouted and repeated. After
a moment, clapping broke out again.

'Oh, that is the raffle,' Muriel said.

Couples made their way back across the lawns towards the marquee, but
she and Rex walked on.

'Do you want to go and see if you have won a bottle of rich old ruby port
or something?' he asked. 'Let's sit down here, or will it spoil your dress?'

She did not even glance at the stone seat, but sat down at once.

'Are you warm enough?' He rearranged her lace stole round her shoulders. Her diamonds shone in the moonlight, and he put his warm hand to
her throat and touched them.

'Heavenly!' he said. 'You have some lovely jewels, ma'am.'

'Perhaps he is going to steal them,' she thought, in a flash of panic and
candour with herself. 'I must have been deluded to think he just wanted
to be with me.' But his hand turned over and lay palm down against her
beating throat. 'Or he will strangle me first,' she thought, putting nothing
past him.

'Why did you ask me to come tonight?' he asked. 'You don't like me, do
you?'

She closed her eyes.

'Do you?' he persisted. 'So often seen your face go smooth and expressionless at things I've said.'

'I don't understand men like you.'

'What sort of man am I then?'

She had an impulse to flatter him, though it was strange for her to flatter
any man. 'Although I'm older than you, you make me feel inexperienced
and immature.'

'It wasn't that,' he said. 'You were just plainly looking down your nose at me, ma'am.'

'Don't call me "ma'am",' she whispered.

'What then?'

For a moment she didn't answer and then murmured, 'I don't know.'

'Mustn't call you "Muriel". Not respectful in one so young, so junior. Mrs Evans, then?'

He slid his hand down her throat and under her armpit. She began to tremble, and at this he leant forward and kissed her.

'I might call you "darling",' he suggested. 'I wonder how that would sound.'

'This is absurd,' she said shakily. 'We must go back.'

'Back to the marquee, or back to where we were before tonight?'

'Both.'

'Just as you say, my dear.' He moved away from her, but she did not move. He let the humiliation of this sink into her for a moment, then took her hands. Her fingers twisted restlessly in his, but fastening and not freeing themselves. 'Nothing so avid as a married woman,' he thought complacently and began to kiss her and embrace her in ways of the most extravagant vulgarity such as she had not encountered outside literature.

In the Hand and Flowers, political discussion, though not really raging, was of enough strength to redden cheeks.

There were two periods of acrimony during the evening, Mrs Brimmer knew. The first was soon after opening-time, when the regulars came in fresh from the six o'clock news and such disasters as it had announced. Later, some of the contentious went home to their supper: others stayed and played darts. By eight o'clock, a different clientele, more genial, out for the evening, had begun to arrive. Politics, at this stage, were tabu. Towards closing-time, however, geniality might wear thin and argument erupt in one place after another. Mrs Brimmer, leaning on the bar, or going ponderously down into the cellar to bring up the half-slopped pots of beer, was always brief or silent unless describing her indigestion, but towards ten o'clock she would sometimes say abruptly: 'I'm Labour anyway,' as in a few minutes she would say 'Time now, gentlemen.' Mrs Brimmer held one or two unexpected opinions which were all the same ground inextricably into her personality. Another of her beliefs which she often made clear was that women should not go into public houses. She served them silently and grudgingly and would have horse-whipped every one, she often said. She really did not approve of drinking at all, apart from the gin-and-pep she sometimes took to shift her wind. However, having lived in the pub as a wife, she duly carried on as a widow.

'What they want is to have us all equal,' Miss Despenser said, 'and the only way to do that is to level everyone *down*. Not to raise everyone *up*. No, it's down, down, down all the time. When we're finally in the gutter, then we shall have true democracy.'

'But surely . . . ' said Hugh Baseden.

'When I was young everyone was better off and do you know why?'

'Well . . . '

'Because we all knew our proper places. No one was ashamed to serve. Why, my mother's maid was like a sister to her. Two sisters. Peas in a pod.'

'That's right.' Mrs Brimmer nodded.

'But when she had helped your mother to dress, she didn't go to the dance with her. She stayed and tidied the bedroom,' Hester said. She glanced at Hugh, who looked gravely back in agreement. Some of his gravity, however, was his anxiety at Hester's having drunk too much.

'She didn't want to go. That is what I am saying. She didn't want to go. That is why she was so happy.'

'My mother was in service,' one of the dominoes players said. 'Happiest days of her life, she reckoned. No worries. All found.'

'There you are, you see,' Miss Despenser said.

'It's wrong to be happy like that . . . not to have your own life,' Hester said. At the back of her mind, she felt a great sense of injustice somewhere, of sacrifices which ought not to be asked or made. 'Kow-towing,' she murmured and, looking flushed and furious, sipped her sherry.

'Kow-towing fiddlededee,' Miss Despenser said. 'You talk as if the educated classes exist for nothing.'

Mrs Brimmer drew her blouse away from her creased chest, glanced down mysteriously, blowing gently between her breasts, then fanned herself. 'I hear Charlie's gone,' she said.

'He's gone, has he?' asked the gaitered gamekeeper. His setters stretched by the fire, blinking their bloody eyes, nosing their private parts.

'So Les Salter said when he came with his club money.'

'I said to the missus I reckon old Charlie's going at last. I said that only last night when I saw the lamp upstairs.'

'That's right.'

'When was that?'

'This morning. They sent along for Mrs Brown about eight o'clock. He'd just gone then.'

'Would you like a drink?' Hugh asked Miss Despenser.

'Most kind.'

'What may I get you?'

'Mrs Brimmer knows.'

He stood awkwardly before Hester. 'The same?' 'If I take her back drunk,

I take the blame, too, I suppose,' he thought. To his relief she shook her head.

'How are you getting home?' he asked quietly.

'I shall look after her,' Miss Despenser said, and she laid her hand on Hester's arm. Hester looked down at it with loathing. Under the shiny, loose skin the high veins seemed to writhe and knot themselves as if separately alive. Nothing was said. He turned to the bar and watched Mrs Brimmer reluctantly pouring out the drinks.

'He is rather familiar,' Miss Despenser said. 'After all, he is not quite in the same position as you. You could spend the night with me if you are nervous.'

To be saved for one night from her dreams would be so very wonderful, she thought. She and Hester could sit up until morning and talk. Her dreams were usually distressing. There was one in which her father kept entering the library, always from the same door, crossing the room, disappearing, only to come in again in the same way, with the dread inevitability of dreams. Then there was the one in which her mother told her to pull down her clothes, but her skirts shrank and shrank. Because of her nightmares, she had tried to sleep in the daytime, for bad dreams come in the dark; but to be awake in the quiet house – especially as it seemed to be only *just* quiet – was frightening, too.

'I will pop a hot-bottle in your bed,' she promised. 'You are not to think it will be a trouble.'

'I must go home. There is no reason why I should not.'

Miss Despenser bent her head. 'I dare say you think me very frumpish,' she said. 'Can't be helped. We all come to it. Most kind,' she said again to Hugh, but gave Mrs Brimmer a sharp glance as a Guinness only was placed before her. Mrs Brimmer was once more glancing nonchalantly inside her blouse.

'Is she cooking something down there?' Hugh muttered, as he sat down beside Hester, and then in an even lower voice asked: 'May I walk home with you?'

'But how can I get rid of her?' Hester asked, and felt soiled by her disloyalty.

'Time, gentlemen, if you please.' Mrs Brimmer went to the door and opened it, letting in cool air and moths.

'I will see you home,' Miss Despenser told Hester. 'But let *him* get on his way first.' She slowly drained her Guinness, keeping her eyes shut. When she opened them, Hugh Baseden was still there. 'Good-night!' she bade him. Froth was drying on her moustached upper lip, and Hugh looked away from her as he spoke.

'I am taking Hester back to the school. May we see you home first?'

'Good-*night!*' said Mrs Brimmer, not caring who went with whom, as long as all went without delay.

They set off together, and Miss Despenser was sullen and her course vague and veering. Once she stumbled against the high bank and, hoping to steady herself, put her hand down into a patch of nettles. She righted herself and wandered on, rubbing her inflamed wrist, drawing herself obstinately away from Hugh when he tried to support her. But when they reached her house she allowed him to take her key and open the door. He switched on the light, and she sat down abruptly on a chair in the hall. When Hester said good-night, she just nodded without lifting her head to see her go and stared at the cat who seemed to have waited for her to come home before he squatted in a corner and began to wet the carpet. She did not rebuke him but sat still for a long time, and at last tears began to slant out of her eyes and down the sides of her face. 'Not since Linda died!' she thought. For Hester, that stranger to her, had come up out of a mist or a dream to confront her with loneliness. Unsteadily, she stood up and crossed the hall. The looking-glass was filmed with damp and dust, but she could see herself dimly in it. Clutching the back of a chair she rocked to and fro, staring. 'It is what I am,' she told herself. 'It is what I live with.' Her vision seemed to slide and slip like colours in a kaleidoscope. 'Pussy,' she called. 'Naughty pussy! Now where are you?' He came swaying out of the kitchen, paw before paw, coat rippling, pupils only a dark slit, tail curved. 'I am master here,' he seemed to say.

'Who was that tipsy, titupping little person?' Hugh Baseden asked.

'I met her once when I was wandering around. She is mad, I think.'

'The stench in that house! Is she a witch?'

'I expect so.'

'I didn't know what to think when you walked in with her.'

'I have to go somewhere.'

'Do ... *they* ... know?'

'Neither know nor care.'

They climbed the bank and began to cross the field towards the wood. 'You must be very lonely,' he said. 'I have often thought that. I suppose they're very nice, though so terribly set in their complacent ways. And when they do do something enjoyable ... this dance, I mean ... they leave you at home.'

'I didn't want to go – like Miss Despenser's mother's maid.'

'And Robert's a kind chap, but such a very dry old stick. Very fussy to work for.'

'Very fussy,' Hester panted, breathless from the steep field-path.

'Of course, he's your uncle. I shouldn't have said that ... '

'My cousin ... my cousin.'

'He has some rather old-maidish ways, you know ... peering over his glasses, taking pills ...'

'And the barometer!' Hester was astonished to hear herself saying. 'Tapping it at least three times a day. Why not just take the weather as it comes?'

They entered the warm wood and this time she was not afraid.

'*She* is the dominant one, of course,' Hugh said.

Hester thought: 'Perhaps I was only scared not to be in love with someone; anybody.' She was confused by her sudden sensations of irritability towards Robert. 'My head!' she said, and stumbled along over the tree roots, pressing both hands to her temples.

'I will find you some of Rex's famous hangover pills when we get back. It was funny about Rex going tonight.'

'Funny?'

'I thought Madam's view of him was very dark indeed.' He took Hester's elbow and guided her out of the way of some low branches. 'Nearly there,' he said.

The air was thinner and cooler outside the wood. They came to the churchyard and the neat Despenser graves.

Muriel had creamed her face and was weeping. Robert was silent with frightening displeasure.

'I don't want to see him again,' she cried.

He took the cuff-links out of his shirt and put them back into their velvet-padded box. He said: 'That is what you cannot help doing. It is a little awkwardness you have created for us all.'

'He might resign.'

'But he won't, and there is no reason why he should. You will find he is quite unperturbed. It will have meant nothing to him,' Robert added cruelly. 'When he remembers, and if it amuses him, he may take advantage of the situation to discomfit us. It is dreadfully late to be crying so,' he said fretfully. 'I am very tired, and he will see your red eyes in the morning and purr more than ever.'

'Robert, you are rather working this up. By the way you are speaking I might have committed adultery.'

'I think you might, if you hadn't suddenly heard "God Save the Queen". Your patriotism made you stand up – even if it *was* in one another's arms.'

'Oh, the brittle wit! How dare you? We had suddenly realised that the dance was over.'

'Time had stood still.'

She began angrily to splash cold water on her eyes. When she was in bed, she said shakily: 'After all, *you* don't make love to me.'

He got neatly into bed and lay down as far from her as he could, his back turned.

'Do you?' she wept.

'You know I do not, and you know why I do not.'

'If I didn't like it, perhaps that was your fault. Did you ever think of that?'

'Very often. I surveyed every explanation in turn. Then I became rather bored and thought "so be it".'

'I know I was wrong tonight . . . though really sillier than wrong.'

'You made us both look absurd and started a ridiculous scandal by your behaviour. Everyone missed you. I suppose it was an arranged thing between you . . . I remember your insistence on having him there. How long, if you wouldn't mind telling me, has this romance been flourishing?' He spoke stiffly, lying with his back to her. He was anxious to be reassured, to shake off the insecurity which results from a serious deviation in one we have trusted.

'You shall not say such a thing,' she cried.

He had gone too far in his suspicions, and her amazed rejection of them was so genuine that he now went too far in his relief; although he only gravely said: 'I apologise.' 'This dreadful conversation!' he thought. 'The cold phrases of hatred – "I apologise." "How dare you!" "You *know* why."'

'If it was just a sudden ill-judged thing,' he said, 'I can understand better. Anything else – plotting, lying – would not have been like you.'

She lay on her back and stared up through the darkness; said 'Thank you' in a far-away voice.

'Oh, don't cry again.' He turned over and touched her hair.

'We were so happy,' she cried.

'I don't think we were very happy.'

'I was.'

He meant his silence to punish her. To explain – she thought – everything; to simplify everything and press the punishment back upon him, she said: 'If Hester had never come here! If we could be as we were!'

'She had no part in this. She was utterly innocent.'

'Her innocence has been like a poison to us. It has corrupted us both.' In her mind she seemed to step back from the thought of their married life, as if she recoiled physically from an unexpected horror. She said: 'It is like the time when I found the adders lying under the ferns.'

'What is like that?' he asked. His head lay on his crooked arm, and he stared into the darkness where there was less to see than behind his closed lids.

'To realise my ignorance about you; to discover our estrangement – this tangle of secrets; and to know that I can behave as I did tonight . . . '

'Don't cry, Muriel.'

'Why do you call me "Muriel"? You have never done so until now, until lately.' 'Until Hester came,' both thought.

'She . . . Hester, I mean . . . has made no difference to us. I'm not in love with her, if that is any comfort . . . if you want to hear such embarrassing things really said aloud.' He spoke coldly and angrily and with a sense of treachery to himself, as if she had forced from him some alien oath. 'She has changed nothing . . . only shown us what existed, exists.'

'We should be very grateful for that.'

Her burst of anger was a relief from tears.

'If I can never love her again,' he thought, 'why is it Hester's fault? It is she, Muriel, who destroyed it, let it slip from her and then, in trying to have it back again, broke it for ever.' Lying so close to her, he let this monstrous treason against her form in the darkness. Then he felt her lift herself up on one elbow. She was wiping her eyes. Crying was over, then? But, more dread to him even than her weeping, she put out her hand and touched his arm and he wondered if she had sensed the fissure widening, separating her from him, in his heart – the hard knowledge of non-love. She began to throw words into this abyss as if to close it before too late. 'Robert, forgive me! I will try. I will do everything. I am sorry. I cannot bear it.'

The words worked no magic, and continued into unseemliness, he thought. This reserve had changed to cold-heartedness, and he wondered how he could ever change it back again. He turned over and put his arms round her.

'Let us try again!' she begged, and she pressed her burning eyes against his shoulder. He moved his head back a little, for her hair had fallen against his mouth.

'We will both try!' he whispered. 'I will try very hard.' 'But will it be any use?' he wondered.

Robert, in the days that followed, wondered if it were the mildness of his nature which enabled him to find the suppression of love more easy than the suppression of non-love. No concentration could cure him of his lack of feeling towards Muriel, and, to ward off his indifference to her, he began, without knowing it, to catalogue her virtues. In this way, he always had a ready antidote for the irritations she caused him, and quickly smothered thoughts of her coldness with remembrances of her kindness to animals and that servants loved her. Against her sarcasm he recalled her loyalty, and tried to acknowledge her steadfastness when beset by her lack of humour.

At first, as if a true understanding were between them, Muriel went through her days in chastened peace of mind, submissive and forgiving. Emotion had tired her and she seemed weakly convalescent, her mind on such little things, as if she only waited for the time to pass. At night, the resentment she fought during the day poisoned her dreams, so that, lying beside Robert with her heart full of love for him, she dreaded to fall asleep and so out of love again – would wake trembling or tearful at his dream-betrayals, carrying imaginary wrongs beyond the dawn, to discolour all the morning.

Bravely, she set out to enchant him all over again, as she had done so many years ago, but disheartened now, frightened, and lacking the equipment of romanticism, energy, curiosity. 'For I did not have him once for all,' she thought sadly, arranging her pink dress against the red carpet and her white hands on the tapestry; glancing timidly at him, who did not look in her direction. Her voice lost its edge when she spoke to him, but only Hester noticed the new warmth, and was embarrassed.

'It will soon be Speech Day,' Muriel said. 'Will last year's hat do, Robert? Or would that look as if the school were going downhill?'

'I should buy a new one – for your sake, not the school's. I can't imagine parents remembering a hat from one year to the next.'

'Hester and I can't agree with that.'

Hester did not raise her eyes.

For the first time, Muriel was self-conscious at Speech Day, watched the great marquee going up, arranged flowers, and finally pinned on her new cartwheel hat, feeling unusual sensations of flurried dread. 'Exquisite!' Rex whispered, passing her as she crossed the hall. Until that moment, the evening of the dance, for him, might never have been. He was as heedless as a bird snatching at berries along a hedgerow.

Muriel stood beside Robert and shook hands with the parents and felt that beneath their admiration these people did not like her; fathers were over-awed and mothers were doubtful – unsure as to whether she really loved their sons as they deserved. Hester watched her; Rex watched her; Robert looked away from her; tiredness overtook her.

In the evening, she telephoned Beatrice – her only friend, she now felt; though more than a friend: perhaps an extension of her own personality and her own experiences (sometimes sullying) greedily grafted on to the weaker parts of Beatrice's nature. 'Oh God, let her not be out!' she prayed, imagining the telephone ringing and ringing in the empty house. But Beatrice, breathless from hurrying, soon answered and lost her mystery in doing so, became accessible, too easily summoned.

'I was in the garden. How did it go, darling? I thought of you. Was the hat right? Did Robert love it?'

'He didn't say he didn't.'

'And tea and everything? And Robert's speech?'

'Yes. Beatrice, if I call in, will you come for a drive before dinner? My head aches. The last ones have only just gone away.'

'Oh, parents!' she said later. They drove along the lanes, down the hill past the Hand and Flowers, where Mrs Brimmer stood at the doorway in the sun. 'Perhaps I just hate them because they have children,' Muriel said.

The car was open and the soft air flowed over them, lifting their hair, but none of the peace of the evening reached Muriel, who drove fast, noticed nothing, frowned at the road ahead. 'You've had children, Beatrice, and you cannot *know* ...'

'Darling, you are overtired ...'

'No. For years it has been so improbable that I should ever have a child that I stopped thinking about it ... I might have been shocked, perhaps, to find myself pregnant ... but now, just lately, knowing for sure that I never could be, that in *this* lifetime, and for *this* woman, it couldn't ever happen, I feel panicky, want to go back, be different, have another chance. I can't explain.' She changed gear badly, was driving carelessly.

'Do slow down,' Beatrice said.

'I'm sorry.'

'I never think about having children now,' Beatrice said. 'All the business bores me enormously, like some hobby one has discarded. When I hear of younger women having them, I even feel slightly surprised, for it all seems so finished with and *démodé*. They think they are being so clever and can't know how I lack interest. I just think, "Goodness me, are people still doing *that?*"'

'But you'll have grandchildren and then you'll be caught up in it again.'

'I suppose so.' She looked smug.

'Where are we going?' Muriel asked. 'I *ought* to be going home.'

She drove on, brushing the cow-parsley in the ditch, swerving as a bird flew up suddenly from some horse-droppings on the road.

'Very sorry! Then the holidays will soon come,' she said, as if continuing the same plaint, 'the three of us left alone together.'

'Has nothing been done about her going?'

'There is nowhere for her to go.'

'You should go away yourself. I would come with you, if you liked. You need a holiday.'

'And leave them together?'

'Oh, no, of course.'

They laughed shakily. Muriel said: 'It is as well one still has a sense of humour.'

*

'Thank you, Hester, for all your help,' Robert said. He handed her a drink and, taking up his own, asked if she had seen Muriel.

'No.' She had watched her driving away, but thought that Muriel could explain her own comings and goings.

'And I heard her asking Hugh in for a drink. You look very smart, Hester.' But it was too robustly said, not tender. 'I suppose it all went off all right. At any rate, it went off. Muriel is splendid at that sort of thing. Never complains, as most women would, although I can see it all seems a great deal of nonsense to her.'

Before Hugh came, Robert was called away to the telephone and Hester was left alone. The day had tired and confused her, for she had never been quite sure of her duties. Ashamed to stand idle, she had tried to attach herself to the other workers, but Matron's campaign of defence had not included her. She had managed to hand a few cups of tea and annoyed the senior boys by doing so. Few things are so fatiguing as standing by to help and not being called upon, and now her feet, her back, even her teeth were aching. She drank her sherry and put the glass on the chimneypiece. Wavering clumsily, her hand touched a china figure and knocked it into the hearth. She gave a quick glance at the door, then stooped down to see what damage was done. Muriel's favourite Dresden girl lay in the fender, an arm carrying a gilt basket of strawberries was broken off at the elbow. Hester prayed for time, as if that could make the figure whole again; but in a school there are so many footsteps and any she could hear above the beating blood in her head might be Robert's or Muriel's coming to this room. She pushed the figure behind a bowl of flowers and put the broken piece in her pocket. If she were ever granted a few undisturbed moments she was sure she could have mended it; but now, although no one came and the waiting was unbearable, she could not be certain of being alone. She tried to find a nonchalant pose, sitting on the window-seat, far from the fireplace: then saw her sherry glass still there, incriminatingly near to and drawing attention to the empty place. She went to fetch it and on her way back to the window-seat thought of refilling it, to give a more natural look to her pose. As she was lifting the decanter, Hugh came in.

Her trembling guilt, the sherry slopped over the table, worried him. 'They are turning her into a secret drinker,' he thought; but her confusion touched him immeasurably, for he knew similar sensations, and had learnt new refinements of them at Muriel's hands. 'We are always mopping up for this girl,' he thought, as he dabbed at the table with his handkerchief. Her misery had gone so far beyond accountable bounds that he began to wonder how much she had drunk.

'Where is everyone?' he asked. He passed his handkerchief under the bottom of the glass before he gave it to her.

'Robert is telephoning.'

'And ... Madam?' For Muriel set up such awkwardnesses in people that they could sometimes not even give her her proper name.

'Went out in the car.'

'Who went out in the car?' Robert asked, as he came from the hall.

In Hester's shattered face, her lips moved stiffly, as if from some rigor, and at last formed the name.

'Oh, I wondered where she was. She'll be back. Sherry, Hugh?' Robert's bustling about could not conceal his perplexity. 'If people are liars, who makes them be?' he was wondering. 'Everything went off well, Hugh,' his voice wavered upwards. 'Nothing untoward? No one insulted Matron? Mrs Vallance seemed incensed at something.'

'The wretched boy's cricket-boot. She kept saying she would much rather both were lost than only one.'

'People often say that – particularly about gloves,' Muriel said, hurrying into the room. She went to the mirror and smoothed her hair. 'Sorry, Robert! Sorry, Hugh! Oh, and Hester, too! I didn't see you hiding in the window-seat. I went for a little drive with Beatrice. May I have a drink, darling; and, Hugh, your glass is empty. God, what a day! Never mind, another year until the next one. Darling, Hugh's glass! Dinner is cold and can wait for us for once. I went into the Science Room, Hugh, just to see if you had been up to anything sinister, and I was charmed. The heavenly demonstration of cross-pollination. I do think you are to be congratulated.'

Hugh gazed intently into his glass as Robert filled it. He looked as if he were parched with thirst, but sherry was a long way from his thoughts. He knew he was being ridiculed but could not sort it out sufficiently to make an answer. 'Meaningless innuendo,' he decided. 'And the very worst kind, too; because it finishes the game.'

'I did Botany at school,' Muriel said. 'That was considered ladylike even in those days – particularly in those days, when we drew no conclusions from it. Purple loosestrife seemed to have nothing in common with us.'

'Muriel!' Robert protested. 'Your Victorian girlhood doesn't convince us, you know.'

She went close to the mirrored over-mantel, leant forward to her reflection and once more smoothed her hair. Hester watched in terror the long white hands moving then from hair to flowers, tidying them, too. Then the room froze. Muriel picked up the Dresden figure, seemed surprised by genuine grief, paused; then turned to face them, looking dazed and puzzled.

'What a beautiful ... thing!' Hugh said, stepping forward, as if she were only asking him to admire it. 'The dress is just like real lace.'

'Robert!' Muriel cried, ignoring Hugh. 'Her grief is out of all proportion,'

Hester thought, remembering the same stunned look of wives in old news-reels, waiting at pit-heads as the stretchers were carried away, or of mothers lifting their babies across the rubble of bombed streets.

Robert asked sharply – as if he foresaw hell for all of them: 'How did that happen?' He took the china figure and examined it. Muriel turned back and began to search the chimneypiece.

'Is it broken?' Hugh asked, but no one answered. He was accustomed to that. Hester began to tremble, and clutched the fragment in her pocket as though she might be searched.

'It must be there,' Robert said. 'One of the maids must have done it without knowing, or they would have told you.'

Hester, falsely, went over and looked into the flower-bowl.

'Not there?' Muriel asked. 'No.'

'Quite a clean break,' Robert said. 'It could be mended easily.'

'If we find the other piece,' said Muriel.

'What is it we are looking for?' Hugh asked. 'I shall have to question the maids,' Muriel said. 'It has been hidden purposely. They have never deceived me before.' She was proud of her relationship with domestic staff, to whom she was always generous and considerate: they saw a side of her which was hidden from most people and they were loyal to her. She delayed the task of questioning them, refilled her glass with sherry and as she drank it went on searching, lifting cushions and rugs and thrusting her fingers down the sides of stuffed chairs until the backs of her hands looked bruised.

Hugh did not dine with them, and Muriel said nothing during the meal. When dishes were brought in, she helped herself and ate without raising her eyes, feeling awkwardness with the maid and guilt at her own suspicions.

After dinner, Hester went out into the garden and walked in an opposite direction to the church – down an azalea walk to a ferny grotto. The dark, dusty leaves parted and disclosed a little Gothic summer-house, which was locked so that the boys should not damage it. No one came there – the dark rockiness of the place was chilling, the clay paths slippery in wet weather; the creaking trees were clotted with rooks' nests, and the rooks themselves filled the air with commotion, restlessly calling, circling, dropping again and again to the branches.

Robert had brought her here on her first day when he had shown her round; he had taken a key from his pocket and unlocked the door for her. The cave-smell was unpleasant to breathe, but she had marvelled aloud at the interior. The walls and domed roof were encrusted with shells in fan patterns set in cement. Light from the coloured glass in the windows shone in patches.

Now she could only stand on tiptoe at the door and look through the wire-covered glass-panel. The piece of china from her pocket she forced through the wire and broken pane. It struck the stone floor inside.

'Were you trying to get in?' Hugh asked her; shouting rather, above the noise of the rooks.

'No, it is always locked.'

'Did I surprise you? I saw you come this way when I was down at the nets with some of the boys. I meant to ask you before dinner if you'd come for a walk, but there was all that rumpus about the ornament – put it out of my mind; I mean I hadn't a chance. Of course, she has some nice things – Madam, Muriel, that is – and she thinks a lot of them: naturally.'

'They were her mother's.'

'Nice diamonds, too, Rex was saying.'

'Yes.'

Hugh began to perceive that Hester lacked interest in Muriel's possessions.

'Never having had anything very valuable myself,' he said, 'it is hard for me to understand anyone being as upset as she was tonight.'

'It is because she hasn't anything valuable,' Hester said. 'And she knows it.'

'Children, you mean?'

'Partly.'

They walked down the winding path. Two boys were kneeling by some flint steps, looking for lizards under the stones. Hugh had a little patronising chat with them, then he and Hester walked on again. The boys exchanged slow winks.

'Did you ever see that horrible old baggage again?' Hugh asked. 'The one with the cat.'

'No. Not again.'

'Are you happy here?'

'Not very.'

This was so promising that he made no answer until they reached the seat in the laurel walk where Muriel and Beatrice had sat and talked; then, when he was sitting at Hester's side, he asked, 'Why aren't you happy?' Looking round carefully, he made sure there were no boys about, and took her hand.

'I am in the way, you see,' Hester said gravely. 'I ought not to be here.'

When he took her other hand and drew nearer to her, she seemed not to notice. Although her indifference was in a sense discouraging to him, it allowed him to proceed without hindrance. He kissed her, but still looking rather mopishly before her, she said: 'I didn't want to harm anyone. Not even someone I hate.'

'You couldn't harm anyone,' he said. 'You are so entirely gentle.'

Some boys shouted in the distance, and he moved promptly aside, leant forward, his elbows on his knees, in an attitude of serious but impersonal discussion. But the voices faded and no one came. A bell rang, and he muttered, 'Thank God for that,' and turned again to Hester and took her in his arms.

In the morning, Muriel questioned the maids, Lucy and Sylvia. One showed transparent surprise and concern; the other haughty offendedness: and since both reacted in their own ways as their innocence dictated, Muriel said no more. She often boasted that she knew at once when people were lying, not realising how little this endeared her to anyone, least of all to Hester who, never very honest in the easiest of times, was lately finding it almost impossible to tell the truth.

One thing Hester was determined on and it was to avoid being left alone with Muriel. She managed this all morning and was about to manage it after lunch as she followed Robert to his study, when Muriel, letting her reach the door, said: 'Oh, Hester! If you wouldn't mind . . . I won't keep you a moment.'

Robert walked on as if he had not heard; but by the time he reached his study, his agitation was so great, he was so sure of what Muriel would inflict on the girl, that he went out into the hall again and stood guiltily at the table pretending to read *The Times*.

The voices on the other side of the door were separated by long silences; the blurred murmurings seemed without consequence or meaning. Then he heard Hester crying. The sobs came in a rush towards the door and in a panic he hurried back to his study and sat down at his desk. He heard footsteps in the hall, and was so sure that they were coming to him and felt so anxious to be ready to deal with disaster – fidgeting busily with papers, continually clearing his throat – that he did not listen, and when at last he realised that the house was silent, he could not tell in which direction Hester had gone.

At three o'clock, he gave a Latin lesson. Afterwards, he returned to his study. She was not there, and the typewriter was still covered. He put down his books and went to look for Muriel; but Muriel, he was told, had gone to a meeting in the village. He spent an idle, worried afternoon, and Hester did not appear. 'Another man,' he thought, 'could get away from this, could leave the women and go to work!' He was forced to remain, always morbidly aware of the atmosphere in the house.

Muriel returned in the early evening, said, 'Hello, Robert!' very casually, as she took her afternoon's post from the hall-table and walked into the drawing-room.

'Where is Hester?'

She read her letters attentively. 'I can't tell you. I went out soon after lunch.'

'Not soon enough.'

She had to raise her head then.

'What have you done to her? You made her cry.'

'From no sense of shame, either, I'm afraid. Only from chagrin at being found out.'

'I suppose she *did* break that damned thing.'

'Exactly.'

'She was afraid to tell you. You shouldn't frighten her so.'

'She stood there and listened to me saying that I should question Lucy and Sylvia.'

'Did you know then that she had done it?'

'I wasn't sure, although she is so clumsy that one's thoughts naturally fly to her.'

'You make her clumsy, you know.'

'Yes, I dare say it is my fault.'

'I know she doesn't always speak the truth and I worry sometimes that she should be driven to deceit.'

'Driven? You choose melodramatic words, Robert. And I can't imagine anyone driving anyone into such fantastic lunatic deceptions as your Hester's.'

'You must have upset her very much.'

'Yes, as you say, I made her cry. I am glad I did not make Lucy cry. I am glad I took their word at once.'

'But where is Hester now?'

Muriel put aside her letters with a sigh of weariness. 'I do not know, Robert. I do not know. You have seen her since I.'

'But I haven't. I left her here with you.'

'The last I saw of her, she was coming to you for the key.'

'What key?'

'The key to the Shell House. Where she had hidden the piece of china. I sent her to fetch it and to get the key from you.'

'That was her punishment, was it? To have to face me, as she was, and make that pathetic little confession, then go out, humiliated, to pick up the bits? And you can do that to someone just because they have broken some china.'

'She has broken more than china for me.'

'The deepest destruction is done with finesse, not clumsiness. She couldn't hold a candle to you. I must go to look for her.'

'He will find her weeping in her room and console her, take sides against me,' Muriel thought. She said: 'I am at the end of this marriage, Robert. I cannot bear any more of it.'

'I will ask Hugh,' he said. 'Perhaps he will have seen her.'

'Why Hugh?'

'Because I think he is in love with her.'

'Is that so? I wouldn't have thought it of him. You need not speak so angrily. Poor young man, I don't suppose he has any idea of how he is trespassing. Anyone else would know; but he's a little extra stupid.' Once again, she desired to strike him, did so with words instead. 'I expect she is just sulking in her bedroom, so I shouldn't fuss.'

But Hester was not in her room, and those who were discreetly questioned had not seen her.

Fortune struck blindingly at Miss Despenser. All fell into place and she saw that, given the right ingredients and patience, heart's desire at last will come, like risen bread, to proving point. She had despaired in loneliness, then conquered her despair, up to that stage of no-feeling, where the mind goes joggety-jog on little errands of the will, each minute measured out in a tiny sip. 'For time heals all,' she told herself. 'At the end of life, we should be quite healed, and so go whole to dissolution.'

Mrs Brimmer, towards two o'clock, had mysteriously run out of both Guinness and Madeira; could only suggest a mild-and-bitter, and then the bitter had given out. The men sniggered. 'You know I don't like cold drinks,' Miss Despenser complained. 'You should write to the brewers!'

'I will,' Mrs Brimmer said, and they laughed again.

'Mother would be shocked,' Miss Despenser thought, as she wandered home. 'The way they speak nowadays.'

It seemed siesta-time in the lanes. Only the bees moved. But the house was buzzing with activity. Green and dark-blue flies were delirious over the plates of cat's food in the kitchen. In sudden disgust with her life, Miss Despenser took them all up and threw them – dishes, too – into the dustbin, and started a furious zigzagging as she lifted the lid.

At that moment, Hester rang the bell.

'What luck!' said Miss Despenser when she opened the door. 'You came just at the right time. I was doing a bit of spring-cleaning and I shall be glad to knock off and have a chat. You will cheer me up, I know you.'

Hester, trembling, swollen-eyed, entered the house. She bore her nausea for the sake of Muriel's punishment, knowing she could not hope to hurt her without sacrificing herself; had even contemplated, in a brief moment of rage, the supreme sacrifice; for no greater hatred could she show than that.

'I knew it would be a red-letter day,' Miss Despenser said and handed

Hester a postcard, 'when this came this morning. I don't often have anything in the post,' she explained simply. It was a printed invitation from a
girls' school. 'Tennis Match,' Hester read. 'Past *v*. Present. 2.15 sharp.' 'What
is Asboga?' she asked dully, and pressed her fingers to her burning eyes.

'Abbey School, Brighton, Old Girls' Association,' Miss Despenser said.
'Linda and I were both Asbogs. Though she could only stand a term there.
It was the happiest time I ever had, although at times we pined for one
another. The food was so good. I don't think you could better that food
anywhere. On Fridays, we had a red jelly with bananas sliced up in it. Every
Friday. We looked forward to it, I can tell you. What is the food like where
you are? What did you have for luncheon today, for instance?'

Hester thought, then said: 'A sort of shepherd's pie.'

'My favourite! And after?'

'Oh, dear, I don't know.'

'But it can only have been half an hour ago.'

'I think it was apple ... something with apple ...' She began to cry
again.

'Now, chin up! Surely you don't grizzle over your food, like poor Linda?
She once cried over an apple-charlotte. She cried all afternoon without
stopping. My father made her sit there till tea-time. She ate it in the end.
He had a will of iron. I advise you to eat up in the beginning ...'

'I don't want to answer questions, that's all,' Hester said.

'You look peaky. Come along, hop on to the sofa, legs up! I'll make you
a cup of tea.'

Hester lay down, the dusty plush against her cheek. Misery obliterated
her. 'Someone take over, take charge, take care!' She wept for a little while,
then fell asleep.

Miss Despenser was a long time getting the tea ready. She worked happily, but slowly, in her usual state of afternoon muzziness.

After dinner, Robert found Hugh walking about the grounds and asked if
he had seen Hester.

'No, I was looking for her.'

'She didn't come to dinner, and I am rather anxious.'

'Has there been some upset?' Hugh asked at once.

'Yes. Why do you ask?'

'She seemed fairly miserable last night. We went for a walk, you know.
Is she in her room?'

'No. Of course, we looked there first. I'll stroll about and keep my eyes
open.'

When he had shaken off Hugh, Robert went quickly up the path to the
Shell House and unlocked the door. It swung open with a grating sound.

The piece of china lay on the dusty floor, proving nothing but what Muriel had said, that Hester had delivered herself into her hands.

He began an aimless search of the grounds, for he could not think where Hester might go, or what she did in her spare time. Some of the boys watched him with excitement, for they were sure he was out on some mysterious investigation and they wondered if school monotony might be enlivened after prayers next day by the announcement of some appalling scandal – some of the lordly ones found smoking in the shrubbery, or the copy of *Lady Chatterley's Lover* unearthed. When he was seen to be walking more quickly towards the churchyard, as if struck by a sudden idea, he was watched intently by one boy, Terence Mooney, who always made his beer in the little shed by the church. His father was a brewer – Mooney's Sunshine Ales – and Terry's school-life was an everlasting misery in consequence. 'You must know how to make it,' the boys said. 'Surely your old man told you. Well, write and ask him, then.' He had pretended to write to ask, and the boys gathered round and watched him open his next letter from home – 'Darling, I hope you are happy and your earache better. Don't talk after lights out, but get all the rest you can.' . . . 'Did he say anything?' 'Yes, of course.' 'Well, what?' 'Well, he says I mustn't say. It's a family secret.' 'Well, you're his family, aren't you? Can't he tell you?' 'Yes.' 'Well, get on, then. We don't want to know how you do it. We just want to drink it.' 'It takes time. It has to ferment, you see.' 'All right, we'll give you time.' They arranged to give him a week. He studied encyclopaedias. He did not sleep. He stole potatoes and brewed concoctions. These never tasted right to him, or to most of the boys, who made it clear that they would never touch Mooney's beer when they left school and could choose. Terry lived in wretched unpopularity, busy, furtive; he segregated his parents on Speech Day, and now, watching Robert, wondered if he would be expelled.

'Mr Baseden's prowling about, too,' a boy said. 'He went through the churchyard a few minutes ago.'

'They might be going for walks,' poor Mooney said.

'Not them. They keep looking round.'

It did not occur to them that masters could have anything but boys in their minds.

Hugh went to the Hand and Flowers, but neither Miss Despenser nor Hester was there. 'I'm not breaking my heart, either,' Mrs Brimmer said as she drew his beer. He drank it quickly and hurried back up the lane to the stucco villa.

'No, there's no one there,' Miss Despenser told Hester, who had heard the knocking on the door. 'I often fancy the same thing; but nobody calls here. Perhaps Pussy jumped down off my bed. It wouldn't be anyone.'

But at the second knock, Hester went to the window. Hugh, stepping back from the porch, saw her behind the dusty pane. She had a fan of old photographs in her hand and her face was stained with tears.

'Yes. It is Hugh Baseden,' she said, and he could see her lips moving as she still stared at him.

'Then draw the curtains. How dare he trespass here! Peering and prying!'

Hester – dreamy with weakness – moved towards the hall and opened the door. She was at a stage of recovery from grief – the air was vacant, silence enfolded her, and when she put out her hand to the wall to steady herself after the effort of opening the door, the wall seemed to bend, to slope away from her; and it was as if Hugh's hand as she touched it dissolved, vanished.

He lifted her and carried her to a chair in the hall. 'Put your head down,' he told her. She obeyed. Her hand with the photographs swung against the floor. Pussy came up and walked in a figure-of-eight round her feet. Hugh pushed him aside. 'And now, Paul Pry, you can leave my house at once,' Miss Despenser said. 'I was just coming into the hall when I saw what you did to Pussy. You peer through my windows, force your way in, are cruel to my cat and goodness knows what you have done to this poor girl. Sit up, Hester! The blood will run to your head.'

Hester sat up and Hugh pushed her head down again.

'You blockhead!' Miss Despenser shouted. 'She will faint, you great dunce, if you are not careful.'

He knelt down before Hester and held her head against him.

'She was all right until you came,' Miss Despenser said. 'I wish you would go away again.'

'What are these?' Hugh asked, gently taking the photographs from Hester.

'They are mine. I am showing them to her,' Miss Despenser said. 'We haven't nearly finished yet.' She sprang forward and snatched up one of the photographs he had dropped. 'How dare you throw my things on the floor, you blundering oaf! That is my sister.' She looked, with a change to tenderness, at the yellowed card, the girl with the vapid smile, the hand resting on a carved pedestal behind which a backcloth of roses and pillars met the carpet unevenly.

'Are you well enough to come home?' Hugh asked Hester. 'Shall I get a car?'

'I can't go home.'

'No, she can't go home.'

'What is wrong?' Hugh asked softly, kneeling by her, rocking her gently in his arms.

'It is out of the question,' Miss Despenser said. 'Now you must run along. I am sorry I cannot invite you to dinner.' She fought bravely, but by now she knew that she was going to lose. He had forgotten her, as an adversary, while he listened to Hester's story.

'Get up off your knees!' Miss Despenser tried to interrupt them. 'You exhibitionist.'

'I don't know why I did,' Hester was moaning. 'I lost my nerve. She makes me behave badly. I hate her. Oh, I hate her.' Her mouth squared like a howling child's, then she began to beat her forehead with her hands.

'There you are, you see,' said Miss Despenser.

'If you would only marry me!' said Hugh, and at once began to cloud the proposal with doubts and apologies. 'I know so little about girls – no time to learn ... I had to work so hard, and I've so little money. I'm awfully dull, I know ...'

'As dull as ditchwater,' Miss Despenser said, but her remarks were now automatic. She had covered her retreat with them, and exhausted, with her efforts and her disappointment, could say no more. She took a pace back in the shadowy hall and when at last Hugh stood up and helped Hester to do so, she closed her eyes and could watch no longer.

'Good-bye,' Hester said, turning to her. 'I'm sorry, and thank you. I had better go back after all.'

Miss Despenser kept her eyes shut; a hard tear was under each lid.

Hugh looked away from Hester for the first time and saw the old woman's wedge-shaped face, so angrily grieved, her down-turned mouth. With the palm of her hand she was pressing to her skirt the photograph of her dead sister. From his own timid loneliness, he had knowledge of such a poverty of love. He said: 'Thank you for taking care of her.' The tragic mask could not move, or the eyes open. When Hester and Hugh had gone, she lifted her lids and two tears dropped out and made tracks down her face to her chin. She picked up the cat and wiped her wet face on his fur, then she gathered up the photographs and crammed them back into the mother-o'-pearl-inlaid box.

Not long after, just as Mrs Brimmer at the Hand and Flowers was saying: 'Well, we choked her off, gentlemen,' Miss Despenser entered the bar. 'So sorry I am late. Some visitors called,' she said cheerily.

'A pleasure, I'm sure,' Mrs Brimmer replied. 'And now last orders, if you please.'

At the school, Hester was enveloped by tact – Muriel, relieved at her re-appearance, seemed unconcerned and talked of trivial things, though lapsing sometimes into sad preoccupation. Robert's lack of allusion was almost imbecilic. Hugh, suddenly masterful, had arranged with him that no words should pass and they did not, although sometimes Hester felt swollen with the rehearsed explanations she was not allowed to make.

As day after day went by, poor little Mooney began at last to wonder if he had escaped expulsion; but Robert's abstracted ways prolonged the boys' uneasiness. Dissociation became the policy under this cloud – the copy of *Lady Chatterley's Lover*, or Latin cribs, lost their value; the shrubbery, or Hell's Kitchen, where the older ones smoked, was deserted.

One day, after lunch, when Robert had said Grace he still stood there, as if he had more to say. They paused and turned their faces towards him, candid, innocent. Only Mooney looked down desperately at his plate – the five prune-stones at its edge: *this* year.

The announcement of Hugh's and Hester's engagement was a tremendous relief. Robert's attempt at joviality brought forth sycophantic cheers and smiles. They were all in a good humour, especially as one wedding present would do for both. 'It is better for them not to marry "outside" people,' the head boy explained. 'Now what we want is for Matron to marry Mr Wigmore!'

Hugh's first biology class of the afternoon was in a mood of refreshment and good humour.

'Congratulations, sir.'

'Thank you, Palmer,'

'Congratulations, sir.'

'I will take Palmer as spokesman for all of you,' Hugh said firmly. 'Page fifty-one.' They opened their books.

'So that's the solution,' Beatrice said. 'You were quite right to be patient and let things work their own way out.'

'I don't know that I did that,' Muriel said. 'And it has taken a long time and she hasn't gone yet.'

'She seems too moony, too dull a girl to fall in love, be fallen in love with.'

'Is love the prerogative of the bright ones? He is very dull himself, you know, and it is a good thing if two uninteresting people marry and keep their dullness to themselves. Though she has changed a little for the better – looks less *driven*, and doesn't knock things over quite as much as she used; can sometimes drink a glass of water without spilling it.'

'Well, if marriage stops her being clumsy it will be something.' Then Beatrice asked slyly: 'How has Robert taken it?'

'Nobly. He arranged Hugh's new job for him and still has nobody to take his place.'

'I meant – about Hester.'

'Oh, Hester!' Muriel's voice was light with annoyance. 'I think I imagined a great deal of that.' If Hester were going, her own agitation would sink; then she wanted her old life again, her picture of serene marriage, of Robert's devotion to her. She regretted having confided in Beatrice, who made past miseries more real by her knowledge of them. To turn the conversation she said: 'I will give her a lovely wedding ... I suppose that she has some friends she can invite – school-friends if nothing better. I have chosen the dress-material. Just think, Beatrice, when we were married we wore those hideous short frocks. It would be our luck to strike that fashion. I wouldn't let anyone see my wedding photographs for all the world.' With tender condescension they recalled the nineteen-twenties and the gay and gentle girlishness of their natures then.

Muriel began to feel energy and optimism, as the holidays and the wedding grew nearer. She worked to bring to life one imagined scene, the beginning of peace for her; foresaw Hester and Hugh going down the steps to the car – 'She was married from my house,' she would tell people.

'She was like a daughter to me' – and when the car had gone (for ever, for ever) down the drive, she and Robert would turn and go up the confetti-littered steps to begin their new – or, rather, their old – life, together and alone.

She worked on the wedding and discussed it incessantly. 'Suppose it rains!' Robert said abruptly one night. Muriel was sitting up in bed while he undressed. She was brushing her hair and at his words parted it from her face, looked up at him in perplexity. 'Are you angry about it, then?'

'Angry? I only said "Suppose it rains!"'

'You sounded so sarcastic.'

He got into bed and closed his eyes at once. Smoothing her hair back, she dropped the brush to the floor and put out the light. 'You do love me, Robert?' she asked in her meekest voice.

'Yes, dear.'

'You aren't still angry with me about Hester? It has turned out well in the end for her.'

'I hope so.'

'He will be very good to her, I am quite sure.'

'Yes, I am sure, too. Good-night, Muriel.'

'Good-night, Robert.'

He turned over and seemed to fall asleep: yet she doubted if he did so, and lay and listened for a long while to his regular, unbroken breathing. Once, to test him, she touched him gently with the back of her hand, but he did not turn to her as years ago he would have done. 'I cannot make him come to me,' she thought in a panic. 'I cannot get my own way.' She became wide awake with a longing for him to make love to her; to prove his need for her; so that she could claim his attention; and so dominate him; but at last wished only to contend with her own desires, unusual and humiliating as they were to her. She lay close to him and masked her shame with a pretence of sleep. When he did not, would not, stir, her tenderness hardened to resentment. She raised herself and looked down at him. His profile was stern; his hair ruffled; he breathed steadily. 'He cannot be asleep,' she thought, as she bent over him, put her cheek to his brow, no longer dissembling or hiding her desire.

His stillness defeated her and after a while, hollowed and exhausted by her experience, she turned away and lay down on her side, listening to her thunderous heart-beat, feeling giddy. 'If I could be young again!' she thought. 'If I could be young!'

Two thrushes were singing in the garden before she fell asleep. The night had dishevelled her, her hair was tangled on the creased pillow, her body damp in the hot bed. But in her dreams, a less disordered Muriel took command. She dreamed that she was making Hester's wedding cake – white and glistering it rose before her, a sacrificial cake, pagoda-shaped in tier on tier, with arcades of sugar pillars, garlanded friezes. Delicate as hoar-rimed ferns she made the fronded wreaths of flowers and leaves. It blossomed as she worked her magic on it with the splendid virtuosity of dreams. 'Yes, that is how it will be!' she thought. 'And no one must ever touch it or break it.' She had surprised herself with her own skill, and, standing back to view her work, felt assuaged, triumphant, but bereft, too, as artists are when their work is done and gone for good.

'Taking Mother Out'

'Give the credit where it is due,' Mrs Crouch said, smiling at her son.

We had, of course, been marvelling at her youthfulness. Every gesture she made, even the most simple, seemed calculated to defy old age. She constantly drew our attention to her eighty years, referred to herself as an old fogey; insisted on this when we were obliged to demur. And then insisted on insisting. We offered her a drink. She became husky, Marie Lloydish, a little *broad*. Her glass of gin she turned into a music-hall act. A further little speech was made over a cigarette, my brother waiting with his lighter flaring ready, while she launched off into an explanation about herself: how she liked a bit of fun, liked young people, was as old as she felt, merely.

I glanced at her son; but not as if he were anything within my, or anybody's, reach. He was flashy, cynical, one of those men who knows about everything; makes sinister implications of rumours in the City, panic in the Cabinet; hints at inside information; has seen everything, seen through everything; known everybody, loved nobody; bought everything, at a special price; and sold it again, at a great profit. His mother admired him of all her children the most. She displayed him, was indebted to him, gave credit to him, as she was doing now.

He looked in her direction and smiled, a little bored with the elderly bird-watcher, who had sat down beside him to describe without pause his day on the marshes. He was right to be bored by the bird-watcher – a relation of ours, who menaced our every summer.

The evening light enhances those marshes. We sipped our drinks, narrowed our eyes, gazing down over the green flatness where masts in the middle of a field seemed to indicate the estuary. Little silences fell over us from time to time. The gentle vista before us, the gradual cadences, the close-cropped grass tufted with rough weeds which the slow-moving sheep had left, untidy little sheets of water, far off the glitter of the sea – all of this held our attention, even from one another, for English people love a view. Only the bird-watcher droned on.

Mrs Crouch twirled her glass, brushed at her skirt, examined her rings, wondering, I guessed, what the Spotted Crake had to do with her and how remarkably she carried her age. She decided to begin a counter-conversation and turned to my brother, raising her voice, for she was a little deaf and usually shouted.

'I hope, my dear, you won't think I tie Roy to my apron-strings. As a matter of fact, I am always saying to him, Roy, I say, you ought to be taking out a beautiful young blonde instead of your old mother. But he won't have it. Of course, I love my little outings, going out and meeting young people. When I'm asked how it is I carry my age so well, I say it's being with young people, and most of all being with Roy. He won't *let* me settle down. Come along, Mother, he says, let's go off on a binge.' She savoured this word, chuckling. My brother fidgeted gloomily with his wrist-watch. Roy Crouch fidgeted with his, too.

'No,' said the bird-watcher, as if contradicting himself, 'not a common sight, but a remarkable one, the male bird sitting on the nest. No mistaking that, even at a distance, through field-glasses. The female is smaller and duller.'

'Quite,' said Roy nastily.

'I've had a full life,' his mother was saying. My brother swallowed and glanced out across the salt-marshes.

'Did you ever see a Richard's Pipit?' Roy suddenly asked.

'No,' said the bird-watcher shortly. 'Did you?'

'Yes.'

The bird-watcher turned right round in his chair and stared at him. He could not call him a liar, but he said: 'Then you were very fortunate, sir. May I enquire where?'

'In Norfolk,' Roy said carelessly.

'Very fortunate,' the bird-watcher repeated, still glaring.

'I think that's why Roy likes to take me out, because I enjoy myself.'

'I expect so,' my brother agreed.

I refilled glasses. The bird-watcher recovered. He began to talk of the Water-Rail, how he had lain in a bed of reeds and counted seven pairs that morning. A wonderful sight. Perhaps not Richard's Pipits, you bounder, he seemed to imply. But a wonderful sight all the same.

'Talking of wonderful sights,' said Roy, getting into his stride, 'I was staying near the Severn Estuary in the spring and saw a very unusual thing – rather a romantic sight . . . ' He laughed apologetically. 'I happened to look out of my bedroom window one night when it was quite dark and I could see something moving down in the water-meadows, something rippling' – he rippled his fingers, to show us. 'Something that shimmered' – his hand shimmered. 'I stood very still and watched, hardly able to believe my eyes, but at last I realised what it was.' He looked at the bird-watcher and at me. My brother was out of this conversation.

'But I really don't think,' Mrs Crouch was telling him, 'that the new tunes are half so jolly as the old ...'

'And what do you think it was?' Roy asked us.

We did not know.

We did not know, we said.

'Eels,' he said impressively, 'young eels, or rather, I should say "elvers",' he corrected himself. 'I shall never forget that sight. It was ghostly, unreal. In a silver flood, they rippled through the grass in the moonlight, through a little stream and then on up the slope ... beautiful. They come up from the sea, you know. Every spring. I've heard people say they *couldn't* travel across land, but there it was, I saw with my own eyes.'

My brother was nearly asleep. Mrs Crouch said suddenly, testily, 'What are you all nodding your heads so solemnly about?'

'Eels,' I said lightly.

'Eels? Oh, eels! Why, only last night some friends of ours, a Mr and Mrs Sibley, were telling us about an experience they had when they were staying near the Severn Estuary. They were going to bed one night and Mr Sibley happened to look out of the window, and he suddenly called out to Mrs Sibley, "Just come and look at this," he said. "There's something moving down there on the grass," and Mrs Sibley said, "Frank, do you know what I think those are? I do believe they're eels, young eels" – I forget the name she gave to them. What was that word, Roy?'

'No one has a drink,' I cried, running frantically from one glass to another. The bird-watcher looked gravely, peacefully, at the view.

'Thank you, dear,' said Mrs Crouch. 'I am not at all sure that I haven't had too much already. What was that word, Roy? I have it at the tip of my tongue.'

'Elvers,' he muttered, and took a great swallow at his gin. He looked dejected, worn, as old as his mother almost. They might have been husband and wife.

Spry Old Character

The Home For The Blind absorbed the surplus of that rural charity – so much more pleasant to give than to receive – the cakes left over from the Women's Institute party, and concerts which could no longer tempt appetites more than satisfied by homely monologues and the post-mistress's zither. Fruit and vegetables from the Harvest Festival seemed not richer from their blessing, but vitiated by being too much arranged, too much stared at. The bread in the shape of a corn-sheaf tasted of incense, and, with its mainly visual appeal, was wasted on the blind.

No week went by without some dispiriting jollity being forced upon him. This week, it was a choir of schoolgirls singing 'Orpheus with His Lute'. 'Which drives me finally up the wall,' Harry decided, and clapped his great horny hands together at the end with relief. 'Your *nails*, Harry!' Matron had said earlier, as if he were a child; and, like a child, he winced each time the scissors touched him. 'You've been biting them again. I shall have to get very cross with you.' He imagined her irritating smile; false teeth like china, no doubt; thin lips. He was on the wrong side of her from the start; had asked her to read out to him the runners at Newmarket. 'You old terror! I shall do nothing of the kind. I'm not having that sort of thing here.' He was helpless. Reading with his hands he regarded as a miracle and beyond him. He had steered clear of books when he could see, and they held even less attraction now that tedious lessons, as well as indifference, stood in the way; and the *Sporting Life* was not set in Braille, he soon discovered.

His request had scandalised, for – he had soon decided – only the virtuous lose their sight: perhaps as a further test of their saintly patience. None of his friends – the Boys – had ever known such a calamity, and rebelliousness, as if at some clerical error, hardened his heart. Set down in this institution after his sister's death, he was a fish out of water. 'I'm just not the type,' he thought, over and over again.

The great house, in its park; the village; the surrounding countryside – which Harry called 'the rural set-up' – was visually unimaginable to him. His nearest experience of it was Hampstead Heath or the view (ignored) from Goodwood Racecourse. Country to him was negative: simply, a place where there was not a town. The large rooms of the Home unnerved him. In his sister's house, he could not go far wrong, edging round the table which took up most of the space; and the heat from the fire, the clock ticking on the dresser had given him his bearings. When she had died he was helpless. The Home had appealed to him as a wonderful alternative to his own picture of himself out in the street with a tray of matches and a card pinned to his breast with some words such as 'On My Beam Ends' or, simply, 'Blind'. 'You'll have the company of others like you,' his neighbours had told him. This was not so. He found himself in a society whose existence he had never, in his old egotism, contemplated and whose ways soon lowered his vitality. He had nothing in common with these faded seamstresses; the prophet-like lay-preacher; an old piano-tuner who believed he was the reincarnation of Beethoven; elderly people who had lived more than half a dim life-time in dark drapers' shops in country towns. Blind they might not have been; for they found their way about the house, its grounds, the village, with pride and confidence. Indoors, they bickered about the wireless; for the ladies liked a nice domestic play and thought some of the variety programmes 'suggestive'. The racing results were always switched to something different, hastily, before they could contaminate the air.

'I once went to a race-meeting,' Miss Arbuthnot admitted. She had been a governess in Russia in the Tsarist days and had taken tea with Rasputin: now she overrode her companions with her past grandeur. No one knew, perhaps she least of all, what bizarre experience might be related next. 'It was at Ascot after the last war. I mean the one before that. I went as chaperone to Lady Allegra Faringdon and one of the Ponsonby cousins.'

'Did you see the King and Queen drive down the Course?' asked the sycophantic Mrs Hussey. 'What a picture that must be!'

'It is quite a pageant of English life. The cream of the cream, as one might say; but, dear, dear me! What a tiring way to spend a day! My poor feet! I wore some pale grey buckskin shoes, and how they *drew*. I dare say they would look very old-fashioned nowadays, but then they were quite à *la*.' She gave her silvery, trilling laugh. '"Well, I have been once," I used to say. "I know what it is like, and I know that I give the preference to Henley, even if the crowd there is not so brilliant. Oh, yes, give me Henley any day."'

No one would be likely to give her any such thing ever again, but this occurred only to Harry.

'Did you have any luck – with the horses, I mean?' he asked, breaking his sullen silence with his coarse, breathy voice. Exasperation and nostalgia forced him to speak, although to do so invited ridicule. He was driven to broach the subject as lovers are often driven to mention the beloved's name, even in casual conversation with unworthy people.

'Do you mean betting?'

'What else do you go for?' he asked huffily.

'Well, certainly not for that, I hope. For the spectacle, the occasion – a brilliant opening to the London season.'

No one thought – their indignation was so centred upon Harry – that she spoke less as a governess than as a duchess. She coloured their lives with her extravagances; whereas Harry only underlined their plight; stumbling, cursing, spilling food, he had brought the word 'blindness' into their midst – a threat to their courage.

'Cantankerous old virgin!' he thought. 'Trying to come it over me.' A spinster to him was a figure of fun; but now he, not she, sat humble and grumpy and rejected.

That evening at the concert, Miss Arbuthnot, with the advantage of her cultured life behind her ('Ah! Chaliapin in "Boris"! After that, one is never quite the same person again'), sat in the front row and led and tempered the applause. A humorous song in country dialect wound up the evening, and her fluting laugh gave the cue for broad-minded appreciation. Then chairs scraped back and talk broke out. Harry tapped his way to a corner and sat there alone.

The girls, told to mingle, to bring their sunshine into these dark lives, began nervously to hand round buns, unsure of how far the blind could help themselves. They were desperately tactful. ('I made the most frightful *faux pas*,' they would chatter in the bus going home. 'Dropped the most appalling brick. Wasn't it all depressing? Poor old things! But it doesn't bear thinking of, of course.')

One girl, obediently, came towards Harry.

'Would you like a cake?'

'That's very kind of you, missie.'

She held the plate out awkwardly, but he made no movement towards it.

'Shall I . . . may I give you one?'

'I should maybe knock them all on the floor if I start feeling about,' he said gloomily.

She put a cake into his hand and looked away as the crumbs began to fall on his waistcoat and knees, fearing that he might guess the direction of her glance; for the blind, she had been told, develop the other senses in uncanny ways.

Her young voice was a pleasure to him. He was growing used to voices either elderly or condescending. Hoping to detain her a little longer, he said: 'You all sang very nice indeed.'

'I'm so glad you enjoyed it.'

He thought: 'I'd only have run a mile from it given half a chance.'

'I'm fond of a nice voice,' he said. 'My mother was a singer.'

'Oh, really?' She had not intended to sound so incredulous, but her affectation of brightness had grown out of hand.

'She was a big figure on the Halls – in more ways than just the one. A fine great bust and thighs she had, but small feet. Collins' Music Hall and the Met ... I dare say you heard of them?'

'I can't really say I have.'

'She had her name on the bills – Lottie Throstle. That was her stage name, and a funny, old-fashioned name it must sound nowadays, but they liked to have something out of the usual run. Louie Breakspear her real name was. I expect you've heard your mum and dad speak of Lottie Throstle.'

'I can't remember ...'

'She was a good old sort.' ('She'd have had you taped,' he thought. 'I can hear her now ... "Ay can't say, ay'm sure."') '"Slip Round the Corner, Charlie", that was her song. Did you ever hear that one?' ('"No, ay can't say ay hev,"' he answered for her. 'No, I thought not. Orpheus and his sodding lute's more your ticket.')

'No, I haven't.' She glanced desperately about her.

'What colour dress you got on, miss?'

'White.'

'Well, don't be shy! Nothing wrong with a white dress at your age. When you're fat and forty I should advise thinking twice about it. You all got white dresses on?'

'Yes.'

'Must look like the Virgins' Outing,' he thought. 'What a sight! Never came my way, of course, before now. No one ever served up twenty-five virgins in white to me in those days; showing common sense on their part, no doubt.'

His rough hand groped forward and rasped against her silk frock.

'That's nice material! I like nice material. My sister Lily who died was a dressmaker ...'

The girl, rigid, turned her head sharply aside. He smelt the sudden sweat of fear and embarrassment on her skin and drew back his hand.

'Now, young lady, we can't let you monopolise Mr Breakspear,' Matron said, coming swiftly across the room. 'Here's Miss Wilcox to have a chat with you, Harry. Miss Wilcox is the choir-mistress. She brings the girls here every year to give us this wonderful experience. You know, Miss Wilcox, Harry is quite the naughtiest of all my old darlings. He thinks we treat him so badly. Oh, yes, you do, Harry. You grumble from morning till night. And so lazy! Such a lovely basket he was going to make, but he lost all interest in it in next to no time.'

Sullenly, he sat beside Miss Wilcox. When coffee was brought to him, he spilt it purposely. He had no pride in overcoming difficulties as the others had. His waistcoat was evidence of this. He was angry that Matron had mentioned his basket-work; for a very deep shame had overtaken him when they tried to teach him such a craft. He saw a picture of his humiliation, as if through his friends' eyes – the poor old codger, broken, helpless, back to the bottom class at school. 'You want to be independent,' the teacher had said, seeing him slumped there, idle with misery. He thought they did not understand the meaning of the word.

'You haven't been here long?' Miss Wilcox enquired kindly.

'No, only since my sister, Lily, died. I went to live along with her when I lost my wife. I've been a widower nineteen years now. She was a good old sort, my wife.'

'I'm sure she was.'

'Why's she so sure,' he wondered, 'when she never as much as clapped eyes on her? She could have been a terrible old tartar for all she knows.'

But he liked to talk, and none of the others would ever listen to him. He engaged Miss Wilcox, determined to prevent her escaping.

'I lost my sight three years ago, on account of a kick I had on the head from a horse. I used to be a horse-dealer at one time.' Then he remembered that no one spoke about being blind. This apparently trivial matter was never discussed.

'How very interesting!'

'I made a packet of money in those days. At one time I was a driver on the old horse-buses ... You could see those animals dragging up Highgate Hill with their noses on the ground nearly. I bought an old mare off of them for a couple of quid, and turned her out on a bit of grass I used to rent. Time I'd fed her up and got her coat nice with dandelion leaves and clover, I sold her for twenty pounds. Everything I touched went right for me in those days. She was the one who kicked me on the head. Francie, we called her. I always wished I could tell the wife what the doctors said. If I'd have said to her: "You know, Florrie, what they hold Francie did to me all those years ago" she would never have believed me. But that's what they reckoned. Delayed action they reckoned it was.'

'Extraordinary!' Miss Wilcox murmured.

'Now, you old chatterbox!' Matron said. 'We're going to sing "Jerusalem", all together, before the girls go home. And none of your nonsense, Harry. He's such an old rascal about hymns, Miss Wilcox.'

Once, he had refused to join in, believing that hymn-singing was a matter of personal choice, and not *his* choice. Now, he knew that the blind are always religious, as they are cheerful, industrious and independent. He no longer argued, but stood up clumsily, feet apart, hands clasped over his paunch, and moved his lips feebly until the music stopped.

In the first weeks of his blindness, he had suffered attacks of hysteria, as wave upon wave of terror and frustration swept across him. 'Your language!' his sister would say, her hand checking the wheel of the sewing-machine. 'Why don't we go round to the Lion for a beer?' She would button up his overcoat for him, saying: 'I can't bear to see you fidgeting with your clothes.' When he had put on his old bowler-hat, they would go along the street arm-in-arm, 'Good-evening, Mrs Simpson. That was Mrs Simpson went by, Harry.' She used no tact or Montessori methods on him. In the pub, she would say: 'Mind out, you! Let Harry sit down. How would *you* like to be blind?' They were all glad to see him. They read out the winners and prices for him. He knew the scene so well that he had no need to look at it, and the sensation of panic would be eased from him.

Now a deeper despair showed him daily the real tragedy of his blindness. This orderly, aseptic world was not only new to him, but beyond his imagining. Food and talk had lost their richness: central-heating provided no warmth: he crouched over radiators with his hands spread over the pipes, his head aching with the dryness of the air. No one buttoned his coat for him. He tapped his way round with his stick, often hitting out viciously and swearing. 'There are ladies present,' he was told, and, indeed, this was so. They lowered the atmosphere with little jealousies and edged remarks and irritated with their arguments about birds ('I could not mistake a chaffinch's song, Mrs Hussey, being country-bred-and-born') or about Royalty ('But both Lady Mary and Lady May Cambridge were bridesmaids to the Duchess of York'). They always remembered 'as if it were yesterday', although begging pardon for contradicting. Morale was very high, as it so often is in a community where tragedy is present. Harry was reminded of the Blitz and Cockney resilience and understatement. Although a Cockney himself he detested understatement. Some Irish strain in him allowed his mind to dwell on the mournful, to spread alarm and despondency and to envisage with clarity the possibilities of defeat. When he confessed to fear, the Boys had relished the joke. 'That'll be the day!' they said. He found the burden of their morale very tiring. 'The war's bad enough in itself,' he had thought; as now he thought: 'Surely it's bad enough being blind,' when he was expected to sing hymns and alter all his ways as well.

After the concert, his luck seemed to change; at first, though, to deteriorate. The still, moist winter weather drew the other inmates out on walks about the village. Only Miss Arbuthnot remained indoors with a slight cold. In the end, the sense of nervousness and irritation she induced in Harry drove him out, too. He wandered alone, a little scared, down the drive and out on to the high road. He followed the brick wall along and turned with it into a narrower lane with a softer surface.

The hedges dripped with moisture although it was not raining. There was a resinous scent in the air which was all about that neighbourhood and pronounced healthy by Matron, who snuffed it up enthusiastically as if she were a war-horse smelling battle. Harry's tread was now muffled by pine-needles and once a fir-cone dropped on his shoulder, startling him wretchedly. Every sound in the hedgerow unnerved him: he imagined small, bright-eyed animals watching his progress. From not following the curve of the hedge sharply enough, he ran his face against wet hawthorn twigs. He felt giddiness, as if he were wandering in a circle. 'Bad enough being out by myself in the country, let alone being blind, too,' he thought, as he stumbled in a rut.

He could imagine Matron when he returned – if he returned – 'Why, Harry, you naughty old thing, going off like that! Why didn't you go with Mr Thomas, who knows the neighbourhood so well and could have told you the names of all the birds you heard, and made it nice and interesting!'

The only birds he, Harry, could recognise – and he did not wish to recognise any – were jackdaws (and they were really rooks), who seemed to congregate above him, throughout his walk, wheeling and cawing in an offensive manner; perhaps disputing over him, he thought morbidly; staking their claims before he dropped.

Then suddenly he lost hedge and ditch. He was treading on turf and the air had widened. He felt a great space about him and the wind blowing, as if he were on a sea-cliff, which he knew he could not be in Oxfordshire. With a sense of being confronted by an immense drop – a blind man's vertigo – he dared not take a pace forward, but stood swaying a little, near to tears. He heard rough breathing and a large dog jumped upon him. In terror, he thrashed about with his stick, the tears now pouring from his eyes which had no other function.

He heard a woman's voice calling and the squelch of the wet turf as she ran towards him across what he had imagined to be the middle of the air. She beat the dog away and took Harry's arm.

'You all right, dear? He's plastered you up properly, but it'll brush off when it's dry.'

'I don't know where I am,' Harry said, fumbling for his handkerchief.

'It's the common where the bus stops.' She pulled his handkerchief from his pocket and gave it to him. 'That's our bus over there.'

'You a conductress then?'

'That's right, dear. You're from that Home, are you? It's on the route and we can give you a lift.'

'I don't have any coppers on me.'

'You needn't worry about that. Just take my arm and we're nearly there. It's a scandal the way they let you wander about.'

'The others manage better nor I. I'm not one for the country. It always gives me the wind-up.'

At the gates of the Home she helped him down, saying: 'Any time, dear. Only too pleased. Take care of yourself. Bye-bye!'

No one had noticed his absence and he concealed his adventure. One of the daily cleaners, with whom he felt more confidence than with the resident staff, brushed his coat for him.

After this, the lane, which had held such terror, was his escape-route. The buses came every hour, and he would sometimes be waiting there; or the drivers would see him stumbling across the common and would sound the horn in welcome. Sitting in the bus before it drew out, he could enjoy the only normal conversation of his day.

'A shilling each way Flighty Frances! That's not much for a man of your substance, Harry.'

'It's just I fancy the name. I had an old mare of the name of Francie. Time was, no doubt, I'd have had a fiver on it. Now I'm left about as free of money as a toad of fleas.'

He would try to roll his own cigarettes, but tore the paper and spilt the tobacco, until the bus-drivers learnt to help him. In their company he opened out, became garrulous, waggish, his old manner returning. He came to know one from another and to call each by his name. Their camaraderie opened up to him garage gossip, feuds at the depot, a new language, a new life. His relationship with them was not one of equality, for they had too much to give, and he nothing. This he sensed and, while taking their badinage and imagining their winks, he played up his part – the lowering rôle of a proper old character – and extracted what he could from it, even to the extent of hinting and scrounging. His fumblings with his cigarette-making became more piteous than was necessary.

'Oh, for goodness' sake, have a proper cigarette ... messing about like that.'

'That's all I got the lolly for, mate.'

'Whose fault's that – if you've got to drink yourself silly every night.'

'I haven't had a pint since I come down here.'

'Well, where's your money gone to – wild living, I suppose? And women.'

'Now don't you start taking the mike out of me, Fred.' He used their names a great deal – the first pride he had felt since his blindness was in distinguishing Fred from Syd or Lil from Marg. The women had more individuality to him, with wider variety of inflection and vocabulary and tone; and the different scents of their powder and their hair.

'Supposing Flighty Frances comes in, what are you going to do with your winnings, Harry? Take us all out for a beer?'

'I'll do that,' he said. 'I forget the taste of it myself. I could do with a nice brown. It's the price of it, though, and how to find my way back afterwards, and all them old codgers sitting round fanning theirselves each time I free a belch. Very off-hand they can be with their ways.'

'What do you do all day?'

The driver felt a curiosity about a life so different from his own, imagined a work-house with old people groping about, arms extended, as if playing Blind Man's Buff.

'We have a nice listen to the wireless-set – a lot of music which I never liked the sound of anyway – and plays about sets of people carrying on as if they need their arses kicked. You never met a breed of people like these customers on the wireless; what they get into a rare consternation about is nobody's business. Then we might have some old army gent give a talk about abroad and the rum ways they get into over there, but personally I've got my own troubles so I lie back and get in a bit of shut-eye. The other night we had a wagon-load of virgins up there singing hymns.'

He played to the gallery, which repaid him with cigarettes and *bonhomie*. His repartee became so strained that sometimes he almost waited to hear Flo, his late wife, say sharply: 'That's enough now, Harry. It's about time we heard something from someone else.' He had always talked too much; was a bad listener; almost a non-listener, for he simply waited without patience for others to stop talking that he might cap their story. 'Well, hurry up, hurry up!' he would think. 'Get a move on with it, man. I got something to say myself on those lines. If you go drivelling on much longer, chances are I'll forget it.'

'No, what I'd do, say this horse comes in, bar the fact I'd only make about seven bob all told, but what I'd do is take the bus down to the fair on Saturday. I like a nice lively fair.'

'What, and have a go on the coco-nut shies?'

'I wouldn't mind, Fred,' he boasted.

'You can come along with me and Charlie, Saturday evening,' Fred said, adding with an ungraciousness he did not intend: 'Makes no odds to us.'

'Well, I don't know,' Harry said. 'Have to see what's fixed up for Saturday. I'll let you know tomorrow.'

'All right, Harry. We'll get one of the boys to pick you up at the gates Saturday after tea, and we can put you on the last bus along with all those coco-nuts you're going to knock down.'

They left him at the gates. He lifted his white stick in farewell and then walked up the drive, slashing out at the rhododendron-hedge and whistling shrilly. Now he was in for a spell of his old difficulty – currying favour. He would not have admitted to Fred that he could not come and go as he pleased, that for the rest of the day he must fawn on Matron and prepare his request. This he overdid, as a child would, arousing suspicion. He lowered himself in his own eyes by praising the minced meat and going into ecstasies over the prunes and custard. His unctuous voice was a deep abasement to him and an insult to Matron's intelligence. 'My, that's what I call a meal, quite a pre-war touch about it. Now, say I have another go at that basket-work, ma'am?'

'What are you up to today, Harry?'

'Me?'

'Yes, you.'

Later, the wind drove gusts of fair-music up the hill. Miss Arbuthnot complained; but Harry could not hear it. Missing so much that the others heard was an added worry to him lately; for to lose hearing as well would finish him as a person, and leave him at the mercy of his own thoughts which had always bored him. His tongue did his thinking for him: other people's talk struck words from him like a light from a match; his phrases were quick and ready-made and soon forgotten; but he feared a silence and they filled it.

Matron found him alone, after the basket-making class was over. He was involved in a great tangle of withies. His enormous hands engrained with dirt looked so ill-adapted to the task that Matron, stringent as she was about the difficulties of others, found them wretchedly pathetic. So few men of action came her way; the burly, the ham-handed ended up in other backwaters she supposed, with gout and dropsy and high blood-pressure. She felt, as Harry himself felt, that he was not the type. He was certainly ill-matched to his present task of managing the intractable, and even dangerous, tangle of cane.

'When is your birthday, Harry?' she asked; for she was interested in astrology and quite surprised how many Cancer subjects came her way.

'April the twenty-first. Why?'

'Taurus the Bull,' she said.

He began to bristle indignantly, then remembered his purpose and bent his head humbly, a poor broken bull with a lance in his neck.

'You mean,' some instinct led him to say, 'I'm like a bull in a china shop?'

Her contrition was a miracle. He listened to her hurried explanations with a glow in his heart.

'I only thought you meant I was clumsy about the place,' he said. 'I don't seem to cotton-on to half what the others say and I keep spilling my dinner.'

'But, Harry ...'

'I've had my sight longer than them, and it takes more getting used to doing without it,' he went on, and might have been inspired. 'When you've been lucky to have your eyes so long as me, it takes some settling to.'

'You've still got yours,' hung in the air. He managed to insinuate the idea
and seem innocent of the thought; but he had lost his innocence and was
as cagey as a child. His late wife would have said: 'All right, you can come
off it now, Harry.' Matron said: 'We only want to make you happy, you
know; though sometimes you're such an old reprobate.'

After that, he had to endure the impatience of being coaxed to do what
he desired, and coquetry was not in his line. He became unsure of himself
and the trend of the conversation, and with a Cockney adroitness let the
idea of the fair simmer in Matron's mind, undisturbed. Busy again with his
basket-work, he let one of the osiers snap back and hit him across the face.
'I'm no spoil-sport, Harry,' she said. This daunted him; in all his life he had
found that sport was spoiled by those who claimed this to be their last
intention. He awaited all the rest of the phrases – 'I should hate to be a wet
blanket', and 'Goodness knows I don't want to criticise'. In his agitation,
he took up the picking-knife to cut an end of cane and cut into the pad of
his thumb. At first, he felt no pain; but the neatness with which the blade
divided his flesh alarmed him. He missed his sight when he needed to feel
pain. Blood, crawling between his thumb and fingers, put him into a panic
and he imagined the bone laid bare, and his head swam. Pain, coming
through slowly, reassured him more than Matron could.

For the rest of the evening, he sat alone in his corner by the radiator,
and the steady throbbing of his bandaged thumb kept him company, mixed
as it was – and, no doubt, in Matron's mind too – with the promise of the
fair. 'I should insist on their bringing you back,' she had said. 'There's the
rough element to contend with on a Saturday night.' In other years he had
been – proudly – a large part of the rough element himself.

After supper, Miss Arbuthnot too, reminded by the distant sounds of the
roundabouts, began to discuss the rough element – which, in her experience, as in all her experiences, was exaggerated beyond anything Harry had
ever known. Spinster-like, she described a teeming, Hogarthian scene of
pick-pockets, drunkards and what she called, contradictorily, 'undesirable
women'. 'Oh, once, I dare say, these fairs were very picturesque ... the may-
poles and the Morris-dancing; and so vividly I remember the colourful
peasants I saw at the fair at Nidjni Novgorod ... such beautiful embroidery.
But now, what is there left of such a life? So drearily commercial as all our
pleasures are.'

She drove their inclinations into the corral: now no one cared to go to
the fair; except Harry, worldly-wise, crouched over his radiator, nursing his
poor hand, with his own inner vision still intact.

In the Home there was an aristocracy, never – from decency – mentioned, of those who had once, and even perhaps recently, seen, over those
blind from birth. The aristocracy claimed no more than the privilege of

kindness and of tact and was tempered by the deftness and efficiency of those who had had longest to adapt themselves. Miss Arbuthnot, blinded, Harry imagined, by her own needlework, was the eyes of them all: for she had great inventiveness and authority and could touch up a scene with the skill of an artist. Harry, finding her vision unacceptable, had nothing of his own to take its place; only the pigheaded reiteration 'It isn't like that' – the fair, the races, the saloon bar.

'I used to like a roundabout when I was a girl,' Mrs Hussey said timidly.

'Well, there you have it!' said Miss Arbuthnot. 'All we have salvaged of the picturesque. The last of a traditional art, in fact. For instance, the carved horses with their bright designs.'

'It was going round, I liked,' Mrs Hussey said.

With a tug, as of a flag unfurling, an old memory spread out across Harry's mind. He recalled himself as a boy, coming home from school with one of his friends, along the banks of a canal. It was growing dark. His child's eyes had recorded the scene, which his busy life had overlaid and preserved: now, unexpectedly laid bare, it was more vivid than anything he had witnessed since. Sensually, he evoked the magic of that time of day, with the earth about to heel over into darkness; the canal steaming faintly; cranes at a menacing angle across the sky. He and the other boy walked in single file, on the muddy path which was hoof-printed by barge-horses. The tufted grass on each side was untidy and hoary with moisture; reeds, at the water's edge, lisped together. Now, in his mind, he followed this path with a painful intensity, fearing an interruption. Almost slyly, he tracked down the boy he had been, who, exposed like a lens, unconsciously took the imprint of the moment and the place. Now, outside the scene, as if a third person, he walked behind the boys along the path; saw one, then the other, stoop and pick up a stone and skim it across the water. Without speaking, they climbed on the stacks of planks when they came to a timber-yard. The air had seemed to brace itself against distant thunder. The canal's surface wrinkled in a sudden breeze, then drops of rain spread rings upon it. The boys, trying the door of a long shed, found it unlocked and crept inside to shelter, wiping their wet hands down their trousers. Rain drove against the windows in a flurry and the thunder came nearer. They stood close to one another just inside the door. The shapes which filled the shed, set out so neatly in rows, became recognisable after a while as roundabout horses, newly carved and as yet unpainted. Harry moved among them, ran his hand down their smooth backs, and breathed the smell of the wood. They were drawn up in ranks, pale and strange horses, awaiting their trappings and decorations and flowing tails.

The two boys spoke softly to one another; their voices muted – for the wood-shavings and the sawdust, which lay everywhere like snow, had a muffling effect: nervousness filled them. Harry forced himself to stare at the horses as if to hypnotise them, to check them rearing and bearing down; and became convinced of their hostility. Moving his eyes watchfully, he was always just too late to see a nostril quiver or a head turn; though feeling that this happened.

The rain fell into the timber-yard as if the sky had collapsed, drumming upon the roof of the shed and hissing into the canal. It was dark now, and they thought of their homes. When the horses were swallowed by shadows, the boys were too afraid to speak and strained their ears for the sound of a movement. Lightning broke across the shed, and the creatures seemed to rear up from the darkness, and all their eyes flashed glassily.

The boys, pelting along the footpath, slipping in the squelching mud, their wet fringes plastered to their foreheads, began after a while to feel their fear recede. The canal was covered with bubbles, sucked at the banks and swirled into rat-holes. Beyond the allotments was the first street-lamp, and the boys leant against it to take a deep breath and to wipe the rain from their faces. 'That was only their glass eyes,' Harry had said; and there, under the lamp-post, the memory ended. He could not pursue himself home; but was obliged to take leave of his boyhood there – the child holding his wet jacket across his chest. The evening was lying vaguely before him, with perhaps a box on the ears from Lottie Throstle, for getting his books wet; or had she fetched the tin-bath in from the wall in the yard and let him soak his feet in mustard-water? She had had her moods and they defeated his memory.

Miss Arbuthnot was still talking of traditional art and craftsmanship and, rather to her vexation, was upheld in her views by the piano-tuner.

Harry leant sleepily against the radiator, tired from the mental strain of recollection – that patient stalking of his boyhood, tiring to one who had never dwelt on the past or reconsidered a scene. The intensity of the experience was so new to him that he was dazed by it; enriched; and awed by the idea of more treasure lying idle and at his disposal.

That night, nursing his throbbing hand to his chest, the pain easing him by giving a different focus to his distress, he slept his first deep and unbroken sleep since his sister's death.

On Saturday, as it grew dark, he waited for the bus at the top of the drive. His bowler hat was tilted forward, as if to match his feeling of jaunty anticipation; his scarf was tucked into his coat. Muffled-up, stooping, with his head thrust from side to side, his reddened, screwed-up eyes turned upwards, he looked like a great tortoise balancing on its hind legs – and one burdened by the extra carapace of blindness.

At tea, he had excited envy in some of the inmates when he at last overcame superstition enough to mention the fair. Miss Arbuthnot had doubled her scorn, but felt herself up against curiosity and surprise and the beginning of a reassessment, in most of their minds, of Harry's character. He had left behind a little stir of conjecture.

He heard the bus coming down the lane and stood ready, his stick raised, to hail it. The unseen headlights spread out, silhouetting him.

'You been hurting your hand?' the conductress asked, helping him into a seat.

'I just cut it. Is that old Fred up in front?'

'No, that's Evan. Fred's been on a different route, but he said to tell you he'd be waiting for you at the depot along with Jock and Charlie.'

Fred's heart sank when he saw Harry climbing down from the bus and smiling like a child. Saddling his friends with the old geezer for an evening was too much of a responsibility, and constraint and false heartiness marked the beginning of the outing. He had explained and apologised over and over again for the impulse which had brought Harry into the party.

'Why, that's all right, Fred,' they had assured him.

He thought that a beer or two at the Wheatsheaf would make them feel better; but Harry, after so much enforced abstinence, found the drink go to his head with swift effect; became boastful, swaggering; invited laughter and threw in a few coarse jests for good measure. Sitting by the fire, his coat trailing about him, he looked a shocking old character, Fred thought. The beer dripped on to his knees; his waistcoat bulged above the straining fly-buttons, looped with the tarnished chain of a watch he kept winding and holding to his ear although he could no longer read it. Every so often he knocked his bowler-hat straight with his stick – a slick, music-hall gesture. Cocky and garrulous, he attracted attention from those not yet tired of his behaviour or responsible for it, as Fred was. They offered cigarettes and more drink. When at last he was persuaded to go, he lurched into a table, slopping beer from glasses.

Down the wide main street the fair booths were set out. Their lights spread upwards through the yellowing leaves of the trees. The tunes of competing roundabouts engulfed them in a confusion of sound. They stopped at a stall for a plateful of whelks and were joined by another bus-driver and his wife, whose shrill, peacock laughter flew out above all the other sounds.

'How are you keeping, Harry?' she asked. She was eating some pink candy-floss on a stick, and her lips and the inside of her mouth were crimson from it. Harry could smell the sickly, raspberry smell of her breath.

'Quite nicely, thanks. I had a bit of a cold, but I can't complain.'

'Ever such a lot of colds about,' she said vaguely.

'And lately I seem to be troubled with my hearing.' He could not forgo this chance to talk of himself.

'Well, never mind. Can't have it all ways, I suppose.'

'*He* doesn't have it many ways,' Fred thought.

'You ought to take me through the Haunted House, you know, Harry. I can't get anyone else to.'

'You don't want to go along with an old codger like me.'

'I wouldn't trust him in the dark, Vi,' Fred said.

'I'll risk it.'

She sensed his apprehension as they turned towards the sideshow. From behind the canvas façade with its painted skeletons came the sound of wheels running on a track, and spasms of wild laughter. Harry tripped over a cable and she took his arm. 'You're a real old sport,' she told him. She paid at the entrance and helped him into a little car like a toast-rack. They sat close together. She finished her candy, threw away the stick and began to lick her fingers. 'I've got good care of you,' she said. 'It's only a bit of kids' fun.'

The car started forward, jolting at sharp bends, where sheeted ghosts leant over them and luminous skulls shone in the darkness. Vi out-laughed everyone, screaming into Harry's ear and gripping his arm with both hands.

'It isn't much for *you*,' she gasped sympathetically at each horrific sight; but the jerking, the swift running-on, the narrow – he guessed – avoidance of unseen obstacles, had made him tremble. The close smell was frightening and when, as part of the macabre adventure, synthetic cobwebs trailed over his face and bony fingers touched his shoulder, he ducked his head fearfully.

'Well, you are an old baby,' Vi said.

They came out into the light and the crowds again, and she put up her raspberry lips and kissed his cheek.

Her behaviour troubled him. She seemed to rehearse flirtatiousness with him for its own sake – unless it were to excite her audience. She expected no consequence from her coquetry, as if his blindness had made him less than a man. Her husband rarely spoke and never to her, and Harry could not see his indifferent look.

With ostentatious care, Vi guided him through the crowds, her arm in his, so closely that he could feel her bosom against his elbow. He was tired now; physically, and with the strain of being at everybody's mercy and of trying to take his colour from other people. His senses, with their extra burden, were fatigued. The braying music cuffed his ears until he longed to clap his hands over them: his uncertain stumblings had made his step drag; drifting smells began to nauseate him – shell-fish, petrol and Vi's raspberry breath.

At the coco-nut shy, she was shriller than ever. She stood inside the net, over the ladies' line, and screamed each time she missed, and, in piteous baby-talk, when a coco-nut rocked and did not fall, accused the proprietor of trickery.

Her husband had walked on, yawning, heedless of her importunities – for she *had* to have a coco-nut, just as she had *had* to have her fortune told and her turn on the swing-boats. Jock and Charlie followed, and they were lost in the crowd. Fred stayed and watched Vi's anger growing. When he knocked down a coco-nut, she claimed it at once as a trophy. She liked to leave a fair laden with such tributes to her sexual prowess.

'Well, it's just too bad,' Fred said, 'because I'm taking it home to my wife.'

'You're mean. Isn't he mean, Harry?'

Fred, coming closer to her, said softly as he held the coco-nut to his ear and rattled the milk: 'You can have it on one condition.'

'What's that?'

'You guess,' he said.

She turned her head quickly. 'Harry, you'll get a coco-nut for me, won't you?'

She ran her hands up under the lapels of his coat in a film-actressy way and rearranged his scarf.

'That's right, Harry,' Fred said. 'You told me the other day you were going to have a try. You can't do worse than Vi.' Her fury relaxed him. He threw the coco-nut from one hand to the other and whistled softly, watching her.

Harry was aware that he was being put to some use; but the childish smile he had worn all the evening did not change: it expressed anxiety and the hope to please. Only by pleasing could he live; by complying – as clown, as eunuch – he earned the scraps and shreds they threw to him, the odds and ends left over from their everyday life.

Fred and Vi filled his arms with the wooden balls and led him to the front of the booth. Vi took his stick and stepped back. Someone behind her whispered: 'He's blind. How dreadful!' and she turned and said: 'Real spry old character, isn't he?' in a proprietary voice. More people pressed up to watch, murmuring sympathetically.

'Aim straight ahead,' Fred was saying, and the man in charge was adding his advice. Harry's smile wrinkled up his face and his scarred-looking eyes. 'How's that?' he cried, flinging his arm up violently. The crowd encouraged him, desperately anxious that he should be successful. He threw again.

Fred stepped back, close to Vi, who avoided his glance. Staring ahead, still whistling, he put his hand out and gripped her wrist. She turned her arm furiously, but no one noticed.

'You've been asking for something all the evening, haven't you?' he asked her in a light conversational tone. 'One of these days you're going to get it, see? That's right, Harry!' he shouted. 'That was a near one! Proper old character. You can't help admiring him.'

Vi's hand was still. She looked coolly in front of her; but he could sense a change of pulse, an excitement in her; and almost nodded to himself when she began to twist her fingers in his, with a vicious lasciviousness he had foreseen.

A cheer went up as Harry went near to his target. 'Next round on the house,' the owner said. Harry's smile changed to a desperate grin. His bowler-hat was crooked, and all of his movements were impeded by his heavy overcoat. Noise shifted and roared round him until he felt giddy and began to sweat.

Insanely, the roundabout horses rose and plunged, as if spurred on by the music and the lateness of the hour; sparks spluttered from the electric cars. Above the trees, the sky was bruised with a reddish stain, a polluted light, like a miasma given off by the fair.

The rough good-will of the crowd went to Harry's head, and he began to clown and boast as if he were drunk. Fred and Vi seemed to have vanished. Their voices were lost. He could hear only the roundabout and the thud of the wooden balls as he threw them against the canvas screen, and he feared the moment when his act was over and he must turn, empty-handed, hoping to be claimed.

First Death of Her Life

Suddenly tears poured from her eyes. She rested her forehead against her mother's hand, and let the tears soak into the counterpane.

'Dear Mr Wilson,' she began, for her mind was always composing letters, 'I shall not be at the shop for the next four days, as my mother has passed away and I shall not be available until after the funeral. My mother passed away very peacefully ... '

The nurse came in. She took her patient's wrist for a moment, replaced it, removed a jar of forced lilac from beside the bed as if this were no longer necessary and went out again.

The girl kneeling by the bed had looked up.

'Dear Mr Wilson,' she resumed, her face returning to the counterpane, 'My mother has died. I shall come back to work the day after tomorrow. Yours sincerely, Lucy Mayhew.'

Her father was late. She imagined him hurrying from work, bicycling through the darkening streets, dogged, hunched-up, slush thrown up by his wheels. Her mother did not move. She stroked her hand with its loose gold ring, the calloused palms, the fine, long fingers. Then she stood up stiffly, her knees bruised from the waxed floor, and went to the window.

Snowflakes turned idly, drifting down over the hospital gardens. It was four o'clock in the afternoon and already the day seemed over. So few sounds came from this muffled and discoloured world. In the hospital itself there was a deep silence.

Her thoughts came to her in words, as if her mind spoke them first, understood them later. She tried to think of her childhood: little scenes, she selected, to prove how they had loved one another. Other scenes, especially last week's quarrel, she chose to forget, not knowing that in this moment she sent them away for ever. Only loving-kindness remained.

But, all the same, intolerable pictures broke through – her mother at the sink; her mother ironing; her mother standing between the lace curtains staring out at the dreary street with a wounded look in her eyes; her mother tying the same lace curtains with yellow ribbons; attempts at lightness, gaiety, which came to nothing; her mother gathering her huge black cat to her, burying her face in its fur and a great shivering sigh – of despair, of boredom – escaping her.

She no longer sighed. She lay very still and sometimes took a little sip of air. Her arms were neatly at her side. Her eyes, which all day long had been turned to the white lilac, were closed. Her cheekbone rose sharply from her bruised, exhausted face. She smelt faintly of wine.

A small lilac-flower floated on a glass of champagne, now discarded on the table at her side.

The champagne, with which they hoped to stretch out the thread of her life minute by minute; the lilac; the room of her own, coming to her at the end of a life of drabness and denial, just as, all along the mean street where they lived, the dying and the dead might claim a life-time's savings from the bereaved.

'She is no longer there,' Lucy thought, standing beside the bed.

All day her mother had stared at the white lilac; now she had sunk away. Outside, beyond the hospital gardens, mist settled over the town, blurred the street-lamps.

The nurse returned with the matron. Ready to be on her best behaviour, Lucy tautened. In her heart she trusted her mother to die without frightening her, and when the matron, deftly drawing Lucy's head to rest on her own shoulder, said in her calm voice: 'She has gone,' she felt she had met this happening half-way.

A little bustle began, quick footsteps along the empty passages, and for a moment she was left alone with her dead mother. She laid her hand timidly on her soft dark hair, so often touched, played with when she was a little girl, standing on a stool behind her mother's chair while she sewed.

There was still the smell of wine and the hospital smell. It was growing dark in the room. She went to the dressing-table and took her mother's handbag, very worn and shiny, and a book, a library book which she had chosen carefully for her, believing she would read it.

Then she had a quick sip from the glass on the table, a mouthful of champagne, which she had never tasted before, and, looking wounded and aloof, walked down the middle of the corridor, feeling the nurses falling away to left and right.

Opening the glass doors on to the snowy gardens, she thought that it was like the end of a film. But no music rose up and engulfed her. Instead there was her father turning in at the gates. He propped his bicycle against the wall and began to run clumsily across the wet gravel.

Gravement Endommagé

The car devoured the road, but the lines of poplars were without end. The shadow of sagging telegraph wires scalloped the middle of the road, the vaguer shadows of the pretty telegraph posts pleased Louise. They were essentially French, she thought – like, perhaps, lilies of the valley: spare, neatly budded.

The poplars dwindled at intervals and gave place to ruined buildings and pock-marked walls; a landscape of broken stone, faded Dubonnet advertisements. Afterwards, the trees began again.

When they came to a town, the cobblestones, laid fan-wise, slowed up the driving. Outside cafés, the chairs were all empty. Plane trees in the squares half-hid the flaking walls of houses with crooked jalousies and frail balconies, like twisted bird-cages. All had slipped, subsided.

'But it is so *dead!*' Louise complained, wanting to get to Paris, to take out from her cases her crumpled frocks, shake them out, hang them up. She dreamt of that; she had clung to the idea across the Channel. Because she was sick before the boat moved, Richard thought she was sick deliberately, as a form of revenge. But seasickness ran in her family. Her mother had always been prostrated immediately – as soon (as she so often had said) as her foot touched the deck. It would have seemed an insult to her mother's memory for Louise not to have worked herself up into a queasy panic at the very beginning. Richard, seeing walls sliding past port-holes and then sky, finished his drink quickly and went up on deck. Hardier women than Louise leant over the rails, their scarves flapping, watching the coast of France come up. The strong air had made him hungry, but when they had driven away from the harbour and had stopped for luncheon, Louise would only sip brandy, looking away from his plate.

'But we can never get to Paris by dinner-time,' he said, when they were in the car again. 'Especially driving on the wrong side of the road all the way.'

'There is nowhere between here and there,' she said with authority. 'And I want to *settle*.'

He knew her 'settling'. Photographs of the children spread about, champagne sent up, maids running down corridors with her frocks on their arms,

powder spilt everywhere, the bathroom full of bottles and jars. He would
have to sit down to telephone a list of names. Her friends would come in
for drinks. They would have done better, so far as he could see, to have
stayed in London.

'But if we are pushed for time ... Why kill ourselves? ... After all, this
is a holiday ... I do remember ... There is a place I stayed at that time ...
When I first knew you ...' Only parts of what he said reached her. The rest
was blown away.

'You are deliberately going slow,' she said.

'I think more of my car than to drive it fast along these roads.'

'You think more of your car than of your wife.'

He had no answer. He could not say that at least his car never betrayed
him, let him down, embarrassed him, because it constantly did and might
again at any moment.

'You planned this delay without consulting me. You planned to spend
this night in some god-forsaken place and sink into your private nostalgia
while my frocks crease and crease ...' Her voice mounted up like a wave,
trembled, broke.

The holiday was really to set things to rights between them. Lately, trivial bickering had hardened into direct animosity. Relatives put this down
to, on his part, overwork, and, on hers, fatigue from the war, during which
she had lived, after their London house was bombed, in a remote village
with the children. She had nothing to say of those years but that they were
not funny. She clung to the children and they to her. He was not, as he
said – at first indulgently but more lately with irritation – in the picture.
She knit them closer and closer to her, and he was quite excluded. He tried
to understand that there must be, after the war, much that was new in her,
after so long a gap, one that she would not fill up for him, or discuss. A new
quirk was her preoccupation with fashion. To her, it was a race in which
she must be first, so she looked *outré* always, never normal. If any of her
friends struck a new note before her, she by-passed and cancelled out that
particular foible. Men never liked her clothes, and women only admired
them. She did not dress for men. Years of almost exclusively feminine society had set up cold antagonisms. Yes, hardship had made her superficial,
icily frivolous. For one thing, she now must never be alone. She drank too
much. In the night, he knew, she turned and turned, sighing in her sleep,
dreaming bad dreams, wherein she could no longer choose her company.
When he made love to her, she recoiled in astonishment, as if she could
not believe such things could happen.

He had once thought she would be so happy to leave the village, that
by comparison her life in London after the war would seem wonderful. But
boredom had made her carping, fidgety. Instead of being thankful for what

she had, she complained at the slightest discomfort. She raised her standards above what they had ever been; drove maids, who needed little driving, to give notice; was harried, piteous, unrelaxed. Although she was known as a wonderful hostess, guests wonderfully enjoying themselves felt – they could not say why – wary, and listened, as if for a creaking of ice beneath their gaiety.

Her doctor, advising the holiday, was only conventional in his optimism. If anyone were benefited by it, it would be the children, stopping at home with their grandmother – for a while, out of the arena. What Richard needed was a holiday away from Louise, and what Louise needed was a holiday from herself, from the very thing she must always take along, the dull carapace of her own dissatisfaction, her chronic unsunniness.

The drive seemed endless, because it was so monotonous. War had exhaled a vapour of despair over all the scene. Grass grew over grief, trying to hide collapse, to cover some of the wounds. One generation hoped to contend with the failure of another.

Late in the afternoon, they came to a town he remembered. The small cathedral stood like torn lacework against the sky. Birds settled in rows on the empty windows. Nettles grew in the aisle, and stone figures, impaled on rusty spikes of wire, were crumbling away.

But it looks too old a piece of wreckage, he thought. That must be the war before last. Two generations, ruined, lay side by side. Among them, people went on bicycles, to and fro, between the improvised shops and scarred dwellings.

'After wars, when there is so little time for patching up before the next explosion, what hope is there?' he began.

She didn't answer, stared out of the window, the car jolting so that her teeth chattered.

When Richard was alone in the hotel bedroom, he tried, by spreading about some of Louise's belongings, to make the place seem less temporary. He felt guilty at having had his own way, at keeping her from Paris until the next day and delaying her in this dismal place. It was destined to be, so far as they were concerned, one of those provincial backgrounds, fleeting, meaningless, that travellers erase from experience – the different hotel rooms run together to form one room, this room, any room.

When he had put the pink jars and bottles out in a row above the hand basin, he became dubious. She would perhaps sweep them all back into her case, saying, 'Why unpack before we reach Paris?' and he would find that he had worsened the situation, after all, as he so often did, meaning to better it.

His one piece of selfishness – this halt on the way – she had stubbornly resisted, and now she had gone off to buy picture-postcards for the children, as if no one would think of them if she did not.

Because he often wondered how she looked when he was not there, if her face ever smoothed, he went to the window, hoping to see her coming down the little street. He wanted to catch in advance, to be prepared for, her mood. But she was not moody nowadays. A dreadful consistency discoloured her behaviour.

He pulled the shutters apart and was faced with a waste of fallen masonry, worse now that it was seen from above, and unrecognisable. The humped-up, dark cathedral stood in an untidy space, as if the little shops and cafés he remembered had receded in awe. Dust flowed along the streets, spilling from ruined walls across pavements. Rusty grasses covered debris and everywhere the air was unclean with grit. Dust, he thought, leaning on the iron rail above window-boxes full of shepherd's-purse – dust has the connotation of despair. In the end, shall we go up in a great swirl of it? He imagined something like the moon's surface, pock-marked, cratered, dry, deserted. When he was young, he had not despaired. Then, autumn leaves, not dust, had blown about these streets; chimes dropped like water, uneven, inconsequential, over rooftops; and the lime trees yellowed along neat boulevards. Yet, in the entrancement of nostalgia, he remembered, at best, an imperfect happiness and, for the most part, an agony of conjecture and expectancy. Crossing the vestibule of this very hotel, he had turned; his eyes had always sought the letter-rack. The Channel lay between him and his love, who with her timid smile, her mild grimace, had moaned that she could not put pen to paper, was illiterate, never had news; though loving him inordinately, could not spell, never had postage stamps; her ink dried as it approached the page; her parents interrupted. Yes, she had loved him to excess but had seldom written, and now went off in the dust and squalor for picture-postcards for their children.

At the window, waiting for her to appear, he felt that the dust and destruction had pinned down his courage. Day after day had left its residue, sifting down through him – cynicism and despair. He wondered what damage he had wreaked upon her.

Across the street, which once had been narrow and now was open to the sky, a nun went slowly, carrying bread under her arm. The wind plucked her veil. A thin cat followed her. They picked their way across the rubble. The cat stopped once and lifted a paw, licked it carefully, and put it back into the grit. The faint sound of trowel on stone rang out, desultory, hopeless, a frail weapon against so convincing a destruction. That piteous tap, tap turned him away from the window. He could not bear the futility of the sound, or the thought of the monstrous task ahead, and now feared, more than all he could imagine, the sight of his wife hurrying back down the street, frowning, the picture-postcards in her hand.

Louise was late. Richard sat drinking Pernod at a table in the bar where he could see her come into the hotel. There was only the barman to talk to. Rather clouded with drink, Richard leant on his elbow, describing the town as it had been. The barman, who was Australian, knew only too well. After the '14–'18 war, he had put his savings into a small café across the road. 'I knew it,' Richard said eagerly, forgetting the lacuna in both years and buildings, the gap over which the nun, the cat had picked their way.

'I'll get the compensation some day,' the Australian said, wiping the bar. 'Start again. Something different.'

When a waiter came for drinks, the barman spoke in slow but confident French, probably different from an Englishman's French, Richard thought, though he could not be sure; a Frenchman would know.

'She gets later and later,' he said solemnly.

'Well, if she doesn't come, that's what she's bound to do,' the barman agreed.

'It was a shock to me, the damage to this town.'

'Twelve months ago, you ought to have seen it,' the barman said.

'That's the human characteristic – patience, building up.'

'You might say the same of ants.'

'Making from something nothing,' Richard said. 'I'll take another Pernod.'

The ringing sound of the trowel was in his ears. He saw plodding humanity piling up the bricks again, hanging sacking over the empty windows, temporising, camping-out in the shadow of even greater disaster, raking ashes, the vision lost. He felt terribly sorry for humanity, as if he did not belong to it. The Pernod shifted him away and made him solitary. Then he thought of Louise and that he must go to look for her. Sometimes she punished him by staying away unaccountably, but knowing that did not lessen his anxiety. He wished that they were at peace together, that the war between them might be over for ever, for if he did not have her, he did not have all he had yearned for; steadied himself with, fighting in the jungle; holding fast, for her, to life; disavowing (with terrible concentration) any danger to her.

He wondered, watching the barman's placid polishing of another man's glasses, if they could begin again, he and Louise, with nothing, from scratch, abandoning the past.

'First I must find her,' he thought. His drinking would double her fury if she had been lingering to punish him, punishing herself with enforced idling in those unfestive streets; a little scared, he imagined; hesitantly casual.

She came as he was putting a foot unsteadily to the floor. She stood at the door with an unexpectant look. When he smiled and greeted her, she tried to give two different smiles at once – one for the barman to see (controlled, marital), the other less a smile than a negation of it ('I see nothing to smile about').

'Darling, what will you have?'

She surveyed the row of bottles hesitantly, but her hesitation was for the barman's benefit. Richard knew her pause meant an unwillingness to drink in such company, in such a mood, and that in a minute she would say 'A dry Martini', because once he had told her she should not drink gin abroad. She sat down beside him in silence.

'A nice dry Martini?' he suddenly asked, thinking of the man with the trowel, the nun with the bread, the battered cathedral, everybody's poor start. Again she tried to convey two meanings; to the barman that she was casual about her Martini, to her husband that she was casual about him.

Richard's head was swimming. He patted his wife's knee.

'Did you get the postcards all right?'

'Of course.' Her glance brushed his hand off her knee.

'Cheers!' She held her glass at half-mast very briefly, spoke in the most annulling way, drank. Those deep lines from her nose to her mouth met the glass.

'Cheers, my darling!' he said, watching her. Her annoyance froze the silence.

Oh, from the most unpromising material, he thought, but he did seem to see some glimmer ahead, if only of his own patience, his own perseverance, which appeared, in this frame of mind, in this place, a small demand upon him.

The Idea of Age

When I was a child, people's ages did not matter; but age mattered. Against the serious idea of age I did not match the grown-ups I knew – who had all an ageless quality – though time unspun itself from year to year. Christmases lay far apart from one another, birthdays even farther; but that time was running on was shown in many ways. I 'shot out' of my frocks, as my mother put it. By the time that I was ten, I had begun to discard things from my heart and to fasten my attention on certain people whose personalities affected me in a heady and delicious way.

Though the years drew me upwards at a great pace, as if they were full of a hurried, *growing* warmth, the seasons still held. Summers netted me in bliss, endlessly. Winter did not promise spring. But when the spring came, I felt that it was there for ever. I had no dread that a few days would filch it from me, and in fact a few days were much when every day was endless.

In the summer holidays, when we went to the country, the spell of the long August days was coloured, intensified, by the fascinations of Mrs Vivaldi. My first thought when we arrived at the guest-house in Buckinghamshire was to look for some sign of *her* arrival – a garden hat hanging in the porch, or books from Mudie's. She came there, she made it clear, to rusticate (a word she herself used, which put a little flushed constraint upon the ladies who kept the guest-house, who felt it to be derogatory); she came to rest from the demands of London; and she did seem to be always very tired.

I remember so many of the clothes she wore, for they seemed to me unusual and beautiful. A large hat of coarse hessian sacking was surprisingly lined under the brim with gold lamé, which threw a light over her pale face. In the evenings, panels heavy with steel-bead embroidery swung away from her as she walked. She was not content to appeal only to one's sight, with her floating scarves, her fringes and tassels, but made claims upon the other senses, with scents of carnations and jasmine, with the rustling of moiré petticoats and the more solid sound of heavy amber and ivory bracelets sliding together on her wrists. Once, when we were sitting in the garden on a still afternoon, she narrowed her hand and wriggled it out of the bracelets and tried them on me. They were warm and heavy, alive like flesh. I felt this to be one of the situations I would enjoy in retrospect but find unendurable at the time. Embarrassed, inadequate, I turned the bracelets on my arm; but she had closed her eyes in the sun.

I realise now that she was not very young. Her pretty ash-blond hair had begun to have less blond, more ash; her powdered-over face was lined. Then I did not think of her as being any age. I drifted after her about house and garden, beset by her magic, endeavouring to make my mark on her.

One evening in the drawing-room she recited, for the guests, the Balcony Scene from *Romeo and Juliet* – all three parts – sitting on the end of the sofa, with her pearls laced through her fingers, her bronze shoes with pointed toes neatly together. Another evening, in that same room, she turned on the wireless and fixed the headphones over my ears (pieces of sponge lessened the pressure), and very far off, through a tinkling, scuffling, crackling atmosphere, I heard Edith Sitwell reciting through a megaphone. Mrs Vivaldi impressed me with the historical nature of the occasion. She made historical occasions seem very rare and to be fastened on to. Since then, life has been one historical occasion after another, but I remember that scene clearly and the lamplight in the room with all the beautiful china. The two ladies who kept the guest-house had come down in the world and brought cupboards full of Crown Derby with them. The wireless-set, with its coils and wires, was on a mosaic-topped table that, one day, my brother stumbled against and broke. It disintegrated almost into powder, and my mother wept. Mrs Vivaldi walked with her in the garden. I saw them going under the rose-arches – the fair head and the dark – both very tall. I thought they looked like ladies in a book by Miss Braddon.

One afternoon I was alone in the drawing-room when Mrs Vivaldi came in from the garden with a basketful of sweet-peas. As if the heat were suddenly too much for her, she sat down quite upright, in a chair, with the basket beside her, and closed her eyes.

The room was cool and shadowy, with blinds half-drawn to spare the threadbare carpet. The house seemed like a hollow shell; its subfusc life had flowed out into the garden, to the croquet lawn, to the shade of the mulberry tree, where elderly shapes sagged in deck chairs, half-covered with newspapers.

I knew that Mrs Vivaldi had not seen me. I was reading, sitting in my ungainly way on the floor, with my body slewed round so that my elbows and my book rested on the seat of a chair. Down there among the legs of furniture, I seemed only part of the overcrowded room. As I read, I ate sweets out of a rather grubby paper bag. Nothing could, I felt, have been more peaceful than that afternoon. The clock ticked, sweets dissolved in my cheek. The scent of the flowers Mrs Vivaldi had brought in began to mix with the clove smell of pinks outside. From the lawn came only an occasional grim word or two – the word 'partner' most of all, in tones of exhortation or apology – and the solid sound of the mallet on the ball. The last smells of luncheon had faded, and the last distant clatter of washing-up. Alone in the room with Mrs Vivaldi, I enjoyed the drowsy afternoon with every sense and also with peaceful feelings of devotion. I liked to be there while she slept. I had her presence without needing to make her love me, which was tiring.

Her presence must have been enough, for I remember that I sat with my back to her and only once or twice turned to glance in her direction. My book was about a large family of motherless children. I did not grudge children in books their mothers, but I did not want them to run the risk, which haunted me, of losing them. It was safer if their mother had already gone before the book began, and the wound healed, and I always tried to choose stories in which this had happened.

From time to time I glanced a little beyond the book and fell into reverie. I tried to imagine my own mother, who had gone out walking that afternoon, alone in the cherry orchard that ran down from hilltop to valley. Her restlessness often sent her off on long walks, too long for me to enjoy. I always lagged behind, thinking of my book, of the large, motherless family. In the cherry orchard it would be hot and scented, with bees scrambling into flowers, and faded-blue butterflies all over the chicory and heliotrope. But I found that I could not imagine her walking there alone; it seemed an incomplete picture that did not contain me. The reality was in this room, with its half-drawn blinds, its large gros-point picture of a cavalier saying good-bye to his lady. (Behind him, a soldier said good-bye in a less affecting way to a servant.) The plush-covered chairs, the Sèvres urns were so familiar to me, so present, as never to fade. It was one of those stamped scenes, heeled down into my experience, which cannot link up with others, or move forward, or change. Like a dream, it was separate, inviolable, and could be preserved. Then I suddenly thought that I should not have let my mother go out alone. It was a revolutionary thought, suggesting that children have some protection to offer to grown-ups. I did not know from what I should have protected her; perhaps just from her lonely walk that hot afternoon. I felt an unwelcome stir of pity. Until now I had thought that being adult put one beyond the slur of being pitiable.

I tried to return to my book, to draw all those children round me for safety, but in my disturbed mind I began to feel that Mrs Vivaldi was not asleep. A wasp zigzagged round the room and went abruptly, accidentally, out of the window. It did not leave the same peace behind, but unease. I could see myself – with *her* eyes – hunched up over my book, my frock crumpled under me, as I endlessly sorted out and chose and ate and brooded over my bag of sweets. I felt that I had intruded and it was no longer a natural thing to be indoors on such a day. If she was awake, I must get up and speak to her.

Her hand supported her head, her white elbow was on the plush arm of the chair. In that dark red chair she seemed very white and fair and I could see long blue veins branching down the inside of her arm.

As I went towards her, I saw, through the slats of her parted fingers, her lashes move. I stood in front of her, holding out the bag of sweets, but she did not stir. Yet so sure was I that she was awake that I did not know how to move away or leave her. Just as my hand wavered uncertainly, her hand fell from her face. She opened her eyes and made a little movement of her mouth, too delicate to be called a yawn. She smiled. 'I must have dropped off for a moment,' she said. She glanced at the basket of flowers, at the clock, then at my bag of sweets.

'How kind of you!' she murmured, shaking her head, increasing my awkwardness. I took a few steps to one side, feeling I was looming over her.

'So you were here all the time?' she asked. 'And I asleep. How dreadful I must have looked.' She put her hand to the plaited hair at the nape of her neck. 'Only young people should be seen asleep.'

She was always underlining my youth, emphasising her own age. I wanted to say, 'You looked beautiful,' but I felt clumsy and absurd. I smiled foolishly and wandered out into the garden, leaving my book in the room. The painted balls lay over the lawn. The syringa made the paths untidy with dropped blossom. Everyone's afternoon was going forward but mine. Interrupted, I did not know where to take it up. I began to wonder how old Mrs Vivaldi was. Standing by the buddleia tree, I watched the drunken butterflies clinging to the flowers, staggering about the branches. Why did she pretend? I asked myself. I knew that children were not worth acting for. No one bothered to keep it up before us; the voices changed, the faces yielded. We were a worthless audience. That she should dissemble for me made me feel very sad and responsible. I was burdened with what I had not said to comfort her.

I hid there by the buddleia a long time, until I heard my mother coming up the path, back from her walk. I dreaded now more than ever that her step would drag, as sometimes it did, or that she would sigh. I came out half-fearfully from behind the buddleia tree.

She was humming to herself, and when she saw me, she handed me a large bunch of wild strawberries, the stalks warm from her hand. She sat down on the grass under the tree, and, lifting her long arms, smoothed her hair, pressing in the hair-pins more firmly. She said: 'So you crept out of that stuffy little room after all?'

I ate the warm, gritty strawberries one by one, and my thoughts hovered all over her as the butterflies hovered over the tree. My shadow bent across her, as my love did.

Nods & Becks & Wreathèd Smiles

'I was *hours* with Jennifer,' Mrs Miller said, and she lifted the lump of sugar out of her coffee to see how much of it had melted. 'I went in at ten o'clock at night, and she didn't arrive until after tea the next day.'

Mrs Graham, not really attending, had a sudden vision of Jennifer, quite grown up, stepping out of a cab with all her luggage, just as it was getting dark. Such pictures were constantly insinuating themselves into her mind, were sharply visual, more actual than this scene in the teashop in the High Street among her friends, from whose conversation she often retracted painfully, to whose behaviour she usually reacted absurdly.

'... and dares to tell me there are no such things as labour pains,' Mrs Miller was saying. '"It's all psychology," he said, and I said, "So are too many things nowadays."'

Mrs Howard said, 'He told me just to relax. Well, I relaxed like mad and I still had to have seven stitches.'

Her voice had risen in her indignation, and Mrs Miller gave a little sideways warning glance at a man at the corner table, who had turned up his coat collar and was rustling his newspaper.

'Well, it was certainly the worst experience I ever had,' Mrs Howard said emphatically. 'I hope never to go through—'

'I thought neuralgia was worse,' Mrs Graham forgot herself enough to say.

At first, they were too surprised to speak. After all, *men* could have neuralgia. Then Mrs Miller gave her own special little laugh. It was light as thistledown. It meant that Mrs Graham only said that to be different, probably because she was a vegetarian. And was always so superior, so. *right* about everything – had said that there wouldn't be a war at the time of Munich, when they were sitting in this very café surrounded by the dried fruit and the tinned food they had been so frantically buying, and the next year, when they *hadn't* bought the fruit, she *had*.

'My God, Dolly! What *have* you done?' Mrs Miller suddenly exclaimed.

Groping tragically before her, like Oedipus going into exile, Mrs Fisher came stumbling towards them, a bandage over one eye, her hat crooked.

They all scraped their chairs back, making room for her.

'Conjunctivitis,' she said faintly.

'You poor darling! Is it infectious?' Mrs Howard asked all in one breath.

'It's the same as pinkeye,' Mrs Miller said.

'In a more virulent form,' Dolly Fisher added. 'Coffee,' she said to the waitress. 'Nothing to eat. What's that you've got, Laura?'

'A scone, dear,' Mrs Miller said.

'I thought you'd given it up.'

'Oh, I did – for at least three weeks. It didn't do any good.'

'A scone and butter,' Dolly Fisher said to the waitress when she brought the coffee.

'Wherever did you pick *that* up?' Mrs Miller went on, and her voice made the affliction sound very sordid indeed.

'I've been run down,' Dolly said.

'You don't get it from being run down. You pick it up.' Mrs Miller spread margarine over half a scone and popped it into her mouth.

'Oh, I'm late!' said Mrs Liddell. She put down her empty shopping basket and pulled up a chair. 'I haven't started yet. I wonder is there any fish about?'

'There *was* some halibut,' Mrs Miller said. 'I went for mine as soon as I'd taken Arthur to the station.'

'Oh, dear! Wasn't there anything else?'

'I seem to remember some sprats.'

'But, Dolly, dear! What have you done?'

'She's picked up pinkeye from somewhere,' Mrs Howard said. From somewhere not very nice, she implied.

Oedipus sat munching her scone. 'It's the worst pain I think I ever had,' she said defiantly.

The man at the corner table stood up hastily and called for his bill.

'Now what are you hiding from us?' Mrs Miller asked Mrs Liddell, who blushed and said, 'Oh, of course, none of you've seen it. Hughie gave it to me.'

She had been hiding nothing but had turned her hand a great deal in the light and now laid it in the middle of the table, as if she were pooling it.

'What a lovely ring!' they cried.

'For my birthday.' She drew it off and let it lie in the palm of her hand.

'Oh, do let me!' Mrs Miller begged. 'If my poor old hands aren't too fat.'

The ring was, after all, rather loose on her.

'It's so unusual!' Mrs Howard said. 'I wonder where on earth he got it.'

'It really has character,' Mrs Miller announced, after long consideration and turning her hand this way and that to catch the light. 'Yes, it really has. And it's *your* ring.' She passed it back to Mrs Liddell. 'Clever Hughie!'

'That will be the day,' Oedipus said, 'when Sidney gives me a ring for *my* birthday.'

'It's a very old ring, he said,' Mrs Liddell began.

'What of it?' Mrs Miller said generously. 'You will often get far better value with second-hand things.'

'Last year, he gave me a set of saucepans we had to have anyhow.'

'Cheer up, Dolly, we're all in the same boat. None of *our* husbands gives us rings.'

'I shall have to go,' Mrs Liddell said, finishing her coffee quickly. She had had her little triumph and now must hurry with it to the fishmonger's.

'I must come, too,' said Oedipus. They left together, and Dolly went off down the High Street towards the hills of Cithaeron.

'Well!' Mrs Miller said. 'Fancy Hughie!' She gave her famous laugh.

They looked at one another.

'It was a very beautiful ring,' said Mrs Graham, who always liked to be different.

Mrs Miller put down her cup. 'I wouldn't have it as a gift,' she said. 'Personally.'

A Sad Garden

The wall running round the small garden was pitted with hundreds of holes, and rusty nails flying little rags were to be seen in the spaces between the espaliers, the branches like candelabra, the glossy leaves, the long rough brown pears, the thin-skinned yellow and the mottled ones which lay against the bricks.

'There is no one to eat the fruit,' said Sybil. 'Take what you want.' She handed her sister-in-law a small ripe William and sauntered away down the garden.

'Well, I certainly will,' said Kathy, following eagerly after, 'I could do with some for bottling.'

'Take them, then. Take them.' Sybil sat down on a stone seat at the end of the path. The day was nearly gone, but the brick wall still gave out its warmth. 'Mind the wasps, Audrey,' she said. 'They're getting sleepy.' ('Audrey!' she thought, watching her little niece coming carefully up the path. 'What a stupid name!')

The garden was filled with the smell of rotting fruit. Pears lay about on the paths and wasps tunnelled into their ripeness. Audrey stepped timidly over them. She was all white and clean – face, serge coat and socks. Her mother held the William pear in her gloved hand. 'You shall have it when we get home,' she promised. 'Not in that coat, dear.'

Sybil sighed sharply.

'Well, if you really mean it, I could slip back home for the big garden-basket,' Kathy went on. She was doubtful always and nervous with her sister-in-law. The others had long ago given up calling on Sybil.

'She's had trouble,' they admitted. 'We can grant her that. But she makes no effort.'

Kathy was the only one who was too kind-hearted to give in. Every week she called. 'You see, she's all on her own,' she would tell the others. 'We've got one another, but she's lost everything – husband and son. I try to think what that would mean to me.' (Not that she had a son; but she had Audrey.)

'She was like it before,' they reminded her. 'Before ever Ralph died. Or Adam. Always queer, always moody and lazy and rude. She thinks she's too clever for us. After all, it's safer to be ordinary.'

Kathy would try to explain, excuse, forgive, and they would never listen to her, for it was instinct which guided them, not reason. 'She led Ralph the hell of a dance, anyway,' they would always conclude.

Kathy glanced at Sybil now, sitting there on the stone seat, leaning back against the wall, with her eyes half-closed and a suggestion about her of power ill-concealed, of sarcasm, of immunity from human contact. Kathy – the others said she was deficient in instinct – saw nothing she could dislike; merely a tired woman who was lonely. There was nothing against her, except that she had once been brave when she should have been overcome and had spoken of her only child with too much indifference – and as for leading Ralph a dance, she had merely laughed at him sometimes and admired him, it seemed, somewhat less than they had always done at home.

'Well, fetch your basket,' she was saying.

Kathy hesitated. 'Coming, Audrey?'

'Oh, she can stay,' said Sybil.

'Well, mind your socks, then they'll be clean for school tomorrow. I'll be back in a minute or two. Be a good girl.'

Audrey had no idea of being anything else. She sat down timidly on the edge of the seat and watched her mother disappear round the side of the house.

Sybil looked at her without enthusiasm.

'Do you like school?' she asked suddenly, harshly.

'Yes, thank you, Auntie.'

Sybil's fingers wandered over the seat as if from habit until the tops of them lay at last in the rough grooves of some carved initials – the letters A. K. R. She had smacked him for that, for always cutting his name into other people's property, had taken away his chisel. When she did that, he had stared at her in hatred, wild, beautiful, a stain on his mouth from the blackberries or some purple fruit, and a stain of anger on his cheeks. Her fingers gripped the seat.

'So you like school and never play truant?'

'Oh, no, Auntie.' A little shocked giggle. The child swung her feet, looking down placidly at her clean socks.

'Thank God I never had a daughter,' thought Sybil.

'Would you like some fruit?'

'Mummy said not to in this coat.'

'What *would* you like?' Sybil asked in exasperation, thrusting her hair back with a gesture of impatience.

The child looked puzzled.

'A swing? Would you like a swing?'

Audrey's mouth shaped a 'No', but, seeing her aunt's look, she changed her mind and smiled and nodded, feigning delight.

She sat down on the swing and put her shiny shoes primly together. Even the seat of the swing was carved with initials. She knew that they were her cousin's and that he was dead, that it had been his swing; she remembered him refusing to allow her to sit on it. She did so now with pleasurable guilt, looking primly round at the clump of Michaelmas daisies, as if she half expected him to come bursting from them in anger. She allowed herself to rock gently to and fro.

Aunt Sybil stopped on her way to the house.

'Can't you go higher than that?' she said, and she took the seat in two hands, drew it back to her and then thrust it far away, so that Audrey went high up into the leaves and fruit. Birds rose off the top of the tree in a panic.

'That's how Adam used to go,' Sybil shouted as Audrey flew down again. 'Right up into the leaves. He used to kick the pears down with his feet.'

'I don't ... I don't ...' cried Audrey.

As she flew down, Sybil put her hands in the small of her back and thrust her away again. 'Higher, higher,' Adam used to shout. He was full of wickedness and devilry. She went on pushing without thinking of Audrey. The garden was darkening. A question-mark of white smoke rose from the quenched bonfire beside the rubbish-heap.

'There you go. There you go,' she cried. And she thought, 'But what a boring little girl. "Yes, Mummy. No, thank you, Auntie." I'd never have Adam tied to my apron strings. I'd push him out into the world. Push him!' She gave a vehemence to her thought and Audrey with her hair streaming among the branches flew dizzily away. Frantically now her aunt pushed her, crying: 'There you go. There you go.'

The child, whiter than ever, was unable to speak, to cry out. She sensed something terribly wrong and yet something which was inevitable and not surprising. Each time she dropped to earth, a wave of darkness hit her face and then she would fly up again in a wild agony. A strand of hair caught in some twigs and was torn from her head.

Sybil stood squarely on the grass. As the swing came down, she put up her hands and with the tips of her fingers and yet with all her strength, she pushed. She had lost consciousness and control and cried out each time exultingly: 'There you go. There you go' – until all her body was trembling.

Kathy came screaming up the path.

Shadows of the World

'I don't call this the real country,' she said. 'People only *sleep* here.'

From the window, she watched the cars going by from the station. There was almost a stream of traffic, for the London train was in.

'And not always with whom they should,' George Eliot agreed. His name was something he had to carry off. He tried to be the first with the jokes and never showed his weariness. His parents were the most unliterary people and had chosen his name because it had somehow sprung to their minds, sounding right, and familiar. Taking that in his stride had originated his flamboyance, his separateness. He made his mark in many dubious ways; but the ways *were* only dubious and sometimes he was given the benefit of the doubt. As a bachelor, he was a standby to dissatisfied wives and only the wives knew – and would not say – how inadequate he turned out to be.

'There go the Fletchers,' Ida said. 'What a mass of silverware they have on that car! They were sitting bolt upright and not speaking to one another.'

'How could you see? She would scarcely have her head on his shoulder just driving back from the station.'

'Nor on any other occasion. Nor his on hers.'

'Come away from the window and talk to me. What time will Leonard come?'

'Who could know but Leonard? He might have caught that train and stepped aside on the way.'

'For a drink?'

'It might be that even,' she said, brightly insinuating.

She turned her back to the window, but stayed where she was. The branches of trees with their young leaves came close to the house and threw a greenish shadow over the walls inside. The colours of the spring evening were intense rather than brilliant: the lilac was heaped up against sky of the same purple. A house nearby had a sharp outline, as if before rain; but there had been neither rain nor sun for several days. Swallows flew low so that she could see their pale, neat bellies as they flickered about the eaves. In the wood, cuckoos answered one another, at long intervals, haltingly; one had its summer stammer already; its explosive, broken cry.

'The peonies almost open! How it all hastens by and vanishes!' Ida said, working herself up for a storm of her own.

'Why not have a drink?' George asked. He had come in for that, and because it looked like being a dark and thundery evening. No golf.

'I hate our lives,' she cried. 'We fritter our time away.'

She looked round the room, at the rather grubby roughcast walls, little pictures hanging crooked, the red-brick fireplace with its littered grate, its dusty logs. 'Everything goes wrong with what I do,' she thought. 'This room has simply no character. It looks raw, bleak, dull.' Studying pictures in magazines it all seemed easy enough, but her colour schemes became confused, something always obtruded. If she followed elaborate recipes, what resulted was nothing like the photograph in the cookery-book. Her enthusiasms scarcely deserved the name. Her piano-playing, to which she resorted in boredom, remained sketchy and improvised in the bass. Resolutions, too, soon abated. Slimming-exercises, diets, taking the children to church, were all abandoned. Only dull habit remained, she thought. When her daughter wished to learn to play the violin, she refused. 'You will want to give it up after a couple of lessons. You will never practise,' she said, thinking only of her experience of herself; for Virginia was a tenacious child.

'A drink ... ?' George began once more. Though they were old friends he did not feel like going to what she called the cocktail cabinet and helping himself.

'I have nothing,' she said moodily and dramatically. He looked surprised and alarmed. 'The empty days,' she continued, to his great relief, 'the long, empty days.'

'Oh hell, I thought for one moment you meant the drink situation.'

'Have what you want,' she said ungraciously, impatiently.

'Those damn cuckoos!' He laughed, pausing with the bottle in his hand pointing at her like a gun, his head on one side.

She persisted in her mood, pacing the room, trying to claim his whole attention. Vexed, frustrated, she was baulked by his indifference.

'You have the children,' he said. 'This nice home.' He glanced at the crooked pictures, at some fallen petals lying round a jar of flowers.

As if he were a conjuror, the door opened and Virginia came in. She looked like a Japanese doll, with her white face, her straight black hair with the curved fringe, and her brightly patterned frock. At the back of the house, life was gayer. In the maid's sitting-room she and the nineteen-year-old girl from the village gossiped and giggled. She held the edges of the sheets to the sewing-machine while Nancy turned the handle, putting sides to middle. ('All the sheets are going at once,' Ida had said bitterly, as if even household linen conspired against her.) The whir of the sewing-machine interrupted their discussions and they sucked sweets instead. The stuffy room smelt of pear-drops. But at seven, Nancy said: 'Hey, you! Go on. Bed. Hop it.'

'Where's Laurie?'

'Out in the shed, I dare say, with the cat. You can just run quick and see whether there's any kittens yet, but mind, when I say quick I don't mean your usual hanging about.'

Virginia pressed her elbows to her sides. The oppressive evening menaced her with thunder and lightning, now with the horror of birth. Her mother had special feelings of the same kind; could forecast storms by her headaches; was sick at the smell of lilies; could not eat shell-fish, and fainted at the sight of blood. She over-reacted to the common things of life, even in physical ways, with giddiness and rashes on her skin. She taught her family to reverence her allergies and foibles and they were constantly discussed.

'I don't want to go,' Virginia had said.

'Then say good-night to your mother,' Nancy said, as if she had no better alternative to offer.

Virginia did not want that either, but stood obediently at the door, with her suspicious, upward look at them, at George and Ida.

Out in the shed, Laurie hung over the cat's basket, absorbed, though a little frightened. His cat, Moira, swaying with her weight of kittens, trampled the basket, crying. When Laurie stroked her head, she stopped, turning her golden eyes on him, appeased. She seemed as nervous as he, and as un-instructed. Maternity wrought an immediate, almost a comical change in her. The first kitten was born, silent, still. Laurie feared that it was dead. It looked so un-kittenish – livid, slimed-over, more blue than black. But at once, Moira became definite and authoritative: she licked and cuffed, treating brutally the poor clambering thing with its trailing navel-cord, its mouth pursed up like a flower-bud. Fantastic, at last alive, it tried to lift on its stringy neck the nodding weight of its head. Its paws were more hands than paws, with frail claws out-stretched, and piteously it raked the air with them.

Laurie imagined the edged cold after the warm; the discomforts of breathing. Surely, he thought, the poor creature felt, if not through its sealed eyes, then through its shivering body, the harsh, belabouring light, after such utter darkness.

Moira was arrogant in maternity, no uncertainty beset her now. When the kitten was cleaned, she lay down on her side awaiting the others, purring a little. She seemed contemptuous of Laurie and gave him only an occasional, unseeing glance. At the approach of each birth, she seemed to gather herself up, took on a suspicious look, with eyes narrowed. When she had cleaned them, the kittens were indistinguishable from her own black body, her thrust-out satiny legs. They clambered feebly over the mound of her belly, even before the last was born: their pink hands frailly felt the air: splayed out on dampish legs, they looked old and burdened creatures: they mewed wretchedly, resenting the bitter, cuffing, hard-edged world in which they were – the unrocking, unyielding stubbornness of it. Black, like their mother, they had bare-looking patches which would one day, Laurie thought, be white feet, white bibs. He looked forward for them. They peopled his home. He thought of them opening their eyes at last and playing; putting on mock terror at the sound of a footfall; arching their spines, cavorting, curveting about the legs of the furniture.

The stream of cars had dwindled and run out. The beech-leaves against the sloe-coloured sky looked more lucent; the birdsong which had suddenly increased in urgency and hysteria as suddenly ceased. Only a single thrush went on and its notes echoed in the silence, the intent air vibrated with the sound.

Thirty miles from London, the village had a preponderance of middle-sized houses. They lay at the end of short but curving drives, embowered in flowering trees. At this time of the year, the landscape was clotted with greenish creamy blossom – pear, white lilac, guelder-rose. Later, as it all faded, a faint grubbiness, a litter of petals seemed a total collapse. But there always were a great many birds: green woodpeckers appeared on the suburban-looking lawns; owls cried in the night. When the rain came it fell through layers of leaves, loosening gravel, staining the white roughcast houses and vibrating on sun-porches and greenhouses.

Ida was unusually placed in being able to see the road. Only rather low beech-hedges separated her. The cars reminded her of fish going by in shoals. At the week-ends when there were parties she would stand waiting by the window to be sure that plenty of her friends had gone by, not caring to be early. Like shoals of fish, they all headed one way, arrived at one destination (where there would be plenty to drink); turned homewards at last in unison.

Ida drank little, although sometimes at parties, because of her very indifference, she would accept glasses haphazardly with no knowledge of her mounting foolishness. She scorned and resented the way her acquaintance revolved round, took their pattern from, so much alcohol. For one thing, the cost dismayed her. She loved clothes, or rather new clothes, and her own clothes. It seemed that dozens of bottles of gin stood between her and all the things she wanted. George, who knew her so well, had no idea of her ill-will each time he filled his glass, which he did while she was saying good-night to Virginia.

Sounds of knives and forks being put out came from the dining-room. Virginia, opening the door, had let in a steaminess from the kitchen, a smell of mint.

'Ask Nancy not to *race* the potatoes like that,' Ida said. 'Good-night, darling one.' She drew the child to her as if she were a springing young tree; Virginia leant, but did not move her feet. Her mother used endearments a great deal: sometimes to put an edge to displeasure. '*Darling*, how *could* you be so stupid!'

'I don't know if I should wait dinner for Leonard,' she said to George, who was just raising his replenished glass. 'You'll stay, won't you?'

'Well, I will then. Do you mean Leonard just may not come home?'

She had a desire to lay waste something, if only George's complacency, 'He may not come home to *me*.'

'Then, dear, you are wondrous cool. Where else should he go?'

'To Isabel's, I expect.'

'Isabel?'

'Oh, you must know,' she said impatiently, surprised at her own tone.

'At the Fletchers' party, you mean? But parties are nothing. Everyone forgets the next day.'

'Do they?'

She went to the window again, rapping her finger-nails on the glass. She felt isolated, because she did not forget the next day. Her own romantic hopes remained, and the young man at the party who had said 'You don't belong', and pressed his knuckles steadily against her thigh as they stood in the porch waiting for cars, who promised – so falsely – to seek her out again, was real to her, her brooding mood enlarged, improved him. She had taken no heed of Leonard all that evening; given no thoughts to him. But some impression had been formed, as if her mind had photographed, without her knowledge, the picture of Leonard and Isabel intently talking. Now her dissatisfaction printed the negative. What had been to her advantage that evening, suddenly infuriated her.

'I'm sure it's nothing,' George assured her. 'Your imagination. Just one of those village things.'

She had imagined the young man sitting in this room with her. The fire was lit; flames had consumed the cigarette-ends and litter. The house was silent, the walls receded into shadow. They watched the fire . . .

'I thought I heard thunder,' George said, hoping to turn the conversation, and also quietly, one-handedly, filling his glass.

'I feel it in my head,' Ida said, putting her hand across her eyes. When she heard footsteps on the road, she could not resist looking out again. She felt like the Lady of Shalott. 'Shadows of the world appear,' she thought. She imagined the young man, riding down between the hedges. But it was

Isabel, going along the road in her old tweed coat with her dejected spaniel on a lead.

Virginia took off her vest and hung it over the mirror. Her nail-scissors and a silver comb she put in a drawer away from the lightning. Naked, she was thin and long-legged, her side marked with a neat appendix-scar. Her spine was silky, downy. She dropped her nightgown over her head and stood, legs apart, elbows up like wings, trying to do up buttons at the back.

Outside, the sky seemed to congeal cruelly, charged with lead. At the first sound of thunder splitting across the roof, she jumped into bed and lay under the thin coverings, quite rigid, as if she were dead.

The birth of the fourth, the last kitten, was a triumph. Creamy and blond tortoiseshell, it was distinguished and mysterious from the beginning, suggesting an elegant grandparent on one side or the other. Larger than the others, longer-haired, somehow complete at once, blind but not helpless, it put the finishing touches to the basket, decorated Moira's maternity.

Laurie shifted from his squatting position, feeling stiff, the pattern of wicker-work dented into one knee. He was relieved and exhilarated. Leaving benign, smug Moira, he went to put his bicycle away, for a few spots of rain had fallen on the path.

'Well, we won't wait,' Ida said. The sight of Isabel had strangely frustrated her. 'I'll tell Nancy, and Laurie must go to bed.' She thought: 'Better to dine alone with George than have him drinking all this gin.'

'Where *is* Laurie?'

'With his cat. She's having kittens.'

She put her hand on the bell and, when Nancy came, gave orders for dinner to be served. 'And tell Laurie it's bedtime.'

'Four kittens,' Nancy said. 'Isn't that lovely?'

'Thank you, Nancy,' Ida said in her quelling way.

'Whatever will you do with them?' George asked. 'Four kittens.'

'Do? What do you imagine? Need we go into details?'

The rain, suddenly released, fell like knives into the flower-beds; bounced and danced on the paths. Different scents steamed up from the earth: the drenched lilac looked as if it would topple over with the weight of its saturated blossom.

Just as Nancy announced with her touch of sarcasm that dinner was served, Leonard's car swept into the drive. They heard him slamming the garage-doors together. George drained his glass and put it reluctantly on the table. Leonard came running up from the garage, his head down and his shoulders stained dark with the rain.

The Light of Day

'And so she has borne you another son,' said the doctor raising his voice
a little, as one who quotes the Bible. He sat sideways to their breakfast table
to show that he was just off.

'Yes, we may use that word again,' the father agreed. 'It is odd that
women do not *bear* their daughters, only have them.'

Sitting in his wife's place, he began to pour out tea and handed the cups
clumsily so that they rocked in their saucers. Overhead, floor-boards
creaked, and at intervals the newly-born broke into paroxysms of despair
as if it were being thrashed. Neither of the men seemed to hear this, sipping at their tea, passing their hands with a harsh sound across their
unshaven chins.

The little maid brought in the children to their breakfast. They suffered
the doctor's jocularity passively, used to it, for he was good with children.
Their bibs were tied, milk poured.

'It is here,' the boy said suddenly, pointing his spoon to the ceiling.
'Crying like a real baby.'

The girl listened, food at a standstill in her mouth. When her brother said
those words 'It is here', the truth dawned in her and she understood that it
had been necessary to make that point about its being a real baby, because
it had been an unreal one for so long. She came out of her daze and excitement broke loose in her. Wrenching down her mouthful, she began to cry.

The young maid tried to comfort her, but she was flurried herself. This
event she had so secretly dreaded was now over and, in her relief, she could
scarcely believe, after all the novels she had read, the stories she had heard,
that the first thing to waken her had been that curious cry. 'One of the children,' her trained ear had warned her, the selective ear which had ignored
the car arriving, the footsteps on the stairs, the doors opening and shutting.
But the sound, so strident and protesting, was not from one of the peacefully sleeping children. It was the new one, the dreaded one. The little boy
turned then and murmured in his sleep, flinging an arm across the pillow;
but the girl sat up in bed and said: 'There is a baby crying in this house,'
and listened, very still, the breeze from the window lifting her light hair up
and back from her face.

'Another cup?' the father now asked the doctor.

'No, I'll be away. Cheer up, lass,' he said, passing the little girl's chair, putting his hand on her head, until she ducked away. 'No tears today, you know,' he added vaguely, and went on into the hall where he looked round sleepily for his hat and his case.

Upstairs, the baby was being bathed. Against the rush of air on his body, he had furiously protested, now he resisted the flow of water over his limbs. By the fire, flannel faintly scorched, waiting for him.

'Then there'll be a nice cup of tea for you,' the old nurse was saying, for it is all cups of tea when a baby is born.

The mother lay back drowsily, high on her pillows, feeling like a great battered boat washed up on the shore, empty, discarded. 'Enjoy this moment,' she told herself, 'before life breaks over you again. Enjoy the soothing peace, the sloughed-off responsibilities, the handing over to others. A whole moment of bliss ... '

'You did well,' she wanted someone to say, as if she were an actress on a first night. Soon flowers would begin to come, the husband's first, the six pink roses all lolling to one side of the wrong sort of vase.

'I saw him born almost,' she thought. 'I propped myself up and watched him take his first breath, lying there, splayed out, mottled, veiled with a pearly film. His great chest arched up, his face darkened, the cry burst from him. "It is *vile* being born," he seemed to cry, the cold air leaping at him.'

'When can the children come?' she asked drowsily.

'Not till he's bathed and dressed and you've had your tea. Plenty of time for them.'

'But they want to see him *new*.'

'He won't change much in half an hour.'

But he was changed already – his folded mauve fists emerging from the frilled sleeve, his hair like damp feathers brushed up.

'There he is then,' cried the nurse, enchanted at her work.

There he was, frilled, feather-stitched and ribboned, rushed into the uniform of civilisation, so quickly tamed, altered, made to conform. His head bobbed grotesquely, weakly, his lashless eyes turned to the light.

'And *there* he is,' the nurse continued, 'and there he *is* then.'

And she twisted him in his shawl and laid him down beside his mother in the bed.

'God, I'm so tired,' the mother thought, bored. She forced her thumb into his fist, examined the little nails, stroked with the back of a finger the damp and silken hair, the tender cheek, breathed in the smell of him. Then her eyes drooped heavily, her body seemed dragged down backwards, into sleep.

'You must take him away, nurse,' she said. 'Show him to the children. I'm ... ' She began to succumb to the heavy weight of sleepiness; but the nurse believed that mothers like to have their babies nestling beside them for a little while after they are born; the sight of this pleased her always and put the finishing touches to the birth, she thought.

Just as she was slipping away, down a fast stream of sleep, the door was tapped and the husband came in, shaved now and carrying tea.

'I am just off,' he announced. 'All is well downstairs.'

Waking again, she suddenly asked, wailing a little: 'But is it *really* well? And did they have their cod-liver oil?'

'Now, now,' soothed the nurse, thinking of the milk.

'Yes, they had it,' he said, and he bent over his new son with conventional clucking noises, making a fool of himself, they all thought. The baby began to cram tiny fingers into his mouth. The nurse stirred the tea, standing by.

The husband knew he was being dismissed. It was his third time of being a father. He bent over and kissed his wife. 'You did well,' he said, and she smiled peacefully, for nothing could hold her back now. She went swiftly, feet first, it seemed; sliding, falling, swimming, into darkness. Beside her, his mouth closing upon, then relinquishing, his bent knuckles, the baby turned his eyes with a look of wonder to the light outside.

Swan-moving

The village stood high in scarred and quarried country. The hillside had been broken into in many places, and some of the wounds, untended, were covered with coarse weeds. Other English villages, with a good foundation of thatched cottages and leafy lanes, improve on their conscious beauty with loving care. Grass verges are shaved neatly, flowers over-hang walls and fruit trees, lime-washed to their chins, stand in orchards full of daffodils. This village lacked even the knowledge of its own ugliness and nothing was done consciously in any direction. Gardens, in which scarcely a blade of grass remained, were littered with chicken-droppings and feathers. On the common, round which the cottages stood, pieces of old bicycles rusted among nettles. Tin cans floated in the muddy water which filled – in winter-time – the deep hollows. In one, an iron bedstead was half submerged. On this, the biggest pond, a swan was found one morning circling disconsolately among the rubbish.

Nights, for a long time, had been muffled with fog. By mid-afternoon, the sky would have begun to congeal in a phlegmy discoloration and then the village was cut off and abandoned to its own squalor.

The swan, arriving unseen, stayed so until late in the morning when the fog shifted and began to roll down the hillside, leaving the crown of the hill standing in an uncertain light. Children, coming out to play on the common, saw what their fathers bicycling to work could not have seen. They crowded the edge of the pond and one boy threw a stick at the swan, trying to make it fly. That was the first and last unkindness the bird ever suffered in the village. The children discovered that more response came when food was thrown, and soon the pond and the trodden grass around were littered with crusts of bread and bacon-rinds, orange-peel and apple-cores. Even in its charity the village was backward and untidy, yet the swan, coming to it out of the fog and remaining as it did, stirred its imagination and pride. On the market bus and in the pub and post office it was the subject of conjecture and theory. Whence had it flown, they wondered, and in what direction? Was it maimed and could fly no farther? Flattered as they were, the villagers could not believe that the muddy pond had ever been its true objective, heart's desire. They talked about the swan and worried over it. The Vicar referred to it in his sermon on the Mysterious Ways of the Lord.

After a week or two – the swan still circling on his muddy pond – strangers were seen about the village, which was becoming a popular diversion from the ennui of the Sunday walk. Mrs Wheatley, at the Stag and Hounds, began to serve afternoon teas. Her son and some of his workmates removed the rusting bedstead from the pond and threw it into a bluebell wood. Eyes so long indifferent became critical and much was suddenly seen to be wrong. A committee was formed to put the common in order and was given its title – The Local Amenities Enhancement Council – by the Vicar, who had a gift for words. To encourage beauty, a prize was offered for the neatest cottage-garden and a notice-board was set up beside the pond with the words 'Rubbish Prohibited'.

It was the first time that the village had worked together on any project. The swan – the unacknowledged instigator – took all for granted, seemed indifferent to amenities, but grew noticeably less aloof; for now he would wait at the edge of the common for the children to come from school. Fussy about his food, he would peck about and reject most of it. His first meal of the day was at half-past six when the men bicycled off to work at the brick-kilns. They would throw pieces from their 'slicers' or lunch-packets. Later, the children, going to school, showered down all the crusts they had had no need for at breakfast, but the swan trod among them at the water's edge or avoided them as they floated on the pond.

Wet weather, dark days, did not suit his looks. Not quite fully grown, he still had some of his dark plumage and this was stained by the orange clay in the water. Standing forlornly and unsteadily in the mud, he seemed stiff with misery and perhaps rheumatism.

'Old chap looks rough,' the men would say anxiously, coming from work. When strangers arrived on those days and appeared amused or made disparaging remarks, the children suffered a painful indignation – a foretaste of parenthood.

But as the spring came and the wild cherry blossomed above the quarries, the swan began to dazzle with the same white brilliance. The flowers grew in the cottage-gardens. They did not blossom well from so stamped-down and untended a soil, but a few wallflowers of a ghastly yellow were bedded out. Hand-written notices swung on gates and fences announcing 'Lemonade – A Penny Per Glass' or 'Cut Flowers – Sixpence the Bunch'.

The swan, preening himself daily into greater beauty, was in himself a lesson, an example in seemliness, and the village began to preen and trim itself, too; but with neither habit nor aptitude for grace. Fair weather, throughout that spring, encouraged a refurbishing, a hurried business with buckets of white-wash and pots of paint. This fermenting creativeness had strange results. So many white curtains were taken down to appear later on clothes-lines, a dull but curious green or indigo or raspberry. Garments – even underclothes – of the same colour hung beside them; for a bowl of dye is usually a great temptation. Few of the experiments were an improvement and most, in their new self-consciousness, went too far; yet, insidiously, the idea of charm spread through the village. A guilty tawdriness was its expression, naive and peasant-like, but here without steadying ritual or tradition. The Vicar, having once despaired at apathy, now winced at exuberance, at red, white and blue rabbit-hutches, the new neon-lighting outside the Stag and Hounds and one of his sidesmen wearing a daffodil in his button-hole at Evensong. He tried to control the general mood of recklessness, but its infection was at its height and beyond him.

In the midst of the wonderful weather, and because of it, the villagers could not avoid the knowledge that there had been summers – especially after such a spring – when the water in the pond had dwindled and gone, leaving a patch of cracked earth and rusty tins. Already it seemed to have receded, and nightly inspection of its level took place, a grave ceremony, like the inspection of a wicket, and confined to the men. They would report back to their women and the news spread among the children – the water was down a quarter of an inch perhaps, or more, or seemed to remain the same. They all watched the sky for rain.

By the beginning of June when the swan had been with them for nearly six months, the water had fallen so low that a meeting was called. When it was over the men went off on their bicycles to look for better accommodation for the swan, who seemed too negligent to do so for himself.

The nearest stretch of water was over a mile away – a deep, clear pond in a buttercup field. Having inspected it, the men went home, and the next evening a great crowd came out on the common to watch the swan moving.

The Vicar drove up in his little car which he left on the road. He walked down to the water's edge, in clerical-collar and his shirt-sleeves and wearing an old baize apron that he had borrowed from his manservant. The swan was coaxed out of the water with pieces of sponge-cake. The men moved forward slowly, the Vicar motioning them in to form a half-circle. Very gently and in silence they closed in on the swan. At this moment of great tension, Mrs Wheatley from the Stag and Hounds – unstable woman – suddenly screamed and was shushed and nudged by her neighbours.

The Vicar gathered up the swan against his apron and held him tenderly in his arms. In a most graceful and affectionate movement the bird curved his shining neck against the Vicar's shoulder. His lower feathers, his spread,

webbed feet dripped dirty water as he was carried up the bank towards the
car, the crowd surging after.

The swan sat on the front seat beside the Vicar and the manservant sat
behind. When they drove away, the crowd waved and cheered as if seeing
off bride and bridegroom. The swan surveyed them with indifference. His
feet were splayed out in an ungainly way on a piece of sacking and, as the
car moved forward, he crooked his neck and began to cleanse from his
plumage the trace of human hands.

Men leapt on to their bicycles with their children across the bars or
perched behind. The Vicar drove slowly and the procession went away
down the side of the common, past the Stag and Hounds where the bar had
been left entirely in the hands of the village dipsomaniac, who had strange
visions of his own and was not tempted from his vocation by such a happening, but had the decency, long remembered to his credit, to come out
and lift his glass as they all went by.

They streamed on between high hedges and ditches full of cow-parsley
and Queen Anne's Lace, the swan now turning his head, his beak parting
and closing as if he were thirsty or afraid. The Vicar watched the road and
the manservant watched the swan. The bicyclists kept up – a noisy throng;
some had bunches of buttercups pinned to their caps. When the car was
slowed up by cows crossing the road, the bicyclists came up to the car
window and looked in approvingly.

'Sits up in the manner born,' one said, with pride.

When they moved on down the lane, which was steaming and smelling
strongly of cow-pats, the swan began to lurch about unsteadily. He turned
his head and gave the Vicar a long and strange glance, and the manservant
leant forward protectively. Then the beak sank into the great rounded
breast and the eyes were covered, as if he slept.

The Vicar stopped the car at the field-gate and stepped out to face the
throng, his hand raised high. 'I want all done in silence now,' he said.
'Nothing to confuse him, so stand afar off.' So important was the occasion
that he fell easily into biblical oratory and might have added 'All of ye'
without knowing or being noticed.

They stood afar off among the polished grasses. It was an evening of
great peace. The shadows were long ovals under the elm trees. Cows
moved slowly through the yellow fields and the water of the pond, still as
a glass, reflected a mackerel sky.

The Vicar and the manservant lifted the swan from his seat in the car
and carried him to the edge of the pond, where they put him tenderly to
the breast of the water, then stood aside.

It was a moment of great emotion, like the launching of a ship. The bird
took to the pond and became two swans. In this clear water his reflection

could be seen for the first time and his foolish-looking feet paddling along. 'Look!' cried a little boy and his father put a hand over his mouth to silence him.

The swan went forward in great majesty, as if at last conscious of his true nature, and his wake spread out and followed like a train.

The Vicar lifted his hand for a second and then touched his eyes. As he came back up the bank, his shoes wet, his baize apron plastered with clay, his parishioners – if such most of them could be called from the fact of living in the same parish – looked at him with respect. He had appeared to them a natural leader, a man of courage and decision.

They returned to the village and crowded into the Stag and Hounds. Some of them took their beer outside and looked over the common to the empty pond. Their lives had been touched so lightly by magic that perhaps only the seeds of a legend were left, or less – no trace at all, but they felt easeful, thinking of the swan in its new home. The Vicar, who would have been an embarrassed man in the Stag and Hounds and no longer a leader, went home and began to prepare his sermon – 'Cast your bread upon the waters.'

The swan, when they had all gone, swam about for a while, plunging his beak deep into the water and ruffling his feathers. Then he came to the pond's edge, and out of the water. He stood there preening himself, an heraldic swan with wings half-lifted. At last, with a tottering run, clumsy, seeming off-balance with his huge breast-bone thrust forward and his neck out-stretched, he made a great commotion with his wings and took the air. As he rose level with the setting sun his feathers were golden. Then he went higher and became a grey shape. The scent of far-off water came to him and he flew on, away from that countryside for ever.

A Red-letter Day

The hedgerow was beaded with silver. In the fog, the leaves dripped with a deadly intensity, as if each falling drop were a drop of acid.

Through the mist, cabs came suddenly face-to-face with one another, passing and re-passing, between station and school. Backing into the hedges – twigs, withered berries striking the windows – the drivers leant out to exchange remarks, incomprehensible to their passengers, who felt oddly at their mercy. Town parents especially shrank from this malevolent landscape, wastes of rotting cabbages, flint cottages with rakish privies, rubbish heaps, grey napkins drooping on clothes-lines, the soil like plum-cake. Even turning in at the rather superior school-gates, the mossy stone, the smell of fungus, still dismayed them. Then, as the building itself came into view, they could see Matron standing at the top of the steps, fantastically white, shaming nature, her hands laid affectionately upon the shoulders of such boys as could not resist her. The weather was put in its place. The day would take its course.

Tory was in one of the last of the cabs. Having no man to exert authority for her, she must merely take her turn, standing on the slimy pavement waiting for a car to come back empty. She stamped her feet, feeling the damp creeping through her shoes. When she left home, she had thought herself suitably dressed; even for such an early hour her hat was surely plain enough? One after another she had tried on and had come out in the end leaving hats all over the bed, so that it resembled a new grave with its mound of wreathed flowers.

One other woman was on her own. Tory eyed her with distaste. Her sons (for surely she had more than one? She looked as if she had what is often called a teeming womb; was like a woman in a pageant symbolising maternity), her many sons would never feel the lack of a father, for she was large enough to be both to them. Yes, Tory thought, she would have them out on the lawn, bowling at them by the hour, coach them at mathematics, oil their bats, dubbin their boots, tan their backsides (she was working herself up into a hatred of this woman, who seemed to be all that she herself was not), one love-affair in her life, or, rather, mating. 'She has probably eaten her husband now that her child-bearing days are over. He would never have dared to have asked for a divorce, as mine did.' She carried still her 'mother's bag' – the vast thing which, full of napkins, bibs, bottles of orange-juice, accompanies babies out to tea. Tory wondered what was in it now. Sensible things, a Bradshaw, ration-books, a bag of biscuits, large clean handkerchiefs, a tablet of soap and aspirins.

A jolly manner. "'I love young people. I feed on them,'" Tory thought spitefully. The furs on her shoulders made her even larger; they clasped paws across her great authoritative back, like hands across the ocean. Tory lifted her muff to hide her smile.

Nervous dread made her feel fretful and vicious. In *her* life, all was frail, precarious; emotions fleeting, relationships fragmentary. Her life with her husband had suddenly loosened and dissolved, her love for her son was painful, shadowed by guilt – the guilt of having nothing solid to offer, of having grown up and forgotten, of adventuring still, away from her child, of not being able to resist those emotional adventures, the tenuous grasping after life; by the very look of her attracting those delicious secret glances, glimpses, whispers, the challenge, the excitement; not deeply sexual, for she was flirtatious; 'but not,' she thought, watching Mrs Hay-Hardy rearranging her furs on her shoulders, 'not a great feather-bed of oblivion. Between Edward and me there is no premise of love, none at all, nothing taken for granted, as between most sons and mothers, but all tentative, agonised. We are indeed amateurs, both of us. No tradition behind us, no gift for the job. All we achieve is too hard come by. We try too piteously to please one another, and if we do, feel frightened by the miracle of it. I do indeed love him above all others. Above all others, but not exclusively.'

Here a taxi swerved against the kerb, palpitated as she stepped forward quickly, triumphantly, before Mrs Hay-Hardy (whose name she did not yet know), and settled herself in the back.

'Could we share?' Mrs Hay-Hardy asked, her voice confident, melodious; one foot definitely on the running-board. Tory smiled and moved over much farther than was necessary, as if such a teeming womb could scarcely be accommodated on the seat beside her.

Shifting her furs on her shoulders, settling herself, Mrs Hay-Hardy glanced out through the filming windows, undaunted by the weather, which would clear, she said; would lift. Oh, she was confident that it would lift by midday.

'One is up so early, it seems midday now,' Tory complained.

But Mrs Hay-Hardy had not risen until six, so that naturally it still seemed only eleven to her, as it was.

'She will share the fare,' Tory thought. 'Down to the last penny. There will be a loud and forthright woman's argument. She will count out coppers and make a fuss.'

This did happen. At the top of the steps, Matron still waited with the three Hay-Hardys grouped about her, and Edward, who blushed and whitened alternately with terrible excitement, a little to one side.

To this wonderful customer, this profitable womb, the headmaster's wife herself came into the hall. Her husband had sent her, instructing her with deft cynicism from behind his detective novel, himself one of those gods who rarely descend, except, like Zeus, in a very private capacity.

'This is the moment I marked off on the calendar,' Edward thought. 'Here it is. Every night we threw one of our pebbles out of the window; a day gone.' The little stones had dropped back on to the gravel under the window, quite lost, untraceable, the days of their lives.

As smooth as minnows were Mrs Lancaster's phrases of welcome; she had soothed so many mothers, mothered so many boys. Her words swam all one way, in unison, but her heart never moved. Matron was always nervous; the results of her work were so much on the surface, so checked over. The rest of the staff could hide their inefficiency, or shift their responsibility; she could not. If Mrs Hay-Hardy cried: 'Dear boy, your teeth!' to her first-born as she did now, it was Matron's work she criticised and Matron flushed. And Mrs Lancaster flushed for Matron; and Derrick Hay-Hardy flushed for his mother.

'Perhaps I am not a born mother,' Tory thought, going down the steps with Edward. They would walk back to the Crown for lunch, she said. Edward pressed her arm as the taxi, bulging with Hay-Hardys, went away again down the drive.

'Do you mean you wanted to go with them?' she asked.

'No.'

'Don't you like them?'

'No.'

'But why?'

'They don't like me.'

Unbearable news for any mother, for surely all the world loves one's child, one's only child? Doubt set in, a little nagging toothache of doubt. 'You *are* happy?' she wanted to ask. 'I've looked forward so much to this,' she said instead. 'So much.'

He stared ahead. All round the gate-posts drops of moisture fell from one leaf to another, the stone gryphons were hunched up in misery.

'But I imagined it being a different day,' Tory added. 'Quite different.'

'It will be nice to get something different to eat,' Edward said.

They walked down the road towards the Crown as if they could not make any progress in their conversation until they had reached this point.

'You *are* warm enough at night?' Tory asked, when at last they were sitting in the hotel dining-room. She could feel her question sliding away off him.

'Yes,' he said absently and then, bringing himself back to the earlier, distant politeness, added: 'Stifling hot.'

'Stifling? But surely you have plenty of fresh air?'

'*I* do,' he said reassuringly. 'My bed's just under the window. Perishing. I have to keep my head under the bedclothes or I get ear-ache.'

'I am asking for all this,' she thought. When the waiter brought her pink gin, she drank it quickly, conscious that Mrs Hay-Hardy across the hotel dining-room was pouring out a nice glass of water for herself. She was so full of jokes that Tory felt she had perhaps brought a collection of them along with her in her shopping-bag. Laughter ran round and round their table above the glasses of water. Edward turned once and she glimpsed the faintest quiver under one eye, and an answering quiver on the middle Hay-Hardy's face.

She felt exasperated. Cold had settled in her, her mouth, her heart too, felt stiff.

'What would you like to do after lunch?' she asked.

'We could look round the shops,' Edward said, nibbling away at his bread as if to keep hunger at arm's length.

The shops were in the Market Square. At the draper's, the hats were steadily coming round into fashion again. 'I could astonish everyone with one of these,' Tory thought, setting her own hat right by her reflection in the window. Bales of apron-print rose on both sides, a wax-faced little boy wore a stiff suit, its price-ticket dangling from his yellow, broken fingers, his painted blue eyes turned mildly upon the street. Edward gave him a look of contempt and went to the shop-door. Breathing on the glass in a little space among suspended bibs and jabots and parlourmaids' caps, he watched the cages flying over-head between cashier and counter.

The Hay-Hardys streamed by, heading for the open country.

Most minutely, Tory and Edward examined the draper's shop, the bicycle shop, the family grocer's. There was nothing to buy. They were just reading the postcards in the newsagent's window when Edward's best friend greeted them. His father, a clergyman, snatched off his hat and clapped it to his chest at the sight of Tory. When she turned back to the postcards, she could see how unsuitable they were – jokes about bloomers, about twins; a great seaside world of fat men in striped bathing-suits; enormous women trotted down to the sea's edge; crabs humorously nipped their behinds; farcical situations arose over bathing-machines, and little boys had trouble with their water. She blushed.

The afternoon seemed to give a little sigh, stirred itself and shook down a spattering of rain over the pavements. Beyond the Market Square, the countryside, which had absorbed the Hay-Hardys, lowered at them.

'Is there anything you want?' Tory asked desperately, coveting the warm interiors of the shops.

'I could do with a new puncture outfit,' Edward said.

They went back to the bicycle shop. 'My God, it's only three o'clock,' Tory despaired, glancing secretly under her glove at her watch.

The Museum Room at the Guildhall was not gay, but at least there were Roman remains, a few instruments of torture, and half a mammoth's jaw-bone. Tory sat down on a seat among all the broken terra-cotta and took out a cigarette. Edward wandered away.

'No smoking, please,' the attendant said, coming out from behind a case of stuffed deer.

'Oh, please!' Tory begged. She sat primly on the chair, her feet together, and when she looked up at him, her violet eyes flashed with tears.

The attendant struck a match for her and his hand curving round it trembled a little.

'It's the insurance,' he apologised. 'I'll have this later, if I may,' and he put the cigarette she had given him very carefully in his breast-pocket, as if it were a lock of her hair.

'Do you have to stay here all day long with these dull little broken jugs and things?' she asked, looking round.

He forgave her at once for belittling his life's work, only pointing out his pride, the fine mosaic on the wall.

'But floor should be lying down,' she said naively; not innocently.

Edward came tip-toeing back.

'You see that quite delightful floor hanging up there,' she said. 'This gentleman will tell you all about it. My son adores Greek Mythology,' she explained.

'Your son!' he repeated, affecting gallant disbelief, his glance stripping ten or fifteen years from her. 'This happens to be a Byzantine Mosaic,' he said, and looked reproachfully at it for not being what it could not be. Edward listened grudgingly. His mother had forced him into similar situations at other times, in the Armoury of the Tower of London, once at Kew. It was as if she kindled in men a little flicker of interest and admiration which her son must keep fanned, for she would not. Boredom drew her away again, yet her charm must still hold sway. So now Edward listened crossly to the story of the Byzantine Mosaic as he had last holidays minutely observed the chasing on Henry VIII's breast-plate, and in utter exasperation the holidays before that watched curlews through field-glasses ('Edward is so very keen on birds') for the whole of a hot day while Tory dozed elegantly in the heather.

'Ordinary days perhaps are better,' Edward thought. Sinking down through him were the lees of despair, which must, at all costs, be hidden from his mother. He glanced up at every clock they passed and wondered about his friends. Alone with his mother, he felt unsafe, wounded and wounding; saw himself in relation to the outside world, oppressed by responsibility. Thoughts of the future and even, as they stood in the church porch to shelter from another little gust of rain, of death, seemed to alight on him, brushed him, disturbed him, as they would not do if he were at school, herded and safe.

Tory sat down on a seat and read a notice about Missionaries, chafing her hands inside her muff while all her bracelets jingled softly.

Flapping, black, in his cassock, a clergyman came hurrying through the graveyard, between the dripping umbrella trees. Edward stepped guiltily outside the porch as if he had been trespassing.

'Good-afternoon,' the Vicar said.

'Good-afternoon,' Tory replied. She looked up from blowing the fur of her muff into little divisions, and her smile broke warmly, beautifully, over the dark afternoon.

Then: 'The weather!' both began ruefully, broke off and hesitated, then laughed at one another.

It was wonderful; now they would soon be saying good-bye. It was over. The day they had longed for was almost over; the polite little tea among the chintz, the wheel-back chairs of the Copper Kettle; Tory frosty and imperious with the waitresses, and once, Edward beginning: 'Father ...' at which she looked up sharply before she could gather together the careful indifference she always assumed at this name. Edward faltered. 'He sent me a parcel.' 'How nice!' Tory said, laying ice all over his heart. Her cup was cracked. She called the waitress. She could not drink tea from riveted china, however prettily painted. The waitress went sulkily away. All round them sat other little boys with their parents. Tory's bracelets tinkled as she clasped her hands tightly together and leant forward. 'And how,' she asked, brightly, indifferently, 'how is your father's wife?'

Now the taxi turned in at the school-gates. Suddenly, the day withdrew; there were lights in the ground-floor windows. She thought of going back in the train, a lonely evening. She would take a drink up to her bedroom and sip it while she did her hair, the gas-fire roaring in its white ribs, Edward's photograph beside her bed.

The Hay-Hardys were unloading at the foot of the steps; flushed from their country walk and all their laughter, they seemed to swarm and shout.

Edward got out of the taxi and stood looking up at Tory, his new puncture outfit clasped tightly in his hand. Uncertainly, awaiting a cue from her, he tried to begin his good-bye.

Warm, musky-scented, softly rustling, with the sound of her bracelets, the touch of her fur, she leant and kissed him.

'So lovely, darling!' she murmured. She had no cue to give him. Mrs Hay-Hardy had gone into the school to have a word with Matron, so she must find her own way of saying farewell.

They smiled gaily, as if they were greeting one another.

'See you soon.'

'Yes, see you soon.'

'Good-bye, then, darling.'

'Good-bye.'

She slammed the door and, as the car moved off, leant to the windows and waved. He stood there uncertainly, waving back, radiant with relief; then, as she disappeared round the curve of the drive, ran quickly up the steps to find his friends and safety.

The Beginning of a Story

They could hear the breathing through the wall. Ronny sat watching Marian, who had her fingers in her ears as she read. Sometimes he leant forward and reached for a log and put it on the fire, and for a second her eyes would dwell on his movements, on his young, bony wrist shot out of his sleeve, and then, like a lighthouse swinging its beam away, she would withdraw her attention and go back to her book.

A long pause in the breathing would make them glance at one another questioningly, and then, as it was hoarsely resumed, they would fall away from one another again, he to his silent building of the fire and she to her solemn reading of *Lady Audley's Secret*.

He thought of his mother, Enid, in the next room, sitting at her own mother's deathbed, and he tried to imagine her feelings, but her behaviour had been so calm all through his grandmother's illness that he could not. It is different for the older ones, he thought, for they are used to people dying. More readily, he could picture his father at the pub, accepting drinks and easy sympathy. 'Nothing I can do,' he would be saying. 'You only feel in the way.' Tomorrow night, perhaps, 'A happy release' would be his comfortable refrain, and solemnly, over their beer, they would all agree.

Once, Marian said to Ronny, 'Why don't you get something to do?'

'Such as what?'

'Oh, don't ask me. It's not my affair.' These last few days, Marian liked, as often as she could, to dissociate herself from the family. As soon as the grandmother became ill, the other lodger, a girl from the same factory as Marian, had left. Marian had stayed on, but with her fingers stuck in her ears, or going about with a blank immunity, polite and distant to Enid. They were landlady and lodger to one another, no more, Marian constantly implied.

'Well, you could make some tea,' she said at last to Ronny, feeling exasperation at his silent contemplation of her. He moved obediently and began to unhook cups from the dresser without a sound, setting them carefully in their saucers on a tray – the pink-and-gilt one with the moss-rose for Marian, a large white one with a gold clover-leaf for his mother.

'You take it in to her,' he said when the tea was ready. He had a reason

for asking her, wishing to test his belief that Marian was afraid to go into
that other room. She guessed this, and snapped her book shut.

'Lazy little swine,' she said, and took up his mother's cup.

Enid rose as Marian opened the door. The room was bright and warm. It
was the front room, and the Sunday furniture had been moved to make
space for the bed. The old woman was half sitting up, but her head was
thrown back upon a heap of pillows. Her arms were stretched out over the
counterpane, just as her daughter had arranged them. Her mouth, without
teeth, was a grey cavern. Except for the breathing, she might have been
dead.

Enid had been sitting up with her for nights, and she stood stiffly now,
holding the cup of tea, her eyes dark with fatigue. I ought to offer, thought
Marian, but I'd be terrified to be left alone in here.

She went back to Ronny, who looked at her now with respect added to
all the other expressions on his face. His father had come back from the
pub and was spreading his hairy hands over the fire to get warm. He was
beery and lugubrious. They were all afraid of Enid. At any sound from the
other room, they flicked glances at one another.

'Poor old gel,' said Ronny's father over and over again. 'Might as well get
to bed, Marian. No need for you to make yourself ill.'

Ronny found his father's way of speaking and his look at the girl intolerable.

Marian had been waiting for someone to make the suggestion. 'Well ...'
She hesitated. 'No sense, I suppose ...'

'That's right,' said the older man.

She went out to the sink in the scullery and slipped her shoulders out
of her blouse. She soaped a flannel under the icy water and passed it quickly
over her throat, gathering up her hair at the back to wash her neck, curving one arm, then the other, over her head as she soaped her armpits.

Ronny and his father sat beside the fire, listening to the water splashing
into the bowl. When they heard the wooden sound as Marian pulled at the
roller towel, the older man glanced at the door and moved, stirred by the
thought of the young girl.

It was one of the moments of hatred that the son often felt for him, but
it seemed to make no impression on his father.

Marian came in, fresh, her face shiny, her blouse carelessly buttoned.
'Well, good-night,' she said, and opened the door behind which stairs led
up to the little bedrooms. 'If you want me, you know where I am.'

There was no sophistication in either man to see the ambiguity of her
words; they simply took them to mean what she intended.

The door closed, and they heard her creak upstairs and overhead. They went on sitting by the fire and neither spoke. Occasional faint beer smells came from the father. It did not occur to him to go into the other room to his wife. Ronny took the tea-things into the scullery and washed up. It was dark out there and lit by a very small oil lamp. He remained there for as long as he thought he could without being questioned. The tap dripped into the sink. He smelled the soap she had used. He could no longer hear the breathing.

Marian lay between the rough twill sheets, shivering. Her feet were like ice, although she had rolled them in her cardigan. The only hot-water bottle was in the bed downstairs. She hated this house but had no energy to move from it. Or had she stayed because of that sickened curiosity that always forced her to linger by hearses while coffins were carried out? 'Ron, too,' she thought. 'It isn't right for us. We're young. In the morning, I'm not fit for work. If only Enid knew how the girls at the factory went on: "What's happening now?" "The blinds down yet?" "How awful for you!"' She drew up her knees, yawned, and crossed her arms on her breast. The young slip into the first attitude with beautiful ease and relaxation.

Because the house had been so quiet for days, the sound of a door bursting open, a chair scraped hurriedly back, shocked Marian out of sleep, and she lay trembling, her feet still entangled in the cardigan. She felt that it was about half-way through the night, but could not be sure. She heard Ron stumbling upstairs, tapping on her door. She put on her raincoat over her night-gown and went out to him.

'It's Gran,' he said. 'She's gone.'

'What had I better do?' she asked in panic, with no example before her of how she should behave. He had wakened her but did not know why.

'Ron!' Enid came to the bottom of the stairs and called up. The light from the room behind her threw a faint nimbus around her head.

'Yes, Mother,' he said, looking down at her.

'Did you wake Marian?'

'Yes.' He answered guiltily, but evidently she thought his action right and proper.

'You will have to go for Mrs Turner,' his mother said.

'Why?'

'She – she's expecting you.'

'In the middle of the night?'

'Yes. Right away – now.' She turned away from the bottom of the stairs.

'Who is Mrs Turner?' Marian whispered.

'I think— She lays people out.' Ronny felt shame and uneasiness at his words, which seemed to him crude, obscene.

The girl covered her face with her hands. 'Oh, life's horrible.'

'No, it's death, not life.'

'Don't leave me.'

'Come with me, then.'

'Is it far?'

'No, not far. Hurry.'

'Stand there by the door while I get ready.'

Marian moved into the dark bedroom, and he stood leaning against the door-frame, waiting, with his arms folded across his chest. She came back quickly, wearing the raincoat, a scarf tied over her head.

They went downstairs into the bright kitchen, where Enid stood fixing candles into brass holders while her husband poured some brandy from an almost empty bottle into a glass. Enid drowned the brandy with warm water from the kettle and drank it off swiftly, her dark eyes expressionless.

'Give some to the children,' she said, without thinking. They stiffened at the word 'children' but took their brandy-and-water and sipped it.

'It's a cold night,' said Enid. 'Now go quickly.'

'Marian's coming with me.'

'So I see,' said Enid. Her husband drank the last spoonful from the bottle, neat. 'The end house, Lorne Street, right-hand side, by the Rose and Crown,' she said, turning back to the other room.

The fumes of the brandy kindled in Ron's and Marian's breasts. 'Remember that,' he said. 'The end house.' He unlatched the back door.

'Next the Rose and Crown,' she added. They slipped out into the beautiful, shocking air of the night.

When Ronny shone his torch down, they could see the yellow hands of the leaves lying on the dark, wet pavements. Now there was only a flick of moisture in the air. He had taken her arm, and they walked alone in the streets, which flowed like black rivers. She wished that they might go on for ever and never turn back towards that house. Or she would like it to be broad daylight, so that she could be at work, giggling about it all with the girls. ('Go on, Marian!' 'How awful for you!')

His arm was pressed against her ribs. Sometimes she shivered from the cold and squeezed him to her. Down streets and around corners they went. Not far away, goods trains shunted up and down. Once, she stumbled over a kerb, and in saving her he felt the sweet curve of her breast against his arm and walked gaily and with elation, filled with excitement and delight, swinging the beam of the torch from side to side, thinking it was the happiest evening of his life, seeing the future opening out suddenly, like a fan, revealing all at once the wonder of human relationships.

'The Rose and Crown,' she whispered. The building was shuttered for

the night, the beer smells all washed away by the rain, the signboard creaking in the wind.

'The next house then.' She felt tensed up, but he was relaxed and
confident.

'I've forgotten the name,' she said.

'Turner.'

They went up a short path on to a dark porch and knocked at the door.
After a moment, a window at the front of the house was thrown up and a
woman's voice called out. They stepped back into the garden and looked
up.

'Who is it?' the voice asked.

'We're from Mrs Baker's,' Ron said.

'Poor soul! She's gone then, at last. How's your mother?'

Ronnie considered this and then said, 'She's tired.'

'She will be. Wait there, and I'll come along with you.' She disappeared
and the window was slammed down.

'She seemed an ordinary sort of woman,' whispered Marian.

They drew back into the shelter of the porch and waited. No sounds
came from the house, but a smell of stuffiness seemed to drift out through
the letter slot in the door.

'Suppose she goes back to bed and leaves us here?' Marian asked, and
began to giggle. She put her mouth against his shoulder to stifle the little
giggles, and he put his arm around her. She lifted her paper-white face in
the darkness and they kissed. The word 'bliss' came into his mind, and he
tasted it slowly on his tongue, as if it were a sweet food. Platitudes began
to come true for them, but they could not consider them as such.

Suddenly, a step sounded on the other side of the door, bolts were slid
back with difficulty, a chain rattled.

'Here we are!' said the brisk voice. The woman stepped out into the
porch, putting on a pair of fur gloves and looking up at the night sky and
the flocks of curdy, scudding clouds. 'It's a sad time,' she said. 'A very sad
time for your poor mum and dad. Come on, then, lad, you lead the way.
Quick, sharp!'

And now the footsteps of the three of them rang out metallically upon
the paving-stones as they walked between the dark and eyeless cliffs of the
houses.

Oasis of Gaiety

After luncheon, Dosie took off her shoes and danced all round the room. Her feet were plump and arched, and the varnish on her toe nails shone through her stockings.

Her mother was sitting on the floor playing roulette with some of her friends. She was always called Auntie except by Dosie, who 'darlinged' her in the tetchy manner of two women living in the same house, and by her son, Thomas, who stolidly said 'Mother', a *démodé* word, Auntie felt – half insulting.

On Sunday afternoons, most of Auntie's 'set' returned to their families when the mid-day champagne was finished. They scattered to the other houses round the golf course, to doze on loggias, snap at their children, and wonder where their gaiety had fled. Only Mrs Wilson, who was a widow and dreaded her empty house, Ricky Jimpson, and the goatish Fergy Burns stayed on. More intimate than a member of the family, more inside than a friend, Fergy supported Auntie's idea of herself better than anyone else did, and, at times and in ways that he knew she couldn't mind, he sided with Dosie and Thomas against her.

In some of the less remote parts of Surrey, where the nineteen-twenties are perpetuated, such pockets of stale and elderly gaiety remain. They are blank as the surrounding landscape of fir trees and tarnished water.

Sunshine, especially blinding to the players after so much champagne, slanted into the room, which looked preserved, sealed off. Pinkish-grey cretonnes, ruched cushions with tassels, piles of gramophone-records, and a velvet Maurice Chevalier doll recalled the stage-sets of those forgotten comedies about weekends in the country and domestic imbroglio.

Auntie's marmoset sat on the arm of a chair, looking down sadly at the players and eating grapes, which he peeled with delicate, worn fingers and sharp teeth. His name was Rizzio. Auntie loved to name her possessions, everything – her car (called the Bitch, a favourite word of her youth), her fur coat, the rather noisy cistern in the WC. Even some of her old cardigans and shawls had nicknames and personalities. Her friends seemed not to find this tiresome. They played the game strenuously and sometimes sent Christmas presents to the inanimate objects. In exchange for all the fun and champagne they were required only to assist the fantasy and preserve the past. Auntie thought of herself as a 'sport' and a 'scream'. (No one knew how her nickname had originated, for neither niece nor nephew had ever appeared to substantiate it.) 'I did have a lovely heyday,' she would say in her husky voice. 'Girls of Dosie's age have never had anything.' But Dosie had had two husbands already, not to count the incidentals, as Thomas said.

Thomas was her much younger brother, something of an incidental flowering himself. 'Auntie's last bit of nonsense,' people called him. Fifteen years and their different worlds separated brother and sister. He was of a more serious generation and seemed curiously practical, disabused, unemotional. His military service was a life beyond their imagination. They (pitying him, though recoiling from him) vaguely envisaged hutted sites at Aldershot, and boorish figures at football on muddy playing-fields with mists rising. Occasionally, at week-ends, he arrived, wearing sour-smelling khaki, which seemed to rub almost raw his neck and wrists. He would clump into the pub in his great Army boots and drink mild-and-bitter at his mother's expense, cagey about laying down a halfpenny of his own.

He made Fergy feel uneasy. Fergy had, Auntie often said, an impossible conscience. Watching bullocks being driven into a slaughterhouse had once taken him off steak for a month, and now, when he saw Thomas in khaki, he could only remember his own undergraduate days, gilded youth, fun with fireworks and chamber-pots, débutantes arriving in May Week, driving his red MG to the Beetle and Wedge for the Sunday-morning session. But Thomas had no MG. He had only the 7.26 back to Aldershot. If he ever had any gaiety, his mother did not discover it: if he had any friends, he did not bring them forward. Auntie was, Fergy thought, a little mean with him, a little on the tight side. She used endearments to him, but as if in utter consternation. He was an uncouth cuckoo in her nest. His hands made excruciating sounds on the silk cushions. Often, in bars, she would slip him a pound to pay his way, yet here he was, this afternoon, making as neat and secret a little pile as one would wish to see.

He played with florins, doubling them slowly, giving change where required, tucking notes into the breast pocket of his battle-dress, carefully buttoning them away as if no one was to be trusted. He had a rather breathy concentration, as he had had as a child, crouching over snakes-and-ladders; his hands, scooping up the coins, looked, Auntie thought, like great paws.

Only Mrs Wilson's concentration could match his, but she had none of his stealthy deliberation. She had lost a packet, she proclaimed, but no one listened. She kept putting her hand in her bag and raking about, bringing out only a handkerchief, with which she touched the corners of her mouth.

The others seemed to her quite indifferent to the fortunes of the game –
Fergy, for instance, who was the banker, pushing Thomas's winnings across
to him with no change of expression and no hesitation in his flow of talk.

Auntie gave a tiny glance of dislike at her son as he slipped some coins
into his pocket. She could imagine him counting them all up, going back
in the train. In her annoyance, she added a brutish look to his face. She
sighed, but it was almost imperceptible and quite unperceived, the slightest intake of breath, as she glanced round at her friends, the darlings, who
preserved her world, drinking her whisky, switching the radio away from
the news to something gayer, and fortifying her against the dreary post-war
world her son so typified. Mrs Wilson, also, was a little dreary. Although
trying gallantly, she had no real flair for recklessness and easily became
drunk, when she would talk about her late husband and what a nice home
they had had.

'Oh, Dosie, do sit down!' Auntie said.

Dosie was another who could not drink. She would become gayer and
gayer and more and more taunting to poor Ricky Jimpson. Now she was
dancing on his winnings. He smiled wanly. After the game, he would happily give her the lot, but while he was playing, it was sacred.

What Dosie herself gave for all she had from him was something to conjecture. Speculation, beginning with the obviously shameful, had latterly
run into a maze of contradictions. Perhaps – and this was even more
derogatory – she did only bestow taunts and abuse. She behaved like a very
wilful child, as if to underline the fact that Ricky was old enough to be her
father. Rather grey-faced (he had, he thought, a duodenal ulcer, and the
vast quantity of whisky he drank was agony to him), he would sit and smile
at her naughty ways, and sometimes when she clapped her hands, as if she
pretended he was her slave, he would show that this was not pretence but
very truth, and hurry to carry out her wishes.

Dosie, with one hand on the piano to steady herself, went through some
of the *barre* exercises she had learnt as a child at ballet class. Her joints
snapped and crackled with a sound like a fire kindling.

'You are a deadly lot,' she suddenly said, and yawned out at the garden.
'Put ten shillings on *rouge* for me, Ricky. I always win if you do it.'

At least she doesn't lose if it isn't her money, Mrs Wilson thought, wondering if she could ever, in a rallying way, make such a request of Fergy.

The hot afternoon, following the champagne, made them all drowsy.
Only Ricky Jimpson sat up trimly. Fergy, looking at Mrs Wilson's bosom,
which her décolleté blouse too generously tendered, thought that in no
time it would be all she had to offer. He imagined her placing it on, perhaps *zéro* – her last gesture.

Quite frightful, Auntie thought, the way Thomas's brow furrowed because he had lost two shillings. He was transparently sulky, like a little boy. All those baked beans in canteens made him stodgy and impossible. She hadn't visualised having such a son, or such a world for him to live in.

'We can really do nothing for young people,' she had once told Mrs Wilson. 'Nothing, nowadays, but try to preserve for them some of the old days, keep up our standards and give them an inkling of what things used to be, make a little oasis of gaiety for them.' That had been during what she called 'the late war'. Thomas was home from school for the Christmas holidays. With tarnished pre-war tinsel Auntie was decorating the Christmas tree, though to this, as to most things, Thomas was quite indifferent. He had spent the holidays bicycling slowly round and round the lawn on the white, rimed grass. In the evenings, when his mother's friends came for drinks, he collected his books and went noticeably to his room. The books, on mathematics, were dull but mercifully concerned with things as they were, and this he preferred to all the talk about the tarnished, pre-war days. He could not feel that the present day was any of his doing. For the grown-ups to scorn what they had bequeathed to him seemed tactless. He ignored those conversations until his face looked mulish and immune. His mother arranged for his adenoids to be removed, but he continued to be closed-up and unresponsive.

Dosie was so different; she might almost be called a ringleader. She made her mother feel younger than ever – 'really more like a sister,' Auntie said, showing that this was a joke by saying it with a Cockney accent. Oh, Dosie was the liveliest girl, except that sometimes she went too far. The oasis of gaiety her mother provided became obviously too small and she was inclined then to go off into the desert and cry havoc. But Auntie thought her daughter mischievous, not desperate.

'Either play or not,' she told her sharply, for sometimes the girl irritated her.

But Dosie, at the French windows, took no notice. She could feel the sun striking through her thin frock, and she seemed to unfold in the warmth, like a flower. In the borders, lilies stood to attention in the shimmering air, their petals glazed and dusty with pollen. The scent was wonderful.

'I shall bathe in the pool,' she said, over her shoulder. The pool – a long rectangle of water thick with plants – was deep and Dosie had never learnt to swim, had always floundered wildly.

Only Ricky Jimpson remonstrated.

'She can't swim,' Auntie said, dismissing her daughter's nonsense. 'Does anyone *want* to go on playing?'

Mrs Wilson certainly did not. She had never believed in last desperate flings, throwing good money after bad. In games of chance there was no certainty but that she would lose; even the law of averages worked against her. What she wanted now was a cup of tea and aspirins, for champagne agreed with her no better than roulette. She felt lost. Her widowhood undermined her and she no longer felt loved.

But who was loved – in this room, for instance? Mrs Wilson often thought that her husband would not have dared to die if he had known she would drift into such company. 'What *you* need, darling, is a nice, cosy woman friend,' Fergy had said years ago when she had reacted in bewilderment to his automatic embrace. He had relinquished her at once, in a weary, bored way, and ignored her coldly ever since. His heartless perception frightened her. Despite her acceptance of – even clinging to – their kind of life, and her acquiescence in every madness, every racket, she had not disguised from him that what she wanted was her dull, good husband back and a nice evening with the wireless; perhaps, too, a middle-aged woman friend to go shopping with, to talk about slimming and recipes. Auntie never discussed those things. She was the kind of woman men liked. She amused them with her scatter-brained chatter and innuendo and the fantasy she wove, the stories she told, about herself. When she was with women, she rested. Mrs Wilson could not imagine her feeling unsafe, or panicking when the house emptied. She seemed self-reliant and efficient. She and Dosie sometimes quarrelled, or appeared to be quarrelling, with lots of 'But, *darling!*' and '*Must* you be such a fool, sweetie?' Yet only Thomas, the symbol of the post-war world, was really an affront. Him she could not assimilate. He was the grit that nothing turned into a pearl – neither gaiety nor champagne. He remained blank, impervious. He took his life quite seriously, made no jokes about the Army, was silent when his mother said, 'Oh, *why* go? Catch the last train or wait until morning. In fact, why don't you desert? Dosie and I could hide you in the attic. It would be the greatest fun. Or be ill. Get some awful soldier's disease.'

Dosie was blocking the sunlight from the room, and Mrs Wilson suddenly felt goose flesh on her arms and cramp in her legs from sitting on the floor.

Ricky Jimpson put his winnings in his pocket without a glance at them. He sat, bent slightly forward, with one hand pressed to his waist. He smiled brilliantly if he caught anybody's eye, but his face soon reassembled itself to its look of static melancholy. The smile was an abrupt disorganisation. His eyes rarely followed Dosie. He seemed rather to be listening to her, even when she was silent. He was conscious of her in some other way than visually. His spirit *attended* to her, caught up in pain though he was.

The roulette cloth was folded and put away. The marmoset was busy tearing one of the cushion tassels. Then, to Mrs Wilson's relief, the door opened and a maid pushed in a trolley with a jazzy black-and-orange pottery tea-set and some rolled-up bread and butter.

Dosie wandered out across the gravelled path in her stockinged feet. The garden, the golf course beyond it, and all the other wistaria-covered, balconied Edwardian villas at its perimeter seemed to slant and swoon in the heat. Her exasperation weakened and dispersed. She always felt herself leaving other people behind; they lagged after her recklessness. Even in making love, she felt the same isolation – that she was speeding on into a country where no one would pursue her. Each kiss was an act of division. 'Follow me!' she willed 'them' – a succession of them, all shadowy. They could not follow, or know to what cold distances she withdrew. Her punishment for them was mischief, spite, a little gay cruelty, but nothing drastic. She had no beauty, for there was none to inherit, but she was a bold and noticeable woman.

When Fergy joined her in the garden, he put his arm across her shoulders and they walked down the path towards the pool. Water-lilies lay picturesquely on the green surface. The oblong of water was bordered by ornamental grasses in which dragonflies glinted. A concrete gnome was fishing at the edge.

They stood looking at the water, lulled by the heat and the beauty of the afternoon. When he slipped his arm closer round her, she felt herself preparing, as of old, for flight. Waywardly, she moved from him. She stripped seeds off a tall grass, viciously, and scattered them on the water. Goldfish rose, then sank away dejectedly.

'Let us throw in this bloody little dwarf,' Dosie said, 'and you can cry for help. They will think I am drowning.' She began to rock the gnome from side to side. Small brown frogs like crumpled leaves leapt away into the grass.

'Auntie dotes on the little creature,' Fergy said. 'She has a special nickname for him.'

'So have I.'

Together they lifted the gnome and threw him out towards the centre of the pool.

'I always loathed the little beast,' Dosie said.

'Help!' Fergy cried. 'For God's sake, help!'

Dosie watched the house, her face alight, her eyebrows lifted in anticipation. Rings widened and faded on the water.

Ricky Jimpson dashed through the French windows and ran towards the pool, his face whiter than ever, his hand to his side. When he saw them both standing there, he stopped. His look of desperation vanished. He smiled his brilliant, dutiful smile, but, receiving one of his rare glances, Dosie saw in his eyes utter affliction, forlornness.

*

That evening, Thomas, on his way back to Aldershot, met Syd at the top
of the station subway; as per usual arrangement, Syd had said when they
parted the day before. Their greeting was brief and they went in silence
towards the restaurant, shouldering their way along the crowded platform.
In the bar, they ordered two halves of mild-and-bitter and two pieces of
pork-pie.

Syd pushed back his greasy beret and scratched his head. Then he broke
open the pie to examine the inside – the pink gristle and tough grey jelly.

'What they been up to this time?' he asked.

'The usual capering about. My mother was rather lit up last night and
kept doing the Charleston.'

'Go on!'

'But I suppose that's better than the Highland fling,' Thomas said. 'Pass
the mustard.'

Syd, whose own mother rarely moved more than, very ponderously,
from sink to gas stove, was fascinated. 'Like to've seen it,' he said. 'From a
distance.'

'What did you do?' Thomas asked.

'Went to the Palais Saturday night along with Viv. Never got up till
twelve this morning, then went round the local. Bit of a read this afternoon, then went for a stroll along with Viv. You know, up by the allotments.
Had a nice lie-down in the long grass. She put her elbow in a cow-pat.
Laugh!' He threw back his head and laughed there and then.

'Same again,' Thomas said to the barmaid. 'Want some more pie, Syd?'

'No, ta. I had me tea.'

'I made thirty-four bob,' Thomas said, tapping his breast pocket.

'You can make mine a pint then,' Syd said. But Thomas didn't say anything. They always drank halves. He looked at Syd and wondered what his
mother would say of him. He often wondered that. But she would never
have the chance. He looked quite fiercely round the ugly restaurant room,
with its chromium tables, ringed and sticky, thick china, glass domes over
the museum-pieces of pork pie. The look of the place calmed him, as Syd's
company did – something he could grasp, *his* world.

'Don't know how they stick that life, week after week,' Thomas said. 'My
sister threw a garden ornament in the pond – pretended she'd fallen in herself. A sort of dwarf,' he added vaguely.

'What for?' Syd asked.

'I think she was fed up,' Thomas said, trying to understand. But he lived
in two irreconcilable worlds.

Syd only said, 'Rum. Could they fish it out again?'

'No one tried. We had tea then.' He gave up trying to explain what he
did not comprehend, and finished his beer.

'Better get a move on,' Syd said, using as few consonants as possible.
'Yes, I suppose so.' Thomas looked at the clock.
'The old familiar faces.'
'You're right,' Thomas agreed contentedly.

Plenty Good Fiesta

Long, long ago, during the Spanish Civil War, Fernando came to live with us for a short time. Nowadays, refugees are part of the world's landscape, but he was much less a refugee than an ambassador. He had come to England with other children from the bombed cities of Spain. They lived in a camp near our home, and were always about the country lanes – graceful, swarthy children. Young as they were, fear had come closer to them than to us, and they seemed like our futures walking towards us. Fernando was the one my husband and I knew most intimately. Because of his nervous habits, which shock had caused, the other children teased him; and the camp doctor asked us if we would take him into our home until he recovered. I knew nothing about him except what the doctor told me – that his father, a schoolmaster, was in hiding, his mother in prison, and his one brother, grown-up, had been killed by the Fascists. Nine years old, forlorn, speaking no word of English, he had achieved a jaunty gaiety to cover up his naturally clinging disposition. I imagined him a 'spoilt' child (though kindness could no more spoil him than evil had) – much petted, the baby of the family, born to his mother in her middle age.

Although he found himself among strangers in a strange country, he gave no measuring glances, showed no surprise or hesitancy; he walked into our house purposefully, carrying in a paper bag some girls' underwear he had been given, a cherished Fair Isle jersey, and a handful of glass marbles. Pride was in each step he took.

Neither my husband nor I can speak Spanish, but the dictionary on the dinner table was unnecessary. Fernando reached for what he needed. He pushed back his chair and went round the table, spearing with his fork whatever took his fancy. Never over everyday things did we feel lack of language a barrier; only over subtler things, emotional nuances or matters of reassurance.

He was a robust child with beautiful ways of walking and moving. His dark cheeks were always suffused with rose, an unusual warmth in such a dusky skin. His black hair was curly and untidy, but on formal occasions he combed it under the bath tap in a great rush of cold water.

His appearance was then quite changed. The long damp fringe level above his eyes gave him a sinister look.

Along with the girls' underwear, he had been given a pair of heavy boots. It was summer, but he would not discard these for the sandals we gave him.

He was never timid or ingratiating, as, in his strange position, he might have been. Only once was he disobedient. I found him striking a box of matches, one by one. Because he always dropped the matches as soon as they flared, he had been told not to touch them. This time, he had used up the whole box. He threw down the last match as I arrived, and smiled. 'Is quite all right,' he said in one breath. It was his first English phrase. He did not know the meaning but took it to be reassuring, as it was what I said when he dropped a plate, or, once, when he wet his bed. For his pidgin English we must have been to blame, as he knew no word when he first came to us. He began to talk like a stage Chinaman. 'Plenty bad,' he explained when he was discovered stoning the sign of the Cyclists' Touring Club, which, with its whirling arrangement of legs, he took to be the Fascist swastika.

He sometimes had a male swagger, hands in pockets, his trousers tight across his buttocks. He would whistle, shrug his shoulders, behave in a pre-cociously cheeky manner to me. He had, especially, a startlingly adult wink, with his finger to the side of his nose. Slowly, laden with meaning, his lid would drop. He would do this in company, across a room at me, suggesting a dubious complicity. I wondered if he had watched his grown-up brother in his conquering days, as he had later watched him killed.

His male arrogance was mingled with a strong maternal tenderness. He loved to push our baby in the pram along the lanes, the blond baby sitting up smiling at him as Fernando strode along singing the songs of Republican Spain. For he never forgot that he was Spanish. He accepted our life with grace and courtesy, but he did not become English. He admired the best we had to offer – the Fair Isle jersey, the boots, our babies, the English countryside – but he was always the proud and formal Catalan. He was for the Republic, against the Fascists, politically conscious, loyal. He also spat as he passed the church; in his country the *iglesia* had often concealed machine-guns. He even cleaned his mouth at the sight of the Baptist Chapel.

Fernando's anger, when it occurred, was a ceremonious anger. His gaiety, which was the gayest gaiety I ever encountered, had some of the same formality. In England, gaiety is informal, spasmodic. We do not reserve it for special occasions, and at Christmas it is sometimes a dogged duty. We did not have Fernando with us for Christmas. But we did have him for the *fiesta*.

One afternoon, we took Fernando and the baby for a drive. Not far from home we came to a village where a little fair was set out on the green – a few caravans, a roundabout, sideshows, swing boats. Fernando, in the back seat, began to wave his arms, and cried, '*Fiesta! Fiesta!*' As we had to get back for the baby's six-o'clock feeding (and even that seemed un-Spanish, dogged), we could only promise to return to the fair next day. '*Mañana.*' He nodded with satisfaction.

Late that night, as my husband and I were thinking of going to bed, we heard Fernando's boots on the landing, then the sound of water running from the bathroom tap. We ran upstairs to see what he was doing. He was dressed in the Fair Isle jersey, his wet hair flattened to his brow. 'For the *fiesta,*' he said. Dismayed by memories of Ernest Hemingway, of bulls charging through the streets at dawn, and wine running in the gutters, I wondered how to explain. In England, I said, the fiesta does not begin until daytime. Dazed, a little scornful, he was led back to his bed.

Very early in the morning, I awoke to the sound of the boots and the rushing water. Again I explained. Puzzled, Fernando watched my husband go to work. ('In England, we do not stop work for the *fiesta.*') Because he spent such a disconsolate morning, and from a kind of national guilt, I let him strike match after match. Thoughts of the modest village fair lowered me.

As it was Saturday, my husband came home at noon, and we all got into the car and drove off after lunch. I was as flattened and subdued as Fernando's hair. Over my shoulder, the baby bobbed its head at him. Long strings of dribble festooned me. Fernando spoke Catalan baby talk, winked, whistled, sang. He was lifted to a pitch of excitement that filled us with gloom and despair. We drove into the village, and the fair was gone.

There were no words to cover our horror. We thanked God for His arrangements about the Tower of Babel, which seemed now a piece of long-term wisdom. We smiled reassuringly and said, 'Is quite all right.' As if he knew where we were going, my husband drove confidently down the lanes, made enquiries at village shops. No one could help. After a long time, we found a few caravans on a dirty fairground, outside a market town. Drearily set amid mud and cinders, they looked shabby and unclean compared with those we had seen the day before.

Fernando put a hand apprehensively to his fringe, as if about to enter Windsor Castle. I wished I had not read that book by Hemingway. It was so full of local colour, of which Britain seemed to have none (save the Fair Isle jersey).

The baby's eyes stretched in terror at the panic of music forced by steam out of the roundabout. Fernando, with his hand still on his fringe, burst from the car. Utterly dejected, my husband and I made our way down the cinder path.

I think that one of the most touching things I have read about a war was by Gertrude Stein, who remarked how the look of her French village altered in 1939. The elder brothers and the fathers went off to the front, and suddenly the lanes were full of little boys riding bicycles too big for them, standing on the pedals, their elbows in the air. I do not know if Fernando's brother had a bicycle and there was the same brief period of riding it, but it was now revealed to us that the great force and passion of Fernando's life was to own one – or at least to ride one for a while, pretending ownership. Ignoring the rest of the fair, he made for the children's roundabout, where, among peacocks, racing cars, airplanes, and gilded horses, he could see a stationary bicycle with movable pedals.

Excitement exploded in him. His hair, beginning to curl again, bounded on his forehead. The few people who were about glanced from the blond baby to the impassioned Spaniard with amusement. Self-consciously, we led him to the bicycle. The other children, used to their fairy-cycles and tricycles, preferred the more exotic birds or the airplanes.

The rides – in those days – were a penny, and lasted perhaps for three minutes. Two shillings' worth covered about an hour and a half, for there were gaps while the man waited for more customers. My husband and I stood watching, taking turns holding the baby. At first Fernando waved as he passed us, but later forgot. He gazed into the distance, pedalling rapidly, grave, absorbed. His eyes narrowed, and he leant to an imagined camber of the road.

What distances in Catalonia, we wondered, did he cover? What goal achieve? Sometimes, impatiently, because of fool drivers, he rang the bell, sometimes seemed to stiffen his whole body, bear down on the pedals, braking for unseen obstacles, though the roundabout took him merrily on.

He became a character to the man in charge and to some of the onlookers, but he was oblivious of them. Each time the roundabout ran down, the bronchial music wheezed off into a trailing sigh, he would hand in another penny in a peremptory, irritable way, checked in his dream, and sit steady, tense, waiting. Once, catching my eye, he looked quickly aside, as if the sight of me violated his privacy.

At the end, when his money was spent, he climbed down. He stumbled towards us, seeming drunk. He did not speak.

We drove off through the drab town, with its queue already outside the cinema, and then into the quiet, lovely countryside. The fields were tented with cornstooks. A picture of peace. The baby slept now. Fernando, gorged with pleasure, replete, dulled, sat with his head jogging against the side of the car. Awkwardly, I was silent, too, thinking of the bullfights, the *corrida*, a mounting, vinous excitement.

When we reached home, I turned to look at Fernando. He seemed drowsy and blissful. He smiled his fine smile. 'Plenty good *bicicleta*,' he said, nodding. 'Plenty good *fiesta*.'

Simone

From four until six-thirty Ethel was alone. Four o'clock was good, with the fire built up to last and a cup of tea in her hand. Mrs Dring left the key under the mat, lest the priest should call, or the doctor – the doctor with sleeping-tablets, the priest with the political pamphlets she could not understand. 'Dull stuff,' she thought, reaching for her library book as the door closed on Mrs Dring at four o'clock, and 'cosy' she would murmur, glancing round the room, which moved in the shifting firelight, and seemed alive. After an hour, though, it had stilled and grown lifeless, and she had begun that agonising time of watching the hand of the clock, so nerve-destroying to the bedridden.

'When Fred comes, we'll have a good laugh about Mrs Dring's boy – must remember to tell him that.'

She arranged the simple anecdote with the touch of an artist, laying a little emphasis here and there, not exactly exaggerating ... She knew Fred's life was dull, that she imprisoned him, made impossible demands. She wanted to tell him one evening to go out for a game of darts, but the evening was what she had looked forward to in anguish all day long, and she had never been able to make the sacrifice, but postponed it day after day.

'He's out all the time, meeting people,' she thought resentfully. 'Has a drink with his dinner. That's more than I have.'

She knew the funny stories were an attempt to compensate him. She garnished, embellished, wrested from Mrs Dring what gossip she could, and her prize was never more than his wan smile, his laugh which cheated neither of them.

'Good old Fred,' she would think, around five o'clock. 'Coming straight from work of an evening. Not many men like that.'

She finicked with her library books, Mrs Dring always said. Liked a nice love story, but nothing sexy. Could never remember what she had read. Would not have books about children; threw them aside at any mention of childbirth or pregnancy. Could not abide stories of foreign countries, or anything historical, or detective tales, or violence, or adventure.

'Oh, I've had this one before, Mrs Dring, and this one's about China. You know I like a nice novel. Surely ...'

If she whined, Mrs Dring wouldn't tell her what the young lady at the library said or what she was wearing, and so she bit off the words and sighed, foreseeing that blank time after tea, without a book even.

By five-thirty, she was thinking that she must come down to reading pamphlets; but they were across the room out of reach. Her eyes kept swivelling back to them in an exasperated way. The little books with their dull covers became dreadfully desirable.

The fire creaked and whispered. Some coals fell together with a shudder. The shadows on the wall grew still. The room seemed to be dying slowly, and the clock was running down.

'It will be like this all my life,' she thought, in one of those obliterating, dark waves of panic which came to her, as if she were in the condemned cell.

Confronted with the inevitable reality, frustration beat her down, hatred filled her; but it was a painful hatred, undefined. In her world there was only Fred. She could not hate him. And she loved and pitied herself.

'I love him, for he is all I have, and I could never repay him for all his goodness.'

The easy tears flowed down the sides of her face. She would not have understood that often we do hate those in whose debt we stand deeply, who are all we have. It was life she hated, she sometimes decided, life itself; but that was like blaming God, the priest said.

She lay there, aching all down her back, the bed needing smoothing, the mirror over the fireplace (painted with bulrushes in one corner) hanging crookedly. She looked from that to the pamphlets in despair.

'Fred *must* come,' she thought. 'He must come soon.'

She tried to imagine him running down the steps outside the office, flinging himself on a bus, knowing as he did that one minute less of her agony and frustration, her discomforts, the crooked bulrushes, her empty mind, was like one minute less on the rack, meant one wrenched-out gasp of irritation the less.

'I can't expect him for ten minutes,' she began. 'Oh, please God, don't let him stop to buy a paper!'

She closed her eyes and counted sixty slowly, and to her triumph more than a minute had passed when she looked at the clock. By six-thirty, the fire needed tending. She lay breathing deeply but unevenly, awaiting the sound of the key scratching at the lock.

When he came – ten minutes later than usual – she was exhausted.

'Sorry I'm late, old girl.'

She turned her face away from him, the tears running out of the corners of her eyes.

'But I brought a little surprise. A lady to see you.'

Ethel's face was wet, pink and crushed-up like an overblown rose in the rain.

He opened the door so that she could see. In walked a cat.

'A Siamese,' he said proudly.

The cat walked into the room and trod delicately across the carpet towards the fire. Ethel watched it. It was not a cat to her yet. It was ten minutes of anxiety and desperation. Fred took off his coat and shut the door. He shifted the coals in the fire, made a little draught between them, and threw on some kindling wood. The fire snapped and crackled into life again. When he had fondled the cat, he went to his wife and kissed her.

'Pleased with your present? I thought it would be company for you.'

'Where did you get it from?'

'One of my customers gave it to me. It's quite valuable. I just stopped to pick her up on the way home.'

'Which customer?'

'Old Hussey. He breeds them. It's quite trained. A nice clean cat.'

He lifted it and dropped it on the bed. Ethel put out her hand and stroked it. For a second, and only just that once, she felt love for the creature. It was oyster-coloured, with chocolate legs and ears, its head smoky, its eyes a deep gentian. She took one of its little suede paws – it was cold and the claws curved out wickedly.

Fred left the cat lying there on her chest, and they watched one another.

'What do you feel like for supper?' he asked her.

'You didn't plump up my cushions.'

'Sorry. Shall I open a tin of sardines?'

'If you like. I'm not hungry.'

'I thought of calling her Simone.'

'Why?'

He seemed not to notice the suspicion, the antagonism in her voice. 'I don't know. I've always liked that name. French. Sounds gay.'

As he opened the sardine-tin, the cat began to make small nervous movements, sniffing the air, lifting its paws and treading the bedspread.

'You'll pull the threads,' Ethel said.

It leapt from the bed and wove its way ecstatically between Fred's legs. He gave it a sardine and the oil in a saucer, and later, while he smoked his pipe, it lay on his lap with its half-closed eyes fixed contemplatively on Ethel. When Fred went out to make tea, it stood by the closed door and wailed.

'Worse than a baby,' he said happily.

Ethel said nothing.

It was the same in the morning. For a while, it cried by the door after he had left.

'Well,' said Mrs Dring. 'It's more like a baby than a cat.'

'What did you get from the library?'

'A nice Warwick Deeping and this *Pride and Prejudice*. A funny title, I know, but the young lady said she enjoyed the film.'

'But it's old-fashioned!' Ethel cried. 'Oh, never mind. The other one looks all right – if I haven't read it before, that is.'

All day, the cat remained by the fire. When Mrs Dring went at four o'clock, it sprang on to the bed and sat hunched up, staring at Ethel. When she put out her hand to touch its mushroom-coloured fur, it gave a quick scratch at her wrist, and its eyes changed to slits. It watched her and oppressed her.

'Well, Simone!' said Fred, coming eagerly into the room promptly at six-thirty. 'How's she been?'

'All right,' said Ethel dully.

After supper, she told Fred a funny story about Mrs Dring and the green-grocer. He laughed and stroked Simone, who lay stretched against his waistcoat.

'She's getting fatter,' he said.

Ethel struggled against her growing hatred of the cat. She felt, though, that the hatred had always been there in the room with her and had merely taken the form of a cat. The fact that it seemed to love Fred so passionately made her struggle more difficult. Every evening it lay on his shoulder, and every morning it cried when he went away; but during those hours between four and six-thirty, it seemed to turn the whole weight of its attention upon Ethel, so that she could not read or relax, and the time seemed longer than ever.

One afternoon, she begged Mrs Dring to shut the cat outside the door, but for two hours and a half the animal wailed, while Ethel, on the other side of the door, wept madly from nerves at the sound.

Fred came home to find both of them distracted.

'Mrs Dring shut her out by mistake,' Ethel explained.

'Poor old Simone. Did she want her mother, then? You must tell Mrs Dring to make quite sure before she goes another time.'

The next day the cat remained by the fire, but Ethel fancied that now it had that grudge against her and hated her that much more.

'Perhaps I am going mad,' she began to think. 'Afraid of a cat!' Yes, she was sure the cat was watching her, waiting for some change.

'Oh, don't bring me books about France,' she said one morning to Mrs Dring. 'I can't bear anything about France. It's worse than China. Why can't people write books about their own country? Showing off.'

'Look at that cat!' Mrs Dring replied. 'More like a human being – sitting there looking out of the window.'

Fred appeared not to notice that between his wife and the cat there was only this uneasy bond – the nervous watching of one another. 'Pussy', she called it, never 'Simone'. She did not fondle it, and it lay out of her reach always at the foot of the bed.

'If I fell asleep!' she thought. 'If I fell asleep while I was alone with it!' She kept herself rigidly from dozing and would not read.

From the priest, the doctor – her only visitors – she hid the secret of her fear and hatred with cunning answers. When they asked her why she was less well than before, she evaded them with trivial reasons – neuralgia, she admitted, the headaches – but she crumbled the aspirins she was given into the bedclothes, afraid to be lulled off her guard by them. She fell into the habit of nursing her cheek with her hand; the pain seemed real to her. After a while, she herself believed that it was there. She guessed that they were all watching her, thinking her half-mad, waiting for her to say, 'I am afraid of the cat,' so that then they would know, and Fred would be free.

Then one afternoon, with rain lashing at the window, the fire smoking a little, her strength suddenly cracked. She could play the game no longer. As the hands of the clock crawled, limped round after one another, the weakness began to break her. She sobbed without covering her face, her mouth squared with distress, like a child's. The cat watched, moving its tail evenly from side to side like a pendulum. Knowing herself beaten, Ethel staked everything on seeking to propitiate it.

'Pussy!' she sobbed. 'Good pussy!'

It crept up the bed towards her, so that she could reach it with her hand, timidly pleading with it. It growled at her a little and, as she snatched back her hand in terror, sprang forward and drew its claws down her cheek.

Fred found her sobbing hysterically, with blood smeared on her face, and the cat licking a paw in a corner.

'What is it, old girl? What on earth has happened?'

'The cat,' she cried, for she had been driven past the thought of the asylum and no longer cared. 'I hate it! I can't have it! Please, Fred, I can't have it here any longer!'

'But, dear, it was only to please you. If you don't like her, she shall go at once. Some people don't like them, I know; but why didn't you say so before?' He wiped her cheek gently with his handkerchief. 'Vicious little devil! Buck up, old girl. What shall we have for supper?'

'When will you take her away?'

'Tomorrow.'

'Tonight.'

In her urgency, she gripped his wrist until her fingers whitened.

'First thing tomorrow. I'll leave a bit early and drop her in on the way to work. I can tell old Hussey she hasn't settled.'

'Tonight. Please go tonight.'

He wiped away sweat from her forehead and upper lip. She seemed exhausted with shock.

'All right.' He patted her hair and straightened himself. Then he began to whistle and put on his overcoat. Without a word, he picked up the cat and tucked it into his breast. He put a large piece of coal on the fire and then wiped his fingers on his navy trousers and grinned. 'Shan't be long.'

'Yes, be long,' she said suddenly. 'Call in and have a game of darts ... be a change for you ... don't hurry back.'

He stopped by the door, looking surprised.

'Please!'

'All right, I'll see.'

When he had gone, she lay back and closed her eyes, and smiled. She heard him going downstairs. Hatred was taken away; only love remained, and she felt unbelievably happy.

As they met the cool air, the cat went close to his breast, patted his chin with her soft paw. He fingered one of the silky ears and ran his lips for a second across her head; then he thrust her deeper into his coat and went quickly down the road to the bus-stop.

I Live in a World of Make-believe

At the end of the village, the house which was of a dazzling whiteness in summer now stood sulphurous and dark against the snow, the plaster discoloured and flocky like ill-washed woollens, and the formal garden and the shrubbery a mass of strange humps. But none of this was without grandeur to Mrs Miller, who fretted as she drew the curtains in her smaller house across the road.

Her view was across the lane and clean through the wrought-iron gates. Beyond these gates a life went on which absorbed and entranced her – the chauffeur brought his shining car to the front steps; a uniformed nanny emerged into the lane with the pram, from which white fur mittens vaguely waved; a bowed and earthy gardener threw maize over the frosty ground; and cockerels – magnificent with their glistering plumage, their crimson combs – danced forward savagely, printing their dagger-like tracks over the snow.

Symbols of all that seemed worth while in life passed and crossed on that gravelled courtyard – symbols of order and of plenty, of service, of the lesser devoted to the superior, and wages paid by the week; not, as Mrs Miller paid her own charwoman, by the hour.

Since children make friends simply and quickly (being less on their dignity, less fearful of rebuff, than adults), in no time, as soon as the Millers moved in, their little boy had insinuated himself into the Big House, was riding the little girl's pony, had invaded nursery tea and even (for this he was scolded by his mother) Lady Luna's solitary breakfast. His mother scolded, but listened to the description of Lady Luna pouring coffee for herself at one end of the cleared and deserted table at half-past nine of a morning, the white-and-red room rosy with a great fire, and, said Timmy Miller, 'a good invention, a little cage on the table where you put bread in and it comes out toast.'

'That's nothing,' his mother said discontentedly, 'your granny has one just the same. And remember, I won't have you bothering over there at all hours of the day.'

Then the telephone rang and a light, inconsequential voice said: 'Oh, you can't know me, my dear. I am Lady Luna from just across the road. We should so love it if you could come over for tea.'

So the telephone bridged the narrow lane and dismissed for Mrs Miller those intricacies of card-leaving she had often pondered in bed at night. She pondered many things at night, all those things that worried her – her husband, for instance, saying 'front room' instead of 'lounge' in the smaller house they had graduated from, and now her faint suspicion that 'lounge' itself no longer did.

'I wish we had more books ...'

'Books?' he echoed, looking worried at once. 'What for?'

'For all those built-in shelves. I'd like to call that room the library.'

'What's it matter what it's called?'

'Books are such an expensive item and I don't fancy them second-hand. You can't tell where they've been nor what they harbour.'

'That's right,' he agreed; for he always agreed; worried, depressed as they are – the husbands of ambitious women.

'And we ought to get an electric toaster. We waste bread' (she was using an argument he would like) 'toasting it like that out in the kitchen.'

He knew she would remain discontented for ever, comparing life, as she did, with accounts of Edwardian house parties she had read in novels; so that each day was wrong from the start with its three boiled eggs instead of the great dishes on the sideboard (lifting one lid after another – the mushrooms, the devilled kidneys, the fish kedgeree – and casting remarks of great brilliance over one shoulder to those who sat at the table slitting open with silver knives invitations to weddings, to garden parties and balls). That fantasy, in all her experience, was most nearly approached by the house across the road, and she lingered over drawing the curtains at tea-time; so Lady Luna's voice on the telephone sent her hastening to her wardrobe to survey her potentialities.

While she painted her nails she assembled and had in readiness a few phrases against awkward pauses in the conversation, of which, had she known, there would be none with Lady Luna, whose murmurings were gentle and continuous like those of doves in summer. For Lady Luna asked questions which she did not intend should be answered; she cooed, murmured and agreed; without sympathy, she uttered sympathetic phrases; and always her eyes had a flitting, heedless restlessness, like the darting, purposeless motions of little fishes.

In the shadow of all this her child, Constance, sat still and unperturbed; looking well-bred, no doubt, thought Mrs Miller, deprived of her chosen phrases; well-bred, but plain, colourless and straight-haired; not cute, as she would have liked a little girl of her own to be.

Mrs Miller felt insulted by the flowing, indifferent talk of her hostess and by the tea itself, over which no trouble had been expended. She felt vaguely that had she also been titled the cake would have contained cream;

not knowing that if the Queen of England Herself (a phrase she often used) had been expected, the same dry little rock buns with their swollen, burnt currants would have been proffered.

After tea, Nanny brought in the baby and proved a better hostess than her mistress, with her compliments on Timmy Miller's good colour; and what a pity Constance did not fill out in the same way, she said, and then, dandling the vaguely stamping, whimpering baby, her fingers in his closed fists, astonished Mrs Miller, who did not talk often to nannies, by saying: 'We're a little constipated today, I'm afraid, and that makes us fretty and cross. We shall have to try a spoonful of the prune purée at bedtime. Shan't we, darling?' The baby put his feet down emphatically but without control; his chin was wet with dribble and his eyes stared.

Meanwhile Lady Luna had lapsed into a drowsy silence as if, her murmurings done, she waited only for her guest to go. Her carefully tended but worn-out little face looked still and empty.

'Manners!' thought Mrs Miller, her colour rising. Only her son (and children have their own private agonies) noted this.

'And you are sure you will not have a sherry?' Lady Luna asked suddenly in the hall. 'For the road,' she added, pleased with the contemporary phraseology she acquired so spasmodically and used too late.

That evening there was nothing of all Lady Luna's talk which Mrs Miller could remember or pass on to her husband when he came home. He had brought the electric toaster, for the sake of peace and quiet, but even that fact could not smooth out the gathers on her brow.

'Did you have a nice tea?' he asked at last.

She made a bitter, scoffing noise, and presently said: 'Buns I'd not hand to a charwoman.'

'Then you will have to put her to shame with some of your nice confections,' he said gently; tenderly jocular, as if to a sick and peevish child.

'I'm not likely to ask her. Timmy, it's your bedtime.'

The little boy looked up from his game, the dice rattling still in the egg-cup in his hand. This rather grubby little hand was dreadfully pathetic, his father suddenly decided.

'Good-night, old chap,' he said kindly.

The boy looked strained, his eyes widened by tears he could scarcely keep back.

'Why? Why won't you ask her?' he began.

Mrs Miller reached for a piece of embroidery, and her husband thought that the only time she appeared relaxed or casual was when she was working herself up into a great storm of anger. She chose a strand of green silk and began to embroider an eye in a peacock's tail. The three of them watched and listened to the needle passing through the linen.

'Your mother,' said Mrs Miller quietly, and as if she were not talking of herself, 'has no cook, nor house-parlourmaid, nor nanny ...'

They waited still.

'She has only herself,' she continued, 'to scrub the floors and bake ...'

She produced a formidable vision of vast flagged floors and great bread ovens, her husband thought.

'And wash and mend,' she concluded. She drew her needle out to the length of the silk and, looking up at them, smiled bravely.

'But doesn't Mrs Wilson do the scrubbing?' Mr Miller asked, as if to erase this picture of intolerable human suffering.

He could not understand the intricacies of housewifery, Mrs Miller implied by her brief look and her silence.

'But ...'

'Yes, Timmy?'

'I wish ...'

'Don't stammer, dear. Would you like shredded-wheat for your supper?'

'Yes, please.'

Dreadful, his father thought, seeing a child biding his time, trying to weather his mother's caprice and bitterness. Too young to be learning worldly wisdom, that unengaging quality.

Mrs Miller, like a good mother, laid aside her embroidery and went to see her child to bed. His father could not help him. He went quietly away to his shredded-wheat.

'Yet, *she* suffers, too,' Mr Miller suddenly thought. '*We* suffer because of *her* suffering. Whatever she lacks in life, whatever she fails to grasp, *we* pay for.' For himself, he no longer cared, but he did not like to see his little boy going to bed so quietly, with his requests weighing heavily in him until a suitable occasion for cajolery arose.

When Mrs Miller came back, he wanted to say to her, 'Let me show you something true for one moment. Let me help you look into your son's heart, or your own even. And if you are always to measure your condition against other people's, let it not be for ever against people who do not exist. For life will never be what you have imagined. Not for five minutes even.'

As a girl she had been affected. 'I live in a world of make-believe,' she would laugh, boastfully, as one laughs when confessing to well-loved weaknesses.

He said nothing. He watched her unhappy eyes and mouth as she sewed. Then it occurred to him that all the time she really intended asking Lady Luna and the child to tea, that she was making a weapon of her reluctance so that she might drive them all to a frenzy with it when the time came. He could not determine how he knew this, but years of living with her had shown him that none of the simple, obvious things about her was true (her calmness covered fury, her fury was deliberately indulged and delighted in), so that when he saw the forthright, he looked at once much deeper than that and through mazes of deception came usually to the reverse.

As she sewed, her eyes darted often to one thing after another in the room, and he thought that she must be measuring these things with the eyes of Lady Luna, who might see them thus if she came to tea. She seemed to dwell most upon those shelves where once the people of the house had kept their books, and where now china was carefully spaced out; but with a poor effect – it could not be denied.

The next day he brought home a row of old sermons bound in calf and gilded richly. She was pleased, and for once allowed herself to show her pleasure. 'I dare say they're quite clean, and it isn't as if we shall be reading them. I've always said books are the making of a room.' And her eyes travelled to the next empty shelf, along which she rearranged some china.

So Mr Miller began to collect books – sets of books with heavily gilded spines, in calf, in marbled paper, to tone in with the room, which slowly came to look, Mrs Miller said, more like a library every day. Coming home in the train he would even dip into these volumes and read a little, but the long 'f's' worried him and tried his patience.

'I suppose I must ask that woman over one day sometime,' she said one evening, and although her voice was fretful, her eyes rested with satisfaction on her cosy room. 'What about asking them for sherry?'

At once he could foresee how poor Timmy would be hastened into bed, nagged at and scolded, then later, to make up for it, allowed to sit up with a plateful of pieces from the snacks, rejected from downstairs, broken cheese straws and scorched almonds.

'It would be nice for Timmy to have the little girl to tea,' he began, as she had known he would.

'I won't have people to tea while I have to carry in my own tea-pot,' she cried. Her voice rang tragically as she envisaged this disgrace.

He knew that another man would have laughed, but there was no laughter left in him, because his son was involved.

One of his friends had put his head in a gas oven and come by a peaceful end that way. This incident had made a great impression upon Mr Miller, who imagined in every detail himself doing the same thing. 'You could make it quite comfortable with a cushion,' he now thought. 'Just be relaxed, breathe deeply, not fight against it, pretend you're at the dentist's without that hateful spinning back into consciousness with the taste of blood in your mouth and the voice saying, "Rinse, please."'

'What are you thinking?' his wife suddenly asked.

'About the dentist, dear.'

'Well, I can't see anything to smile about in that,' she said restlessly, and she threw aside her library book, which was morbid.

In the morning she telephoned Lady Luna to ask her to tea at the end of the week.

'But how lovely!' cried Lady Luna. 'Constance will be delighted.'

Her rapturous acceptance was overdone, Mrs Miller thought. In one who obviously had far more exciting engagements this enthusiasm seemed automatic, even absent-minded. But Timmy went to school happy the next day, and Mrs Miller called in the sweep so that she could be sure the chimney would not smoke.

On Thursday she did not sit down all day, she told her husband in the evening. She was a great one for not sitting down all day, not touching a morsel of food, never sleeping a wink all night and hearing every quarter of an hour strike from midnight until dawn.

In the larder tiny éclairs and meringues cooled on wire trays, silver was polished, apple jelly spooned carefully into cut-glass, rosettes of pink icing piped in the middle of biscuits. Two branches of white lilac stood leafless in a jar under the sink, the coolest, safest place, and were given an aspirin tablet every time Mrs Miller thought of it. The drawn-thread tray-cloth was dipped into sugar and water and ironed damp.

'You'll be too worn out by tomorrow to enjoy yourself,' Mr Miller observed as he drank tinned soup.

'I don't expect to enjoy myself,' his wife replied, for once truthful. 'I've got a splitting head.'

'Well, have some supper, old girl.'

'I couldn't bring myself to. And, Robert, I do wish you wouldn't call me "old girl". Even when we're by ourselves. It isn't very kind.' Her mouth dropped, her voice quivered.

'I meant it kindly. Have a drop of gin.'

'Of course not. You know I only drink in company. To be sociable. I don't really care for it at all, the taste is so nasty. I can't understand people going so mad over it, when it's so expensive, too. Think what you could do with the money.'

He couldn't really think of anything, so he went on with his soup.

'Oh, my back's breaking,' she continued. 'What with leaning over that bath washing Timmy, and then the sink all day ... ' He scarcely listened. Her head was splitting and her back was breaking and, still wearing an apron, she perched for a moment on the arm of a chair and cheered him on as he ate his supper.

'She ought to have gone on the stage,' he thought. 'She'd have had them crying their eyes out.'

She was late to bed. She put her hair into curlers and creamed her hands, then, wearing a pair of cotton gloves, got into bed and lay there, twitching slightly with fatigue, and going back over the day's work and forward over tomorrow's. As she took it for granted that her husband was lying beside her doing the same, she felt no hesitation in making her observations aloud from time to time.

Yet in spite of the hell she had made of the house for two days, when Timmy came from school next day at half-past three he found his mother good-humoured and at ease, the worst over, wearing her best shoes, but a tweed suit which would show Lady Luna that she regarded the occasion as of little importance. He was warmed by her good humour, responding at once to her mood with the intolerable sensitivity of those who live with the quick-tempered. He inspected, with Constance's eyes, the little biscuits, the pale meringues. Two of the best apple logs were laid on the bright fire. The lilac was seen to be magnificent now that it had been taken from under the sink, and the rows of books looked as if they had been in the family for years.

Mrs Miller stood by the window, feeling like a good producer who knows that every detail has been attended to, every difficulty foreseen, and who can await the lifting of the curtain with confidence and even pleasure.

'I wish it could always be like this,' thought Timmy vaguely.

And then – it was twenty to four – the gate creaked and Auntie Flo appeared with little Valerie and came waving and calling up the path.

Across the road Nanny was rinsing out pillow-slips in Sanitas. At twelve that morning, just as the music mistress arrived, Constance, practising scales in the schoolroom, paled and then vomited all over the piano and into her lap.

While Nanny sponged the keys and changed Constance's blouse and skirt, Lady Luna took Miss Hayday, who was fond of painting, to see a Gainsborough of her great-great-grandmother in the drawing-room.

Constance, so suddenly ill, was quite as suddenly restored, and it would be a pity, her mother said, to have brought Miss Hayday from one end of the village to another for nothing. So, a little late, they sat down to the lesson, in a room still smelling rather of sick, only partly covered up by disinfectant, and Constance, in a clean blouse, started off on her arpeggios, her tongue between her lips, her straight hair falling forward over her shoulders, and Miss Hayday, sitting beside her on an upright chair, breathing in a panic-stricken way into a little scented handkerchief.

Afterwards Constance ate a good lunch, and while she did so her mother remarked a great deal on the way children are down one moment and up the next. After this Constance went to lie on her bed with a book, and very soon was sick again, this time all over the pink eiderdown.

Auntie Flo was Mr Miller's sister, and she had come on the bus with an oilcloth bag containing a dozen eggs and a jar of pickled cabbage. She seemed so very pleased to see her sister-in-law and called 'Yoo-hoo' through the letter-box, always being full of high spirits.

'Oh, God, how could'st Thou?' Mrs Miller cried in silent anguish as she opened the door. Her world swayed and crashed at the thought of mingling together Auntie Flo and Lady Luna. Even her neck was flushed as she gave her cheek to be kissed, and Timmy watched her with anxiety.

Auntie Flo never talked, she always shouted, and she shouted now. 'Take them eggs into the scullery for your auntie, Valerie. No, leave your pixie on, that's a good girl. She's had the ring-worm. All over now, of course, but the hair doesn't seem to grow very quick. Never mind. Well, this is lovely, dear. A lovely home.'

Mrs Miller had begun to sweat. One absurd excuse after another for getting rid of Auntie Flo swept through her panic-confused mind – such as taking her to one side and saying she awaited the doctor ('They suspect a touch of cancer'), or a lover, or children with diphtheria coming to tea. While she thought, she smiled frostily at Valerie and glanced continually towards the window.

Valerie sat on the edge of a chair, swinging her legs and fidgeting with a loose tooth, and she seemed to have the smirk on her of a child who knows it is the apple of its mother's eye.

Auntie Flo rattled on.

'And although I say it, she really does talk lovely since she went to the private school. It's worth every penny of the money, not a penny of it would I begrudge them, the lovely way she talks now. My next-door neighbour, she said to me only yesterday, "Mrs Shaw," she said, "doesn't your Valerie talk lovely now she goes to the private school? I was saying to Will last night," she said, "doesn't young Valerie next door talk lovely, you'd never credit it ...."'

Mrs Miller, her throat choked with tears, looked out of the window, wringing her hands. 'I must get rid of her. I must get rid of her. In five more minutes she must be out of this house, and her horrifying little Valerie with her.'

At half-past five Lady Luna lowered the bound volume of *Little Folks* she had had as a child and stopped reading aloud in the middle of the story.

'Oh, my God!' she said to Constance, who was now properly in bed eating arrowroot mould. 'We ought to've gone to tea across the road. I'll have to telephone.'

'Oh, not till the bottom of the page,' Constance wailed, taking advantage of her indisposition.

Her mother agreed without argument, for the story lulled her nerves with beautiful nostalgia for her own cosy childhood, when nobody had ever heard of the Labour Government and servants were grateful for their jobs.

Timmy lay still, too rigid with apprehension to draw his cold feet up into a warmer place in the bed. Downstairs his parents quarrelled. They quarrelled all the time Mrs Miller was getting supper; the dissenting voices swelled or diminished as doors were opened or closed, and the argument went on from room to room.

'You let my own sister go away without even a cup of tea,' cried Mr Miller, 'after her coming all that way to see you, out of the kindness of her heart.'

'The child had ringworm. She had no business to have come ...'

'You know full well you let her go because you're such a bloody snob; she wasn't good enough to meet her ladyship ...'

'How dare you swear at me!'

'It's just about time someone did, to knock some sense into your empty head ... Damn fine friends, too, without the manners of a ...'

'Don't shout!'

'I'll shout as much as I bloody well please.' He became exhilarated with his success. He had never answered her back before, and she was frightened, he could see.

Her head wheeled and hammered. She sat down at the table with her arms before her and put her head down on them and began to cry.

The thought of Timmy hearing this deflated Mr Miller. He put a hand on her shoulder, hoping to steady her.

'Poor old Flo,' he conceded. 'I suppose she is a bit of a rough diamond.'

'It was the ringworm,' Mrs Miller sobbed into her sleeve.

'All right. All right. Let's get on with some supper and have a nice quiet sit-down by the fire.'

'I don't know what to have for supper.' For her plans had not extended beyond tea-time.

'Well, we can make do with something – a bit of cold meat out there, and a nice jar of pickled cabbage, I saw. That'll be a change. Now don't go off again. What's the matter now? The boy'll hear you.'

She went out into the kitchen and held her handkerchief under the cold water and then put it to her aching forehead.

'And there's all these nice cakes,' her tactless husband went on. 'We can follow up with some of these.'

'All right,' she said meekly.

His very air was one of mastery and decision; even cutting his meat, forking pickled cabbage on to his plate, he seemed different, she thought.

She was very subdued. She ate nothing, her head ached so. When the telephone rang, she started and began to tremble.

There was the cool, inconsequential voice.

'My dear, it's Winifred Luna, I know you will never forgive me. We've had such a day ... Constance vomiting the whole time ... and Cook's afternoon off ... it simply is one thing after another with children ... they're up one minute and down the next ... what Nanny and I have had to put up with this day ... but now she has had an enormous amount of arrowroot mould and gone fast to sleep, like a baby, though my babies were never so marvellous as all that about sleeping ... and Nanny and I are just exhausted ... and on top of it all the dreadful feeling that you are not going to forgive my rudeness and thoughtlessness ... but I expect you will be very understanding and give us just one more chance. Perhaps we could pop over tomorrow, instead ...'

'Of course,' said Mrs Miller faintly, and smiled wanly into the telephone.

'Then that will be lovely. Constance will be so delighted. It will quite cheer her up.'

When Mrs Miller put down the receiver, she went on standing there, her eyes closed, her wrist to her brow, her mouth dragged tragically down. 'Sarah Bernhardt,' thought her husband, eating one éclair after another.

Madame Olga

Ronald Ives once more took the train from Victoria to the place of all his seaside holidays in Kent. To travel first class did not – would not for many years – occur to him.

On most of those journeys to Eastgate his widowed mother, whose brother lived in that town, had been with him. When she had died he had thought of nowhere else to go, even after her brother had died too. He had simply taken a bedroom in a boarding-house farther down the same road. Fernbank. This was his destination.

His mother had died without knowing about Madame Olga, who was the purpose of his visit. In a way, her death had left him less grieved than at a loose end. Their life together had gone on too long for his good. On that first holiday without her, he had wandered about aimlessly until he had been driven by rain into a shopping-and-pleasure arcade. It was on that day, there, that he met Madame Olga.

Speeding through Kent on this later occasion, the train rattled and jolted and he wondered if it would be derailed. He was a nervous man but hoped to hide his anxiety by softly humming and glancing about him. He wore spectacles, nicely polished like his shoes. His mouth drooped, pouchy from many small disappointments, and he did not look like a man who had only a week before come into a large fortune.

He knew that there were people to whom seventy-five thousand pounds would not seem to be a large fortune. He had never met any of them and did not expect to.

He wondered if his mixed emotions might be described as a depressed excitement and decided that it would be a contradiction of words. Yet his heart gave a lift, then a lurch, when they ran into the steep chalk cutting, through the tunnel, out of it and, slowing down, into the echoing, fish-smelling station, Eastgate Central.

Arrival at a known resort out of season has a strangeness that those who have been there only on holidays, with all the pavements crowded with sauntering people, noise, traffic, can imagine.

Ronald, in a taxi on his way to Fernbank, saw a changed territory – the ice-cream parlours closed, the beach deserted and the town taken over by the elderly, who sat lonely in half-glazed shelters or walked, in tweeds, with dogs.

Along the windy esplanade, the sand had blown up over the lawns. The sea was a long way out. He passed the Grand Hotel, the Connaught, the Marston Towers. Then, farther on, and nearly into bed-and-breakfast land, the taxi took a turn-off by the bowling green and drove to Mrs Plaistow's 'Fernbank'.

Mr and Mrs Plaistow were decorating, and Ronald had been warned that being out of season he would have to muck in as best he could – ever so welcome all the same. Here was a different atmosphere, too. He remembered the summer jollity of the other guests, those dining-room jokes and the end-of-holidays photographs of them all taken on the front steps, with glimpses of wet, sandy swim-suits draped from window-sills above. This afternoon he was given a cup of tea in the kitchen while Mrs Plaistow tried to find out why he was there.

'I felt I was due for a bit of a change. Four days at Mrs Plaistow's will do the trick, set me up,' he said. 'I suppose I've been overdoing it a bit.' He told them of his new responsibilities: until last year he had been an assistant in a grocery shop, but now was promoted to manager of a smaller branch of the same firm. He wished, he said, that his mother might have known of his success, but it had come too late for that.

Mrs Plaistow believed scarcely a word of what he was saying. She was convinced that he was giving her false reasons or, at best, being suspiciously reticent.

What Ronald was being reticent about was his fortune – but only because he needed time to come to terms with it, to understand its implications before all the other smarter people did. He was relieved that he had signed a form debarring any disclosure of his name. Although never having expected to win, he had protected himself.

Mrs Plaistow, not being satisfied by his explanation (for he did not look at all off-colour to her), began to wonder if the opposite of what he had told her might not be true, if he had not in fact lost his job and was looking around for something else, perhaps in Eastgate. Lest he should be unable to pay his bill, she decided to be very careful about the catering. She made the decorating an excuse for cold ham and beetroot that evening.

Later, coming back probably earlier than expected from a stroll to the darkened Esplanade Gardens, he smelled onions being fried in the kitchen, imagining steaks lying ready for the pan. But he was not to be put out by such a thing. He called 'Good-night' cheerily from the foot of the stairs and went on up to his cold bedroom. Looking around it he had again the strange sensation of both depression and excitement.

In the morning he set out to walk to Madame Olga's.

In summer the arcade was usually crowded, with voices echoing and mingling with the din from the jukebox at 'The Burger 'n' Beans' and the shrieks of laughter coming from the Hall of Mirrors. Ronald had not imagined half the shops and all the amusements being closed for the winter.

Half-way down the arcade was a cheap jewellery shop that during the season had a souvenir stall outside it. Now the stall had been taken away, and the jeweller's window was revealed, with its display of engagement rings and alarm clocks. Next to the shop was a door giving on to stairs that led to a flat above the shop. There had been a card taped to the glass panel on the door: 'Madame Olga. Palmist and Clairvoyant. First Floor.'

The card had gone and the door was locked.

'I'm afraid Madame Olga's folded up,' the jeweller said.

In a flash, Ronald saw as a vivid picture that rather frail figure bent double in some sort of predicament, for 'predicament' was implicit in the jeweller's voice.

'Financially. Also healthwise.' The jeweller was engraving a silver-plated tray with an electrically driven machine. 'Forgive me. This needs my concentration.'

But Ronald lingered.

At last the jeweller swung the instrument aside and looked across at Ronald. 'What were we saying? Ah, Madame Olga. As she was known. She won't be returning, I'm afraid. In fact I've already let the flat to a so-called Japanese masseuse for the next season. It may work. It may not. Eastgate has always been a place for family holidays. Now it's changed in every way. They seem to go to Ostend and Boulogne and all that these days. Unfortunately, the Ostenders and so on don't reciprocate.'

'I've been coming to Eastgate for many years,' Ronald said. 'Twenty odd, or maybe more.'

'Loyalty is a rare quality in this day and age.' The jeweller screwed a glass in one eye and began to examine the inside of a watch.

'And in time, one holiday, came to consult Madame Olga,' Ronald said. 'I found her predictions uncannily exact.'

The jeweller took the glass from his eye so that his face could better express amazement.

'"Promotion in my employment," she said.'

The jeweller shrugged. After all, most people, unless utter numbskulls, got some sort of promotion as their lives went on. Nothing so very surprising about that. 'You *did* say "predictions", though,' he reminded Ronald, stressing the plural.

'That I should travel abroad ...'

'And ...?'

'Only months later I went with our local football team's Supporters' Club to France. Day trip. I'm keen on football, always turn out for the Club, even week-nights, but that was a trying day. People were sick on the pavements of Dieppe. I wished I'd stayed at home. But, you see, the prediction came true. And there was also a question of my kidney.'

'Ah, yes,' the jeweller said resignedly, screwing in the glass again, thinking the man strange, to say the least.

'I passed a small stone. Madame Olga had warned me of an internal upset. She was reassuring about it and said that there was nothing to worry about – and so it turned out.'

'Nothing marvellous *so* far,' the jeweller thought.

'With *her* insight, or foresight, I should have thought the world would have been flocking up those stairs,' Ronald said.

'There certainly was no flocking.'

'Have you any idea of her whereabouts?'

'When she fell ill – it was some form of schizophrenia or kleptomania, one of those nervous disorders that make you keep twitching your mouth and blinking your eyes, also a persistent cough – well, she was certainly not herself and couldn't have inspired much confidence in clients. Some cousin or other came and took off the bits of furniture and *she* went into the convalescent home at the end of the esplanade. All this was some months ago.'

'They might be able to put me on the track,' Ronald said brightly. 'I can't thank you enough.'

'Her name, by the way,' the jeweller called after him, 'is Lacey. Winnie Lacey. That's the name to ask for.'

When Ronald had left, the jeweller smiled to himself. 'There goes a man who very badly needs to know the answer to something further,' he thought ...

At the convalescent home, where frizzy-haired women in short, quilted dressing gowns stared at him, Ronald was at last told by a reception secretary that, as far as was now known, Miss W. Lacey now resided at Number 178 Dover Road in the care of a relation.

'A cousin,' Ronald said.

'Might well be,' said the secretary.

Ronald thanked her and left. Afterwards, walking to Dover Road, which ran through a squalid part of town beyond the station, away from the sea front, he tried to imagine the visit before him, as he had tried for days – to rehearse, to improve.

*

'And as soon as I heard the news, though I was stunned, it was *you* who came into my mind,' he would say. They would talk. He would tell her how all the things she had foretold had come about, and come about so soon. Then he would put the envelope with the cheque in discreetly in her hand, thank her, and slip away. Having found out her real name, he had already written out the cheque, except for the actual amount, which even now he had not decided. His fortune had made money seem unreal to him: suddenly there were zeros at the ends of sums that pitched them into fantasy. All of his life's careful calculations were nonsense now. He thought that one hundred pounds would be quite a handsome present, fifty adequate, even ten a mark of grace. But he had not made this journey simply to give someone ten pounds. Gratitude had no price, he decided. Madame Olga had protected him from great areas of depression, as when he had thought someone else – young Tarrystone, for instance – would get the branch managership, be promoted over his head. But Madame Olga had said no, that was not to be. And the trouble with the kidney stone: remembering her gentle warning, he had gone at once to his doctor, and all had been well. Yet she, Madame Olga, had been unable to help herself, it seemed, if what the jeweller and the convalescent home had said were true. She was in need; how much need he could not know until perhaps too late. He would scarcely (according to the sort of plight he found her in) sit down in front of her and fill in the cheque. He was still undecided about the matter when he came at last to Dover Road. Terraces of shabby Victorian houses on either side, small shops. He suddenly stopped by the piece of blank wall, took the cheque from his wallet and, resting it against the wall, filled in, *One thousand pounds only.*

Of course Madame Olga has no memory of him. A shaking hand flew to her lips in terror when he asked if he might come in and talk for a while.

'It's past – it's all in the past,' she insisted. 'I gave it up. I take in alterations now instead.'

But very soon she realised that he was nervous, too: that he had the mild face of a man who had never done anyone any harm, never would. She backed into the passage, seemed to fade into its darkness, opened a door on a room untidy only with sewing things: otherwise neat, but dismal.

'Do you remember my promotion – the question of my promotion?' Ronald asked, as she gathered up some tacked material from a chair so that he might sit down.

No, she remembered nothing, was obviously determined not to. Her offer of tea Ronald accepted, and he watched her quietly preparing it. If not exactly folded up, she was bowed slightly – not from age, for he guessed her to be in her forties, as he was himself, but from frailty or too much stooping over a sewing-machine. In spite of fragility, pallor, she was a not unattractive woman. There was a difference about her that he had noted at once – her hair, which in the arcade days had been an unvarying black, had now at least two inches of greyish-brown at the parting and around her brow. He thought the lighter colour would be more becoming when the hard black had finally grown out. Perhaps he had stared at her for too long, and she had been conscious of it in her uncanny way for, waiting for the kettle to boil on the gas ring, and with her back to him, she touched her hair and said, 'I am surprised you recognised me.'

He knew that in any other place he would not have, but *here* he had expected to find her.

'Of course, my hair was quite black then. That was my mother's idea. She thought the black hair leant more to the occult. "Whoever heard of a mouse-coloured clairvoyant?" she used to say.'

Having warmed the tea-pot, she set out some biscuits on a flowered plate.

'My mother was a medium, a spiritualist. She died five years ago.'

'My own mother passed on – a little more recently than that. It merely *seems* longer,' Ronald said.

When the tea had drawn, they sat and drank it and talked about their dominant mothers and how they missed them.

'I have my cousin upstairs,' Madame Olga said. 'Mavis Lacey. By the way, *my* name is Lacey too. Winnie. But of course you must have known that.'

He had described to her, while still standing outside the front door, how he had managed to track her down. It was then that the fear had come over her face. 'But Mavis has her own life,' she went on now. 'Bingo and that. I could never go out alone and she does – sometimes, since I was ill, a little walk down to the shops makes me feel nervous. But I see my clients.' She glanced down at a skirt with a pinned-up hem and then away from it with a look of distaste.

'Is it ... remunerative?' Ronald asked.

'Well, I am slow at it so far. Everything takes too long. And sometimes things go wrong and have to be done again.' She looked upset, as if some such calamity had recently happened.

Ronald had taken against Mavis and her selfish bingo-playing. 'You need a little cheering up after an illness,' he said.

He declined a biscuit. She nibbled at one as if it were a curious thing she had never tried before.

'Well, now, about the promise of promotion you held out to me,' he began.

She got up quickly to refill the tea-pot in her hand, staring at him.

'I travelled abroad. I had a kidney stone,' he went on.

*

He felt weak and confused. He accepted another cup of tea and sat back, easy, relaxed, as he had seldom been in his life. 'You have some uncanny genius, no doubt of that.'

'No longer. I am tired.'

'The virtue has gone out of you,' he said, not quite knowing what he meant. 'You have given all of yourself. No one can do more. And there must come a time for packing it all in.'

As well as being interested in football (and of course football pools) he was now a member of the local Chamber of Commerce, and there was a man there who was always proposing votes of thanks and putting forward amendments and who spoke in a way that Ronald admired and often tried to copy. 'We are all subject to our human condition,' he added.

'I *do* believe the palm shows certain characteristics,' she said in a rather defiant voice, and then she looked straight at him and said, 'but not the future; not the future, Mr ... '

'Ives. Ronald Ives.'

'No, the future, Mr Ives, is hidden from us all, and that is as it should be. Sometimes, though, just taking someone's hand and talking about the lines on it, sort of vibrations seemed to come through. "To someone like this, such and such might happen," you'd think. If I sensed something terrible, I never mentioned it, and if I worried you about a kidney stone, I apologise. That wasn't like me.'

The word 'candour' came into his mind. It was a word he had always admired; he believed he admired the quality itself and did so, as most people do, with reserve. He looked at Madame Olga with even greater interest. So her genius had been intermittent. It was not everybody's hand, or the touching of it, that had inspired her.

'There were times, I remember,' she said, 'when I felt dreadful things – that they might soon die. After they'd gone I'd go to the window and watch them going up the arcade, full of ideas about what I'd told them – about their lines of success, upwards emotional trends and so on, and they looked pleased with themselves, I thought. Probably treated it all as a bit of a joke, I thought, something to tell people back home. But I couldn't shake off the feeling of terror. I hope I was always wrong. But then of course ...' and she smiled so brightly, so warmly, 'sometimes I had just the opposite feeling. Instead of thinking, "They are going to die soon," I'd be sure they would suddenly find their feet.'

'As I did.'

'I loved that happening. I could say it, come right out with it, and I'm very glad it was true for you. You see, this the first time I've ever found out if I was right or wrong. Are you sure you won't have a biscuit?'

'I think I'll allow myself to be tempted after all,' he said. 'Since you twisted my arm.' That was one of the Chamber-of-Commerce man's phrases.

'To be quite honest,' she went on, 'those sorts of feelings about people were very few and far between. If it hadn't been for my mother, I'd have been doing *this* all my life, I suppose.' She made a gesture towards the sewing-machine and sighed. 'I should never have set the Thames on fire, as they say. It was interesting in the arcade, though such a short season. I couldn't make do. Then fell ill.'

'What form did your indisposition take?' He remembered the jeweller's sinister if muddled implications. 'Or perhaps I shouldn't ask?'

She tapped her chest. 'Bronchial,' she said. 'It wouldn't shake off and was very lowering. I became quite depressed, all on my own here.'

She was wearing a hand-knitted jersey of rust-colour wool. The only other time he had seen her she had worn a flowing red dress with bead embroidery.

'In a way, I suppose I was dominated by my mother,' she said – as if the idea suddenly, in his company, had occurred to her.

'And perhaps I was too,' he said.

They talked for a while of those two strong characters who had marred their lives, and they spoke in admiration and with a sense of loss.

Suddenly he realised that it was past five o'clock. 'I've kept you from your work for more than half the afternoon,' he said, and remembered her saying how slow she was at it.

'You're not to worry about that. Mrs Mason's alterations can wait another day. She goes on diets, you see, so I am forever taking in or letting out.'

'Very trying. I can understand that.'

'Well, it's my living now.' And she grinned, as Madame Olga would not have allowed herself to do.

'A fourth thing you said ...' he began and now she looked not frightened, just waiting to hear. 'You spoke of a fortune. That's hard enough for anyone in my walk of life to take in; although, of course, what's a fortune to one is just peanuts to another. However, my football pools came up.'

'Why, it's like a fairy story,' she said, with wonderment unsuitable to an ex-clairvoyant. Her pleasure for him, her childish excitement, was unlike anything he had ever known. She – still like a child – did not even ask him how much.

He was reluctant to go away, to end their conversation, without finding out far more about her that he wanted to know – about her childhood, her father (not yet mentioned), the sort of people who had visited her in the arcade, her mother's séances.

'What about a bite out this evening?' he suggested.

'A bite out?'

'I believe the Dolphin puts on quite a presentable dinner.'

She hesitated, and he believed she was worrying about clothes. His mother's first words on receiving an invitation had always been, 'But I've nothing to wear.'

'We can just be informal – go on with our chat,' he said.

'I should like it more than anything,' she said, having remembered a white mohair coat that her cousin, with persuasion or bribes, might lend her.

At the door he took her thin hand. 'I shall call at, say, seven-thirty. I'll get a taxi.'

She flushed with pleasure and he smiled from the same emotion.

Walking back to Fernbank, he took the cheque from his wallet, tore it into little pieces and dropped them into a litter-bin. He felt ashamed that he had ever thought of giving her money – and relieved, so relieved, that he had not.

The Ambush

A few weeks after the funeral, Catherine went back to stay with the Ingrams. Uncertain, during those weeks, how much grief was suitable to her – for she and Noël had not been officially engaged and in the eyes of the world she saw her status as mourner undecided – she had shown no sign of sorrow, for one tear might release the rest and one word commit her to too many others. Her fortitude was prodigious, even alone after the funeral when all that she had keyed herself up to was over. She avoided the drawer where his letters were; the air about her, at the art school by day and with her parents at home, was full of warnings and tensions. She felt jolted and stunned, as if she had been in his car at the time of the accident, and she walked about slowly and carefully, suffering from a stiffness of her limbs and a sensation of vertigo. By the end of the first month her effort had told on her – the energy spent in fending off other people and the sympathy they might offer, the holding back of tears, left her weak and apathetic. The boredom of her grief was not its easiest part to bear – the irritation of having nothing but her loss ever enter her mind now, when once she had had so many thoughts, dulled all her days and her dreams at night. Her parents were thankful when she took herself off to the Ingrams and they could come down from their tightrope and relax.

Mrs Ingram met her at the station. Catherine saw her first, standing on the platform, scanning the carriages as the doors began to open. She was wearing a mauve gingham frock and her white hair was blown back from her forehead and from that plane below her high cheekbone which Noël had had, too, and which made, Catherine thought, those two faces the most beautiful she had ever known.

'I am here,' she said, setting down her suitcase for a moment while she was kissed.

'Dear Catherine, I am so glad you came before it was dark.' Her seemingly meaningless phrases were often found, later, to have some meaning after all.

A soldier, for Mrs Ingram's sake, not Catherine's, had lifted the suitcase and was carrying it out to the station-yard. A wake of devotion always followed her and Catherine joined her own homage to the rest.

They got into Mrs Ingram's tinny little shopping car and drove away through the red-brick Thames-side village and down darkening lanes scented with elder-blossom.

'Esmé is still with us,' Mrs Ingram said. 'I wanted you to come before his leave was over.'

Esmé was Noël's elder brother, adored first-born, whom Catherine had heard of for years, resented somewhat on Noël's account and seen fleetingly at the funeral, to which he had come from abroad.

'You will be someone young for him,' Mrs Ingram said.

She drove as if she were a goddess in a chariot, her white hands confident, her head erect. Sometimes she waved to children who pressed back against the hedges, staring.

They turned through iron gates into the tunnel of trees leading up to the house; a haze of gnats danced under the bitten leaves; cow-parsley was grey in the shadows. The drive ended suddenly and they were under the high façade of the house with its rows of Georgian windows diminishing in height at each storey and the panelled door and rounded fanlight. Lights were on on the ground floor and a young man came out of the house and down the steps towards them.

Not quite up to the shock of seeing even a slight resemblance to Noël, Catherine was obliged to look up at what she had steadfastly at the funeral ignored. This brother had the same eyes, shrewd and alert, lines from laughter beneath them – for as a family they seemed to have laughed a great deal. When Mrs Ingram did so, she became even more beautiful – a rare thing in a woman; laughter enlivened her features and never disorganised them. Esmé was heavier than Noël; his features less defined; his colour paler. The beautiful flatness under the cheekbone he lacked. Catherine could imagine him in middle-age rather puffy under the eyes and stout and inactive and even, later, gouty as his father had been.

Catherine saw the house in the last of the light – perhaps its most magical time. It was ashen and flat against the dark trees. Beyond the lawns the river slid by and she could hear and smell the tumbling water at the weir. Moths followed them into the lighted hall. Damp had drained colour from great patches of the crimson walls, but the room was in brilliant contrast to outside. The tall clock only tocked, never ticked, Noël had said. On a table was a disarray of flowers and baskets and vases, for Mrs Ingram had left for the station in the middle of building a great pyramid of honeysuckle and peonies. She now, leading Catherine to her room, looked back regretfully at her interrupted work. 'Could not Esmé have fetched me, then?' Catherine wondered, apologetic as always. 'Or wouldn't he?'

From her bedroom's two long windows she would be able to see the river when it was daylight again.

'I hope the weir won't disturb you,' Mrs Ingram said, as if Catherine had never stayed in the house before. 'I never hear it now.'

When Esmé had brought in the suitcase and gone, Mrs Ingram embraced Catherine again. 'So lovely that you are here,' she murmured. 'Come down soon and have a drink after your long journey.'

She looked round the room, pulled at a curtain and rearranged some white geraniums in a pewter mug before she left Catherine alone.

The girl had the most extraordinary feeling of dizziness from so much sudden beauty – the beauty of Mrs Ingram herself whose footsteps were now light and hastening on the oak staircase, and the house and garden and this room scented with pinks and sounding of the river.

On the wall above the writing-table hung a water-colour drawing of Esmé and Noël as children – vaguely done, insipidly pretty and not worthy of their mother's room. They sat on a sofa together and had a picture-book open across their knees. The smocking on their blouses was painstakingly tinted in and Esmé's tawny curls were carefully high-lighted though nothing much could be made of Noël's straight black hair. His eyes were round and unseeing and bright as forget-me-nots. Fond drawing by a relative, Catherine thought. She herself had never drawn Noël, either fondly or objectively. The nearest she had got to that, she reflected, was once sketching his foot when he was lying on the lawn after swimming. She had been drawing the gable of the boathouse and branches of a chestnut tree and, for some reason turning to look at him, began on a corner of the paper to draw his foot with its bony ankle and raised veins. Then he had slapped one foot against the other to chase off a fly. She had rubbed out the sketch, blown at the paper and quickly covered up the smudge with a clump of rushes. She had trembled as if hoping to hide some misdemeanour, but was calm again when he stood up and came to look at her drawing. She had added an imaginary dragonfly above the rushes and then, at his request, a heron. What became of the drawing she could not now recall.

Mrs Ingram was in the hall when Catherine went downstairs. The uncarpeted staircase could be an ordeal, so much of it exposed to the hall, and now Mrs Ingram looking up and smiling as she stripped leaves from the peonies. Voices echoed here, and whatever Esmé said as he came from the library carrying a decanter was lost to Catherine.

She took her glass of whisky and Esmé pulled a chair out from the table for her where she could watch Mrs Ingram's flower-arranging. A pale grey-hound lay on a window-seat, and Esmé sat down beside it, fingering its silky ears.

'Other women I know do the flowers in the morning,' he said.

'You need not stay with me.'

She tore some leaves from a stalk with an asperity to match her voice, an asperity Catherine had never heard before, but which she always had felt to be a dreaded possibility in people as decisive as Mrs Ingram.

Esmé sat far back in the shadows stroking the dog's ears, not replying.

This hall was at the heart of the house – open to the garden in fine weather, a place for casual conversations and chance meetings. The last time Catherine was there it had been filled with wreaths, cushions of carnations propped against chair-legs, Mrs Ingram's hoop of roses and camellias lying on the table. It had had a drab symmetry about it, with its suggestion of flowers bought by the dozen, and Catherine had seen the glance it received, the weary contempt with which it was put aside as beyond improving.

Now Mrs Ingram carried the big soup tureen of flowers and stood it against the wall, stepped back to view it while Esmé yawned and clapped his hands, then called to his dog and went out into the garden.

Mrs Ingram sank into a chair the moment he had gone as if she had no need now to be busy.

'I shall send you to bed soon,' she told Catherine. 'You look tired after your journey.' And then as Catherine was obediently finishing her whisky she asked, 'How are you getting over Noël?'

At home, no one had dared to say this name and Catherine was unprepared to hear it and could think of no reply.

'Don't defer it, or try to pay off in instalments,' Mrs Ingram said. 'One only pays more in the end.' She sat so still with her elbow among the litter of leaves on the table and her cheek resting on her hand. 'I knew you would take it in this way, poor Catherine, and that is why I asked you to come here.' She gave the smile that was always so much remembered when Catherine had left her and was trying to reassemble the look of her, feature by feature, in her mind. The smile was the only uncertain thing about her, wavering, pleading; deep lines broke up the smoothness of her face and her regality – the Blue Persian look, Noël had called it – vanished.

'I love her,' Catherine thought. 'I could never withstand her, no matter what she wanted of me.'

When she was in bed, she wondered why such a thought had come to her, when there was no longer anything Mrs Ingram could want of her, no longer anything she could ask her to relinquish. Strangeness and the physical beauty of the place overtook her. She was under this roof again, but the old reason for being there was gone. Listening to the weir, lying in the flower-scented room, between the cool sheets (Mrs Ingram's linen was glassier than anyone else's, she thought), she fell under the spell of the family again, although the one of it she loved was dead. Missing him, it was in this place she wanted to be, no other.

She heard Esmé crossing the gravel again and calling in a low voice to the dog.

In the morning, the garden, drenched with dew, flashed with rainbow colours; the meadows on the other side of the river gently steamed. The sun had already warmed the carpet under the windows. Catherine stood there barefoot looking down on the dazzling scene. She could hear the grating sound of oars in rowlocks before Esmé appeared round the river-bend under the silvery willows. She watched him coming up from the boathouse. His footprints were dark on the dewy grass and the dog's paw-prints ran in circles about them. He was especially tender with his dog, would be with all animals and with children, as some bachelors are, she guessed.

When Catherine had stayed in the house on other occasions, Mrs Ingram had always had breakfast in bed. She had a clever way of not being seen coming downstairs, but of being discovered later very busy about the house, at her desk or coming from the kitchen with a list in her hand, as if she had been about since daybreak, the reins gathered in her hands for hours. This morning, Catherine, coming downstairs, was surprised to hear Mrs Ingram and Esmé talking in the dining-room. 'If you object, I can go to *his* place instead.' That was Esmé. Then his mother said quickly, 'I don't object ...' and paused, as if she were about to add a second clause that would take the meaning from the first. She got as far as saying 'but' and then heard the footsteps in the hall and Catherine came into the room to a tense silence and rearranged expressions.

Mrs Ingram was standing by the window, drinking coffee. Esmé rose from the table and, doing so, scattered some pages of a letter over the carpet. His mother glanced, then glanced away. 'She really does look as if she has been up since dawn,' Catherine thought. 'Perhaps *she* doesn't sleep, either.'

The warmth of Mrs Ingram's smile welcomed her and Catherine regretted the stiffness and timidity of her own that answered it. She felt full of a jerky vagueness, and the beginning of a fear that the house with its associations might undermine her and expose some nerve in an intolerable way. She was constantly alarmed at the possibility of behaving badly and trembled to think of the presumption of not holding back a grief that Mrs Ingram herself seemed able to contain. The strain was not merely of never being herself, but of not knowing who she any longer was.

She took a chair opposite Esmé's and Mrs Ingram came back to the table to pour out coffee, but without sitting down.

'Are you going out sketching this morning?' she asked Catherine; for that was how she had spent her mornings on other visits.

Catherine stared down at her boiled egg as if she were wondering what curious object she had been given, so dismayed was her expression. Esmé, who had put away his letter, looked across at her but wished that he had not. There was a sign of a crack in her sedate composure.

She said: 'Yes, I think I will do that.'

'Then we shall all meet at luncheon.'

Mrs Ingram was brisk, as if now Catherine was disposed of for the morning. This was unlike her, Esmé thought: but his mother was definitely up to something and he wondered for whom ill was boded, Catherine or himself. Some wonderful ill, no doubt, he thought; done for one's good; a great, bracing, visionary ill. 'Even if I want to paint again,' Catherine thought, 'I don't want to be in the painting *mood* – so exposed and inviting.' She had brought her painting materials with her and knew that she must rouse herself to work again and better here, perhaps, than at her own home with its too patent watchfulness, the irritating parental concentration upon her and all her doings and the secret discussions she could imagine just as if she had overheard them. 'Now she is painting again. Such a good sign. We will pretend not to have noticed.'

So after breakfast she went down to the river and along the bank until she reached the lock. Much about the Thames valley is Victorian – the canopied steamers and the red-brick lock-keepers' houses and the little shelters with spiked edges to their wooden roofs like miniature railway platforms. The garden beds of marguerites, calceolarias, were edged with whitewashed stones and slung about with whitened chains; all was neat and two-dimensional, like a primitive painting, captivating, bright and unconvincing.

Beyond the lock was a stretch of river, darkened and smothered by dusty, summer chestnuts; the oily, olive-green water slid by, was brown when the sun went in; a boat tied up in the rushes had no reflection. The other bank, in contrast, was silvery with aspens and willows, with shifting white leaves and light.

She sat on the bank and unpacked her water-colours. The sun was strong now, the light banal, she thought fretfully, narrowing her eyes to blur what she saw too sharply and with too many irrelevances. She felt a deep reluctance to begin painting on this lulled and buzzing mid-morning, and felt too that she had been expelled, excluded from Mrs Ingram's presence where she wanted to be, and sent off to do her painting as a child might be sent to practise scales.

She slapped at the horse-flies biting her bare legs. They were always a plague – the towing-path flies – and on other summer days Noël had sat beside her and waved them away with his handkerchief while she painted. Her irritation suddenly heeled over into grief and she dropped her brush, stunned, appalled, as the monstrous pain leapt upon her. Her painting – the faint washes of grey and green which had lifted the paper – dried in the sun, the jar of water was scarcely coloured. She rested her elbows on the drawing-board and covered her eyes with her hands, waiting for this moment to pass. Esmé, going along the tow-path to the pub, saw her before she heard his footsteps and would have turned back, but as he hesitated he thought that she had heard him. He was a reticent man but could see no reason for turning his back on sorrow, so against his inclination he went over to her. His dog, following him, sniffed at the paint water and stretched himself out in the shade of some rushes.

Catherine kept her head bent, and began to pack up her painting things as Esmé sat down beside her. She had not been crying. Her face was pale, but her cheekbones were red where her hands had pressed against them. In a few seconds this colour receded and she seemed more in command of herself.

She unpinned the drawing-paper from the board and tore it across.

'Not a good morning?' he asked.

'I am bitten to death by horse-flies.'

'Come with me to the pub and have a drink. I will carry all the paraphernalia.'

He had Noël's voice, though he talked too rapidly and stumbled over words. His tongue was not quick enough to keep up with his desire to have the words done with and his part of the conversation over. His manner of speaking was, from nervousness, over-decisive and just when he meant to be tender he sounded stern.

They walked along the towing-path in silence until they reached the Rose and Crown – there, the bar was empty until a woman came through from the kitchen, drying her hands, to serve them. She drew the beer and went back to her cooking. Catherine and Esmé sat on the varnished window-seat and looked out at the river. Conversation was uneasy between them. What they had in common was felt by both to be tabu and he, from lack of interest and living abroad, had no idea of what sort of girl she was. This morning, he began to be moved by her forlornness and blamed his mother for letting her mope: something strenuous and gay should surely have been arranged – though he could not think what.

'Would you like to play darts?' he asked her. She did not in the least want to play darts and did not know how, but his solicitude was so masked, his voice was so abrupt that she timidly agreed. He was patient and encouraging as her darts struck the brick wall, once a tin lamp-shade, but rarely the board, until, as part of her haphazard throwing – and she had no idea that such a thing could happen – two darts landed together in the bull's-eye. She glowed at his amazement and praise. He called in the landlord's wife to draw them some more beer and to see Catherine's score and said that he had never done such a thing in his life and would never do it.

'But I didn't *know*,' Catherine said happily. 'They might just as easily have gone out of the window.' She could not have imagined that doing something well in a game could be so stimulating.

They left the pub and walked back along the towing-path. Mrs Ingram was sitting on the steps in the sun and she, too, listened to Esmé's account of Catherine's first game of darts and she smiled radiantly, as if this was the nicest, gayest thing that could happen. At luncheon, the three of them were drawn together: by some simple magic, which Catherine could not understand, Mrs Ingram no longer seemed cross or embarrassed with her son, but rather as if she were acquiescing to some delightful plan he had for the future. Only when they were drinking coffee on the terrace and Esmé suggested an afternoon on the river did she detach herself from them again, making too many excuses – a little headache and a letter to write and a vague notion that one of her friends might call. She would not let them delay one moment. They must go alone and if they wanted tea it could be packed for them.

Catherine was disappointed, for it was Mrs Ingram she loved and admired, not Esmé and Esmé himself looked sulky again. He watched his mother going away from them along the terrace and his eyes were full of contempt, as if he knew some secret she had, which he despised. He stood up and said, 'Well, then,' in a hearty voice, trying to seem gaily anticipatory, but not managing it.

Mrs Ingram had a small motor launch which was used for visiting her friends up and down the river, and in this, sitting beside one another in wicker chairs, Esmé and Catherine drove sedately under the summer darkness of the trees. The easy gaiety had gone and Catherine felt helplessly that Mrs Ingram had pushed her off alone with Esmé against his inclination, and she was puzzled to think what motive she could have for doing such a thing. If it was simply to be rid of her, then she need never have invited her; that she might be trying to lay the foundations of something deeper between Esmé and Catherine than this slight acquaintance they had was not in character with her rôle of possessive mother. Noël had once said: 'It is lucky for you that you love me, not Esmé. Mamma never allows any girls within yards of her darling. They are just to be devoted to one another.' Equally, that Mrs Ingram simply had, as she said, a headache was unthinkable. She was not a woman who would be likely to have headaches or confess to such frailty if she had. She was ordinarily so proudly direct that excuses were alien to her. She would not deign to dissemble or explain. When she did so, Catherine felt uneasily compelled to wonder why.

Some cloud was between mother and son. In other circumstances, Catherine would have thought that it gathered from Mrs Ingram's jealousy. Her coldness might have been caused by Catherine and Esmé wishing to escape together, not from the reverse. For the second time that day Esmé set out to dispel the melancholy his mother had induced in Catherine. She recognised along the river features of the landscape she had discovered with Noël, and Esmé pointed them out to her as if she had never seen them before. Soon, his discourse became more than a commentary upon the river banks and the late Victorian and Edwardian houses, gabled and balconied, the rustic summer-houses, the lawns with urns of geraniums and flag-poles, and weeping copper-beeches, and began to be an excursion back through time; for here, he said, Noël had rammed the boat into the mooring-posts ('Yes, he told me,' Catherine whispered), and on that island disturbed a wasps' nest in a hollow tree.

They were held up outside the lock, and at last the keeper came out and opened the gates. The peace and heat inside the lock were intense. As the water went down, Catherine, grasping a slimy chain, looked long at Esmé who stood up with the painter over a bollard and was lighting a cigarette. The most veiled of men, she suddenly thought him; his in some ways handsome face expressionless with discretion, the speed of his talk overcoming his reluctance to talk at all, and his easiness, his courtesy – with the lock-keeper at this moment – proclaiming almost that beyond this he was far removed and could not love, be loved, or have any exchange at all that courtesy or kindness did not dictate.

Beyond the lock, she found herself thinking: 'We shall have to come back through it,' in an echo of the triumph with which she used to say this aloud to Noël. Each lock had prolonged their aloneness, as indeed it prolonged her time with Esmé, but it was so much as an echo of an old thought that it came to her that she found herself telling Esmé now how once it had been.

At first, she thought his courtesy had deserted him. 'Oh, look, a kingfisher,' he said.

She looked in the wrong place and it was gone. 'Another thing about the river,' he said. 'We can quite safely bring our unhappiness here. No one can reach it or be contaminated by it, as on dry land. I have felt that I was in quarantine with it these last weeks.'

'But at home . . . ?' Catherine began.

'No, I don't think we can be safe there,' he said rapidly. 'I mean that other people would not be safe from us.'

'I wonder if your mother wishes now that she hadn't invited me.'

'My dear little Cathy, what an odd thing to wonder. Or should I not call you "Cathy"?'

'I liked to hear it.' She had blushed with pleasure and surprise. 'I wondered if the sight of me depresses her,' she said humbly. 'I suppose that we have only Noël in common. By the fact of just being myself I can only go on and on reminding her of him.'

'You remind her of yourself and that she loves you. The dead can become too important, just by dying. Any ordeal is yours surely? Coming back to the house and the river and so much obviously that only you and Noël knew about.' He spoke rather aloofly, to imply that being in love was not in his province, though he acknowledged it in hers. 'But I understand,' he added, 'that it was probably now or never.'

'I shouldn't have liked it to be never. I love it here, being with your mother and seeing the house again – the *beautiful* house . . . '

'Yes, I think it is the only nice one on the river,' he said. He turned the boat round in mid-stream. 'All of those rose-red villas with their fretwork balconies and the conservatories and so much wistaria . . . yet I miss it when I'm away, and it comes at me with a dismaying, not wholly depressing rush, when I return. Living in one place all of one's youth makes being an expatriate very difficult. I think I shall go and live in London for a bit before I go abroad again. Go by instalments, as it were. It may halve the pains of departure. I must tell Mamma. Until I have done so, know nothing of it, please.'

'Of course not,' Catherine whispered.

'Has Esmé said anything to you about leaving here?' Mrs Ingram asked Catherine a day or two later.

'No.'

'Wide-eyed surprise, poorly done,' thought Mrs Ingram. 'I know he feels concerned about leaving me and may not like to mention it; but he will have to go in the end. He mustn't be tied to my apron-strings for ever.'

'Apron-strings' had too homely a connotation altogether – Esmé and his mother were not just pottering cosily about a kitchen. So fine that they were invisible were the threads with which she drew him to her: it was by the most delicate influence that she had had him break off his long-ago engagement and had later tried to stop him from going abroad, though seeming all the time to speed him on his way. 'I know that she sometimes does wrong,' Catherine thought. 'But I love her and I should be happy if she cared to dominate me, too.' She had wanted to be her daughter-in-law and part of the enchantment. She and Noël would have lived nearby, and come often to the house. 'The children are coming to luncheon,' Mrs Ingram would say. Once, the summer before, Catherine, sitting out on the steps in front of the house, had heard Mrs Ingram in the hall, telephoning a friend. 'Do come over. I shall be alone. The children are going to the cinema.' Bliss

had flowed through Catherine. She had shut her eyes, feeling the sun, hearing the sounds of the garden – the birds and insects and the weir. Yes, it was
bliss in those days, she thought, and she still sensed the magic of this quieter
house, though the river was more melancholy to her and the family diminished and Mrs Ingram's composure no longer completely holding.

Someone called Freddie began to be talked of – a friend of Esmé's, a
painter, of whose painting Mrs Ingram disapproved. She compared it
unfavourably with Catherine's. It had, she said, that detestable ingredient,
virtuosity. 'It allows one to see how clever he has been, and that should
never be. I don't want to see the wheels go round or to feel called upon to
shout "Bravo", as if he were some sweating Italian tenor. One should really
feel, "How easy it must be! How effortless!" I should think – don't you,
Catherine? – that an artist must seem too proud to have tried, too careless
to have thought of succeeding.' Esmé said nothing, so Catherine could not
judge if he agreed.

Freddie was expected for luncheon, but did not come.

'Perhaps he didn't feel hungry today,' Mrs Ingram said.

So Freddie himself was out of favour along with his paintings, Catherine
thought. Mrs Ingram had glanced at Esmé when she had spoken and his
face betrayed him by its impassivity.

In the afternoon, Catherine made another attempt to paint, in a tangled
part of the garden behind the old stables. In the shade, the nettles and
docks were a dark and bitter green and this greenness seemed to tinge the
curdy white flowers of elder and cow-parsley. She became gradually
absorbed in the shapes and the textures of the leaves – the feathery, the
ribbed and spade-like, the giant fern weighted down by a heavy snail. She
was pleased with what she was doing and just painting in a bright poppy
among the green and silvery green, for contrast, when she saw a snake lying
on the path before her at the edge of the shade. It was green, too, of an
olive-green to enhance her picture and in a curious way she realised this
before she took fright, tiptoeing backwards away from it until she felt safe
to turn and run.

She sped up the steps and into the hall, calling for Esmé, then the
wonderful sunny slumbrance of the house checked her and she felt
disconcerted. A young man came to the drawing-room door, saying, 'I
wanted Esmé, too.'

'Oh, I am glad, for Esmé's sake, that he came at last,' thought Catherine,
pulling up too suddenly and slipping on a rug.

'Scatter-rugs they call these in America,' said Freddie, coming to steady
her. 'A good name. I should like to scatter them all in the river.'

He seemed a very neat young man at a first glance. His suit exactly
matched his fawn hair and his blue bow-tie matched his pullover and

socks. His voice and his Cockney accent were pert and gay, his small eyes very bright. A second impression revealed his bitten nails and dirty shoes and the fact that his slight build and his clothes made him seem more boyish than he was.

'You sound as if you wanted Esmé in a great hurry,' he said.

'Yes, I saw a snake round by the stables and I think it is an adder.'

'Isn't there a gardener or something?' Freddie asked, looking vaguely out at the terrace.

'I just thought of Esmé first. I left all my painting things there.'

'I shouldn't think a snake would harm them. Did you want me to kill it or something?' he asked reluctantly.

'You see, I am sure they are deadly.'

'Is that supposed to encourage me?'

He went into the back hall and chose a walking-stick from the umbrella-stand. 'Oh, dear, this isn't really up my street. I just hope it's gone away by now. It would have been much better if you had asked a gardener.'

They set out towards the stables and he said: 'My name is Freddie Bassett. I was expected to lunch. Was there much hard feeling?'

'I am a guest. It isn't for me to say.'

'So there was! I ran out of petrol miles from anywhere. So what could I do?'

'You could have telephoned, I suppose.'

'Splendid! I knew I was right to try the story out on you first. You spotted the flaw as Mrs Ingram would have done. How can I get round that one? I telephoned, but the silly girl at the exchange said there was no reply. I don't know what these girls are coming to.'

'No one would believe you.'

'Mrs Ingram will not dare to say so. All right, then, I lost my way.'

'This way,' said Catherine coldly, taking another path.

'As a matter of fact, I did.' He seemed surprised to find himself speaking the truth. 'I stopped for a quick one and fell in with a little party. You know how that can be done – complete strangers, but something happens, there is some clemency in the smoke-haze, so that they seem the dearest companions one ever had, one almost weeps with gratitude that they are so sympathetic, so much one's own sort. So helpful in helping one to forget anxiety. I could not tear myself away from them and now I have forgotten them and shall never see them again – only similar ones. When it was closing-time we stayed on, because the landlord was the same sort as well. I felt dreadfully guilty about Esmé and they were all so sympathetic and so full of condolences and advice about what his mother would say. They came out to see me off and wish me good luck. Then I took the wrong road.'

'Wouldn't it have been better not to have come at all?'

'Surely not? I can stay to dinner instead.'

Catherine felt frightened. 'I am not his accomplice,' she thought. 'It is nothing to do with me.'

'Do you know when Esmé went out?' he asked. 'I want to say that I arrived the minute after.'

'I didn't know that he had gone.'

'He has taken his mother to a meeting. I hope it is a nice long one and that my head will feel better before she comes back.'

They crossed the stables courtyard and Catherine peered through the archway at the path where her painting things were lying beside her folding stool.

'Have I really got to?' Freddie asked. 'Oughtn't I to be wearing puttees or something? I am sure it has kindly gone away.'

But the snake had only moved farther into the sun. Catherine shrank back and for some strange reason put her hands over her ears. 'Oh, Lord!' grumbled Freddie, going forward with the stick held high. Catherine stayed in the courtyard. She heard the stick beating the ground and Freddie swearing, but she would not look. When he came back, he was carrying the stool and the drawing-board and his face was white. 'I take it you don't want to go on with this at the moment,' he said, handing her the unfinished watercolour without glancing at it. 'I just left it there – the snake.'

'You did kill it?'

'Yes, I suddenly went mad with fear. It was a dreadful thing to ask someone from London to do. Are you the girl Noël was engaged to?'

'We weren't engaged.'

'And now, I understand, Mamma wants you to marry Esmé?'

'I think you are rude and absurd,' Catherine said. 'It is none of my business, but I don't know how Esmé can tolerate you.'

She hurried on ahead of him and turned the corner of the house. There was Esmé walking on the lawn, his head down, his hands in his pockets. He paced up and down dejectedly. When he saw Catherine he smiled and then his smile warmed and he came forward eagerly, quite transformed by the sight of Freddie trailing behind, carrying the folding stool.

'It was a poor grass snake,' Mrs Ingram said. 'It would have done no harm to anyone and great good to the garden.'

'I am just a Cockney. How should I know?' said Freddie. 'I did as I was told.'

Catherine could only keep saying how sorry she was.

'I am surprised at you,' Mrs Ingram said teasingly. 'So meticulous in your painting, and to make such a mistake.'

It seemed to be Catherine who had failed. Freddie was triumphantly eating dinner instead of lunch, although Catherine would have staked a great deal against such a possibility. She had listened to his long apology with outraged astonishment ... 'tramping along in the blazing heat with my little petrol can in my hand ... I went all round some village looking for the Post Office. Wonderful honeysuckle all over it and jars of bull's-eyes in the window. I should have thought there would be some regulation against calling them that, when they are nothing of the kind ... '

'He is putting off the weak part of his story, about the telephone,' Catherine thought with interest.

' ... the phone-box was just outside the door and the exchange itself just inside by the bacon-slicing machine. The same pop-eyed old codger who was selling the bull's-eyes went to the switchboard. Twice he got the wrong number. "Skates the Fishmongers here" was one. The third time I truly thought would be lucky, but there was no reply. "There is always someone there. There are hundreds of servants. They are moneyed folk," I said. "Comfortably *placed*, as you might say." "I dare say," he said, sarcastically, as if I were a child, or drunk. "All the same, they're not answering."'

Esmé bent down and stroked his dog, trying to hide a smile.

'You *might* have answered,' Freddie whined complainingly. 'After I had trudged so far and had such a horrible time and my hands were so *sore* with carrying the petrol can.' He glanced at them, wincing.

'It *is* only pretending, isn't it?' said Mrs Ingram, her voice as sweet as honey. As if she thought that Freddie was over-exciting himself, she changed the conversation.

So Freddie triumphed. He triumphed over his headache and he stayed to dinner and Catherine thought that he would manage to stay the night as well. Esmé was quiet and full of a peace that Catherine could understand. She remembered the contentment of saying those words to herself, 'We are under the same roof.' She had known how beautiful it can be to come to the close of the day and lie down in bed, thinking those words. Then the house itself became haunted, enchanted, spellbound with love.

Her heart began to ache again and her throat almost shut. The flesh is endlessly martyred by grief, humiliated by nausea and vomitings, bothered and alarmed; breath checked and the heart belaboured; the eyes stabbed viciously until they unload their tears and the tongue as bitter as if it had tasted poison. 'This Freddie does not know,' Catherine thought, and she felt pity for Esmé and kinship with him.

Dinner was soon over, for there was hardly any conversation to prolong it. Once Mrs Ingram said to Freddie: 'Catherine paints, too,' and Freddie answered, 'So I saw.'

Beset by midges they drank coffee out on the terrace above the steps.

'An irritating noise,' Freddie said, referring to the weir, and Catherine thought, 'So it is. The sound is what you are yourself at the moment: if you are in despair, it sounds despairing; tumultuous if you are angry; romantic when you are in love.'

Esmé and Freddie never exchanged remarks or glances and when Mrs Ingram went indoors Catherine felt herself so much in the way that she followed her and was conscious of their nervous silence as she walked away.

Mrs Ingram came from the back hall carrying a bunch of roses. 'I was going to ask you if you would like to come, but don't if you aren't up to it. To Noël's grave, I mean. No, you would rather not, I am sure,' she said quickly. 'It is difficult to guess how other people feel about such a thing. I know it is old-fashioned and unimaginative of me, but I feel comforted when I go there.'

Catherine did not know herself how she felt or would feel, but she went with Mrs Ingram and carried the roses for her. They walked slowly along the scented lane to the church by the river; then through the lych-gate under the limes. She began to be afraid. She remembered the churchyard carpeted with wreaths and the raw earth mounded up ready for its dreadful purpose; the groups of black figures standing, as if stunned, among the graves and the lime trees only just in leaf which now were ready to flower. She wondered if she would have to face some overpowering monument, for death is alien enough in itself without some of the things which are done afterwards as being appropriate. She hung back on the gravel path as she had done once before and Mrs Ingram, humming peacefully, her pink cardigan hung over her shoulders, stepped quickly across the grass. Following her, raising her eyes only to look at a safely eighteenth-century headstone with a cherub's head and wings and saffron rosettes of lichen all over the crumbling stone, Catherine saw the name 'Ingram' with a sense of shock. But there were groves of Ingrams, among them Noël's father, who was to share the roses. Unlike most of the other riverside families, this had kept its bones in one place for at least two hundred years. The last Ingram had, Catherine was relieved to find, only a simple white wooden cross with his name painted in black. She faced this steadily, feeling that she had been spared an awkwardness. 'Only until the ground has sunk,' Mrs Ingram said, throwing away stale water and going to fetch fresh.

Catherine took a step back, as if she might otherwise sink with the earth. She felt obscenity, not peace, around her.

'I suppose that little liar will be staying the night,' said Mrs Ingram, returning from the water tap. 'I can't pretend that I fancy having him under my roof.'

She knelt down and began to strip leaves off the roses and break off the big blood-red thorns.

'When her plans have failed, there are always the flowers to do,' Catherine thought. 'The night I arrived, I suppose that she left them until late as an excuse for sending Esmé to the station – to make us be together from the start. But Esmé wouldn't fall in with the plan – a new habit in him, I should think.'

Then the words 'my darling Noël' broke across her reflections. For a second, she wondered if she had said them aloud, caught on the in-breath of a sob. But Mrs Ingram finished the flowers calmly and then they walked home along the towing-path. The river was bronze in the sunset and the fluffy meadow-grasses filled with a pinkish light.

Esmé and Freddie were still sitting on the terrace. Freddie was now in Mrs Ingram's wicker chaise-longue, his hands clasped behind his head and his legs stretched out comfortably. Esmé sat, rather awkwardly, with his greyhound across his lap. They both struggled to rise when they saw Mrs Ingram and Catherine crossing the lawn, but Mrs Ingram ignored them and went round the house by a side-way and Catherine followed her.

Catherine went up to bed and stood by the open window, looking out into the dark garden. A misty moonlight furred the grass, like rime, and white ghosts rose off the weir. 'I have been to the churchyard,' she thought, 'and now I have had enough.'

She drew one of the heavy velvet curtains round her like a cloak. 'I cannot *not* feel when I am here,' she thought. 'Especially when I am so *meant* to feel.' Was not Mrs Ingram, she wondered, trying to make her realise the extent of her loss, as if nothing could be accomplished until this was done or any other part of her plan proceeded with.

Mrs Ingram came in to say good-night and found Catherine wound up in the curtain.

'So Freddie went – as if he overheard me and meant to prove me wrong.'

She came to the window and they both looked out at the garden, listening to the weir.

On the blanched terrace below Esmé's greyhound appeared, then Esmé. He went down the steps and was lost in the dark garden. Sometimes he reminded Catherine of his brother. Family likenesses in gestures are stranger than those of feature or build and often more poignant and she had sometimes been moved by such a slight thing as the inclination of his head as he walked, so mysteriously the same as Noël.

'He is going away next week,' Mrs Ingram said.

'And I,' said Catherine quickly. 'I must go too.' She was struggling with tears and her voice was rough and abrupt. She breathed very steadily and presently the tears receded and she said: 'I must get back to work, you know. I must ...'

'What makes it difficult for living here may make it good for painting,' Mrs Ingram said.

'Too beautiful,' Catherine began. She put her hands over her face and tears ran down her wrists and the insides of her arms. Mrs Ingram waited, as if she were measuring the fall of tears and knew when the limit of grief was reached and only then put out her hand and touched Catherine's shoulder.

'You see, I can't stay. You do see?' Her heart had been twice ambushed in this house and now she was desperate to escape. Yet did Mrs Ingram understand? She said nothing. She simply took Catherine in her arms and kissed her – but with a welcoming, a gathering-in gesture as if to one who has come home at last rather than to someone preparing to go away.

The Blush

They were the same age – Mrs Allen and the woman who came every day to do the housework. 'I shall never have children now,' Mrs Allen had begun to tell herself. Something had not come true; the essential part of her life. She had always imagined her children in fleeting scenes and intimations; that was how they had come to her, like snatches of a film. She had seen them plainly, their chins tilted up as she tied on their bibs at meal-times; their naked bodies had darted in and out of the water-sprinkler on the lawn; and she had listened to their voices in the garden and in the mornings from their beds. She had even cried a little dreaming of the day when the eldest boy would go off to boarding-school; she pictured the train going out of the station; she raised her hand and her throat contracted and her lips trembled as she smiled. The years passing by had slowly filched from her the reality of these scenes – the gay sounds; the grave peace she had longed for; even the pride of grief.

She listened – as they worked together in the kitchen – to Mrs Lacey's troubles with her family, her grumblings about her grown-up son who would not get up till dinner-time on Sundays and then expected his mother to have cleaned his shoes for him; about the girl of eighteen who was a hairdresser and too full of dainty ways which she picked up from the women's magazines, and the adolescent girl who moped and glowered and answered back.

'My children wouldn't have turned out like that,' Mrs Allen thought, as she made her murmured replies. 'The more you do for some, the more you may,' said Mrs Lacey. But from gossip in the village which Mrs Allen heard, she had done all too little. The children, one night after another, for years and years, had had to run out for parcels of fish and chips while their mother sat in the Horse and Jockey drinking brown ale. On summer evenings, when they were younger, they had hung about outside the pub: when they were bored they pressed their foreheads to the window and looked in at the dark little bar, hearing the jolly laughter, their mother's the loudest of all. Seeing their faces, she would swing at once from the violence of hilarity to that of extreme annoyance and, although ginger-beer and packets of potato crisps would be handed out through the window, her anger went out with them and threatened the children as they ate and drank.

'And she doesn't always care who she goes there *with*,' Mrs Allen's gardener told her.

'She works hard and deserves a little pleasure – she has her anxieties,' said Mrs Allen, who, alas, had none.

She had never been inside the Horse and Jockey, although it was nearer to her house than the Chequers at the other end of the village where she and her husband went sometimes for a glass of sherry on Sunday mornings. The Horse and Jockey attracted a different set of customers – for instance, people who sat down and drank, at tables all round the wall. At the Chequers no one ever sat down, but stood and sipped and chatted as at a cocktail party, and luncheons and dinners were served, which made it so much more respectable: no children hung about outside, because they were all at home with their nannies.

Sometimes in the evenings – so many of them – when her husband was kept late in London, Mrs Allen wished that she could go down to the Chequers and drink a glass of sherry and exchange a little conversation with someone; but she was too shy to open the door and go in alone: she imagined heads turning, a surprised welcome from her friends, who would all be safely in married pairs; and then, when she left, eyes meeting with unspoken messages and conjecture in the air.

Mrs Lacey left her at midday and then there was gardening to do and the dog to be taken for a walk. After six o'clock, she began to pace restlessly about the house, glancing at the clocks in one room after another, listening for her husband's car – the sound she knew so well because she had awaited it for such a large part of her married life. She would hear, at last, the tyres turning on the soft gravel, the door being slammed, then his footsteps hurrying towards the porch. She knew that it was a wasteful way of spending her years – and, looking back, she was unable to tell one of them from another – but she could not think what else she might do. Humphrey went on earning more and more money and there was no stopping him now. Her acquaintances, in wretched quandaries about where the next term's school-fees were to come from, would turn to her and say cruelly: 'Oh, *you're* all right, Ruth. You've no idea what you are spared.'

And Mrs Lacey would be glad when Maureen could leave school and 'get out earning'. '"I've got my geometry to do," she says, when it's time to wash up the tea-things. "I'll geometry you, my girl," I said. "When I was your age, I was out earning."'

Mrs Allen was fascinated by the life going on in that house and the children seemed real to her, although she had never seen them. Only Mr Lacey remained blurred and unimaginable. No one knew him. He worked in the town in the valley, six miles away, and he kept himself to himself; had never been known to show his face in the Horse and Jockey. 'I've got my own set,' Mrs Lacey said airily. 'After all, he's nearly twenty years older than me. I'll make sure neither of my girls follow my mistake. "I'd rather see you dead at my feet," I said to Vera.' Ron's young lady was lucky; having Ron, she added. Mrs Allen found this strange, for Ron had always been painted so black; was, she had been led to believe, oafish, ungrateful, greedy and slow to put his hands in his pockets if there was any paying out to do. There was also the matter of his shoe-cleaning, for no young woman would do what his mother did for him – or said she did. Always, Mrs Lacey would sigh and say: 'Goodness me, if only I was their age and knew what I know now.'

She was an envious woman: she envied Mrs Allen her pretty house and her clothes and she envied her own daughters their youth. 'If I had your figure,' she would say to Mrs Allen. Her own had gone: what else could be expected, she asked, when she had had three children? Mrs Allen thought, too, of all the brown ale she drank at the Horse and Jockey and of the rem- iniscences of meals past which came so much into her conversations. Whatever the cause was, her flesh, slackly corseted, shook as she trod heav- ily about the kitchen. In summer, with bare arms and legs she looked larger than ever. Although her skin was very white, the impression she gave was at once colourful – from her orange hair and bright lips and the floral pat- terns that she always wore. Her red-painted toe-nails poked through the straps of her fancy sandals; turquoise-blue beads were wound round her throat.

Humphrey Allen had never seen her; he had always left for the station before she arrived, and that was a good thing, his wife thought. When she spoke of Mrs Lacey, she wondered if he visualised a neat, homely woman in a clean white overall. She did not deliberately mislead him, but she took advantage of his indifference. Her relationship with Mrs Lacey and the intimacy of their conversations in the kitchen he would not have approved, and the sight of those calloused feet with their chipped nail- varnish and yellowing heels would have sickened him.

One Monday morning, Mrs Lacey was later than usual. She was never very punctual and had many excuses about flat bicycle-tyres or Maureen being poorly. Mrs Allen, waiting for her, sorted out all the washing. When she took another look at the clock, she decided that it was far too late for her to be expected at all. For some time lately Mrs Lacey had seemed ill and depressed; her eyelids, which were chronically rather inflamed, had been more angrily red than ever and, at the sink or ironing-board, she would fall into unusual silences, was absent-minded and full of sighs. She had always liked to talk about the 'change' and did so more than ever as if with a desperate hopefulness.

'I'm sorry, but I was ever so sick,' she told Mrs Allen, when she arrived the next morning. 'I still feel queerish. Such heartburn. I don't like the signs, I can tell you. All I crave is pickled walnuts, just the same as I did with Maureen. I don't like the signs one bit. I feel I'll throw myself into the river if I'm taken that way again.'

Mrs Allen felt stunned and antagonistic. 'Surely not at your age,' she said crossly.

'You can't be more astonished than me,' Mrs Lacey said, belching loudly. 'Oh, pardon. I'm afraid I can't help myself.'

Not being able to help herself, she continued to belch and hiccough as she turned on taps and shook soap-powder into the washing-up bowl. It was because of this that Mrs Allen decided to take the dog for a walk. Feeling consciously fastidious and aloof she made her way across the fields, trying to disengage her thoughts from Mrs Lacey and her troubles; but unable to. 'Poor woman,' she thought again and again with bitter animosity.

She turned back when she noticed how the sky had darkened with racing, sharp-edged clouds. Before she could reach home, the rain began. Her hair, soaking wet, shrank into tight curls against her head; her woollen suit smelt like a damp animal. 'Oh, I am drenched,' she called out, as she threw open the kitchen door.

She knew at once that Mrs Lacey had gone, that she must have put on her coat and left almost as soon as Mrs Allen had started out on her walk, for nothing was done; the washing-up was hardly started and the floor was unswept. Among the stacked-up crockery a note was propped; she had come over funny, felt dizzy and, leaving her apologies and respects, had gone.

Angrily, but methodically, Mrs Allen set about making good the wasted morning. By afternoon, the grim look was fixed upon her face. 'How dare she?' she found herself whispering, without allowing herself to wonder what it was the woman had dared.

She had her own little ways of cosseting herself through the lonely hours, comforts which were growing more important to her as she grew older, so that the time would come when not to have her cup of tea at four-thirty would seem a prelude to disaster. This afternoon, disorganised as it already was, she fell out of her usual habit and instead of carrying the tray to the low table by the fire, she poured out her tea in the kitchen and drank it there, leaning tiredly against the dresser. Then she went upstairs to make herself tidy. She was trying to brush her frizzed hair smooth again when she heard the door bell ringing.

When she opened the door, she saw quite plainly a look of astonishment take the place of anxiety on the man's face. Something about herself surprised him, was not what he had expected. 'Mrs Allen?' he asked uncertainly and the astonishment remained when she had answered him.

'Well, I'm calling about the wife,' he said. 'Mrs Lacey that works here.'

'I was worried about her,' said Mrs Allen.

She knew that she must face the embarrassment of hearing about Mrs Lacey's condition and invited the man into her husband's study, where she thought he might look less out-of-place than in her brocade-smothered drawing-room. He looked about him resentfully and glared down at the floor which his wife had polished. With this thought in his mind, he said abruptly: 'It's all taken its toll.'

He sat down on a leather couch with his cap and his bicycle-clips beside him.

'I came home to my tea and found her in bed, crying,' he said. This was true. Mrs Lacey had succumbed to despair and gone to lie down. Feeling better at four o'clock, she went downstairs to find some food to comfort herself with; but the slice of dough-cake was ill-chosen and brought on more heartburn and floods of bitter tears.

'If she carries on here for a while, it's all got to be very different,' Mr Lacey said threateningly. He was nervous at saying what he must and could only bring out the words with the impetus of anger. 'You may or may not know that she's expecting.'

'Yes,' said Mrs Allen humbly. 'This morning she told me that she thought . . .'

'There's no "thought" about it. It's as plain as a pikestaff.' Yet in his eyes she could see disbelief and bafflement and he frowned and looked down again at the polished floor.

Twenty years older than his wife – or so his wife had said – he really, to Mrs Allen, looked quite ageless, a crooked, bow-legged little man who might have been a jockey once. The expression about his blue eyes was like a child's: he was both stubborn and pathetic.

Mrs Allen's fat spaniel came into the room and went straight to the stranger's chair and began to sniff at his corduroy trousers.

'It's too much for her,' Mr Lacey said. 'It's too much to expect.'

To Mrs Allen's horror she saw the blue eyes filling with tears. Hoping to hide his emotion, he bent down and fondled the dog, making playful thrusts at it with his fist closed.

He was a man utterly, bewilderedly at sea. His married life had been too much for him, with so much in it that he could not understand.

'Now I know, I will do what I can,' Mrs Allen told him. 'I will try to get someone else in to do the rough.'

'It's the late nights that are the trouble,' he said. 'She comes in dog-tired. Night after night. It's not good enough. "Let them stay at home and mind their own children once in a while," I told her. "We don't need the money."'

'I can't understand,' Mrs Allen began. She was at sea herself now, but felt perilously near a barbarous, unknown shore and was afraid to make any movement towards it.

'I earn good money. For her to come out at all was only for extras. She likes new clothes. In the daytimes I never had any objection. Then all these cocktail parties begin. It beats me how people can drink like it night after night and pay out for someone else to mind their kids. Perhaps you're thinking that it's not my business, but I'm the one who has to sit at home alone till all hours and get my own supper and see next to nothing of my wife. I'm boiling over some nights. Once I nearly rushed out when I heard the car stop down the road. I wanted to tell your husband what I thought of you both.'

'My husband?' murmured Mrs Allen.

'What am I supposed to have, I would have asked him? Is she my wife or your sitter-in? Bringing her back at this time of night. And it's no use saying she could have refused. She never would.'

Mrs Allen's quietness at last defeated him and dispelled the anger he had tried to rouse in himself. The look of her, too, filled him with doubts, her grave, uncertain demeanour and the shock her age had been to him. He had imagined someone so much younger and – because of the cocktail parties – flighty. Instead, he recognised something of himself in her, a yearning disappointment. He picked up his cap and his bicycle-clips and sat looking down at them, turning them round in his hands. 'I had to come,' he said.

'Yes,' said Mrs Allen.

'So you won't ask her again?' he pleaded. 'It isn't right for her. Not now.'

'No, I won't,' Mrs Allen promised and she stood up as he did and walked over to the door. He stooped and gave the spaniel a final pat. 'You'll excuse my coming, I hope.'

'Of course.'

'It was no use saying any more to her. Whatever she's asked, she won't refuse. It's her way.'

Mrs Allen shut the front door after him and stood in the hall, listening to him wheeling his bicycle across the gravel. Then she felt herself beginning to blush. She was glad that she was alone, for she could feel her face, her throat, even the tops of her arms burning, and she went over to a looking-glass and studied with great interest this strange phenomenon.

The Letter-writers

At eleven o'clock, Emily went down to the village to fetch the lobsters. The heat unsteadied the air, light shimmered and glanced off leaves and telegraph wires and the flag on the church tower spreading out in a small breeze, then dropping, wavered against the sky, as if it were flapping under water.

She wore an old cotton frock, and meant to change it at the last moment, when the food was all ready and the table laid. Over her bare arms, the warm air flowed, her skirt seemed to divide as she walked, pressed in a hollow between her legs, like drapery on a statue. The sun seemed to touch her bones – her spine, her shoulder-blades, her skull. In her thoughts, she walked nakedly, picking her way, over dry-as-dust cow-dung, along the lane. All over the hedges, trumpets of large white convolvulus were turned upwards towards the sky – the first flowers she could remember; something about them had, in her early childhood, surprised her with astonishment and awe, a sense of magic that had lasted, like so little else, repeating itself again and again, most of the summers of her forty years.

From the wide-open windows of the village school came the sound of a tinny piano. 'We'll rant, and we'll roar, like true British sailors,' sang all the little girls.

Emily, smiling to herself as she passed by, had thoughts so delightful that she began to tidy them into sentences to put in a letter to Edmund. Her days were not full or busy and the gathering in of little things to write to him about took up a large part of her time. She would have made a paragraph or two about the children singing, the hot weather – so rare in England – the scent of the lime and privet blossom, the pieces of tin glinting among the branches of the cherry trees. But the instinctive thought was at once checked by the truth that there would be no letter-writing that evening after all. She stood before an alarming crisis, one that she had hoped to avoid for as long as ever she lived; the crisis of meeting for the first time the person whom she knew best in the world.

'What will he be like?' did not worry her. She knew what he was like. If he turned out differently, it would be a mistake. She would be getting a false impression of him and she would know that it was temporary and would fade. She was more afraid of herself, and wondered if he would know how to discount the temporary, and false, in her. Too much was at stake and, for herself, she would not have taken the risk. 'I agree that we have gone beyond meeting now. It would be retracing our steps,' he had once written to her. 'Although, perhaps if we were ever in the same country, it would be absurd to make a point of *not* meeting.' This, however, was what she had done when she went to Italy the next year.

In Rome, some instinct of self-preservation kept her from giving him her aunt's address there. She would telephone, she thought; but each time she tried to – her heart banging erratically within a suddenly hollow breast – she was checked by thoughts of the booby-trap lying before her. In the end, she skirted it. She discovered the little street where he lived, and felt the strangeness of reading its name, which she had written hundreds of times on envelopes. Walking past his house on the opposite pavement, she had glanced timidly at the peeling apricot-coloured plaster. The truth of the situation made her feel quite faint. It was frightening, like seeing a ghost in reverse – the insubstantial suddenly solidifying into a patchy and shabby reality. At the window on the first floor, one of the shutters was open; there was the darkness of the room beyond, an edge of yellow curtain and, hanging over the back of a chair set near the window, what looked like a white skirt. Even if Edmund himself threw open the other shutter and came out on to the balcony, he would never have known that the woman across the road was one of his dearest friends, but, all the same, she hastened away from the neighbourhood. At dinner, her aunt thought she might be ill. Her visitors from England so often were – from the heat and sight-seeing and the change of diet.

The odd thing to Emily about the escapade was its vanishing from her mind – the house became its own ghost again, the house of her imagination, lying on the other side of the road, where she had always pictured it, with its plaster unspoilt and Edmund inside in his tidied-up room, writing to her.

He had not chided her when she sent a letter from a safer place, explaining her lack of courage – and explain it she could, so fluently, half-touchingly yet wholly amusingly – on paper. He teased her gently, understanding her decision. In him, curiosity and adventurousness would have overcome his hesitation. Disillusionment would have deprived him of less than it might have deprived her; her letters were a relaxation to him; to her, his were an excitement, and her fingers often trembled as she tore open their envelopes.

They had written to one another for ten years. She had admired his novels since she was a young woman, but would not have thought of writing to tell him so; that he could conceivably be interested in the opinion of a complete stranger did not occur to her. Yet, sometimes, she felt that without her as their reader the novels could not have had a fair existence. She was so sensitive to what he wrote, that she felt her own reading half-created it. Her triumph at the end of each book had something added of a sense of accomplishment on her part. She felt it, to a lesser degree, with some other writers, but they were dead; if they had been living, she would not have written to them, either.

Then one day she read in a magazine an essay he had written about the boyhood of Tennyson. His conjecture on some point she could confirm, for she had letters from one of the poet's brothers. She looked for them among her grandfather's papers and (she was never impulsive save when the impulse was generosity) sent them to Edmund, with a little note to tell him that they were a present to repay some of the pleasure his books had given her.

Edmund, who loved old letters and papers of every kind, found these especially delightful. So the first of many letters from him came to her, beginning, 'Dear Miss Fairchild'. His handwriting was very large and untidy and difficult to decipher, and this always pleased her, because his letters took longer to read; the enjoyment was drawn out, and often a word or two had to be puzzled over for days. Back, again and again, she would go to the letter, trying to take the problem by surprise – and that was usually how she solved it.

Sometimes, she wondered why he wrote to her – and was flattered when he asked for a letter to cheer him up when he was depressed, or to calm him when he was unhappy. Although he could not any longer work well in England – for a dullness came over him, from the climate and old, vex-atious associations – he still liked to have some foothold there, and Emily's letters refreshed his memories.

At first, he thought her a novelist manqué, then he realised that letter-writing is an art by itself, a different kind of skill, though with perhaps a similar motive – and one at which Englishwomen have excelled.

As she wrote, the landscape, flowers, children, cats and dogs, sprang to life memorably. He knew her neighbours and her relation to them, and also knew people, who were dead now, whom she had loved. He called them by their Christian names when he wrote to her and re-evoked them for her, so that, being allowed at last to mention them, she felt that they became light and free again in her mind, and not an intolerable suppression, as they had been for years.

Coming to the village, on this hot morning, she was more agitated than she could ever remember being, and she began to blame Edmund for creating such an ordeal. She was angry with herself for acquiescing, when he had suggested that he, being at last in England for a week or two, should come to see her. 'For an hour, or three at most. I want to look at the flowers in the *very* garden, and stroke the cat, and peep between the curtains at Mrs Waterlow going by.'

'He knows too much about me, so where can we begin?' she wondered. She had confided such intimacies in him. At that distance, he was as safe as the confessional, with the added freedom from hearing any words said aloud. She had written to his mind only. He seemed to have no face, and certainly no voice. Although photographs had once passed between them, they had seemed meaningless.

She had been so safe with him. They could not have wounded one another, but now they might. In ten years, there had been no inadvertent hurts, of rivalry, jealousy, or neglect. It had not occurred to either to wonder if the other would sometime cease to write; the letters would come, as surely as the sun.

'But will they now?' Emily was wondering.

She turned the familiar bend of the road and the sea lay glittering below – its wrinkled surface looking solid and without movement, like a great sheet of metal. Now and then a light breeze came off the water and rasped together the dried grasses on the banks; when it dropped, the late morning silence held, drugging the brain and slowing the limbs.

For years, Emily had looked into mirrors only to see if her hair were tidy or her petticoat showing below her dress. This morning, she tried to take herself by surprise, to see herself as a stranger might, but failed.

He would expect a younger woman from the photograph of some years back. Since that was taken, wings of white hair at her temples had given her a different appearance. The photograph would not, in any case, show how poor her complexion was, unevenly pitted, from an illness when she was a child. As a girl, she had looked at her reflection and thought 'No one will ever want to marry me' and no one had.

When she went back to the living-room, the cat was walking about, smelling lobster in the air; baulked, troubled by desire, he went restlessly about the little room, the pupils of his eyes two thin lines of suspicion and contempt. But the lobster was high up on the dresser, above the Rockingham cups, and covered with a piece of muslin.

Emily went over to the table and touched the knives and forks, shook the salt in the cellar nicely level, lifted a wine-glass to the light. She poured out a glass of sherry and stood, well back from the window – looking out between hollyhocks at the lane.

Unless the train was late, he should be there. At any moment, the station taxi would come slowly along the lane and stop, with terrible inevitability, outside the cottage. She wondered how tall he was – how would he measure against the hollyhocks? Would he be obliged to stoop under the low oak beams?

The sherry heartened her a little – at least, her hands stopped shaking – and she filled her glass again. The wine was cooling in a bucket down the well and she thought that perhaps it was time to fetch it in, or it might be too cold to taste.

The well had pretty little ferns of a very bright green growing out of the bricks at its sides, and when she lifted the cover, the ice-cold air struck her. She was unused to drinking much, and the glasses of sherry had, first, steadied her; then, almost numbed her. With difficulty, she drew up the bucket; but her movements were clumsy and uncertain, and greenish slime came off the rope on to her clean dress. Her hair fell forward untidily. Far, far below, as if at the wrong end of a telescope, she saw her own tiny face looking back at her. As she was taking the bottle of wine from the bucket, she heard a crash inside the cottage.

She knew what must have happened, but she felt too muddled to act quickly. When she opened the door of the living-room she saw, as she expected, the cat and the lobster and the Rockingham cups spread in disorder about the floor.

She grabbed the cat first – though the damage was done now – and ran to the front door to throw him out into the garden; but, opening the door, was confronted by Edmund, whose arm was raised, just about to pull on the old iron bell. At the sight of the distraught woman with untidy hair and her eyes full of tears, he took a pace back.

'There's no lunch,' she said quickly. 'Nothing.' The cat struggled against her shoulder, frantic for the remains of the lobster, and a long scratch slowly ripened across her cheek; then the cat bounded from her and sat down behind the hollyhocks to wash his paws.

'How do you do,' Emily said. She took her hand away from his almost as soon as she touched him and put it up to her cheek, brushing blood across her face.

'Let us go in and bathe you,' he suggested.

'Oh, no, please don't bother. It is nothing at all. But, yes, of course, come in. I'm afraid . . .' She was incoherent and he could not follow what she was saying.

At the sight of the lobster and the china on the floor, he understood a little. All the same, she seemed to him to be rather drunk.

'Such wonderful cups and saucers,' he said, going down on his knees and filling his hands with fragments. 'I don't know how you can bear it.'

'It's nothing. It doesn't matter. It's the lobster that matters. There is nothing else in the house.'

'Eggs?' he suggested.

'I don't get the eggs till Friday,' she said wildly.

'Well, cheese.'

'It's gone hard and sweaty. The weather's so ...'

'Not that it isn't too hot to eat anything,' he said quickly. 'Hotter than Rome. And I was longing for an English drizzle.'

'We had a little shower on Monday evening. Did you get that in London?'

'Monday? No, Sunday we had a few spots.'

'It was Monday here, I remember. The gardens needed it, but it didn't do much good.'

He looked round for somewhere to put the broken china. 'No, I suppose not.'

'It hardly penetrated. Do put that in the waste-paper basket.'

'This cup is fairly neatly broken in half, it could be riveted. I can take it back to London with me.'

'I won't hear of it. But it is so kind ... I suppose the cat may as well have the remains of this – though not straight away. He must be shown that I am cross with him. Oh, dear, and I fetched it last thing from the village so that it should be fresh. But that's not much use to you, as it's turned out.'

She disappeared into the kitchen with her hands full of lobster shells.

He looked round the room and so much of it seemed familiar to him. A stout woman passing by in the lane and trying to see in through the window might be Mrs Waterlow herself, who came so amusingly into Emily's letters.

He hoped things were soon going to get better, for he had never seen anyone so distracted as Emily when he arrived. He had been prepared for shyness, and had thought he could deal with that, but her frenzied look, with the blood on her face and the bits of lobster in her hands, made him feel that he had done some damage which, like the china, was quite beyond his repairing.

She was a long time gone, but shouted from the kitchen that he must take a glass of sherry, as he was glad to do.

'May I bring some out to you?' he asked.

'No, no thank you. Just pour it out and I will come.'

When she returned at last, he saw that she had washed her face and combed her hair. What the great stain all across her skirt was, he could not guess. She was carrying a little dish of sardines, all neatly wedged together as they had been lying in their tin.

'It is so dreadful,' she began. 'You will never forget being given a tin of sardines, but they will go better with the wine than the baked beans, which is the only other thing I can find.'

'I am *very* fond of sardines,' he said.

She put the dish on the table and then, for the first time, looked at him. He was of medium height after all, with broader shoulders than she had imagined. His hair was a surprise to her. From his photograph, she had imagined it white – he was, after all, ten years older than she – but instead, it was blond and bleached by the sun. 'And I always thought I was writing to a white-haired man,' she thought.

Her look lasted only a second or two and then she drank her sherry quickly, with her eyes cast down.

'I hope you forgive me for coming here,' he said gravely. Only by seriousness could he hope to bring them back to the relationship in which they really stood. He approached her so fearfully, but she shied away.

'Of course,' she said. 'It is *so* nice. After all these years. But I am sure you must be starving. Will you sit here?'

'How are we to continue?' he wondered.

She was garrulous with small talk through lunch, pausing only to take up her wine-glass. Then, at the end, when she had handed him his coffee, she failed. There was no more to say, not a word more to be wrung out of the weather, or the restaurant in Rome they had found they had in common, or the annoyances of travel – the train that was late and the cabin that was stuffy. Worn-out, she still cast about for a subject to embark on. The silence was unendurable. If it continued, might he not suddenly say, 'You are so different from all I had imagined,' or their eyes might meet and they would see in one another's nakedness and total loss.

'I *did* say Wednesday,' said Mrs Waterlow.

'No, Thursday,' Emily insisted. If she could not bar the doorway with forbidding arms, she did so with malevolent thoughts. Gentle and patient neighbour she had always been and Mrs Waterlow, who had the sharp nose of the total abstainer and could smell alcohol on Emily's breath, was quite astonished.

The front door of the cottage opened straight into the living-room and Edmund was exposed to Mrs Waterlow, sitting forward in his chair, staring into a coffee-cup.

'I'll just leave the poster for the Jumble Sale then,' said Mrs Waterlow. 'We shall have to talk about the refreshments another time. I think, don't you, that half a pound of tea does fifty people. Mrs Harris will see to the slab cake. But if you're busy, I mustn't keep you. Though since I am here, I wonder if I could look up something in your Encyclopaedia. I won't interrupt. I promise.'

'May I introduce Mr Fabry?' Emily said, for Mrs Waterlow was somehow or other in the room.

'Not Mr *Edmund* Fabry?'

Edmund, still holding his coffee-cup and saucer, managed to stand up quickly and shake hands.

'The author? I could recognise you from your photo. Oh, my daughter will be so interested. I must write at once to tell her. I'm afraid I've never read any of your books.'

Edmund found this, as he always found it, unanswerable. He gave an apologetic murmur, and smiled ingratiatingly.

'But I always read the reviews of them in the Sunday papers.' Mrs Waterlow went on, 'I'm afraid we're rather a booky family.'

So far, she had said nothing to which he could find any reply. Emily stood helplessly beside him, saying nothing. She was not wringing her hands, but he thought that if they had not been clasped so tightly together, that was what would have happened.

'You've *really* kept Mr Fabry in the dark, Emily,' said Mrs Waterlow.

'Not so *you* to *me*,' Edmund thought. He had met her many times before in Emily's letters, already knew that her family was 'booky' and had had her preposterous opinions on many things.

She was a woman of fifty-five, whose children had grown up and gone thankfully away. They left their mother almost permanently, it seemed to them, behind the tea-urn at the village hall – and a good watching-place it was. She had, as Emily once put it, the over-alert look of a ventriloquist's dummy. Her head, cocked slightly, turned to and fro between Emily and Edmund. 'Dyed hair,' she thought, glancing away from him. She was often wrong about people.

'Now, don't let me interrupt you. You get on with your coffee. I'll just sit quiet in my corner and bury myself in the Encyclopaedia.'

'Would you like some coffee?' Emily asked. 'I'm afraid it may be rather cold.'

'If there *is* some going begging, nothing would be nicer. "Shuva to Tom-Tom", that's the one I want.' She pulled out the Encyclopaedia and rather ostentatiously pretended to wipe dust from her fingers.

She has presence of mind, Edmund decided, watching her turn the pages with speed, and authority. She has really thought of something to look up. He was sure that he could not have done so as quickly himself. He wondered what it was that she had hit upon. She had come to a page of photographs of Tapestry and began to study them intently. There appeared to be pages of close print on the subject. So clever, Edmund thought.

She knew that he was staring at her and looked up and smiled; her finger marking the place. 'To settle an argument,' she said. 'I'm afraid we are a very argumentative family.'

Edmund bowed.

A silence fell. He and Emily looked at one another, but she looked away first. She sat on the arm of a chair, as if she were waiting to spring up to see Mrs Waterlow out – as indeed she was.

The hot afternoon was a spell they had fallen under. A bluebottle zig-zagged about the room, hit the window-pane, then went suddenly out of the door. A petal dropped off a geranium on the window-sill; occasionally – but not often enough for Edmund – a page was turned, the thin paper rustling silkily over. Edmund drew his wrist out of his sleeve and glanced secretly at his watch, and Emily saw him do it. It was a long journey he had made to see her, and soon he must be returning.

Mrs Waterlow looked up again. She had an amused smile, as if they were a couple of shy children whom she had just introduced to one another. 'Oh, dear, why the silence? I'm not listening, you know. You will make me feel that I am in the way.'

You preposterous old trollop, Edmund thought viciously. He leant back, put his finger-tips together and said, looking across at Emily, 'Did I tell you that cousin Joseph had a nasty accident? Out bicycling. *Both* of them, you know. Such a deprivation. No heir, either. But Constance very soon con-soled herself. With one of the Army padres out there. They were discovered by Joseph's batman in the most unusual circumstances. The Orient's insidious influence, I suppose. So strangely exotic for Constance, though.' He guessed – though he did not look – that Mrs Waterlow had flushed and, pretending not to be listening, was struggling hard *not* to flush.

'Cousin Constance's Thousand and One Nights,' he said. 'The padre had courage. Like engaging with a boa-constrictor, I'd have thought.'

If only Emily had not looked so alarmed. He began to warm to his inventions, which grew more macabre and outrageous – and, as he did so, he could hear the pages turning quickly and at last the book was closed with a loud thump. 'That's clinched *that* argument,' said Mrs Waterlow. 'Hubert is so often inaccurate, but won't have it that he can ever be wrong.' She tried to sound unconcerned, but her face was set in lines of disapproval.

'You are triumphant, then?' Edmund asked and he stood up and held out his hand.

When she had gone, Emily closed the door and leant against it. She looked exhausted.

'Thank you,' she said. 'She would never have gone otherwise. And now it is nearly time for *you* to go.'

'I am sorry about Cousin Joseph. I could think of no other way.'

In Emily's letters, Mrs Waterlow had been funny; but she was not in real life and he wondered how Emily could suffer so much, before transforming it.

'My dear, if you are sorry I came, then I am sorry, too.'

'Don't say anything. Don't talk of it,' she begged him, standing with her hands pressed hard against the door behind her. She shrank from words, thinking of the scars they leave, which she would be left to tend when he had gone. If he spoke the truth, she could not bear it; if he tried to muffle it with tenderness, she would look upon it as pity. He had made such efforts, she knew; but he could never have protected her from herself.

He, facing her, turned his eyes for a moment towards the window; then he looked back at her. He said nothing; but she knew that he had seen the station-car drawing to a standstill beyond the hollyhocks.

'You have to go?' she asked.

He nodded.

Perhaps the worst has happened, she thought. I have fallen in love with him – the one thing from which I felt I was completely safe.

Before she moved aside from the door, she said quickly, as if the words were red-hot coals over which she must pick her way – 'If you write to me again, will you leave out today, and let it be as if you had not moved out of Rome?'

'Perhaps I didn't,' he said.

At the door, he took her hand and held it against his cheek for a second – a gesture both consoling and conciliatory.

When he had gone, she carried her grief decently upstairs to her little bedroom and there allowed herself some tears.

When they were dried and over, she sat down by the open window.

She had not noticed how clouds had been crowding into the sky. A wind had sprung up and bushes and branches were jigging and swaying.

The hollyhocks nodded together. A spot of rain as big as a halfpenny dropped on to the stone sill, others fell over leaves down below, and a sharp cool smell began to rise at once from the earth.

She put her head out of the window, her elbows on the outside sill. The soft rain, falling steadily now, calmed her. Down below in the garden the cat wove its way through a flower-bed. At the door, he began to cry piteously to be let in and she shut the window a little and went downstairs. It was dark in the living-room; the two windows were fringed with dripping leaves; there were shadows and silence.

While she was washing up, the cat, turning a figure-of-eight round her feet, brushed her legs with his wet fur. She began to talk to him, as she often did, for they were alone so much together. 'If you were a dog,' she said, 'we could go for a nice walk in the rain.'

As it was, she gave him his supper and took an apple for herself. Walking about, eating it, she tidied the room. The sound of the rain in the garden was very peaceful. She carried her writing things to the table by the window and there, in the last of the light, dipped her goose-quill pen in the ink, and wrote, in her fine and flowing hand, her address, and then, 'Dear Edmund'.

A Troubled State of Mind

In the old part of the town, between the castle and the cathedral, were some steep and cobbled streets whose pavements were broken open by the roots of plane trees. The tall and narrow houses stood back, beyond the walls of gardens and courtyards, but there were glimpses of them through wrought-iron gates. The quiet here was something that country people found unbelievable. Except for the times when the cathedral bells were ringing, the silence was broken only by the rooks in the castle trees or, as on this afternoon, by the sound of rain.

Lalage left the car in the garage at the foot of the hill and the two girls – Lalage herself and her step-daughter, Sophy – walked as quickly as they could towards home, carrying the smaller pieces of Sophy's luggage, Lalage, already hostess-like (Sophy thought), bowed over to one side with the weight of the bigger suitcase, and the other arm thrust out shoulder-high to right her balance.

The road narrowed gradually to less than a car's width and rain ran fast down the cobbles, swirling into drains. Reaching the gate in the wall, Sophy swung her skis off her back and turned the iron handle. The scraping, rusty sound of it was suddenly remembered and was as strange to her as anything else in a world where every familiar thing had moved into a pattern too fantastic ever – she was sure – to be dealt with or understood. She and Lalla, for instance, going in through this gate as they had done so often before; but Sophy now at a loss to guess what might be waiting for her inside, in her own home.

Her father, Colonel Vellacott, had always loved Italy and everything Italian and had tried to make a Venetian courtyard in wet England. Its sadness was appalling, Sophy thought. The paving-stones were dark with rain and drops fell heavily from the vine and the magnolia, off statues and urns and, in a sudden gust of wind, rattled like bullets on the broad fig-leaves by the wall. In the seats of some iron chairs puddles reflected the cloudy sky.

'John will be back for dinner,' Lalage said, as they picked their way across the wet stones – 'He had to go because he was in the chair.'

Ah yes, 'John', of course, Sophy thought.

The front door opened and Miss Sully came out to take the case from

Lalage, primly eager to wring all she could from the peculiar situation. 'It is just like old times,' she said to Sophy, 'when Madam used to come to stay with you in the holidays and I used to listen to hear the gate so that I could run out with a welcome.'

'Madam' had been a shock and a calculated one, Sophy thought. She smiled and shook hands. 'In the old days, you always said we had grown. Not any more, I hope.'

'Grown *up*, I should say.'

'Isn't she brown?' said Lalla.

'As brown as a berry.'

They went into the dark hall where the Italian influence continued in glass and marble, trailing leaves and a wrought-iron screen which served no purpose. Nothing visible had been altered since Sophy was here last, a year ago, but everything invisible had been. At Sophy's bedroom door, Miss Sully turned away, with promises of tea in five minutes and a fire in the drawing-room. Sophy, standing in the middle of the room, looking about her, but not at Lalla, asked: 'How do you get on with *her?*'

'As I always did, trying to be as nice as pie, wearing myself out, really, but not getting anywhere. She is, as we always found her, a mystery woman.'

'Kind . . . ' Sophy began.

'Kindness itself. Thoughtful, considerate, efficient. But what lies underneath, who knows? Something does. She's learning Italian now.'

'Perhaps that's what's underneath. Not enough goes on here for her. She's too intelligent to be a housekeeper, and too ambitious.'

'Then why go on?'

Sophy could not now say 'I think because she hoped to marry my father'. She had sometimes thought it in the past and suddenly wondered if she had ever told Lalla. She felt that she must have done, for she had told her everything, though she no longer could.

'What was Switzerland *like?*' Lalla asked. 'I mean really.'

'It went on too long.'

Sophy put her fingers to the locks of her suitcase, about to spring them open, and then could not be bothered, and straightened her back, thinking, 'She will wonder why, if I found it too long, I did not come back earlier, as I could have done, and should have done and would have done, if it had not been for *that.*' It was always 'that' in her mind – the marriage of her father and her dearest friend. The other questions – Sophy's questions – that hovered between them were too unseemly to be spoken – for instance 'why?' and 'how?' and 'where did it begin?' The only question in the least possible Sophy was turning over in her mind and beginning to make a shape of it in words, when Lalla, before it could be spoken, answered it.

Since early girlhood, they had often found their thoughts arriving at the same point without the promptings of speech.

'I am so happy, you know,' Lalla said. 'It is all so lovely in this house and now to have you in it with me at last! Though,' she added quickly, 'it is you who have always been here and I who has at last arrived.'

'But, Lalla dear, you always seemed *part* of the house to me. We never called the spare room anything but "Lalla's room". When other people came to stay, it seemed wrong to me that they should hang their clothes in your cupboard.'

Then she suddenly bent down and unclicked her suitcase after all, to have something to do with her trembling fingers, and wondered, 'What is the spare room called now? I have made another booby-trap for us, where there already were too many.'

'Did you notice,' Lalage asked, as if she had not heard, 'how eagerly Miss Sully ran out to greet you? She has been quite excited all the week.'

'I can understand that.' Sophy lifted the lid of the suitcase and looked gloomily at her creased and folded clothes. 'She loves situations and she wanted to see how I was facing this one.'

'Yes, to see if you were jealous of me, hoping perhaps that life here from now on would be full of interesting little scenes between us, something to sustain and nourish her while she chops the parsley – which she does – doesn't she? – with not just *kitchen* venom?'

'She will analyse everything we say and fit it into her conception of our relationship.'

'She has already tried to haunt me with your mother – so beautiful she was and you are growing up to be her image.'

Sophy lifted her head from the unpacking and could not help giving a quick look into the mirror before her. 'How absurd!' she said. 'If she could throw up a woman so long dead, how impatiently she must have waited for *me* to throw *myself* up.'

'She longs for incidents. I am sure she will hover to see who pours out the tea and whether, from habit, you will go to your old place at the table.'

This was brave of Lalage and seemed to clear the air.

'It is a good thing,' Sophy said, 'that you and I have read so many novels. The hackneyed dangers we should be safe from.'

'We shall be safe *together*,' Lalla said. 'Loving one another,' she added, so quietly that she seemed to be talking to herself.

'Demurrings and deprecations will not escape notice either,' said Sophy. 'Saying "*you* do it, please", or "you go first". We must beware of every one of those. I will be a straightforward daughter to you, I think. It may be ageing for you, but I think it will be safer than for us to try to be like sisters.

I thought of that in Switzerland, and I decided that a daughter has privileges and a rôle to play, which a younger or inferior sister has not.'

'As long as I am never called "Mamma".'

Miss Sully, hovering at the foot of the stairs, heard laughter as the bedroom door opened and Lalage's voice saying with great gaiety, 'Who – a year ago – would have believed that we could come to this?'

They were on the stairs now, and Miss Sully hurried back to the kitchen for the hot scones. She wanted to watch the approach to the tea table.

This turned out to be disappointing. Sophy went straight to the drawing-room window and, with her back turned to the room, said, 'Since last I saw you, Lalla, I've given up milk and sugar. What Father used to call "puppy-fat" turned out just to be fat.'

'Then I must do the same,' said Lalla and sat down before the tray and took up the tea-pot. 'And every time John goes out, we will have those slimming meals I am always reading about at the hairdresser's – meagre things like tomato jellies and stuffed cucumbers and lettuce juice. Meanwhile, you could have a scone, couldn't you?'

Sophy turned from the window and sat down in a chair, opposite the one where she had always sat before.

'Only this time,' she said.

Miss Sully, having very slowly put a log on the fire and rearranged the tongs, was now obliged to go. At the door, she heard Sophy say, 'Just to celebrate the occasion.'

By the time Colonel Vellacott returned from his meeting, a mode of behaviour was established between the two girls. It had often been tried out in their minds during their separation, suggested and explored with nervous tact in their letters to one another.

He found them by the drawing-room fire, Lalage winding wool from Sophy's outstretched hands. Kneeling on the rug, Sophy rocked from side to side, and swayed her arms, turning her wrists deftly as the wool slipped off them. So often, bemused and patient, she had held Lalla's wool for her: the knitting craze came and went, jerseys were seldom finished and, if they were, were sorry things. From past experience, neither had high hopes for this new skein.

'A charming sight,' Colonel Vellacott said. They had settled down together already, he was relieved to see. It was like bringing a new dog into a house where another had reigned alone for a long time. The scene might have been prearranged – the girls were so tangled up in wool that they could not extricate themselves and the kisses he gave each on the top of her head were almost simultaneous, Lalla hardly first at all.

'That's *that* over,' he thought, and for no reason felt self-congratulatory. 'That', for him, was his embarrassment. Now, it was as easy as could be to talk about Switzerland and Sophy most brilliantly took the lead with her descriptions of the school and the lunacy of its inhabitants.

'Don't!' Lalage half-sobbed, gasping with laughter, and wiped her eyes on the ball of wool.

'Ah, you are going into fits,' her husband said. He remembered all the holiday laughter in this house, Lalla's cries of 'Don't' and her collapsed state, his teasing of them both and his mocking echoes of their girlish phrases. He had felt in those days wonderfully indulgent. 'Bring Lalla back with you,' he always told Sophy. 'It is sad for you to be alone – and sad for her, too.' Lalla – the poor orphan child – lived with an aunt, but was more often, in school holidays, at Ancaster, with Sophy.

'Now, Lalla!' he said, in a severe voice. He leant back in his chair and folded his arms with a show of excessive patience. 'If you snort again, you must be sent away.'

'Oh, please, I *ache*,' she implored Sophy, holding the ball of wool tight to her ribs, her beautiful eyes glittering with tears.

'Oh, please, I *ache*, Sophy,' said Colonel Vellacott.

'I am only telling you what happened,' Sophy said, with what Lalla called her straight face.

'The experience seems to have been worth every penny,' her father said. 'Yes, I am truly finished.'

The end of the wool slipped from her fingers, she sank back on her heels and looked up at her father, at last returning his gaze, smiling with love and delight, but with a reserve of mischief, too, and that pleased him most of all, it was what gave reality to her warm-heartedness. If she were dissembling her gaiety and friendliness, she would not have dissembled *that*, he thought. It would not have occurred to her as a necessary ingredient of mirth.

Sophy kept up her spirits throughout dinner and then flagged. It was her long journey, the other two said and she agreed. 'And you miss the clarity of that air,' her father added.

But there were other exhaustions she could less easily endure and the chief was, she saw, that she had cast herself in a rôle that would take too much from her.

She remembered – and this was after she had said good-night and gone to her room – long ago and when her mother was alive, she herself perhaps five or six years old, being taken on a train journey, from Edinburgh, her mother's old home it may have been. Kneeling in her corner seat, breathing on the window, breathing and wiping, in stupefying boredom, she had begun suddenly to talk in baby talk, demanding, for no reason she could now recall, in a lispy, whiny voice that had never been her own, a 'chocky bikky'. Her mother, gently remonstrating, had made publicly clear that this odd voice was to be regarded as a game. 'Icky chocky bikky,' Sophy had insisted, pouting. It was then that she had first realised her own power of mimicry; power it was and went to her head. She had become the nauseating infant she impersonated. Other people in the compartment took the lead from her mother and laughed. Sophy herself had pretended not to hear this and turned her back and breathed on the window again, but soon she could not help herself. 'Pitty gee-gees,' she said, pointing. When she had tired of talking, she let her eyelids droop and began to suck her thumb as she had scornfully watched other children doing. Her mother, who knew that things were going too far, but was never brisk with her in public, tried to distract her attention, but could not. The performance had been tiring, like playing Lady Macbeth with heart and soul and, in the end, Sophy had become sickened by her own creation, caught in its tentacles and quite unable to escape. Everyone else was tired, too; she knew that her mother was desperate and that glances were exchanged; but she seemed powerless to end the misery. It was too late to speak suddenly in her own voice. What voice was it, and what things did it say? She could remember putting her forehead to the cool window-pane and counting to herself, 'One, two, then three and then I'll speak again as I used and they will all know the other voice has gone.' But her shyness was too great, she was too committed to the other character and had no way of breaking loose from it. Badgered, exhausted and embarrassed, she had at last burst into tears, taking refuge, as she wept, against her mother's arm. 'Over-tired,' the grown-ups said. 'Such a long journey. She's stood up to it very well.'

Lalla and her father had said good-night and used the same words, though now the climate was to blame as well. They were no more true than when she was a child. The acting had exhausted her, and nothing else. She could have cried, as she had when a young girl, 'Oh, my darling Mamma, why did you have to die?' The words were so loud in her head and her breast that she might have said them aloud. They returned with the aching familiarity of a long time ago, when she had lain in bed after lights-out at boarding-school, or on their first Christmas Eve alone, with her father trying to remember everything her mother had always done, so that Sophy should not be deprived of one sprig of holly or Christmas-tree candle. In the end, unbelievably, the words had become a habit and lost their pain. Her life without her mother was different from before, but it was, after all, the same life. If Mamma had been here, she sometimes thought, accepting that she could not be.

This evening the phrase sprang at her with a sudden freshness, the first time for years. She sat down on the edge of her bed and her hands dropped into her lap, palms upwards in a gesture of hopeless inertia. 'If she were alive,' she thought, 'she would be downstairs with Father, and Lalla here with me, as she ought to be. Or not under this roof at all. And I should be relieved of this tiring pretence, that won't end with the end of the train journey, as it did before. It will be there waiting for me in the morning and all the mornings after – having to be gay and unselfconscious – as if it were a perfectly normal thing for one's father to marry one's school-friend – fifty-three and eighteen and all plotted and planned with me safely out of the way in a foreign country,' she added, feeling self-pity. 'I must be gracious and hand over my home and my place in it and have, day in, day out, my constant companion chosen for me.'

Sometimes, at school, Lalla had stolen marches on her. She could remember well the case of the borrowed treasure and the broken promise, the forgotten appointment, the betrayed confidence. Many instances came to her mind from the dark place where they had long ago been thrust impatiently away.

'I must get away,' she thought, and her hands sprang to life and were clenched tight, drumming on her knees. 'I must run away from my own home, as soon as I have come back to it.' In Switzerland, she had longed for it so much, in that clear air her father had mentioned, faced for months at a time with the monotony of the snow, and the dark trees that never shed their leaves, as trees ought, she was sure. 'Write to me about England,' she had begged her father and Lalage. 'Describe a nice drizzle, a beautiful muggy evening with the fallen leaves sticking to the pavements. You describe it for me, though; not I to you.'

Instead, they had written to say that they were getting married. They had met several times in London, for both had been lonely, missing Sophy. In their loneliness they had flown together, and clung, and wished to remain so for ever. The loneliness had been much stressed – orphan and widower, as they constantly referred to themselves. Companionship (and Sophy was to share in this, too) and common interests (both liked going to plays, but seldom did so) were enlarged upon. Love itself was not once mentioned and Sophy was glad that it was not. She was to fly home for the wedding – very quiet, just the three of them and Lalage's aunt. But Sophy would not go. She was on her way up to a chalet for the winter sports and had made arrangements which she could not confuse. She knew that they were glad to have her stay in Switzerland and she was glad to do so, although she was sure that if she had not gone there in the first place, she could have prevented things from reaching such a pass.

Her bedroom, above her father's, overlooked the courtyard and when she heard footsteps out there, she went across to the window and looked out. It was almost dark. Lalage and her father were going for a walk in the rain. He opened the courtyard door into the street and as Lalage passed through it, put his hand on her shoulder.

'Ah, yes, and bedtime, too,' Sophy thought, turning away. 'Beyond one's imagination, thank God. I hope I can hide my revulsion from her. I dare say there's nothing to stop her having a baby even. It is perfectly possible.'

Their footsteps and voices faded away down the street. The drizzle continued, and downstairs Miss Sully was singing 'Oh, what a Beautiful Morning'.

'I must get a job,' Sophy thought. 'Without a day's delay.'

'Sophy's job' was soon a great topic of conversation.

Colonel Vellacott was full of facetious suggestions. At every meal some new one came to mind, and Sophy grinned, and wondered if her face would crack in two, as her heart must.

'Oh, hush, I can't hear of it,' Lalage would beg her husband, and stuff her fingers in her ears. 'Sophy, please! You will make me think you are running away from *me* and it will be as Miss Sully predicted.' She kept her hands pressed to her cheekbones, ready to make herself deaf again, if necessary. Her bracelets slid down her thin arms to her elbows. Her eyes were full of pleading.

'Affected,' Sophy thought. 'She used not to be. Father loves it.'

'I always meant to get a job,' she said. 'I couldn't have just stayed here and looked after the house – which Miss Sully does much better anyhow.' But this was dangerous ground and she stepped from it quickly. 'I should have taken the Secretarial course with you, Lalla, if Father hadn't made me go to Switzerland first.'

'*Made?*' said Colonel Vellacott.

'Persuaded, then.'

'Your French was horrible.'

'Well, "made" me, then.'

'You'd have loathed the Secretarial School,' Lalla said complacently. 'I hated every moment.'

'And was glad to leave it and get married,' Sophy thought. 'So it was typing and shorthand that drove you to it. He hasn't, after all, a spectacular enough amount of money to be married for. And love? If you love him, you show none of it. Perhaps I inhibit you and force you to keep it for when you are alone. In which case, the sooner I go, the better.'

She felt absurdly in the way, but also shut out that they should turn to secrecy because of her.

It was not easy to slip away from Lalage, her too-constant companion, but, one morning, she managed to, and set out, as if on an illicit errand, through wet alleyways towards the Market Place. It had rained for all of the fortnight she had been at home, but had this morning stopped. The clouds had lifted and broken open and bright light, though not yet quite sunshine, poured down over the puddles and dripping eaves. Slate roofs dried rapidly and pavements steamed. It was the end of April.

'We begin the second of May,' said the Principal of the Secretarial School in Market Street. She underlined this date on the application form. 'Your father will complete this for you.' She thought it strange for the girl to come there on her own, making enquiries. Sophy stared at her hands, which were a dark plum colour, scarred from broken chilblains. Clumsy as they were, she used them affectedly, drawing attention to them with hooked fingers as she wrote, and then by twisting round an engagement ring of dull little diamonds.

'I know your father very well,' Miss Priestley said. 'Although I don't suppose he would be able to place *me*. I was a reporter once upon a time on the *Ancaster Herald* and used to cover some of the Court cases when he was on the bench. And my late fiancé was in his regiment in the war. He didn't come back,' she added, in an affectedly casual voice she had learnt at the cinema.

'I'm so sorry,' Sophy murmured.

'Yes, we had been engaged for eleven years. But you don't want to listen to all my sad affairs.'

Although this was true, Sophy felt obliged to make a sound which she hoped suggested denial as well as a certain amount of discouragement. 'If only there were something amusing in this,' she thought. 'Something with which to decorate the plain statement when I tell them at lunch.' But there was not: the bereaved Miss Priestley with her chilblains was saddening and unattractive and the office was stuffy and untidy, not a good example to the pupils.

The sun was shining when Sophy stood, dazed by its brightness, on the steps in Market Street. The Town Hall clock struck twelve. She hurried back home and was there before Lalla returned from the hairdresser's.

'Just *see* what they've done,' was Lalla's piteous cry at luncheon. They had always done the same thing and Sophy only briefly glanced.

'Why don't you tell them?' asked Colonel Vellacott and seemed to have an edge of exasperation to his voice.

'I tell them and tell them. As smooth as smooth, I always say. Not a kink or a curl or I shall be so cross.'

'It will settle down,' Sophy said. 'It always does.'

They had just finished what Miss Sully called 'chicken and all the trimmings'.

'They've caught that man,' Miss Sully said, as she lifted the dishes off the table. 'They gave it out on the one o'clock news.'

'What man?' asked Lalla, still fidgeting with her hair.

'The one that assaulted that little boy and then smothered him.'

'Oh dear!' Lalage frowned.

'I shouldn't have mentioned it, only I thought you'd like to know. It isn't very nice at meal-times, I'm afraid.' She stacked the plates and carried them away.

'This is a very rum Baba,' said Colonel Vellacott, as he always did when given this pudding, and Sophy felt the usual embarrassment, wondering – as she was also used to wondering – just how tedious her friend found this heavy jocularity. Then she remembered that her father was much more Lalage's responsibility. The old situation was reversed. It should be Lalla's task to try to prevent the inevitable phrases, to turn the conversations as deftly as she could as the stale quip rose ominously before them.

'And I shall enjoy seeing how she does it, as time goes on,' she thought. At present, Lalla was merely smiling her bright, usual smile, a guest's smile, vaguely willing.

'I met someone this morning who knows you, Father,' Sophy suddenly told him, deciding that as any kind of approach to her embarrassment would lead to it, this would do as well as any. 'In fact, I did not so much meet her as go to see her.'

Colonel Vellacott waited – with the calm of a man who has nothing to fear – for the mystery to unfold, but Lalla stopped eating, put her fork down on her plate and glanced anxiously at Sophy, who went on: 'Though she says you would never be able to place *her. Can* you place someone called Miss Priestley, who has a secretarial school – no, college, so sorry – in Market Street?'

'No. She is right. I can't.'

'Is she from your past?' Lalla asked. 'Poor Miss Priestley! I am glad that I am in your present.'

'No, she simply wrote down in shorthand things you said in Court,' Sophy explained. 'And her fiancé was in the regiment and was killed, but I don't think she blamed you for it.'

'It was generous of her. Especially as I survived. I should have thought she would have resented that.'

'Why did you go to see her?' Lalla asked, taking up her fork again.

'She is going to teach me to be a secretary.'

'Oh no! Then I shall come too, I won't be left here on my own. May I go, too, John?'

'You know that we agreed not to be sisters,' Sophy told her. 'You have to learn to be my mamma and stay at home while I go off to school.'

'I shall be lonely.'

'Mothers are. Though perhaps they get used to it, and even rather like it in the end.'

'Why did you go about the business in so odd a way?' her father asked. 'There was no necessity to be secretive. If you wanted to do it at all, you should have said so.'

'I said, and said.'

'We thought you were joking.'

'Yes, I knew you thought that.'

'And I might have been consulted, I should have thought. I could have done much better for you than this Miss Whatshername, of whom I certainly have never heard.'

'Then why did you do nothing?'

'Now, Sophy, don't try to be cool with me. You are only just home from Switzerland and there was all the time in the world to make arrangements.'

'I never like to do things at a leisurely pace,' Sophy said, looking calmly at him. 'One may as well get on with life.' As you did, her voice implied.

'But we know nothing of this Miss Thingummy. She seems a strange end to your education.'

'It is what I want, Father.'

Lalla, murmuring 'coffee', left the room.

'I was bringing it,' said Miss Sully, who was never caught out. The tray was in her hands.

Instead of going ahead to the drawing-room, Lalla ran upstairs murmuring 'handkerchief'.

In the dining-room Colonel Vellacott and his daughter were arguing. 'Unlike you, Sophy,' Miss Sully heard.

'I've put the coffee in the drawing-room,' she said, then hurried forward to rearrange the fire. But there was nothing for her to listen to but the sound of their chairs being pushed back. 'Madam will be down directly,' she added.

This was unanswerable and unanswered. Sophy crossed the hall to the drawing-room and without sitting down, carelessly poured out her father's coffee and her own. She took hers over to the window-seat and began to sip it, lifting the cup only a little from its brimming saucer. She supposed that Lalla was upstairs, waiting for them to finish their quarrel.

Displeased and austere Colonel Vellacott remained for days, wearing what Sophy called his Doge's face. With Lalage, too, and in private, he was reserved. Rebellion was in the air – a youthful contagion that he intended should not spread. Don't *you* go running to some Miss Thingummy, or even worse, his mood seemed to warn her.

That Sophy's action was hardly drastic he constantly reminded himself, but her way of taking it had been cold and secretive. For her to earn her own living was nothing other than he intended and desired, but it seemed to him that there was no desperate need and that for a month or two she might have helped him out with Lalla. 'Helped me out' was his own phrase. He had seen what he called 'Bride's despondency' in Lalage's eyes, in spite of her bright smiles and her laughter. He did not know how to cheer her up; his time was so much given over to public work and there was no theatre here in Ancaster. She was lonely and suffering reaction from the sudden adventure of their courtship and wedding. He could not hide his anxiety that the house was dull and silent and – with all his Italian décor long ago perfected – too completed. She had simply taken over what was there and had had nothing to contribute. Although he was pleased with what he had done, he began to wonder if it was what a bride would hope for. 'One day, we will have a change,' he had promised, but could not bring himself to move one fern or sconce. She had insisted – not knowing what was good for her – that nothing should be touched and that she loved it exactly as it was.

Sophy's home-coming had raised her spirits and he himself had felt freer and happier and less anxious. He looked forward to entering the house when he returned from his meetings. People who have had the best of both worlds are the crossest of all when the best in one is lost, and he knew this and scolded himself, but the Doge's face remained and, inhibited by his new habit of sternness, he found himself unable to make love to Lalage. The marriage, Miss Sully thought, was crumbling even more quickly than she had predicted.

At Miss Priestley's, Sophy was by far the eldest girl and the slowest one at learning, too. Miserably, she bowed her head over the abominable hooks and dots of her shorthand, or touch-typed rows of percentage signs or fractions where should have been 'Dear Sirs, We beg to confirm receipt of your esteemed order.'

The other girls had left school at sixteen and seemed as quick as birds with their taking down and reading back, always put their carbon paper in the right way round and never typed addresses on upside-down envelopes.

The class-rooms were on the first floor of the old house, a building now given over to offices. The boards were bare and the long tables were ribbed and splintered and ink-stained. Miss Priestley felt the cold and even in May the windows were kept shut, so that the air was chalk-laden and smelt of lead pencils and glue and india-rubber and girls. The windows faced south, over the top branches of budding lilac trees. Below was a tangled garden into which Sophy found herself more and more inclined to stare. At twelve and four, the heavy notes of the Town Hall clock descended on the roof tops in the most gracious – Sophy thought – signal of release. She was the first to have her books closed, knowing before the chimes began that they

were imminent; she could feel the air growing tense and the clock gathering itself to strike, and her face would put on its bright, good-bye look,
turned expectantly towards Miss Priestley for dismissal.

Then, being free, she was suddenly loth to go home to Lalla's 'I knew
you'd hate it!' The other girls clustered together and showed one another
their work, but Sophy took down her jacket from its peg. She knew that
the others exchanged looks when she left them and when she called out
'good-bye' only one or two answered her, and then in a surprised tone as
if it were strange of her to address them.

Sometimes, instead of going home to tea, she would buy an evening
paper and read it in a little café in Market Street. The idea of punishment
being in the air, it suited her to think of her teacup on the tray at home,
unfilled. There, in the Oak Beams Tea Shop, she met Graham Dennis
again. He was working in a solicitor's office nearby and had so grown up
that she had not recognised him.

The Dennises' parties were famous in Ancaster, and Sophy had been going
to them for as long as she could remember. Mrs Dennis always described
herself as putting herself out for her young people and was not content with
Christmas and birthday parties. There were Hallowe'en parties and garden
parties, and parties at the New Year and on Guy Fawkes' Day. Her husband
could find no escape. If there were not children bobbing for apples in the
hall, they were playing charades in several rooms, or hunting for treasure
all over the house. 'I shall rope Herbert in,' Mrs Dennis told her friends,
who, rather aggrieved because she put themselves so much to shame, wondered how she could manage it. Herbert had been roped in to let off
fireworks or be Father Christmas. Lately, as Denise and Graham were no
longer children, he was roped in to make claret cup or dance with an odd
girl out.

Sophy remembered even the first parties, when she was a little girl. After
the exquisite orderliness of her own home, the great, shabby, untidy house
with its lighted windows and its noise infected her with delicious excitement.

Mrs Dennis was always kindness itself. 'You are only young once,' she
often told her children and their friends and made sure that, as well as
youth, they had as many other delights lavished on them as she could find
time and money to bestow. At the back of her mind, she knew that the two
most important parties of all would come at the end: even in nursery days,
watching the little ones departing with their balloons and presents, she felt
that she was only rehearsing for the culmination of it all – Denise's wedding and Graham's twenty-first birthday. Now, both were looming in the
same year and 'loom' was her own word for their approach. She was

confident that she would surpass herself – the Dennis wedding would be talked about for years; but, for the last time of many, Denise would say, as she drove away: 'Thank you for doing it all.' Beyond, lay a blank future for her mother. But first would come Graham's twenty-first birthday and any champagne left over from that would come in later for the wedding. Only one thing perplexed her, as they went over the list of invitations. Lalage, when staying with Sophy, as she so often was, had always been invited too. For years and years, she had attended the Dennis parties.

'We couldn't leave her out now,' Mrs Dennis said.

'And how possibly ask her?' Graham said. 'Husbands and wives go to parties together. You'd have to ask that old man.'

'He is only your father's age,' Mrs Dennis said, but she knew that that was what Graham meant. It was an awkward situation. She realised that she and Herbert were only at the parties themselves in order to see that the food and drink were plentiful and available. Herbert knew his place and preferring it, made off to his study as soon as he was able, and Mrs Dennis was always in and out of the kitchen.

'How sad to leave her out, after all these years, poor girl,' she said.

Lalage felt both sad and embarrassed when Sophy's invitation came. Her husband, watching her show of unconcern, realised for the first-time the consequences of their romance. The marriage, surviving important hazards, seemed now as likely as not to founder upon trivial matters, on this invitation, for instance, and others that would follow. Lalage had been ardent and generous in her love, to come first in someone's life exalted her and, radiant and incredulous, she had given herself in gratitude. Yet, at the sight of an invitation to a party, she appeared to falter, she glanced away and was confused and could not hide her feeling that she had placed herself in a special position with her contemporaries, was being markedly pushed by them into the ranks of the middle-aged.

Sophy, her father realised, was no longer making things easier, but worsening them. The sooner she could go away and leave them, the better for them all. He could perfectly see this now and wondered how he could hasten what he had so lately tried to prevent.

'As you seem so sure about your typing and shorthand,' he said one day, with a great show of tolerance, 'and are really settled to it, I am quite willing for you to do the thing properly, to go up to London and train at some reputable place.'

But Sophy had not settled to her shorthand and typing; every day she fell back, as the other girls progressed; and now she no longer wanted to go away from Ancaster, having at the twenty-first birthday party fallen in love with Graham Dennis.

Graham and Sophy had rediscovered one another, as young people do who have lived in the same neighbourhood for years and then been separated by school, so that, meeting in the holidays, they seem almost total strangers. Violent changes of height and voice and manner were bewildering and shyness descended. Now, with all the changes made – as they thought – quite grown-up and likely to remain the same for ever, they could sum one another up, and come to a conclusion. Sophy and Graham concluded that they were in love, that they must always have loved, though first immaturity and then separation had hindered their acceptance of the fact.

To Colonel Vellacott, Graham's National Service had not made the man of him it should. Nonchalant and without ambition, he had spent the two years cheerfully peeling potatoes or drinking in the Naafi. Promotion had seemed to him quite as undesirable as it was unlikely. To Colonel Vellacott's questions, on their first meeting after some years, he gave unsatisfactory answers. Nor did Colonel Vellacott like his clothes – his dirty cord trousers and suede shoes and vivid pullovers. Particularly he disliked – and in a cathedral city it was out of place, as Graham himself was – the car he drove. It was an old London taxi painted yellow, with window-boxes and lace curtains. Once, Graham had had written across the back, 'Do not laugh, madam, your daughter may be inside.' In love, and serious at last, he had painted this over.

Even so, that *his* daughter should be inside annoyed Colonel Vellacott considerably.

'Lots of young men have cars like it,' Sophy told him. 'It isn't smart to have a new one. The older and funnier the better.'

'Not in a place like this.'

'We can't *help* living in a place like this. And I think it's amusing. You were young once yourself, remember.'

Lalage, who could not easily escape these much dreaded discussions, turned aside.

Sophy and Lalla found their so gallantly planned relationship beginning to wear threadbare. It was difficult to keep up, especially as it was so unproductive of incredulity in others – its primary aim. Their affection for one another was too easily taken for granted and few of their friends or acquaintances seemed to find it at all remarkable. Their laughter about the hackneyed jealousies that might have threatened them was joined in by their guests, who – so infectious was the gaiety – did not realise how much of relief it contained.

Sophy was the first to find the ordeal going on too long. It had become a mere routine of good behaviour, with no congratulation in it for herself.

Miss Sully thought, observing the minute omens, that soon the situation would have more piquancy. Lalla seemed dull and puzzled, with nothing to do but mend her clothes, change her library books and water all the ferns – too often, for they began to droop and rot away.

One morning, when Colonel Vellacott was in Court and Sophy at her Typing School, Lalage, feeling more restless than ever, wandered into the kitchen, where Miss Sully was making stuffing for green peppers. Lalla sat on a corner of the table and watched, picking up bits of parsley and chewing them, holding pepper-seeds on the tip of her tongue until it tingled.

Miss Sully, mixing raisins and rice, was talking of the days when she was companion to an old lady whose footman had interfered with one of the gardener's boys. She brought in many a Freudian phrase along with those of the cheapest newspapers and her voice dropped to its cathedral hush as it did when she talked of sex. One side of her neck was a bright red. Deftly her fingers worked and when she took up a large knife and began to chop some mushrooms, she abandoned herself almost obscenely to the job. 'What's for pudding?' Lalla asked, like a little girl, as soon as there was quiet again. It had never occurred to her that she might order meals herself. She had once timidly put forward a suggestion that Colonel Vellacott would like jugged hare, but had been told that hare was out of season.

'Well, what *shall* we have?' Miss Sully asked, suddenly indulgent. The names of puddings at once went from Lalla's head, although Miss Sully had such a repertoire of them – there was Cabinet Pudding and High Church Pudding and Guardsman's Pudding and even Railway Pudding – they were mostly sponge mixtures, differing with a dash of spice or jam, or a handful of candied peel. Lalla could never remember which was which.

'What about rice pudding?' she asked. 'I haven't had that since I was at school.'

'Well, we can't very well have rice two courses running, can we?' Miss Sully asked, laughing gently and pointing at the dish of peppers, now ready for the oven. 'And you will have to give me plenty of warning for rice pudding, because the grain must soak at least an hour, you know.'

Lalage hadn't known.

'Is there anything I can do?' she asked, jumping down from the table. It was only eleven o'clock.

'Well, now, you could run the ribbon through the hem of Miss Sophy's petticoat. I know she'll be wanting it this evening. Then I can get on with some scones for tea.' ('Without you under my feet,' she seemed to imply.) By the time she had told Lalla where to find the petticoat and then the ribbon and the bodkin, she thought that she could have done the job herself.

'The shiny side of the ribbon facing you, mind,' she warned her, thinking, 'Really, she's as useless as a little doll.'

When Lalla had finished that small task, she carried the petticoat to Sophy's room and laid it carefully on the bed, hoping she would be touched and grateful when she discovered it there. 'And I would do anything for her,' she thought, 'if there were anything else to do.'

She went over to the window and looked down into the courtyard – so still and full of heat and the scent of honeysuckle this sunny morning. On the wall below her was the starry jasmine that framed her own bedroom window. She leant out, resting her elbows on the rough stone sill, feeling insecurely attached to space and time – the seconds would never tick on till luncheon, or the silence be broken, or the sun ever again go in.

It was the room behind her that overcame, at last, her sense of unreality – though she had turned her back upon it, she felt it awaiting her attention – Sophy's room, where Sophy shut the door on all that she pretended downstairs and where she was confronted by her own thoughts, which she kept imprisoned in this place. They were almost palpably imprisoned, Lalla suddenly felt, and she spun round quickly from the window as if to catch them unawares.

The room was menacing to her now and laden with treachery, its air heavy with secrets. The clock ticked slyly and a curtain lifted slowly and sank back full of warning. It was an alien territory and one where Lalla knew she had no right to be. Even the way the towels hung by the basin expressed hostility, she thought, and so did the truculent angle of the looking-glass. It did not seem too fanciful to imagine mute things infected by Sophy's own antagonism.

A letter addressed to Graham lay on the writing-table, the envelope unsealed and the pages sticking out from it as if as a reminder that they were to be added to, or something else enclosed.

In terror, Lalla thought, I could find out if I cared to, just where I stand with her and why, for weeks, she has shrugged me aside in that bright, cold way.

She recoiled and then, almost immediately, stepped quickly forward and drew the pages from the envelope, very careful to make no sound, lest Miss Sully, far below in the kitchen, would prick up her ears and sense the treachery.

'It is the worst thing people can do to one another,' she told herself, 'and I knew nothing about myself, when I believed that I could not.'

The first lines – Sophy's lament at Graham's absence for five whole days – Lalla passed over. She was looking only for her own name and, sure that she would find it, turned to the second page.

'Father, of course, will disapprove and say that I should not go, for he gets more stuffy and morose each day. Anyone young is what he can't bear nowadays, and all that we two do is vulgar and absurd. I wish that Lalla would try to be a wife to him and not a romping schoolgirl still. I should think he would like to be quiet for a while and serious, and so should I. To see him all the time exposed to her high spirits – that gather *me* in, but exclude him – and in any case they are far beyond his powers – is quite painful. He is less and less in the house, and when he is, is so sour and gruff. But he can't – so far – be gruff with *her*, so is with me instead. Where can it end? But all the same, I'll brave his wrath and tell him that I'll go away with you.'

There was no more. Very gently, Lalla folded the pages and put them inside the envelope. Then she tiptoed from the room. Her heart beat so loudly that she thought it would betray her. Her hands were icy-cold, and hurt, as if they had touched poison.

She tried to eat luncheon, but failed. The sight of the dish of peppers reminded her of how short a time ago she had been sitting in the kitchen, bored and restless, but still innocent and loving.

Perhaps it is a baby already, Sophy thought, when Lalla, too sick to stay, had left the room. She now had her father to herself and in a nonchalant voice said: 'Graham and I think of going to France in August, as soon as Denise's wedding is over!'

'You couldn't choose a worse month,' said Colonel Vellacott and threw down his napkin and stood up. 'I'm worried about Lalla. I think I'll go up to her.' Sophy sat alone. Her eyebrows were raised and she looked down at her plate with an air of surprise and curiosity.

Afterwards she went to her bedroom. The petticoat threaded with its scarlet ribbon lay on the bed, and she wondered if Lalla had done it. She could imagine her trying to while away her mornings with one trivial task after another, spending as long upon them as she could. She pictured her standing in this sunny room, with the petticoat over her arm, feeling lonely and out-of-place. Then a fearful intuition sprang upon Sophy and she swung round and looked for the letter she had so carelessly left on the table. It lay there, just as she expected, and with a trembling hand she picked it up and stared at it. 'I have been read,' it seemed to say.

Miss Sully could now watch things worsening daily. The laughter had worn off: it was strange to her that it had lasted so long.

Lalla recovered from her sickness, but was dispirited. Her attitude towards her husband changed, was appealing and conciliatory and over-anxious. With Sophy she was reserved. They had drawn a long way apart and the distance was clouded with suspicions and mistrust.

Colonel Vellacott, as the letter had stated, was less and less in the house, and when she was alone, Lalla paced up and down, clasping her hands tight to her breast, and then the other words of the letter echoed over and over in her mind, with burning emphasis – 'Where can it end? Where can it end?'

'You are run down,' her husband told her. He was wonderfully solicitous, yet bored. She seemed unreal to him, but he would do his best for her. This summer he was feeling his age; marriage had drawn too much attention to it, and so much youth in the house underlined it. Once, he had thought it would have the opposite effect.

'You need a holiday, poor Lalla. And you shall have one. In September I should be able to get away for a couple of weeks. How would you like to go to Florence?'

Yes, she would like to go to Florence and she smiled and nodded; but she thought, 'I am not really used to him *here*, and now I must try to get used to him in a foreign country.'

She tried hard to be more wifely to him, but when she made attempts at serious discussion, he smiled so fondly, so indulgently, that she was aggravated. Sophy watched her attempts with grim understanding. 'I know what *this* is all about,' she thought.

So they were all going abroad – Lalla and her husband sedately to Florence, and Sophy and Graham, full of secrecy and excitement, to France. There was a great difference, Lalla thought.

'I neglect you shamefully,' said Colonel Vellacott. 'I promise I will mend my ways after our holiday. I will come off some of my committees.'

'But couldn't I go with you?' Lalla asked. 'I should be so interested to hear you speak. Just this once?'

'You would be bored to death and, in any case, I'm afraid tonight's meeting is in camera.'

To her own distress, her eyes filled with tears. She was most dreadfully sorry for herself and grieved that no one else was.

She knew that the tears were a pity and that he would think her more childish than ever. 'Where will it end?' she wondered, as he patted her cheek, saying 'good-bye'.

Sophy was out with Graham, Miss Sully listening to a Murder play on the wireless in her sitting-room. 'I could teach myself Italian, perhaps,' Lalla thought, and she went to the study and looked along the shelves, but, though there were many books written in Italian, she could find none to teach the language to her. One was expected to know it already.

'In Florence, they will all gabble away and leave me out of it,' she thought, growing sorrier and sorrier for herself. 'It really is too bad.' Now, they were to be joined in Italy by Major and Mrs Mallett, old friends of the

Colonel's, a pleasant elderly couple, who still regarded the Colonel as of a younger generation.

'They are only going because he would be so bored with just me,' Lalla thought, crossly. 'Oh, I have been complaisant for too long,' she decided. 'I have tried hard and given in and got nowhere.'

She thought that, instead of meekly waiting up for him, she would go up to bed, without telling Miss Sully even. She would turn out the lights and if she were not asleep when he came home, she would pretend to be.

A long drawn-out scream came from Miss Sully's wireless-set as Lalla crossed the hall and went softly upstairs.

When she awoke it was dark and she was still alone. She got out of bed and went to the window. Lamplight shone over leaves in the street beyond the wall and fell over the courtyard. The statues and urns looked blanched. In the centre was an ornamental stand for plants. Its wrought-iron lilies threw slanting shadows across the paving-stones; she could even see the shadows of the fuchsia blossoms – real flowers, these – swinging upon the ground.

It was a romantic place in this light, and she knelt by the window looking down at it, quite awake now and refreshed by her sleep. Then she saw that Sophy and Graham found the place romantic too. She had not noticed them at first, under the dark wall, clasped close together, as still as the tree beyond them. But before Lalla could turn away, she saw them move – they swayed lightly, like the fuchsia blossoms, as if rocked by the same faint air, of which they were so heedless.

She went back to bed and lay down and drew the covers over her, her eyes wide open to the darkness. 'Defend me from envy, God,' she prayed. But the poison of it gathered in her against her will and when it had filled her and she was overflowing with despair, tears broke in her like waves. Even Miss Sully, coming upstairs when the play was over, could hear her.

The True Primitive

Lily had not considered culture – as a word or anything else – until she fell in love. As soon as that happened it, culture, descended on her. It was as if all the books Mr Ransome had ever read were thrown at her one after the other – Voltaire, Tolstoi, Balzac – the sharp names came at her, brutal spondees, brutally pronounced. She thought, though, that she hated Dostoievski most of all. 'Yes, Dad,' Mr Ransome's two sons continually said, agreeing to rate Zola higher than Dickens if he wished them to, promising to remember what he had told them about Michelangelo. Painters' names were also part of the attack, but Lily thought they sounded gentler. She had felt curiosity about someone called Leonardo when first she heard him mentioned and had wondered if he were Harry's cousin. When she asked Harry he laughed and referred her to his father, which meant three-quarters of an hour wasted, sitting in the kitchen listening, and then it was too late for them to go for their walk. Trembling with frustrated desire, she had learnt her lesson; she asked no more questions and sat sullenly quiet whenever the enemy names began again.

Only winter courting seemed to be allowed: then, with the Thames valley giving off impenetrable vapours or taking in, day after day, torrents of rain until the river rose and spread over the fields, Harry was free to take her out; except, of course, for his two evenings at the Art School. They held hands coming back in the bus from the cinema, kissed beneath dripping trees in the muddy lane, choked and whispered in the fog.

'Silly notion, venturing out tonight,' Mr Ransome would tell them. 'You've no right, letting her catch her death, Harry.'

'I think it's easing up now,' Lily would say. 'Just the clearing-up shower. And a spot or two of rain doesn't do anyone any harm.'

Mr Ransome, with a daunting-looking book open in front of him, would be hurriedly unfolding his spectacles.

'We ought to be going,' Lily whispered.

'Man is a political animal,' boomed Mr Ransome, wanting to throw as many words at them as he could before they escaped, but Lily had gone, was through the scullery and already standing in the wet garden and Harry sent an apologetic smile back at his father and followed her.

'Good Lord,' said Lily. 'Once he gets going.'

'He's a wonderful old man,' Harry said.

'You're both afraid of him, I think – you and Godfrey.'

'We *respect* him,' Harry said sententiously. 'He's been a good father and since Mother died he has no one to read to in the evenings. He misses that.'

'She did the best thing, dying,' Lily thought.

Mr Ransome was a lock-keeper. He and his sons lived in a red-brick cottage at the side of the lock. On hot summer afternoons, the garden was what people going through in their boats called a riot of colour. The primary colours assaulted the eye – salvias, geraniums, lobelias, calceolarias were made all the more dazzling by everything being whitewashed that Mr Ransome could lay his brush on – flower-tubs, step-edges, the boulders round flower-beds, the swinging chains round the little lawns. In wintertime, it seemed that it could not really have been so bright.

Now, when all the locks down the river were closed, the cottage was lost in a cauldron of steam and the sad sound of the weir came drearily through the fog. Mr Ransome wondered how Harry and Lily could prefer the sodden lanes to a nice fire and a book to read beside it. He read so much about great passions, of men and women crossing continents because of love, and enduring hardship and peril, not just the discomforts of a dark, wet night – but he could not see Harry and Lily go out without feeling utter exasperation at their fecklessness.

'It will be lovely when the summer comes,' Lily sometimes said; but Harry knew that it would not be, if by 'lovely' she meant they would have long evenings together in the golden meadows or walking along the towing-path. 'He does like us to get out with our sketching, Godfrey and me,' he said.

'I don't mind. We can go miles away. You can sketch with one hand and I'll sit beside you and hold the other.'

'We couldn't very well do that, you see, because Dad likes to come out with us.'

'I can't think why you bother with it when you've got such a nice job.'

Harry knew why he bothered. His father, self-taught painter, had once had a picture hung in a local exhibition – an oil-painting, moreover. 'I jib at nothing,' he had explained. The bright, varnished scene hung in the parlour now. 'It was not for sale,' he said, when no one bought it. Jibbing at nothing, he had used a great deal of paint and had, in some way, caught the hard, venomous colours of his own garden. 'The Towing Path of A Sunday' was inscribed carefully on the frame. The white chains stood out thickly, like icing piped on the canvas; the chestnut trees had pink cones of blossom stuck about them and dropped down sharp ovals of shadow on the emerald grass. 'If I had of had tuition,' Mr Ransome so often said. He would see to it, he added, that his sons should not look back and have to say the same. In their earliest days they had been given paint-boxes and sketching-blocks; he had taken them to London to the National Gallery and shown them the Virgin of the Rocks and, standing in front of it, lectured them on Leonardo. They had not known which was most painful – their embarrassment or their shame at their own disloyalty in suffering it. Young as they were at the time, they realised that he was much stared at – the thin, fierce man with his square beard and so old-fashioned clothes – but they could not help feeling that he deserved it, booming away as he did in the echoing gallery. They even began to think that he expected to be noticed and took pleasure from it.

Harry and Godfrey, articled in respectable offices in the nearby town, were not quite yet a disappointment to him; for many great men mature late, their father reminded them, reach their height after middle-age: Voltaire, for one. They went on with their art classes at evening school and were painstaking enough in their desire to please; but, sometimes, looking at them and then at their feeble paintings, Mr Ransome could not help thinking that passion was missing from them.

'They are not on fire,' he mourned. 'As I have been.'

Then Harry met Lily and seemed, to his father, to be less on fire than ever. 'But it will come,' he encouraged his sons. It must come. What had been in him so powerful a desire, so bitterly a failed attempt, could not be wasted, must be passed on, and in greater strength, too, if things were to turn out as he considered just.

Lily, impinging on his plan with her sly, mincing manner, her pout and her impatient sighs, was the eternal female enemy. He had built a bastion, a treasure-house for his sons, with all the great names they had heard from the cradle, the learning he had struggled for to make their inheritance. It had come too easily, he realised now, and Harry would rather spend an evening talking inanities, lowering his mind to Lily's level. His attitude towards her was vexing, suggesting that he was willing, eager to learn something from her and even that she might be able to teach it: suppliant, receptive he was with her; yet it was surely for him to instruct, who knew so much, and dominate, being a man, and to concede, whatsoever he felt inclined to concede; not beg for favours.

Mr Ransome thought of his own happy married life – the woman, so gentle and conciliatory, listening to him as he read. Into those readings he had put the expression of his pleasure at being able to share with her the best he had discovered. She had sat and sewed and, when she raised her eyes to look for her scissors, she would also glance across at him and he, conscious of her doing so, would pause to meet this glance, knowing that

it would be full of humble gratitude. She had never been able to comprehend half of what he had offered her, she had muddled the great names and
once dozed off after a few pages of Stendhal; but something, he thought,
must have seeped into her, something of the lofty music of prose, as she listened, evening after evening of her married life. Now he missed her and so
much of the sound of his own voice that had gone with her.

How different was Lily. The moment he began to read aloud, or even to
quote something, down came her eyelids to half-mast. An invisible curtain
dropped over her and behind it she was without any response, as if heavily drugged. He would have liked to have stuck pins in her to see if she
would cry out: instead, he assaulted her – indecently, she thought, and that
was why she would not listen – with Cicero and Goethe, Ibsen and
Nietzsche and a French poet, one of his specials, called Bawdyleer. Having
removed herself, as it were, she would then glance at the clock, wind a curl
round her finger and suddenly loosen it to spring back against her cheek.
Distracted by this, Harry would murmur, 'Yes, Dad, I remember you telling
us.' So Mr Ransome had lost them both. 'Come here,' Lily seemed to be
enticing his son. 'Come behind my invisible curtain and we can think of
other things and play with my hair and be alone together.'

Sometimes, but very rarely, Mr Ransome would manage to catch her
unawares and force one of the names on her before she had time to bring
down the curtain. Then her manner was rude and retaliatory instead of
vague. 'And who, pray, is Dosty what's-his-name when he's at home?' She
knew that Mr Ransome was her enemy and felt not only malice in his attitude towards her, but something she might have defined as obscenity if she
had known the meaning of the word.

He – for he was at heart puritanical – had once or twice delighted to
indulge in a bout of broad-mindedness. She should learn that he and some
of the great thinkers of the world could face the truth unflinchingly and
even some of the words the truth must be described in. To the pure, he said,
all things are pure: he watched Lily's look of prim annoyance, implying that
to her they obviously were not. He was defeated, however, by the silence
that fell – Lily's and his son's. His remark, made to seem blatant by being
isolated and ignored, repeated itself in his own head and he felt his cheeks
and brow darkening. He did not want to appear to have any impurity in his
own mind and quickly bent down and rearranged the coals on the fire.

The spring was beginning; the puddles along the rutted lanes were blue,
reflecting the bright sky, and lilac trees in cottage-gardens bore buds as
small as grape-pips. Although the darkness fell later, the interval of daylight
after tea was of no use to Lily, for Mr Ransome had his two sons out, white-
washing and weeding and trimming. 'We shall have no time to do it once
the season has begun,' he said.

'But what about us?' Lily asked Harry.

'I can't help but give him a hand of an evening. It wouldn't be right to leave it all to Godfrey.'

'It sounds as if the summer's going to be just as bad as the winter.'

All along, Harry had known it would be worse.

In the summer, the lock was always full, boats jostled together, smart women in motor launches stared through their dark glasses at men in rowing-boats wearing braces and knotted handkerchiefs on their heads: in the narrowness of the lock they were all resentful of their proximity to one another, and were glad, when the water had finished rising or falling, to see the gates opening slowly. The locks were an ordeal to be negotiated, not made easier by the passers-by on the tow-path who stopped to watch them lying exposed below and hoped that they would ram their craft into the gates, or take the paint off one of the white launches.

Steamers came through at intervals and then the lock was a well of noise with someone thumping at the piano in the saloon and cheery messages thrown from deck to towing-path; glasses of beer were held up to tantalise and the funny man of the party, wearing a yachting cap, sang 'A life on the ocean wave is better than going to sea'.

The pretty stretch of river with its willows hanging down to the water and the brilliance of the lock garden brought artists, with folding stools and easels, who took up much of Mr Ransome's time. Such an odd character they thought him, forgetting – as, of all people, the English should not – that characters are encouraged at the cost of their families' destruction. He showed them his own painting of the same scene and they were enraptured, they called him a true primitive and talked of the Douanier Rousseau.

On summer evenings, after days of advising these amateur artists, talking about himself, bringing in a great deal about Leonardo, Mr Ransome behaved as if he had been drinking too much. He boasted, belaboured his sons with words and then, from too much excitement, surrendered to self-pity. It suddenly seemed to him that he had wasted his life: he had seen this on the face of one stranger after another. 'You,' they had been thinking, 'a man who has all the great Masters at his finger-tips and can summon from memory one thundering phrase after another, who would expect to find you in such a backwater, living so humbly?'

'You two, my sons, shall make up for me,' he told them. 'Then I have not lived in vain.' 'I am the teacher of athletes,' he intoned. 'He that by me spreads a wider breast than my own proves the width of my own. He most knows my style who learns under it to destroy the teacher.'

'Yes, Father,' said his sons.

'Walt Whitman,' he added, giving credit where credit was due.

Lily, who had given up working in a shop to become a laundress, now had Saturday afternoons free. The full significance of this she told Harry when they were lingering over, postponing from minute to minute, their farewell embrace in the dark lane near her home. To draw apart was so painful to them that, as soon as they attempted it, they suffered too much and flew together again for comfort.

'It must be gone eleven,' she said. 'Dad's tongue will curdle the milk. But guess what, though. Did you realise?'

'Realise what?' he mumbled, and lifted her hair from her shoulders and kissed underneath it, along the back of her neck, with busy little nibbling kisses. In a curious and contradictory way, she felt that he was so intent on her that she no longer existed.

'Why, Saturday afternoons, of course,' she said. 'You'll be free: now I'll be free as well.' She could not help noticing that the kissing stopped at once.

'Well, you do know week-ends in the season I have to give Dad a hand,' Harry said.

'It isn't the season yet. We'll have a fortnight before that. I can meet you any time after dinner. Sooner the better,' she whispered and raised herself on tiptoe and put her warm mouth against his. He was unhappy and she became angry.

'Say about tea-time,' he suggested.

'Why not earlier?'

She knew, although of course she could not see, that he was blushing.

'Ever since we were little, Dad's liked us to be together on Saturday afternoons.'

'What for, pray?'

'Just to have a quiet time together. It's a family custom.'

Now she could feel him blushing.

'If you ask me, he's round the bend,' she said loudly. 'And even if you don't ask me, he is.'

She pushed Harry away and began to walk down the lane towards her home. He followed her. 'And so are you,' she added. She did not turn her head as she spoke, but the words came back to him clearly. 'No wonder that girl Vera Webster gave up going out with Godfrey. She could see the way the wind was blowing. "Dad likes this and Dad likes that." I'm sick and tired of Dad and one of these days I'll tell him so. "You and your Bawdyleer," I'll say, "you boring old ..."' her voice rose and trembled, '"codger,"' she cried. 'And you, too.' She had reached her gate, threw it open and hurried up the path.

'Saturday tea-time then?' he called after her anxiously.

'Saturday nothing,' she shouted back, and she lifted the latch and went in boldly to face her father's sarcasm.

'You're in early this morning,' he said. 'The milkman hasn't been yet.'

The next day her beautiful anger had dissolved. She had enjoyed it while she indulged in it, but now her words haunted and alarmed her. Perhaps they had meant the end of Harry's love for her and, so, of all her hopes. Her future life with him dissolved – a whole council-house full of day-dreams; trousseau, wedding presents, pots and pans, dainty supper-dishes, baby-clothes; cradle, even a kitten asleep on a cushion. She imagined him going to work and then on to his evening class, his head tilted proudly back, the stain of anger on his cheeks. The day after would be Saturday and if it turned out that he had taken her at her furious word, she could not endure to go on living.

'Not going out with Harry?' her mother asked her, when Lily began to wash her hair at the kitchen sink on Saturday afternoon.

'I think love's sweet song has run into a few discords,' her father said. 'Very hoity-toity words coming up the path the night before last.'

Lily poured a jug of water over her head and so her tears were hidden.

By four o'clock her hair was quite dry. Harry had not come. She was rest-less and felt herself watched by her mother and father. Soon she decided that there was, after all, nothing to stop her walking along the towing-path for a breath of fresh air. It was a public way and there was no one who could stop her. It would be a sorry thing if, just because of Harry Ransome, she could never walk along the river bank again.

It was a bright and blowy evening. She met no one. At every bend in the lane, she expected to see Harry come hastening, full of apologies, towards her. Then she came to the river and still no one was in sight. The water was high, after the winter's rain, and flowed fast, covered with bub-bles, bearing away scum and twigs and last year's leaves. The sound and look of it completed her depression.

With her head turned towards the river and not in the direction of the cottage, she walked along the lock-side. She went on beyond it a little way and then turned and sauntered back. The kitchen window was dark, but from the parlour a light fell faintly through the wooden shutters which had been drawn across the outside of the window. This seemed quite strange to Lily, for it would not be dark for some hours to come and in all the months she had known Harry she had never seen anyone go into the parlour except to fetch a book. She remembered Harry's shame and reluctance when she had tried to make plans for this afternoon and an unreasonable suspicion overtook her that he was in that shuttered room making love to someone, that he had known beforehand that he would be doing so, and knowing, had gone on kissing Lily; though he had had, she admitted, the decency to blush. She stepped quietly on to the little plot of grass and hesi-tated, glancing round her. There was no one in sight and not a sound except for the river. She went softly across to the window and listened there; but there was a shameful silence from within. Her heart beating with great violence unnerved her and only the extreme tension of her jealousy enabled her to lay her hand on the shutter and move it gently towards her.

The light in the room was not so very bright; but standing upright in a strange stiff pose with hand on hip and one knee slightly bent, she could see Mr Ransome facing her not two yards away, his beard jutting forward and his expression fixed. A rosy glow from an oil-stove close beside him fell over his completely naked body.

Their eyes met, his widened with surprise, Lily's with horror. Then she slammed back the shutter and leant against it for a moment, sick and trembling. Through the narrow slit between the shutters she had not seen the two sons, sitting unwillingly but dutifully behind their easels. Terror, in any case, had quite put the thought of Harry out of her mind. She was afraid that Mr Ransome would come leaping out of the house after her and chase her down the towing-path, naked and mad as he was, shouting Balzac and Voltaire after her. She summoned all her strength and turned and ran across the lawn, as fast as she could go, away from the cottage, and her legs were as heavy as lead, as if she were running in a nightmare.

The Rose, The Mauve, The White

In the morning, Charles went down the garden to practise calling for three cheers. When he came to the place farthest of all from the house and near to the lake, he paused among clumps of rhubarb and mounds of lawn-clippings, and glanced about him. His voice had broken years before, but was still uncertain in volume; sometimes it wavered, and lost its way and he could never predict if it would follow his intention or not. If his voice was to come out in a great bellow or perhaps frenziedly high-pitched, people would turn towards him in surprise, even astonishment, but how, if it sank too low, would he claim anyone's attention after the boisterous confusions of 'Auld Lang Syne'? He could hardly be held responsible for it, he felt, and had often wished that he might climb to the top of a mountain and there, alone, make its acquaintance and come to terms with it. As he could not, this morning in the garden at home, he put on what he hoped was an expression of exultant gaiety, snatched off his spectacles and, waving them in the air, cried out: 'And now three cheers for Mrs Frensham-Bowater.' He was about to begin 'Hip, hip, hooray', when a bush nearby was filled with laughter; all the branches were disturbed with mirth. Then there were two splashes as his little sisters leapt into the lake for safety. 'And now three cheers for Charles,' they called, as they swam as fast as they could away from the bank.

If he went after them, he could only stand at the edge of the water and shake his fist or make some other ineffectual protest, so he put his spectacles on again and walked slowly back to the house. It was a set-back to the day, with Natalie arriving that afternoon and likely to hear at once from the twins how foolishly he had behaved.

'Mother, could you make them be quiet?' he asked desperately, finding her at work in the rose-garden. When he told her the story, she threw back her head and laughed for what seemed to him to be about five minutes. 'Oh, poor old Charles. I wish I'd been in hiding, too.' He had known he would have to bear this or something like it, but was obliged to pay the price; and at long last she said: 'I will see to it that their lips are sealed; their cunning chops shut up.'

'But are you sure you can?'

'I think I know how to manage my own children. See how obedient you yourself have grown. I cross my heart they shall not breathe a word of it in front of Natalie.'

He thanked her coldly and walked away. In spite of his gratitude, he thought: 'She is so dreadfully chummy and slangy. I wish she wouldn't be. And why say just "Natalie" when there are two girls coming? I think she tries to be "knowing" as well,' he decided.

Two girls were coming. His sister, Katie, was picking sweet-peas for the room these school-friends were to share with her.

'You are supposed to cut those with scissors,' Charles said. The ones she couldn't strip off, she was breaking with her teeth. 'What time are they coming?'

'In the station-taxi at half-past three.'

'Shall I come with you to meet them?'

'No, of course not. Why should you?'

Katie was sixteen and a year younger than Charles. It is a very feminine age and she wanted her friends to herself. At school they slept in the same bedroom, as they would here. They were used to closing the door upon a bower of secrets and intrigue and diary-writing; knew how to keep their jokes to themselves and their conversations as incomprehensible as possible to other people. When Charles's friends came to stay, Katie did not encroach on them, and now she had no intention of letting him spoil that delightful drive back from the station: she could not imagine what her friends would think of her if she did.

So after luncheon she went down alone in the big, musty-smelling taxi. The platform of the country station was quite deserted: a porter was whistling in the office, keeping out of the hot sun. She walked up and down, reading the notices of Estate Agents posted along the fence and all the advertisements of auction-sales. She imagined the train coming nearer to her with every passing second; yet it seemed unbelievable that it would really soon materialise out of the distance, bringing Frances and Natalie.

They would have the compartment to themselves at this time of the day on the branch line and she felt a little wistful thinking that they were together and having fun and she was all alone, waiting for them. They would be trying out dance-steps, swaying and staggering as the train rocked; dropping at last, weak with laughter, full-length on the seats. Then, having been here to stay with Katie on other occasions, as they came near to the end of their journey they would begin to point out landmarks and haul down their luggage from the rack – carefully, because in the suitcases were the dresses for this evening's dance.

The signal fell with a sharp clatter making Katie jump. 'Now where shall I be standing when the train stops?' she wondered, feeling self-conscious suddenly and full of responsibility. 'Not here, right on top of the gents' lavatory of all places. Perhaps by the entrance.' Nonchalantly, she strolled away.

The porter came out of the office, still whistling, and stared up the line. Smoke, bowing and nodding like a plume on a horse's head, came round a bend in the distance and Katie, watching it, felt sick and anxious. 'They won't enjoy themselves at all,' she thought. 'I wish I hadn't asked them. They will find it dreadfully dull at home and the dance is bound to be a failure. It will be babyish with awful things like "The Dashing White Sergeant" and "The Gay Gordons". They will think Charles is a bore and the twins a bloody nuisance.'

But the moment they stepped out of the train all her constraint vanished. They caught her up into the midst of their laughter. 'You can't think what happened,' they said. 'You'll never believe what happened at Paddington.' The ridiculous story never did quite come clear, they were so incoherent with giggling. Katie smiled in a grown-up way. She was just out of it for the moment, but would soon be in the swim again.

As they drove up the station-slope towards the village, they were full of anticipation and excitement. 'And where is Charles?' asked Natalie, smoothing her dark hair.

Tea was such great fun, their mother, Myra Pollard, told herself: though one moment she felt rejuvenated; the next minute, as old as the world. She had a habit of talking to herself, as to another person who was deeply interested in all her reactions: and the gist of these conversations was often apparent on her face.

'They keep one young oneself – all these young people,' she thought as she was pouring out the tea. Yet the next second, her cheek resting on her hand as she watched them putting away great swags and wadges and gobbets of starch, she sighed; for she had not felt as they all felt, eager and full of nonsense, for years and years. To them, though they were polite, she was of no account, the tea pourer-out, the starch-provider, simply. It was people of her own generation who said that Charles and she were like brother and sister – not those of Charles's generation, to whom the idea would have seemed absurd.

Frances and Natalie were as considerate as could be and even strove to be a little woman-to-womanly with her. 'Did you ever find your bracelet, Mrs Pollard? Do you remember you'd lost it when we were here last time? At a ... a dance, wasn't it?' Natalie faltered. Of course, Katie's mother went to dances, too. Indeed, why not? Grotesque though they must be. She was glad that her own parents were more sedate and did not try to ape the young.

'I wish *we* could go to a ball,' said Lucy, one of the twins.

'Your time will come,' their mother said. She laid her hand to the side of the silver tea-pot as if to warm and comfort herself.

'Oh, do you remember that boy, Sandy, in the elimination dance?' Katie suddenly exploded.

Frances, who was all beaky and spectacly, Mrs Pollard thought, exploded with her.

'The one who was wearing a kilt?' Natalie asked, with more composure. She wondered if Charles was thinking that she must be older than the other girls and indeed she was, by two and a half months.

'Will Mrs Frensham-Bowater be there?' Lucy asked.

Her sly glance, with eyelids half-lowered, was for Caroline's – her twin's – benefit.

'Of course, Mrs Frensham-Bowater always organises the dance,' their mother said briskly, and changed the subject.

Charles was grateful to her for keeping her promise; but all the same he had had an irritating afternoon. The twins, baulked in one direction, found other ways of exasperating him. When he came out of the house with his gun under his arm, they had clapped their hands over their ears and fled shrieking to the house. 'Charles is pointing his gun at us,' they shouted. 'Don't be bloody silly,' he shouted back. 'Charles swore,' they cried.

'What an unholy gap between Katie and me and those little perishers,' he thought. 'Whatever did Mother and Father imagine they were up to? What can the neighbours have thought of them – at their time of life?' He shied away from the idea of sexual love between the middle-aged; though it was ludicrous, evidence of it was constantly to be seen.

'Did you shoot anything?' his mother asked him.

'There wasn't anything to shoot.' He had known there wouldn't be and had only walked about in the woods with his gun for something to do until the taxi came.

'And the girl next door?' Frances asked. 'I have forgotten her name. Will she be going to the dance tonight?'

'Oh, Deirdre,' said Caroline to Lucy.

'Yes, Deirdre,' Lucy said, staring across the table at Charles.

'No, she has gone to school in Switzerland,' said Katie.

'Poor Charles!' the twins said softly.

'Why not try to be your age?' he asked them in a voice which would, he hoped, sound intimidating to them, but nonchalant to everybody else.

'Have you had nice holidays?' Mrs Pollard asked, looking from Frances to Natalie, then thinking that she was being far too hostessy and middle-aged, she said without waiting for their answer, 'I do adore your sweater, Natalie.'

'Jesus bids us shine, with a pure, clear light,' Caroline began to sing, as she spread honey on her bread.

'Not at the table,' said her mother.

'What shall we do now?' Katie asked after tea. She was beginning to feel her responsibility again. There was no doubt that everything was very different from school; there were Frances and Natalie drawn very close together from sharing the same situation; and she, apart, in the predicament of hostess. It was now that she began to see her home through their eyes – the purple-brick house looked heavy and ugly now that the sun had gone behind a cloud; the south wall was covered by a magnolia tree; there were one or two big, cream flowers among the dark leaves: doves were walking about on the slate roof; some of the windows reflected the blue sky and moving clouds. To Katie, it was like being shown a photograph which she did not immediately recognise – unevocative, as were the photographs of their mothers in the dormitory at school – they seldom glanced at them from the beginning of term to the end.

They sat down on the grass at the edge of the orchard and began to search for four-leaf clovers. Their conversation consisted mostly of derogatory remarks about themselves – they were hopeless at dancing, each one said; could never think what to say to their partners; and they had all washed their hair that morning and now could do simply nothing with it.

'So lucky having red hair, Katie. How I envy you.'

'But it's horrible. I hate it.'

'It's so striking. Isn't it, Frances?'

'Well, yours is, too, in a different way. It's this awful mousiness of mine I can't abide.'

'You can't call it mousy: it's chestnut.'

It was just a game they played and when they had finished with their hair they began on the shape of their hands. There was never any unkindness in anything they said. They were exploring themselves more than each other.

The twins wandered about the garden, shaking milk in jars to make butter: every few minutes they stopped to compare the curd they had collected. They had been doing this tirelessly for days, but were near the time when that game would seem dull and done with and they would never play it again. This evening, they marched about the lawn, chanting a meaningless song.

The older girls were discussing whether they would rather be deaf or blind. Frances lay on her stomach watching the children and wondering if they were not lucky to be so free of care and without the great ordeal of the dance ahead of them.

'Deaf any day,' said Katie.

'Oh, no!' said Natalie. 'Only think how cut off you'd be from other people; and no one is ever as nice to the deaf or has much patience with them. Everyone is kinder to the blind.'

'But imagine never seeing any of this ever again,' said Frances. Tears came up painfully in Katie's eyes. 'This garden, that lovely magnolia tree, sunsets. Never to be able to read *Jane Eyre* again.'

'You could read it in Braille,' Katie said.

'It wouldn't be the same. You know it wouldn't be. Oh, it would be appalling ... I can't contemplate it ... I really can't.'

Anyone who reminded them that the choice might not arise would have been deeply resented.

'I suppose we had better go in and iron our frocks,' Katie said. No one had found a four-leaf clover.

'Where is Charles?' Natalie asked.

'The Lord knows,' said Katie.

Frances was silent as they went towards the house. She could feel the dance coming nearer to her.

'The house is full of girls,' Charles told his father. George Pollard left the car in the drive and went indoors. 'And steam,' he said.

Natalie, Frances and Katie had been in the bathroom for nearly an hour and could hardly see one another across the room. Bath-salts, hoarded from Christmas, scented the steam and now, still wearing their shower-caps, they were standing on damp towels and shaking their Christmas talcum powder over their stomachs and shoulders.

'Will you do my back and under my arms?' asked Katie, handing to Frances the tin of Rose Geranium. 'And then I will do yours.'

'What a lovely smell. It's so much nicer than mine,' said Frances, dredging Katie as thoroughly as if she were a fillet of fish being prepared for the frying-pan.

'Don't be too long, girls!' Mrs Pollard called, tapping at the door. She tried to make her voice sound gay and indulgent. 'The twins are waiting to come in and it's rather past their bedtime.' She wondered crossly if Katie's friends were allowed to monopolise bathrooms like that in their own homes. Katie was plainly showing off and would have to be taken aside and told so.

'Just coming,' they shouted.

At last they opened the door and thundered along the passage to their bedroom where they began to make the kind of untidiness they had left behind them in the bathroom.

Yvette, the French mother's-help, whose unenviable task it now was to supervise the twins' going to bed, flung open the bathroom window and kicked all the wet towels to one side. 'They will be clean, certainly,' she was thinking. 'But they will not be chic.' She had seen before the net frocks, the strings of coral, the shining faces.

She rinsed the dregs of mauve crystals from the bath and called out to the twins. The worst part of her day was about to begin.

'This is the best part of the day,' George said. He shut the bedroom door and took his drink over to the window. Myra was sitting at her dressing-table. She had taken off her ear-rings to give her ears a little rest and was gently massaging the reddened lobes. She said: 'It doesn't seem a year since that other dance, when we quarrelled about letting Katie go to it.'

'She was too young. And still is.'

'There were girls of thirteen there.'

'Well, that's no affair of mine, thank God.'

'I wonder if Ronnie what's-his-name will be sober. For the MC of a young people's dance I consider he was pretty high last time. He always has drunk unmercifully.'

'What the devil's this?' George asked. He had gone into his dressing-room and now came back with his safety-razor in his hand.

'Oh, the girls must have borrowed it.'

'Very hospitable guests they are, to be sure. They manage to make me feel quite at home.'

'Don't fuss. You were young yourself once.'

She dotted lipstick over her cheekbones and he watched her through the looking-glass, arrested by the strange sight. The incredulous expression made her smile, eyebrows raised, she was ready to tease. He tilted her face back towards him and kissed her quickly on the mouth.

'You look absurd,' he said.

As soon as she was released, she leant to the mirror again and began to smooth the dots of colour over her cheeks until they were merged into the most delicate flush. 'A clever girl,' he said, finishing his drink.

The girls were still not dressed when a boy called Benedict Nightingale arrived in his father's car – and dinner-jacket, George decided. 'Katie's first beau,' he told himself, 'come calling for her.' He felt quite irritable as he took the boy into the drawing-room.

'They won't be long,' he said, without conviction.

'Don't be too long, girls,' Myra called again in her low, controlled and unexasperated voice. She stopped to tap on their bedroom door before she went downstairs; then, knowing that Charles would be having trouble with his tie, she went in to his rescue.

'What about a drink?' George asked Benedict reluctantly.

'No thank you, sir.'

'Cigarette?'

'No thank you, sir.'

'I don't know what they can be doing all this time. Now what the hell's happening up there?'

The twins were trying to get into Katie's bedroom to pry into adolescent secrets, and the girls, still in their petticoats, held the door against them. From the other side of it Lucy and Caroline banged with their fists and kicked until dragged away at last by Yvette.

'Now we shall be late,' said Katie.

They lifted their frocks and dropped them over their heads, their talcumed armpits showed white as they raised their elbows to hook themselves at the back. Frances tied Natalie's sash, Natalie fastened Katie's bracelet.

'Is this all right? Does it hang down? You're sure? Am I done up?' they asked.

'Oh, yes, yes, yes, I mean no,' they all answered at once, not one of them attending.

'*This* is what *I'm* allowed,' said Katie, smudging on lipstick, stretching her mouth as she had seen her mother do. 'So pale, I'm wasting my time.'

Natalie twisted her bracelet, shook back her hair: she hummed; did a glissade across the clothes-strewn floor, her skirts floating about her. She was away, gone, in Charles's arms already. She held her scented arm to her face and breathed deeply and smiled.

Frances stood uncertainly in the middle of the room. 'I am the one who will be asked to dance last of all,' she thought, cold with the certainty of her failure. 'Katie and Natalie will go flying away and I shall be left there on my own, knowing nobody. The time will go slowly and I shall wish that I were dead.' She turned to the long looking-glass and smoothed her frock. 'I hate my bosoms,' she suddenly said. 'They are too wide apart.'

'Nonsense, that's how they're supposed to be,' Katie said, as brisk as any nanny.

'Give those girls a shout, Charles,' George said and helped himself to another drink.

But they were coming downstairs. They had left the room with its beds covered with clothes, its floor strewn with tissue-paper. They descended; the rose, the mauve, the white. Like a bunch of sweet-peas they looked, George thought.

'What a pretty frock, Frances,' Myra said, beginning with the worst. 'Poor pet,' she thought, and Frances guessed the thought, smiling primly and saying thank you.

'And such a lovely colour, Natalie,' Myra went on.

'But is it, though?' Natalie asked anxiously. 'And don't my shoes clash terribly? I think I look quite bleak in it, and it is last year's, really.'

Myra had scarcely wanted to go into all that. 'Now, Katie,' she began to say, as soon as she could. 'I don't think your friends know Benedict. And when you have introduced them we must be on our way. Your father and I have to go out to dinner after we've taken you to the dance. So who's to go with whom?'

That was what Frances had wondered. The worst part of being a guest was not being told enough about arrangements. One was left in a shifting haze of conjecture.

Benedict had come to attention as the girls came in and now he stepped forward and said with admirable firmness: 'I will take Katie in my car.' Then he was forced to add: 'I would have room for someone else in the back.'

'That's me,' thought Frances.

'Good! Now don't crush your dresses, girls,' said Myra. 'Gather them up – so – from the back of the skirt. Have you got everything?'

'Of course, Mother,' said Katie. 'We aren't children,' she thought.

Four hours later, Charles let go of Natalie's hand and took a pace forward from the circle of 'Auld Lang Syne'. 'Three cheers for Mrs Frensham-Bowater,' he shouted. 'Hip, hip, hooray!'

Myra, standing in the entrance hall with the other parents, tried to look unconcerned. She knew that Charles had been nervous all along of doing that little duty and she was thankful that it was safely over. And that meant that the dance was over, too.

With the first bars of 'God Save the Queen', they all became rigid, pained-looking, arms to their sides and heads erect; but the moment it was over, the laughter and excitement enlived their faces again. They began to drift reluctantly towards the hall.

'How pretty the girls are,' the mothers said to one another. 'Goodness, how they grow up. That isn't Madge's girl, surely, in the yellow organza? They change from day to day at this age.'

'Was it lovely?' Myra asked Katie.

'So lovely! Oh and someone spilt fruit-cup all down poor Natalie's front.'

'Oh, no!' said Myra.

'She doesn't care though.'

'But her mother . . . I feel so responsible.'

'Oh, her mother's awfully understanding. She won't give a damn.' ('Unlike you,' Katie's voice seemed to imply.) 'It was last year's, anyway.'

Benedict was hovering at Katie's shoulder.

'Charles had torn the hem already, anyway,' Katie said.

'But how on earth?'

'They won a prize in the River Dance.'

Myra had not the faintest idea what a River Dance was and said so.

'The boys have to run across some chalk lines carrying their partners and he tore her skirt when he picked her up. She's no light weight, I can assure you.'

'I hope it hasn't been rowdy,' Myra said, but this remark was far too silly to receive an answer.

Frances had attached herself to Charles and Natalie, so that she would not seem to leave the floor alone; but she knew that Mrs Pollard had seen her standing there by the door, without a partner, and for the last waltz of all things. To be seen by her hostess in such a predicament underlined her failure.

'Did you enjoy it, Frances?' Myra asked. And wasn't that the only way to put her question, Frances thought, the one she was so very anxious to know – 'Did you dance much?'

'We had better go back as we came,' Myra said. 'Have you all got everything? Well then, you go on, Benedict dear, with Frances and Katie, and we will follow.'

'I wish she wouldn't say "dear" to boys,' Katie thought. 'And she doesn't trust us, I suppose, to come on after. I hope that Benedict hasn't noticed that she doesn't trust him: he will think it is his driving, or worse, that she is thoroughly evil-minded. Goodness knows what she got up to in her young days to have such dreadful ideas in her head.'

The untidy room was waiting for them. Five hours earlier, they had not looked beyond the dance or imagined a time after it.

'Well, I don't think that poor boy, Roland, will thank you much for asking him in your party,' Frances said. 'He was wondering how he would ever get away from me.'

She thought, as many grown-up women think, that by saying a thing herself she prevented people from thinking it. She had also read a great many nostalgic novels about girls of long ago spending hours in the cloakroom at dances and in her usual spirit of defiance she had refused to go there at all, had stuck the humiliation out and even when she might have taken her chance with the others in the Paul Jones had stuck that out, too.

'He told me he thought you danced very well,' Katie said.

This made matters worse for Frances. So it wasn't just the dancing, but something very much more important – her personality, or lack of it; her plainness – what she was burdened with for the rest of her life, in fact.

Natalie seemed loth to take off her frock, stained and torn though it now was. She floated about the room, spreading the skirt about her as she hummed and swayed and shook her hair. She would not be back on earth again until morning.

'Here is your safety-pin, Katie,' said Frances.

'And here, with many thanks, your necklace safe and sound.'

The trinkets they had borrowed from one another were handed back; they unhooked one another; examined their stockings for ladders. Katie took a pair of socks out of her brassiere.

One by one, they got into bed. Natalie sat up writing her diary and Katie thought hers could wait till morning. Benedict's amusing sayings would be quite safe till then and by tomorrow the cloud that had been over the evening might have dispersed. The next day, when they were swimming in the lake, or cleaning out the rabbits or making walnut fudge, surely Frances would be re-established among them, not cut off by her lack of success as she now was, taking the edge off Benedict's remembered wit, making Katie's heart ache just when it was beginning to behave as she had always believed a heart should.

Turning in Benedict's arms as they danced she had sometimes caught Frances's eyes as she stood there alone or with some other forlorn and unclaimed girl. Katie had felt treachery in the smile she had been bound to give – the most difficult of smiles, for it had to contain so much, the assurance that the dance was only a dance and nothing very much to miss, a suggestion of regret at her – Katie's – foolishness in taking part in it and surprise that she of all people had been chosen. 'It is soon over,' she tried to signal to Frances. 'You are yourself. I love you. I will soon come back.'

And Frances had received the smiles and nodded. 'There are other things in the world,' she tried to believe.

'Shall we have a picnic tomorrow?' Katie asked. She snuggled down into bed and stared up at the ceiling.

'Let's have one day at a time,' said Natalie. She had filled in the space in her diary and now locked the book up with a little key that hung on a chain round her neck.

'Do put out the light before the moths come in,' said Frances.

They could hear Katie's parents talking quietly in the next room. Frances thought: 'I expect she is saying, "Poor Frances. I'm afraid she didn't get many dances; but I am sure that Katie did what she could for her. It would really have been kinder not to have invited her."' The unbroken murmuring continued on the other side of the wall and Frances longed for it to stop. She thought: 'She is forever working things out in her mind, and cruelly lets people guess what they are. It would be no worse if she said them out loud.' She had prayed that before Myra came to fetch them from the dance it would all be over; 'God Save the Queen' safely sung and her own shame at last behind her. As the last waltz began, she had longed for someone to claim her – any spotty, clammy-handed boy would do. Benedict and Katie had hovered by her, Benedict impatient to be away, but Katie reluctant to leave her friend alone at such a crucial moment. 'Please go,' Frances had told them and just as they danced away, Myra had appeared in the doorway, looking tired but watchful, her eyes everywhere – Katie accounted for, Charles, Natalie, then a little encouraging smile and nod to Frances herself, trying to shrink out of sight on the perimeter of the gaiety. 'As I expected,' her eyes said.

Gradually, the murmurings from the other room petered out and the house became silent. Then, in Charles's room across the landing, Natalie heard a shoe drop with a thud on the floor and presently another. 'Sitting on the edge of the bed, dreaming,' she thought. She lay awake, smiling in the darkness and stroking her smooth arms long after the other two had fallen asleep.

Better Not

After tea, the little conservatory was the only place with any sunshine. Helen left the table and went out to see what the children were doing: partly that, and partly because the thought of Lecky going had suddenly put something solid in her throat.

She stood there in the sunshine, breathing slowly to relax herself. 'If you sing,' she thought. 'I heard that somewhere, or read it. Begin to hum, then you find you are singing and all the knots in your throat are untied ...'

She watched Vicky going down the path on her tricycle and she began to hum. She couldn't think of a tune and when Lecky came out to be with her she was buzzing away like a blue-bottle; and it was true, her throat had straightened out and she could even say, 'Ah, you're all leaving me now.'

He knew her too well to think for one moment that she was humming because she was contented or serene.

In the stuffy warmth he narrowed his eyes like a cat and folded his arms across his chest. The sunshine arrested time and induced day-dreaming. They stood very still.

'What time tomorrow?' she asked.

'Ten o'clock from King's Cross.'

'King's Cross. That station suggests Infinity, Forster says. Do you remember?'

Yes, the long evenings before Vicky was born, Helen sewing in the rocking-chair, tipping back and forth, while he read – right through Forster, some Meredith, the beginnings of Henry James. Most bachelors attach themselves to some family and this was his. He had presented christening mugs, stood at the font on Sunday afternoons, remembered birthdays, read to the wife when her husband was away, partnered her young sister at dances, filled the fourteenth chair and, only last week, signed Harry's will before he went away.

'Embarkation leave,' mused Helen. 'Sometimes they come back again and have another. But mine won't.' She began to hum again. A washed-out butterfly expended itself upon the panes.

'Put it out, Lecky,' she cried. 'I can't bear touching them.'

'A vile way of spending one's life, certainly,' he agreed. He caught the butterfly in his handkerchief and threw it out the open door.

'Nearly Vicky's bedtime,' she said. The children's bedtime. After that began the worst part of the day. You would pour yourself a drink, perhaps. 'Ah, this is gay,' you would think, kicking the coals on the fire, watching the sparks fly. The gin rolls on the tongue, a little oily. You go to the window to have a last look at the day and stand there, wringing your hands like a woman in a play. And at night you lay down calmly and quietly in the big double bed. Another day gone. A sense of achievement in this. Going cheerfully towards the grave.

'What are you thinking?' he asked her.

'About being a butterfly and not having very long to live. What it's like,' she lied.

Outside, Vicky's fat legs went slowly up and down as she tricycled along the path. For a moment a young boy was visible, jumping across flower-beds with a pole.

'There's my skinny one,' she laughed, and he was gone.

It was a boring little garden, and old-fashioned – full of colourless hydrangeas and snails and tongue ferns, with those curly glazed earthenware edgings to the paths.

'Those frightful pink Dorothy Perkins,' Lecky said, filled with gloom as he looked at them. There was some association of thought there, but it eluded them.

'Yes, I must soon put Vicky to bed,' she said again, sensing his depression and wishing she had not said that about King's Cross and Infinity.

But it was warm and pleasant in a rather stuffy way and she was too lazy to move. Birds flew down suddenly from the eaves outside. The white shelves with their peeling paint were empty save for a tin of Daisy-Killer and a bleached euonymus clattering its dry leaves in a tiny draught.

'It has been ...' he began, but that could not be continued. He frowned through the window at Vicky as if she were annoying him, going up and down so placidly.

Did he love Helen? The burden of some emotion towards her oppressed him this evening. He was hastened into this emotion by the flight of these last few hours of his last leave. To go away, see her, perhaps, no more, after all these years of kind companionship, to say nothing, explain nothing, all of this suddenly unthinkable. Which was the *more* unthinkable was what he had to decide.

She felt the pressure of his attention and stirred uncomfortably, leaning her cheek against a warm pane which she dusted first with her handkerchief. She picked up a dead wasp by its wing and examined it. Its small body was drawn round, concaved, in an attitude of pain, which seemed human, universal. But the face! She looked at it more closely. Beautiful, it was, fantastic and frightening, like a Japanese mask.

'I shall be lonely,' she sighed. 'With Harry gone, you gone. The children are sweet, but they are not really *company*.'

He imagined himself in a tent on a rainy day, the soaking canvas taut and heavy. If he were to put up his hand to touch that canvas, some deluge would begin, which he would have no power to stop. 'But I *know* that,' he warned himself. 'I *know* that.'

All the same, he suddenly turned, his lips parted, and he began: 'Helen!'

She frowned and reddened, with displeasure, he thought. He observed this with a sense of complete panic. Then she put up her hand and rapped the window with her knuckles.

'Vicky!' she cried sharply. 'Off that garden at once!'

They watched the child smile with guilt and go slowly away, up the garden, with bent head, towards more mischief.

Then they looked at one another and smiled, too. The relief made them laugh. It ran sweetly through them.

'Now I really *must*,' she said. 'I really must put her to bed.'

Summer Schools

Sitting outside on the sill, the cat watched Melanie through the window. The shallow arc between the tips of his ears, his baleful stare, and his hunched-up body blown feathery by the wind, gave him the look of a barn-owl. Sometimes, a strong gust nearly knocked him off balance and bent his whiskers crooked. Catching Melanie's eye, he opened his mouth wide in his furious, striped face, showed his fangs and let out a piteous mew instead of a roar.

Melanie put a finger in her book and padded across the room in her stockinged feet. When she opened the French windows, the gale swept into the room and the fire began to smoke. Now that he was allowed to come in, the cat began a show caprice; half in, he arched his back and rubbed against the step, purring loudly. Some leaves blew across the floor.

'Either in or out, you fool,' Melanie said impatiently. Still holding the door, she put her foot under the cat's belly and half-pushed, half-lifted him into the room.

The French windows had warped, like all the other wooden parts of the house. There were altogether too many causes for irritation, Melanie thought. When she had managed to slam the door shut, she stood there for a moment, looking out at the garden, until she had felt the full abhorrence of the scene. Her revulsion was so complete as to be almost unbelievable; the sensation became ecstatic.

On the veranda, a piece of newspaper had wrapped itself, quivering frenziedly, round a post. A macrocarpa-hedge tossed about in the wind; the giant hydrangea by the gate was full of bus-tickets, for here was the terminus, the very end of the esplanade. The butt and end, Melanie thought, of all the long-drawn-out tedium of the English holiday resort. Across the road a broken bank covered with spiky grass hid most of the sands, but she could imagine them clearly, brown and ribbed, littered with bits of cuttle-fish and mussel-shells. The sea – far out – was staved with white.

Melanie waited as a bowed-over, mufflered man, exercising a dog, then a duffel-coated woman with a brace of poodles on leads completed the scene. Satisfied, she turned back to the fire. It was all as bad as could be and on a bright day it was hardly better, for the hard glitter of the sun seemed unable to lift the spirits. It was usually windy.

The creaking sound of the rain, its fitful and exasperated drumming on the window, she listened to carefully. In one place at the end of the veranda, it dropped more heavily and steadily: she could hear it as if the noise were in her own breast. The cat – Ursula's – rubbed its cold fur against her legs and she pushed him away crossly, but he always returned.

'A day for indoors,' Ursula said gaily. She carried in the tea-tray, and set down a covered dish on the hearth with the smug triumph of one giving a great treat.

'I am to be won over with buttered scones,' Melanie thought sulkily. The sulky expression was one that her face, with its heavy brows and full mouth, fell into easily. 'One of Miss Rogers's nasty looks,' her pupils called it, finding it not alarming, but depressing. Ursula, two years younger, was plumper, brighter, more alert. Neither was beautiful.

'Oh, sod that cat of yours,' Melanie said. He was now mewing at the French windows to be let out. Melanie's swearing was something new since their father had died – an act of desperation, such as a child might make. Father would turn in his grave, Ursula often said. Let him turn, said Melanie. 'Who will look after him while you're away?' she asked, nodding at the cat. Ursula put him outside again and came back to pour out the tea. 'How do you mean, look after him? Surely you don't mind. I'll order the fish. You'll only have to cook it and give it to him.'

'I shan't be here.'

The idea had suddenly occurred, born of vindictiveness and envy. For Pamela had no right to invite Ursula to stay there on her own. Melanie was only two years their senior; they had all been at the same school. Apart from all that, the two sisters always spent their holidays together; in fact, had never been separated. To Melanie, the invitation seemed staggering, insolent, and Ursula's decision to accept it could hardly be believed. She had read out the letter at breakfast one morning and Melanie, on her way out of the room to fetch more milk, had simply said, 'How extraordinary,' her light, scornful voice dismissing the subject. Only a sense of time pass-ing and middle-age approaching had given Ursula the courage (or effrontery) to renew the subject. For the first time that either she or Melanie could remember, her energy and enthusiasm overcame the smoth-ering effect of her sister's lethargy.

'She means to go,' Melanie told herself. Her sensation of impotence was poison to her. She had a bitter taste in her mouth, and chafed her hands as if they were frozen. If Ursula were truly going, though, Melanie deter-mined that the departure should be made as difficult as possible. Long before she could set out for the station she should be worn out with the obstacles she had had to overcome.

'You can't expect me to stay here on my own just in order to look after your cat.'

And lest Ursula should ask where she was going before she had had time to make her plans, she got up quickly and went upstairs.

The cat was to stay in kennels and Ursula grieved about it. Her grief Melanie brushed aside as absurd, although she was at the same time inclined to allow Ursula a sense of guilt. 'A dog one can at least take with one,' she told her. She had decided that the cat reflected something of Ursula's own nature – too feminine (although it was a tom); it might be driven, though not led, and the refusal to co-operate mixed, as it was, with cowardice resulted in slyness.

The weather had not improved. They could remember the holidays beginning in this way so often, with everything – rain, flowers, bushes – aslant in the wind. 'It will be pretty miserable at Pamela's,' Melanie thought. She could imagine that house and its surroundings – a parade of new shops nearby, a tennis club, enormous suburban pubs at the corners of roads. She was forever adding something derogatory to the list. 'Dentists' houses always depress me,' she said. 'I don't think I could stay in one – with all that going on under the same roof.'

What awaited herself was much vaguer.

'It will be like being at school – though having to run to the bell instead of ringing it,' Ursula said, when she had picked up the prospectus for the Summer Lecture Course. 'A pity you can't just go to the discussions and not stay there. Breakfast 8.15,' she read. 'Oh, Lord. The Victorian Novel. Trollope, 9.30.'

Melanie, in silence, held out her hand for the prospectus and Ursula gave it to her. She did not see it again.

'Will you want Mother's fur?' she asked, when she began to pack. 'I just thought ... evenings, you know, it might be useful ...'

'I shall have evenings, too,' Melanie reminded her.

Their mother could not have guessed what a matter of contention her ermine wrap would turn out to be when she was dead.

'How is Melanie?' Pamela asked.

'Oh, she's well. She's gone on a little holiday, too.'

'I'm so glad. I should have liked to have asked her to come with you,' Pamela lied. 'But there's only this single bed.'

Ursula went over to the window. The spare room was at the back of the house and looked across some recreation grounds – a wooden pavilion, a bowling-green; and tennis courts – just as Melanie had said there would be.

That evening, there was the pub.

All afternoon the front-door bell had rung, and Pamela and Ursula, sitting in the drawing-room upstairs, could hear the crackle of Miss Potter's starched overall as she crossed the hall to answer it. Patients murmured nervously when they entered, but shouted cheerful good-byes as they left, going full tilt down the gravelled drive and slamming the gate after them.

'I'm sorry about the bell,' Pamela said. 'At first, I thought it would send me out of my mind, but now it's no worse than a clock striking.'

Ursula thought it extraordinary that she had changed so much since their schooldays. It was difficult to find anything to talk about. The books they had once so passionately discussed were at the very bottom of the glass-fronted case, beneath text-books on dentistry and Book Club editions, and Ursula, finding Katherine Mansfield's Journal covered with dust, felt estranged. Perhaps Pamela had become a good cook instead, she thought, for there were plenty of books on that.

Melanie would have scorned the room, with its radiogram and cocktail cabinet and the matching sofa and chairs. The ash-trays were painted with bright sayings in foreign languages; there were piles of fashion magazines that later – much later, Ursula guessed – would be put in the waiting-room downstairs. The parchment lamp-shades were stuck over with wine labels and the lamps were made out of Chianti bottles. The motif of drinking was prevalent, from a rueful yet humorous viewpoint. When Pamela opened the cigarette-box it played 'The More we are Together', and Ursula wondered if the clock would call 'Prosit' when it struck six.

'That's the last patient,' Pamela said. 'Mike will come up panting for a drink.'

Her full skirt, printed with a jumble of luggage-labels, flew out wide as she made a dash to the cocktail cabinet. She was as eager to be ready with everything as if she were opening a pub.

Panic now mingled with the feeling of estrangement, as Ursula listened to the footsteps on the stairs. 'Hello, there, Ursula,' said Mike as he threw open the door. 'And how are you? Long time, no see, indeed.'

'Not since our wedding,' Pamela reminded him.

'Well, what will you be after taking?' Mike asked. He slapped his hands together, ready for action, took up a bottle and held it to the light.

'I suppose he feels uneasy because I am a schoolmistress,' Ursula thought; 'And perhaps also – lest I shall think Pam married beneath her.'

Pamela put out the glasses and some amusing bottle-openers and corkscrews. Ursula remembered staying with her as a girl, had a clear picture of the gloomy dining-room: a dusty, cut-glass decanter, containing the dregs of some dark, unidentified liquid had stood in the centre of the great sideboard, its position never shifting an inch to the right or left. From that imprisoning house and those oppressive parents, Mike had rescued his betrothed and, though she had shed Katherine Mansfield somewhere on the way, she seemed as gay as could be that she had escaped.

Now she kissed her husband, took her drink and went downstairs – to turn the waiting-room back into a dining-room, she said. Mike's uneasiness increased. He was clearly longing for her to return.

'You must be a brave man,' Ursula said suddenly. 'I remember Pam's mother and father and how nervous I was when I stayed there. Even when we were quite well on in our teens, we were made to lie down after luncheon, in a darkened room for ages and ages. "And no reading, dears," her mother always said as we went upstairs. At home, we never rested – or only when we were little children, but I pretended that we did, in case Pam's mother should think badly of mine. They seemed so very stern. To snatch away their only daughter must have needed courage.'

For the first time, he looked directly at her. In his eyes was a timid expression. He may have been conscious of this and anxious to hide it, for almost immediately he glanced away.

'I girded on my armour,' he said, 'and rode up to the portcullis and demanded her. That was all there was to it.'

She smiled, thinking, 'So this room is the end of a fairy tale.'

'Astonishing good health, my dear,' Mike said, lifting his glass.

Melanie took her coffee and, summoning all her courage, went to sit down beside Mrs Rybeck, who gave her a staving-off smile, a slight shake of her head as she knitted, her lips moving silently. When she came to the end of the row, she apologised, and jotted down on her knitting-pattern whatever it was she had been counting.

'What a stimulating evening,' Melanie said.

'Have you not heard George Barnes lecture before?' Mrs Rybeck was obviously going to be condescending again, but Melanie was determined to endure it. Then – what she had hoped – Professor Rybeck came in. She felt breathless and self-conscious as he approached.

'Darling!' he murmured, touching his wife's hair, then bowed to Melanie.

'Miss Rogers,' his wife reminded him quickly. 'At St Winifred's, you know, where Ethel's girls were.'

'Yes, of course I know Miss Rogers,' he said.

His dark hair receded from a forehead that seemed always moist, as were his dark and mournful eyes. As soon as they heard his voice – low, catarrhal and with such gentle inflections – some of the women, who had been sitting in a group by the window, got up and came over to him.

'Professor Rybeck,' one said. 'We are beside ourselves with excitement about your lecture tomorrow.'

'Miss Rogers was just saying that she thought highly of George's talk this evening,' said Mrs Rybeck.

'Ah, George!' her husband said softly. 'I think George likes to think he has us all by the ears. Young men do. But we mustn't let him sharpen his wits on us till we ourselves are blunt. None the less, he knows his Thackeray.'

Melanie considered herself less esteemed for having mentioned him.

'How I love *Middlemarch*,' some woman said. 'I think it is my favourite novel.'

'Then I only hope I do it justice tomorrow,' Professor Rybeck said. Although he seemed full of confidence, he smiled humbly. Nothing was too much trouble.

Pamela had insisted that the three of them should squeeze into the front of the car and Ursula, squashed up in the middle, sat with rounded shoulders and her legs tucked to one side. She was worried about the creases in her skirt. The wireless was on very loud and both Pamela and Mike joined in the Prize Song from *Die Meistersinger*. Ursula was glad when they reached the Swan.

The car-park was full. This pub was where everybody went, Pamela explained; 'at the moment,' she added. In the garden, the striped umbrellas above the tables had been furled; the baskets of geraniums over the porch were swinging in the wind.

'Astonishingly horrid evening,' Mike said, when some of his acquaintances greeted him. 'This is Pam's friend, Ursula. Ursie, this is Jock' – or Jean or Eve or Bill. Ursula lost track. They all knew one another and Mike and Pam seemed popular. 'Don't look now, the worst has happened,' someone had said in a loud voice when Mike opened the door of the saloon bar.

Ursula was made much of. From time to time, most of them were obliged to bring out some dull relation or duty-guest. ('Not really one of us'), and it was a mark of friendliness to do one's best to help with other people's problems – even the most tiresome of old crones would be attended to; and Ursula, although plump and prematurely grey, was only too ready to smile and join in the fun.

'You're one of us, I can see,' someone complimented her.

'Cheers!' said Ursula before she drank. Melanie would have shivered with distaste.

'We are all going on to Hilly's,' Pam called to Mike across the bar at closing-time.

This moving-on was the occasion for a little change-round of passengers and, instead of being squeezed in between Pamela and Mike, Ursula was taken across the car-park by a man called Guy.

'Daddy will give you a scarf for your head,' he promised, opening the door of his open car. The scarf tucked inside his shirt was yellow, patterned with horses and when he took it off and tied it round Ursula's head, the silk was warm to her cheeks.

They drove very fast along the darkening roads and were the first to arrive.

'Poor frozen girl,' said Guy when he had swung the car round on the gravelled sweep in front of the house and brought it up within an inch of the grass verge. With the driving off his mind, he could turn his attention to Ursula and he took one of her goosefleshy arms between his hands and began to chafe it. 'What we need is a drink,' he said. 'Where the hell have they all got to?'

She guessed that to drive fast and to arrive first was something he had to do and, for his sake and to help on the amiability of the evening, she was glad that he had managed it.

'You're sure it's the right house?' she asked.

'Dead sure, my darling.'

She had never been called 'darling' by a man and, however meaningless the endearment, it added something to her self-esteem, as their arriving first had added something to his.

She untied the scarf and gave it back to him. He had flicked on his cigarette lighter and was looking for something in the dash-pocket. For a moment, while the small glow lasted, she could study his face. It was like a ventriloquist's dummy's – small, alert, yet blank; the features gave the appearance of having been neatly painted.

He found the packet of cigarettes; then he put the scarf round his neck and tied it carefully. 'Someone's coming,' he said. 'They must have double-crossed us and had one somewhere on the way.'

'You drove fastest, that's all,' she said, playing her part in the game.

'Sorry if it alarmed you, sweetheart.' He leant over and kissed her quickly, just before the first of the cars came round the curve of the drive.

'That's the first evening gone,' Ursula thought, when later, she lay in bed, rather muzzily going over what had happened. She could remember the drawing-room at Hilly's. She had sat on a cushion on the floor and music from a gramophone above her had spilled over her head, so that she had seen people's mouths opening and shutting but had not been able to hear the matching conversations. In many ways the room – though it was larger – had seemed like Pamela's, with pub signs instead of bottle labels on the lamp-shades. Her sense of time had soon left her and her sense of place grew vaguer, but some details irritated her because she could not evade them – particularly a warming-pan hanging by the fireplace in which she confronted her distorted reflection.

There had seemed no reason why the evening should ever end and no way of setting going all the complications of departure. Although she was tired, she had neither wanted to leave or to stay. She was living a tiny life within herself, sitting there on the cushion; sipping and smiling and glancing about her. Mike had come across the room to her. She turned to tilt back her head to look up into his face but at once felt giddy and had to be content with staring at his knees, at the pin stripes curving baggily, a thin stripe, then a wider, more feathery one. She began to count them, but Mike had come to take her home to bye-byes he said, stretching out a hand. 'If I can only do this, I can do anything,' Ursula thought, trying to rise and keep her balance. 'I was silly to sit so low down in the first place,' she decided. 'I think my foot has gone to sleep,' she explained and smiled confidingly at his knees. His grip on her arm was strong; although appearing to be extending a hand in gallantry, he was really taking her weight and steadying her, too. She had realised this, even at the time and later, lying safe in bed at last, she felt wonderfully grateful for his kindness, and did not at all mind sharing such a secret with him.

Pamela had put a large jug of water by her bed. An hour earlier, it had seemed unnecessary, but now water was all she wanted in the world. She sat up and drank, with a steady, relentless rhythm, as animals drink. Then she slid back into the warm bedclothes and tried to reconstruct in her mind that drive with Guy and became, in doing so, two people, the story teller and the listener; belittling his endearments, only to reassure herself about them. The sports car, the young man (he was not very old, she told herself), the summer darkness, in spite of its being so windy, were all things that other young girls she had known had taken for granted, at Oxford and elsewhere, and she herself had been denied. They seemed all the more miraculous for having been done without for so long.

Of recent years she had often tried to escape the memory of two maiden-ladies who had lived near her home when she and Melanie were girls. So sharp-tongued and cross-looking, they had seemed then as old as could be, yet may have been no more than in their fifties, she now thought. Frumpish and eccentric, at war with one another as well as all their neighbours, they were to be seen tramping the lanes, single-file and in silence, with their dogs. To the girls, they were the most appalling and unenviable creatures, smelling of vinegar, Melanie had said. The recollection of them so long after they were dead disturbed Ursula and depressed her, for she could see how she and Melanie had taken a turning in their direction, yet scarcely anything as definite as this, for there had been no action, no decision; simply, the road they had been on had always, it seemed, been bending in that direction. In no time at all, would they not be copies of those other old ladies? The Misses Rogers, the neighbours would think of them, feeling pity and nervousness. The elder Miss Rogers would be alarmingly abrupt, with her sarcastic voice and old-fashioned swear-words. 'They won't be afraid of me,' Ursula decided; but had no comfort from the thought. People would think her bullied and would be sorry. She, the plumper one, with her cat and timid smiles, would give biscuits to children when Melanie's back was turned. Inseparable, yet alien to one another, they would become. Forewarned as she was, she felt herself drifting towards that fate and was afraid when she woke at night and thought of it.

Her first drowsiness had worn off and her thirst kept her wakeful. She lay and wondered about the details of Pamela's escape from her parents' sad house and all that had threatened her there – watchfulness, suspicion, envy and capricious humours; much of the kind of thing she herself suffered from Melanie. Pamela's life now was bright and silly, and perhaps she had run away from the best part of herself; but there was nothing in the future to menace her as Ursula was menaced by her own picture of the elderly Misses Rogers.

'But *surely*,' insisted the strained and domineering voice. The woman gripped the back of the chair in front of her and stared up at Professor Rybeck on the platform.

At the end of his lecture, he had asked for questions or discussions. To begin with, everyone had seemed too stunned with admiration to make an effort; there were flutterings and murmurings, but for some time no one stood up. Calmly, he waited, sitting there smiling, eyes half-closed and his head cocked a little as if he were listening to secret music, or applause. His arms were crossed over his chest and his legs were crossed too, and one foot swayed back and forth rhythmically.

The minute Mr Brundle stood up, other people wanted to. He was an elderly, earnest man, who had been doggedly on the track of culture since his youth. His vanity hid from him the half-stifled yawns he evoked, the glassy look of those who, though caught, refused to listen and also his way of melting away to one victim any group of people he approached. Even Professor Rybeck looked restless, as Mr Brundle began now to pound away at his theory. Then others, in disagreement or exasperation, began to jump to their feet, or made sharp comments, interrupting; even shot their arms into the air, like schoolchildren. World Peace they might have been arguing about, not George Eliot's Dorothea Casaubon.

'Please, please,' said Professor Rybeck, in his melodious protesting voice. 'Now, Mrs Thomas, let us hear you.'

'But *surely*,' Mrs Thomas said again.

'Wouldn't it be time to say?' asked Mrs Wetherby – she sounded diffident and had blushed; she had never spoken in the presence of so many people before, but wanted badly to make her mark on the Professor. She was too shy to stand upright and leant forward, lifting her bottom a couple of inches from the chair. Doing so, she dropped her notebook and pencil, her stole slipped off and when she bent down to pick it up she also snatched at some large, tortoise-shell pins that had fallen out of her hair. By the time she had done all this, her chance was gone and she had made her mark in the wrong way. The one and only clergyman in the room had sprung to his feet and, knowing all the tricks needed to command, had snatched off his spectacles and held them high in the air while, for some reason no one was clear about, he denounced Samuel Butler.

'I think, Comrade ... Professor, I should say,' Mr Brundle interrupted. 'If we might return but briefly to the subject ... '

Melanie closed her eyes and thought how insufferable people became about what has cost them too much to possess – education, money, or even good health.

'Lightly come or not at all, is what I like,' she told herself crossly and, when she opened her eyes, glanced up at Professor Rybeck, who smiled with such placid condescension as the ding-dong argument went on between clergyman and atheist (for literature – Victorian or otherwise – had been discarded) and then she looked for Mrs Rybeck and found her sitting at the end of the second row, still knitting. She gave, somehow, an impression of not being one of the audience, seemed apart from them, pre-occupied with her own thoughts, lending her presence only, like a baby-sitter or the invigilator at an examination – well accustomed to the admiration her husband had from other women of her own age, she made it clear that she was one with him in all he did and thought; their agreement, she implied, had come about many years ago and needed no more discussion, and if the women cared to ask her any of the questions he had no time to answer, then she could give the authorised replies. With all this settled, her placidity, like his, was almost startling to other people, their smiling lips (not eyes), their capacity for waiting for others to finish speaking (and it was far removed from the act of listening), is often to be found in the mothers of large families. Yet she was childless. She had only the Professor, and the socks she knitted were for him. She is more goddessy than motherly, Melanie thought.

'We are summoned to the banqueting-hall,' said the Professor, raising his hand in the air, as a bell began to ring. This was the warning that lunch would be ready in ten minutes, the Secretary had told them all when they arrived, and 'warning' was a word she had chosen well. The smell of minced beef and cabbage came along passages towards them. To Melanie it was unnoticeable, part of daily life, like other tedious affairs; one disposed of the food, as of any other small annoyance, there were jugs of water to wash it down and slices of bread cut hours before that one could crumble as one listened to one's neighbour.

One of Melanie's neighbours was an elementary school-teacher to whom she tried not to be patronising. On her other side was a Belgian woman whose vivacity was intolerable. She was like a bad caricature of a foreigner, primly sporty and full of gay phrases. 'Mon Dieu, we have had it, chums,' she said, lifting the water-jug and finding it empty. The machine-gun rattle of consonants vibrated in Melanie's head long after she was alone. 'Oh, là, là!' the woman sometimes cried, as if she were a cheeky French maid in an old-fashioned farce.

'You think "Meedlemahtch" is a good book?' she asked Melanie. They all discussed novels at meal-times too; for they were what they had in common.

Melanie was startled, for Professor Rybeck had spent most of the morning explaining its greatness. 'It is one of the great English novels,' she said.

'As great as Charles Morgan, you think? In the same class?'

Melanie looked suspicious and would not answer.

'It is such a funny book. I read it last night and laughed so much.'

'And will read *War and Peace* between tea and dinner, I suppose,' the elementary school-teacher murmured. 'Oh dear, how disgusting!' She pushed a very pale, boiled caterpillar to the side of her plate. 'If that happened to one of our little darlings at school dinner, the mother would write at once to her M.P.'

At Melanie's school, the girls would have hidden the creature under a fork in order not to spoil anyone else's appetite, but she did not say so.

'A *funny* book?' she repeated, turning back to the Belgian woman.

'Yes, I like it so much when she thinks that the really delightful marriage must be that where your husband was a sort of father, and could teach you Hebrew if you wished it. Oh, là, là! For heaven's sake.'

'Then she did read a page or two,' said the woman on Melanie's other side.

A dreadful sadness and sense of loss had settled over Melanie when she herself had read those words. They had not seemed absurd to her; she had felt tears pressing at the back of her eyes. So often, she had longed for protection and compassion, to be instructed and concentrated upon; as if she were a girl again, yet with a new excitement in the air.

As they made their way towards the door, when lunch was over, she could see Professor Rybeck standing there talking to one or two of his admirers. Long before she drew near to him, Melanie found another

direction to glance in. What she intended for unconcern, he took for deliberate hostility and wondered at what point of his lecture he had managed
to offend her so.

In a purposeless way, she wandered into the garden. The Georgian
house – a boys' preparatory-school in the term-time – stood among dark
rhododendron bushes and silver birches. Paths led in many directions
through the shrubberies, yet all converged upon the lake – a depressing
stretch of water, as bleary as an old looking-glass, shadowed by trees and
broken by clumps of reeds.

The pain of loneliness was a worse burden to her here than it had ever
been at home and she knew – her behaviour as she was leaving the dining-
room had reminded her – that the fault was in herself.

'Don't think that I will make excuses to speak to you,' she had wanted
to imply. 'I am not so easily dazzled as these other women.' 'But I wanted
him to speak to me,' she thought, 'and perhaps I only feared that he would
not.'

She sat down on the bank above the water and thought about the
Professor. She could even imagine his lustrous eyes turned upon her, as he
listened.

'I give false impressions,' she struggled to explain to him. 'In my heart ...
I am ... '

'I know what you are,' he said gently. 'I knew at once.'

The relief would be enormous. She was sure of that. She could live the
rest of her life on the memory of that moment.

'But he is a fraud,' the other, destructive voice in her insisted, the voice
that had ruined so much for her. 'He is not a fraud,' she said firmly; her lips
moved; she needed to be so definite with herself. 'Perhaps he cannot find
the balance between integrity and priggishness.'

'Is that all?' asked the other voice.

The dialogue faded out and she sighed, thinking: 'I wish I hadn't come.
I feel so much worse here than I do at home.'

Coming round the lake's edge towards her was the atrocious little Mr
Brundle. She pretended not to have seen him and got to her feet and went
off in the other direction.

By the afternoon post came a letter from Ursula, saying how dull she was
and that Melanie had been so right about it all – and that comforted her
a little.

Ursula was polishing a glass on a cloth printed with a chart of vintage years
for champagne. Although she was drunk, she wondered at the usefulness
of this as a reference. It would be strange to go home again to a black telephone, white sheets and drying-up cloths on which there was nothing at

all to read, not a recipe for a cocktail or a cheerful slogan.

On the draining-board two white tablets fizzed, as they rose and fell in a glass of water. The noise seemed very loud to her and she was glad when the tablets dissolved and there was silence.

'There you are,' Guy said, handing the glass to her. The water still spat and sparkled and she drank it slowly, gasping between sips.

'Pamela will wonder where I am,' she said. She put the glass on the draining-board and sat down with a bump on one of the kitchen chairs. She had insisted on washing the two glasses before she went home, and had devoted herself to doing so with single-mindedness; but Guy had been right, and she gave in. Everything she had to do had become difficult – going home, climbing the stairs, undressing. 'I shall just have to sit on this chair and let time pass,' she decided. 'It will pass,' she promised herself, 'and it mends all in the end.'

'Where did we go after that Club?' she suddenly asked frowning.

'Nowhere,' said Guy. 'On our way back to Pamela's we stopped here for a drink. That's all.'

'Ah, yes!'

She remembered the outside of this bungalow and a wooden gate with the name 'Hereiam'. It had been quite dark when they walked up the stony path to the front door. Now, it seemed the middle of the night. 'I think you gave me too much whisky,' she said, with a faint, reproachful smile.

'As a matter of fact, I gave you none. It was ginger-ale you were drinking.'

She considered this and then lifted her eyes to look at him and asked anxiously: 'Then had I had ... was I ... ?'

'You were very sweet.'

She accepted this gravely. He put his hands under her arms and brought her to her feet and she rested the side of her face against his waistcoat and stayed very still, as if she were counting his heart-beats. These, like the fizzing drink, also sounded much too loud.

'I didn't wash the other glass,' she said.

'Mrs Lamb can do it in the morning.'

She went from one tremulous attempt at defence to another, wanting to blow her nose, or light a cigarette or put something tidy. In the sitting-room, earlier, when he had sat down beside her on the sofa, she had sprung up and gone rapidly across the room to look for an ash-tray. 'Who is this?' she had asked, picking up a framed photograph and holding it at arm's length, as if to ward him off. 'Girl friend,' he said briefly, drinking his whisky and watching her manoeuvres with amusement.

'Haven't you ever wanted to get married?' she had asked.

'Sometimes. Have you?'

'Oh, sometimes ... I dare say,' she answered vaguely.

Now, in the kitchen, he had caught her at last, she was clasped in his arms and feeling odd, she told him.

'I know. There's some coffee nearly ready in the other room. That will do untold good.'

What a dreadful man he is, really, in spite of his tenderness, she thought. So hollow and vulgar that I don't know what Melanie would say.

She was startled for a moment, wondering if she had murmured this aloud; for, suddenly, his heartbeat had become noisier – from anger, she was afraid.

'You are very kind,' she said appeasingly. 'I am not really used to drinking as much as people do here – not used to drinking at all.'

'What *are* you used to?'

'Just being rather dull, you know – my sister and I.'

His way of lifting her chin up and kissing her was too accomplished and she was reminded of the way in which he drove the car. She was sure that there was something here she should resent. Perhaps he was patronising her; for the kiss had come too soon after her remark about the dullness of her life. I can bring *some* excitement into it, he may have thought.

Without releasing her, he managed to stretch an arm and put out the light. 'I can't bear to see you frowning,' he explained. 'Why frown anyway?'

'That coffee ... but then I mustn't stay for it, after all. Pamela will be wondering ...'

'Pam will understand.'

'Oh, I hope not.'

She frowned more than ever and shut her eyes tightly although the room was completely dark.

Melanie sat on the edge of the bed, coughing. She was wondering if she had suddenly got T.B. and kept looking anxiously at her handkerchief.

The sun was shining, though not into her room. From the window, she could see Professor Rybeck sitting underneath the Wellingtonia with an assortment of his worshippers. From his gestures, Melanie could tell that it was he who was talking, and talking continuously. The hand rose and fell and made languid spirals as he unfolded his theme, or else cut the air decisively into slices. Mrs Rybeck was, of course, knitting. By her very presence, sitting a little apart from her husband, like a woman minding a stall on a fairground, she attracted passers-by. Melanie watched the Belgian woman now approaching, to say her few words about the knitting, then having paid her fee, to pass on to listen to the Professor.

Desperately, Melanie wished to be down there listening, too; but she had no knowledge of how to join them. Crossing the grass, she would attract too much attention. Ah, *she* cannot keep away, people would think, turning to watch her. She must be in love with the Professor after all, like the other women; but perhaps more secretly, more devouringly.

She had stopped coughing and forgotten tuberculosis for the moment, as she tried to work out some more casual way than crossing the lawn. She might emerge less noticeably from the shrubbery behind the Wellingtonia, if only she could be there in the first place.

She took a clean handkerchief from a drawer and smoothed her hair before the looking-glass; and then a bell rang for tea and, when she went back to the window, the group under the tree was breaking up. Mrs Rybeck was rolling up her knitting and they were all laughing.

'I shall see him at tea,' Melanie thought. She could picture him bowing to her, coldly, and with the suggestion that it was she who disliked him rather than he who disliked her. 'I could never put things right now,' she decided.

She wondered what Ursula would be doing at this minute. Perhaps sitting in Pamela's little back garden having tea, while, at the front of the house, the patients came and went. She had said that she would be glad to be at home again, for Pamela had changed and they had nothing left in common. 'And coming here hasn't been a success, either,' Melanie thought, as she went downstairs to tea. She blamed Ursula very much for having made things so dull for them both. There must be ways of showing her how mistaken she had been, ways of preventing anything of the kind happening again.

'Miss Rogers,' said the Professor with unusual gaiety. They had almost collided at the drawing-room door. 'Have you been out enjoying the sun?'

She blushed and was so angry that she should that she said quite curtly, 'No, I was writing letters in my room.'

He stood quickly aside to let her pass and she did so without a glance at him.

Their holiday was over. On her way back from the station, Ursula called at the kennels for the cat and Melanie, watching her come up the garden path, could see the creature clawing frantically at her shoulder, trying to hoist himself out of her grasp. The taxi-driver followed with the suitcase.

Melanie had intended to be the last home and had even caught a later train than was convenient, in order not to have to be waiting there for her sister. After all her planning, she was angry to have found the house empty.

'Have you been home long?' Ursula asked rather breathlessly. She put the cat down and looked round. Obviously Melanie had not, for her suitcase still stood in the hall and not a letter had been opened.

'Only a minute or two,' said Melanie.

'That cat's in a huff with me. Trying to punish me for going away, I suppose. He's quite plump though. He looks well, doesn't he? Oh, it's so lovely to be home.'

She went to the hall-table and shuffled the letters, then threw them on one side. Melanie had said nothing.

'Aren't *you* glad to be home?' Ursula asked her.

'No, I don't think so.'

'Well I'm glad you had a good time. It was a change for you.'

'Yes.'

'And now let's have some tea.'

She went into the kitchen and, still wearing her hat, began to get out the cups and saucers. 'They didn't leave any bread,' she called out. 'Oh, yes, it's all right, I've found it.' She began to sing, then stopped to chatter to the cat, then sang again.

Melanie had been in the house over an hour and had done nothing.

'I'm so glad you had a good time,' Ursula said again, when they were having tea.

'I'm sorry you didn't.'

'It was a mistake going there, trying to renew an old friendship. You'd have hated the house.'

'You'd have liked *mine*. Grey stone, Georgian, trees and a lake.'

'Romantic,' Ursula said and did not notice that Melanie locked her hands together in rather a theatrical gesture.

'Pam seems complacent. She's scored over me, having a husband. Perhaps that's why she invited me.'

'What did you do all the time?'

'Just nothing. Shopped in the morning – every morning – the house-wife's round – butcher, baker, candlestick maker. "I'm afraid the piece of skirt was rather gristly, Mr Bones." That sort of thing. She would fetch half a pound of butter one day and go back for another half-pound the next morning – just for the fun of it. One day, she said, "I think we'll have some hock for supper." I thought she was talking about wine, but it turned out to be some bacon – not very nice. Not very nice of me to talk like this, either.'

However dull it had been, she seemed quite excited as she described it; her cheeks were bright and her hands restless.

'We went to the cinema once, to see a Western,' she added. 'Mike is very fond of Westerns.'

'How dreadful for you.'

Ursula nodded.

'Well, that's their life,' she said. 'I was glad all the time that you were not there. Darling puss, so now you've forgiven me.'

To show his forgiveness, the cat jumped on to her lap and began dough-punching, his extended claws catching the threads of her skirt.

'Tell me about *you*,' Ursula said. She poured out some more tea to sip while Melanie had her turn; but to her surprise Melanie frowned and looked away.

'Is something the matter?'

'I can't talk about it yet, or get used to not being there. This still seems unreal to me. You must give me time.'

She got up, knocked over the cream jug and went out of the room. Ursula mopped up the milk with her napkin and then leant back and closed her eyes. Her moment's consternation at Melanie's behaviour had passed; she even forgot it. The cat relaxed, too, and, curled up against her, slept.

Melanie was a long time unpacking and did nothing towards getting supper. She went for a walk along the sea road and watched the sunset on the water. The tide was out and the wet sands were covered with a pink light. She dramatised her solitary walk and was in a worse turmoil when she reached home.

'Your cough is bad,' Ursula said when they had finished supper.

'Is it?' Melanie said absent-mindedly.

'Something has happened, hasn't it?' Ursula asked her, and then looked down quickly, as if she were confused.

'The end of the world,' said Melanie.

'You've fallen in love?' Ursula lifted her head and stared at her.

'To have to go back to school next week and face those bloody children – and go on facing them, for ever and for ever – or other ones exactly like them ... the idea suddenly appals me.'

Her bitterness was so true, and Ursula could hear her own doom in her sister's words. She had never allowed herself to have thoughts of that kind.

'But can't you ... can't he?' she began.

'We can't meet again. We never shall. So it *is* the end of the world, you see,' said Melanie. The scene gave her both relief and anguish. Her true parting with Professor Rybeck (he had looked up from *The Times* and nodded as she crossed the hall) was obliterated for ever. She could more easily bear the agonised account she now gave to Ursula and she would bear it – their noble resolve, their last illicit embrace.

'He's married, you mean?' Ursula asked bluntly.

'Yes, married.'

Mrs Rybeck, insensitively knitting at the execution of their hopes, appeared as an evil creature, tenacious and sinister.

'But to say good-bye for ever ...' Ursula protested. 'We only have one life ... would it be wicked, after all?'

'What could there be ... clandestine meetings and sordid arrangements?'

Ursula looked ashamed.

'I should ruin his career,' said Melanie.

'Yes, I see. You could write to one another, though.'

'Write!' Melanie repeated in a voice as light as air. 'I think I will go to bed now. I feel exhausted.'

'Yes, do, and I will bring you a hot drink.' As Melanie began to go upstairs, Ursula said, 'I am very sorry, you know.'

While she was waiting for the milk to rise in the pan, she tried to rearrange her thoughts, especially to exclude (now that there was so much nobility in the house) her own squalid – though hazily recollected – escapade. Hers was a more optimistic nature than Melanie's and she was confident of soon putting such memories out of her mind.

When she took the hot milk upstairs, her sister was sitting up in bed reading a volume of Keats' letters. 'He gave it to me as I came away,' she explained, laying the book on the bedside table, where it was always to remain.

'We have got this to live with now,' Ursula thought, 'and it will be with us for ever, I can see – the reason and the excuse for everything. It will even grow; there will be more and more of it, as time goes on. When we are those two elderly Misses Rogers we are growing into it will still be there. "Miss Melanie, who has such a sharp tongue," people will say. "Poor thing ... a tragic love-affair a long way back." I shall forget there was a time when we did not have it with us.'

Melanie drank her milk and put out the light; then she lay down calmly and closed her eyes and prepared herself for her dreams. Until they came, she imagined walking by the lake, as she had done, that afternoon, only a few days ago; but instead of Mr Brundle coming into the scene, Professor Rybeck appeared. He walked towards her swiftly, as if by assignation. Then they sat down and looked at the tarnished water – and she added a few swans for them to watch. After a long delicious silence, she began to speak. Yet words were not really necessary. She had hardly begun the attempt; her lips shaped the beginning of a sentence – 'I am ...' and then he took her hand and held it to his cheek. 'I know what you are,' he said. 'I knew at the very beginning.'

Although they had parted for ever, she realised that she was now at peace – she felt ennobled and enriched, and saw herself thus, reflected from her sister's eyes, and she was conscious of Ursula's solemn wonder and assured by it.

Perhaps a Family Failing

Of course, Mrs Cotterell cried. Watery-eyed, on the arm of the bride-groom's father, she smiled in a bewildered way to left and right, coming down the aisle. Outside, on the church steps, she quickly dashed the tears away as she faced the camera, still arm-in-arm with Mr Midwinter, a man she detested.

He turned towards her and gave a great meaningless laugh just as the camera clicked and Mrs Cotterell had his ginny breath blown full in her face. Even in church he had to smell like that, she thought, and the grim words, 'Like father, like son', disturbed her mind once more.

Below them, at the kerb's edge, Geoff was already helping his bride into the car. The solemnity of the service had not touched him. In the vestry, he had been as jaunty as ever, made his wife blush and was hushed by his mother, a frail, pensive creature, who had much, Mrs Cotterell thought, to be frail and pensive about.

It was Saturday morning and the bridal car moved off slowly among the other traffic. Mrs Cotterell watched until the white-ribboned motor disappeared.

The bridesmaids, one pink, one apple-green, were getting into the next car. Lissport was a busy place on Saturdays and to many of the women it was part of the morning's shopping-outing to be able to stand for a minute or two to watch a bride coming out of the church. Feeling nervous and self-conscious, Mrs Cotterell, who had often herself stood and watched and criticised, crossed the pavement to the car. She was anxious to be home and wondered if everything was all right there. She had come away in a flurry of confused directions, leaving two of her neighbours slicing beetroot and sticking blanched almonds into the trifles. She was relieved that the reception was her own affair, that she could be sure that there would be no drunkenness, no rowdy behaviour and suggestive speeches, as there had been at Geoff's sister's wedding last year. One glass of port to drink a toast to the bride and bridegroom she had agreed to. For the rest she hoped that by now her kindly neighbours had mixed the orange cordial.

*

Mrs Cotterell cried again, much harder, when Beryl came downstairs in her going-away suit, and kissed her and thanked her (as if her mother were a hostess, not her own flesh and blood, Mrs Cotterell thought sorrowfully) and with composure got into Geoff's little car, to which Mr Midwinter had tied an empty sardine-tin.

Then everyone else turned to Mrs Cotterell and thanked her and praised the food and Beryl's looks and dress. It had all gone off all right, they said, making a great hazard of it. 'You'll miss her,' the women told her. 'I know what it's like,' some added.

The bridesmaids took off their flower wreaths and put on their coats. Geoff's brothers, Les and Ron, were taking them out for the evening. 'Not long till opening-time,' they said.

Mrs Cotterell went back into the house, to survey the wedding presents, and the broken wedding cake, with the trellis work icing she had done so lovingly, crumbled all over the table. Beryl's bouquet was stuck in a vase, waiting to be taken tomorrow to poor Grandma in hospital.

In the kitchen, the faithful neighbours were still hard at work, washing up the piles of plates stained with beetroot and mustard and tomato sauce.

'She's gone,' Mrs Cotterell whispered into her crumpled handkerchief as her husband came in and put his arm round her.

'Soon be opening-time,' Geoff said, driving along the busy road to Seaferry. He had long ago stopped the car, taken the sardine-tin off the back axle and thrown it over a hedge. 'Silly old fool, Dad,' he had said fondly. 'Won't ever act his age.'

Beryl thought so, too, but decided not to reopen that old discussion at such a time. For weeks, she had thought and talked and dreamt of the wedding, studied the advice to brides in women's magazines, on make-up, etiquette and Geoff's marital rights – which he must, she learnt, not be allowed to anticipate. 'Stop it, Geoff!' she had often said firmly. 'I happen to want you to respect me, thank you very much.' Unfortunately for her, Geoff was not the respectful kind, although, in his easy-going way, he consented to the celibacy – one of her girlish whims – and had even allowed the gratifying of his desires to be postponed from Easter until early summer, because she had suddenly decided she wanted sweet-peas in the bridesmaids' bouquets.

To the women's magazines Beryl now felt she owed everything; she had had faith in their advice and seen it justified. I expect Geoff's getting excited, she thought. She was really quite excited herself.

'Now where are you going?' she asked, as he swerved suddenly off the road. It was perfectly plain that he was going into a public house, whose front door he had seen flung open just as he was about to pass it by.

'Well, here it is,' he said. 'The White Horse. The very first pub to have the privilege of serving a drink to Mr and Mrs Geoffrey Midwinter.'

This pleased her, although she wanted to get to the hotel as quickly as she could, to unpack her trousseau, before it creased too badly.

It was a dull little bar, smelling frowsty. The landlord was glumly watchful, as if they might suddenly get out of hand, or steal one of his cracked ash-trays.

Geoff, however, was in high spirits, and raised his pint pot and winked at his wife. 'Well, here's in anticipation,' he said. She looked demurely at her gin and orange, but she smiled. She loved him dearly. She was quite convinced of this, for she had filled in a questionnaire on the subject of love in one of her magazines, and had scored eighteen out of twenty, with a rating of 'You and Cleopatra share the honours'. Only his obsession with public houses worried her, but she was sure that – once she had him away from the influence of his father and brothers – she would be able to break the habit.

At six o'clock Mr Midwinter took his thirst and his derogatory opinions about the wedding down to the saloon bar of the Starter's Orders. His rueful face, as he described the jugs of orangeade, convulsed his friends. 'Poor Geoff, what's he thinking of, marrying into a lot like that?' asked the barmaid.

'Won't make no difference to Geoff,' said his father. 'Geoff's like his dad. Not given to asking anybody's by-your-leave when he feels like a pint.'

Mrs Midwinter had stayed at home alone. It had not occurred to her husband that she might be feeling flat after the day's excitement. She would not have remarked on it herself, knowing the problem was insoluble. He could not have taken her to a cinèma, because Saturday evening was sacred to drinking, and although she would have liked to go with him for a glass of stout, she knew why she could not. He always drank in the Men Only bar at the Starter's Orders. 'Well, you don't want me drinking with a lot of prostitutes, do you?' he often asked, and left her no choice, as was his habit.

Beryl had never stayed in an hotel before, and she was full of admiration at the commanding tone Geoff adopted as they entered the hall of the Seaferry Arms.

'Just one before we go up?' he enquired, looking towards the bar.

'Later, dear,' she said firmly. 'Let's unpack and tidy ourselves first; then we can have a drink before dinner.' The word 'dinner' depressed him. It threatened to waste a great deal of Saturday evening drinking time.

From their bedroom window they could see a bleak stretch of promenade, grey and gritty. The few people down there either fought their way against the gale, with their heads bowed and coats clutched to their breasts, or seemed tumbled along with the wind at their heels. The sun, having shone on the bride, had long ago gone in and it seemed inconceivable that it would ever come out again.

'No strolling along the prom tonight,' said Geoff.

'Isn't it a shame? It's the only thing that's gone wrong.'

Beryl began to hang up and spread about the filmy, lacy, ribboned lingerie with which she had for long planned to tease and entice her husband.

'The time you take,' he said. He had soon tipped everything out of his own case into a drawer. 'What's this?' he asked, picking up something of mauve chiffon.

'My nightgown,' she said primly.

'What ever for?'

'Don't be common.' She always affected disapproval when he teased her.

'What about a little anticipation here and now?' he suggested.

'Oh, don't be so silly. It's broad daylight.'

'Right. Well, I'm just going to spy out the lie of the land. Back in a minute,' he said.

She was quite content to potter about the bedroom, laying traps for his seduction; but when she was ready at last, she realised that he had been away a long time. She stood by the window, wondering what to do, knowing that it was time for them to go in to dinner. After a while, she decided that she would have to find him and, feeling nervous and self-conscious, she went along the quiet landing and down the stairs. Her common sense took her towards the sound of voices and laughter and, as soon as she opened the door of the bar, she was given a wonderful welcome from all the new friends Geoff had suddenly made.

'It seems ever so flat, doesn't it?' Mrs Cotterell said. All of the washing-up was done, but she was too tired to make a start on packing up the presents.

'It's the reaction,' her husband said solemnly.

Voices from a play on the wireless mingled with their own, but were ignored. Mrs Cotterell had her feet in a bowl of hot water. New shoes had given her agony. Beryl, better informed, had practised wearing hers about the house for days before.

'Haven't done my corns any good,' Mrs Cotterell mourned. Her feet ached and throbbed, and so did her heart.

'It all went off well, though, didn't it?' she asked, as she had asked him a dozen times before.

'Thanks to you,' he said dutifully. He was clearing out the budgerigar's cage and the bird was sitting on his bald head, blinking and chattering.

Mrs Cotterell stared at her husband. She suddenly saw him as a completely absurd figure, and she trembled with anger and self-pity. Something ought to have been done for her on such an evening, she thought, some effort should have been made to console and reward her. Instead, she was left to soak her feet and listen to a lot of North Country accents on the radio. She stretched out her hand and switched them off.

'What ever's wrong, Mother?'

'I can't stand any more of that "By goom" and "Nowt" and "Eee, lad". It reminds me of that nasty cousin Rose of yours.'

'But we always listen to the play on a Saturday.'

'This Saturday isn't like other Saturdays.' She snatched her handkerchief out of her cuff and dabbed her eyes.

Mr Cotterell leant forward and patted her knee and the budgerigar flew from his head and perched on her shoulder.

'That's right, Joey, you go to Mother. She wants a bit of cheering-up.'

'I'm not his mother, if you don't mind, and I don't want cheering-up from a bird.'

'One thing I know is you're overtired. I've seen it coming. You wouldn't care to put on your coat and stroll down to the Public for a glass of port, would you?'

'Don't be ridiculous,' she said.

After dinner, they drank their coffee, all alone in the dreary lounge of the Seaferry Arms, and then Beryl went to bed. She had secret things to do to her hair and her face. 'I'll just pour you out another cup,' she said. 'Then, when you've drunk it, you can come up.'

'Right,' he said solemnly, nodding his head.

'Don't be long, darling.'

When she had gone, he sat and stared at the cupful of black coffee and then got up and made his way back to the bar.

All of his before-dinner cronies had left and a completely different set of people stood round the bar. He ordered some beer and looked about him.

'Turned chilly,' said the man next to him.

'Yes. Disappointing,' he agreed. To make friends was the easiest thing in the world. In no time, he was at the heart of it all again.

At ten o'clock, Beryl, provocative in chiffon, as the magazines would have described her, burst into tears of rage. She could hear the laughter – so much louder now, towards closing-time – downstairs in the bar and knew that the sound of it had drawn Geoff back. She was powerless – so transparently tricked out to tempt him – to do anything but lie and wait until, at bar's emptying, he should remember her and stumble upstairs to bed.

It was not the first happy evening Geoff had spent in the bar of the Seaferry Arms. He had called there with the team, after cricket-matches in the nearby villages. Seaferry was only twenty miles from home. Those summer evenings had all merged into one another, as drinking evenings should – and this one was merging with them. 'I'm glad I came,' he thought, rocking slightly as he stood by the bar with two of his new friends. He couldn't remember having met nicer people. They were a very gay married couple. The wife had a miniature poodle who had already wetted three times on the carpet. 'She can't help it, can you, angel?' her mistress protested. 'She's quite neurotic; aren't you, precious thing?'

Doris – as Geoff had been told to call her – was a heavy jolly woman. The bones of her stays showed through her frock, her necklace of jet beads was powdered with cigarette ash. She clutched a large, shiny handbag and had snatched from it a pound note, which she began to wave in the air, trying to catch the barmaid's eye. 'I say, miss! What's her name, Ted? Oh, yes. I say, Maisie! Same again, there's a dear girl.'

It was nearly closing-time, and a frenzied reordering was going on. The street door was pushed open and a man and woman with a murderous-looking bull terrier came in. 'You stay there,' the man said to the woman and the dog, and he left them and began to force his way towards the bar.

'Miss! Maisie!' Doris called frantically. Her poodle, venturing between people's legs, made another puddle under a table and approached the bull terrier.

'I say, Doris, call Zoë back,' said her husband. 'And put that money away. I told you I'll get these.'

'I insist. They're on me.'

'Could you call your dog back?' the owner of the bull terrier asked them. 'We don't want any trouble.'

'Come, Zoë, pet!' Doris called. 'He wouldn't hurt her, though. She's a bitch. Maisie! Oh, there's a dear. Same again, love. Large ones.'

Suddenly, a dreadful commotion broke out. Doris was nearly knocked off her stool as Zoë came flying back to her for protection, with the bull terrier at her throat. She screamed and knocked over somebody's gin.

Geoff, who had been standing by the bar in a pleasurable haze, watching the barmaid, was, in spite of his feeling of unreality, the first to spring to life and pounce upon the bull terrier and grab his collar. The dog bit his hand, but he was too drunk to feel much pain. Before anyone could snatch Zoë out of danger, the barmaid lifted the jug of water and meaning to pour it over the bull terrier, flung it instead over Geoff. The shock made him loosen his grip and the fight began again. A second time he grabbed at the collar and had his hand bitten once more; but now – belatedly, everyone else thought – the two dog-owners came to his help. Zoë, with every likelihood of being even more neurotic in the future, was put, shivering, in her mistress's arms, the bull terrier was secured to his lead in disgrace, and Maisie called Time.

After some recriminations between themselves, the dog-owners thanked and congratulated Geoff. 'Couldn't get near them,' they said. 'The bar was so crowded. Couldn't make head or tail of what was going on.'

'Sorry you got so wet,' said Doris.

The bull terrier's owner felt rather ashamed of himself when he saw how pale Geoff was. 'You all right?' he asked. 'You look a bit shaken up.'

Geoff examined his hand. There was very little blood, but he was beginning to be aware of the pain and felt giddy. He shook his head, but could not answer. Something dripped from his hair on to his forehead, and when he dabbed it with his handkerchief, he was astonished to see water and not blood.

'You got far to go?' the man asked him. 'Where's your home?'

'Lissport.'

'That's our way, too, if you want a lift.' Whether Geoff had a car or not, the man thought he was in no condition to drive it; although, whether from shock or alcohol or both, it was difficult to decide.

'I'd *like* a lift,' Geoff murmured drowsily. 'Many thanks.'

'No, any thanks are due to *you*.'

'Doesn't it seem strange without Geoff?' Mrs Midwinter asked her husband. He was back from the Starter's Orders, had taken off his collar and tie and was staring gloomily at the dying fire.

'Les and Ron home yet?' he asked.

'No, they won't be till half-past twelve. They've gone to the dance at the Town Hall.'

'Half-past twelve! It's scandalous the way they carry on. Drinking themselves silly, I've no doubt at all. Getting decent girls into trouble.'

'It's only a dance, Dad.'

'*And* their last one. I'm not having it. Coming home drunk on a Sunday morning and lying in bed till all hours to get over it. When was either of them last at Chapel? Will you tell me that?'

Mrs Midwinter sighed and folded up her knitting.

'I can't picture why Geoff turned from Chapel like that.' Mr Midwinter seemed utterly depressed about his sons, as he often was at this time on a Saturday night.

'Well, he was courting ...'

'First time I've been in a church was today, and I was not impressed.'

'I thought it was lovely, and you looked your part just as if you did it every day.'

'I wasn't worried about my part. Sort of thing like that makes no demands on me. What I didn't like was the service, to which I took exception, and that namby-pamby parson's voice. To me, the whole thing was – insincere.'

Mrs Midwinter held up her hand to silence him. 'There's a car stopping outside. It can't be the boys yet.'

From the street, they both heard Geoff's voice shouting good-bye, then a car door was slammed, and the iron gate opened with a whining sound.

'Dad, it's Geoff!' Mrs Midwinter whispered. 'There must have been an accident. Something's happened to Beryl.'

'Well, he sounded cheerful enough about it.'

They could hear Geoff coming unsteadily up the garden path. When Mrs Midwinter threw open the door, he stood blinking at the sudden light, and swaying.

'Geoff! What ever's wrong?'

'I've got wet, Mum, and I've hurt my hand,' Geoff said.

Good-bye, Good-bye

On his last evening in England he broke two promises – one, that he would dine with his brother, and another, older promise made to a woman whom he loved. When he and Catherine had tried, years before, to put an end to this impermissible love for one another the best they could decide was to give it no nourishment and let it wither if it would. 'No messages,' she had said when they parted, 'no letters.' His letters had always incapacitated her: on days when she received them, she moved slowly at her work, possessed by his words, deaf to any others, from husband or children or friends. 'I don't want to know how you are getting on,' she told him, 'or to think of you in any particular place. You might die: you might marry. I never want to know. I want you to stop, here, for ever.' (*Then, there*, an autumn night, a railway station.) As his train moved off he saw that her face had a look of utter perplexity, as if the meaning of her future were beyond her comprehension. The look had stayed in his mind and was in his imagination this evening as he walked from the bus-stop in the village and out on the sea-road towards the house. This house, which she rented each summer for the children's holidays, was where they had sometimes been together. The recklessness, the deceit which, in London, they suppressed, they had indulged here, as if a different sort of behaviour were allowed at the sea-side. Returning to her husband, who had no part in those holidays, she would at once feel so mortified and so uneasily ashamed, that their few meetings were humiliating to them both and full of recriminations and despair; and it was after such a summer that they had parted – for ever, both had believed.

The road under the sea-wall was sheltered. Inland, sheep cropped the salt-marshes where he and Catherine had walked in the evening when the children were in bed. When it was dark, they would kiss and say good-bye, then kiss again. He would walk back to the village along this sea-road and she would tiptoe into the house, so that the children's nurse would not be wakened or discover how late she had stayed out.

Memories agitated him as he walked along the road. The landscape seemed to have awaited him, to have kept itself unchanged to pain him now with a great sense of strangeness. He had no hopes for this visit, no

vestige of confidence in it, knew that it was mistakenly made and fraught
with all perils – her anger, her grief, her embarrassment. In him, love
could not be reawakened, for it had not slept. He did not know what risk
faced her; how she had dealt with her sadness, or laid him away in his
absence. He was compelled to find out, to discover if he were quick or
dead in her mind, and to see if the look – the perplexed expression – had
hardened on her face, or vanished. But as he came round a bend in the
road and saw the chimneys of the house and the beginning of the garden,
he was so appalled by his venture that he walked more slowly and longed
to turn back. He thought: 'She will be changed, look different, wear new
clothes I have never seen, the children will be older, and, oh God,' he
prayed, his heart swerving at the sudden idea, 'let there be no more! Let
her not have had more children! Let her not have filled her life that
way!'

He stopped in the road and listened for children's voices in the garden
but in the still evening the bleating of sheep was the only sound. High up
on the orchard trees red apples shone in the sun. An old net sagged across
the tennis-lawn. The gabled, hideous house with its verandas and balconies
came into view. At the open windows, faded curtains flapped over the
newly-cleaned tennis-shoes bleaching on sills and sandy swim-suits and
towels hung out to dry. The house, which looked as if it had been burst
asunder, and left with all its doors ajar, had a vacant – though only lately
vacant – appearance.

In the conservatory-porch a tabby cat was sleeping on a shelf among
flower-pots and tennis-racquets. A book lying open had all its pages arched
up in the sun and a bunch of wild flowers were dying on a ledge. He pressed
the bell and away at the back of the house heard it ringing. The heat under
the dusty panes made him feel faint and he stepped back from it, away from
the door. As he did so, a girl leant from an upstairs window and called
down to him. 'Do you want Mother?'

Hit by the irony of the words, the shock of seeing Catherine's eyes looking down at him, he could not answer her at once. Her daughter did not
wait for his reply. 'She's on the beach. They're all there. I'm just going, too.
One moment!' She moved from sight, he heard her running downstairs,
then she came to the door.

'You are Sarah?' he said.

'Yes.'

'Oh, Catherine's eyes, those eyes!' he thought. 'The miracle, but the
enormity, that they should come again; clearer, more beautiful' – he would
not think it. 'You don't remember me. I am Peter Lord.'

'I remember the name. I remember *you* now. I had only forgotten. You
came here once and helped us with a picnic on the beach; lit a fire, do you

remember that? It's what they are all doing at this moment. I was waiting for a friend.' She hesitated, looked towards the gate. 'But they didn't come.'

'"They" because she will not say "he",' Peter thought. 'The embarrassments of the English language!' She was bright with some disappointment.

'Shall we go down together and find them?' she asked; then, in the patronising tone young people use when they try to carry on conversations with their elders on equal terms, she asked: 'Let me see, you went abroad, didn't you? Wasn't it South America?'

'South Africa.'

'I always get those two muddled. And now you have come back home again?'

'For a short time. I am off in the morning.'

'Oh, what a pity; but Mother *will* be pleased that you came to say goodbye.'

They crossed the road and climbed the bank to the top of the sea-wall. There they paused. The tide was out and the wet sand far down the beach reflected a pink light from the sun, which was going down in an explosive, Turneresque brilliance above the sand-hillocks. Farther along, they could see figures busily bringing driftwood to a fire and two children at the sea's edge were digging in the sand.

Seeing Peter and Sarah on the skyline, one of the group waved, then turned away again.

'He thinks you are my friend,' Sarah said. She wore Catherine's anxious look. 'That's Chris. Do you remember Chris? He is fifteen – nearly two years younger than me.'

'Yes, I remember him.' Peter was feeling tired now, rather puffed by keeping up with her across a stretch of hot white sand in which his feet sank at every step. This sand, seldom washed by the sea, was full of dried seaweed and bits of old newspapers. Clumps of spiky reed grew in it and sea-poppies and thistles.

'Who are all those other children?' he asked. He stopped and took off his shoes and socks, rolled his trousers above his ankles. 'A fine sight,' he thought crossly. 'Completely ridiculous.'

'Our friends,' said Sarah, turning and waiting for him.

He could see Catherine. She was apart from the others and was bending over a picnic-basket. When Sarah called to her, she turned and, still kneeling in the sand, looked up towards them, her arm shading her eyes. The incredulous look was on her face as if it had never left it and at the sight of the agitation she could not hide from her children and their friends, he realised the full cruelty of his treachery. She took his hand, and recovered enough to hide shock beneath a show of superficial surprise, glossing over the grotesque situation with an hostessy condescension.

'Are you on leave?' Her voice indicated his rôle of old friend of the family.

'No, my father died. I had to come over in a hurry.'

'I am sorry. Graham will be sad when he hears that.'

'So I am to be her husband's comrade, too!' he thought.

As if she were in her drawing-room she invited him to sit down, but before he could do so, the younger children had run up from the sea and stood on either side of their mother, staring in curiosity at him and awaiting an explanation.

They were all variations of her, her four sons and daughters, and these two, a boy and a girl, with their unguarded, childish gaze, were more like her than the other two whose defined features were brightly masked to preserve the secrets of adolescence.

'Lucy, this is Mr Lord. He gave you your fairy-tale book that you love so much.'

'Yes, I do.'

'And this is Ricky.'

'What did you give *me*?' the boy asked.

'I'm sure I don't know. Perhaps you were to share the book.'

'No, it is only mine,' Lucy said certainly.

'He gave you lots of things,' said Catherine.

'More than me?'

'No, Lucy, I am sure not.'

'I think *I* only had the book.'

'This isn't a nice conversation. You should think of other things than what you are given. Go and help Chris to find some firewood. You can't enjoy the fire and the supper if you do nothing to help.'

The children wandered off, but back to the edge of the sea. They left a vacuum. She had tried to fill it with what he disliked and had always thought of as 'fussing with the children' – the children whom he had half-loved, for having her likeness, and half-resented, for not being his, for taking her attention from him and forbidding their life together.

'They've grown,' he said.

'Yes, of course.'

She put her hand deep in the sand, burying it in coolness. He watched her, remembering how once long ago she had done that and he had made a tunnel with his own hand and clasped hers and they had sat in silence, their fingers entwined beneath the sand. Such far-off lovers' games seemed utterly sad now, utterly forlorn, dead, their meaning brushed away like dust.

'Why did you come?' she whispered, her eyes fixed on the young ones building their fire; but fearing his answer, she caught her breath and called to her son. 'Chris, darling, bring the others over to meet Mr Lord.'

They came over, polite and estranged, willing to be kind. Chris hadn't remembered, but now he did. He introduced his friends, the same bright, polite boys and girls as himself. The boys called him 'sir', the girls smiled warmly and encouragingly. 'You are quite welcome, don't feel out of it – the fun, the lovely evening – just because you are old,' their smiles said.

They diminished Catherine. They were all taller. She seemed to Peter now to be set apart as 'mother', their voices were protective to her, undemanding. (Once they had clamoured for her attention, claimed every second. 'Look at me, Mummy! Look at me!') They had set her firmly in her present rôle and, instinctively, they made her part quite clear to Peter.

They returned to the fire. Chris was peeling sticks and sharpening the ends so that they could hold sausages over the fire to cook.

'What about the children?' Sarah asked. 'How long are you staying, Mother?'

This was Catherine's dilemma which she had been pondering as she sat there with her hand buried in the sand.

'They can stay up,' she said. 'We will all stay. It will be a special treat for the little ones and they can sleep late in the morning. You others shall have a party on your own another night.'

She looked away from Sarah and her voice was gentle, for she knew that *this* could not be Sarah's special night, that the girl was desperate with disappointment. 'This evening is nothing,' Catherine tried to imply. 'There will be so many others for you.'

'We always like it better if you are here,' Sarah said. 'I was wondering about the children.' She dreaded that her mother should feel old or left out, and she often was alone on these long holidays. Peter's presence lightened the load of responsibility she felt towards her. For an hour or two, Catherine had someone of her own and Sarah could let go of her, could turn back to her own secrets, aloof, in love.

'Has she a confidante among the other girls?' Catherine wondered. Remembering her own girlhood she did not hope to be confided in herself; the very last, she knew – even if first to know, before Sarah sometimes, yet still the last of all to be told.

If she had taken Lucy and Ricky home to bed, Peter would have gone with her. Then they would be alone and nothing could prevent him from talking to her. To stay where she was not much wanted and to endure an evening of social exchanges before the children – painful though it must be – would be less menacing than that.

She turned to the picnic-basket, put a loaf of bread on a board and began to cut it into slices. 'You haven't changed much,' she said. 'Are you happy in South Africa and is the work interesting? How is your brother?'

'I had no intention of coming here, but suddenly, this morning, it seemed so unreasonable, so falsely dramatic – our promise.'

'No, sensible.'

'I'm sorry I gave no warning.'

'You could have telephoned,' she said lightly, her back turned to him.

'You would have said "No".'

She wrapped the slices of bread in a napkin and put them back in the hamper. 'Being needlessly busy,' he thought. 'Fussing with the children, anything to exclude me.'

'You *would* have said "No", wouldn't you?'

'Yes, of course.'

'You haven't changed either,' he said at last, dutifully.

She was smoothing her hair, thinking, 'I don't know what I look like.' She wished that she could glance in a mirror, or that she had done so before she had left the house.

In her brown hair, some strands, coarser than the others, were silver. Fine lines crossed her forehead, and deeper ones curved from the corners of her eyes.

'Graham all right?' he asked.

'Yes, very well. Very busy. He gets tired.'

'And bloody cross, I bet,' Peter thought. He imagined the tetchy, pompous little man, returning from the city, briefcase full of documents and stomach full of bile.

'And is he as rich as ever?' he asked.

'I've noticed no difference,' Catherine said angrily. 'Have *you* prospered? You always had such money-troubles.'

'Father's dying should help.'

He had always refused to see Graham as anything but a monstrous begetter of money and children, and showed himself up in contrast – the bachelor beyond the gates, without home or family, whose schemes came to nothing as his love-making came to nothing, neither bearing fruit. His insistence on her wealth was partly from a feeling that she had shared too much with her husband and he could not bear her to share any more, not even anxieties about money.

'They are nice children,' he said, looking on the sunnier side of her marriage. 'A great credit to you.'

'Thank you.' Her eyes filled with tears and at that moment Sarah, standing by the fire, turned and looked curiously at her, then at Peter.

The fire was burning high and the young people moved about it continually as if performing some ceremony. As the sun went down, shadows fell across the beach from the sea-wall, cooling the sand quickly. Catherine spread out a rug for Peter to sit on and then sat down herself on a corner of it, as far from him as she could.

'Come by the fire,' Chris shouted to her.

'It is too smoky for her,' said Sarah.

'Not on the other side.'

'It blows about.'

Catherine had not asked her the one question she had dreaded – 'He didn't come then?' – and so in turn she would protect her mother. She, Sarah, no longer prayed for him to come, for her thoughts of him were angry now. Absorbed in this anger, she asked only that no one should speak of him. Waiting for him and the gradual loss of hope had been destructive, and a corrosive indignation worked on her love; it became non-love, then nothing.

'Is that Ronnie coming?' Chris asked, mopping his eyes with a hand-kerchief, waving away smoke.

A figure in the dusk appeared on the sea-wall, then a dog followed and flew down through the sand, crashed over the stretch of loose shingle to the wet, runnelled sands where the children worked, murmuring and intent, over their digging. Lucy cried out as the dog bounded towards her and a man's voice – nothing like Ronnie's – called the dog back.

Sarah was glad that she had not moved forward to wave or made any mistake. Standing quite still by the fire, she had kept her patience; but all the carefully-tended hatred had vanished in those few seconds, love had come hurrying back with hope and forgiving. 'It is worse for her now,' Catherine thought, and she felt hostility towards men. 'As it is worse for me.'

The man and the dog disappeared. Lucy and Ricky, disturbed into real-isation of the darkness falling, began to trail up from the sea. The water between the hard ribs of sand felt cold to their bare feet and they came up to the bonfire and stood watching it, at the fringe of their elders and bet-ters who laughed and danced and waved their speared sausages in the air to cool.

'Let them cook their own,' said Catherine, and Chris handed the little ones two sticks and fixed on the sausages for them. They stood by the fire holding the sticks waveringly over the flames. Once, Ricky's nervousness broke into a laugh, his serious expression disintegrated into excited pleas-ure. 'It will never cook like that,' Chris said. 'Keep it to the hot part of the fire.' He sighed affectedly and murmured 'Pesky kids' to one of the girls, who said haughtily: 'I think they're sweet.'

'They're all yours, then,' said lordly Chris.

'I never had anything like this when I was young,' Peter said. 'I didn't even know any girls.'

The children had their feast and Catherine and Peter sat and watched them; even, Catherine thought, in Peter's case, sat in judgement on them – 'as if he were their father and jealous of their youth, saying "*I* didn't have this or do that when *I* was a boy; but was made to do such and such, and go without et cetera, and be grateful for nothing. And look at me ..." If he were their father, that is how he would be; if he had not come back to me this evening, I should never have thought such a thing of him. How I loved you, my darling, darling. The passion of tears, the groping bewilderment of being without you, the rhythm of long boredom and abrupt grief, that I endured because of you; then my prayers, my prayers especially that Sarah shall have a happier time, and a more fortunate love.'

The children brought them sausages wrapped in bread. The young girls were attentive to Catherine. 'I *adore* your jersey,' one said, and Catherine would not conceal her pleasure. 'But it's so old. It's Chris's, really.'

'Then you shouldn't let him have it back,' the girl said. '*He* couldn't look so nice in it.'

'All right!' said Chris. 'You may cook your own sausages now. Didn't you know that the whole family wear my old cast-offs?'

'Not I,' said Sarah.

'Not I,' said Lucy.

Peter had glanced at the jersey in annoyance. He was beginning, Catherine knew, to harden against Chris, identifying him with his father, comparing himself and his own lost opportunities with the boy and the life lying before him. When Chris brought sausages, said 'For you, sir', he refused to eat.

'Then coffee,' Catherine suggested, beginning to unscrew a flask.

'Oh, dear, it is so cold,' Lucy cried, and she flung herself against Catherine's thighs, burrowing under her arm.

'Steady, my love, I can't pour out,' Catherine said, and she held the flask and the cup high out of reach and for the first time looked truly at Peter and laughed.

'Come to me, then,' he said, and he lifted Lucy away and held her to him. She lolled against him, her salty, sticky hair touching his cheek. 'That isn't good for you,' he said, taking the half-eaten sausage, which was pink inside, uncooked, and throwing it away across the sand.

'Fishes will eat it,' Ricky said. 'When the tide comes up.'

'Coffee!' Catherine called out and they came over to fetch it, then went back to gather round the dying fire. The girls began to sing, one of their school songs, which the boys did not know and Chris said: 'What a filthy row.'

'Did you read that fairy book to me when I was in bed?' Lucy asked Peter drowsily.

'I don't know.'

'Yes, you did.'

'Do you remember then?'

'No, Mummy told me.'

Then Catherine had talked of him! He had often wanted to talk to someone about *her*, to say her name. In Africa, he had nicknamed a little native girl – his servant's child – 'Catherine', for the sake of saying the name occasionally. 'Good-morning, Catherine' or 'What a pretty frock, Catherine!' The child could not understand English. He might, he had sometimes thought, have said anything, out loud, bold and clear. 'I cannot forget you, Catherine, and my life is useless without you.'

Lucy had crawled inside his jacket for warmth, he rubbed her cold, sandy legs, held her bare feet, and once kissed her forehead. Catherine sipped her coffee, looking away from this display of tenderness, thinking: 'A barren evening. Nothing said; nothing felt, but pain. The wheel starting to creak again, starting to revolve in agony.'

'If any ... regrets ... have arisen from my visit,' Peter said, trying to speak obscurely, above Lucy's head in two senses, 'I couldn't blame myself more or detest my own egotism.'

'There is no need to say anything,' she said hurriedly. 'No need at all. I would rather you didn't.'

'Are you ... ?'

'No,' she interrupted him, afraid of what Lucy might hear. 'Am I what?' she wondered. 'I am in love with you still. In love, certainly. And there isn't a way out and never will be now.'

Her eyes might say this without Lucy knowing, and she turned to him so that before he went away he could be a witness to her constancy; but their situation was changed now; the observant eyes of the children were on them, Sarah's, the other girls', and Chris, brusque and guarded, goodness knew what thoughts *he* had about her.

'I shall soon have to go,' Peter said and as he glanced at his watch, Lucy pushed herself closer to him, almost asleep.

Singing together now, the girls and boys were beginning to pack up – one of the girls turned cartwheels, and Sarah suddenly spun round, her bell-like skirt flying out.

'Are you staying at the pub?' Catherine asked.

'No, I am catching the last bus, then the last train.'

'The last train,' Lucy murmured cosily, as if there were no such thing save in a story he was telling her.

Catherine shivered.

'Are you sure you won't write to me?' Peter asked her, as quietly as he could. 'Or let me write to you?'

'Quite sure.'

'She will,' said Lucy. 'She writes to Sarah and Chris every day when they are at school.'

'Then there wouldn't be time for me,' said Peter.

Catherine packed the basket wishing that she might pack up the evening, too, and all that it had brought to the light, but it lay untidily about them. The children ran to and fro, clearing up, exhilarated by the darkness and the sound of the sea, the tide coming up across the sands, one wave unrolling under the spray of the next. The boys took the baskets and the girls looked the beach over, as if it were a room in some home of their own which they wished to leave tidy until they returned.

'Who will remember the evening?' Catherine wondered. 'Perhaps only he and I, and Sarah.' Little Ricky had attached himself to the others as they left the beach. He walked beside Sarah, clinging to her skirt. Peter had Lucy on his back, his shoes dangling by their laces round his neck as he walked unsteadily on the cold, loose sand.

'We live only once,' he said.

'Of course,' said Lucy, awake now and laughing. She wriggled her sandy feet, trying to force them into the pockets of his jacket.

'Lucy, sit still or walk,' her mother said sharply.

A little surprised, she sat still for a bit and then, when she could see the house, the lights going on as the others went indoors, she slipped down and ran away from Peter, down the bank and across the lane.

Catherine and Peter sat down just below the sea-wall and put on their shoes.

'Will you forgive me?' he asked.

'I might have done the same.'

'There is far too much to say for us to begin talking.'

'And no time,' she said. She fastened her sandals, then looked up at the sky, as if she were scanning it anxiously for some weather-sign, but he knew that she was waiting for tears to recede, her head high, breath held. If he kissed her, she would fail, would break, weep, betray herself to the children. 'To have thought of her so long, imagined, dreamed, called that child "Catherine" for her sake, started at the sight of her name printed in a book, pretended her voice to myself, called her in my sleep, and now sit close to her and it is almost over.' He stood up and took her hand, helping her to her feet.

In the lane the children were trying one another's bicycles, the lamp light swung over the road and hedges. Lucy was crying and Sarah attempted to comfort her, but impatiently. 'The same old story,' she told her mother. 'Stayed up too late.'

'Yes, she did.'

'I didn't undo my sand-castle,' Lucy roared.

'Hush, dear. It doesn't matter.'

'I like to undo it. You know I like to undo it and now the sea will get it.'

'It doesn't matter.'

'Don't *say* it doesn't matter.'

'Peter, do borrow Chris's bicycle. You can leave it at the pub and he can fetch it tomorrow.'

'I like the walk.'

'I am not leaving her like that,' he thought, 'not bicycling off up the road with a mob of adolescents.'

'Good-bye, and thank you for the picnic,' the children began to say, coming one after another to shake hands with Catherine.

'You should have *reminded* me,' shrieked Lucy, at the end of her tether.

'Oh, Christ . . . ' said Chris.

'Chris, I won't have that,' said Catherine.

'Good-bye, and thank you so much.'

'I hope you will come again.'

'Good-bye, good-bye,' Chris shouted.

They swung on to their bicycles and began to ride away, turning often to wave.

'Good-bye, Fanny! Good-bye, Sue!' Chris shouted.

The voices came back, as the lights bobbed along the lane. 'Good-bye, Sarah! Good-bye, Chris!'

Sarah called once, then she shook hands with Peter and turned towards the house, gathering up Ricky, who was swinging on the gate as if hypnotised, too tired to make the next step.

'Good-bye, Catherine, or I shall miss the bus.'

'Yes. Good-bye, Peter.'

'Take care of yourself. And *you* take care of her,' he said to Chris with bright jocularity, as he began to walk away down the road.

'What, my dear old mum?' Chris said, and flung his arm across her shoulder so that she staggered slightly. Then, hearing a faint cry in the distance he rushed from her into the middle of the road and shouted again, his hands cupped to his mouth. 'Good-bye, good-bye.'

For Thine is the Power

Coming down the hill in the bus. The tyres lick the hot road. Four o'clock is dazzling. Down the new roads of the estate, the houses ranked shoulder to shoulder; thin trees let down into the asphalt; double daisies, dirty pink, dirty white, with dirt scraped up round them, in the new gardens descending the hill.

Eva moued, fringing her mauve ticket, her case lying squarely on her lap. When you opened it, out flew the smell of cardboard and egg sandwiches and rubber soles.

'—noon miss. G'bye miss.' Some of her class shuffling by her down on the gangway, getting off the bus. Once by, sniggering behind hands. In the front panel her reflection, striped silk dress, felt hat, glasses. Eva. What others saw. The children. Shooting up their arms in class. 'Miss! Miss!' She hated them, really, thinking she loved them. And they hated her, drawing her with bits of chalk on bridges and blank walls among obscenities, plaguing her subtly with their sycophancy. 'Miss! Miss!' It rang in her ears at night. At night, lying in bed, dividing up the day into what she had approved and what she had not. Condemning what she was denied and sentimentalising what she dared not condemn. Closing her mind firmly, snapping it up, on little shafts of truth which threatened it. (That it was odd her headache kept her away from week-night service when the old Vicar was taking them. But was clear as a bell on young Mr Beaver's nights.)

'Craigie Avenue.' The bus still but shuddering while she pushed her way out, case held in front.

Up in the avenue laburnums were out. She didn't see them, going on with her head bent, the pain beginning again as soon as she stood up, the pain descending again through her body, like tiredness drawn down to one point, crystallised, her body a shaft for the pain to drop down. She dragged up the hill in the heat, between rowan trees and the board fences of gardens. At Abercrombie she trailed up the path and opened the door. Empty house, you could tell at once, by the smell and sound of it and the tick of the clock. Her tea laid on a corner of the plush cloth. Slices of bread-and-butter, curling up at the edges; the stub-end of a cucumber; the waxen-looking cake dotted with sultanas. She made tea, reaching her horoscope in the paper. Step out today; sign letters; grasp opportunities. That's what she ought to do.

She dropped sugar in – three. 'I'm sweet enough already,' Ada would say, shaking her head. Ada. 'I thought you *knew*.' That was another of the things she was always saying, having shattered your world. The one before Mr Beaver, who left and got married, took another living, anyway. 'She's *sweet*. I thought you *knew*.'

And this morning, drinking tea at eleven, elbows on the *Daily Sketch*, while the children raced and shrieked across the asphalt and the whistle blew. In a corner, whispering together.

'Well,' said Eva, blushes engulfing her. 'He said something about ovaries.' Her voice swerved.

'Who is it?'

'Dr Petrie.'

The eyes lengthening, surveying her above the cup of tea.

'I'm surprised you went to him.'

'Oh, why?' He ... he's oldish, and *nice* – as nice as he could be, I suppose.'

'Oh, I expect he's *nice*. That's hardly the point when one's reputation's involved.'

'I don't see ...' After all, Ada had made her go, worrying about her cancer. And one day, seeing it on the surgery door – Gerald Petrie, M.R.C.S. – she had swung it suddenly in, not knowing how she would ever say it, but had, with his help.

'In Manchester, I think,' said Ada. 'Pretty serious for him. Interfering with one of his patients. A young girl. Wonder he wasn't struck off. But I quite thought you *knew*.'

And now she had to go again. This evening. Her hands were damp over the bread-and-butter. That sort of man. And he seemed so kind. Too kind, perhaps. Visions of the forbidden made her inside plunge wildly. She drank her tea and fetched her Chain Library book. The sweet, tasteless tea and the sweet, tasteless story.

At half-past five she went and washed and got ready. Mrs Profitt came back.

'Just off to the doctor's about my indigestion,' said Eva.

'I'm surprised he never gave you no peppermint,' Mrs Profitt said, unrolling a haddock on the draining-board. 'Always gives me a bottle. That shifts it like nothing else I know.'

'Perhaps he will, then,' said Eva, setting off, scarlet at her own duplicity.

The shadows, longer, deeper now, lying down the avenue. There it was, as soon as she put her feet to the ground, the pain gathering itself together, like an animal that has lain in wait. That pounced on her as she stood on hot afternoons, the whistle round her neck on the teeming playground.

So she took the quick cut over the fields to the town, the grass short and slippery and full of thistles. The unemployed walked here with dogs and prams, listless and oppressed. Plumes of smoke rose stiffly off the town in the valley.

In the waiting-room she sat with cold hands and feet, her nostrils sickened by the rich smell of the *Sketch*, the *Tatler*, her bowels turned to water, it seemed, by nervousness and dread.

'Any improvement?' he asked, the man going grey in the white room with the brown linoleum, signalling her to the chair.

'No.' Her eyes riveted on him, fascinated.

'Oh, come now. Not even a little?'

She shook her head.

'Well, then, I'll examine you today. Unloosen your clothes and lie down, will you?'

He turned away. He began to wash his hands. Behind the screen, shaking, fearful, charged, she unclasped her pink corsets and lay down. The noise her heart. The walls covered with grained paper, imitating wood.

He came and laid his hand on her side, pressing intolerably. As if he were a snake she watched him, horrified. 'How dare he,' she thought. 'In Manchester. I thought you knew. A young girl.' But she wasn't young and his eyes fixed on the wallpaper were vague, impersonal. 'Interfering with one of his patients.' The way thoughts leapt up quite uncontrolled. What he had done. And how did she know? Out of what steaming stew of her mind emerged the cool and certain picture of what he had done, might do to her, lying here, defenceless and exposed.

'OK,' he said, moving away, leaving her.

'OK,' he said. Stupidly she fastened her corsets. Back at the desk, couldn't listen. Greying hair and tired voice. 'I love him. I loathe him,' she thought hysterically.

She waited for her medicine and clutching the white, red-sealed parcel set off home, something destroyed in her. Back across the scented fields. The men on allotments. Children shouting. Tomorrow, school, and the children shouting. At the top of the hill a decaying haystack, dark and hacked away. The pain dragged at her. She went and sat down, leaning against the wall of the haystack, facing the valley which began to blossom faintly with lights. She sat there for a long time, until it grew nearly dark, and voices on the other side of the haystack disturbed her. She got up, clasping her bottle of medicine, and walked round the stack to the footpath.

'Silly!' giggled the girl, lying on her back in the darkness of the wall of hay. She rolled her head from side to side teasingly to avoid his kisses, the man pressing her down into the grass with the weight of his body.

Eva reached the footpath. Stumbled back home. How dare they! She felt filthy, just seeing them.

'Did he give you anything?' Mrs Profitt asked, coming in from the kitchen. There was a damp steam of haddock everywhere. 'Well, what's wrong?'

For Eva slumped forward over the table, dropping her parcel, retching up dreadful sobs. 'The filthy, filthy, filthy, filthy ...' she babbled.

'Filthy what?' asked Mrs Profitt.

And then Eva sat up as if she saw visions before her.

'The doctor,' she said quietly. 'He – he – insulted me.'

'Insulted? How?'

'I can't tell you.' She dropped her head and began to sob again on her silk sleeve.

At last Mrs Profitt gasped: 'You don't mean interfered with you?'

'Tried,' said Eva, drumming her fists on the table, blotting out those two under the haystack.

It took no time for Mrs Profitt to turn the gas low and put on her hat.

'See to that haddock. I'm going straight to the police. Dirty monkey! Upsetting a decent girl like you.' Off she went. Eva tormented, the picture of those two writhing on the hay, went and stuck a fork in the fish, moving like a sleepwalker.

'You can't be sorry for a man like that,' said Ada vehemently, drinking her sugarless tea. 'With a wife and children, too. He ought to think of them. And decent girls. Why doesn't he go after his own kind? But they never do.'

'No,' said Eva.

'Well, it's stopped his tricks. Serve him right. He shouldn't abuse his position.'

'What will he do?' Eva asked herself. Wife and children. Going grey a bit at the sides. Kind, but impersonal. 'What have I done? What's left to him?'

Ada's eyes followed her everywhere with a new kind of filthy respect. She put down her cup and picked up a pile of books. 'What's left to him?' she wondered. And then a surge of anger rose up in her, drove the colour up her neck into her face. 'But he shouldn't have done it,' she thought, clenching her fingers up, going downstairs to the class-room. 'Dirty monkey. Serves him right. He shouldn't have done it.'

Poor Girl

Miss Chasty's first pupil was a flirtatious little boy. At seven years, he was alarmingly precocious, and sometimes she thought that he despised his childhood, regarding it as a waiting time which he used only as a rehearsal for adult life. He was already more sophisticated than his young governess and disturbed her with his air of dalliance, the mockery with which he set about his lessons, the preposterous conversations he led her into, guiding her skilfully away from work, confusing her with bizarre conjectures and irreverent ideas, so that she would clasp her hands tightly under the plush table-cloth and pray that his father would not choose such a moment to observe her teaching, coming in abruptly as he sometimes did and signalling to her to continue the lesson.

At those times, his son's eyes were especially lively, fixed cruelly upon his governess as he listened, smiling faintly, to her faltering voice, measuring her timidity. He would answer her questions correctly, but significantly, as if he knew that by his aptitude he rescued her from dismissal. There were many governesses waiting employment, he implied – and this was so at the beginning of the century. He underlined her good fortune at having a pupil who could so easily learn, could display the results of her teaching to such an advantage for the benefit of the rather sombre, pompous figure seated at the window. When his father, apparently satisfied, had left them without a word, the boy's manner changed. He seemed fatigued and too absent-minded to reply to any more questions.

'Hilary!' she would say sharply. 'Are you attending to me?' Her sharpness and her foolishness amused him, coming as he knew they did from the tension of the last ten minutes.

'Why, my dear girl, of course.'

'You must address me by my name.'

'Certainly, dear Florence.'

'Miss Chasty.'

His lips might shape the words, which he was too weary to say.

Sometimes, when she was correcting his sums, he would come round the table to stand beside her, leaning against her heavily, looking closely at her face, not at his book, breathing steadily down his nose so that tendrils of hair wavered on her neck and against her cheeks. His stillness, his concentration on her and his too heavy leaning, worried her. She felt something experimental in his attitude, as if he were not leaning against her at all, but against someone in the future. 'He is only a baby,' she reminded herself, but she would try to shift from him, feeling a vague distaste. She would blush, as if he were a grown man, and her heart could be heard beating quickly. He was aware of this and would take up the corrected book and move back to his place.

Once he proposed to her and she had the feeling that it was a proposal-rehearsal and that he was making use of her, as an actor might ask her to hear his lines.

'You must go on with your work,' she said.

'I can shade in a map and talk as well.'

'Then talk sensibly.'

'You think I am too young, I dare say; but you could wait for me to grow up, I can do that quickly enough.'

'You are far from grown-up at the moment.'

'You only say these things because you think that governesses ought to. I suppose you don't know how governesses go on, because you have never been one until now, and you were too poor to have one of your own when you were young.'

'That is impertinent, Hilary.'

'You once told me your father couldn't afford one.'

'Which is a different way of putting it.'

'I shouldn't have thought they cost much.' He had a way of just making a remark, of breathing it so gently that it was scarcely said, and might conveniently be ignored.

He was a dandified boy. His smooth hair was like a silk cap, combed straight from the crown to a level line above his topaz eyes. His sailor-suits were spotless. The usual boldness changed to an agonised fussiness if his serge sleeve brushed against chalk or if he should slip on the grassy terrace and stain his clothes with green. On their afternoon walks he took no risks and Florence, who had younger brothers, urged him in vain to climb a tree or jump across puddles. At first, she thought him intimidated by his mother or nurse; but soon she realised that his mother entirely indulged him and the nurse had her thoughts all bent upon the new baby; his fussiness was just another part of his grown-upness come too soon.

The house was comfortable, although to Florence rather too sealed-up and overheated after her own damp and draughty home. Her work was not hard and her loneliness only what she had expected. Cut off from the kitchen by her education, she lacked the feuds and camaraderie, gossip and cups of tea, which make life more interesting for the domestic staff.

None of the maids – coming to light the lamp at dusk or laying the schoolroom-table for tea – ever presumed beyond a remark or two about the weather.

One late afternoon, she and Hilary returned from their walk and found the lamps already lit. Florence went to her room to tidy herself before tea. When she came down to the schoolroom, Hilary was already there, sitting on the window-seat and staring out over the park as his father did. The room was bright and warm and a maid had put a white cloth over the plush one and was beginning to lay the table.

The air was full of a heavy scent, dry and musky. To Florence, it smelt quite unlike the eau de cologne she sometimes sprinkled on her handkerchief, when she had a headache, and she disapproved so much that she returned the maid's greeting coldly and bade Hilary open the window.

'Open the window, dear girl?' he said. 'We shall catch our very deaths.'

'You will do as I ask and remember in future how to address me.'

She was angry with the maid – who now seemed to her an immoral creature – and angry to be humiliated before her.

'But why?' asked Hilary.

'I don't approve of my schoolroom being turned into a scented bower.' She kept her back to the room and was trembling, for she had never rebuked a servant before.

'I approve of it,' Hilary said, sniffing loudly.

'I think it's lovely,' the maid said. 'I noticed it as soon as I opened the door.'

'Is this some joke, Hilary?' Florence asked when the girl had gone.

'No. What?'

'This smell in the room?'

'No. You smell of it most, anyhow.' He put his nose to her sleeve and breathed deeply.

It seemed to Florence that this was so, that her clothes had caught the perfume among the folds. She lifted her palms to her face, then went to the window and leant out into the air as far as she could.

'Shall I pour out the tea, dear girl?'

'Yes, please.'

She took her place at the table abstractedly, and as she drank her tea she stared about the room, frowning. When Hilary's mother looked in, as she often did at this time, Florence stood up in a startled way.

'Good-evening, Mrs Wilson. Hilary, put a chair for your mamma.'

'Don't let me disturb you.'

Mrs Wilson sank into the rocking-chair by the fire and gently tipped to and fro.

'Have you finished your tea, darling boy?' she asked. 'Are you going to read me a story from your book? Oh, there is Lady scratching at the door. Let her in for Mamma.'

Hilary opened the door and a bald old pug-dog with bloodshot eyes waddled in.

'Come, Lady! Beautiful one. Come to mistress! What is wrong with her, poor pet lamb?'

The bitch had stepped just inside the room and lifted her head and howled. 'What has frightened her, then? Come, beauty! Coax her with a sponge-cake, Hilary.'

She reached forward to the table to take the dish and doing so noticed Florence's empty teacup. On the rim was a crimson smear, like the imprint of a lip. She gave a sponge-finger to Hilary, who tried to quieten the pug, then she leaned back in her chair and studied Florence again as she had studied her when she engaged her a few weeks earlier. The girl's looks were appropriate enough, appropriate to a clergyman's daughter and a governess. Her square chin looked resolute, her green eyes innocent, her dress was modest and unbecoming. Yet Mrs Wilson could detect an excitability, even feverishness, which she had not noticed before and she wondered if she had mistaken guardedness for innocence and deceit for modesty.

She was reaching this conclusion – rocking back and forth – when she saw Florence's hand stretch out and turn the cup round in its saucer so that the red stain was out of sight.

'What is wrong with Lady?' Hilary asked, for the dog would not be pacified with sponge-fingers, but kept making barking advances farther into the room, then growling in retreat.

'Perhaps she is crying at the new moon,' said Florence and she went to the window and drew back the curtain. As she moved, her skirts rustled. 'If she has silk underwear as well!' Mrs Wilson thought. She had clearly heard the sound of taffetas, and she imagined the drab, shiny alpaca dress concealing frivolity and wantonness.

'Open the door, Hilary,' she said. 'I will take Lady away. Vernon shall give her a run in the park. I think a quiet read for Hilary and then an early bed-time, Miss Chasty. He looks pale this evening.'

'Yes, Mrs Wilson.' Florence stood respectfully by the table, hiding the cup.

'The hypocrisy!' Mrs Wilson thought and she trembled as she crossed the landing and went downstairs.

She hesitated to tell her husband of her uneasiness, knowing his susceptibilities to the kind of women whom his conscience taught him to deplore. Hidden below the apparent urbanity of their married life were old unhappinesses – little acts of treachery and disloyalty which pained her to remember, bruises upon her peace of mind and her pride: letters found, a pretty maid dismissed, an actress who had blackmailed him. As he read the

Lesson in church, looking so perfectly upright and honourable a man, she sometimes thought of his escapades; but not with bitterness or cynicism, only with pain at her memories and a whisper of fear about the future. For some time she had been spared those whispers and had hoped that their marriage had at last achieved its calm. To speak of Florence as she must might both arouse his curiosity and revive the past. Nevertheless, she had her duty to her son to fulfil and her own anger to appease and she opened the library door very determinedly.

'Oliver, I am sorry to interrupt your work, but I must speak to you.'

He put down the *Strand Magazine* quite happily, aware that she was not a sarcastic woman.

Oliver and his son were extraordinarily alike. 'As soon as Hilary has grown a moustache we shall not know them apart,' Mrs Wilson often said, and her husband liked this little joke which made him feel more youthful. He did not know that she added a silent prayer – 'O God, please do not let him *be* like him, though.'

'You seem troubled, Louise.' His voice was rich and authoritative. He enjoyed setting to rights her little domestic flurries and waited indulgently to hear of some tradesman's misdemeanour or servant's laziness.

'Yes, I am troubled about Miss Chasty.'

'Little Miss Mouse? I was rather troubled myself. I noticed two spelling faults in Hilary's botany essay, which she claimed to have corrected. I said nothing before the boy, but I shall acquaint her with it when the opportunity arises.'

'Do you often go to the schoolroom, then?'

'From time to time. I like to be sure that our choice was wise.'

'It was not. It was misguided and unwise.'

'All young people seem slip-shod nowadays.'

'She is more than slip-shod. I believe she should go. I think she is quite brazen. Oh, yes, I should have laughed at that myself if it had been said to me an hour ago, but I have just come from the schoolroom and it occurs to me that now she has settled down and feels more secure – since you pass over her mistakes – she is beginning to take advantage of your leniency and to show herself in her true colours. I felt a sinister atmosphere up there, and I am quite upset and exhausted by it. I went up to hear Hilary's reading. They were finishing tea and the room was full of the most overpowering scent, *her* scent. It was disgusting.'

'Unpleasant?'

'No, not at all. But upsetting.'

'Disturbing?'

She would not look at him or reply, hearing no more indulgence or condescension in his voice, but the quality of warming interest.

'And then I saw her teacup and there was a mark on it – a red smear where her lips had touched it. She did not know I saw it and as soon as she noticed it herself she turned it round, away from me. She is an immoral woman and she has come into our house to teach our son.'

'I have never noticed a trace of artificiality in her looks. It seemed to me that she was rather colourless.'

'She has been sly. This evening she looked quite different, quite flushed and excitable. I know that she had rouged her lips or painted them or whatever those women do.' Her eyes filled with tears.

'I shall observe her for a day or two,' Oliver said, trying to keep antici-pation from his voice.

'I should like her to go at once.'

'Never act rashly. She is entitled to a quarter's notice unless there is definite blame. We should make ourselves very foolish if you have been mistaken. Oh, I know that you are sure; but it has been known for you to misjudge others. I shall take stock of her and decide if she is unsuitable. She is still Miss Mouse to me and I cannot think otherwise until I see the evidence with my own eyes.'

'There was something else as well,' Mrs Wilson said wretchedly.

'And what was that?'

'I would rather not say.' She had changed her mind about further accus-ations. Silk underwear would prove, she guessed, too inflammatory.

'I shall go up ostensibly to mention Hilary's spelling faults.' He could not go fast enough and stood up at once.

'But Hilary is in bed.'

'I could not mention the spelling faults if he were not.'

'Shall I come with you?'

'My dear Louise, why should you? It would look very strange – a depu-tation about two spelling faults.'

'Then don't be long, will you? I hope you won't be long.'

He went to the schoolroom, but there was no one there. Hilary's story-book lay closed upon the table and Miss Chasty's sewing was folded neatly. As he was standing there looking about him and sniffing hard, a maid came in with a tray of crockery.

'Has Master Hilary gone to bed?' he asked, feeling rather foolish and confused.

The only scent in the air was a distinct smell – even a haze – of cigarette smoke.

'Yes, sir.'

'And Miss Chasty – where is she?'

'She went to bed, too, sir.'

'Is she unwell?'

'She spoke of a chronic head, sir.'

The maid stacked the cups and saucers in the cupboard and went out. Nothing was wrong with the room apart from the smell of smoke and Mr Wilson went downstairs. His wife was waiting in the hall. She looked up expectantly, in some relief at seeing him so soon.

'Nothing,' he said dramatically. 'She has gone to bed with a headache. No wonder she looked feverish.'

'You noticed the scent.'

'There was none,' he said. 'No trace. Nothing. Just imagination, dear Louise. I thought that it must be so.'

He went to the library and took up his magazine again, but he was too disturbed to read and thought with impatience of the following day.

Florence could not sleep. She had gone to her room, not with a headache but to escape conversations until she had faced the predicament alone. This she was doing, lying on the honeycomb quilt which, since maids do not wait on governesses, had not been turned down.

The schoolroom this evening seemed to have been wreathed about with a strange miasma; the innocent nature of the place polluted in a way that she could not understand or have explained. Something new, it seemed, had entered the room – the scent had clung about her clothes; the stained cup was her own cup, and her handkerchief with which she had rubbed it clean was still reddened; and finally, as she stared in the mirror, trying to re-establish her personality, the affected little laugh which startled her had come from herself. It had driven her from the room.

'I cannot explain the inexplicable,' she thought wearily and began to prepare herself for bed. Homesickness hit her like a blow on the head. 'Whatever they do to me, I have always my home,' she promised herself. But she could not think who 'they' might be; for no one in this house had threatened her. Mrs Wilson had done no more than irritate her with her commonplace fussing over Hilary and her dog, and Florence was prepared to overcome much more than irritation. Mr Wilson's pomposity, his constant watch on her works, intimidated her, but she knew that all who must earn their living must have fears lest their work should not seem worth the wages. Hilary was easy to manage; she had quickly seen that she could always deflect him from rebelliousness by opening a new subject for conversation; any idea would be a counter-attraction to naughtiness; he wanted her to sharpen his wits upon. 'And is that all that teaching is, or should be?' she had wondered. The servants had been good to her, realising that she would demand nothing of them. She had suffered great loneliness, but had foreseen it as part of her position. Now she felt fear nudging it away. 'I am not lonely any more,' she thought. 'I am not alone any more. And I have lost something.' She said her prayers; then, sitting up in bed, kept the candle alight while she brushed her hair and read the Bible.

'Perhaps I have lost my reason,' she suddenly thought, resting her finger on her place in the Psalms. She lifted her head and saw her shadow stretch up the powdery, rose-sprinkled wall. 'How can I keep that secret?' she wondered. 'When there is no one to help me do it? Only those who are watching to see it happen.'

She was not afraid in her bedroom as she had been in the schoolroom, but her perplexed mind found no replies to its questions. She blew out the candle and tried to fall asleep, but lay and cried for a long time, and yearned to be at home again and comforted in her mother's arms.

In the morning she met kind enquiries. Nurse was so full of solicitude that Florence felt guilty. 'I came up with a warm drink and put my head round the door but you were in the land of Nod so I drank it myself. I should take a grey powder; or I could mix you a gargle. There are a lot of throats about.'

'I am quite better this morning,' said Florence and she felt calmer as she sat down at the schoolroom-table with Hilary. 'Yet, it was all true,' her reason whispered. 'The morning hasn't altered that.'

'You have been crying,' said Hilary. 'Your eyes are red.'

'Sometimes people's eyes are red from other causes – headaches and colds.' She smiled brightly.

'And sometimes from crying, as I said. I should think usually from crying.'

'Page fifty-one,' she said, locking her hands together in her lap.

'Very well.' He opened the book, pressed down the pages and lowered his nose to them, breathing the smell of print. 'He is utterly sensuous,' she thought. 'He extracts every pleasure, every sensation, down to the most trivial.'

They seemed imprisoned in the schoolroom, by the silence of the rest of the house and by the rain outside. Her calm began to break up into frustration and she put her hands behind her chair and pressed them against the hot mesh of the fireguard to steady herself. As she did so, she felt a curious derangement of both mind and body; of desire unsettling her once sluggish peaceful nature, desire horribly defined, though without direction.

'I have soon finished those,' said Hilary, bringing his sums and placing them before her. She glanced at her palms which were criss-crossed deep with crimson where she had pressed them against the fireguard, then she took up her pen and dipped it into the red ink.

'Don't lean against me, Hilary,' she said.

'I love the scent so much.'

It had returned, musky, enveloping, varying as she moved.

She ticked the sums quickly, thinking that she would set Hilary more work and escape for a moment to calm herself – change her clothes or cleanse herself in the rain. Hearing Mr Wilson's footsteps along the passage, she knew that her escape was cut off and raised wild-looking eyes as he came in. He mistook panic for passion, thought that by opening the door suddenly he had caught her out and laid bare her secret, her pathetic adoration.

'Good morning,' he said musically and made his way to the window-seat. 'Don't let me disturb you.' He said this without irony, although he thought: 'So it is that way the wind blows! Poor creature!' He had never found it difficult to imagine women were in love with him.

'I will hear your verbs,' Florence told Hilary, and opened the French Grammar as if she did not know them herself. Her eyes – from so much crying – were a pale and brilliant green, and as the scent drifted in Oliver's direction and he turned to her, she looked fully at him.

'Ah, the still waters!' he thought and stood up suddenly, 'Ils vont,' he corrected Hilary and touched his shoulder as he passed. 'Are you attending to Miss Chasty?'

'Is she attending to me?' Hilary murmured. The risk was worth taking, for neither heard. His father appeared to be sleep-walking and Florence deliberately closed her eyes, as if looking down were not enough to blur the outlines of her desire.

'I find it difficult,' Oliver said to his wife, 'to reconcile your remarks about Miss Chasty with the young woman herself. I have just come from the schoolroom and she was engaged in nothing more immoral than teaching French verbs – that not very well incidentally.'

'But can you explain what I have told you?'

'I can't do that,' he said gaily. 'For who can explain a jealous woman's fancies?' he implied.

He began to spend more time in the schoolroom; from surveillance, he said. Miss Chasty, though not outwardly of an amorous nature, was still not what he had at first supposed. A suppressed wantonness hovered beneath her primness. She was the ideal governess in his eye – irreproachable, yet not unapproachable. As she was so conveniently installed, he could take his time in divining the extent of her willingness; especially as he was growing older and the game was beginning to be worth more than the triumph of winning it. To his wife, he upheld Florence, saw nothing wrong save in her scholarship, which needed to be looked into – this, the explanation for his more frequent visits to the schoolroom. He laughed teasingly at Louise's fancies.

The schoolroom indeed became a focal point of the house – the stronghold of Mr Wilson's desire and his wife's jealousy.

'We are never alone,' said Hilary. 'Either Papa or Mamma is here. Perhaps they wonder if you are good enough for me.'

'Hilary!' His father had heard the last sentence as he opened the door and the first as he hovered outside listening. 'I doubt if my ears deceived me. You will go to your room while you think of a suitable apology and I think of an ample punishment.'

'Shall I take my history book with me or shall I just waste time?'

'I have indicated how to spend your time.'

'That won't take long enough,' said Hilary beneath his breath as he closed the door.

'Meanwhile, I apologise for him,' said his father. He did not go to his customary place by the window, but came to the hearth-rug where Florence stood behind her chair. 'We have indulged him too much and he has been too much with adults. Have there been other occasions?'

'No, indeed, sir.'

'You find him tractable?'

'Oh, yes.'

'And are you happy in your position?'

'Yes.'

As the dreaded, the now so familiar scent began to wreath about the room, she stepped back from him and began to speak rapidly, as urgently as if she were dying and must make some explanation while she could. 'Perhaps, after all, Hilary is right and you do wonder about my competence – and if I can give him all he should have. Perhaps a man would teach him more ... '

She began to feel a curious infraction of the room and of her personality, seemed to lose the true Florence, and the room lightened as if the season had been changed.

'You are mistaken,' he was saying. 'Have I ever given you any hint that we were not satisfied?'

Her timidity had quite dissolved and he was shocked by the sudden boldness of her glance.

'I should rather give you a hint of how well pleased I am.'

'Then why don't you?' she asked.

She leaned back against the chimney-piece and looped about her fingers a long necklace of glittering green beads. 'Where did these come from?' she wondered. She could not remember ever having seen them before, but she could not pursue her bewilderment, for the necklace felt familiar to her hands, much more familiar than the rest of the room.

'When shall I?' he was insisting. 'This evening, perhaps, when Hilary is in bed?'

'Then who is *he*, if Hilary is to be in bed?' she wondered. She glanced at him and smiled again. 'You are extraordinarily alike,' she said. 'You and Hilary.' 'But Hilary is a little boy,' she reminded herself. 'It is silly to confuse the two.'

'We must discuss Hilary's progress,' he said, his voice so burdened with meaning that she began to laugh at him.

'Indeed we must,' she agreed.

'Your necklace is the colour of your eyes.' He took it from her fingers and leant forward, as if to kiss her. Hearing footsteps in the passage, she moved sharply aside, the necklace broke and the beads scattered over the floor.

'Why is Hilary in the garden at this hour?' Mrs Wilson asked. Her husband and the governess were on their knees, gathering up the beads.

'Miss Chasty's necklace broke,' her husband said. She had heard that submissive tone before: his voice lacked authority only when he was caught out in some infidelity.

'I was asking about Hilary. I have just seen him running in the shrubbery without a coat.'

'He was sent to his room for being impertinent to Miss Chasty.'

'Please fetch him at once,' Mrs Wilson told Florence. Her voice always gained in authority what her husband's lacked.

Florence hurried from the room, still holding a handful of beads. She felt badly shaken – as if she had been brought to the edge of some experience which had then retreated beyond her grasp.

'He was told to stay in his room,' Mr Wilson said feebly.

'Why did her beads break?'

'She was fidgeting with them. I think she was nervous. I was making it rather apparent to her that I regarded Hilary's insubordination as proof of too much leniency on her part.'

'I didn't know that she had such a necklace. It is the showiest trash I have ever seen.'

'We cannot blame her for the cheapness of her trinkets. It is rather pathetic.'

'There is nothing pathetic about her. We will continue this in the morning-room and they can continue their lessons, which are, after all, her reason for being here.'

'Oh, they are gone,' said Hilary. His cheeks were pink from the cold outside.

'Why did you not stay in your bedroom as you were told?'

'I had nothing to do. I thought of my apology before I got there. It was: "I am sorry, dear girl, that I spoke too near the point."'

'You could have spent longer and thought of a real apology.'

'Look how long Papa spent and he did not even think of a punishment, which is a much easier thing.'

Several times during the evening Mr Wilson said: 'But you cannot dismiss a girl because her beads break.'

'There have been other things and will be more,' his wife replied.

So that there should not be more that evening, he did not move from the drawing-room where he sat watching her doing her wool-work. For the same reason, Florence left the schoolroom early. She went out and walked rather nervously in the park, feeling remorseful, astonished and upset.

'Did you mend your necklace?' Hilary asked her in the morning.

'I lost the beads.'

'But my poor girl, they must be somewhere.'

She thought: 'There is no reason to suppose that I shall get back what I never had in the first place.'

'Have you got a headache?'

'Yes. Go on with your work, Hilary.'

'Is it from losing the beads?'

'No.'

'Have you a great deal of jewellery I have not seen yet?'

She did not answer and he went on: 'You still have your brooch with your grandmother's plaited hair in it. Was it cut off her head when she was dead?'

'Your work, Hilary.'

'I shudder to think of chopping it off a corpse. You could have some of my hair, now, while I am living.' He fingered it with admiration, regarded a sum aloofly and jotted down his answer. 'Could I cut some of yours?' he asked, bringing his book to be corrected. He whistled softly, close to her, and the tendrils of hair round her ears were gently blown about.

'It is ungentlemanly to whistle,' she said.

'My sums are always right. It shows how I can chatter and subtract at the same time. Any governess would be annoyed by that. I suppose your brothers never whistle.'

'Never.'

'Are they to be clergymen like your father?'

'It is what we hope for one of them.'

'I am to be a famous judge. When you read about me, will you say: "And to think I might have been his wife if I had not been so self-willed"?'

'No, but I hope that I shall feel proud that once I taught you.'

'You sound doubtful.'

He took his book back to the table. 'We are having a quiet morning,' he remarked. 'No one has visited us. Poor Miss Chasty, it is a pity about the necklace,' he murmured, as he took up his pencil again.

Evenings were dangerous to her. 'He said he would come,' she told herself, 'and I allowed him to say so. On what compulsion did I?'

Fearfully, she spent her lonely hours out in the dark garden or in her cold
and candle-lit bedroom. He was under his wife's vigilance and Florence did
not know that he dared not leave the drawing-room. But the vigilance
relaxed, as it does; his carelessness returned and steady rain and bitter cold
drove Florence to warm her chilblains at the schoolroom fire.

Her relationship with Mrs Wilson had changed. A wary hostility took
the place of meekness, and when Mrs Wilson came to the schoolroom at
tea-times, Florence stood up defiantly and cast a look round the room as
if to say: 'Find what you can. There is nothing here.' Mrs Wilson's suspicious ways increased her rebelliousness. 'I have done nothing wrong,' she
told herself. But in her bedroom at night: 'I have done nothing wrong,' she
would think.

'They have quite deserted us,' Hilary said from time to time. 'They have
realised you are worth your weight in gold, dear girl; or perhaps I made it
clear to my father that in this room he is an interloper.'

'Hilary!'

'You want to put yourself in the right in case that door opens suddenly
as it has been doing lately. There, you see! Good-evening, Mamma. I was
just saying that I had scarcely seen you all day.' He drew forward her chair
and held the cushion behind her until she leant back.

'I have been resting.'

'Are you ill, Mamma?'

'I have a headache.'

'I will stroke it for you, dear lady.'

He stood behind her chair and began to smooth her forehead. 'Or shall
I read to you?' he asked, soon tiring of his task, 'Or play the musical-box?'

'No, nothing more, thank you.'

Mrs Wilson looked about her, at the teacups, then at Florence.
Sometimes it seemed to her that her husband was right and that she was
growing fanciful. The innocent appearance of the room lulled her and she
closed her eyes for a while, rocking gently in her chair.

'I dozed off,' she said when she awoke. The table was cleared and Florence
and Hilary sat playing chess, whispering so that they should not disturb her.

'It made a domestic scene for us,' said Hilary. 'Often Miss Chasty and I
feel that we are left too much in solitary bliss.'

The two women smiled and Mrs Wilson shook her head. 'You have too
old a head on your shoulders,' she said. 'What will they say of you when you
go to school?'

'What shall I say of *them*?' he asked bravely, but he lowered his eyes and

kept them lowered. When his mother had gone, he asked Florence: 'Did
you go to school?'

'Yes.'

'Were you unhappy there?'

'No, I was homesick at first.'

'If I don't like it, there will be no point in my staying,' he said hurriedly.
'I can learn anywhere and I don't particularly want the corners knocked off,
as my father once spoke of it. I shouldn't like to play cricket and all those
childish games. Only to do boxing and draw blood,' he added, with sudden
bravado. He laughed excitedly and clenched his fists.

'You would never be good at boxing if you lost your temper.'

'I suppose your brothers told you that. They don't sound very manly to
me. They would be afraid of a good fight and the sight of blood, I dare say.'

'Yes, I dare say. It is bedtime.'

He was whipped up by the excitement he had created from his fears.

'Chess is a woman's game,' he said and upset the board. He took the
cushion from the rocking-chair and kicked it inexpertly across the room.
'I should have thought the door would have opened then,' he said. 'But as
my father doesn't appear to send me to my room, I will go there of my own
accord. It wouldn't have been a punishment at bedtime in any case. When
I am a judge I shall be better at punishments than he is.'

When he had gone, Florence picked up the cushion and the chess-
board. 'I am no good at punishments either,' she thought. She tidied the
room, made up the fire, then sat down in the rocking-chair, thinking of all
the lonely schoolroom evenings of her future. She bent her head over her
needlework – the beaded sachet for her mother's birthday present. When
she looked up she thought the lamp was smoking and she went to the table
and turned down the wick. Then she noticed that the smoke was wreath-
ing upwards from near the fireplace, forming rings which drifted towards
the ceiling and were lost in a haze. She could hear a woman's voice humming softly and the floorboards creaked as if someone were treading up and
down the room impatiently.

She felt in herself a sense of burning impatience and anticipation and
watching the door opening found herself thinking: 'If it is not he, I cannot
bear it.'

He closed the door quietly. 'She has gone to bed,' he said in a lowered
voice. 'For days I dared not come. She has watched me every moment. At
last, this evening, she gave way to a headache. Were you expecting me?'

'Yes.'

'And once I called you Miss Mouse! And you are still Miss Mouse when
I see you about the garden, or at luncheon.'

'In this room I can be by myself. It belongs to us.'

'And not to Hilary as well – ever?' he asked her in amusement.

She gave him a quick and puzzled glance.

'Let no one intrude,' he said hastily. 'It is our room, just as you say.'

She had turned the lamp too low and it began to splutter. 'Firelight is good enough for us,' he said, putting the light out altogether.

When he kissed her, she felt an enormous sense of disappointment, almost as if he were the wrong person embracing her in the dark. His arch masterfulness merely bored her. 'A long wait for so little,' she thought.

He, however, found her entirely seductive. She responded with a sensuous languor, unruffled and at ease like the most perfect hostess.

'Where did you practise this, Miss Mouse?' he asked her. But he did not wait for the reply, fancying that he heard a step on the landing. When his wife opened the door, he was trying desperately to light a taper at the fire. His hand was trembling, and when at last, in the terribly silent room, the flame crept up the spill it simply served to show up Florence's disarray, which, like a sleep-walker, she had not noticed or put right.

She did not see Hilary again, except as a blurred little figure at the schoolroom window – blurred because of her tear-swollen eyes.

She was driven away in the carriage, although Mr Wilson had suggested the station-fly. 'Let us keep her disgrace and her tearfulness to ourselves,' he begged, although he was exhausted by the repetitive burden of his wife's grief.

'*Her* disgrace!'

'My mistake, I have said, was in not taking your accusations about her seriously. I see now that I was in some way bewitched – yes, bewitched, is what it was – acting against my judgement; nay, my very nature. I am astonished that anyone so seemingly meek could have cast such a spell upon me.'

Poor Florence turned her head aside as Williams, the coachman, came to fetch her little trunk and the basket-work holdall. Then she put on her cloak and prepared herself to go downstairs, fearful lest she should meet anyone on the way. Yet her thoughts were even more on her journey's end; for what, she wondered, could she tell her father and how expect him to understand what she could not understand herself?

Her head was bent as she crossed the landing and she hurried past the schoolroom door. At the turn of the staircase she pressed back against the wall to allow someone to pass. She heard laughter and then up the stairs came a young woman and a little girl. The child was clinging to the woman's arm and coaxing her, as sometimes Hilary had tried to coax Florence. 'After lessons,' the woman said firmly, but gaily. She looked ahead, smiling to herself. Her clothes were unlike anything that Florence had ever seen. Later, when she tried to describe them to her mother, she could only remember the shortness of a tunic which scarcely covered the knees, a hat like a helmet drawn down over eyes intensely green and matching a long necklace of glass beads which swung on her flat bosom. As she came up the stairs and drew near to Florence, she was humming softly against the child's pleading: silk rustled against her silken legs and all of the staircase, as Florence quickly descended, was full of fragrance.

In the darkness of the hall a man was watching the two go round the bend of the stairs. The woman must have looked back, for Florence saw him lift his hand in a secretive gesture of understanding.

'It is Hilary, not his father!' she thought. But the figure turned before she could be sure and went into the library.

Outside on the drive Williams was waiting with her luggage stowed away in the carriage. When she had settled herself, she looked up at the schoolroom window and saw Hilary standing there rather forlornly and she could almost imagine him saying: 'My poor dear girl; so you were not good enough for me, after all?'

'When does the new governess arrive?' she asked Williams in a casual voice, that strove to conceal both pride and grief.

'There's nothing fixed as far as I have heard,' he said.

They drove out into the lane.

'When will it be *her* time?' Florence wondered. 'I am glad that I saw her before I left.'

'We are sorry to see you going, miss.' He had heard that the maids were sorry, for she had given them no trouble.

'Thank you, Williams.'

As they went on towards the station, she leant back and looked at the familiar places where she had walked with Hilary. 'I know what I shall tell my father now,' she thought, and she felt peaceful and meek as though beginning to be convalescent after a long illness.

Hare Park

At an early hour, the pale deer moved down from the high slopes of the park towards the lakes. Sunlight gilded the stone deer on the piers of the main gates, where the steward stopped his horse and shouted to the lodge-keeper to take in a line of washing. As he rode on up the great avenue he could not see a twig that was out of place; on either side, stretches of water – one harp-shaped, one heart-shaped – glinted as if they had been polished. The landscape might have been submerged all night and now risen, cleansed and dazzling, as new as the beginning of the world, this April morning.

Along the avenue, the clear shadow of the man and horse slanted across the gravel. To the steward this was a wonderful hour of the day. His master, the Duke, slept late, shut away in the great house, and until the moment when he rose and came out on to the terrace, his steward claimed his possessions for himself, watched *his* pheasants fly up in a flurry disturbed by the horse, as he passed, *his* hare leaping through the grass. When he met any of the estate men, he lifted his crop as affably as the Duke himself.

Farther up the hill, the road forked. The avenue with its lime trees continued up towards the stables, and the second road, treeless, austere, led over the Palladian bridge which spanned the narrow end of the harp lake; and there the house came into view.

The steward took this road, and, looking up at the great building, felt his sense of ownership lessening. The stained, brown sandstone was crowned with a vast green dome. In some weathers it could look frightening; but this morning the sun mellowed it.

The grassland swept right up to the terrace. There were no flowers, no shrubs to spoil the formality. Even the runs along the terrace were empty. Stuck rakishly among the hundreds of chimneys were three television aerials. Holland blinds made blanks of rows of windows, but at one window on the second storey the curtains were parted and a young boy, still in his pyjamas, was looking out.

Arthur was watching his father's steward riding along before the house. The horse dancing like a race-horse seemed to be trying to shake off his own shadow. There was a tremendous certainty about the weather, unlike the apprehensions which had gathered about the day itself. The sun went up in triumph and drenched the park-land with gold. Arthur had a feeling that he was looking down upon an empty stage, awaiting the development of a drama which he wondered if he would ever understand. He imagined, later in the day, cars coming up the drive; the invasion, as his mother named it, beginning – the great house, Hare Park, thrown open to the enemy at half-a-crown a ticket, exposed for the first time in its history to shuffling sightseers, sullied, cheapened. So the Duchess protested. Her husband was robust enough to laugh at her charges and she could not goad him with the sharpness of her tongue. Upon all his money-raising schemes she had poured her scorn. 'You could let them be photographed in our bed at twopence a time,' she cried. 'Or I could pose stark naked on a plinth in the Orangery. I should be no more exposed than I shall be.'

'What would your mamma have said to that?' he asked gravely.

'What would Mamma have said?' had been her theme for months. Once upon a time, Mamma and her friends had supposed that she had married well. Yorkshire had thought it a staggering match. She had gone from the manor house near Harrogate to the great ducal seat in the south; had gone, as now was shown, from gentility and decency, to vulgarity, publicity and flamboyance. Mamma was dead, though, and spared knowledge of such an indecorous traipsing about her daughter's home, of pryings and pokings, ribald comments, names scribbled, souvenirs stolen, germs breathed out.

All the preparations were made. Red ropes made passageways through the rooms, heirlooms were brought out and personal possessions put away. The dogs and their baskets were moved from the library to the gun room. A stall for picture postcards and ice-cream was built in the courtyard, and upon two of the doors hung notices printed 'Ladies' and 'Gentlemen'.

'Ladies! Gentlemen!' said the Duchess. 'What lady or gentleman would wish to spy upon us just because we are poor?' She could hear all the tea-cups of Harrogate tinkling as the cries of pity passed above them, eager and energetic as cries of pity are. 'How dreadful for her! Imagine one's own feelings!' And the coronet and the seat in the Abbey would be forgiven.

Arthur had felt the air about him riven with expectation and dissent. The staff had split apart, as his parents had. The steward, the wood ranger – but not the gardeners – stood close to the Duke. Footmen and housemaids were excited; the butler saddened, but understanding. The housekeeper was in a frenzy of indignation and the Duchess's maid aligned herself fully with Harrogate and almost outdid the Duchess herself in sensibility and distaste. Arthur's tutor, who had begun to see his present employment coming to an end as talk of Eton grew more frequent, was wondering if he might not make himself indispensable in other ways: his attachment to the house, and the knowledge of its history he had come by, fitted him beautifully for the task of Guide or Lecturer. Perhaps Guide and Librarian would be a pleasant combination and might keep him settled for the rest of his life. He became as eager as the Duke to bring in the half-crowns and to have the ice-creams sold. He had written a little guide-book and Arthur's lessons were neglected while he polished up his commentary.

'When they are about the place, you are to keep to the schoolroom or play in the walled garden,' the Duchess had told her son. As for herself, her pianoforte, her painting materials, her tapestry canvas with enough wools to last five years or more, were carried to her sitting-room. She gathered her possessions about her, as if to withstand a long siege.

With feelings totally curious and expectations muddled, Arthur had awaited the day. He sensed surveillance lifting from him, authority rising away from him, as indifferent as the sun going up in the sky. He was sure that neither schoolroom nor walled garden should play any part in his day.

His father now came out on the terrace below. He stood looking across the lakes, his hand resting on the winged foot of a stone Mercury, whose shadow mingled with his own. All along the front of the house the sun was bleaching the statues. Rain-pitted, damp from the dew-fall, with mossy drapery and eye-sockets, they held out their shells and grapes and cornucopias to dry.

'Nothing gives me more pleasure than the notion that every little helps,' the Duke had told the steward. This feeling had led him to what his wife called 'excesses of vulgarity' and which had even slightly estranged those who were sympathetic to him. The steward was obliged to turn his eyes from the litter of paddle-boats on the harp-shaped lake.

The first cars to drive in when the gates were opened came very slowly and looked purposeful and menacing to Arthur – like a funeral procession – but soon the atmosphere became jollier; the car-park filled up; the crowds spread about the terrace, invading the house from all sides, like an army of ants, penetrating in no time the stables and courtyard and lining up for the house itself. The tutor, Mr Gilliat, soon collected his first batch of sightseers and fluently and facetiously began his description of pictures and cabinets and carvings.

Arthur had wandered round into the courtyard. Helpers from the village, selling postcards and refreshments, might have recognised him and he dared not buy an ice-cream and so risk being identified and imprisoned in the walled garden for the afternoon. When the steward came through the courtyard, people looked at him respectfully. A boy beside Arthur nudged him and whispered: 'That's the Duke.'

'No, it isn't,' Arthur said.

'How do you know? He's got a badge on with the coat of arms.'

The boy was running his tongue over his ice-cream cornet, long, slow licks which Arthur watched with increasing irritation. They leant against the warm stone wall. The sun in this enclosed place made them feel drowsy.

'I've shaken my lot off. Gave Dad the slip,' the boy said. He was about Arthur's age. He wore a school blazer with a row of fountain-pens clipped to the pocket. His lapels were covered with little enamel badges. Ice-cream, melting fast, dripped on to his trousers, and he spat on his handkerchief and wiped it off.

'I gave mine the slip, too,' Arthur said.

'They get my goat,' said the boy.

'And mine.'

'Once they're safely inside we might get on a boat. What say?'

The afternoon now seemed to Arthur to have expanded with brilliant promise.

They moved on together as if by a silent arrangement and came to the Orangery which was apart from the house. Crowds shuffled through it, looking at the rows of statues and busts, and nymphs and goddesses and broken-nosed emperors.

'Might as well have a look round as it's free,' said the boy. 'What's your name?'

'Arthur Blanchflower.'

'You're kidding.'

'No I'm not.'

'Well, rather you than me. I bet it takes some living down at school. My name's Derek Beale,' he added with simple pride.

The Orangery smelt of damp stone and a chalky dust filtered down through the sunlight over all the mutilated and dismembered sculpture.

'What a lot of rubbish,' said Derek, and in fact this was so. The statues had become a burden and problem, accumulating through the centuries, breaking and flaking; crumbling, but never quite away. Until today, no one had glanced at them for years. Now they were the object of derision and ribaldry. Laughter echoed round as the crowds drifted through the building.

'Look at this one! He's had his knocked off,' said Derek.

Arthur felt vexed. He had begun to toady to Derek, who had taken the initiative from the start, but he wondered if he was prepared to toady to the extent of disloyalty towards his home.

'Some of the best statues have bits knocked off,' he said. 'Everyone knows that.'

But Derek only went eagerly ahead and now was testing the strength of the armature upholding a disintegrating torso of Aphrodite.

'You're not supposed to touch them,' Arthur said nervously.

'I should bloody care,' said Derek.

Difficulties arose all the afternoon. On the lake, taking turns to manage the little boat, Arthur felt exposed to view from the house.

'What will happen when your father finds you?' he asked Derek.

'I shall tell him where he gets off.'

'Won't he mind that?'

'What he minds or doesn't mind's up to him, isn't it?'

'Yes, I suppose it is.'

'Let's go and chase those deer,' said Derek, when they got out of the boat.

Arthur could see the deer-keeper riding up the avenue. 'There's . . . a man's watching.' He sat down on the grass with his face turned away.

'He can't do anything to you.'

'Yes, he can. He did once before,' Arthur said truthfully.

'What, for chasing the deer?'

'Yes.'

'What did he do?'

'He told my father.'

'What of it? I thought you meant he had used that whip on you.'

Arthur's wits were exhausted with all the day's evasions and the risks he had run. A girl from a nearby riding-stables was walking his pony round at the edge of the lake, giving sixpenny rides to the children – since every little helped, His Grace had said.

'Want a ride?' Derek asked.

'Not much.'

'I'm going to. I've only ever been on a donkey. I shall tell her where she gets off, if she thinks she's going to walk round with me, though. You go first.'

'I don't want to go at all.'

'She'll hold you if you're afraid.'

He was forced to go up and pay his sixpence and the pony recognised him if the girl did not. She insisted on walking beside him.

'They're my orders,' she said. 'I'm responsible. You can take it or leave it.'

He was led round the lake's edge in humiliation. His face burning with embarrassment, he dismounted and threw himself on to the grass while Derek had his turn. Yet, despite the anxieties and indignities, he clung greedily to this casual encounter, his first meeting with another boy, free of the incidence of hovering adults. He tried to make the most of the opportunity to discover a great deal that he needed to know, and doggedly asked his questions and listened with respect to Derek's terse replies.

'You swear a lot, don't you?'

'Yep.'

'Do you like school?' (He could not ask, 'What is school like?')

'No.'

'Do the bigger boys bully you?'

'They better not try it on.'

Derek's father, mother, and auntie were now seen coming away from the house. The boys hid behind a tree until they had disappeared into a tunnel of wistaria which led to a grotto.

'Now they've come out, we can go in,' said Derek. 'You don't have to pay extra so we might as well take a quick butcher's.'

A 'quick butcher's' sounded vaguely brutal to Arthur but he would not demean himself by asking for translations of slang.

'I'll stay out here,' he said. 'It's too hot to go inside. I'm not interested in houses. My father might be in there.'

'If he is, he'll have gone to the front by now. We can hang about at the back so no one sees us.'

'I'd rather not.'

'Are you afraid of your father?'

'No.'

'Well then ...'

He went towards the house as if hypnotised by the older boy. Waiting wretchedly for the appalling moment when he would meet his tutor's eye, and to delay his discovery and disgrace, he stood behind two fat women and tried to merge with their swarm of children.

Mr Gilliat had become rather tangled up and confused with the queue and most people were simply drifting through at their own pace, not listening to him. The group which he had gathered about him stayed only from courtesy and listened with a sense of rebellion, eyeing with envy and reproach those who had escaped. Too slowly they were taken down the long gallery, past one Duchess after another, by Romney, by Gainsborough, by Sargent.

'The mistress of the Third Duke, by Lely,' said Mr Gilliat, standing coyly before the portrait.

'That means they weren't married,' Derek whispered. 'She was breaking the law all right. What a mug, I ask you! She looks like a bloody horse.'

'Lady Constance Considine, the present Duchess, before her marriage,' said Mr Gilliat. They all gazed up at Arthur's mother. 'Lovely gold tints in her hair,' one fat woman said. 'The lace is quite life-like.' 'She looks half asleep,' said someone else, and Arthur bowed his head.

Mr Gilliat drew them on. He was almost hysterical with fatigue and with the failure of all his little jokes. Like cows they herded together, his unworthy audience, gazing blankly, mute and stupid. He felt like taking a stick and whacking their rumps. His domed and nearly bald head glistened with sweat, his hands flapped and gesticulated and he smiled until his face was stiff.

'Proper pansy,' one young woman murmured to another.

All the time Arthur managed to conceal himself behind the fat women; but Mr Gilliat was no longer looking at the crowd, could meet the bovine stares no more.

The Haunted Bedroom with its legend of scandal and tragedy interested only Arthur from whom such frightening stories had been kept. The others stared dully at the worn brocade hangings and at the priedieu where some wanton forebear had been strangled while she was praying – presumably for the forgiveness of her sins. A burden of vice and terror was descending upon poor Arthur. The best that any of his ancestors had done was to be arrogant in battle. They were painted against backgrounds of carnage, standing, with curls blowing and armour shining, among contorted and dying horses.

Mr Gilliat now brought them to the partition chambers. Here, he explained, was an ancient, creaking apparatus which could lift one wall in its entirety so that eighteenth-century house parties might be diverted by having a curtain, as it were, raised without warning to disclose their friends' discomfiture and deshabille. Arthur felt shame to hear of such behaviour and he did not wonder that these rooms were usually locked. Scenes of cruel embarrassment he could imagine, obscene hordes of mockers in night-caps and ruffled wraps jeering at sudden exposure, invading the privacy of their fellows' undressing or praying or making love.

This last possibility Mr Gilliat did not suggest. He merely dwelt laughingly upon the picture of an imaginary lady discovered without her wig – bad enough, thought Arthur.

Derek moved closer to him and murmured: 'Yes, and people might be ... you know.'

'Rather childish,' someone said. 'They might have had something better to do with their time.'

Arthur felt stifled and frightened.

'My feet!' a woman complained.

They were nearly at the end, had wound through the core of the house and now were to descend the other side of the horse-shoe staircase.

'Fancy keeping it clean,' one of the fat women said. She stopped to run a finger along the carved banister and Arthur drew up close behind her.

'Very tiring,' they said, coming out into the fresh air again.

'Where the dickens have you been?' shouted Derek's father, pushing into the crowd. 'Wasting our time; worrying your mother? Don't answer me back, my lad, or you'll get a taste of my hand.'

Disillusioned, Arthur watched the boy pushed on ahead, nagged and ranted at. He took it in silence. He did not tell his father where to get off, but kept his eyes averted. 'Where have you been?' cried his mother. 'We've been beside ourselves.' He straightened the row of fountain-pens in his pocket, looked nervous and meek, did not glance back at Arthur, who could not bear to witness this sudden change in him and turned away in the opposite direction.

The Duchess went to her bath as the last visitors departed. Although she had kept to her room, she felt bruised and buffeted and contaminated. 'The noise!' she said, pressing her fingers to her temples and thrusting back her beautiful golden hair. 'I tried to be brave,' she told her maid.

The Duke was exhilarated as he walked in the grounds with his steward. 'A good day,' he said. 'A nice crowd and no litter.'

The steward picked up an empty cigarette packet.

'I wonder what they all think and why they come, and do they resent my having such a place as this, I wonder?'

The steward could not say: 'No, your Grace, they pity you, and go back to their own homes in relief.'

As the last cars went down the drive, Arthur, watching from the school-room window, felt a sense of isolation coming over him. In the new silence a cuckoo called. Two other birds in a bush below him carried on a boring exchange. He was loth to explore his own loneliness. It was distasteful to him, and the day had done too much.

He did not turn from the window when Mr Gilliat came in.

'What a day!' fussed the tutor. 'Oh, dear, my head! The hoi polloi! One despairs. Have you done your Latin?'

'I couldn't find the book.'

'But' – his voice rose hysterically – 'you should have asked me for it.'

'I couldn't find you either.'

'Someone could have done so. I was not entirely inaccessible. So you have idled your day away? It is too vexing for words. You will have to put your back into it tomorrow to make up. Yes, you really will. To take advantage at a time like this when we all have so much to cope with! More than enough on our hands. All of us tired and trying to do our best, and this is to be our reward, is it? You have fallen short of all your papa would expect of you.'

Arthur stood quite still, watching the deer moving across the park, up towards the wooded slopes for the night. 'I should bloody care,' he said.

You'll Enjoy It When You Get There

'Shyness is *common*,' Rhoda's mother insisted. 'I was never *allowed* to be shy when I was a girl. Your grandparents would soon have put a stop to *that*.'

The stressed words sounded so peevish. Between each sentence she refreshed herself with a sip of invalid's drink, touched her lips with her handkerchief, and then continued.

'Self-consciousness it was always called when I was young, and that is what it is. To imagine that it shows a sense of modesty is absurd. *Modesty.* Why, I have never known a *truly* modest person to be the least bit shy.'

The jaundice, which had discoloured her face and her eyes, seemed as well to wash all her words in poison.

'It's all right for you, Mother,' Rhoda said. 'You can drink. Then anyone can talk.'

Mrs Hobart did not like to be reminded that she drank at all: that she drank immoderately, no one – she herself least of all – would ever have dared to remind her.

Rhoda, who was sitting by the window, nursing her cat, stared down at the gardens in the square and waited huffily for an indignant rebuke. Instead, her mother said wearily: 'Well, you will have a drink, too, before the banquet, and no nonsense. A "girl of eighteen".'

'I hate the taste.'

'I, I, I. I hate this; I loathe that. What do you think would have happened if *I* had considered what *I* liked through all these years. Or the Queen,' she added. 'The poor girl! The rubbish she's been forced to eat and drink in foreign countries. And never jibbed.'

'You and the Queen are different kettles of fish from me,' Rhoda said calmly. Then she threw up the window from the bottom and leant out and waved to her father, who was crossing the road below.

'Please shut that window,' Mrs Hobart said. 'Leaning out and waving, like a housemaid. I despair.' She put the glass of barley-water on one side and said again: 'I despair.'

'There is no need. I will do my best,' said Rhoda. 'Though no one likes to be frightened in quite such a boring way.'

*

She sat in the train opposite her father and wedged in by business-men. In books and films, she thought, people who go on train journeys always get a corner seat.

In a corner, she could have withdrawn into her day-dreaming so much more completely; but she was cramped by the fat men on either side, whose thighs moved against hers when they uncrossed and recrossed their legs, whose newspapers distracted her with their puzzling headlines – for instance 'Bishop Exorcises £5,000 Ghost,' she read. Her father, with his arms folded neatly across his chest, dozed and nodded, and sometimes his lips moved as if he were rehearsing his speech for that evening. They seemed to have been in the train for a long time, and the phlegmy fog, which had pressed to the windows as they left London, was darkening quickly. The dreadful moment of going in to dinner was coming nearer. Her father suddenly woke up and lifted his head. He yawned and winked a watery eye at her, and yawned and yawned again. She sensed that to be taking his daughter instead of his wife to what her mother called the Trade Banquet made it seem rather a spree to him and she wished that she could share his light-heartedness.

Like sleepwalkers, the other people in the compartment, still silent and drowsy, began now to fold their newspapers, look for their tickets, lift down their luggage from the racks. The train's rhythm changed and the lights of the station came running past the windows. All that Rhoda was to see of this Midlands town was the dark, windy space between the station entrance and the great station hotel as they followed a porter across the greasy paving-stones and later, a glimpse from her bedroom window of a timber-yard beside a canal.

When she was alone in the hotel bedroom, she felt more uncertain than ever, oppressed by the null effect of raspberry-coloured damask, the large intolerable pieces of furniture and the silence, which only sounds of far-away plumbing broke, or of distant lifts rising and falling.

She shook out her frock and was hanging it in a cavernous wardrobe when somebody in the corridor outside tapped on the door. 'Is that you, Father?' she called out anxiously. A waiter came in, carrying a tray high in the air. He swirled it round on his fingers and put down a glass of sherry.

'The gentleman in number forty-five ordered it,' he explained.

'Thank you,' Rhoda said timidly, peeping at him round the wardrobe door, 'very much,' she added effusively.

The waiter said, 'Thank *you*, madam,' in a quelling voice, and went away.

Rhoda sniffed at the sherry, and then tipped it into the wash-basin. 'I suppose Father's so used to Mamma,' she thought. She knew the bedroom imbibing that went on, as her mother moved heavily about, getting dressed: every time she came back to her mirror, she would take a drink from the glass beside it.

The hotel room was a vacuum in which even time had no reality to Rhoda. With no watch to tell her, she began to wonder if she had been there alone for ten minutes or an hour and in sudden alarm she ran to the bathroom and turned on taps and hurriedly unpacked.

She put on a little confidence with her pretty frock; but, practising radiant smiles in the looking-glass, she was sure that they were only grimaces. She smoothed on her long white gloves and took up her satin bag, then heard a distant clock, somewhere across the roofs of high buildings, strike the half-hour and knew that she must wait all through the next, matching half-hour for her father to come to fetch her.

As she waited, shivering as she paced about the room, growing more and more goose-fleshed, she saw the reasonableness in her father's thought about the sherry and wished that she had not wasted it and, even more, that she had lain twenty minutes longer in her warm bath.

He came as the clock struck out the hours and, when she ran and opened the door to him, said: 'Heavens, ma'am, how exquisite you look!'

They descended the stairs.

In the reception-room, another waiter circled with a tray of filled glasses. Four people stood drinking by the fire – two middle-aged men, one wearing a mayoral chain, the other a bosomful of medals; and two middle-aged women, stiffly corseted, their hair set in tight curls and ridges. Diamonds shone on their freckled chests and pink carnations slanted heads downwards across their bodices. They look as if they know the ropes, thought Rhoda, paralysed with shyness. They received her kindly, but in surprise. 'Why, where is Ethel?' they asked her father, and they murmured in concern over the jaundice and said how dreary it must be to be on the waggon. 'Especially for her', the tone of their voices seemed to Rhoda to suggest.

A bouquet was taken from a little side table and handed to Rhoda, who held it stiffly at her waist where it contended fiercely with the colour of her dress.

The six of them were, in their importance, shut off from a crowded bar where other guests were drinking cocktails: on this side of the door there was an air of confidence and expectation, of being ahead of the swim, Rhoda thought. She wished passionately, trying to sip away her sherry, that she might spend the entire evening shut away from the hordes of strangers in the bigger room but, only too soon, a huge toast-master, fussing with his white gloves, brought the three couples into line and then threw wide the doors; inclining his head patronisingly to guest after guest, he bawled out some semblance of the names they proffered. As the first ones came reluctantly forward from the gaiety of the bar, Mr Hobart leant towards Rhoda and took the glass from her hand and put it on the tray with the others. 'How do you do,' she whispered, shaking hands with an old gentleman, who was surprised to see that her eyes were filled with tears. 'You are deputising for your dear mother?' he asked. 'And very charmingly you do it, my dear,' he added, and passed on quickly, so that she could brush her wet lashes with her gloved hand.

'Good-evening, Rhoda.' The bracing mockery of this new voice jolted her, the voice of Digby Lycett Senior, as she always called him in her mind – the mind which for months had been conquered and occupied by Digby Lycett Junior. This unexpected appearance was disastrous to her. She felt indignantly that he had no right to be there, so remotely connected was he with the trade the others had in common. 'Nice of you to come,' her father was now telling him. They were old business friends. It was Digby Lycett who sold her father the machinery for making Hobart's Home-made Cookies. It was *loathsome* of you to come, Rhoda thought, unhappily.

She took one gloved hand after another, endlessly – it seemed – confronted by pink carnations and strings of pearls. But the procession dwindled at last – the stragglers, who had lingered over their drinks till the last moment, were rounded up by the toast-master and sent resignedly on their way to the banqueting-hall, where an orchestra was playing 'Some Enchanted Evening' above the noise of chairs being scraped and voices mounting in volume like a gathering wave.

In the reception-room, the Mayor straightened the chain on his breast. One duty done, he was now prepared to go on to the next. All of his movements were certain and automatic; every evening of his life, they implied, he had a hall full of people waiting for him to take his seat.

As she moved towards the door a sense of vertigo and nausea overcame Rhoda, confronted by the long walk to her place and the ranks of pink faces turned towards her. With bag and bouquet and skirt to manage, she felt that she was bundling along with downcast eyes. Before a great heap of flowers on the table, they stopped. The Mayor was humming very softly to the music. He put on his spectacles, peered at the table and then laid his hand on the back of a gilt chair, indicating that here, next to him, Rhoda was to be privileged to sit.

At the doors, waitresses crowded ready to rush forward with *hors d'oeuvres*. The music faded. Without raising her eyes, instinctively, wishing to sink out of sight, Rhoda slid round her chair and sat upon it.

Down crashed the toast-master's gavel as the Mayor, in a challenging voice, began to intone Grace. Mr Hobart put his hand under Rhoda's elbow and brought her, lurching, as she could not help doing, to her feet again. The gilt chair tipped, but he saved it from going over, the bouquet shot under the table and Rhoda prayed that she might follow it.

'Please God, let me faint. Let me never have to look up again and meet anybody's glance.'

'Now you can, young lady,' the Mayor said, helping her down again. Then he turned quickly to the woman on his other side and began a conversation. Rhoda's father had done the same. Sitting between them, she swallowed sardines and olives and her bitter, bitter tears. After a time, her isolation made her defiant. She lifted her head and looked boldly and crossly in front of her, and caught the eye of Digby Lycett Senior, just as he raised a fork to his mouth, and smiled at her, sitting not far across the room, at right angles to her table, where he could perfectly observe her humiliation and record it for his son's interest and amusement later. 'Poor old Rhoda' – she could hear the words, overlaid with laughter.

She ate quickly, as if she had not touched food for weeks. Once, her father, fingering a wine-glass restlessly, caught and held as he was in conversation by the relentless woman at his side, managed to turn his head for a moment and smile at Rhoda. 'All right?' he asked, and nodded his own answer, for it was a great treat for a young girl, he implied – the music, the flowers, the pretty dress, the wine.

Someone *must* talk to me, she thought, for it seemed to her that, through lack of conversation, her expression was growing sullen. She tried to reorganise her features into a look of animation or calm pleasure. She drank a plate of acid-tasting, red soup to its dregs. Chicken followed turbot, as her mother had assured her was inevitable. The Mayor, who went through the same menu nearly every evening, left a great deal on his plate; he scattered it about for a while and then tidied it up: not so Rhoda, who, against a great discomfort of fullness, plodded painstakingly on.

At last, as she was eating some cauliflower, the Mayor turned his moist, purple face towards her. She lifted her eyes to the level of the chain on his breast and agreed with him that she was enjoying herself enormously.

'It is my first visit to Norley,' she said gaily, conscious of Digby Lycett Senior's eyes upon her. She hoped that he would think from her expression that some delicious pleasantry was in progress. To keep the Mayor in conversation she was determined. He should not turn away again and Digby Lycett, Senior or Junior, should not have the impression that she sat in silence and disgrace from the beginning to the end.

'But I have a cat who came from here,' she added.

The Mayor looked startled.

'A Burmese cat. A man in Norley – a Doctor Fisher – breeds them. Do you know Doctor Fisher?'

'I can't say that I do.'

He was plainly unwilling for her to go on. On his other side was feminine flattery and cajolery and he wished to turn back for more, and Rhoda and her cat were of no interest to him.

'Have you ever seen a Burmese cat?' she asked.

He crumbled some bread and looked cross and said that as far as he knew he never had.

'He came to London on the train all by himself in a little basket,' Rhoda said. 'The cat, I mean, of course. Minkie, I call him. Such a darling, you can't imagine.'

She smiled vivaciously for Digby Lycett Senior's benefit; but, try as she might, she could not summon the courage to lift her eyes any higher than the splendid chain on the Mayor's breast, for she shrank from the look of contempt she was afraid he might be wearing.

'They are rather like Siamese cats,' she went on. 'Though they are brown all over and have golden eyes, not blue.'

'Oh?' said the Mayor. He had to lean a little nearer to her as a waitress put a dish of pistachio ice-cream over his left shoulder.

'But rather the same natures, if you know what I mean,' said Rhoda.

'I'm afraid I don't care for cats,' said the Mayor, in the voice of simple pride in which this remark is always made.

'On all your many social commitments,' the woman on his other side said loudly, rescuing him, 'which flavour of ice-cream crops up most often?'

He laughed and turned to her with relief. 'Vanilla,' he said jovially. 'In a ratio of eight to one.'

'Enjoying yourself?' Rhoda's father asked her later, as they danced a foxtrot together. 'I dare say this is the part of the evening that appeals to you – not all those long-winded speeches.'

It appealed to Rhoda because it was nearer to the end, and for no other reason.

'You seemed to be getting on well with the Mayor,' Mr Hobart added.

The Mayor had disappeared. Rhoda could see no sign of his glittering chain and she supposed that he disliked dancing as much as he disliked cats. She prayed that Digby Lycett Senior might not ask her to do the Old Fashioned Waltz which followed. She was afraid of his mocking smile and, ostrich-like, opened her bag and looked inside it as he approached.

Another middle-aged man stepped forward first and asked to have the pleasure in a voice which denied the possibility of there being any. Rhoda guessed that what he meant was 'May I get this duty over and done with, pursued as it is as a mark of the esteem in which I hold your father'. And Rhoda smiled as if she were enchanted, and rose and put herself into his arms, as if he were her lover.

He made the waltz more old-fashioned than she had ever known it, dancing stiffly, keeping his stomach well out of her way, humming, but not saying a word to her. She was up against a great silence this evening: to her it was the measure of her failure. Sorting through her mind for something to say, she rejected remarks about the floor and the band and said instead that she had never been to Norley before. The observation should have led somewhere, she thought; but it did not: it was quite ignored.

'But I have a cat who came from here,' she added. 'A little Burmese cat.'

When he did not answer this, either, she thought that he must be deaf and raised her voice. 'There is a doctor here who breeds them. Perhaps you have come across him – a Doctor Fisher.'

'No, I can't say that I have.'

'He sent the kitten to London by train, in a little basket. So pretty and gay. Minkie, I call him. Have you ever seen a Burmese cat?' She could not wait for his answers, lest they never came. 'They are not a usual sort of cat at all. Rather like a Siamese in many ways, but brown all over and with golden eyes instead of blue. They are similar in nature though, if you can understand what I mean.'

He either could not, or was not prepared to try and at last, mercifully, the music quickened and finally snapped off altogether. Flushed and smiling, she was escorted back to her father who was standing by the bar, looking genial and indulgent.

Her partner's silence seemed precautionary now. He handed her over with a scared look, as if she were some dangerous lunatic. Her father, not noticing this, said: 'You are having quite a success with your Mayor, my dear.'

'My Mayor?'

She turned quickly and looked after the man who had just left her. He was talking to a little group of people; they all had their heads together and were laughing.

'He took that chain off then?' she said, feeling sick and dazed. It was all she had had to distinguish him from the rest of the bald-headed and obese middle-aged men.

'You couldn't expect him to dance with that hanging round his neck – not even in your honour,' her father said. 'And now, I shall fetch you a long, cool drink, for you look as if the dancing has exhausted you.'

Girl Reading

Etta's desire was to belong. Sometimes she felt on the fringe of the family, at other times drawn headily into its very centre. At meal-times – those occasions of argument and hilarity, of thrust and counterstroke, bewildering to her at first – she was especially on her mettle, turning her head alertly from one to another as if watching a fast tennis match. She hoped soon to learn the art of riposte and already used, sometimes unthinkingly, family words and phrases; and had one or two privately treasured memories of even having made them laugh. They delighted in laughing and often did so scoffingly – 'at the expense of those less fortunate' as Etta's mother would sententiously have put it.

Etta and Sarah were school-friends. It was not the first time that Etta had stayed with the Lippmanns in the holidays. Everyone understood that the hospitality would not be returned, for Etta's mother, who was widowed, went out to work each day. Sarah had seen only the outside of the drab terrace house where her friend lived. She had persuaded her elder brother, David, to take her spying there one evening. They drove fifteen miles to Market Swanford and Sarah, with great curiosity, studied the street names until at last she discovered the house itself. No one was about. The street was quite deserted and the two rows of houses facing one another were blank and silent as if waiting for a hearse to appear. 'Do hurry!' Sarah urged her brother. It had been a most dangerous outing and she was thoroughly depressed by it. Curiosity now seemed a trivial sensation compared with the pity she was feeling for her friend's drab life and her shame at having confirmed her own suspicions of it. She was threatened by tears. 'Aren't you going in?' her brother asked in great surprise. 'Hurry, hurry,' she begged him. There had never been any question of her calling at that house.

'She must be very lonely there all through the holidays, poor Etta,' she thought, and could imagine hour after hour in the dark house. Bickerings with the daily help she had already heard of and – Etta trying to put on a brave face and make much of nothing – trips to the public library the highlight of the day, it seemed. No wonder that her holiday reading was always so carefully done, thought Sarah, whereas she herself could never snatch a moment for it except at night in bed.

Sarah had a lively conscience about the seriousness of her friend's private world. Having led her more than once into trouble, at school, she had always afterwards felt a disturbing sense of shame; for Etta's work was more important than her own could ever be, too important to be interrupted by escapades. Sacrifices had been made and scholarships must be won. Once – it was a year ago when they were fifteen and had less sense – Sarah had thought up some rough tomfoolery and Etta's blazer had been torn. She was still haunted by her friend's look of consternation. She had remembered too late, as always – the sacrifices that had been made, the widowed mother sitting year after year at her office desk, the holidays that were never taken and the contriving that had to be done.

Her own mother was so warm and worldly. If she had anxieties she kept them to herself, setting the pace of gaiety, up to date and party-loving. She was popular with her friends' husbands who, in their English way, thought of her comfortably as nearly as good company as a man and full of bright ways as well. Etta felt safer with her than with Mr Lippmann, whose enquiries were often too probing; he touched nerves, his jocularity could be an embarrassment. The boys – Sarah's elder brothers – had their own means of communication which their mother unflaggingly strove to interpret and, on Etta's first visit, she had tried to do so for her, too.

She *was* motherly, although she looked otherwise, the girl decided. Lying in bed at night, in the room she shared with Sarah, Etta would listen to guests driving noisily away or to the Lippmanns returning, full of laughter, from some neighbour's house. Late night door-slamming in the country disturbed only the house's occupants, who all contributed to it. Etta imagined them pottering about downstairs – husband and wife, would hear bottles clinking, laughter, voices raised from room to room, good-night endearments to cats and dogs and at last Mrs Lippmann's running footsteps on the stairs and the sound of her jingling bracelets coming nearer. Outside their door she would pause, listening, wondering if they were asleep already. They never were. 'Come in!' Sarah would shout, hoisting herself up out of the bed clothes on one elbow, her face turned expectantly towards the door, ready for laughter – for something amusing would surely have happened. Mrs Lippmann, sitting on one of the beds, never failed them. When they were children, Sarah said, she brought back *petits fours* from parties; now she brought back *faux pas*. She specialised in little stories against herself – Mummy's Humiliations, Sarah named them – tactless things she had said, never-to-be-remedied remarks which sprang fatally from her lips. Mistakes in identity was her particular line, for she never remembered a face, she declared. Having kissed Sarah, she would bend over Etta to do the same. She smelt of scent and gin and cigarette smoke. After this they would go to sleep. The house would be completely quiet for several hours.

Etta's mother had always had doubts about the suitability of this *ménage*. She knew it only at second hand from her daughter, and Etta said very little about her visits and that little was only in reply to obviously resented questions. But she had a way of looking about her with boredom when she returned, as if she had made the transition unwillingly and incompletely. She hurt her mother – who wished only to do everything in the world for her, having no one else to please or protect.

'I should feel differently if we were able to return the hospitality,' she told Etta. The Lippmanns' generosity depressed her. She knew that it was despicable to feel jealous, left out, kept in the dark, but she tried to rationalise her feelings before Etta. 'I could take a few days off and invite Sarah here,' she suggested.

Etta was unable to hide her consternation and her expression deeply wounded her mother. 'I shouldn't know what to do with her,' she said.

'Couldn't you go for walks? There are the Public Gardens. And take her to the cinema one evening. What do you do at *her* home?'

'Oh, just fool about. Nothing much.' Some afternoons they just lay on their beds and ate sweets, keeping all the windows shut and the wireless on loud, and no one ever disturbed them or told them they ought to be out in the fresh air. Then they had to plan parties and make walnut fudge and deflea the dogs. Making fudge was the only one of these things she could imagine them doing in her own home and they could not do it all the time. As for the dreary Public Gardens, she could not herself endure the asphalt paths and the bandstand and the beds of salvias. She could imagine vividly how dejected Sarah would feel.

Early in these summer holidays, the usual letter had come from Mrs Lippmann. Etta, returning from the library, found that the charwoman had gone early and locked her out. She rang the bell, but the sound died away and left an even more forbidding silence. All the street, where elderly people dozed in stuffy rooms, was quiet. She lifted the flap of the letter-box and called through it. No one stirred or came. She could just glimpse an envelope, lying face up on the doormat, addressed in Mrs Lippmann's large, loopy, confident handwriting. The house-stuffiness wafted through the letter-box. She imagined the kitchen floor slowly drying, for there was a smell of soapy water. A tap was steadily dripping.

She leant against the door, waiting for her mother's return, in a sickness of impatience at the thought of the letter lying there inside. Once or twice, she lifted the flap and had another look at it.

Her mother came home at last, very tired. With an anxious air, she set about cooking supper, which Etta had promised to have ready. The letter was left among her parcels on the kitchen table, and not until they had finished their stewed rhubarb did she send Etta to fetch it. She opened it carefully with the bread knife and deepened the frown on her forehead in preparation for reading it. When she had, she gave Etta a summary of its contents and put forward her objections, her unnerving proposal.

'She wouldn't come,' Etta said. 'She wouldn't leave her dog.'

'But, my dear, she has to leave him when she goes back to school.'

'I know. That's the trouble. In the holidays she likes to be with him as much as possible, to make up for it.'

Mrs Salkeld, who had similar wishes about her daughter, looked sad. 'It is too one-sided,' she gently explained. 'You must try to understand how I feel about it.'

'They're only too glad to have me. I keep Sarah company when they go out.'

They obviously went out a great deal and Mrs Salkeld suspected that they were frivolous. She did not condemn them for that – they must lead their own lives, but those were in a world which Etta would never be able to afford the time or money to inhabit. 'Very well, Musetta,' she said, removing the girl further from her by using her full name – used only on formal and usually menacing occasions.

That night she wept a little from tiredness and depression – from disappointment, too, at the thought of returning in the evenings to the dark and empty house, just as she usually did, but when she had hoped for company. They were not healing tears she shed and they did nothing but add self-contempt to her other distresses.

A week later, Etta went the short distance by train to stay with the Lippmanns. Her happiness soon lost its edge of guilt, and once the train had rattled over the iron bridge that spanned the broad river, she felt safe in a different country. There seemed to be even a different weather, coming from a wider sky, and a riverside glare – for the curves of the railway line brought it close to the even more winding course of the river, whose silver loops could be glimpsed through the trees. There were islands and backwaters and a pale heron standing on a patch of mud.

Sarah was waiting at the little station and Etta stepped down on to the platform as if taking a footing into promised land. Over the station and the gravelly lane outside hung a noonday quiet. On one side were grazing meadows, on the other side the drive gateways of expensive houses. The Gables was indeed gabled and so was its boat-house. It was also turreted and balconied. There was a great deal of woodwork painted glossy white, and a huge-leaved Virginia creeper covered much of the red-brick walls – in the front beds were the salvias and lobelias Etta had thought she hated. Towels and swim-suits hung over balcony rails and a pair of tennis-shoes had been put out on a window-sill to dry. Even though Mr Lippmann and his son, David, went to London every day, the house always had – for Etta – a holiday atmosphere.

The hall door stood open and on the big round table were the stacks of new magazines which seemed to her the symbol of extravagance and luxury. At the back of the house, on the terrace overlooking the river, Mrs Lippmann, wearing tight, lavender pants and a purple shirt, was drinking vodka with a neighbour who had called for a subscription to some charity. Etta was briefly enfolded in scented silk and tinkling bracelets and then released and introduced. Sarah gave her a red, syrupy drink and they sat down on the warm steps among the faded clumps of aubretia and rocked the ice cubes to and fro in their glasses, keeping their eyes narrowed to the sun.

Mrs Lippmann gossiped, leaning back under a fringed chair-umbrella. She enjoyed exposing the frailties of her friends and family, although she would have been the first to hurry to their aid in trouble. Roger, who was seventeen, had been worse for drink the previous evening, she was saying. Faced with breakfast, his face had been a study of disgust which she now tried to mimic. And David could not eat, either; but from being in love. She raised her eyes to heaven most dramatically, to convey that great patience was demanded of her.

'He eats like a horse,' said Sarah. 'Etta, let's go upstairs.' She took Etta's empty glass and led her back across the lawn, seeming not to care that her mother would without doubt begin to talk about her the moment she had gone.

Rich and vinegary smells of food came from the kitchen as they crossed the hall. (There was a Hungarian cook to whom Mrs Lippmann spoke in German and a Portuguese 'temporary' to whom she spoke in Spanish.) The food was an important part of the holiday to Etta, who had nowhere else eaten *Sauerkraut* or *Apfelstrudel* or cold fried fish, and she went into the dining-room each day with a sense of adventure and anticipation.

On this visit she was also looking forward to the opportunity of making a study of people in love – an opportunity she had not had before. While she unpacked, she questioned Sarah about David's Nora, as she thought of her; but Sarah would only say that she was quite a good sort with dark eyes and an enormous bust, and that as she was coming to dinner that evening, as she nearly always did, Etta would be able to judge for herself.

While they were out on the river all the afternoon – Sarah rowing her in a dinghy along the reedy backwater – Etta's head was full of love in books, even in those holiday set books Sarah never had time for – *Sense and Sensibility* this summer. She felt that she knew what to expect, and her perceptions were sharpened by the change of air and scene, and the disturbing smell of the river, which she snuffed up deeply as if she might be able to store it up in her lungs. 'Mother thinks it is polluted,' Sarah said when Etta lifted a streaming hand from trailing in the water and brought up some slippery weeds and held them to her nose. They laughed at the idea.

Etta, for dinner, put on the liberty silk they wore on Sunday evenings at school and Sarah at once brought out her own hated garment from the back of the cupboard where she had pushed it out of sight on the first day of the holidays. When they appeared downstairs, they looked unbelievably dowdy, Mrs Lippmann thought, turning away for a moment because her eyes had suddenly pricked with tears at the sight of her kind daughter.

Mr Lippmann and David returned from Lloyd's at half-past six and with them brought Nora – a large, calm girl with an air of brittle indifference towards her fiancé which disappointed but did not deceive Etta, who knew enough to remain undeceived by banter. To interpret from it the private tendernesses it hid was part of the mental exercise she was to be engaged in. After all, David would know better than to have his heart on his sleeve, especially in this *dégagé* family where nothing seemed half so funny as falling in love.

After dinner, Etta telephoned her mother, who had perhaps been waiting for the call, as the receiver was lifted immediately. Etta imagined her standing in the dark and narrow hall with its smell of umbrellas and furniture polish.

'I thought you would like to know I arrived safely.'

'What have you been doing?'

'Sarah and I went to the river. We have just finished dinner.' Spicy smells still hung about the house. Etta guessed that her mother would have had half a tin of sardines and put the other half by for her breakfast. She felt sad for her and guilty herself. Most of her thoughts about her mother were deformed by guilt.

'What have you been doing?' she asked.

'Oh, the usual,' her mother said brightly. 'I am just turning the collars and cuffs of your winter blouses. By the way, don't forget to pay Mrs Lippmann for the telephone call.'

'No. I shall have to go now. I just thought . . .'

'Yes, of course, dear. Well, have a lovely time.'

'We are going for a swim when our dinner has gone down.'

'Be careful of cramp, won't you? But I mustn't fuss from this distance. I know you are in good hands. Give my kind regards to Mrs Lippmann and Sarah, will you, please. I must get back to your blouses.'

'I wish you wouldn't bother. You must be tired.'

'I am perfectly happy doing it,' Mrs Salkeld said. But if that were so, it was unnecessary, Etta thought, for her to add, as she did: 'And someone has to do it.'

She went dully back to the others. Roger was strumming on a guitar, but he blushed and put it away when Etta came into the room.

As the days went quickly by, Etta thought that she was belonging more this time than ever before. Mr Lippmann, a genial patriarch, often patted her head when passing, in confirmation of her existence, and Mrs Lippmann let her run errands. Roger almost wistfully sought her company, while Sarah disdainfully discouraged him; for they had their own employments, she implied; her friend – 'my best friend', as she introduced Etta to lesser ones or adults – could hardly be expected to want the society of schoolboys. Although he was a year older than themselves, being a boy he was less sophisticated, she explained. She and Etta considered themselves to be rather worldly-wise – Etta having learnt from literature and Sarah from putting two and two together, her favourite pastime. Her parents seemed to her to behave with the innocence of children, unconscious of their motives, so continually betraying themselves to her experienced eye, when knowing more would have made them guarded. She had similarly put two and two together about Roger's behaviour to Etta, but she kept these con-clusions to herself – partly from not wanting to make her friend feel self-conscious and partly – for she scorned self-deception – from what she recognised to be jealousy. She and Etta were very well as they were, she thought.

Etta herself was too much absorbed by the idea of love to ever think of being loved. In this house, she had her first chance of seeing it at first hand and she studied David and Nora with such passionate speculation that their loving seemed less their own than hers. At first, she admitted to her-self that she was disappointed. Their behaviour fell short of what she required of them; they lacked a romantic attitude to one another and Nora was neither touching nor glorious – neither Viola nor Rosalind. In Etta's mind to be either was satisfactory; to be boisterous and complacent was not. Nora was simply a plump and genial girl with a large bust and a faint moustache. She could not be expected to inspire David with much gal-lantry and, in spite of all the red roses he brought her from London, he was not above telling her that she was getting fat. Gaily retaliatory, she would threaten him with the bouquet, waving it about his head, her huge engage-ment ring catching the light, flashing with different colours, her eyes flashing too.

Sometimes, there was what Etta's mother would have called 'horseplay', and Etta herself deplored the noise, the dishevelled romping. 'We know quite well what it's instead of,' said Sarah. 'But I sometimes wonder if they do. They would surely cut it out if they did.'

As intent as a bird-watcher, Etta observed them, but was puzzled that they behaved like birds, making such a display of their courtship, an absurd-looking frolic out of a serious matter. She waited in vain for a sigh or secret glance. At night, in the room she shared with Sarah, she wanted to talk about them more than Sarah, who felt that her own family was the last possible source of glamour or enlightenment. Discussing her brides-maid's dress was the most she would be drawn into and that subject Etta felt was devoid of romance. She was not much interested in mere weddings and thought them rather banal and public celebrations. 'With an overskirt of embroidered net,' said Sarah in her decisive voice. 'How nice if you could be a bridesmaid, too; but she has all those awful Greenbaum cousins. As ugly as sin, but not to be left out.' Etta was inattentive to her. With all her studious nature she had set herself to study love and study it she would. She made the most of what the holiday offered and when the exponents were absent she fell back on the textbooks – *Tess of the D'Urbervilles* and *Wuthering Heights* at that time.

To Roger she seemed to fall constantly into the same pose, as she sat on the river bank, bare feet tucked sideways, one arm cradling a book, the other outstretched to pluck – as if to aid her concentration – at blades of grass. Her face remained pale, for it was always in shadow, bent over her book. Beside her, glistening with oil, Sarah spread out her body to the sun. She was content to lie for hour after hour with no object but to change the colour of her skin and with thoughts crossing her mind as seldom as clouds passed overhead – and in as desultory a way when they did so. Sometimes, she took a book out with her, but nothing happened to it except that it became smothered with oil. Etta, who found sunbathing boring and ener-vating, read steadily on – her straight, pale hair hanging forward as if to seclude her, to screen her from the curious eyes of passers-by – shaken by passions of the imagination as she was. Voices from boats came clearly across the water, but she did not heed them. People going languidly by in punts shaded their eyes and admired the scarlet geraniums and the green-ness of the grass. When motor cruisers passed, their wash jogged against the mooring stage and swayed into the boat-house, whose lacy fretwork trim-mings had just been repainted glossy white.

Sitting there, alone by the boat-house at the end of the grass bank, Roger read, too; but less diligently than Etta. Each time a boat went by, he looked up and watched it out of sight. A swan borne towards him on a wake, sitting neatly on top of its reflection, held his attention. Then his place on the page was lost. Anyhow, the sun fell too blindingly upon it. He would glance again at Etta and briefly, with distaste, at his indolent, spread-eagled sister, who had rolled over on to her stomach to give her shiny back, criss-crossed from the grass, its share of sunlight. So the afternoons passed, and they would never have such long ones in their lives again.

Evenings were more social. The terrace with its fringed umbrellas – symbols of gaiety to Etta – became the gathering place. Etta, listening intently, continued her study of love, and as intently Roger studied her and the very emotion which in those others so engrossed her.

'You look still too pale,' Mr Lippmann told her one evening. He put his hands to her face and tilted it to the sun.

'You shan't leave us until there are roses in those cheeks.' He implied that only in his garden did sun and air give their full benefit. The thought was there and Etta shared it. 'Too much of a bookworm, I'm afraid,' he added and took one of her textbooks which she carried everywhere for safety, lest she should be left on her own for a few moments. '*Tess of the D'Urbervilles*,' read out Mr Lippmann. 'Isn't it deep? Isn't it on the morbid side?' Roger was kicking rhythmically at a table leg in glum embarrassment. 'This won't do you any good at all, my dear little girl. This won't put the roses in your cheeks.'

'You are doing that,' his daughter told him – for Etta was blushing as she always did when Mr Lippmann spoke to her.

'What's a nice book, Babs?' he asked his wife, as she came out on to the terrace. 'Can't you find a nice story for this child?' The house must be full, he was sure, of wonderfully therapeutic novels if only he knew where to lay hands on them. 'Roger, you're our bookworm. Look out a nice story-book for your guest. This one won't do her eyes any good.' Buying books with small print was a false economy, he thought, and bound to land one in large bills from an eye specialist before long. 'A very short-sighted policy,' he explained genially when he had given them a little lecture to which no one listened.

His wife was trying to separate some slippery cubes of ice and Sarah sprawled in a cane chair with her eyes shut. She was making the most of the setting sun, as Etta was making the most of romance.

'We like the same books,' Roger said to his father. 'So she can choose as well as I could.'

Etta was just beginning to feel a sense of surprised gratitude, had half turned to look in his direction when the betrothed came through the French windows and claimed her attention.

'In time for a lovely drink,' Mrs Lippmann said to Nora.

'She is too fat already,' said David.

Nora swung round and caught his wrists and held them threateningly. 'If you say that once more, I'll ... I'll just ...' He freed himself and pulled her close. She gasped and panted, but leant heavily against him. 'Promise!' she said.

'Promise what?'

'You won't ever say it again?'

He laughed at her mockingly.

They were less the centre of attention than they thought – Mr Lippmann was smiling, but rather at the lovely evening and that the day in London was over; Mrs Lippmann, impeded by the cardigan hanging over her shoulders, was mixing something in a glass jug and Sarah had her eyes closed against the evening sun. Only Etta, in some bewilderment, heeded them. Roger, who had his own ideas about love, turned his head scornfully.

Sarah opened her eyes for a moment and stared at Nora, in her mind measuring against her the wedding dress she had been designing. She is too fat for satin, she decided, shutting her eyes again and disregarding the bridal gown for the time being. She returned to thoughts of her own dress, adding a little of what she called 'back interest' (though lesser bridesmaids would no doubt obscure it from the congregation – or audience) in the form of long velvet ribbons in turquoise ... or rose? She drew her brows together and with her eyes still shut said, 'All the colours of the rainbow aren't very many, are they?'

'Now, Etta dear, what will you have to drink?' asked Mrs Lippmann.

Just as she was beginning to ask for some tomato juice, Mr Lippmann interrupted. He interrupted a great deal, for there were a great many things to be put right, it seemed to him. 'Now, Mommy, you should give her a glass of sherry with an egg beaten up in it. Roger, run and fetch a nice egg and a whisk, too ... all right, Babsie dear, I shall do it myself ... don't worry, child,' he said, turning to Etta and seeing her look of alarm. 'It is no trouble to me. I shall do this for you every evening that you are here. We shall watch the roses growing in your cheeks, shan't we, Mommy?'

He prepared the drink with a great deal of clumsy fuss and sat back to watch her drinking it, smiling to himself, as if the roses were already blossoming. 'Good, good!' he murmured, nodding at her as she drained the glass. Every evening, she thought, hoping that he would forget; but horrible though the drink had been, it was also reassuring; their concern for her was reassuring. She preferred it to the cold anxiety of her mother hovering with pills and thermometer.

'Yes,' said Mr Lippmann, 'we shall see. We shall see. I think your parents won't know you.' He puffed out his cheeks and sketched with a curving gesture the bosom she would soon have. He always forgot that her father was dead. It was quite fixed in his mind that he was simply a fellow who had obviously not made the grade; not everybody could. Roger bit his tongue hard, as if by doing so he could curb his father's. 'I must remind him again,' Sarah and her mother were both thinking.

The last day of the visit had an unexpected hazard as well as its own sadness, for Mrs Salkeld had written to say that her employer would lend her his car for the afternoon. When she had made a business call for him in the neighbourhood she would arrive to fetch Etta at about four o'clock.

'She is really to leave us, Mommy?' asked Mr Lippmann at breakfast, folding his newspaper and turning his attention on his family before hurrying to the station. He examined Etta's face and nodded. 'Next time you stay longer and we make rosy apples of these.' He patted her cheeks and ruffled her hair. 'You tell your Mommy and Dadda next time you stay a whole week.'

'She *has* stayed a whole week,' said Sarah.

'Then a fortnight, a month.'

He kissed his wife, made a gesture as if blessing them all, with his newspaper raised above his head, and went from the room at a trot. 'Thank goodness', thought Sarah, 'that he won't be here this afternoon to make kind enquiries about *her* husband.'

When she was alone with Etta, she said, 'I'm sorry about that mistake he keeps making.'

'I don't mind,' Etta said truthfully, 'I am only embarrassed because I know that you are.' That's *nothing*, she thought; but the day ahead was a different matter.

As time passed, Mrs Lippmann also appeared to be suffering from tension. She went upstairs and changed her matador pants for a linen skirt. She tidied up the terrace and told Roger to take his bathing things off his window-sill. As soon as she had stubbed out a cigarette, she emptied and dusted the ash-tray. She was conscious that Sarah was trying to see her with another's eyes.

'Oh, do stop taking photographs,' Sarah said tetchily to Roger, who had been clicking away with his camera all morning. He obeyed her only because he feared to draw attention to his activities. He had just taken what he hoped would be a very beautiful study of Etta in a typical pose – sitting on the river bank with a book in her lap. She had lifted her eyes and was gazing across the water if she were pondering whatever she had been reading. In fact, she had been arrested by thoughts of David and Nora and, although her eyes followed the print, the scene she saw did not correspond with the lines she read. She turned her head and looked at the willow trees on the far bank, the clumps of borage from which moorhens launched themselves. 'Perhaps next time that I see them, they'll be married and it will all be over,' she thought. The evening before, there had been a great deal of high-spirited sparring about between them. Offence meant and offence taken they assured one another. 'If you do that once more . . . I am absolutely serious,' cried Nora. 'You are trying not to laugh,' David said. 'I'm not. I am absolutely serious.' 'It will end in tears,' Roger had muttered contemptuously. Even good-tempered Mrs Lippmann had looked down her long nose disapprovingly. And that was the last, Etta supposed, that she would see of love for a long time. She was left once again with books. She returned to the one she was reading.

Roger had flung himself on to the grass nearby, appearing to trip over a tussock of grass and collapse. He tried to think of some opening remark which might lead to a discussion of the book. In the end, he asked abruptly, 'Do you like that?' She sat brooding over it, chewing the side of her finger. She nodded without looking up and, with a similar automatic gesture, she waved away a persistent wasp. He leant forward and clapped his hands together smartly and was relieved to see the wasp drop dead into the grass, although he would rather it had stung him first. Etta, however, had not noticed this brave deed.

The day passed wretchedly for him; each hour was more filled with the doom of her departure than the last. He worked hard to conceal his feelings, in which no one took an interest. He knew that it was all he could do, although no good could come from his succeeding. He took a few more secret photographs from his bedroom window, and then he sat down and wrote a short letter to her, explaining his love.

At four o'clock, her mother came. He saw at once that Etta was nervous and he guessed that she tried to conceal her nervousness behind a much jauntier manner to her mother than was customary. It would be a bad hour, Roger decided.

His own mother, in spite of her linen skirt, was gawdy and exotic beside Mrs Salkeld, who wore a navy-blue suit which looked as if it had been sponged and pressed a hundred times – a depressing process unknown to Mrs Lippmann. The pink-rimmed spectacles that Mrs Salkeld wore seemed to reflect a little colour on to her cheekbones, with the result that she looked slightly indignant about something or other. However, she smiled a great deal, and only Etta guessed what an effort it was to her to do so. Mrs Lippmann gave her a chair where she might have a view of the river and she sat down, making a point of not looking round the room, and smoothed her gloves. Her jewellery was real but very small.

'If we have tea in the garden, the wasps get into Anna's rose-petal jam,' said Mrs Lippmann. Etta was not at her best, she felt – not helping at all. She was aligning herself too staunchly with the Lippmanns, so that her mother seemed a stranger to her, as well. 'You see, I am at home here,' she implied, as she jumped up to fetch things or hand things round. She was a little daring in her familiarity.

Mrs Salkeld had contrived the visit because she wanted to understand and hoped to approve of her daughter's friends. Seeing the lawns, the light reflected from the water, later this large, bright room, and the beautiful poppy-seed cake the Hungarian cook had made for tea, she understood completely and felt pained. She could see then, with Etta's eyes, their own dark, narrow house, and she thought of the lonely hours she spent there reading on days of imprisoning rain. The Lippmanns would even have better weather, she thought bitterly. The bitterness affected her enjoyment of the poppy-seed cake. She had, as puritanical people often have, a sweet tooth. She ate the cake with a casual air, determined not to praise.

'You are so kind to spare Etta to us,' said Mrs Lippmann.

'*You* are kind to invite her,' Mrs Salkeld replied, and then for Etta's sake, added: 'She loves to come to you.'

Etta looked self-consciously down at her feet.

'No, I don't smoke,' her mother said primly. 'Thank you.'

Mrs Lippmann seemed to decide not to, either, but very soon her hand stole out and took a cigarette – while she was not looking, thought Roger, who was having some amusement from watching his mother on her best behaviour. Wherever she was, the shagreen cigarette case and the gold lighter were nearby. Ash-trays never were. He got up and fetched one before Etta could do so.

The girls' school was being discussed – one of the few topics the two mothers had in common. Mrs Lippmann had never taken it seriously. She laughed at the uniform and despised the staff – an attitude she might at least have hidden from her daughter, Mrs Salkeld felt. The tea-trolley was being wheeled away and her eyes followed the remains of the poppy-seed cake. She had planned a special supper for Etta to return to, but she felt now that it was no use. The things of the mind had left room for an echo. It sounded with every footstep or spoken word in that house where not enough was going on. She began to wonder if there were things of the heart and not the mind that Etta fastened upon so desperately when she was reading. Or was her desire to be in a different place? Lowood was a worse one – she could raise her eyes and look round her own room in relief; Pemberley was better and she would benefit from the change. 'But how can I help her?' she asked herself in anguish. 'What possible change – and radical it must be – can I ever find the strength to effect?' People had thought her wonderful to have made her own life and brought up her child alone. She had kept their heads above water and it had taken all her resources to do so.

Her lips began to refuse the sherry Mrs Lippmann suggested and then, to her surprise and Etta's astonishment, she said 'yes' instead.

It was very early to have suggested it, Mrs Lippmann thought, but it would seem to put an end to the afternoon. Conversation had been as hard work as she had anticipated and she longed for a dry martini to stop her from yawning, as she was sure it would; but something about Mrs Salkeld seemed to discourage gin drinking.

'Mother, it isn't half-past five yet,' said Sarah.

'Darling, don't be rude to your mummy. I know perfectly well what the time is.' ('Who better?' she wondered.) 'And this isn't a public house, you know.'

She had flushed a little and was lighting another cigarette. Her bracelets jangled against the decanter as she handed Mrs Salkeld her glass of sherry, saying, 'Young people are so stuffy,' with an air of complicity.

Etta, who had never seen her mother drinking sherry before, watched nervously, as if she might not know how to do it. Mrs Salkeld – remembering the flavour from Christmas mornings many years ago and – more faintly – from her mother's party trifle – sipped cautiously. In an obscure way she was doing this for Etta's sake. 'It may speed her on her way,' thought Mrs Lippmann, playing idly with her charm bracelet, having run out of conversation.

When Mrs Salkeld rose to go, she looked round the room once more as if to fix it in her memory – the setting where she would imagine her daughter on future occasions.

'And come again soon, there's a darling girl,' said Mrs Lippmann, putting her arm round Etta's shoulder as they walked towards the car. Etta, unused to but not ungrateful for embraces, leant awkwardly against her. Roger, staring at the gravel, came behind carrying the suitcase.

'I have wasted my return ticket,' Etta said.

'Well, that's not the end of the world,' her mother said briskly. She thought, but did not say, that perhaps they could claim the amount if they wrote to British Railways and explained.

Mrs Lippmann's easy affection meant so much less than her own stiff endearments, but she resented it all the same and when she was begged, with enormous warmth, to visit them all again soon her smile was a prim twisting of her lips.

The air was bright with summer sounds, voices across the water and rooks up in the elm trees. Roger stood back listening in a dream to the good-byes and thank yous. Nor was *this* the end of the world, he told himself. Etta would come again and, better than that, they would also grow older and so be less at the mercy of circumstances. He would be in a position to command his life and turn occasions to his own advantage. Meanwhile, he had done what he could. None the less, he felt such dejection, such an overwhelming conviction that it was the end of the world after all, that he could not watch the car go down the drive, and he turned and walked quickly – rudely, off-handedly, his mother thought – back to the house.

Mrs Salkeld, driving homewards in the lowering sun, knew that Etta had tears in her eyes. 'I'm glad you enjoyed yourself,' she said. Without waiting for an answer, she added: 'They are very charming people.' She had

always suspected charm and rarely spoke of it, but in this case the adjec-
tive seemed called for.

Mr Lippmann would be coming back from London about now, Etta was
thinking. 'And David will bring Nora. They will all be on the terrace
having drinks – dry martinis, not sherry.'

She was grateful to her mother about the sherry and understood that it
had been an effort towards meeting Mrs Lippmann's world half-way, and
on the way back, she had not murmured one word of criticism – for their
worldliness or extravagance or the vulgar opulence of their furnishings. She
had even made a kind remark about them.

I might buy her a new dress, Mrs Salkeld thought – something like the
one Sarah was wearing. Though it does seem a criminal waste when she has
all her good school clothes to wear out.

They had come on to the main road, and evening traffic streamed by. In
the distance the gas holder looked pearl grey and the smoke from factories
was pink in the sunset. They were nearly home. Etta, who had blinked her
tears back from her eyes, took a sharp breath, almost a sigh.

Their own street with its tall houses was in shadow. 'I wish we had a cat,'
said Etta, as she got out of the car and saw the next door tabby looking
through the garden railings. She imagined burying her face in its warm fur,
it loving only her. To her surprise, her mother said: 'Why not?' Briskly, she
went up the steps and turned the key with its familiar grating sound in the
lock. The house, with its smell – familiar, too – of floor polish and stuffiness, looked secretive. Mrs Salkeld, hardly noticing this, hurried to the
kitchen to put the casserole of chicken in the oven.

Etta carried her suitcase upstairs. On the dressing-table was a jar of
marigolds. She was touched by this – just when she did not want to be
touched. She turned her back on them and opened her case. On the top
was the book she had left on the terrace. Roger had brought it to her at the
last moment. Taking it now, she found a letter inside. Simply 'Etta' was
written on the envelope.

Roger had felt that he had done all he was capable of and that was to
write in the letter those things he could not have brought himself to say,
even if he had had an opportunity. No love letter could have been less
anticipated and Etta read it twice before she could realise that it was neither a joke nor a mistake. It was the most extraordinary happening of her
life, the most incredible.

Her breathing grew slower and deeper as she sat staring before her,
pondering her mounting sense of power. It was as if the whole Lippmann
family – Nora as well – had proposed to her. To marry Roger – a long, long
time ahead though she must wait to do so – would be the best possible way
of belonging.

She got up stiffly – for her limbs now seemed too clumsy a part of her body with its fly-away heart and giddy head – she went over to the dressing-table and stared at herself in the glass. 'I am I,' she thought, but she could not believe it. She stared and stared, but could not take in the tantalising idea.

After a while, she began to unpack. The room was a place of transit, her temporary residence. When she had made it tidy, she went downstairs to thank her mother for the marigolds.

The Prerogative of Love

Where the lawn was in shadow from the house, the watering-spray flung dazzling aigrettes into the air. The scent of the wet earth, the sound of dripping rose-leaves was delicious.

The round marble table was abandoned in the sun, a butterfly hovered above it, both blindingly white. Too hot, Lillah had decided, and had taken her chair and her sewing into the shade; but the damage was done, and she began to feel giddy. Mrs Hatton made her go upstairs and drink salt water and lie on her bed.

'It's a swine, isn't it?' the gardener said, meaning the weather. He was speaking to the postman, who crunched by on the gravel drive with letters in his hand.

'Too sudden,' the postman agreed, stopping for a moment, watching the other man work, the brown hand moving slow as a toad among the geraniums, tweaking up tiny weeds. 'A criminal colour, that bright red,' he said. 'Hurts my eyes to look at it. I always preferred the white ones.'

He continued slowly up the drive, hoping to be seen from the house by Mrs Hatton the cook, and offered tea.

No one saw him, for the curtains, hardly stirring, were drawn across the open windows. He stepped into the hall and laid the letters on the brass tray on the table. He suffered a fit of noisy coughing, stood with bowed head after it, listening, but heard not a sound and made off down the drive again.

The letters – what Lillah would call a tradesman's lot – stayed there until Richard came home. It was six o'clock then and hardly any cooler. The cats lay on the stone floor like cast-off furs. One of them got up and stretched and came towards him, its sides hanging, very thin, for it did not fancy its food in this weather. Listlessly, it rubbed its head against his leg, smelt the streets of London on his shoes and wandered, repelled, back to its place and flopped again.

Mrs Hatton, neat as a new pin, came down the back stairs to the kitchen, having napped and tidied up and now, ready for the fray, pinned a clean, folded napkin round her head, as if it were a Stilton cheese. She took the grey and white fish off the ice and, looking grim, began to fillet.

All her movements were slow, so that she should not get hot. She even sang under her breath; although yearningly – for a Wiltshire woman – about Galway Bay.

'I'm afraid you'll have to hold the fort,' Lillah told her husband. 'I'll try again later, but at the moment I can't put my feet to the ground.'

She lay on the bed, wrapped in a white kimono. The bedroom was cool to Richard, after the hot pavements and the asphyxiating train. His clothes clung to him, he felt that this room was no place for him and longed to plunge into the river, a long dive between the silken, trailing weeds. But Lillah said there would not be time.

She had nothing to do all day but keep herself cool, he thought, and she had not even managed that. He held the curtain aside, so that at least he could look at the river. It flowed by at the foot of the garden, beyond the urns of geraniums where the lawn sloped down to the mooring-stage. On the evenings when there was dinghy-racing from the club, white sails clustered there, tipping and rocking, caught in the sheltered curve of river without wind. There was none tonight. There was no breath of air.

'Too late to put the Foresters off,' Lillah said. 'I suppose.'

Although actressy in so many other ways, she lacked the old trouper's temperament, and her audiences – even such a loyal one as the Foresters – were not considered first if she were out of humour.

'Do you mean you won't come down at all?' he asked in consternation.

'Of course, I'll try. I did a little while ago. You must leave me as long as you can, please, darling. Every minute I think it must get cooler, that the dizziness will go.'

She sighed and stirred, then stretched her arm towards him. It looked imploring, but as he moved towards her was withdrawn. She crooked it under her head, and stared up at the ceiling.

'A quick wash, then,' he said, turning to the door.

'Did Mrs Hatton put the wine on ice, I wonder,' Lillah said, not exactly giving him instructions to go and find out, but getting that effect.

Richard went to the kitchen as soon as he could, and found that Mrs Hatton had remembered the wine. She was well forward, she said. And it was certainly hot, she agreed, but nothing to the climate in some parts of the world.

Once upon a time, she had made what she called 'the round trip', on a legacy from an employer, and travel had changed her life. She had returned to another kitchen, but so enriched that her mind was forever roaming, as she stirred and whisked and sieved. 'Bermuda, you'd like, sir,' she once told Richard, as he was setting off for a short holiday in Suffolk.

'The heat's knocked Madam,' she remarked, and took up some steak and began to knock that. 'I got her to drink some salt water. We always did that in India, I told her. "It will put back what you've perspired," I said.' She had indeed told Lillah this and Lillah had disdained to listen, drinking quickly to prevent more of such homely hints. 'You learn to respect the sun when you've been in the tropics,' Mrs Hatton informed Richard.

'No doubt you do,' he said. 'I never was east of Biarritz in all my life.'

'If Madam wants help dressing, I can spare a minute. I'm quite nicely forward.'

'We can always rely on you,' he said hurriedly, looking about him in a flustered manner, forgetting what on earth it was that had suddenly come into his mind while she was talking.

'The ice is in the drawing-room on the tray,' she said.

She could even recapture and read thoughts that had flown from him. She was always more attuned to the master of the house than to the mistress. 'I laid it all out ready.'

'Yes, you think of everything.'

'It's simple enough when you're on your own. It's when there are two of you that things get overlooked.'

'I could have swum, after all,' Richard thought.

But that moment he heard a car coming up the drive, and went out to the hall door to greet the Foresters, relieved to know that at last Lillah had decided to get up again and dress.

A small, open car swung round the circle of gravel in front of the house and, alone in it, bare-shouldered, with hair knotted up on top, Lillah's niece, Arabella, looked as if she were naked, she might have been sitting up in her bath.

'I won't stop a second if you would rather not,' she said, as the car pulled up.

'I thought you were stark naked,' Richard said, opening the door and looking with interest at her small, white frock – which was sparsely patterned with strawberries – and at her shining, tanned legs.

'I'll only come in for a minute,' she said, when she had jumped out of the car. She put her thin arms round his neck and kissed him. They were very long arms, he thought, and seemed to have been flung over his head like a lasso. Then she stepped back and hauled out of the car a large wicker hamper.

'Are you picnicking?' he asked.

She looked surprised. 'This is only my make-up,' she explained. 'Don't worry, darling. I shan't stay the night. But I must have it with me. My cigarettes are in it.'

'And your shoes?' he asked, for she was crossing the gravel barefoot.

'Maybe,' she said, nodding. 'Oh, it's cool!' She stood in the hall and let out a deep breath. 'I've been in some bogus-looking pub all day long wearing a chinchilla coat – one of those snobbish photographs; playing darts with the locals, draped in fur and choked with pearls and all the mates grinning and enjoying the joke. So hot.'

'Lillah's not been well all day.'

'Oh, poor old thing. I'll tell you what, Richard – though I promise not to stay one moment – can I just slake my thirst before I go? Oh, you've got people coming,' she said, passing the open dining-room door, seeing the table. 'That settles it. I'll run out the back way with my empty glass the minute they arrive.'

Richard wished that Lillah had been down to answer for him and he poured out the drink quickly and handed it to Arabella.

She picked up ice with her fingers and dropped it into her glass and took another piece and ran it round the nape of her neck and up and down the insides of her arms. 'What's wrong with her?' she asked.

'The heat, you know.'

'Oh, I *know*. A chinchilla coat, if you please. Oh, I told you. I'll just dash up and say good-bye to her. Who's coming?'

'The Foresters. John and Helen.'

'Well, do give them my love.'

She ran upstairs, still holding the lump of ice in her fist, and Richard stood staring in a disturbed way at her wicker basket lying on a chair.

Lillah, whose bedroom, at the back of the house, overlooked the river, had not heard the car and answered rather suspiciously when Arabella knocked on the door.

She was at the dressing-table powdering her white shoulders, and turned, looking far from welcoming, to be kissed and then leant towards the glass again and wiped the lipstick off her cheek.

'What are you up to, Arabella?'

'I've been at Henley all day long, playing darts in a pub and wearing fur coats. I was just going home, when I thought that being in striking distance, I would look in for a drink.'

She sat down on a brocade-covered chair and sucked her ice cube. 'I'm not staying a minute, though.'

'How is your mother?'

'Oh, you're not well, Richard was saying. I'm so sorry. I was quite forgetting. I expect it's the heat. I know *I've* sweltered all day long. Guess what I had for lunch. A cheese sandwich. But not to worry, I'll be home in an hour and a half with any luck. You look so wonderfully cool, Lillah. It's the most elegant dress. The Poor Man's Lady Diana Duff Cooper,

Mother and I always call you. Don't let me hinder you, but I must shake out my hair.'

She wandered round the room, looking for somewhere to put the piece of melting ice and at last threw it out of the window. Then she took the pins from her bright hair and shook it against her bare shoulders.

'I like the colour of your hair today,' Lillah said.

'Oh, thank you. And I simply dote on yours.'

'Well, mine is always the same.'

Lillah leant close to the looking-glass, fixing on some ear-rings.

'Yes, of course, darling,' her niece murmured, face hidden now under a tent of hair, rubbing her scalp. Before Lillah had put on the second ear-ring, she saw Arabella stretch out a hand and take up one of her hair-brushes.

'You don't mind, do you?' she asked, and began to brush with great energy.

'Well, as a matter of fact, I do rather,' Lillah replied.

Back under her hair and brushing until it crackled, the girl seemed not to hear.

'Haven't you one of your own?' Lillah asked, making an impatient movement to gain the girl's attention. 'I thought that models carried the lot wherever they went.'

She felt giddy again – rage hitting her, as the sun had.

Arabella swept the hair back from her face and smiled at her aunt. 'I left the lot downstairs with Uncle Richard,' she replied.

'But you should have put us off,' Helen Forester protested.

'Of course you should,' her husband added.

'For goodness' sake, we're old enough friends by now ...' his wife went on.

'Lillah wouldn't hear of it. She says she feels so much better now and I shall be in trouble for ever having mentioned it. She'll be down in a moment. This is Arabella's, her niece's,' he explained, as he moved the wicker basket from a chair so that Helen Forester could sit down. 'She's a model in London and just looked in on her way home from some job.'

He thought that John Forester seemed to brace himself, and that well he might.

'Forgive me, please,' Lillah said, coming across the hall to the open door of the drawing-room. She stretched out her arms to them and put her cheek first to Helen's then John's, a heavy ear-ring swung against each face in turn. 'I've felt so stupid all day long. I couldn't lift my silly head.'

'You should have put us off,' said Helen. 'I was telling Richard ...'

'But I had looked forward to seeing you so much, and now I have seen you I'm myself again. Mrs Hatton' – she lowered her voice – 'insisted on my going to bed. She's a very strict disciplinarian.'

She saw John looking towards the door and turned round.

'This is my niece, Arabella, who's just dropped in,' she said, staring down at the girl's bare feet.

Arabella's hair was now looped smoothly against her cheeks, like the youthful Queen Victoria's. She had also, her aunt noticed, helped herself very liberally to Lillah's scent.

'We met when I was a little girl,' Arabella said demurely. 'I know you can't remember me, because I was fat and had pigtails and a great brace on my teeth. I must look different now.'

'You must indeed,' John Forester said.

She smiled and came farther into the room. 'You're the Labrador breeders, aren't you?' she asked.

'Where are your shoes, dear girl?' asked Lillah, trying to get a tone of asperity across to Arabella, but so that the Foresters would not detect it.

'It's hardly worth putting them on now when I'm just going. I don't care to drive with shoes on.'

'You left your drink,' said Richard, handing it to her.

'Thank you, darling, I'll thrust it down and be off. I promised to be out of the back door before you arrived,' she told John Forester.

'You silly girl,' said Lillah lightly. She took the drink that Richard had poured out quickly, before, he hoped, she could put them all in the wrong, as she often did, by asking for something without gin. She laid her hand on his shoulder for a moment, where it looked very pale against the dark cloth, and Richard covered it quickly with his own. He smiled questioningly and she nodded.

'Isn't that a beautiful dress of Lillah's?' Helen asked, slightly embarrassed to find herself caught staring at them.

'It's my beautiful wife in it,' Richard said.

'But I meant that, too,' Helen said, too willing for words to agree, not to seem restrained by hearing another woman praised.

Arabella was telling John Forester about the chinchilla coat and the game of darts, and he seemed entranced. 'And guess what I had for lunch,' she asked.

'Isn't it a heavenly frock Lillah's wearing?' Helen asked him. 'Doesn't it suit her wonderfully?' To bring Lillah's beauty to the notice of her husband was even greater generosity, she thought, and she looked almost transfigured with the pleasure of finding her friend so lovely.

John's attention was turned from Arabella rather slowly, his eyes moved almost unseeingly to where they were directed. 'Perfect,' he said.

'A cheese sandwich,' said Arabella. 'Just imagine.'

'I suppose you live on air,' he said, his glance, enlivened, returning quickly to her. He was much taken by the rounded thinness of her arms, slim even where they joined the shoulders. If they had been alone, he would have made some excuse to touch them, perhaps patting her in a fatherly way as he begged her not to starve herself or, more youthfully, wondering if he could circle them between finger and thumb.

'I eat like a horse,' she said. 'Worse – for I'm carnivorous. And the bloodier the better.'

'What a gigantic cineraria,' Helen said in an admiring voice.

'It is rather ghastly, but dear Mrs Hatton gave it to me on my birthday and I have to have it about, not to hurt her feelings. It's just the sort of thing she adores.'

Helen decided not to like cinerarias in future.

John was looking at Arabella's diminishing drink with anguish. Evenings alone with Richard and Lillah were never so entrancing to him as they were to his wife. Admiration was such a large ingredient of Helen's simple good-nature. She did not feel, as he did, that some attempt should be made on their own behalf. She basks in the shade, he thought. The tops of her arms, he suddenly noticed, were very freckled and their flabbiness flattened against her sides.

What would happen to them all if the girl didn't soon go, Richard wondered. Especially, he wondered, what would happen to him.

Then Lillah – not to be put in the wrong by this ravenous girl, warmly said, 'Arabella, may I ask Mrs Hatton to do a little concocting? You *will* stay?'

'I simply *couldn't*. I know only too well how it is in kitchens. Sometimes I take a man home to dinner without warning and there may be only two cutlets.' John seemed to have drawn her eyes back to his, and to his devouring attention she addressed herself. 'Mother and I hiss over them all the time they are cooking. "Let *me* be the vegetarian this time. You were yesterday." But Mother's so noble. She usually manages to get the poached egg for herself and makes long, long apologies for never eating meat. She goes into it rather too much. She went on and on to one man, and a lot later he came again and this time I had managed to get the egg, and Mother ate her cutlet with great enjoyment. "You've changed over, you two," he said.'

For some reason, John burst into sycophantic laughter, then he tilted his glass and finished his gin.

'You will think we live on cutlets,' Arabella said a few seconds later, and after that there was silence.

'Well, nothing is settled,' Richard thought. 'She hasn't answered one way or another.' He felt that their evening was nearly on the rocks. Adoration cleft the conversation in two – John's of Arabella, Helen's of Lillah – and he began to pour out more drinks, since the continuing silence and John's empty glass made it impossible not to. Lillah, thinking of Mrs Hatton and even more, no doubt, of social patterns she despised, would be impatient. 'Everyone drunk before dinner,' she had said so often, driving home from other people's houses. 'I have never known a claret so thrown away,' or 'That poor withered old soufflé.'

'I'll tell you what, Lillah,' Arabella said in her most childish voice, 'let me go and reconnoitre. I'll see how things are with Mrs Hatton. It's for me to bear the brunt.'

Lillah moved quickly to prevent her, tried to say something to detain her, but the girl had sped across the hall. John was touched to see that the soles of her feet were dirty.

'Oh dear,' Lillah said. 'I'm so sorry.'

'Such a beautiful girl,' said Helen.

'That family has more than its fair share of looks, I always think,' Richard said, smiling at his wife. John looked at her, too, almost for the first time that evening – and saw resemblances between the two faces – the niece's, the aunt's. He had not known Lillah in the early years of her marriage, and he wondered if Richard had had such luck long ago – an Arabella-like bride, whom time had changed and paled and quietened, but whose erstwhile beauty still quite clearly bewitched him.

'Oh, dear,' Lillah said again. 'I hope she is not lifting the lids off the saucepans and asking questions.'

Richard, seeing Mrs Hatton crossing the hall with a grim stride, going to rearrange her table, closed the door.

'How are the roses this year, John?' he asked.

Having upset all but one of them under that roof, hindered dinner, made an awkward number at the table and talked too much, Arabella, towards the end of the meal, suddenly shivered. Leaning forward, chafing the tops of her arms, she studied the centrepiece of fruit and took out an apple from underneath, so that the pyramid collapsed, a peach rolled across the table and cherries were scattered.

'It will be a chilly run back,' she said. 'Perhaps I should make a start.' For at last the day was cool.

The others were still eating a kirsch-flavoured confection that Mrs Hatton had sampled in California. Much praised it had been by Helen, who spooned it up lovingly. She would describe it later to her humbler friends and would expect them to listen spellbound.

Arabella was up now and darted round the table with a kiss for each of them. Lillah, receiving hers last, kept her head bent, and John pushed back his chair, dropped his napkin, knocked a spoon and some cherries on the floor. Richard went to the door and opened it.

'Don't stir, anybody,' Arabella said.

'It's true that we haven't finished dinner,' Lillah said. ('And I consider she had every right to say it,' Helen told John afterwards.)

'Don't come out, Richard. Please not to. Lillah, may I borrow a sweater? I'll be frozen driving home.'

'There's a cardigan on the hall settle,' her aunt said, and seemed with the most delicate gesture to draw Richard's attention to his place at the table. He returned to it and passing Lillah's chair, patted her shoulder – with such a touch of understanding, Helen thought.

'There's lipstick on your face,' she told her husband.

'On all your faces, if I may say so,' Lillah said, having removed it from her own.

'Such a lively girl,' Helen said uncertainly. After all, it was Lillah's own sister's child and so had every claim to praise.

'Delightful,' John said in a more definite tone. 'She reminds me how scatter-brained I was myself when I was young.' He listened to the car being started, then throwing up gravel as it tore away.

'We envy the young, that's what it is,' Richard thought sadly. 'It is natural for us to harden against them.'

'My poor sister was widowed at twenty-three,' Lillah said; as if this could be the explanation of her niece's behaviour. She gazed at the scattered cherries on the white cloth, then added: 'Her life was haphazard, at the best of times.'

'My aunt is a perfectionist,' Arabella had said a little while ago. She had spoken to Helen, and as if Lillah herself were not present.

This had often been said of her before, but now she would have liked to disclaim the label, seeing herself, in Arabella's eyes, too much absorbed by trifles, restricted and neurotic. 'It must be Mrs Hatton who is the perfectionist,' she had said. 'It was all left to her.' Helen had once more, boringly, been praising something.

Haphazard though her sister's life was, she had this daughter in it, and close enough they seemed to Lillah whenever she saw them together. And the Foresters had children, too, though grown-up now and gone away.

'Rather a disrupted evening,' Lillah said apologetically as her guests were going, and had hardly the patience to listen to their protestations, their expressions of delight. She and Richard went down the steps with them on to the dark drive and stood together as the car drove away, each lifting a hand briefly in farewell, then turning back towards the house, which still threw out from its walls the stored warmth of the day. He took her arm as they went up the steps.

'You were wonderful,' he said.

'Well, it is over.'

'You must feel exhausted.'

'That dreadful girl,' she said.

*

Helen looked back as the car turned into the lane, and saw Richard and Lillah at the top of the steps, in the light from the hall. Until they were out of the drive, she had said nothing, and even now kept her voice low, as if the still air might waft it back towards the house.

'How in love they are,' she said. 'Every time I see them they seem more so.' Which touched her most she hardly knew – Richard's gallantry, or Lillah, who inspired it. 'I loved the stuffed vine-leaves. I've so often read about them in books. I suppose Mrs Hatton picked that up in the Middle East. What a pretty touch – those tiny flowers in the finger-bowls. What were they? I meant to ask. I don't think the niece was welcome. I'm sure I shouldn't have been so smooth about it as Lillah was. If Mrs Hatton complained, you couldn't blame her. I must try that with the vine-leaves. See what I can do. I suppose you would need to blanch them first. I was longing to ask, but didn't quite like to.'

She was really talking to herself.

Those treasure-hunts we used to go on, all about these very lanes, John suddenly remembered. Lovely summer evenings just like this one, tearing like demented things about the countryside, diving into the river in the early hours, parking cars at the edges of woods.

He kept his thoughts to himself, as if they were secrets of his own, and then he remembered that Helen had been there too. She had once swum across the river fully dressed, for a bet. It was difficult to believe.

'A really beautiful frock,' she was saying.

'Unusual,' he replied. 'Not much of it.' He suddenly laughed.

'I meant Lillah's.'

Presently she sighed and said: 'He's so wonderful to her always.'

John knew the pattern – the excited admiration invariably turned to dissatisfaction in the end – one of the reasons why these evenings ruffled him.

'I'm sure that to him she's as beautiful as on the day they married,' she went on.

'Still a very fine woman,' he replied.

'Is it because they've never had children, I wonder? The glamour wasn't worn off by all those nursery troubles. All their love kept for one another.'

'It is better to have children,' John said.

'Well, of course. Who ever'd deny it? You know I didn't think that. But I wondered if it had drawn them closer together, *not* having them. They never seem to take one another for granted.' 'As we do,' she left unspoken, though her sigh was explicit.

'Well, we mustn't compare ourselves with *them*,' he said rather smartly. 'And who are we to be talking about love? They're the ones. They're famous for it, after all. It's their prerogative.'

The Thames Spread Out

Nothing could have been lovelier, Rose thought. For most of the day she stayed on the little balcony, looking out over the flooded fields. Although it was Friday, Gilbert had not come and she was sure now that he would not come, and was shaken with laughter at the idea of him rowing out to her from the railway station, across the river and meadows, bowler-hatted and red with exasperation.

This day was usually her busiest of the week, when she stopped pottering and worked methodically to make the ramshackle villa and herself clean and tidy. By four o'clock she would be ready, and Gilbert, who was punctual over his illicit escapades as with everything else, would soon after drive down the lane. Perhaps escapade was altogether too exciting a word for the homely ways they had drifted into. She fussed over his little ailments far more than his wife had ever done, not because she loved him more, or indeed at all, but because her position was more precarious.

On Saturday mornings he left her, having broken his long journey from the North, as he told his wife. He often thought how furious she would have been if she had known that the break was only twenty miles from London, where they lived.

As soon as he left her on Saturdays, Rose went down to the shops by the station, cashed the cheque he had given her, and bought some little treats for herself to while away the weekend – a few slices of smoked salmon, chocolate peppermint-creams, and magazines. She loved the rest of that day. Gilbert had gone – she could shut herself in and be cosy till he came again.

Only the faintest of regrets ruffled her comfort – little faults in herself that depressed her slightly but could easily be rectified later on. She was shamefully lazy, she knew, and self-indulgent. All the time she meant to save money, but never did. Gilbert was not very generous. His Friday nights were expensive and he knew it and very rarely gave Rose a present. She really had nothing.

Her fur coat, which she had worn all day as she leant over the balcony rail watching the seagulls on the floodwater, was shabby and baggy; he had given it to her years ago at the beginning of their liaison when she was still working for him. It was squirrel, and his wife would not have been seen dead in it.

He certainly won't come now, Rose decided, looking at the forsaken water. There had really never been the slightest likelihood of it, and that was just as well, she thought, catching sight of herself in a glass as she was making a cup of tea. A dark band showed at the parting of her golden hair and she had run out of peroxide.

Some young boy had come in a rowing-boat that morning – a Boy Scout, perhaps – and had offered to do her shopping. She had wrapped some money in the shopping-list and let it down in a basket from the bedroom window. Later he had brought back a loaf of bread and some milk, a pound of sausages and cigarettes, a dozen candles. She would have liked a half-bottle of gin, but had not liked to write it down. The peroxide she had quite forgotten.

She made tea on the primus stove Gilbert had bought for their river picnics. These were in July always, when his wife went to stay with her mother in the Channel Islands. Then he moved in with Rose for a whole fortnight; from niggardly motives made love to her excessively, became irritable, felt cramped in the uncomfortable little house and exasperated by the way it was falling to pieces. The primus stove was hardly ever used. It was too often raining, or they were in bed, or both. Rose was afraid it would blow up, but now, with the floodwater in the downstairs rooms, she had to overcome her fears or go without tea.

The sun was beginning to set and she knew how soon it got dark these winter days. She took her cup of tea and went out on to the balcony to watch. Every ten years or so, the Thames in that place would rise too high, brim over its banks and cover the fields for miles, changing the landscape utterly. The course of the river itself she could trace here and there from lines of willow trees or other landmarks she knew.

Beyond, on what before had been the other bank, a little train was crossing the floods. The raised track was still a foot or two above river level. Puffing along, reflected in the water, it curved away into the distance and disappeared among the poplar trees by the church. There, all the gravestones were submerged, and the inn had the river flowing in through the front door and out of the back.

'Thames-side Venice,' a newspaper reporter had called it. The children loved it, and now Rose saw two young boys rowing by on the pink water. The sun had slipped down through the mist, was very low, behind some grey trees blobbed with mistletoe; but the light on the water was very beautiful. The white seabirds scarcely moved and a row of swans went in single file down a footpath whose high railing-tops on either side broke the surface of the water.

Rose sipped her tea and watched, intent on having the most of every second of the fading loveliness – the silence and the reflections and the light, and then the silence broken by a cat crying far away or a shout coming thinly across the cold air.

'I'm glad he didn't come,' she said aloud.

At this hour, other men, husbands, those who had not sent their families away, would be returning. The train was at the station and they would take to their boats and row homewards, right up to their staircases, tying up to the newel-post and greeted from above by their children. Rose imagined them all as lake dwellers and hoped that they were enjoying the adventure.

She was curious about her neighbours – the few of them scattered along the river bank. She wondered about them when she passed by on her way to the shops, but she had never spoken to them or been inside their houses, and she had never wished to do so. Her solitariness suited her and her position was too informal. She would not embarrass other people by her situation.

But she made up stories to herself about some of them, especially about the people at the white house nearby who came only at week-ends. They seemed very gay, and laughter and music went on till late on Saturday nights. From where she was, she could just see the eaves of their boat-house sticking out of the river, but the house itself lay farther back and out of sight.

It was growing dark very fast, and the water, a moment or two earlier rosy, whitened as the sun went down. Under the high woods, out of the wind, the fields were frozen, their black and glassy surface littered with broken ice that boys had thrown.

Suddenly, at last, Rose could bear no more. The strangeness overcame her and she went inside and washed her cup and saucer in the bathroom basin and emptied the tea-pot over the banisters into the flooded passageway.

A swan had come in through the front door. Looking austere and suspicious, he turned his head about, circled aloofly, and returned to the garden. It was weird, Rose thought. This was a word she often used. So many things were to her either weird or intriguing.

The sunset, for instance, had been intriguing, but the sudden beginning of the long evening, the swan coming indoors, the smell of the water lying down there was very weird. She drew the curtains across the balcony doors. They would not meet and she clipped them together with a clothes-peg to keep the darkness hidden.

The bedroom was crowded with furniture and rolled-up matting rescued from downstairs, and looked like a corner of a junk shop. Nothing was new or matched another thing. It had all no doubt been bought off old barrows or hunted for in attics, so that the house could be called furnished when it was let. Wicker uncurled from the legs of an armchair and caught Rose's stockings as she passed by, and in the mornings when she made the bed she picked up dozens of blond feathers from the eiderdown.

It was the first time she had ever had a house to herself. After years of living with her married sister, it had seemed wonderful to put the frying-pan on her own stove and fry her own sausages in it, and she had felt a little self-conscious, as if she were playing at keeping house and did so before an audience, as in the imaginary games of her childhood.

For a time she could not be quite natural on her own. Look at me all the way round, from any angle, I really am a housewife. You won't catch me out, she often thought. But no one was ever there but Gilbert, and he, indifferent to the intriguing notion of her keeping house, sat with his back to her and read his pink newspaper.

In the end the magic had gone, she tired of her rôle, and the home was not one, she saw, that anyone could take a pride in, especially this evening, with candlelight making the crowded room macabre.

'I shall never get the place straight afterwards,' she said. She talked to herself a great deal nowadays.

She had forgotten the beauty of the flooded landscape and was overcome by wretchedness. The woman at the post office had warned her of the filth the receding water would leave behind, the smell that lingered, the stained walls and woodwork, and doors half twisted off their hinges.

Earlier that week, as she watched the rockery slowly going under, then the lower boughs of shrubs and very soon the higher ones, Rose had felt apprehensive. She had never had any experience in the least like it. Yet, when the worst happened and the house was invaded, perched up above it, enisled, as if she were hibernating in these unusual surroundings, she had begun to feel elated instead.

Her sister, worried to death from reading about the Thames-side Venice in the newspapers, wrote to ask her to stay. The letter had come by boat and was taken up in a basket through the bedroom window. 'Roy and I wish you would come back for good, you know that,' Beryl had written. The children missed her. They had been told that she had gone away to work, and the same story did for the neighbours, but they were less likely to think it true.

Roy said that his sister-in-law was wasting herself and ruining her chances. Once a girl takes up with married men, he had told his wife, she will find herself drifting from one to the other and she'll never get married herself. This Beryl left out of the letter.

Rose had been frank about her plans but, wary from long practice of secret affairs, had kept Gilbert's name to herself. 'The man I'm going out with,' she had called him at the beginning, and so she still wrote of him. She would have made someone a good wife, her brother-in-law often said, knowing what men liked. The house was pleasanter when she was there and the children were easier to manage.

A letter must be written to still her sister's fears. All day, Rose had put it off, but now began to look for some writing-paper. The wardrobe door swung open as she crossed the room and she saw her reflection in the blurred glass front. 'My hair!' she thought. She had a suspicion that she might be beginning to let herself go, a serious mistake for one in her position.

When she had found the paper and a bottle of green ink, she cleared a corner of the table and began to write. 'Dear B, you'd laugh if you could see me at this minute.'

She glanced round the room and then, smiling to herself, began to describe it. She was a born letter-writer, Beryl said, and she tried consciously to display her talent.

The church clock struck seven. The chimes had a different sound, coming across water instead of grassy meadows. She paused, listened, her chin on her hand and her eyes straying to the curtained door. She thought now that she could hear something moving on the water outside and went to the window and parted the curtains.

Below her, she could see two figures in a punt, one standing and using the pole, the other sitting down and fanning torchlight back and forth across the darkness.

'Going next door,' she thought, as she sat down again and dipped her pen into the ink. 'It's up to the second stair now,' she wrote, and then had to jump up, to go and see. Last thing at night, first thing in the morning, and a dozen times a day she would go out to the landing to see if the water had risen or fallen.

The house was open to anyone and the keys of the upstairs rooms had long ago been lost. The swan had come in and so might rats. Nervously, she peered over the banisters.

The water was disturbed and was slapping the threshold and swaying against the staircase. She could hear laughter and then a man's voice echoing up the well of the staircase, calling out to ask if she were safe. 'Quite safe and well?' the voice persisted. Torchlight ran up the walls and vanished, and a boat grated against some steps outside.

'Yes, I'm all right,' she called. 'Who is it?'

'Next door.'

The light came bobbing back across the threshold. Holding the torch was a young man, wading carefully through the water, his trousers rolled up above his pale knees. He came to the bottom of the stairs and looked up at her. His smile was the beginning of laughter, and he seemed to be deeply enjoying the novelties of the situation.

'Are you all alone?' he asked. Then he hurried over the indiscretion and, giving her no time to reply, said, 'Don't you mind being up there? We saw the light.'

She was tempted to say that she did mind. Then perhaps he would come up the stairs and talk to her for a little while. 'No, I don't mind,' she replied.

'We saw your light,' he said again. 'I just wondered if you were all right. "She might be lying there ill for all we know," I said to Tony.' ('Dead,' he had really said.) '"We'd better make sure," I said.'

They were both a little drunk. So endearing, Rose found this. It was a long time since she had been with anyone who was in the least intoxicated; Gilbert dully carried his drink and often remarked upon the fact.

'We went to get some whisky.'

He seemed not to notice the cold, standing there in the icy water.

'What fun,' she said. She smiled back at him. As she leant over the ban- isters, he spotlighted her with the torch and could see the top of her breasts, white against the green of her jersey as she bent towards him.

A jolly nice bosom, he thought. She seemed to be what he and Tony called a proper auntie. I shall bring out the maternal in her, he thought, and between the banister slats examined her pretty legs. So many plump women have slim ankles. He had often noticed this.

'Why don't you come with us?' he said. 'I can carry you to the boat.'

'Don't be silly. More like I'd have to carry you.'

'Well, paddle, then. It's not cold. It's lovely in.'

She had put her hand up to her hair, so he knew that she would come; but, before, would go through all the feminine excuses about her appear- ance.

'There's only us,' he said. 'You look very nice to me. What my brother thinks is of no importance. I can't stand in this water much longer, though.' He held out his arms.

'I'll take off my stockings, then.'

She went quickly back to her room. When she had rolled off her stock- ings and put them into her coat pocket, screwed up the top of the ink-bottle, she took up her shoes and blew out the candles. The hardly started letter was left lying on the table.

'I *could* do with a drink,' she said. 'I didn't like to ask that errand-boy to fetch some gin. Breaking the law, I suppose.'

The torchlight led her down the stairs, and there the young man took her shoes from her and put them in his pockets. He steadied her with his arm as she hitched up her skirt and stepped down into the icy water.

'Oh, my God,' she gasped and began to giggle, wading on tiptoe towards the doorway.

'Got her?' Tony shouted. He was sitting in the boat, holding on to the rustic-work porch.

If it all comes away in his hands, Gilbert will go mad, Rose thought, smiling in the darkness.

They helped her into the boat, and Tony, letting go of the porch, gave her a cigarette, lighting it first and putting it into her mouth with the intimacy which comes easily in time of peril or exultation.

'You can put your stockings on now,' said the young man whom Tony called Roger. 'No more paddling. We row straight in through the French windows to the landing-stage at the foot of the stairs.'

Tony gave a final push at the rustic-work porch and swung the punt towards the next-door garden. Bottles jingled against one another under the seat, and when Roger had wiped Rose's feet with a damp handkerchief, he reached for a whisky bottle, took off the wrapping-paper, and let it blow away across the water.

'Keep the cold out,' he urged Rose, trying to hold the bottle to her lips. 'Your teeth are chattering. Never mind, nearly there, and we've a wonderful oilstove going upstairs.'

As the boat swayed, whisky trickled over her chin; then she put her hands over his and, steadying them, took a long drink.

'I'll bet she's been a barmaid,' thought Roger.

'Jolly boating weather,' Tony sang, and the punt slipped over the still water, and the white house next door came into sight.

'Isn't it lovely?' Rose murmured.

'Not to be missed,' said Roger.

The next morning she slept late. It was nearly noon before she was properly awake, and any errand-boys who might have called her from below had gone away unanswered. Even when she was wide awake at last, she lay in bed staring at the curtains pinned across the window, striving to remember all she could of the evening before.

In bright moonlight they had brought her home in the boat and their singing must have carried a long way across the water. I don't care if the boat capsizes, she had thought.

When she waded indoors they called good-night; and she went upstairs and, still with wet bare feet, watched from the window until they were out of sight.

Quite clearly across the water, she heard Roger say, 'Well, that worked out all right, didn't it?'

A moment later, a gust of laughter came back to her, and she had won-

dered uneasily if they were laughing at her. But they were high-spirited
boys, she reminded herself. They would laugh at anything. Perhaps Tony
had let go of the punt pole.

Before her return home, there must have been hours and hours of sitting
on the floor and drinking in what they called 'Mamma's bedroom'. An oil-
stove threw a shifting daisy pattern on the ceiling, and two pink candles had
been burning on the dressing-table – must surely have burnt themselves out.
'How long was I there?' she wondered. 'And how did we pass the time?'
While it was happening it had seemed one of the loveliest evenings of her
life and she was sorry to have forgotten a moment of it.

The peach-coloured bedroom was draped with satin, and a trail of wet footprints went back and forth across the white carpet. Mamma's wedding
photograph was on a little table, and Rose had at one point suddenly asked,
'Whatever would your mother say about this?' By 'this' she meant herself being
there, not the empty bottles and the cigarette smoke and the dirty glasses.

'We'll clear up afterwards,' Roger said. The other bedrooms were full of
furniture from downstairs. They had been sent from London to rescue it.

Now it was Saturday morning and she could not walk down to the shops
to buy her little week-end treats. Today there was no cheque to cash, and
for the first time she realised how much she was at Gilbert's mercy.

She got out of bed and began to search the room for money, found thirty
shillings in one bag, some pennies dusty with face powder in another, half
a crown in her mackintosh pocket, and a florin in a broken cup on the
chest of drawers. She could survive the week until he came again, just as
she could survive until Monday on stale bread and the rest of the sausages.

Yes, I can survive all right, she told herself briskly, and pulled off her
nightgown and began to dress.

A glimpse in the wardrobe mirror as she crossed the room depressed her.
She was getting too fat and her sister would see a difference in her.

'But when?' she wondered. There was the unfinished letter on the table.
When she had made herself a cup of tea she would make an effort to write
it. I shall go on surviving and surviving, and growing fatter and fatter, she
thought, and her lips were pressed together and her eyes flickered because
she was frightened.

She lit the primus stove and then unpegged the curtains and opened the
balcony windows. Outside, a great change had taken place while she slept.
The floods were subsiding. Along the bank of the railway tracks she could
see grass, and in the garden the tops of shrubs and bushes had come up for
a breath of air and were steaming in the sunshine. She remembered that
last night, as the two young men punted away, she had heard one of them
say, 'The water's going down,' and she had felt regret, as if a party were
nearing its end.

It was going down more rapidly than it had risen, draining away into the earth, evaporating into the air, hastening down gratings. The adventure was nearly over and in its diminuendo had become an exasperation. What had been so beautiful yesterday was now an inconvenience, and Rose, on her island, would have to drink her tea without milk.

Surely those two dear boys will come, she thought. They had concerned themselves about her last night when they did not know her; it seemed more likely that they would do so today. She so convinced herself of this that, in the middle of sipping her tea, she went into the bathroom to make something of her face.

But they did not come and the day went slowly. She watched from the window and it was a dull, watery world she saw. The crisis was over and the seabirds beginning to fly away. She finished writing her letter and propped it up against the clock, which had stopped.

When it was dark she pinned the curtains together again and sat down at the table, simply staring in front of her; at the back of her mind, listening. In the warm living-room of her sister's house, the children in dressing-gowns would be eating their supper by the fire; Roy, home from a football match, would be lying back in his chair. Their faces would be turned intently to the blue-white shifting screen of the television.

Rose's was another world, candlelit, silent, lifeless. The church clock chimed seven and she got up and wound up her own clock and set it right; then sat down again, stiffly, with her hand laid palm downwards on the table like an old woman.

They asked me for fun, she told herself. It was just a boyish lark – quite understandable; a joke they wouldn't dream of repeating. If I ever see them again, other week-ends, they'll nod, maybe, and smile; that's all; not that, if their mother's with them. At their age, they never look back or do the same thing twice.

As she had come towards middle-age, she had developed a sentimental fondness for young men – especially those she called the undergraduate type, spoilt, reckless, gay, with long scarves twisted round their necks. Roger had, as he predicted, brought out the maternal in her. Humbly, with great enjoyment, she had listened to their banter, the family jokes, a language hardly understood by her, whom they had briskly teased but gallantly drawn in. So the hours must have passed.

Their mother won't be best pleased about that carpet, she thought, and she got up and took the last cigarette from the packet.

All of Sunday the waters receded. Morning and evening the church bells rang across the meadows in which ridges and hillocks of sodden grass stood up. One or two cars splashed down the lane during the afternoon, keeping to the crown of the road and making a great wash.

By Monday morning the garden path was high and nearly dry. Rose looked over the banisters at the wet, muddy entrance and found it difficult to believe that the swan had ever swum about down there. It was all over.

She could go out now and post her letter and fetch what she wanted from the shops; and on Friday Gilbert would come, and on all the Fridays after, she supposed, though she could never be quite sure. So she would survive from year to year, and one day soon would begin a diet and perhaps save some money for her old age.

It was like being in prison, she thought of the last few days. Sunday had been endless and she had cried a little and gone to bed early, but remained awake, yet on other Sundays she most often stayed indoors all day or pottered about the garden, and had always been contented.

Now she was set free and she put on her coat, took the letter from the shelf, and looked out of the window once more to make sure that it was really safe to go out and walk on the earth again. And that really was the sum of her freedom – for the first time the truth of it dawned in her. She could go out and walk to the shops, like a prisoner on parole, and spend the money Gilbert had given her, or save it if she could, and then she would turn back and return, for there was nothing else to do.

The clock ticked – a sound she knew too well. There were other sounds which were driven into her existence – the church bells and the milkman's rattle – and they no longer sufficed and had begun to torment her. Her contentment with them had come to an end.

The exciting thought occurred to her that it was in her power to fly away from them for ever. Nothing could stop her.

For a moment she stood quite still, her head tilted as if she were listening, and then she suddenly turned her handbag upside down and tipped the money on to the table. 'What will Gilbert do?' she wondered, as she counted the coins. He would never have visualised her doing anything impulsive, would stand in the porch bewildered, amazed that she did not open the door at once and, when he had sorted out his own key and let himself in, his face would be a picture, she thought.

'I'd like to see it,' she said aloud, and scooped up the money and dropped it back into her bag. Where would he break his journey that night? she wondered. Or would he perhaps go petulantly home to his wife?

She was smiling as she quickly packed her suitcase, almost shook with laughter when she slammed the door and set off down the muddy path. Such a dreadful mess she had left behind her.

She felt warm in her fur coat as she picked her way down the lane. The floods had shifted the gravel about and made deep ruts, the hedgerows were laced with scum; but the valley was recovering, cows were being driven back to the pastures and hundreds of birds were out scavenging.

The letter was still in Rose's hand but, as she stopped for a moment by a stile to rest, she suddenly screwed it up and tossed it over the hedge, knowing she would reach Beryl first.

In a Different Light

The boat brought people and took others away. In summer it came three times a week to the island, and the sisters, sitting outside the waterfront café, would watch it appearing round the point. It came with the most beautiful inevitability – however late. Quayside life would begin to stir and, as the deep sound of the ship's hooter came across the bay, little boats would put out from the shore. They were low on the water, with packed and standing people holding aloft baskets, trying to wave good-bye. The same boats, on their return journey, were watched more critically. Exposed and bewildered, and perhaps sick and tired as well, the newcomers stepped on to the broken marble of the waterfront and looked about them, shading their eyes from the sun and the fierce bright-ness of the white buildings. Their baggage would be seized by old men or young boys with handcarts and donkeys, and they would follow it on foot as if dazed with the suddenness of their arrival, wiping away sweat and trying to smack down flies.

After a time, the scene was peaceful again, the empty boats hardly moving on the water and, looking out to sea, Jane and Barbara would watch the ship making its wide curve before disappearing round the head-land.

Then they would go to a *taverna* and choose their fish (except on Sundays, the boat came at about noon), and when it was cooked and eaten, they would walk slowly up the hillside track, through the herb-scented scrub, to Jane's cottage.

'I shall never go home to England now. I feel it in my bones,' Jane said once. 'Every time the boat goes back to Athens, I think that.'

'But you still say "home",' her sister said.

'I didn't mean to. *This* is home. The other's Blighty – I can't imagine it any more. Do they still have those double-decker buses?'

Her husband – an expatriate painter, as Barbara's husband, Leonard, always referred to him – had died that spring and Barbara had come from England to be with her sister for a time and eventually to take her home – for she believed that what Jane had written in letters could soon be rea-soned away; and so she had sent the children to their grandmother, drawn all her savings from the bank and had arrived on the island ready to clasp her younger sister in her arms and soon restore her to her proper place.

'There is nothing to keep you,' she had pleaded on her first evening on the island. There had been a sudden, brilliant sunset and afterwards it was dark and warm. The streets smelt of honeysuckle and carnations. Their sandals slapped quietly on the flagstones. They spoke in low voices and were greeted softly by passers-by. 'There is nothing to keep you,' Barbara repeated.

The next day, they climbed the hillside to Alan's grave in the cluttered little cemetery above the sea; but even standing there, Jane did not weep or seem particularly moved. She turned, instead, to look downwards at the sea and she took a deep breath – almost a satisfied, a triumphant breath, thought Barbara.

'I'm afraid I have come all this way for nothing,' she wrote to Leonard. 'But I will stay on a little as you suggest.'

Day by day, she lost her usual pallor and became almost as brown as Jane, and she slept long and deeply at night. Her letters were insincere, for she could only write of how much money she had wasted on the journey and how many people she had inconvenienced at home.

On one of their usual mornings at the café, they waited to see the boat come in from Athens. They had bought a basket of artichokes and some paraffin oil, and now sat under a bamboo awning drinking coffee. The boat appeared far out; it rounded the headland and they watched it curving in towards the harbour. A few people collected by the water's edge with their baggage – baskets of cheeses, chickens and bunches of flowers.

Barbara sipped her glass of ice-cold water to take away the bitter taste the coffee had.

'The flowers are always dead by the time they get to Athens,' Jane said.

Two rowing-boats put out across the water towards the anchored ship and later, when they were returning, Jane said: 'I never watch them without thinking of the day Alan and I came. The houses seemed to rise higher and higher as we rowed into the harbour, and I felt alien and self-conscious when I stepped ashore – all the village out watching, taking note of my London clothes. My shirt was far too bright for here, but luckily it soon faded.' (She had worn it ever since Barbara's arrival, washing it sometimes at night, but never ironing it and never mending the tear in the sleeve. 'In London, I couldn't have just one shirt,' she had said. 'And that is all I care to have.') 'When we came ashore that day, I had no idea what impression we were making. We were the only visitors – which is how we thought of ourselves then, not knowing that we were here for ever.'

'What will you live on?' Barbara asked. She had given up persuasion at last, convinced now of her sister's obstinacy, of her determination to stay exactly where she was – among people whose language she spoke indifferently – wearing her one shirt till it was threadbare.

'I've got Mother's money.'

'It isn't enough. Mine hardly keeps me in cigarettes.'

Jane put on her sunglasses and turned in her chair to look across the bright water and the approaching boats. She said: 'Don't fuss so much. I can always take summer visitors. You could send them out to me from Blighty. I should like some nice, bewildered-looking visitors like this one. I would take them under my wing.'

There was only one bewildered-looking person on the boat. He was dressed in khaki drill and carried a rucksack which – when he had jumped ashore – he set down so that he could give his hand to an old woman, who was swathed in black and proudly carried a Pan-American travel bag. When he had her safely on land, he bowed and said, '*Khérete.*' She drew her head veil across her mouth and nodded.

'One of our fellow-countrymen,' said Jane, glancing at him without enthusiasm.

He stood looking about him, smilingly refusing to hire a donkey or rent a room or have his rucksack taken from him. Then he appeared to make a great decision and he came over to the café and sat down.

'*Kali méra,*' he said self-consciously.

'Good-morning,' the waiter replied. That, however, was the extent of his English, and confusion arose about what sort of coffee he should order.

Jane, over her shoulder, off-handedly explained.

'You wouldn't *like* having visitors,' Barbara said softly. 'And you wouldn't take them under your wing.'

'I should like their money. That is what would appeal to me about them.'

'You would resent them.'

'Let's go.' Jane jumped up and went inside the café to pay, then she took up the oilcan and handed the artichokes to her sister. As they were passing the Englishman's table, she relented. She stopped to ask him when he had left home.

'A fortnight ago,' he said, pushing the table as he stood up, slopping his glass of water.

'And it was raining, I suppose?'

'Pouring down. It was like another world. And still is, my wife writes to say.'

'You are badly sunburned,' Jane said in a stern voice. 'Spyros will give you some yoghourt to soothe it if you ask.' She nodded towards the café. 'Are you staying at the Amphitryon?'

There was only one hotel on the island – on the other side of the bay from her cottage. She pointed it out to him and gave careful instructions how to reach it, up flights of steps and between orchards of lemon trees.

He watched them walking away, carrying the artichokes and the oilcan, marked out by these as inhabitants, he thought. It was not the kind of shopping that visitors would do.

When Spyros came outside again, he asked him for yoghourt, but was not understood. He shouldered his rucksack and made for the hotel, soon taking a wrong flight of steps and getting lost between the close-packed houses. The sun beat down and the whitewashed walls dazzled him; his shirt under the rucksack was soaked with sweat. He took a map from his pocket and unfolded it and held it up as a screen between the blazing sun and his peeling face. From dark doorways shy children stared at him; old women, shelling peas or spinning, inclined their heads graciously towards him. 'Kali méra,' he repeated gallantly as he passed the open doorways. 'Kali méra sas.' The children smiled and turned aside their heads.

'It is quite wonderful,' he told himself. 'I am here. It is true.' His wife was miles away in a dark world underneath the clouds. He was sorry for her; he told himself he missed her; he forgot her. 'Hibiscus,' he murmured, looking up at a wall. He recognised it from pictures. When he reached the hotel, he would describe everything in his diary – the sea, the boat, the two Englishwomen at the café, the flowers. He had climbed to one of the higher streets and could look down through the leaves of some lemon trees at the harbour. The waterfront was deserted now, for everyone had gone in out of the heat and there was complete human silence over the island – bees buzzed, crickets chirped, a church bell chimed – but there were no voices. At the end of one of the deserted streets, he saw the word 'Amphitryon' written on a board over a doorway and he went towards it in triumph.

Jane and Barbara, at lunch, discussed him – Jane, with an almost Greek sharpness of curiosity and detachment, her sister thought. It was very much like the way she was eating her artichoke – the deft stripping away of leaves, the certainty of the hidden heart being there for the reaching. Licking oil from her fingers, Jane said: 'So his wife writes to tell him about the rain. Complainingly, I dare say. He thinks he is glad to get her letters, but he is gladder to put them out of his mind.'

'This you know,' said Barbara.

'This I know. And he also thinks he is glad to be in Greece. He has to be. I expect he has waited twenty years or more to come here and how can he afford, now that he's here, to dwell on his sunburn and his blistered feet and mosquito bites? I bet he gets frightful diarrhoea, too, poor old thing.'

'Is everyone who comes on the boat such a matter of conjecture?'

'Everyone. Luckily one doesn't know till later, or who could dare to brave it? You noticed the crowds when *you* arrived? Although you were expected and known about, so there was a more critical turnout for you.'

'I thought they were meeting people off the boat, or going back in it themselves.'

'Well, you know better now.'

In the afternoon – as on every afternoon – Jane lay down on the big brass bedstead in her room and went to sleep. Barbara, unused to this habit and scorning it, wrote to her children and then took the track down the hillside to the village to post her letter. In the hot, quiet afternoon the smell of wild sage was overpowering as she brushed against it along the path.

The post office was dark and cool, and inside it sat the Englishman. He had come to buy stamps and had been requested to draw up a chair and have some conversation with the clerk, who had a married sister living in Bermondsey. A boy came in from the café, carrying a swinging tray, with coffee and glasses of water. Barbara stood by while the Englishman was handed his cup and glass. He had risen when she entered, but was curtly motioned to sit down by the clerk, who got up to tear off stamps for Barbara and give her change.

'Roland Bagueley,' the Englishman said slowly and loudly in answer to an earlier question. He took the pad he was offered and wrote his name in capitals.

'From London? Swindon? Falmouth?' asked the clerk.

Barbara, sticking on stamps, lingered. The buckle of her sandal was given some attention.

'London,' said Roland Bagueley. 'A part of London.'

'Hampstead, for instance,' Barbara thought. She picked up her change, put it in her purse and, smiling in his direction, went out. As he once more jumped to his feet, she heard him shouting, 'Hampstead – a part of London called Hampstead.'

She stopped at the café for cigarettes and on her way home printed his name on the packet lest she should forget it. 'Roland Bagueley from Hampstead,' she would tell Jane. She wondered if in the end her sister would go mad, living alone, nourished on such trifles.

In the evening, they met him again. He was sitting outside a waterside *taverna* where they went for dinner. Jane looked disconcerted when he stood up and offered them chairs. She liked conjecture about strangers rather than facts about acquaintances.

They sat down and ordered drinks. 'So you're not visitors here,' he said to Barbara, as Jane was speaking in Greek to the waiter.

'I am, but my sister lives here – Jane Bailey. And I am Barbara Fennell.'

To know their names seemed to gratify him enormously.

'I heard it in the post office this afternoon,' Barbara said when he had introduced himself.

'The clerk knows a little English and hoped to practise it on me. His sister lives in Bermondsey and he supposed that I must know her.'

'And you live in Hampstead. I heard that, too.'

'Yes, I am an architect.'

Jane, returning her attention, nodded as if this much she had already guessed. 'And have you been to Greece before?' she asked.

'No. It is a dream realised after many, many years.'

She put out her foot and tapped Barbara's. 'And are you disappointed in it?' Her questions were peremptory and put him out. She was a small, dark, darting person, often intimidating – even to her sister.

He shook his head, looking puzzled; but what he was puzzled about was not his reactions to Greece, Barbara realised suddenly, but the sight of his name written on the cigarette packet which was lying on the table. Unlike Jane, she was liable to blush and, doing so, puzzled him more.

'*Yassoo*,' he said painstakingly, lifting his glass.

'Oh, good luck,' said Jane, who had just put hers down.

Barbara took the cigarette packet and in rather an affected voice said: 'How amusing! When I heard your name in the post office I wrote it down on this so that I could remember to tell Jane.'

'But why?'

'I thought she would admire my sharpness. No one arrives on this island without being scrutinised, you see; and I am falling into the habit.'

'Wasn't it your wife's lifelong ambition to come to Greece, too?' asked Jane.

'No, Iris likes to spend her holidays with her sister in Buxton.'

'Well, I expect that's very nice, too.'

They went into the *taverna* to choose their fish and when they came outside again the sun was dropping fast into the pinkish water. They watched it go and it was suddenly dark and the air seemed warmer and more still. 'I really wanted to be alone here,' Roland was thinking. The brisk, dark little woman was in no way part of what he had come all this distance for and awaited so long, and about the place itself she seemed imperious and possessive, describing to him how she had chosen it for life. She had traded it for a great deal, he thought – for she was a young woman to make such a decision – and under the influence of ouzo, he began to make a list for her of what she lacked.

'But I have friends here,' she said, dropping a fish's head to a pleading cat and wiping her fingers on a piece of bread.

'Not your own kind.'

'I never found my own kind anywhere – only in my husband.'

'Even everyday things – comforts we take for granted.'

'Like the Underground at rush hours; fog and rain; cocktail parties; wearing hats.'

'There is no water at my hotel – one carafe in my room for drinking, which I'm too nervous to do. I have paid extra for a shower, but nothing comes out of it.'

'Oh, well, the sea is warm now.'

'I wasn't complaining,' he said quickly, wondering if there had been impatience in her voice – even, perhaps, contempt. In fact, he had wanted – and still wanted – everything to be quite different from at home, and had already written almost boastingly to tell his wife about the shower.

'I know that the man who understands how to work the pumps has gone to Athens to have his chest X-rayed,' Jane said. 'He will be back on the boat the day after tomorrow and then you'll be all right.'

'I wasn't complaining,' he said again, thinking, 'Two more days!'

'Can't you imagine England now?' Barbara asked. 'A long light evening and the sound of mowing-machines.' The children would be going to bed; she tried to visualise them – pink faces, fair hair, blue dressing-gowns – and they remained unreal. A barefooted boy, no older than her son, was driving a donkey along the sea front, whacking its rump and making kissing noises at it. Other children were playing in boats under the harbour wall, their voices conspiratorial above the sound of the water peacefully slapping the stone wall.

'I could *sleep* . . . I could sleep,' she said, and covered her face with her hands and yawned. But Jane was perfectly alert – had hardly begun the second half of her waking day.

'It's the air perhaps,' said Roland, trying not to yawn, too.

'It's trying to keep going all day in the heat,' said Jane. 'The air is perfectly invigorating.'

When they had said good-night to Roland and seen him going off in the opposite direction to his waterless hotel, the sisters began the steep climb up the hillside. Pausing for breath and looking back at the harbour lights, Barbara said: 'I'll have to go home soon, I suppose. Next week, perhaps.'

'Well, you are not to think of me. I'm quite all right now. You must do whatever you must. I expect you are missing the children.'

'A little.' All the way along the track, she was treading on the thyme or brushing against sage bushes, freeing the scent of the herbs upon the air. I don't really miss the children, she thought. Each day, I miss them less, not more.

When they reached the cottage, Jane lit two oil-lamps. She gave one to Barbara to take upstairs to bed with her, and sat beside the other to read until two or three o'clock. As she kicked off her sandals and settled down, she said, 'In the morning, I might get out Alan's paints and make a start. I'll teach myself and surprise you all.' Although she had said this before, and in a tone of great decision and determination, nothing had been done.

Barbara went to her bedroom and leant out of the window, breathing the scented air. She was beginning to understand her sister and even to foresee difficulties for herself lying ahead, and imagined herself back home, unsettled by her experience, deprived of the dazzling light, and the deep silence.

There were fewer boats now down in the harbour. She got into bed. Her sunburned body was fiery between the coarse sheets; she felt wonderfully lulled and, turning her cheek at once to the pillow, she let out a long breath like a contented sigh, and fell asleep.

They saw a great deal of Roland, as it was natural to do in that small village – meeting at the *taverna*, the café, the bathing-place below the rocks. Sometimes, on afternoons when Jane was sleeping, Barbara went on excursions with him – to one of the bays to swim and, once, by mules, to a convent at the highest point on the island. There, among lemon trees, they tied up their mules and Roland sat down on the hillside, while Barbara went into the courtyard. It was filled with stocks and roses and the sound of bees. The Reverend Mother came to meet her. She led her into a cool dark room and gave her a spoonful of jam and a glass of water on a tray. She was a plump lively woman with gold teeth and a great smell of garlic. Although they had no words in common, they had plenty of nods and smiles and Barbara had admiring sounds as well – at the *ikons* in the ugly little chapel, at a piece of sacred bone in a box, at the view, and the arum lilies in the courtyard. She bought a lace-edged handkerchief and was given a bunch of stocks. When she took the old nun's hand, it was as hard as leather, and creased; for she had worked in the fields like any peasant. As Barbara left, she heard whispering and giggling above her and, looking up, glimpsed two nuns peeping from a high window. She lifted her flowers to wave; but, as soon as she had turned, they had drawn back out of sight.

Under a lemon tree lay Roland, fast asleep. Not liking to wake him, she sat down a little way off, smelt her bunch of stocks, gazed down at the dark sea with the pale outlines of other islands circling it. He slept on and soon she felt drowsy, too, and stretched herself out among the rock-roses and wild larkspur and dozed a little.

When they awoke, both suddenly stirring at the same moment, it seemed much later, but they had no idea of the time. They pumped some water for the mules in the convent yard and mounted them. It was an odd, holiday companionship they shared, founded on nothing but what had happened in the last few days – the mistakes they had made from not understanding the language, their delight in their new experience and, now, the hazards of riding their mules down a rocky, dried-up river bed. Half-way down it, with a guilty backward glance towards the now hidden convent, Barbara threw away the stocks, which had died in the sun.

When they reached the cottage, they found Jane rummaging among some canvases, as if about to make a start at last. She had washed her hair and it hung straight and wet close to her head and dripped on to her shoulders. She smiled when Barbara told her that they had fallen asleep up on the hillside.

The next afternoon, as soon as lunch in the *taverna* was over, the three of them separated. They went back to their rooms, drew the shutters together, and lay down on their beds. And this they continued to do for the rest of their time on the island.

Barbara and Roland began to count the days they had left. She had chosen a date haphazardly and despairingly. She knew that she ought to go early and she wanted to go later and, between conscience and desire, must find a compromise. Roland's return to England was already arranged, and as it grew nearer he began to sacrifice other projects he had had in mind – Mycenae, Delphi, Perachora. 'I shall go to Perachora next time,' he explained. 'Perhaps in two years' time.' He wondered if his wife had been happy with her sister in Buxton and hoped devoutly that she had been.

Meanwhile, he stayed on the island, sitting lingeringly outside the café talking to the sisters, who could not help wondering, when they were alone, how it was that they could find him both amiable and boring. One day, he brought a photograph of his wife to show them, and they looked at it carefully and said 'Awfully pretty'. An insipid face, they decided.

'You must miss her,' Barbara said.

'She would love it here,' he said and then added, 'Yes, in many ways she'd love it. Then things go wrong and I'm glad, after all, that I'm on my own. The frustrations and misunderstandings about the language. And sometimes the food ... and having no water all that time.'

'Well, it's all put right now,' said Jane. She was really making a start that morning and had brought a sketching-block and a box of water-colours down to the café and was now washing in a grey sky above the tiers of white houses. For the first day, there was no sun. It was hot, though, and a glare came off the sea.

Spyros, bringing them more coffee, looked over Jane's shoulder and said something angrily and rapidly in Greek. She shrugged and pointed at the sky with her brush. He protested, set down their coffee, slopped water over the table, then shrugged too – but crossly, not indifferently – and pushed his way back through the chairs, banging the tray angrily against his knee as he went.

'What was that about?' asked Barbara.

Still washing in grey, Jane said: 'He wanted me to paint a blue sky. Over this island, he says, the sky is always blue. When I pointed out that today it was not and it was today's sky I was painting, he said that people from other islands would misunderstand.'

'Day after day, there are the same illogical arguments,' Barbara said.

'Trivial, silly things happen in Blighty, too.'

Roland, who had been fidgeting with his wife's photograph, flipping it to and fro, glanced at it again and slipped it into his pocket. He was leaving the next day. His holiday was almost over and he felt lost and disconsolate. Dreams had come true, but merely to give birth to others. He had overcome discomfort, his skin was now at terms with the sun as his digestion was with the food, and he had formed new habits, such as sleeping in the afternoons and eating late at night. It was life in Hampstead that had the look of strangeness about it now – the little dinner parties with the lace mats set out on the polished table, coming back from his office to those, or to an evening's gardening, or listening to records while he stuck his holiday photographs in an album. He was an intensely patriotic man and dearly loved the English landscape. 'I could never live anywhere else,' he told himself. He thought it very strange that Jane could, but there was almost nothing about her that he could understand. She was hard, he thought – unlike her sister, whom he found rather girlish and sentimental. He was not greatly drawn to either of them; but they had been part of his holiday and because of that he must feel disturbed at saying good-bye to them.

The cloud at last drifted out to sea and the sun shone in a clear blue sky. Spyros ran out from the café, pointing upwards, smiling triumphantly at Jane.

'Now I can finish my spool of photographs,' Roland said. He took out his camera and began fussing with it. 'If I may; if you will both look up.' He studied the light meter. 'My wife's the photographer, I'm afraid. She has endless patience over everything. I don't understand the gadget.'

So his wife took a positive role occasionally, Barbara thought. From her photograph this was not to be guessed.

'There ... and now if you would ... '

Obediently, they took off their sunglasses and looked up at him and smiled – Jane holding a paint brush and Barbara a coffee-cup.

He left next day on the morning boat. They waited for it at the café. He thought of it as an enemy vessel, coming malignly round the headland; making directly for him, he felt.

He and Barbara had exchanged addresses, for they would meet in England – husbands and wives would be introduced and, in her case, children. There would also be the photographs to be sent on.

They stood on the waterside and watched him stepping into the rowing-boat. He had his rucksack and a large sponge as a present for Iris. Barbara had tears in her eyes – for she could not bear any good-byes, and departures by boat were especially poignant to her. She was also reminded of her own going away in two days' time.

Roland, steadying himself, standing up in the crowded boat, turned to wave. They waved back and called good-bye, as he was rowed out across the harbour. To him, the shape of the island changed as he went farther out from it – the hills spread out and the coast line was seen to be dotted with windmills.

'Well,' Jane began, as they turned away. 'You may be invited once to Hampstead; then you'll have to ask them back, and you'll wish you hadn't to – and Leonard will, even more. "My friend I met in Greece,"' she said mockingly. 'After that, you'll send Christmas cards for a year or two – especially if you can find any with a Greek flavour, which I should think would be unlikely.'

'I know all that. People are different in different surroundings.' Barbara, under her sunglasses, wiped her eyes. 'I cry too easily,' she explained. 'Just as I'm sick too easily.'

'It's a good thing to be easily sick,' said Jane.

It was another kind of poignancy Barbara felt when it was time to go herself. As she left the harbour, she was surprised to see Jane turn and walk away almost at once. She was not the type to stand waving until the boat was out of sight, but her turning away seemed impatient and abrupt. She was soon too far away to be seen and the whole of that little world where she was seemed to lock itself closer and closer together until the expansive waterfront life, with its comings and goings – its landings of fish and sponges, its trotting donkeys, its desultory spectators – could hardly be imagined any more.

Leaning on the rails, she watched until all she could see was the little village against the golden hills and a white speck at the summit of one of them – which was the convent to which she and Roland had ridden on the mules.

Soon the whole island was lost on the horizon; but all the time other islands were coming up on either side – some close, so that she could see more white villages, more blue-domed churches; some distant, misty shapes.

This journey to Athens was the first stage of her journey, which would end next day in England. 'Blighty!' she thought, and she leant over the rails and stared down into the brilliant, wrinkled sea, feeling very strange, both sick and tearful.

Jane went for a walk along the cliffs and after a while noticed a strange dog pacing along with her – sometimes a little in front as if to guide her, and then at her heels as if to comfort her. He had an air of obedience about him, and might have been ordered to keep her company now that her sister had gone. When she sat down to rest, he sat down in front of her and gave her anxious looks.

She felt painfully unsettled. Barbara's visit had made her first loss so much worse. She had come too soon and her departure added the second loss to the earlier one, a second kind of silence to grow used to. 'Which can be done,' she thought.

She looked out to sea, but the boat was out of sight and nothing was left but its faint trail across the water. She made her way back to the cottage and when she reached it, she thanked the dog for his company and shut the door on him. Then she went and lay down on her bed, for it was siesta time.

Sometimes there were holes in the clouds and through these Barbara could peer down from the plane and see a green landscape crossed by slate grey roads. It looked neat and dark and alienating. She had no feeling of coming home and could not believe that she was here. They flew over reservoirs and gravel pits filled with milky water, and then over the Thames itself – a broad reach lined with houseboats and launches and fringed with willows – a very sedate-looking river. Coming in to land, she saw the houses tip suddenly sideways and the fields scudding past, and she imagined her husband somewhere down there, waiting for her.

When at last she saw him, standing outside the customs office – looking pale, she thought – his pleasure at having her back affected her deeply. They drove home slowly and from time to time he took her hand, as if to reassure himself that she was with him again.

'So Jane decided to stay?' he asked.

'I went all that way for nothing.'

'You had to go. And it has done you good.'

'Is everything all right at home?'

'There have been one or two upsets, but never mind now.'

'But I *must* know.'

Gradually she learnt the list of calamities – the children with chickenpox at their grandmother's; the cat who had disappeared (from loneliness? from neglect? she wondered), the tree that had blown down in a gale and the daily help who had given in her notice. She was filled with despair and guilt. 'You should have told me,' she said again and again.

'I wanted you to have your holiday. And I wish I hadn't to tell you now.'

It was a dull, warm night. While she had been away, the summer had come and the trees had grown dark and weighty. All along the lanes was a bitter smell of dusty leaves. They turned into their own drive and she looked about her with a despondent curiosity. The lilac had bloomed and faded in her absence. As they went into the hall together, she put her arms round him, blinded again with tears. 'Oh, thank you, my darling, for managing,' she said.

No letter came from Jane, although Barbara, after her first letter, wrote a second, then a third. Her tan faded in the mild, dark weather, but images of the island stayed vividly in her mind. She fretted for some word from it and about it, feeling – where she now was – less than half alive. Jane's water-colour sketch – of the harbour and the grey sky – which she had brought home with her, was propped up on her desk – a lack-lustre little painting, but all she had.

Her home seemed lack-lustre, too, and she could no longer see what strangers – exclaiming at its beauty – must see, and the gentle view from upstairs windows – the blue-and-green Thames valley which she had always loved – was tame and vapid now.

Leonard thought her merely unsettled by travelling, or else worried about Jane. The children – returning spoiled by their grandmother's indulgence – sensed her inattentiveness and continued their misbehaviour. Serena, who had never lived up to her name, gave way to even more spectacular tantrums. Robert, her brother, simply did damage. Each day he left the mark of destruction on the house. 'It is like having a poltergeist among us,' Barbara said, gathering up the fragments of a lustre jug.

She wondered why she had the strange belief that if only Jane would write, she could find her old contentment and see the island in the right perspective – as merely a place where dwelling was primitive, the weather fairer than at home, and life uncluttered – with no fine china to be broken, no cupboards full of clothes to be looked after and no telephone to keep on ringing. Jane's letter, when it came, would reconcile her, she felt, to all these frustrations and annoyances; Serena would stop casting herself down on the floor howling; Robert would go more carefully about the house, and she would find herself once more enchanted with her surroundings. How any letter could accomplish all this she did not ask herself; but she knew that without it she was left in the air, her visit abroad not finally rounded off. And then the letter came at last and there was news of the island, but no reference to Barbara's ever having been on it. This made it seem more remote to her – a different place.

Sometimes, increasingly, she wondered about Roland Bagueley and how he was faring in Hampstead. His association with the island, the fact of his coming so much into her recollections of it, began to give him an illusory charm; but he, too, was lost in silence – had failed even to send the promised photographs. On an impulse, she wrote to invite him and his wife to lunch on Sunday. This she very soon regretted having done and she began to await their arrival in a state of nervous agitation.

'I wish I hadn't asked them,' she told Leonard at breakfast. 'I don't know why I did. He's boring, really.'

'They won't be here for ever,' he said.

'But why on earth should I inflict such tedium on you?'

'An hour or two of tedium can't hurt anybody.'

He was so equable, she thought; so good-natured. However disastrously things turned out, he would never blame her.

On Sunday, Roland and Iris got out of their car at a quarter to one, just as Robert had shut Serena's fingers in a door and was shouting guilty disclaimers while she was hysterical on the floor. Barbara, with her face hot from the oven and from embarrassment, too, opened the door while Leonard carried the shrieking child to the bathroom.

At first, there was too much to say all at once – introductions, greetings, explanations, apologies – and then, suddenly, standing in the hall with the door shut, there was nothing at all.

'Poor little girl,' said Roland, glancing upstairs.

Only her curiosity quietened Serena. Feeling that she was missing something, she allowed her screams to die down into a tremulous whimpering; she freed herself from her father and appeared on the staircase, with tears over her face and her lips quivering.

'Poor little girl,' Roland said again – and he held out his arms to her as she descended the stairs slowly and suspiciously. She was far from being a shy child, but decided to feign timidity. She skirted the visitors widely and hid her face against Barbara, refusing to be coaxed away from her.

Leonard came downstairs, wearing a jovial and anticipatory look, which even Iris Bagueley's gushing voice did not diminish. 'Delightful!' she kept exclaiming. 'Your *garden.* "Oh," I said to Rollo, "the garden, Rollo! The irises. What a *show.*" Oh, she's a *shy* girl, is she? Who's lost her tongue?'

'I hope she won't talk like this to Robert,' Barbara thought fearfully.

'Have you any animals?' Iris suddenly asked in a low and confidential voice.

'Only guinea-pigs,' Barbara said hesitantly.

'Then have you any objection if Chummy comes in? We take him everywhere and he's such an unhappy boy when he's left in the car. Girlie see doggie?'

Chummy was an evil-looking chow with a curled tail, a rather matted coat, and tongue hanging loose in a wicked wolf's mouth. He was brought through the hall, looking balefully about him. He panted, his ears pricked at every sound, claws pitter-pattered on the parquet floor as he restlessly and scornfully explored the room. Serena clung closer to her mother and her whimpering gathered force.

'Aren't you a Mummy's girl?' asked Iris brightly, tapping her on the head with her gloves.

'Go away!' Serena muttered angrily into her mother's skirt.

Robert, who had been comforting himself with a long drink, sidled in, his face stained with purple juice.

'And here's the son and heir,' said Iris.

She seemed to twinkle at him – her spectacles, ear-rings, necklace and her shiny straw hat – and Robert backed away, scowling.

So far, Roland had said very little, except to demur about the dog's being brought in, and ignored. Now – with a glass of sherry in his hand – he looked across at Barbara and said: 'Yassoo!'

She smiled self-consciously and glanced at him – for the first time, she realised – and saw how utterly unfamiliar he looked in his dark suit – a different person, a different *kind* of person.

'Oh, Rollo and his Greek,' said Iris, laughingly. 'Cheers, my dears. You see, *I* can only say it in English. Before he went away, I thought I should go mad – he was everlastingly going about the house, practising sentences out of his phrase book, quite determined to be able to talk to the natives when he got there. Weren't you, Rollo?'

The nickname, thought Barbara, did not seem to attach itself to him, however constantly it was used; it glanced off him.

He had blushed when his wife spoke of his attempts to learn Greek and said that he had simply wasted his time, and Barbara – with Serena still clinging to her skirt – went on one of her little trips to the kitchen to lift saucepan lids and look into the oven. She had been drinking rather hastily, from nervousness, and felt hot and confused. The thought of finishing off the cooking, dishing-up, the gathering together of them all at the table, oppressed her unbearably.

'*You* didn't feel drawn towards Greece?' Leonard asked Iris when they were in the dining-room at last. It was late. The potatoes had taken so long to brown that Barbara despaired, and several times Iris had peeped at her watch. She had refused a second drink. Then – just when everything was ready – Chummy had wanted to go out and had to be taken and waited for.

Leonard now clashed the carving knife against the steel and Barbara watched anxiously, as he cut off the first slice of beef and, from habit, laid it aside on the dish for himself.

'No,' said Iris. 'I was never taken with the idea. An aunt of mine went deaf from typhoid on the island of Rhodes.'

'A long time ago,' said Roland.

'"Don't drink the water and don't eat the salads," I told Rollo before he went. No, do serve the kiddies first, I implore you.'

'Stop kicking your chair,' said Barbara to Robert, who ignored her. She blushed, hearing in her mind what Iris must be thinking – 'Such behaviour! What spoilt kiddies!' 'You lost your tan,' she said to Roland.

'And you.'

'No, I think "abroad", as I call it, is terribly over-rated,' Iris told them. 'Perhaps we haven't been awfully lucky. Goodness, don't you remember when we went to the Costa Brava, Rollo? The people there. They really were rather ... well ... '

'Mixed,' Roland said quickly. It was the best he could think of in a hurry and doubtless had staved off worse.

'Yes, *mixed*.' She smiled at him gratefully. 'And the *food*.' She closed her eyes.

When she opened them, she seemed encouraged to see the plate of decent English food in front of her, even though she could not have felt proud of the potatoes if *she* had cooked them. 'Delicious,' she said, in a faint and trailing-off voice as she took up her knife and fork.

She may have been pretty when she was younger, Barbara thought. In her mind, she brightened the hair, took off the spectacles, smoothed out the lines of discontent and eye-strain, and was just able to imagine Roland – a shy and unpractised young man – allowing himself to be carried away. In Greece, she had known that he had nothing but solid worth to recommend him. He had been dogged – even about his holiday, until staying on the island – out of the world, out of context – he had achieved an undreamt of air of negligence. They had ridden up to the convent, she reminded herself. Sweating, sunburned, untidy, he had stretched himself out under a tree and fallen asleep, spread-eagled in the dappled light. It was a different man, she thought, glancing at the trim, anxious one who was listening to his wife with an attentiveness he must have wisely acquired to make up for everyone else's lack of it.

These weeks, since his return from the island, must have been worse than hers, she realised – as the rest of his life would be worse. His experience must have been deeper, his brief escape desperately planned and wearily paid for. It was something for her – for Iris – to deride along with the other things. Once he had liked music, he had told Jane in answer to one of her off-hand enquiries: later the sisters had laughed about it, but Barbara could not have laughed now. She could see too clearly the history of discarded interests.

It would have been better to have asked them to dinner, with the children safely in bed, she thought, slipping a clean plate under the
wine-stained table-cloth. Robert had knocked over the glass of wine and
water, which plainly Iris thought he should not have been given.

'And who is a little bit tipsy?' she was saying.

'Are you?' Robert asked.

Her laughter, her effusive ways with them, revealed her hatred of all
children – and these particularly. They were what she did not want to be
reminded of.

'Robert!' said Leonard, warningly.

Ignoring his father, staring at Iris, Robert said, with contempt in his
voice: 'You aren't really laughing. I know.'

'I am,' said Serena. She threw back her head and half closed her eyes
and gave a passable imitation of Iris's trilling laugh.

Affecting not to notice exactly what the child was doing, Barbara said:
'Any more silliness from either of you, and you will be sent upstairs to rest
until you're sensible again.'

'*You* would *like* that, wouldn't you?' Robert said in a low voice, with a
glance at Iris.

'Well, then it is no use,' Barbara said. 'You must go upstairs this minute,
Robert.' She was very nervous lest he should refuse to, and wondered how
she would deal with so much loss of face if he did. To her relief, he slid
down at once from his chair, walked round the table, and as he went out
of the door was heard to say how glad he was to go. 'Horrible old gooseberry
tart,' he chanted loudly, as he stamped upstairs. 'Horrible, beastly old
cream.'

'I'm sorry,' Barbara said.

'Goodness, only a very silly person would take offence at anything a
child says,' said Iris.

'And that is what we are all afraid of one doing,' Leonard thought.

When they had finished lunch, Roland gave Barbara his holiday photographs. 'They're really no good,' he apologised. 'I think the light was too
strong.'

'I told you to allow for that,' said Iris. 'You had the meter.'

Barbara's hands trembled with eagerness when she took the photographs
from him, and her disappointment was great as she looked at one after
another. She and Jane – standing beside donkeys or lemon trees or the
masts of fishing-boats – were blurred albino figures, their pale lips parted;
or marble statues bleached in moonlight. The curving waterfront, the
white village was like a heap of tripe.

'I think the light was far too strong,' he said again.

She could distinguish the café with all the chairs outside, and Spyros's apron like a trail of ectoplasm among them. 'Don't you remember . . . ' she began. She looked up from the photograph and saw that his expression, though gentle, was forbidding.

He was right, of course, she realised. There could be no resurrection of those days – even the photographs had failed.

'Would you like to walk round the garden?' Leonard suggested.

Watched malignly from an upstairs window by Robert, Iris and Roland were shown the garden, flowers were picked for them, Chummy was called off the herbaceous border and shooed away from the guinea-pigs. Soon after three they went away.

'Oh dear,' said Iris, as they drove through the Sunday afternoon traffic, 'my *head*.' She pressed her hands to her forehead. Chummy, sitting up in the back of the car, panted loudly, his tongue lolling out of his mouth. 'Those *children*,' Iris said.

'I must admit they were rather out of hand. What did you think of Barbara?'

'Quite frankly,' said Iris, 'I wasn't terribly impressed.'

Barbara took tea on to the lawn. There was no sun, but it was warm. Robert, having been freed and forgiven, lovingly ate cold gooseberry tart and cream. It was a peaceful tea-time. At the end, Serena, getting up from the grass, asked: 'Can we get down?'

For a little while, she and Robert played amicably together and Barbara and Leonard watched them contentedly.

'I wonder if they're back in Hampstead yet?' she said. 'I'd like to know what they are doing at this moment. They must have finished talking about us by now. I'm sorry about the awful fiasco. I let you in for it.'

'He was quite a decent sort of fellow.'

'But *she*!'

'Yes, she certainly *was* rather . . . '

'Mixed.'

They laughed, and the children, swinging in a hammock, looked across at them. To hear their parents laughing together was a sound they loved very much. Hearing it, they thought they would be good for ever, so that it would never stop. The world then became a settled, a serene place to be in.

'Oh, darling! I'm so glad I have you,' Barbara told Leonard.

The Benefactress

Four widows lived in the almshouses beside the church. On the other side of the wall, their husbands' graves were handy. 'I've just seen to Charlie's,' Mrs Swan called out to Mrs Rippon, who was going down the garden path carrying a bunch of phlox.

They were four robust old ladies, and their relationship with one another was cordial, but formal. Living at close quarters, they kept to themselves, drank their own tea in their own kitchens, used surnames, passed a few remarks, perhaps, when they met by chance in the graveyard or weeding their garden plots or, dressed in their best, waiting for the bus to go to the village and draw their pensions.

The almshouses were Elizabethan, with pretentious high chimneys whose bricks were set in a twist. In an alcove above the two middle front doors was a stone bust of the benefactor who had built the cottages and endowed them for the use of four old people of the parish. He wore a high ruff and a pointed beard, and rain had washed deep sockets to his eyes and pitted his cheeks so that he looked as if he were ravaged by some horrible disease. His name was carved in Latin below the alcove – a foreigner, the old ladies had always supposed.

Outside each front door was a wooden bench where they could have sat in the sun to warm their ageing bones, but this they never did. In fine weather it was much too public, with sightseers in and out of the old church taking photographs. They photographed the almshouses without asking permission, and once Mrs Swan, going down the garden to pick a few gooseberries, had been requested to pose within her porch wearing an old black apron. 'Saucy monkeys,' she had said to her niece's daughter, who was indoors visiting.

She was there again this afternoon, sitting in the greenish light that came through heavily leaded panes and slanted in from the open, leaf-fringed doorway. The path outside was shaded by a yew tree, and Mrs Rippon had passed by it carrying her bunch of phlox.

'That grave's a novelty to her,' Mrs Swan said to her grand-niece when her neighbour was out of hearing. 'It's only human, after all. I know I was over there every day when Charlie had just died.'

The niece, Evie, seemed to stiffen with disdain.

'I wish I could bring her down to earth,' Mrs Swan thought. 'What's wrong with going to the graveyard, I should like to know.'

'I couldn't bring myself to grieve,' she went on. 'Poor man, he did suffer. From here to here they opened him.' She measured off more than a foot of her own stomach, holding her hands there.

'Yes, you've told me,' Evie said, refusing to look.

'"It's a fifty-fifty chance," the doctor said, before he operated.'

As if he would have, Evie thought.

Her mother had told her to take a present to her aunt, and on the way from work she had bought some purple grapes. They were reduced in price, being past their prime, and they lay now on the table in a dish shaped like a cabbage leaf. Dull, and softly dented, they gave a sweet, beery smell to the room. Tiny flies had already gathered round them. They rose for a moment when Mrs Swan waved her hand over the dish, but soon settled again. Grapes were for the dying, she had always believed, and 'deathbed grapes' she called the purple kind. She would rather have had a quarter of a pound of tea.

It was no use Evie glancing up at the clock every few seconds, she thought. The bus would come along no sooner than it was due, if then. It was a wasted afternoon for them both. Mrs Swan could imagine the argument at her niece's house. 'You really ought to go, Evie. No one's been near her for months.' 'Why pick on me?' Evie would ask, and be told that the others had their families to occupy their time. So Evie – as if being so far unmarried and having to live at home were not enough – was made to do the duty visits, give up her free afternoon. No wonder, Mrs Swan thought, that she looked as morose as a hen.

She herself had planned a busy afternoon and had brought from the garden a large striped marrow to be made into jam. It matched the white-and-amber cat who had settled beside it on the sofa, as if for company or camouflage. The cat slept most of its life – at night from custom and by day from boredom. On the sofa now he drowsed, had not quite dropped off, for his eyelids wavered. His front legs were folded under him, like a cow's, his whiskers curled down over his alderman's chains – the bib of white rings on his breast.

Mrs Swan, glancing regretfully at the marrow, noticed him and said mechanically, 'Isn't he a lovely ginger, then?'

The cat at once feigned a deep sleep.

'He must be company,' Evie said.

Mrs Swan was often told this, and, although it was not true, she never disagreed. She was not a person who could make a friend of a cat, and had never found the necessity. They bored one another. She had had him to keep away the mice. Instead, he brought them in and played evil games with them on the hearthrug.

'He's no trouble,' she said.

Mrs Rippon passed the open door without glancing in, on her way back from the churchyard. The clock made a sudden rustling noise and struck four with an old-fashioned chime, and Mrs Swan got up and put the tea-pot by the kitchen range to warm. Evie racked her brains for something to say, and began a tedious description of the bridesmaids' dresses at a wedding she had been to. She thought her aunt could not fail to be grateful for this glimpse of the outside world.

While she waited for the kettle to boil, Mrs Swan took up her knitting. She was making a blanket from little squares sewn together, and there was already a carrier-bag full of them knitted from oddments of drab-coloured wool – a great deal of khaki left over from the war. The needles clicked steadily and she let her eyes move about the room as her thoughts settled like moths on her possessions. She might wash the muslin curtains tomorrow if the weather held. Evie was dropping cigarette ash on to the rag hearthrug, she noticed. She would put it on the clothes-line in the morning, and give it the devil's own beating.

'The two grown-up bridesmaids were in a sort of figured nylon organza,' Evie said. She tried hard to give an accurate picture, but her aunt did not understand the words. The water in the kettle had begun to stir, so she put aside the knitting and finished laying the table. She had some stewed raspberries to eat with the bread and butter. This was her last meal of the day and she always enjoyed it, but she knew that Evie would say 'Nothing for me, Auntie', and light another cigarette.

'In a mauvy-pinky shade, lovely with the sweet-peas,' she was saying.

'The girl's clothes-mad, though it's only natural,' her aunt thought as she poured out the tea and suffered boredom.

Evie lit another cigarette to stop herself yawning, remembering the freedom of stepping on to the bus after these visits, the wonderful release, and the glow of self-righteousness – duty done, sunshine bestowed, vistas widened.

Mrs Swan stood by the wall of her front garden, knitting, as Evie's bus drove off. It was a summer's evening, with a scent of blossom from the trees in the churchyard. The vicarage doves were strutting about the roof, making peaceful sounds, over the tiles white-splashed with their droppings.

Mrs Butcher from the Plough Inn had got off the bus before it turned to go back to the town, taking Evie on it. She walked slowly – looking angrily hot, as red-haired people often do – carrying a cardboard dress-box. It was an awkward shape, and the string cut into her fingers. She had hoped to get into the pub without her husband, Eric, noticing it and, seeing him crossing the yard, she stopped to have a chat with Mrs Swan until he should have disappeared again.

'Lovely evening,' she said.

'Yes, very nice,' Mrs Swan responded cheerfully, although usually the woman passed by without speaking, intent on her own business, full of dissatisfactions and impatience. She drank too much at night and laughed for no reason, Charlie used to say when he returned from his evening glass of bitter. But all day long she was morose.

'You're busy.' Phyllis Butcher nodded at Mrs Swan's knitting, determined not to move on until Eric was back in the bar. She would leave the dressbox in the outside Ladies, until after opening-time. Her husband was more observant about parcels than about clothes. Once a dress was unwrapped, she was safe, and if a customer praised a new one and he glanced at it suspiciously, she would look quite surprised and say, 'Why, it's been hanging in my wardrobe for at least three years.'

'I've got lots of odd wool,' she said, when Mrs Swan explained about the blanket she was making. 'The sweaters and things I've started in my time. I'll bring it round tomorrow.'

'It's very good of you,' said Mrs Swan. 'A different colour makes a change.' 'I'll believe in it when I see it,' she thought, knowing the sort of woman Mrs Butcher was.

Yet she was wrong, for the very next afternoon Mrs Butcher came to the cottage with a great assortment of brightly coloured wool. She sat down in the kitchen and drank a cup of tea. She had been crying, Mrs Swan thought, and presently she began to explain why, stretching her damp handkerchief from corner to corner, and sometimes dabbing her eyes with it.

Mrs Swan sorted the wool and untangled it. The colours excited her, particularly a turquoise blue with a strand of silver twisted in it, and her fingers itched to begin knitting a new square – an adventure she must put off until she had finished one of mottled grey.

Phyllis Butcher's mother was poorly. Listening, Mrs Swan thought it did the woman credit that she should weep.

'I'll have to go up there,' Mrs Butcher said. 'Up north. Real Geordie country,' she added scornfully. 'I hate it there.'

'I was in service in Scotland once,' said Mrs Swan. 'Nice scenery and all, but I was happier when I moved down south. I shouldn't care to go back.' The very thought was tiring. She visualised the road to Scotland, climbing steeply all the way, a long pull uphill, ending in a cold bedroom under the slated turret roof of a castle. 'I saw an eagle once,' she said. 'A wicked great bird. There were stags, too, and cattle with great horns. Five o'clock us girls got up, and some days I could have cried, my hands were so cold.'

'Oh, Consett's not romantic,' Phyllis Butcher said, 'It's all mining round there. I can't stand it, that's a fact, and never could. I know I ought to go more often, but you can't think how it depresses me.'

Eric had put it more strongly – hence the tears. 'Your own mother,' he had said. 'You'll be old and lonely one day yourself, perhaps.'

'I'd rather be taken!' she had cried.

'Mother's not easy,' she told Mrs Swan. When she had drunk her tea, from habit she turned the cup upside down in the saucer and then lifted it up again and examined the tea leaves. There were always birds flying, and she had forgotten what they meant.

'What's her complaint?' Mrs Swan enquired, for she was interested in sickness, and when younger had longed to be a nurse.

'Oh, I don't know. If it's not one thing it's another. The house is full of bottles of medicine. Illness gives me the creeps. She's always been chesty, of course.' She was still studying the cup and, turning it in her hands, had found the promise of a letter and what she thought was a threatened journey. 'I'll go tomorrow,' she said. 'Get things straightened up here and set off in the morning. "Hello, stranger," she'll say when I walk in. That's enough for a start to make me want to turn round and go back the way I came. If she wasn't so catty, I'd go more often. I couldn't do enough for her, if she was only pleasant.'

'Why not go straight away?' Eric had said when she received the letter. 'She might be worse than she makes out.'

'I can't just walk out of the house like that,' she had told him. 'There are all the things I have to do here – arrangements to make.'

To escape his critical eye, she had slipped round with the wool – anything to get out of the house – and had sat in the peaceful little room for over half an hour, trying to improve her self-esteem.

'I should go and get it over with,' Mrs Swan advised, thinking of her niece, Evie, and her bright face when she said good-bye, and her quick, light step going towards the bus-stop.

Phyllis did not see Mrs Swan again until she had returned from the funeral. She had delayed her journey too long, and, as she opened her mother's front gate, bracing herself for the usual sarcastic greeting, she had looked up and seen one of the neighbours drawing the blind over the bedroom window.

She went to stay in a small hotel rather than remain in the house. Eric came up to join her for the funeral, at which she knew the neighbours were watching her and whispering. Their eyes were lowered, their lips set together whenever she turned to look at them, but she guessed what they were saying. They had known her when she was a child, but she had forgotten all of them and their names meant nothing.

She had not pretended to grieve, not even in order to shelter herself
from Eric's words of blame. 'You could just as easily have gone the day
before,' he told her. 'I don't know what these people think of us.'

'And I'm sure I don't care,' she said. But she cared very much, and her
face burned as she walked out of the chapel after the coffin, feeling the hostility of the other women, the neighbours who had sat with her mother and
taken in her meals.

'You'll have to thank them properly,' Eric said. 'Do something to show
your gratitude.'

She refused to speak to them. 'I know what they're like,' she said. 'They
lean over one another's fences all day long and wag their wicked tongues.
Wild horses wouldn't drag me to this place again.'

All the unspoken words had hurt her and those spoken ones of Eric's,
too. She had such a different picture of herself from the one other people
seemed to see, and she was frightened and astounded by glimpses of how
she appeared to them, for they perceived traits she was sure she had never
possessed – or only under the most serious provocation. She thought so
much about herself that it was important to have the thoughts comfortable,
and many desolate hours had been made more bearable by gazing at her
own reflection. Warm-hearted, impulsive, she was sure she was – herself
hardly considered, and then always last, as she bustled about the countryside doing good. 'No one knows what people in this village owe her.' The
words were clear, though the person who said them was only dimly imagined. 'She herself would never tell, but I doubt if there's a cottage in the
parish where there isn't someone with cause to be grateful. In this village,
it's a funny thing, if anyone is in trouble, it's the pub they go to for help,
not the vicarage.' From her bedroom window, she could look across at the
churchyard and would imagine the procession of villagers winding up the
pathway under the chestnut trees, in black for her own funeral. 'There
wasn't a dry eye,' she told herself.

Then Eric's sharp phrases splintered the image – 'Your own mother.' 'You
think only of yourself and what you are going to put on your back.'

She tried not to listen, and could soon comfort herself, just as when she
looked in a mirror and the freckled skin and sandy hair were transfigured
into alabaster and Titian red.

Sitting at lunch in the train, flying past dreary canals and grey fields, she
endured her husband's sullen silence, and buttered bread rolls; buttering
and nibbling, to comfort herself, she stared out at the sour-looking pastures.

She was glad to be back in her own picturesque village. The Thames
valley consoled her, but uncertainty still hovered about her and she wondered if, after all, she had failed her own image of herself. She had not yet
dared to unpack her new dress. It was too bright a colour and she dreaded

Eric's comments. She kept it hidden on top of the wardrobe, although she knew that the pleasure of putting it on for the first time was perhaps the only way there was of dispelling her sadness.

To escape the atmosphere of disapproval, she unravelled one of her old sweaters and took the wool to Mrs Swan, not admitting to herself that, because of past aloofness, there was no other house in the village where she could drop in and exchange a word or two. In the past, an afternoon's shopping had always cured despondency, and, in the evenings, beer and backchat were even better distractions. However, deference to her bereavement seemed to have sobered customers for the time being – the last sort of behaviour to raise her spirits.

Mrs Swan was not alone. She had called Mrs Rippon in from the garden to give her a present of a pot of blackberry jelly, and they were sitting at the table, drinking tea.

Phyllis joined them, nervously praising the look of the jelly and everything else she could see.

'I was sorry to hear of your loss,' said Mrs Swan, whose neighbour kept her eyes averted and suddenly took up the pot of jelly and said good-bye.

'I brought some more wool.' Phyllis saw the half-finished blanket spread over the back of a horsehair sofa, and began to praise that, too, and got up to study it – the uneven stitches and the cobbled-together squares, the drabness already beginning to break into gaudiness since her last visit. She returned to her chair, feeling that the brightness she had brought was symbolic. 'Yes, poor Mother,' she said. She bowed her head and sighed and looked resigned. 'It sounds a dreadful thing to say, but I can't be sorry, for *her* sake. It really was a merciful release.'

That's what young Evie will say about me when I go, Mrs Swan thought. And so it will be, too, for her.

'It's peaceful here,' said Phyllis.

The cat lay asleep by the fender, moving his ears and beating the end of his tail rhythmically against the rug, as if he were in the midst of a dream that bored and angered him. Above the fireplace hung a strip of sticky paper, black with flies, some dead and some dying a wretched death. Others had evaded it, and circled the room slowly and warily.

Phyllis leant forward and sniffed at a vase full of nasturtiums edged with their little round leaves. The smell tantalised her, reminding her of something. Was it mustard, she wondered, or some medicine – or just nasturtiums? They had grown in Consett. Those and dusty, insect-bitten hollyhocks were all she could remember in the shabby strip of garden where her father had kept rabbits.

'Aren't they pretty?' she said, sniffing the flowers again, and then she determined not to praise another thing, lest she should sound condescending. 'That's your husband, isn't it?' she asked, nodding at an old photograph in a frame made of sea shells.

'He had that taken the day he joined up, when he was twenty-five. And he wore a moustache like that till he was fifty. Then he began to go bald, and that great bush looked silly then, he thought, so he shaved it off. He hadn't a hair between his head and Heaven by the time he was sixty.'

'Yes, I remember,' Phyllis said. She supposed she did remember seeing him in the public bar, but she had never bothered to give him a name.

'It's a pity having to leave your mother all that long way away,' Mrs Swan said. 'My own mother's buried down in Bristol and the train fare's out of the question. I'd dearly like to go.' After a pause, she said, 'I expect the flowers were lovely, though it's not an easy time of the year. I find plenty of garden flowers for Charlie, but they're no use for a burial. Gladioli don't make up well and shop roses are exorbitant.'

'We sent carnations, Eric and I.'

She got up to go and stood looking down at the cat, whose dream seemed to have taken a better turn, for he lay relaxed now, with crossed paws and a smile on his face. Phyllis felt peaceful, too.

'Well, come again,' Mrs Swan said, from politeness.

'I really will,' Phyllis promised.

Enlivening Mrs Swan's life became an absorbing pastime and something of which, for once, Eric could not disapprove. Phyllis was always dropping in to the cottage, and found ingenious ways of giving presents tactfully, not knowing that the tact was wasted, since Mrs Swan had grace enough to be pleased with the gifts and to accept them simply, unbothered by motives. She thought of them as charity, and had no objection to that. She only wondered why there was so little of it about nowadays.

'The hens are laying like wildfire,' Phyllis would say. If she met anyone she knew on the way home, she always explained her outing. 'I was just taking a few eggs to poor old Mrs Swan.'

One day she asked her to go back to the Plough for a glass of sherry, but Mrs Swan thought it a mistake for widows to drink. 'I haven't taken any since Charlie died,' she said.

'You're very good to that old lady,' one of the customers told Phyllis.

'I'm not at all. I just like being with her. And she's got no one else. It means a lot to her and costs me nothing.'

'Most people wouldn't bother, all the same.'

'It's a terrible thing, loneliness.'

'There's no need to tell me that.'

The bar had only just opened for the evening, and he was the only customer so far. He was always the first to arrive, and although he came so regularly, Phyllis knew very little about him. He was middle-aged and not very talkative, and never stayed drinking for long. 'Very genuine,' she said, when other people mentioned him. It was an easy label and she made it sound utterly dull.

This evening, instead of opening his newspaper, he seemed inclined to talk. 'Living in lodgings palls in the end,' he said. 'I never married, and it gets lonely, the evenings and weekends. I sometimes think what I'd give to have some nice family where I could drop in when I wanted, and be one of them – remember the children's birthdays, give a hand with the gardening, that sort of thing. Everyone ought to have some family like that where they're just accepted and taken for granted, given pot luck, not a lot of fuss. It's tiring always being a guest. Well, I find it so.'

'It sounds to me as if there's a fairy godfather being wasted,' Phyllis said.

He smiled. 'You feel you'd like to have your stake in someone else's family if you haven't got one of your own. Will you have a drink with me?'

'Thank you very much,' she said brightly. 'I'd like a lager.'

'Well, please do.'

'What a lovely rose,' she said. 'I've always noticed what lovely roses you wear in your buttonhole, Mr ...' Her voice trailed off, as she couldn't remember his name. 'Well, here's all you wish yourself,' she said, and sipped the lager, then wiped her lips on her scented handkerchief.

He had taken the rose from his buttonhole and handed it to her across the bar. 'Out of my landlady's garden,' he said. 'I always look after them for her.'

'Oh, you are sweet!' She twirled the rose in her fingers and then turned to the mirrored panelling behind the bar and, standing on tiptoe to see her reflection above the shelf of bottles, tucked the rose into her blouse.

'That reminds me of that picture – *The Bar at the Folies-Bergère* – one of my favourites,' he said. 'All the bottles, and your reflection, and the rose.'

'Well, how funny you should say that. We had it for our Christmas card one year. Everyone liked it. "Well, we didn't realise they had Bass in those days" – that's what everyone said. "In Paris, too!" There's those bottles on the bar, if you remember. It makes the picture look a bit like an advertisement. Look at my lovely rose, Eric.'

'Good evening, Mr Willis,' Eric said, carrying in a crate of light ale. 'Yes, it's quite a perfect bloom, isn't it? I suppose she cadged it off you.'

'It's a pleasure to give Mrs Butcher something,' Mr Willis replied. 'As far as I have seen, it's usually *she* who does it all.'

Phyllis was happier, gentler than she had been for years. In Mr Willis's eyes she saw her ideal self reflected.

'Oh, I haven't had time to powder my nose,' she would say, scrabbling through her handbag, which she kept on a shelf beneath the bar.

'I suppose you've been off on one of your errands of mercy,' said Mr Willis.

'Don't be silly. I've had a very nice tea party with my old lady in the almshouse. What errand of mercy is there about that? Oh, you really shouldn't. What a gorgeous colour!'

Every evening now, he brought her a rose. When he had left the bar to go back to his lodgings for supper, the other customers teased her. 'Your boy friend stayed late tonight,' Eric would say.

'He's sweet,' she protested. 'No truly. Such lovely old-world manners, and he's so genuine.'

The evening before her birthday, he came in as usual, admired her new blouse, and gave her a yellow rosebud. 'And that may be the last,' he said.

'Oh, you aren't going away!' she exclaimed, looking so disconcerted that he smiled with pleasure.

'No, but the roses have already gone. Unless we have another crop later on.'

'What a relief. You really frightened me. I can do without the roses at a pinch, but we couldn't do without you.'

'You're always kind. I enjoy our chats. I couldn't do without them, either.'

She turned her head away, as if she dared not meet his eyes.

'How's your old lady?' he asked. In the silence that had fallen he was conscious of his heart beating. It was a loud and hollow sound, like an old grandfather clock, and he spoke quickly lest she, too, should hear it. They were alone in the bar, as they so often were for the first quarter of an hour after opening time.

'My old lady?' she repeated, and seemed to be dragging her thoughts back from a long way away. Then she smiled at him. 'Oh, she's very well.'

'Have you seen her lately?'

'Well, not many days go by when I don't pop in.'

But she had not popped in for a long time. There had been other things to occupy her mind, and shopping had become a pleasure again.

'You must be sure to come in tomorrow and have a drink with me,' she said. 'It's my birthday.'

Instead of pinning the rosebud to her blouse, she put it in a glass of water. 'I'll keep it for tomorrow night,' she said.

He leant across the bar and took the rose from the glass and wiped it carefully on his handkerchief. Then, hoping he would not blush, he tucked it into her blouse.

The next morning, two dozen shop roses arrived by messenger.

When the bus turned round at the church and set off on its journey back to the town, Evie always felt marooned. Until it returned, in two hours' time, there was no escape.

It was three o'clock on a late autumn afternoon – soft, misty weather. In the churchyard, graves were lost under the fallen leaves. There were pockets of web on the brambles and unseen strands of it in the air. From the bus-stop, Evie could see her great-aunt at work in the churchyard, raking leaves off the grave. She was wearing a forage cap of emerald-green wool that she had knitted herself, and she had tied a pinafore over her winter coat.

'Well, girl,' she said, when Evie joined her. 'I wasn't expecting you.'

'Mother thought the news ought to come from me,' Evie said. She sat down on a slab of polished granite and gazed at her aunt's astonishing hat. 'I'm getting engaged on Sunday,' she said. 'Norman's bringing his mother and father to tea, and giving me the ring then. It's a diamond with two amethysts.'

'And when's the wedding?'

Evie looked vague. 'Oh, I don't know about that. Both Norman and I favour long engagements.' She stood up quickly, hearing footsteps and not wanting to be seen sitting on a grave.

Phyllis Butcher was taking a short cut through the churchyard on her way from the post office. She nodded as she passed them, hurrying towards the lych-gate.

'*She's* offhand,' Evie said. 'There were two women talking about her on the bus. She was in the telephone box outside the post office as we went by. They were saying that she goes down there nearly every afternoon to ring someone up, although they've got the phone at the pub. I must say she looks the type. Does she still keep pestering you?'

'She hasn't been in since the summer. Fill that vase from the tap over there, will you?'

Evie took the stone urn, which was inscribed 'In Loving Memory', and made her way between graves to the water tap by the church wall. When she came back, the grave was raked free of leaves and Mrs Swan was untying the string round a bunch of bronze chrysanthemums.

'I imagine her one of those people – gushing one moment and cutting you dead the next,' Evie said, her thoughts still on Phyllis Butcher. 'Every time I came last summer, she was stuck there in the kitchen. And putting you under an obligation with all those presents.'

'I didn't see any obligation in it.'

'I told Mother about her, and she was quite annoyed. It wasn't her place to carry on like that.'

'I was sorry for her,' Mrs Swan replied. 'She did me no harm.' She knelt down to arrange the flowers in the urn. 'There, that looks nice, I think. I'm always pleased when the chrysanthemums come. Charlie was so fond of them.'

She straightened her back and pushed stray ends of hair under her cap. 'If you bring the rake, I'll take the basket. We'll make a cup of tea, and you can tell me about your plans.'

They walked slowly to the lych-gate. The last of the yellow leaves were drifting down. On some graves, the chestnut fans lay flat, like outspread hands.

A Dedicated Man

In the dark, raftered dining-room, Silcox counted the coned napkins and, walking among the tables, lifted the lids of the mustard pots and shook salt level in the cellars.

At the beginning of their partnership as waiter and waitress, Edith had liked to make mitres or fleurs-de-lis or water-lilies of the napkins, and Silcox, who thought this great vulgarity, waited until after he had made his proposal and been accepted before he put a stop to it. She had listened meekly. 'Edwardian vulgarity,' he had told her. Taking a roll of bread from the centre of the petalled linen, he whipped the napkin straight, then turned it deftly into a dunce's cap.

Edith always came down a little after Silcox. He left the bedroom in plenty of time for her to change into her black dress and white apron. His proposal had not included marriage or any other intimacy and, although they lay every night side by side in twin beds, they were always decorous in their behaviour, fanatically prim, and he had never so much as seen her take a brush to her hair, as he himself might have said. However, there was no one to say it to, and to the world they were Mr and Mrs Silcox, a plain, respectable couple. Both were ambitious, both had been bent on leaving the hotel where they first met – a glorified boarding-house, Silcox called it. Both, being snobbish, were galled at having to wait on noisy, sunburned people who wore freakish and indecent holiday clothes and could not pronounce *crêpes de volaille*, let alone understand what it meant.

By the time Silcox heard of the vacancy at the Royal George, he had become desperate beyond measure, irritated at every turn by the vulgarities of seaside life. The Royal George was mercifully as inland as anywhere in England can be. The thought of the Home Counties soothed him. He visualised the landscape embowered in flowering trees.

In his interview with the manageress he had been favourably impressed by the tone of the hotel. The Thames flowed by beyond the geranium-bordered lawns; there would be star occasions all summer – the Fourth of June, Henley, Ascot. The dining-room, though it was small, had velvet-cushioned banquettes and wine-lists in padded leather covers. The ash-trays advertised nothing and the flowers had not come out of the garden.

'My wife,' he said repeatedly during the interview. He had been unable to bring her, from consideration to their employer. The manageress respected him for this and for very much else. She could imagine him in tails, and he seemed to wear the grey suit as if it were a regrettable informality he had been unable to escape. He was stately, eyes like a statue's, mouth like a carp's. His deference would have that touch of condescension which would make customers angle for his good will. Those to whom he finally unbent, with a remark about the weather or the compliments of the season, would return again and again, bringing friends to whom they could display their status. 'Maurice always looks after me,' they would say.

Returning to the pandemonium – the tripperish hotel, the glaring sky – he made his proposal to Edith. 'Married couple', the advertisement had stipulated and was a necessary condition, he now understood, for only one bedroom was available. 'It has twin bedsteads, I ascertained,' he said.

Marriage, he explained, could not be considered, as he was married already. Where the person in question (as he spoke of his wife) was at present, he said he did not know. She had been put behind him.

Until that day, he had never spoken to Edith of his personal affairs, although they had worked together for a year. She was reserved herself and embarrassed by this unexpected lapse, though by the proposal itself she felt deeply honoured. It set the seal on his approval of her work.

'I think I am right in saying that it is what matters most to both of us,' he observed, and she nodded. She spoke very little and never smiled.

The manageress of the Royal George, when Edith went for her separate interview, wondered if she were not too grim. At forty-five, her hair was a streaked grey and clipped short like a man's at the back. She had no make-up and there were deep lines about her mouth which had come from the expression of disapproval she so often wore. On the other hand, she was obviously dependable and efficient, would never slop soup or wear dirty cuffs or take crafty nips of gin in the still-room whenever there was a lull. Her predecessor had done these things and been flighty, too.

So Edith and Silcox were engaged. Sternly and without embarrassment they planned arrangements for bedroom privacy. These were simply a matter of one staying in the bathroom while the other dressed or undressed in the bedroom. Edith was first to get into bed and would then turn out the light. Silcox was meanwhile sitting on a laundry basket in his dressing-gown, glancing at his watch until it was time to return. He would get into bed in the dark. He never wished her good-night and hardly admitted to himself that she was there.

Now a week had gone by and the arrangements had worked so smoothly that he was a little surprised this evening that on the stroke of seven o'clock she did not appear. Having checked his tables, he studied the list of bookings and was pleased to note the name of one of his *bêtes noires*. This would put a spur to his pride and lift the evening out of the ordinary ruck. Pleasant people were not the same challenge.

Upstairs, Edith was having to hurry, something she rarely deigned to do. She was even a little excited as she darted about the room, looking for clean cuffs and apron, fresh dress preservers and some pewter-coloured stockings, and she kept pausing to glance at a photograph on the chest of drawers. It was postcard size and in a worn leather frame and was of an adolescent boy wearing a school blazer.

When she had gone back to the bedroom after breakfast she saw the photograph for the first time. Silcox had placed it there without a word. She ignored it for a while and then became nervous that one of the maids might question her about it, and it was this reason she gave Silcox for having asked him who it was.

'Our son,' he said.

He deemed it expedient, he added, that he should be a family man. The fact would increase their air of dependability and give them background and reality and solid worth. The boy was at a public school, he went on, and did not divulge to his friends the nature of his parents' profession. Silcox, Edith realised with respect, was so snobbish that he looked down upon himself.

'How old is he?' she asked in an abrupt tone.

'He is seventeen and working for the Advanced Level.'

Edith did not know what this was and wondered how she could manage to support the fantasy.

'We shall say nothing ourselves,' said Silcox, 'as we are not in the habit of discussing our private affairs. But he is there if wanted.'

'What shall we ... what is his name?'

'Julian,' Silcox said and his voice sounded rich and musical.

Edith looked with some wonder at the face in the photograph. It was a very ordinary face and she could imagine the maids conjecturing at length as to whom he took after.

'Who is he really?' she asked.

'A young relative,' said Silcox.

In Edith's new life there were one or two difficulties – one was trying to remember not to fidget with the wedding ring as if she were not used to wearing it, and another was being obliged to call Silcox 'Maurice'. This she thought unseemly, like all familiarities, and to be constant in it required continual vigilance. He, being her superior, had called her Edith from the start.

Sleeping beside him at night worried her less. The routine of privacy was established and sleep itself was negative and came immediately to both of them after long hours of being on their feet. They might have felt more sense of intimacy sitting beside one another in deckchairs in broad daylight, for then there would be the pitfalls of conversation. (How far to encroach? How much interest to show that could be shown without appearing inquisitive?)

Edith was one of those women who seem to know from childhood that the attraction of men is no part of their equipment, and from then on to have supported nature in what it had done for them, by exaggerating the gruffness and the gracelessness and becoming after a time sexless. She strode heavily in shoes a size too large, her off-duty coat and skirt were as sensible as some old nanny's walking-out attire. She was not much interested in people, although she did her duty towards them and wrote each week to her married sister in Australia: and was generous to her at Christmas. Her letters, clearly written as they were, were still practically unreadable – so full of facts and times: where she took the bus to on her day off and the whole route described, where this road forked and that branched off and what p.m. she entered this or that café to progress from the grapefruit to the trifle of the *table d'hôte* (five and sixpence). Very poor service usually, she wrote – odd knives and forks left on the table while she drank her coffee, for no one took any pride nowadays.

Edith had no relations other than her sister; her world was peopled with hotel staff and customers. With the staff she was distant and sometimes grim if they were careless in their work, and with her customers she was distant and respectful. She hardly responded to them, although there were a very few – usually gay young men or courtly and jovial elderly ones – to whom she behaved protectively, as nannyish as she looked when she wore her outdoor clothes.

The other person in her life – Silcox – was simply to her the Establishment. She had never worked with anyone she respected more – in her mind, he was always a waiter and she always thought of him dressed as a waiter. On his day off, he seemed lowered by wearing the clothes of an ordinary man. Having to turn her eyes away from him when she glimpsed him in a dressing-gown was really no worse. They were not man and woman in one another's eyes, and hardly even human beings.

No difficulties they were beset with in their early days at the Royal George could spoil the pleasures of their work. The serenity of the dining-room, the elaborate food which made demands upon them (to turn something over in flaming brandy in a chafing-dish crowned Silcox's evening), the superiority of the clientele and the glacial table linen. They had suffered horrors from common people and this escape to elegance was precious to them both. The hazards that threatened were not connected with their work, over which both had mastery from the beginning, but with their private lives. It was agonising to Edith to realise that now they were expected to spend their free time together. On the first day off they took a bus to another hotel along the river and there had luncheon. Silcox modelled his behaviour on that of his own most difficult customers, and seemed to be retaliating by doing so. He was very lordly and full of knowledge and criticism. Edith, who was used to shopping ladies' luncheons in cafés, became nervous and alarmed. When she next wrote to her sister, she left this expedition altogether out of the letter and described instead some of the menus she had served at the Royal George, with prices. Nowadays, there was, for the first time in her life, an enormous amount that had to be left out of the letters.

She was dreading their next free day and was relieved when Silcox suggested that they should make a habit of taking the train to London together and there separating. If they came back on the same train in the evening, no suspicions would be roused.

In London, she enjoyed wandering round the department stores, looking without surprise or envy at all the frivolous extravagancies. She made notes of prices, thinking that her sister would be interested to compare them with those in Melbourne, and she could spend a whole day over choosing a pair of gloves, going from shop to shop, studying the quality. One day, she intended to visit the Zoo.

Silcox said that he liked to look in the jewellers' windows. In the afternoons, he went to a News Cinema. Going home in the train, he read a newspaper and she looked at the backs of houses and little gardens, and later, fields or woods, staring as if hypnotised.

One morning, when she had returned to their bedroom after breakfast, he surprised her by following her there. This was the time of day when he took a turn about the garden or strolled along by the river.

When he had shut the door, he said quietly, 'I'm afraid I must ask you something. I think it would be better if you were less tidy in here. It struck me this morning that by putting everything away out of sight, you will give rise to suspicion.'

Once, he had been a floor waiter in an hotel and knew, from taking breakfast in to so many married people, what their bedrooms usually looked like. His experience with his own wife he did not refer to.

'I overheard Carrie saying what a tidy pair we were and she had never met anyone like it, not a pin in sight when she came into this room, she said.'

'I respect your intentions,' he said grandly, 'but the last thing to serve our purpose is to appear in any way out of the ordinary. If you could have one or two things lying about – your hairbrush, perhaps – well, I leave it to you – just a pot of something or other on the dressing-table. A wife would never hide everything away in the drawers. Carrie's right, as it is there isn't even a pin to be seen. Nothing to show it's anyone's room at all, except for the photograph.'

Edith blushed and pressed her lips tightly together. She turned away and made no reply. Although she knew that it had been difficult for him to make the suggestion, and sensible and necessary as she saw it to be, she was angry with him. She wondered why his words had so humiliated her, and could find no reason. He had reproved her before about her work – the water-lily napkins, for instance – but he had never angered her.

She waited for him to leave her and then she removed from the drawer a large, harsh-bristled brush, a boxful of studs and safety pins and a pot of Vaseline which she used in cold weather when her lips were chapped. In the early evening, when she came up to change, she found Silcox's brushes beside hers, a shoe-horn dangled from the side of the mirror and his dressing-gown had been taken from his clothes cupboard and was hanging at the back of the door.

She felt very strange about it all and when she went downstairs she tried to direct all her thoughts towards her work.

'He couldn't be anyone else's,' said Carrie Hurt, the maid, looking at the photograph. She had the impertinence to take it up and go over to the window with it, to see it better.

'He is thought to take more after his father's side.' Edith said, tempted to allow the conversation to continue, then wondering why this should be.

'I expect it's his father's side that says it,' Carrie replied. 'Oh, I can see you. The way his hair grows on his forehead. His father's got quite a widow's peak.'

Edith found herself looking over Carrie's shoulder, as if she had never seen the photograph before.

'As a matter of fact, he is a little like my sister's eldest boy,' she conceded. 'His cousin,' she added, feeling wonder at the words.

'Well, you must be proud of him. Such an open face,' Carrie said, replacing the photograph in its right position and passing a duster over the glass.

'Yes,' said Edith. 'He's a good boy.'

She left Carrie and went downstairs and walked in the garden until it was time to go on duty. She went up and down the gravel paths and along by the river, but she could not overcome the excitement which lately disturbed her so, the sensation of shameful pleasure.

By the river's edge, she came upon Silcox, who had taken up fishing in his spare time – a useful excuse for avoiding Edith's company. He stood on the bank, watching the line where it entered the water, and hardly turned his head as Edith approached him.

'Where does he – where does Julian go to in the holidays?' she asked.

'He goes to relatives,' Silcox answered.

She knew that she was interrupting him and that she must move on. As she did, he heard her murmuring anxiously, 'I do so hope they're kind.'

He turned his head quickly and looked after her, but she had gone mooning back across the lawn. The expression of astonishment stayed on his face for a long time after that, and when she took up her position in the dining-room before lunch, he looked at her with concern, but she was her usual forbidding and efficient self again.

'Don't we ever go to see him?' she asked a few days later. 'Won't they think us strange not going?'

'What we do in our free time is no concern of theirs,' he said.

'I only thought they'd think it strange.'

He isn't real, none of it's true, she now constantly reminded herself, for sometimes her feelings of guilt about that abandoned boy grew too acute.

Sometimes, on Sunday outings from school, boys were brought by their parents to have lunch at the hotel, and Edith found herself fussing over them, giving them huge helpings, discussing their appetites with their parents.

'They're all the same at that age,' she would say. 'I know.'

It was so unlike her to chat with the customers and quite against Silcox's code. When he commented disdainfully upon her unusual behaviour, she seemed scarcely to listen to his words. The next Sunday, serving a double portion of ice-cream to a boy, she looked across at his mother and smiled. 'I've got a son myself, madam,' she said. 'I know.'

Silcox, having overheard this, was too enraged to settle down to his fishing that afternoon. He looked for Edith and found her in the bedroom writing a letter to her sister.

'It was a mistake – this about the boy,' he said, taking up the photograph and glaring at it. 'You have not the right touch in such matters. You carry the deception to excess. You go too far.'

'Too far?' she said brightly, but busy writing.

'Our position is established. I think the little flourishes I thought up had their result.'

'But they were all *your* little flourishes,' she said, looking up at him. 'You didn't let *me* think of any, did you?'

He stared back at her and soon her eyes flickered, and she returned to her writing.

'There won't be any more,' he said. 'From me, or from you. Or any more discussion of our affairs, do you understand? Carrie in here every morning gossiping, you chatting to customers, telling them such a pack of lies – as if it were all true, and as if they could possibly be interested. You know as well as I do how unprofessional it is. I should never have credited it of you. Even when we were at that dreadful place at Paignton, you conducted yourself with more dignity.'

'I don't see the harm,' she said mildly.

'And I don't see the necessity. It's courting danger for one thing – to get so involved. We'll keep our affairs to ourselves or else we'll find trouble ahead.

'What time does the post go?'

Without reading her letter through, she pushed it into an envelope. Goodness knows what she has written, he thought. A mercy her sister was far away in Australia.

The photograph – the subject of their contention – he pushed aside, as if he would have liked to be rid of it.

'You don't seem to be paying much attention,' he said. 'I only warn you that you'd better. Unless you hope to make laughing stocks of both of us.'

Before she addressed the envelope, she looked gravely at him for a moment, thinking that perhaps the worst thing that could happen to him, the thing he had always dreaded most, was to be laughed at, to lose his dignity. 'I used to be the same,' she thought, taking up her pen.

'Yes, I made a mistake,' he said. 'I admit it freely. But we shall stand by it, since it's made. We can hardly kill the boy off, now we've got him.'

She jerked round and looked at him, her face even paler than usual, then seemed to gather her wits again and bent her head. Writing rather slowly and unsteadily, she finished addressing the envelope.

'I hope I shan't have further cause for complaint,' he said – rather as if he were her employer, as in fact he always felt himself to be. The last word duly spoken, he left her, but was frowning as he went downstairs. She was behaving oddly, something was not quite right about her and he was apprehensive.

Edith was smiling while she tidied herself before slipping out to the pillar box. 'That's the first tiff we've ever had,' she thought. 'In all our married life.'

'I find *her* all right,' Carrie Hurt said to the still-room maid. 'Not stand-offish, really, when you get to know her.'

'It's him I can't abide.'

'I'm sorry for her. The way he treats her.'

'And can't you tell he's got a temper? You get that feeling, don't you, that for two pins he'd boil over?'

'Yes, I'm sorry for her. When he's not there, she likes to talk. And dotes on that boy of theirs.'

'Funny life it must be, not hardly ever seeing him.'

'She's going to soon, so she was telling me, when it's his birthday. She was showing me the sweater she was knitting for him. She's a lovely knitter.'

Silcox found Edith sitting in a secluded place at the back of the hotel where the staff were allowed to take the air. It was a cobbled courtyard, full of empty beer-crates and strings of tea-towels hung to dry. Pigeons walked up and down the outhouse roofs and the kitchen cat sat at Edith's feet watching them. Edith was knitting a white, cable-stitch sweater and she had a towel across her lap to keep the wool clean.

'I have just overheard that Carrie Hurt and the still-room girl discussing you,' Silcox said, when he had looked round to make sure that there was no one to overhear him. 'What is this nonsense about going to see the boy, or did my ears deceive me?'

'They think we're unnatural. I felt so ashamed about it that I said I'd be going on his birthday.'

'And when is *that*, pray?'

'Next month, the eighteenth. I'll have the sweater done by then.'

She picked up the knitting pattern, studied it frowning.

'Oh, it is, is it? You've got it all cut and dried. But his birthday happens to be in March.'

'You can't choose everything,' she said. She was going on with her knitting and smiling.

'I forbid you to say any more about the boy.'

'You can't, you see. People ask me how he's getting on.'

'I wish I hadn't started the damn fool business.'

'I don't. I'm so glad you did.'

'You'll land us in gaol, do you realise that? And what is this you're knitting?' He knew, from the conversation he had overheard.

'A sweater for him, for Julian.'

'Do you know what?' he said, leaning towards her and almost spitting the words at her, one after the other. 'I think you're going out of your mind. You'll have to go away from here. Maybe we'd both better go, and it will be the parting of the ways.'

'I don't see any cause for that,' said Edith. 'I've never been so happy.'

But her happiness was nearly at an end: even before she could finish knitting the sweater, the spell had been broken.

A letter came from her sister, Hilda, in Melbourne. She wrote much less frequently than Edith and usually only when she had something to boast about – this time it was one of the boys having won a tennis tournament.

'She has always patronised me,' Edith thought. 'I have never harped on in that way about Julian. I don't see why I should have hidden his light under a bushel all these years.'

She sat down at once and wrote a long letter about his different successes. Whatever Hilda's sons may have done, Julian seemed to find it easy to do better. 'We are sending him for a holiday on the Continent as a reward for passing his exams,' she finished up. She was tired of silence and modesty. Those qualities had never brought her any joy, none of the wonderful exhilaration and sense of richness she had now. Her attitude towards life had been too drab and undemanding; she could plainly see this.

She took her letter to the village and posted it. She imagined her sister looking piqued – not puzzled – when she read it.

Silcox was in the bedroom when she returned. A drawer slid quickly shut and he was suddenly busy winding his watch. 'Well, I suppose it's time to put my hand to the wheel,' he said in a voice less cold than it had been of late, as he went out.

Edith was suspicious of this voice, which was too genial, she thought, and she looked round to see if anything of hers had been tampered with. She was especially anxious about her knitting, which was so precious to her; but it was still neatly rolled up and hanging in a clean laundry-bag in her cupboard.

She opened the drawer which Silcox had so smartly closed and found a letter lying on top of a pile of black woollen socks. A photograph was half out of the envelope. Though he had thrust it out of sight when she came into the room, she realised that he had been perfectly easy in his mind about leaving it where it was, for it would be contrary to his opinion of her that she would pry or probe. 'He knows nothing about me,' she thought, taking the photograph to the window so that she could see it better.

She was alarmed at the way her heart began to leap and hammer, and she pressed her hand to her breast and whispered 'Hush' to its loud beating. 'Hush, hush,' she implored it, and sat down on her bed to wait for the giddiness to pass.

When she was steadier, she looked again at the two faces in the photograph. There was no doubt that one of them was Julian's, though older than she had imagined and more defined than in the other photograph – the one that stood always on the chest of drawers.

It was so much like the face of the middle-aged woman whom his arm encircled affectionately, who wore the smug, pleased smile of a mother whose son has been teasing her. She glowed with delight, her lips ready to shape fond remonstrances. She looked a pretty, silly woman and wore a flowered, full-skirted dress, too girlish for her, too tight across the bust. They were standing by the wooden fence of a little garden. Behind them, hollyhocks grew untidily and a line of washing, having flapped in the wind as the camera clicked, hung there, blurred, above their heads. Julian had stared at the photographer, grinning foolishly, almost pulling a face. 'It's all put on,' thought Edith. 'All for effect.'

When her legs stopped trembling, she went again to the drawer and fetched the letter. She could only read a little of it at a time, because the feeling of faintness and nausea came upon her in waves and she would wait, with closed eyes, till each receded. After seeing 'Dear Father' she was as still as a stone, until she could brace herself for more, for the rest of the immaturely written, facetious letter. It contained abrupt and ungracious thanks for a watch he had received for what he referred to as his twenty-first. He seemed, Edith thought, to have expected more. A good time had been had by all, with Mum pushing the boat out to the best of her ability. They were still living in Streatham and he was working in a car showroom, where, he implied, he spent his time envying his customers. Things weren't too easy, although Mum was wonderful, of course. When he could afford to take her out, which he only wished he were able to do more often, she enjoyed herself as if she were a young girl. It was nice of his father to have thought of him, he ended reproachfully.

Carrie Hurt pushed the bedroom door open at the same time as she wrapped on it with her knuckles. 'I was to say would you come down at once, Edith. There's some people in the dining-room already.'

'I shan't be coming down,' Edith said.

'Don't you feel well?'

'Tell him I shan't be coming down.'

Edith turned her head away and remained like that until Carrie had gone. Quietly, she sat and waited for Silcox to arrive. He would do so, she knew, as soon as he could find the manageress or a maid to take his place for a moment. It would offend his pride to allow such a crisis, but he would be too seriously alarmed to prevent it.

Her hatred was now so heavy that it numbed her and she was able to sit, quite calm and patient, waiting for him, rehearsing no speeches, made quite incapable by the suddenness of the calamity and the impossibility of accepting the truth of it.

It was not so very long before she heard his hurrying footsteps. He entered the room as she had thought he would, brimming with pompous indignation. She watched this fade and another sort of anger take its place when he saw the letter in her hand, the photograph on the bed.

'No, your eyes don't deceive you,' she said.

At first, he could think of nothing better to say than 'How dare you!' He said this twice, but as it was clearly inadequate, he stepped forward and grasped her wrists, gripping them tightly, shook her back and forth until her teeth were chattering. Not for years, not since the days of his brief marriage, had he so treated a woman and he had forgotten the overwhelming sensations to be derived from doing so. He released her, but only to hit her across her face with the back of one hand then the other.

Shaken, but unfrightened, she stared at him. 'It was true all the time,' she said. 'He was really yours and you disowned him. Yet you made up that story just to have a reason for putting out the photograph and looking at it every day.'

'Why should I want to do that? He means nothing to me.' He hoped to disconcert her by a quick transition to indifference.

'And his mother – I was supposed to be his mother.' He laughed theatrically at the absurdity of this idea. It was a bad performance. When he had finished being doubled-up, he wiped his eyes and said: 'Excuse me.' The words were breathed on a sigh of exquisite enjoyment.

Coming to the door for the second time, Carrie Hurt waited after knocking. She had been surprised to hear Silcox laughing so loudly as she came along the passage. She had never heard him laugh in any way before and wondered if he had gone suddenly mad. He opened the door to her, looking grave and dignified.

'Yes, I am coming now,' he said.

'They're very busy. I was told to say if you could please . . .'

'I repeat, I am coming now. Edith is unwell and we must manage for today as best we may without her. She will stay here and rest,' he added, turning and saying this directly to Edith and stressing his even tone by a steady look. He would have locked the door upon her if Carrie had not been standing by.

Edith was then alone and began to cry. She chafed her wrists that were still reddened from his grasp, and moved her head from side to side, as if trying to evade the thoughts that crowded on her.

Carrie Hurt returned presently with a glass of brandy. 'It can't do any harm,' she said. 'He told me to leave you alone, but there might be something she wants, I thought.'

She put the glass on the table beside the bed and then went over to draw the curtains. Edith sat still, with her hands clasped in her lap, and waited for her to go.

'My mother has these funny spells,' Carrie told her. Then, noticing the letter lying on the bed, she asked, 'Oh, you haven't had any bad news, have you?'

'Yes,' Edith said.

She leant forward to take the glass, sipped from it and shuddered.

'Not your *boy?*' Carrie whispered.

Edith sighed. It seemed more than a sigh – a frightening sound, seeming to gather all the breath from her body, shuddering expelling it.

'He isn't ill, is he?' Carrie asked, expecting worse – though Silcox, to be sure, had seemed controlled enough. And what had his dreadful laughter meant?

Edith was silent for a moment and took a little more brandy. Then she said, in a forced and rather high-pitched voice: 'He is much worse than ill. He is disgraced.'

'Oh, my God!' said Carrie eagerly.

Edith's eyes rested for a second on the photograph lying beside her on the bed and then she covered it with her hand. 'For theft,' she said, her voice strengthening, 'thieving,' she added.

'Oh dear, I'm ever so sorry,' Carrie said softly. 'I can't believe it. I always said what an open face he'd got. Don't you remember – I always said that? Who could credit it? No one could. Not that I should breathe a word about it to a single soul.'

'Mention it to whoever you like,' Edith said. 'The whole world will know, and may decide where they can lay the blame.'

She drained the glass, her eyes closed. Then, 'There's bad blood there,' she said.

When Silcox had finished his duties, he returned, but the door was locked from inside, and there was no answer when he spoke, saying her name several times in a low voice, his head bent close to the keyhole.

He went away and walked by the river in his waiter's clothes, stared at by all who passed him. When he returned to the hotel, he was stared at there, too. The kitchen porter seemed to be re-assessing him, looked at him curiously and spoke insolently. The still-room maid pressed back against the passage wall as he went by. Others seemed to avoid him.

The bedroom door was still shut, but no longer locked. He stood looking at the empty room, the hairbrush had gone from the dressing-table and only a few coat-hangers swung from the rail in the clothes cupboard. He picked up the brandy glass and was standing there sniffing it when Carrie Hurt, who had enjoyed her afternoon, appeared in the doorway.

'I don't know if you know, she's packed and gone,' she said, 'and had the taxi take her to the train. I thought the brandy would pull her together,' she went on, looking at the glass in Silcox's hand. 'I expect the shock unhinged her and she felt she had to go. Of course, she'd want to see him, whatever happened. It must have been her first thought. I should like to say how sorry I am. You wouldn't wish such a thing on your worst enemy.'

He looked at her in bewilderment and then, seeing her glance, as it swerved from his in embarrassment, suddenly checked by something out of his sight, he walked slowly round the bed and saw there what she was staring at – the waste-paper basket heaped high with her white knitting, all cut into little shreds; even the needles had been broken in two.

Before the new couple arrived, Silcox prepared to leave. Since Edith's departure, he had spoken to no one but his customers, to whom he was as stately as ever – almost devotional he seemed in his duties, bowed over chafing-dish or bottle – almost as if his calling were sacred and he felt himself worthy of it.

On the last morning, he emptied his bedroom cupboard and then the drawers, packing with his usual care. In the bottom drawer, beneath layers of shirts, and rolled up in a damask napkin, he was horrified to discover a dozen silver-plated soup-spoons from the dining-room.

The Little Girl

She looked grave and timid, leaving heavily against her mother's knees, nursing a dirty teddy-bear. This evidence of her clinging nature, the shabby animal contrasted with her expensive clothes and her neatly plaited pigtails. It had comforted her when she felt apprehensive; she was lost without it. Her mother, who cared for appearances, had tried to transfer the devotion to other less shaming toys, this morning in another department of the shop had offered a white fur poodle who could sit up on its hind legs and beg. 'Perhaps I might take it as well,' said Deborah, who had not come down with the last fall of snow, her nanny said.

The poodle now lay wrapped up on the seat beside Mrs Daubeny and Deborah was stroking her teddy's threadbare ears, humming softly to him as she watched the other children – one exuberantly riding a rocking-horse (for the shoe department was as full of diversions as a dentist's waiting room), others walking obediently up and down trying new boots. At one little boy, who screamed and kicked when his feet were measured, Deborah looked with smug distaste. She had never screamed in her life.

'Darling, do stand up,' her mother said. 'You're twisting the seams of my stockings.' Exasperation came easily to her and this showed on her face. Her daughter reminded her of her own Aunt Hester – the clinging vine, as she was called in the family. Despite the difference in age, in both of them timidity was tinged with obstinacy and compliance always had its shadow of censure. So now Deborah, removing herself at once, looked aloof.

An argument over the rocking-horse had begun between two boys. As each was ordered by his mother to give in, neither could. Rough children, Deborah thought, and she hid her teddy-bear in her muff.

'Now, little lady,' said the shop assistant, coming at last. 'Let's sit you up here beside Mummy.' Thinking nothing of the liberty she took, she swung Deborah off her feet and put her into a chair.

'Dancing slippers,' her mother said. 'Bronze kid, with rosettes.' This kind she had worn herself as a child and she could imagine nothing better.

'Hello, Teddy!' the assistant said, shaking his paw. She was good with children, mothers and nannies thought, although most of the children themselves thought that her brain had softened.

'Terribly, terribly precious,' Mrs Daubeny murmured. 'Although he is so d-i-r-t-y.' The moment she had said this, she was angry with herself for being apologetic to a shop-assistant.

Soon, shiny white boxes were heaped on the floor and every kind of dancing slipper but bronze with rosettes was unpacked – white buckskin with little bows, patent leather with buckles, red kid with pink pearl buttons and gold kid with cross-over elastic. Deborah tried them all, walked up and down, and turned about. They all pinched, she said when questioned. Not very badly, though, she added, trying to please.

All the time, she kept kissing Teddy and whispering in his ear and smoothing his knitted jersey, to reassure herself. Some of the rough children were staring at her. The victorious rider of the rocking-horse, bucketing back and forth with maniacal exertion, shouted something derogatory about a pair of red shoes. Deborah, growing pale, tried to remove them. Stupid as she found grown-ups, on the whole she preferred them to other children.

'Try the black ones again,' her mother said. 'What a rude little boy.' She had seen Deborah's look of fear and was depressed by the thought of her passing from one stage to another and never managing to stand on her own feet, always shrinking at every raised tone, never answering back, just as Hester had shrunk and remained silent. The only time she – Hester – had been known to express a definite decision was when she had said 'I will' on the day she had married Uncle Archie who, fortunately, had been a millionaire.

Watching her daughter, as the black slippers were put on over the cream mesh socks, Mrs Daubeny skipped in her imagination over the next fifteen or so years, deleting the unsatisfactory schooldays, finishing and coming-out, the obstinate withdrawals from all forms of competitions – muscular, intellectual, sexual – and hastily, in her mind's eye, threw a white veil over Deborah's composed features and dumped her down before the altar. Having her own way to the last, Deborah carried Teddy instead of stephan-otis.

'Which feel most comfortable?' Mrs Daubeny asked. 'Oh, Lord, Nanny, we had a dreadful morning,' she would say when they got back. Dropping her furs on a chair in the hall, she would discard Deborah and go in search of a decanter.

Deborah looked up anxiously, as if not sure how she could best oblige. Which pair, she wondered, did her mother want her to say was most comfortable? All had associations for her with the dreaded dancing-class, with thoughts of strange children who might ask her name and prance about her and push her on the slippery floor.

'Are *those* all right?'

She nodded.

'You won't, the minute we get home, say that they're too tight?'

She shook her head.

'Very well, then.' Mrs Daubeny's voice sounded grim and threatening. 'Take your plait out of your mouth, dear.'

The assistant tied up the box and put Deborah's hand through a loop in the string and said: 'There you are, little lady. I hope you will wear them to some lovely parties.'

At once, the horrors of Oranges and Lemons sprang into Deborah's mind. She pictured herself hysterically diving under those menacing clasped hands above her, while the owners of them chanted fiendishly – chop, chop, chop, chop. Each escape only delayed the final capture, at last they would have her, trembling and embarrassed, her hair untidy from the struggle, imprisoned, as they had intended from the start. Once, suddenly crazy with fear, she had tried to dive to freedom and had badly grazed her knee on the parquet floor.

Mrs Daubeny smoothed her gloves and graciously thanked the assistant. They set off across soft carpets, through a department all pink and white with lingerie, then one where furs were crouched. The whole room smelled of animals, Deborah thought, stepping slightly aside from an ocelot on a gilt chair. Mrs Daubeny was inclined to linger here and Deborah, forgetting, began to chew her plait again.

The lift was full and as they began to descend Deborah felt stifled, her eyes level with handbags, umbrellas, sharp-edged parcels. She knew, though, that unlike Oranges and Lemons, if she waited patiently enough she would escape from this.

Mrs Daubeny, made discontented with visions of mink and chinchilla, suffering from backache – her old trouble – and thirst, closed her eyes, but opened them at once as some disturbance took place. A large woman had suddenly struck a rather furtive-looking man across the face with her glove. He lost his balance and staggered back with his fingers to his eyes.

'I have never been so insulted,' the woman shouted, too angry to see the absurdity of the phrase. 'How dare you!' She flourished the glove again and the man raised an elbow.

'I've no idea what you mean!' he kept saying. His accent was against him and everybody thought so – he whined and overdid the aggrieved attitude.

An unpleasant man, Mrs Daubeny thought, wondering exactly what he had done, but the indignant woman would not say since there *were* gentlemen present. These – there were two of them – immediately looked dependable and edged forward protectively as all the women shrank back.

'I never did anything.' The shameful protests went on and on. Mrs Daubeny drew Deborah to her and put her gloved hand across her eyes.

'I must ask you to remain here,' the lift attendant said sternly as they touched ground-floor level. Ranks were closed to prevent escape.

'Disgusting!' women murmured to one another. The man's very presence in such a shop was suspect. He carried no parcel and looked impoverished. They had all heard stories of men like him who made nuisances of themselves in cinemas.

'May I pass, please?' Mrs Daubeny said firmly. 'This is no place for a little girl.'

At once a way was made for them. The lift attendant, barring the way until the house detective arrived, allowed them to go through.

'Disgusting,' Mrs Daubeny muttered as she did so.

'I'll have my solicitor on you,' the man cried piteously, his voice croaking with catarrh.

'Solicitor!' Mrs Daubeny thought scornfully. She took Deborah's parcel from her and hurried out through the shop. Then, at the entrance, she stopped to buy the child a pretty handkerchief to take her mind off the unpleasantness. One takes such care, she thought angrily, such care about their friends and their surroundings and then, in a shop of this kind, they are brought face to face with a vulgar brawl. One might just as well take them into a pub on a Saturday night. She felt quite soiled by having stood so close to the squalid little man – a type she had noticed in the Charing Cross Road, furtively turning the pages of Krafft-Ebing or *Oriental Art Poses*.

The air in the street outside seemed blessedly clean and the commissionaire helped them most respectfully into a taxi. 'There, young lady!' he said, settling Deborah as carefully as if he were putting a soufflé into an oven.

'Soon be home,' Mrs Daubeny said, smiling encouragingly at the child, who looked flushed and worried. But presently, as they were driven homewards across the leaf-strewn park, Deborah, staring hard at her mother, said severely: 'I thought that was a horrid lady.'

If she were to brood on it, lasting harm might be done and Nanny must be warned.

'It wasn't a very nice thing to do,' her mother said in her most casual voice.

'I didn't like her when I first saw her,' said Deborah. 'She pushed me and squashed me. She didn't care if I was there or not and she hurt Teddy's bad ear.'

Sitting up primly and nursing the bear, she looked across the yellow park.

'I pinched her bottom very hard,' she said.

As if I Should Care

The imitation suède jacket came by the post at breakfast-time and the girl, with strength from impatience, broke the string with her hands and tore open the parcel. For a moment, she was disappointed. From the time when she had seen the advertisement in a newspaper and had sent off her money, the coat had become real leather in her mind and not this rather creased, ginger-coloured cloth.

'Rita, will you take your granny's tea up?' her mother said. 'It's been poured out this last five minutes.'

Rita put the jacket on and buttoned it up. She went on tiptoe to get what view of herself she could in the little piece of looking-glass on the dresser. 'Yes, it's very nice,' her mother said, sighing. 'But did you hear what I said?'

The sleeves were too long, Rita thought. She took the cup of tea and went upstairs to her grandmother's room. She hated going into it, for it was stuffed with furniture and cardboard boxes and smelt old and fusty. As a very small child, she had played there happily for hours, with her grand-mother's sentimental treasures – scrapbooks and albums and seaside souvenirs. She felt debased by the memory. By now, she had shed her family. Her grandmother had been the first to go.

'There you are,' she said, putting the cup of tea down and standing back, as far away as she could from the old woman in the bed.

'What you all dressed up for?' her grandmother asked. 'Why can't you carry a cup of tea without slopping it?' She spoke in a slurred cracked voice, her lips unmanageable without her false teeth which – Rita knew, but with-held her glance – lay at the bottom of a glass of water on the other side of the bed.

'It's my new jacket,' she said sulkily. The cuffs hung over the backs of her hands, but otherwise it fitted, she thought.

'You only come up here when you want to show yourself off.' Her grand-mother began to drink the tea with an ugly sucking sound; above the rim of the cup, her eyes looked peevish, taking in the new jacket, the bouncy, red-haired girl standing away from the bed, who now said: 'Well, I can't stand here all day. I've got to go to work.'

'How's your father this morning?'

'All right, as far as I know.'

'All right!' her grandmother repeated scornfully.

On her way out of the room, Rita managed to take a glance at herself in the mirrored panel of the wardrobe – the only big looking-glass in the house. As she slammed the door, her grandmother was beginning to say something in a sarcastic voice. She could imagine one of her usual uncouth sayings, such as 'You're getting a bit too big for your boots, my girl.' She had no wish to stay to hear.

Her father was coughing weakly in the front bedroom and she put her head round the door with a false smile for him. 'Just off,' she said cheerily – as if there were nothing at all wrong with him. He nodded gently and rearranged his hands on the bedclothes. 'Be seeing you,' she added uneasily.

'You aren't wearing that new coat to work,' her mother said, when Rita went into the kitchen to fetch her sandwiches, but her voice was neither questioning nor forbidding, simply a meaningless phrase – for, of course, the girl was wearing it and would wear it. She always hacked things on straight-way – another phrase – to get the glory of them new.

Going out, Rita slammed the front door, forgetting her father in the room directly above, and crossed the cobbled road to the edge of the canal. The damp, misty air, the bubbles and the leaves on the slow-moving water seemed not at all melancholy to her; the scene, from the one advantage of being out of doors, uplifted her. She was away from the dark house, and the old and the sick and the dejected. Even to go to work was a relief.

The shop at the corner of the terrace was empty, boarded-up. It had once been the centre of her life, a meeting-place for all the children of the neighbourhood, who were sent there on errands and lingered to play games on the chalked pavement or to skip, chanting strange rhymes, with one end of a rope tied to a lamp-post. It was there, while bouncing a ball high up on the brick wall, that her world had broken. 'My auntie told me,' shouted her confidante, backing away half-fearfully from Rita's blazing anger. 'She knows it's true.' Suddenly Rita, too, knew that it was true. 'So what's the odds?' she shouted back. She turned her attention to the wall, threw the ball viciously against it, caught it, threw it, her wrist twisting smartly, the colour whipped up in her cheeks. If these too-old parents were not her own, she was glad, she thought. To be a hushed-up threat of scandal, the result of misdemeanour by her 'mother's' younger sister, suited her every bit as well.

When she was alone – when her backing-away, excited informant had turned the corner, she had begun to walk alongside the canal, bouncing her ball before her every three or four paces. She wandered on and leant for a long time on the parapet of a bridge, watching a string of barges going slowly underneath it. 'But I didn't want to find out that way,' she thought. The shock had been great and she had been scored off while she suffered it, had been made to look ridiculous. In such a neighbourhood, the truth must have been known by some people from the time of its occurring, and she wondered if they had smiled knowingly at one another when she had spoken of her parents with innocent possessiveness.

After that lingering walk by the canal, she returned home, inimical, her love dead and inhumed, the face of her world altered beyond all recognising; her own face altered, too. She was eleven years old and began to go through a difficult phase, her school-teachers said. She went through it alone, without a word to anyone of her discovery. It was five years ago. Her informant had gone to live in one of the large blocks of flats on the town's outskirts. Most of the young ones had gone. The seedy and sickly and aged remained. Soon the crumbling terrace would be pulled down and only they would care. Rita knew that she would watch the demolition exultingly. She imagined the façade collapsing and the poky rooms exposed, with their faded, varnished wallpapers and their grimy ceilings, and the smell of the canal surging into the ruins.

She was always glad, on her way to work, to cross the iron bridge to the other side of the water. There, were buses and shops, children going to school, the pavements full of hurrying people – not an invalid in sight. Anyone incapable of moving at a brisk pace very sensibly stayed at home until after the rush hour.

She felt exhilarated by the bustle of the world going to work, and her new jacket made it a different morning. She looked for her reflection in shop windows. The shops were opening, but it was still too early for shoppers. They would come later, at what Rita thought of as a less vital time of day.

This less vital time of day began for her soon after she had entered the shabby hairdresser's where she worked, when she had hung her new jacket in the dark cupboard at the back of the shop and put on her overall. As it was Friday, this was dirty.

Her first customer was an elderly woman. Shampooing the yellow-grey hair, she gazed at herself in the looking-glass and made plans with less hope than she would have had an hour earlier.

'Your nails are too long,' the elderly woman complained, flinching.

'Sorry, dear,' Rita said, winking at her friend, Diane, who raised shoulders and eyebrows, as if to say, 'The old ones in their dotage; bear with them if you can.'

The shampooed head was knobbly and poorly off for hair. 'Has it been coming out very much?' Rita asked punishingly. 'I hadn't noticed. Do you?' Rita, in the ascendancy now, made a towel deftly into a turban and said:

'Well, I'm sure it might be worse.' The words, after all, sounded as if they were meant to encourage, but if they failed to do so she was perfectly satisfied.

For the next ten minutes she stood deferentially beside her Senior, handing pins. This young woman, Miss Edmead, was popular with her customers, had soothing ways with them, but the moment Rita relaxed or let her dreamy gaze wander to the street beyond the shop door, she would click her fingers frenziedly, kept waiting one second for a pin.

The day fell into its usual pattern. The air outside thinned, the mistiness drifted away, traffic increased and passers-by walked more slowly, looking in shop windows, carrying heavy baskets, stopping to chat. In the shop, customers came and went every half-hour, and when she was not handing pins and shampooing, Rita swept up hair from the floor or ran to the baker's shop nearby for sticky buns. The girls ate these and, later, their lunch-time sandwiches in a small store-room at the back of the shop. Today, the sky darkened early and rain spattered upon the skylight. As soon as she had eaten her sandwiches, Rita's thoughts went forward towards the evening. The day had reached a turning-point and the rest of it was fit only for wishing away.

'I shall get my jacket wet,' she thought, listening to the rain coming in gusts on the skylight.

The girls, over cups of tea, discussed their customers, who were either 'sweet' or 'catty'. The business was old-fashioned, its clientele those mostly elderly women, who felt that they had wasted their money if, when they left, their hair was not arranged in deep waves and confusions of tight curls. Rita often day-dreamed of laying hands on a head of thick, straight, brilliant hair, imagined the weight of it and the way in which it would fan out in the water as she washed it; young hair, with no scalp showing through.

The afternoon went slowly. Every time the shop door opened, a bell rang and she always looked up. Only the expected came. They struggled out of wet raincoats and were full of rueful remarks about the weather. Beyond them, in the street, the umbrellas went by. Rita tried not to listen to Miss Edmead's small talk – the same soothing, automatic remarks to one customer after another – 'It's always the same, isn't it?', 'What a day to choose!', 'Let's hope it clears up for the week-end.' ... 'Thank you, Rita.' Rita started and passed a hair net. Diane, idle for a while, yawned and yawned. Women, sitting under the driers, sleepily turned the pages of magazines, the rain drummed down, the shop bell occasionally rang, and Diane went on yawning. There was a humming sound and a sense of suspension. The falling rain lulled them, and Miss Edmead, twisting up hair, thrusting in pins, talked as if she could not stop. 'You can't really expect anything else ...' She gave Rita a sharp look, for now she, too, was yawning. 'That's what I always say ...' Rita, patting her mouth with her fist, blinking her watering eyes, thought, 'I couldn't stand too much of this, year in, year out.' It would be some time before she could expect to get married and solve the problem of her employment by having none; nor had she anyone in mind for such a future. Her friend, Derek, would not do. He was too poor and too short.

At last it was closing time and she put on her suède jacket, was again admired in it and, feeling herself the object of envy – which was like wine to her – said good-bye.

Miraculously, it had stopped raining. It was quite dark and blurred; shaggy lights were reflected in the wet road and pavement. She walked along close to the shop windows, sauntering, waiting for Derek, who was already three minutes late. Not once, all day, had she given a thought to what might be happening at home.

Returning late, as she crossed the canal bridge, she could see the lighted upstairs window, and it was then – as it was every night – that her thoughts for the first time turned homewards, and it was as if a blind were drawn over her gaiety.

Her mother greeted her with some more of the accustomed phrases – 'This is a fine time ... while you're under my roof ... piece of my mind ... a sight too big for your boots.'

Rita unhooked a cup from the dresser and poured out some milk. Standing, sipping it, still wearing her jacket, she appeared preoccupied, obviously not listening. This, as was intended, angered her mother more. The phrases tumbled over one another and were forlornly reiterated. Her voice rose until, remembering her husband lying upstairs, she hesitated and turned away. In a despairing way, she began to lay the table ready for the morning.

'What's the use of coming home?' asked Rita. 'You only go for me the minute I put my nose round the door.'

Now her mother took her turn of remaining silent, moving about the room, her lips pressed together. Rita would rather have had the familiar spate of words and her mother realised it. 'How's Dad?' she asked, after a while, her voice gruff and uneasy.

'Much the same.' 'As if you care', the wounded expression said.

I wish I were on the top of a mountain, Rita thought. I would take deep breaths, feel clean and light again. She pictured her real mother like that, living a wild and carefree life among the mountains, in Canada, to which she had emigrated.

'Well, I'm going up,' her mother said. 'And so will you, if you've any sense. I don't know how you expect to do a proper day's work ...' The phrases were a dire temptation to her. 'Say good-night nicely to your father, won't you?' she asked, turning at the door with an appealing look.

Grandmother had always been against the adoption. 'You can't know what you're taking on,' she had told her daughter-in-law. 'Impossible to tell.' Now they knew. 'Like mother, like daughter,' the old woman would say, taking her hot drink up to bed, night after night, and Rita still not home. 'You've spoilt that girl. Nothing to be done now, bar wait for the consequences. Letting her have those dancing-lessons. That began it. That made her wilful.'

Everything went back to the dancing-lessons, years ago, when Rita had been a bouncy little girl with disarming manners. They had been very much resented at the time, for the expense; and, later, for the fact that, after a while, they had changed the child. She had lost the wheedling, simpering ways they had found so endearing and scowled at them instead.

It was after one of the early dancing-lessons that she had learnt of her origins. Unsure of her position after that, she had ceased to boast to her friends about her lessons or anything else; no longer, tossing her curls, swinging her ballet shoes by the ribbons, went out of her way to be seen on Saturday mornings, to be able to say 'I'm just going to dancing', enjoying reactions of envy. From then on, Grandmother's plaint became built into the domestic fabric – 'It started with those dancing-lessons.'

When the world was broken apart, it was her grandmother who seemed to Rita to become her first enemy. At the earliest signs of rebellion – the scowling silences, the ducking when her curls were stroked – the old lady saw signs of bad blood, as she had long expected to. There is no relationship between us, both she and the child thought, though they held their secret. Mother humbly bore the brunt of their differences, and hid them from her husband.

'It's a good thing your granny's gone up to bed. I can smell drink.'

It was this beginning, as soon as Rita opened the kitchen door, that began an evil dialogue. She had taken off her jacket and thrown it over a chair ... 'you haven't had it but a couple of days and look at the way you're treating it ...' and began to comb her hair ... 'all over the breakfast table. I don't know what's come over you ...' She shrugged her shoulders.

Imitation is the sincerest and the most infuriating form of flattery, and Diane's having bought a jacket so much like her own had clouded the day, spoilt the evening. Moments of pleasure there had been, dancing under the arched, smoke-wreathed roof where balloons hung in a net. It was the place where she was always happiest and she found beauty in it which stirred her in the same way as the look of the canal sometimes did, when the lighted street-lamps were reflected in it. The dance hall had a livelier beauty – the girls with their full skirts, their quickly turning profiles as they spun round, their hair flicking from side to side, their lips parted. While she was danc-ing, she forgot her annoyance, but as soon as she sat down at one of the orange-painted tables with Derek or any of what she called 'the Crowd', crossness returned. She scarcely listened to them; she smoked and wagged her head to the music and wondered what she could do – not to get even, but to raise herself far above Diane, right out of her reach, where she would know she could not hope to follow. The balloons had been released and there was the usual horseplay, but she sat still, not turning her head. It was frustrating that whatever was beyond Diane's reach should also be beyond her own.

'I don't know what's come over you,' her mother said again; but she did know. Her real mother had come over her.

Another step was taken towards the evil outcome of their conversa-tion – Rita said: 'I shall please myself, you know.'

'Not under my roof, you won't.' Her mother gripped the edge of the table and leant forward to spit out the words. She dared not raise her voice because of her husband upstairs; instead, she gave a venomous clarity to what she said.

Rita rasped her thumb along the teeth of her comb, looking patiently down.

'You've got to be a better girl,' her mother said, raising her voice just a little, altering her tone. 'You'll only worry your father.'

'It'll be you who'll be worrying him, if you want to make any fuss. I shall still do as I like.'

'All I've got to do, looking after *them*, and you never so much as wash up a cup. What sort of a daughter do you think you are?'

'You know what sort of a daughter I am.' Rita lifted her eyes for a second.

'What do you mean?'

There was a fearful silence. 'It's a relief she's not really my mother,' Rita thought. 'No risk of growing up to be like her – dowdy, grey-faced.' (There was a photograph upstairs of her own mother, the younger sister, a bold laughing girl.) 'My mother and me, we're not a bit like you,' she thought staring across the table, meeting those anxious eyes. 'What do you ever do for me?' she asked. 'To make up for all this. It's not much for anyone young to come back to – it's depressing. As soon as I put the wireless on, you tell me to turn it down. This house! I've never been happy here.'

'You ungrateful girl.' Her mother hadn't the words to express grief and bitter disappointment, only the old and worn-out phrases of blame. 'All we've done for you ... It would break your father's heart if he could hear ...'

'There are other things you don't want him to hear, aren't there? Such as what *I* heard the doctor tell *you* when he came back from the hospital.' The dialogue ahead of her lay in darkness, but each line she spoke revealed another in its time.

Her mother stared at her in a dazed way, then sank down into a chair and covered her face with her hands.

'There's nothing to cry about,' Rita said. 'There's no need to make such a fuss. I shan't go running upstairs to him with the bad news.' Her mother dabbed her eyes. 'Not so long as I get my way about things.'

Her mother struggled to control herself, remembering that she must not cry, especially as it was time for her to go upstairs and that she must do so without tears in her eyes. She breathed deeply to steady herself, then rose and walked past Rita without a word. She climbed the stairs slowly and Rita listened to the dragging steps. 'I hate slow-moving people,' she thought. 'My real mother and me, we walk fast.' She pictured her clicking along a Canadian pavement on high, thin heels.

She lingered in the kitchen, pondering the new relationship she had made with her mother, and putting off looking in to say 'good-night' to her father. She cut a slice of bread, spread it with butter, sprinkled sugar over it and, eating it slowly and with great enjoyment, wandered about the kitchen, making her plans.

The dancing-lessons were quite forgotten when Rita brought home the real suède coat. For kindling caustic comment, it bettered any other fuel. The dancing was regarded as the starting-point of the girl's evil ways; but the suède coat was proof of how far gone she was in them.

'I bought it in a sale,' she said, avoiding her mother's eyes, as she had begun to do. Sometimes, it was a strain keeping her gaze constantly lowered, and she was relieved when she was outside the house and could raise her head and look at the sky and the tall buildings on the other side of the canal.

'Bought it in a sale,' her grandmother repeated. She repeated nearly everything that Rita said, giving her words an extra exposure to ridicule. 'And what with, we should like to know.'

'What do you think? Money.'

'Oh, money, of *course*. I didn't think you'd got it for a handful of glass marbles. We're just interested in where the money came from in the first place.'

'Mother! Leave the girl alone, for pity's sake. It's her business.'

'It's *your* business where she picks her money up, or so I should think … out till all hours of the night. I can see the end of this as plain as I can see this cup in my hand. Well, we've seen it before, haven't we?'

'That will be enough, Mother.' It won't be long, she thought. This can't go on for very long. Her spirit bruised from blackmail, she could only go automatically about her long day's work. She was like a watch-dog, whose power of protection was running out.

Rita felt uplifted when, wearing her new coat, she walked to work in the mornings. She liked to hang it beside Diane's if she could, and cared not at all that the girls made the same insinuations as her grandmother. She wished to be envied, not liked.

She spent her mother's savings quickly. Towards the end of them, she had to put up a fight for what she wanted – going threateningly to the door at the foot of the staircase, knowing that she would soon be called back. She was always relieved when her mother gave in. 'I wouldn't really tell him,' she would think, picking up the money that had been thrown from trembling hands upon the table. 'Not unless she really made me mad.'

'Who rules this house?' her grandmother once asked, unnerved by the calm power her granddaughter now exerted. 'Who rules this house, I'd like to know.'

'I do,' Rita said, and went from the room, leaving her mother to smooth out the matter.

She was happier at work. A little money and her mother's nagging tongue stilled made a world of difference to the day, and the envious hostility of the other girls was much to be desired; but she had lost her ascendancy with the Crowd and was under suspicion. Once or twice there had been quarrels, which made the boys wary, quarrels especially with Diane – rather one-sided quarrels, for Rita for the most part ignored the enquiries about where she had left her mink coat and why she was slumming at the Majestic Dance Hall or the Piazza Coffee Bar. She simply smiled and turned her head, basking in jealousy. 'Oh, pardon me for living,' Diane would shout, deliriously losing her temper.

Derek was puzzled. Rita's money worried him. She bought him cigarettes and gave them patronisingly, and when at last he refused to take any more, she threw the packet into the canal, along which they were walking.

It was a Sunday afternoon and very cold. Through the knotted branches, the sky looked scratched and bleeding and there was a pinkish reflection on the water ahead of them.

'I don't smoke that kind myself,' she said, in reply to his amazed reproach.

She flung her arms out, walked forward airily, fancily, as if on a tight-rope. 'The sky's pretty,' she said. Then her moment of exuberance passed, her arms dropped and she put her hands back in her pockets.

'Better turn back?' he suggested. 'It'll get dark soon.'

And she wore him out with her changing moods.

'*You* can,' she said.

They plodded on. The towing-path ran under an old iron bridge, across whose parapet she had once walked, balancing precariously in her stockinged feet. Someone – she had forgotten who – had dared her to.

Shapes – of the arthritic-looking trees, of the iron girders of the bridge – had become menacing, and the sky was now colourless behind them. The dark indeed came quickly. It piled up behind them and they fled before it, like refugees. Death was behind her, too, and it was from this that she was really fleeing, taking the unwilling Derek along with her. 'I'm no good at anything like that,' she told herself; 'don't know what to do when people are sick.' All day, neighbours had been in and out of the house, trying to comfort and support her mother and giving Rita black looks. 'I can't do anything right,' she thought defensively.

Her mother was grim and brusque; she seemed no longer to fear her daughter, paid no heed to her, was engrossed, dedicated. Her grandmother, however, made up for her with phrases – 'at a time like this ... your poor mother ... never so much as lift a finger.'

'I think I'd like to go to Canada,' Rita said suddenly to Derek.

He walked along, hunched up, his hands in his pockets. He had no warm coat, like Rita's.

'Oh, all right, then; we'll turn back,' she said.

They faced round and saw all the lights of the town against the darkness.

'Why Canada?' he asked at last.

'It sounds nice and lively. Big and clean and everything new. Not like this dirty old place.'

'Well, why not go then? You seem to be all right for money,' he said angrily.

She walked on in silence, thinking, 'I shan't have a penny.'

They came to the terrace of houses alongside the canal. There was a light in her father's room and a car outside the front door.

'I'll have to go in, I suppose,' she said. She crossed the road, away from him, reluctantly. 'See you!' She turned and shouted, her hand on the door knob.

'Hush, girl,' said the doctor, opening the door suddenly to come out. 'Better go in to your mother.'

'Why, has something happened?'

'You'd better run along in. See what you can do for your mother.' Even he seemed to have a poor opinion of her.

'I can't face it,' Rita thought, but she went in, closed the door after her and leant back against it, trying to summon her courage.

Her grandmother sat by the kitchen fire, her screwed-up handkerchief held to her mouth. She stared at Rita, but for once no phrases came to her lips. Then she was suddenly overcome by grief, got up stiffly, and went from the room.

'Oh, Lord, how long does this last?' Rita wondered. She filled the kettle at the tap in the scullery and was bringing it in to set it on the kitchen range when her mother came downstairs.

'What are you doing?'

'Was going to make a cup of tea,' Rita replied.

'Don't overstrain yourself.'

Rita set down the kettle and looked at her mother, who stood very straight on the other side of the table, a letter in her hand.

'All these weeks,' she began, 'you know how wicked you have been. I wouldn't like anyone else in the world to know the wicked things you've done. That was money your father and I scraped and saved ... ' Her voice trembled, and she paused for a moment, looking down at the table, and then at the letter in her hand. 'He knew all the time, poor man. He just thought it would be easier for us to carry on as if he didn't ... so good always ... ' She read the few lines of the letter again with her tear-blurred eyes. 'He put this in his drawer all that time ago, when he came back from the hospital ... all that time ago, the poor man ... Where are you going now?' she asked sharply, her voice changing.

'Nowhere. Just to put out some cups and saucers.'

'You can stay where you are for the time being. I've got something to tell you about yourself that it's about time you knew. There's a shock coming to you, my girl, and you've been deserving one for a long time.'

Rita shrugged her shoulders and sat down on the arm of the chair, staring at the fire glowing between the bars of the grate and listening to the gently humming kettle, hardly at all to what her mother had to say.

'As if I should care,' she thought.

Mr Wharton

The furnished flat in a London suburb fell vacant on a Monday and Hilda
Provis, having collected the key from the agents in the High Street, walked
down the hill towards Number Twenty. It was half-past eleven in the morning and early summer. In the quiet road, houses – some quite large – stood
in dusty gardens full of may trees and laburnums, past blossoming. There
had been no rain for a fortnight and, in the gutters and under garden walls,
drifts of powdery dead petals and seeds had collected. The air had a dry,
polleny smell.

It was a strange land to Hilda, and a great adventure. She was to be here
for a week, to see her daughter settled into the flat; had quite insisted on
coming, had been obliged to insist; for Pat had thought she could manage
very well on her own, had begged her mother not to put herself to so much
trouble, coming so far – from the country near Nottingham, in fact. There
was no need, she had written. But Hilda desperately maintained that there
was.

When Pat first went to work in London, living there in a hostel, Hilda,
left alone and nervous at night, moved to her sister's, thinking that anything was better than seeming to hear burglars all the time; but she and her
brother-in-law did not get on well together, and she longed for a home of
her own and to have her daughter back. It was with a joyful excitement
that she descended the hill this morning and pushed open the heavy gate
of Number Twenty.

It was a tall house with a flight of steps to the front door and below them
a basement area. The garden was neglected, growing only ferns and the
grass between the broken tiles of the path. The lawn at the back was on a
lower level – in fact, the house was found to be built on a hillside. Down
below, beyond the roofs of other houses, was London itself – grey, but for
one or two bone-white church spires, sudden glitterings from windows or
weather vanes struck by the sun, and one green dome floating in haze.

Hilda stood by the side door with the key in her hand and looked down
at the view. It is a panorama, she thought; that really is the word for it. She
could imagine it at night – dazzling it would be. She had never seen anything like it. Life teemed down there – traffic strove to disentangle itself,

Pat pounded her typewriter; but to Hilda it was a lulled and dormant city, under its nearly midday haze, nothing doing, nothing stirring. She could not imagine anything happening beneath those pigeon-coloured roofs going down, street after street, lower and lower into the smoky mist.

After the brilliant out-of-doors, she was hit by cold dismay when she unlocked the door and stepped inside – such darkness, such an unfriendly smell of other people's belongings. The flat was clean, but not up to Hilda's standards. She went from the hall into a kitchen. The previous tenants had left remains – a little flour in a bin, some sugar in a jar, a worn-out dish-cloth and a piece of dirty soap. She disposed of these before taking off her hat. A spider sat in the sink and she swilled it down the drain.

The living-room window looked into the area. She opened it and let in the sound of footsteps on the pavement above. Furniture was either black and in the Jacobean style, or Indian with trellis-work and brass. So many twisted chair-legs needing a polish. A green stain had been allowed to spread from bath taps to plug, but Hilda knew a way of removing it. The bedroom was full of sunshine, for the smeared windows looked out over the lawn at the back and at the panorama beyond it. It smelt of sun-warmed carpet and cushion dust. She opened the windows, and then the drawers of the chest. They were lined with old paper and there were oddments left behind in most of them – curtain-rings, safety-pins, a strip of beading which she could see had fallen off the wardrobe. This she could glue on again, though it was not her duty to do so. Of the two beds, she thought Pat would prefer the one by the window.

In the afternoon, she went shopping. The street where the shops were climbed steeply towards the heath and, turning corners, looking down side streets, she was sometimes surprised by a sudden openness and glimpsed from different sides the city below.

Everything she bought added to her pleasure and excitement. She was reminded of being a bride again. It seemed a long time since she had planned a meal or chosen a piece of fish or done anything on her own. Knowing no one in the shops, she felt shy; but her loneliness was wonderful to her and her slow pace, as she sauntered along, was tuned to it.

The leisurely afternoon was very pleasant. Babies lay awake under the canopies of their perambulators, staring sternly upwards, making purling sounds like doves, or fidgeted, turning their wrists impatiently, arching their backs and thrusting limbs out into the sunshine. Hilda peeped at each one, stooped to look under the canopies, and blew kisses. If she had been child-less herself, she thought she must have looked in another direction. As it was, she just felt momentarily wistful; it was nothing distressing. The young mothers all paused for her, quite patient while they shared their marvels.

Everything glittered in the fine air of this high suburb. A warm rubbery puff of air flowed out from the Underground station at the crossroads; and out of it, too, in a couple of hours, Pat would hasten – on a tide of rush-hour workers, gradually thinning themselves out in different directions, she down the hill under the trees to Number Twenty.

Outside a greengrocer's, on the wide pavement, was a stall of bedding plants and, although her basket was full, Hilda stopped to buy a pot of bright red double daisies. ('Chubby daisies', Pat had called them when she was a little girl.) She was tired, for she had scoured the bath, and polished all the curly furniture, and was not used to doing so much. At her sister's, she was inclined to indispositions and began most days with a health bulletin which was taken in silence – discourteously, she thought. They were selfish people – her sister and brother-in-law – she had long ago decided; too much wrapped up in themselves, in the manner of childless people.

The front door of Number Twenty was open, and there were sounds of life. A toddler with wide-apart legs, napkins dropping, came on to the steps, then an arm swooped after him and lifted him back out of sight. 'I could get to know them,' Hilda thought. 'I could keep an ear open for the baby while they went for a stroll in the evening.' She even chose a pub in which they – whoever they were – could sit and have a quiet drink. She had noticed a nice one on her walk home from the shops; it had a horse-trough outside and a chestnut tree – like a country pub.

The flat was cool and smelt better now. She had discovered that other people's belonging were more interesting than her own – which by now were so familar as to be invisible. She had innovated, improvised with the material to hand and was pleased with the effect. Unpacking her basket, stacking food on bare shelves, she remembered her first home, her first shopping – such a young bride she had been that she had thought of it as running the errands, until the moving truth had dawned on her that she herself must choose, and pay for, and bring home. Again, after all those years, she had a feeling of being watched, of not being entirely spontaneous. Methodically, she put the food away, washed some lettuce, found a saucer for the pot of daisies and began to lay the table for supper. 'Hilda's managing well,' she seemed to hear a voice say. It was as if she were doing everything for the first time.

The evening began to go slowly. She wandered about, waiting for Pat, putting finishing touches, glancing at the clock, straightening pictures ('Too awful,' she thought – heathery moorlands, a rosy glow on the Alps), turning the chipped side of a vase to the wall.

She would have liked to unpack the big suitcase which had arrived from the hostel, but she had done this for her daughter before, and been told that she was interfering.

She sat down in the living-room, and stared out of the window, waiting for Pat's legs to appear above the area. She was by now quite nervous with anticipation, and felt that the girl would never come.

As long-awaited people come in the end as a surprise, so Pat did.

'Hello, dear,' Hilda said, almost shyly, when she had hurried to open the door.

'My *feet!*' Pat said, flopping into a chair, dropping gloves and parcels on the floor. She kicked off her shoes and stared down at her large, bare, mottled feet. Her heaviness – of bone and features – suggested sculpture. *Seated Woman* she might have been, glumly motionless.

'Did you have a bad day?' Hilda asked timidly.

'Oh, I had a bad day all right,' Pat said, as if this went without saying. She leant back now – almost *Reclining Woman* – and shook a lock of hair off her forehead. 'That man!' She yawned and her eyes watered. Even looking at her made Hilda feel weary. The man was Mr Wharton, Pat's employer – a big Masonic Golfer, as she described him. He had a habit of returning from lunch at half-past three and then would dictate letters at a great rate to make up for lost time, and Pat, trying at the end of the day to keep up, was worn out, she said, by the time she left to join the rush-hour traffic. Mr Wharton was a very real person to Hilda, who had never seen him.

'Inconsiderate,' she said, made quite indignant by Pat's long plaint.

'Comes back reeking – face the colour of those daisies.'

'Disgusting,' Hilda murmured, following Pat's glance. 'I bought them this afternoon. "Chubby daisies", you used to call them.'

'Did I?' Pat was not so much in love with herself as a child as her mother was and Hilda always found this indifference strange. 'Expense accounts,' Pat went on, and blew out her lips in contempt. 'Eat and drink themselves stupid, and then go home and tell their wives what a hard day they've had. Well, it all looks very nice,' she said at last, glancing round. 'Even my cardigan smells of his bloody cigars.' She sniffed at her sleeve with distaste. 'You literally can't see across the office.'

A huge man, like a bison, Hilda visualised. She felt great respect for her daughter, cooped up in that blue haze with such a character – managing him, too, with her icy reminders, her appearance at other times of praying for patience, her eyes closed, her pencil tapping her teeth. Hilda could see it all from her descriptions – Pat giving him one of her looks and saying briskly 'Do you mind' when he stood too close to her. It was not a question.

Mother and daughter had changed places, Hilda sometimes thought. She felt like a young girl in the shade of Pat's knowledge of the world. Yet once she herself had worked for her living – serving in a milliner's shop, full of anxieties, trying to oblige, so afraid of displeasing and being dismissed.

To earn one's livelihood is a precarious affair, and even Pat would say, 'Well, if I can hold down a job like that for all these years ...' She held it down firmly, her clever eyes on those who might try to snatch it from her; but she made it sound a desperate business.

'Well, it's nice not to be in that perishing hostel,' she said. Hilda glowed with pleasure when they sat down at the table and Pat began to eat, as if she were quite content to be where she was. 'Canteens!' she said. 'The Lord preserve me from them. Tinned pilchards. Cottage pie. Never again.'

Hilda had been worried for years about the food, especially as she had heard about working girls in London going without lunch – window-shopping or having their hair done instead. 'It will all be different now,' she thought, watching Pat's knife and fork slashing criss-cross at the food which, though not commented on, seemed to be approved. 'I can't at her age,' Hilda thought, 'tell her not to talk with her mouth full' – for all the time the knife and fork were shredding and spearing and popping things into her mouth, Pat was describing Mr Wharton's private life. Hilda found it all trivial and uninteresting. She did not care enough to try to visualise Mr Wharton gardening on Saturday, playing golf on Sundays and going to cocktail parties, of which there seemed to be so many in the Green Belt where he lived. She saw him more clearly in his smoke-filled office.

'I met his wife once,' Pat said. 'She came to call for him and they went out to lunch. Very dowdy. I'll give you a hand,' she added, and stirred slightly as Hilda began to stack up plates.

'No, you sit still. Make the most of it while I'm here.' But Hilda had begun to believe that she would never go. She would make herself so useful.

'I wish I had your figure,' Pat said, watching her mother moving neatly about the room. She said it in a grudging voice, as if Hilda had meanly kept something for herself which she, Pat, would have liked to possess. It was not and had not been the pattern of their lives for this to happen.

Hilda blushed with guilty pleasure. There was something so sedentary about her daughter – not only because of her office job, for as a child she had sat about all the time, reading comics, chewing her handkerchief, twisting her braided hair, very often just lethargically sulking. At this moment, she was slumped back in her chair, eating a banana, the skin of it hanging down in strips over her hand.

'I might bring Mavis Willis back tomorrow evening,' she said. 'She's thinking of sharing the flat with me. Let her have a look round and make up her mind.' She got up and went to the area window and looked meditatively up at the railings.

'Quiet here, isn't it?' she said. She stayed there for a long time, just gazing out of the window, and Hilda, clearing the table, wondered what she was thinking.

Mavis Willis was a young woman of much refinement, and Hilda, watching her eat her supper daintily, was taken by her manners. 'A rather old-fashioned type of girl,' Hilda thought. If she had been asked to, she could not have chosen anyone more suitable to share the flat with her daughter. This one would not lead her into bad company or have wild parties; but Hilda had not been asked, and it was a disappointment to her that the question had not arisen.

When Mavis had been shown round the flat before supper, something in her manner had surprised Hilda; there was a sense of effort she could not define. The girl had gushed without showing much interest, had given the bathroom the briefest glance and had not opened the cupboard where she would be hanging her clothes – the first thing any normal young woman would do.

Now, at supper, she gushed in the same way about Hilda's cooking. Pat's compulsive grumbling about Mr Wharton was resumed, and Mavis joined in. She referred to him as 'H.W.' – which sounded more officey, Hilda decided, listening humbly.

'One of these days, you'll find yourself out of a job,' she told Pat, who had repeated one of her tarter rebukes to her employer – 'I gave him one of my looks and I said to him, "That'll be the day," I said. "When you get back before three o'clock. We'll hang the flags out that day," I said to him.'

Mavis took off her spectacles and began to polish them on a clean handkerchief she had kept tucked in her cuff. She looked down her shiny nose, smiling a little. Her face was pale and glistened unhealthily, and she reminded Hilda of the languid, indoors young women who had sat all day – long days then – in the milliner's workroom, stitching buckram and straw and flowers, hardly moving, sadly cooped up in the stuffy room. She, in the shop itself, had seemed as free as air.

Mavis put back her spectacles and rearranged her hair, and at once she appeared less secretive. She insisted on helping Hilda to wash the dishes, while Pat spent the time looking for cigarettes and then for her lighter.

'I hope Pat won't leave all the work to you, if you come,' Hilda said.

'Oh, she won't.' Mavis wiped a glass and held it up to the light. 'Once we're on our own, she'll be enthusiastic. You know, she'll feel it's more hers and want to take a pride in it. Of course, it's been wonderful for her, having you to settle her in and get it looking so nice. Simply wonderful. You must have done marvels.' She looked vaguely round the kitchen.

'Well, it was in rather a pickle,' Hilda said warmly. 'All I hope is you won't just live on tinned food.'

'You can rest assured we won't.'

'I'm afraid Pat hasn't been brought up to be very domesticated. I did try, but I ended up doing things myself, because it was quicker.'

'Well, it always happens. I know I'd be the same.'

Pat, through the doorway, in the living-room, was looking for an ashtray. She moved clumsily about, knocked into something and swore. Hilda and Mavis glanced at one another and smiled, as if over a child's head.

'What did you think of her?' Pat asked, as soon as she got back from walking with Mavis to the Tube station.

'A nice girl. I thought slightly enigmatic,' said Hilda, who took a pride in finding the right word.

'Well, she's decided to move in next Monday. I said I thought you'd be going back at the weekend.'

'I might stay and clear up on Monday morning. Leave you a little supper, her first night,' Hilda said, and pretended she did not hear a resigned intake of breath from Pat.

'That girl Mavis,' Hilda was thinking, 'perhaps she's no intention of coming; perhaps she's wasting Pat's time.' Yet she sensed something arranged between them, something she could not understand. She used the word 'duplicity' in her mind.

They began to get ready for bed, and when Pat, stout in her dressing-gown, came from the bathroom into the bedroom, she found the room in darkness and her mother peeping through the curtains of the French windows. 'What are you doing, Mother?' she asked, switching on the light.

As guilty as a little girl caught out of bed, Hilda made for hers.

'I really love London,' she said. 'All that panorama, at night, and yet it's so quiet. I sat out there this afternoon for a bit, and it was so peaceful, like being in the country. It's been like a lovely holiday here.'

'It's been good of you to come,' Pat said, in a cautious voice.

When she had switched the light off, her mother turned on her side, put her hands under her cheek, and with faint purring, puffing sounds, fell lightly asleep. Pat lay on her back like a figure on a tomb, and presently began to snore.

On Hilda's last day, it set in wet, and she could not go into the garden again. She went out shopping in the rain, said good-bye to the shop-assistants she had made friends of, and thought how extraordinary it was that the little High Street had become so familiar in such a short time. The view was obscured by mist. But the holiday feeling persisted and at twelve o'clock she entered the saloon bar of the little pub by the water trough and bought herself a glass of sherry. She had never been alone into a bar before,

and was gratified that no one seemed surprised to see her do so. The barmaid was warmly chatty, the landlord courteous; an old man by the fire did
not even raise his head. A stale beery smell pervaded the room, as if everything – the heavy curtains, the varnished furniture, even perhaps the old
man by the fire – was gently fermenting.

'So cosy,' said Hilda.

'A day like this,' the barmaid agreed, scalloping a damp cloth along the
bar.

'A fire's nice.'

'It makes a difference. You live hereabouts?'

Hilda told her about Pat and the flat, and Mavis Willis.

'Nice to have a mother,' the barmaid said.

'I think she appreciates it. But I've enjoyed myself. It's made a lovely
break. I'd like a bottle of sherry to take away, if you please. I'll leave it as
a surprise for the girls – warm them up when they come in wet from work.'

'Well,' said the barmaid, wrapping the bottle in a swirl of pink paper,
'let's hope we see you when you're in these parts again.'

'Good-morning, madam. Thank you,' the landlord added and Hilda,
with her heavy shopping basket, stepped out into the rain. How very pleasant, she was thinking, rather muzzily, as she walked down the hill. The only
pity was not having made friends with the people on the first floor.
Glimpses of the toddler she had had from time to time, heard his little footsteps running overhead; but had not had a word with his mother. That had
been a disappointment.

She made herself a cup of tea when she had hung up her wet coat. The
flat was so dark that afternoon that she had to switch on the lights. The
rain seemed to keep her company, as a coal fire does the very lonely – the
sound of it falling softly into the ferns in the garden, or with a sharp, ringing noise on the dustbin lids outside the door. She could hear the splashing
of cars going by on the road above the window, changing gear to take the
hill.

Although she felt sad, packing her case, she cheered up when she was
putting the finishing touches to the supper table, leaving the sherry on a
tray with a note and two glasses. She watered the double daisy and added
a reminder about it to her note. At three o'clock, she put on her still damp
coat and was ready to go to the station. She locked the door and hid the
key under the dustbin as they had arranged and, feeling melancholy, in
tune with the afternoon, walked with head bowed, carrying her heavy suitcase up the hill to the Underground station.

At four o'clock the rain suddenly stopped. Already on her way back to
Nottingham in the train, Hilda watched the watery sunshine on the fields
and the slate roofs drying. She reminded herself that she was always sad on

train journeys. It's a sensation of fantasy, she decided, having searched for and found the word.

The sunshine was short-lived. The dark purple clouds soon gathered over again and in London, crowds surging towards stations, queueing for buses, were soaked. The pavements steamed in the hissing rain, and taxis were unobtainable, although commissionaires under huge umbrellas stood at kerbs, whistling shrilly and vainly whenever one appeared in the distance.

In a positive deluge, Pat and Mr Wharton drove up to Number Twenty. He, too, had an umbrella, and held it carefully over her as they went down the garden path and round the side of the house.

'*Excusez-moi,*' she said, stooping to get the key from under the dustbin.

'Could be a nice view on a nice day,' he said.

'Could be,' she agreed, putting the key in the door.

Mice and Birds and Boy

'Was this when you were pretty?' William asked, holding the photograph in both hands and raising his eyes to the old lady's with a look of near certainty.

'I was thought to be beautiful,' she said; and she wondered: 'How long ago was that?' Who had been the last person to comment upon her beauty, and how many years ago? She thought that it might have been her husband, from loyalty or from still seeing what was no longer there. He had been dead for over twenty years and her beauty had not, by any means, been the burden of his dying words.

The photograph had faded to a pale coffee-colour, but William could distinguish a cloud of fair hair, a rounded face with lace to the chin, and the drooping, sad expression so many beautiful women have. Poor Mrs May, he thought.

The photographs were all jumbled up in a carved sandalwood box lined with dusty felt. There was a large one, mounted on stiff cardboard, of the big house where Mrs May had lived as a child. It had been pulled down between the wars and in its grounds was built a housing estate, a row of small shops by the bus-stop and a children's playground, with swings and slides. William could look out of the narrow window of the old gardener's lodge where Mrs May lived now and watch the shrieking toddlers climbing the frames, swinging on the swings. He never went to the playground himself now that he was six.

'It was all fields,' Mrs May would often say, following his glance. 'All fields and parkland. I used to ride my pony over it. It was a different world. We had two grooms and seven indoor servants and four gardeners. Yet we were just ordinary people. Everybody had such things in those days.'

'Did every child have a pony?' William asked.

'All *country* children had one,' she said firmly.

His curiosity endeared him to her. It was so long since anyone had asked her a question and been interested in the answer. His curiosity had been the beginning of their friendship. Going out into her overgrown little garden one afternoon, she had found him leaning against the rickety fence staring at her house, which was round in shape and had attracted his attention. It was made of dark flint and had narrow, arched windows and an arched door studded with big square-headed nails. A high twisted chimney-stack rose from the centre of the roof. Surrounded by the looped and tangled growth of the garden – rusty, black-leaved briars and crooked apple trees – the place reminded the boy of a menacing-looking illustration by Arthur Rackham in a book he had at home. Then the door had opened and the witch herself had come out, leaning on a stick. She had untidy white hair and a face cross-hatched with wrinkles; but her eyes weren't witch-like, not black and beady and evil, but large and milky blue and kind, though crows had trodden about them.

'How can your house be round inside?' William asked, in his high, clear voice. She looked about her and then saw his red jersey through the fence and, above it, his bright face with its straight fringe of hair. 'How can rooms be round?' he asked. He came up to the broken gate and stood there.

Beyond a row of old elm trees which hid the lodge from the main road, a double-decker bus went by, taking the women from the estate to Market Swanford for their afternoon's shopping. When it had gone, William turned back to the old lady and said: 'Or are they like this shape?' He made a wedge with his hands.

'You had better come and see,' she said. He opened the gate at once and went in. 'She might pop me into the oven,' he thought.

One room was half a circle, the other two were quarters. All three were dark and crammed with furniture. A mouse streaked across the kitchen floor. The sink was stacked with dirty china, the table littered with odds and ends of food in torn paper wrappings.

'Do you live here alone?' he asked.

'Except for the mice; but I should prefer to be alone.'

'You are more like a hermit than a witch.'

'And would rather be,' she said.

He examined a dish of stewed fruit which had a greenish-grey mantling of mould.

'Pooh! It smells like beer,' he said.

'I meant to throw it away, but it seemed such a criminal waste when the natives are starving everywhere.'

In the sitting-room, with frail and shaking hands, she offered him a chocolate box; there was one chocolate left in it. It was stale and had a bloom on it, and might be poisoned, he thought; but he took it politely and turned it about in his mouth. It was very hard and tasted musty. 'Curiosity killed the cat,' his mother would say, when his body was discovered.

Mrs May began then to tell him about the fields and park and her pony. He felt drowsy and wondered if the poison were taking effect. She had such a beautiful voice – wavering, floating – that he could not believe in his heart that she would do him any harm. The room was airless and he sat in a little spoon-shaped velvet chair and stared up at her, listening to a little of her story, here and there. Living alone, except for the mice, she had no one to blame her when she spilt egg and tea down her front, he supposed; and she had taken full advantage of her freedom. She was really very dirty, he decided dispassionately. But smelt nice. She had the cosy smell that he liked so much about his guinea-pigs – a warm, stuffy, old smell.

'I'd better go,' he said suddenly. 'I might come back again tomorrow.'

She seemed to understand at once, but like all grown-up people was compelled to prolong the leave-taking a little. He answered her questions briefly, anxious to be off once he had made up his mind to go.

'There,' he said, pointing up the hill. 'My house is there.' The gilt weather-vane, veering round, glittered in the sun above the slate roofs.

'Our old stables,' Mrs May said quite excitedly. 'Oh, the memories.'

He shut the gate and sauntered off, between piles of bricks and tiles on the site where more houses were being built. Trees had been left standing here and there, looking strange upon the scarred, untidy landscape. William walked round the foundations of a little house, stood in the middle of a rectangle and tried to imagine a family sitting at a table in the middle of it, but it seemed far too small. The walls were only three bricks high. He walked round them, one foot before the other, his arms lifted to keep his balance. Some workmen shouted at him. They were tiling the roof of a nearby house. He took no notice, made a completed round of the walls and then walked off across the rough grass, where Mrs May had ridden her pony when she was a little girl.

'Do you *hear* me?' his mother said again, her voice shrill, with anxiety and vexation. She even took William's shoulder and shook him. 'You are *not* to talk to strangers.'

His sister, Jennifer, who was ballet-mad, practised an arabesque, and watched the scene without interest, her mind on her own schemes.

William looked gravely at his mother, rubbing his shoulder.

'Do you understand?'

He nodded.

'That's right, remember what your mother told you,' his father said, for the sake of peace.

The next morning, William took a piece of cheese from the larder and a pen-knife and went to the building-site. His mother was having an Italian lesson. Some of the workmen were sitting against a wall in the sun, drinking tea and eating bread and cheese, and William sat down among them, settling himself comfortably with his back against the wall. He cut pieces of cheese against his thumb as the others did and popped them neatly into his mouth. They drew him into solemn conversation, winking at one another above his head. He answered them politely, but knew that they were making fun of him. One wag, going too far, grimacing too obviously, asked: 'And what is your considered opinion of the present emergency?'

'I don't know,' William replied, and he got up and walked away – more in sorrow than in anger, he tried to convey.

He lingered for a while, watching a bulldozer going over the uneven ground, opening wounds in the fields where Mrs May had ridden her pony; then he wandered on towards the main road. Mrs May came out to her front doorstep and dropped an apronful of crumbs on to the path. Thrushes and starlings descended about her.

'So you're back again,' she called. 'I am shortly off to the shops. It will be nice to have a boy go with me.' She went inside, untying her apron.

He tried to swing on the gate, but it was lopsided. When she came out after a long time, she was wearing a torn raincoat, although it was quite hot already. It had no buttons and hung open. Her dirty jersey was held to her flat chest with rows of jet beads.

William noted that they were much stared at as they passed the bus queue and, in the butcher's shop, Mrs May was the subject of the same knowing looks and gravely-kept straight faces that he himself had suffered from the builders. He felt, uncomfortably, that this behaviour was something that children came to expect, but that an older person should neither expect nor tolerate. He could not find words to explain his keen uneasiness on Mrs May's account.

He watched the butcher unhook a drab piece of liver, slap it on the counter and cut off a slice.

'When I think of the saddles of mutton, the sucking pigs ...' said Mrs May vaguely, counting out coppers.

'Yes, I expect so,' said the butcher's wife, with a straight face turned towards her husband.

Outside the shop, Mrs May continued the list. 'And ribs of beef, green goose at Michaelmas,' she chattered on to herself, going past the dairy, the grocer's, the draper's, with quick, herringbone steps. William caught glimpses of themselves reflected in the shop windows, against a pyramid of syrup tins, then a bolt of sprigged cotton.

'And what are *you* going to tell *me*?' Mrs May suddenly asked. 'I can't do all the entertaining, you know. Are you quite warm up there in the stables? Have you beds and chairs and all you need?'

'We have even more beds than we need.'

'Well, don't ask me to imagine it, because I can't. Shall we turn back?

I'll buy an egg at the dairy and I might get some stale bread for the birds. "My only friends," I say to them, as they come to greet me.'

'You have the mice as well.'

'I can't make friends with mice. The mice get on my nerves, as a matter of fact.'

'You could get a cat,' he suggested.

'And seem more like a witch than ever?'

There appeared to be no stale bread at the baker's. At sight of Mrs May, the woman behind the counter seemed to shutter her face; stood waiting with lowered eyes for them to go.

When they reached Mrs May's broken gate – with only the slice of meat and the egg – William would not go in. He ran home as fast as he could over the uneven ground, his heart banging, his throat aching.

When he reached it, the house was quiet and a strange, spicy smell he could not identify came from the kitchen. His mother, as well as her Italian lessons, had taken up Japanese cooking. His sister, returning from ballet class, with her shoes hanging from her neck by their ribbons, found him lying on the floor pushing a toy car back and forth. Her suspicions were roused; for he was pretending to be playing, she was convinced, with an almost cross-eyed effort at concentration. He began to hum unconcernedly. Jennifer's nose wrinkled. 'It smells as if we're going to have that horrid soup with stalks in it.'

'I like it,' he murmured.

'You would. What have you been doing, anyway?'

Still wearing her coat, she practised a few *pliés*.

'Never waste a moment,' he thought.

'Nothing.'

But she was not interested in him; had been once – long ago, it seemed to her, when his birth she hoped would brighten up the house. The nov-elty of him had soon worn off.

'The death duties,' Mrs May explained. Because of them, she could not light a fire until the really chilly days and sometimes had only an egg to eat all day. These death duties William thought of as moral obligations upon which both her father and husband had insisted on discharging while dying – some charitable undertakings, plainly not approved of by Mrs May. He was only puzzled by the varying effect of this upon her day-to-day life; sometimes she was miserably conscious of her poverty, but at other times she bought peppermint creams for herself and William and digestive bis-cuits for the birds.

Every time she opened or shut the garden gate, she explained how she would have had it mended if it were not for the death duties. *The* death duties made them sound a normal sort of procedure, a fairly usual change of heart brought about perhaps by the approach of death and clearly happening not only in Mrs May's family.

The days were beginning to grow chilly, too chilly to be without a fire. The leaves on the great chestnut trees about the building-site turned yellow and fell. William went back to school and called on Mrs May only on Saturday mornings. He did not miss her. His life was suddenly very full and some weeks he did not go at all and she fretted for him, watching from a window like a love-sick girl, postponing her visit to the shops. She missed not only him, but her glimpses – from his conversation – of the strange life going on up in the old stables. His descriptions – in answer to her questions – and what she read into them formed a bewildering picture. She imagined the family sitting round the bench in the old harness room, drinking a thin soup with blades of grass in it – the brisk mother, the gentle, dreamy father and an objectionable little girl who kept getting down from the frugal meal to practise *pas-de-chat* across the old, broken brick floor. She had built the scene from his phrases – 'My mother will be cross if I'm late' (more polite, he thought, than 'My mother will be cross if she knows I came to see you'), and 'My father wouldn't mind.' His sister, it seemed, complained about the soup; apart from this, she only talked of Margot Fonteyn. But confusions came into it – in William's helping to clean silver for a dinner party and having been sent to bed early for spilling ink on a carpet. Silver and carpets were hard to imagine as part of the old stables.

She had forgotten what a family was like, and had never had much chance of learning – only child and childless wife. William was too young to be a satisfactory informant. He was haphazardly selective, interested too much in his own separate affairs, unobservant and forgetful of the adult world; yet she managed to piece something together and it had slowly grown – a continuous story, without direction or catharsis – but could no longer grow if he were not to visit her.

Holding the curtains, her frail hands shook. When he did come, he was enticed to return. On those mornings now, there were always sweets. But her questions tired him, as they tire and antagonise all children, who begin to feel uneasily in the wrong rôle. He had by now satisfied his curiosity about her and was content to let what he did not understand – the death duties, for instance – lie at peace.

'You shall have this when I'm gone,' she began to say, closing the lid of the sandalwood box in which she kept the old photographs. Also promised was her father's sword and scabbard, in which William was more interested, and a stuffed parrot called Bertha – once a childhood pet and still talked to as if no change had taken place.

One morning, she saw him playing on the building-site and went out to the gate and called to him, lured him into the garden and then the house with witch-like tactics, sat him down on the spoon-shaped chair and gave him a bag of sweets.

'And how is your mother?' she enquired. She had a feeling that she detested the woman. William nodded absent-mindedly, poking about in the sweet bag. His hair was like gold silk, she thought.

'People have always lost patience with me,' she said, feeling his attention wandering from her. 'I only had my beauty.'

She was going on to describe how her husband's attention had also wandered, then thought it perhaps an unsuitable subject to discuss with a child. She had never discussed it with anyone else. Such a vague marriage – and her memories of it were vague, too – seemed farther away than her childhood.

A mouse gnawed with a delicate sound in the wainscot and William turned his gaze towards it, waiting for the minutes to pass until the time when he could rise politely from the dusty chair and say good-bye.

'If only he would tell me!' Mrs May thought in despair. 'Tell me what there was for breakfast, for instance, and who said what and who went where, so that I could have something to think about in the evening.'

'Oh, well, the winter will come if it means to,' she said aloud. Rain had swept in a gust upon the window, as if cast upon the little panes in spite. 'Nothing we can do can stop it. Only dig in and make ourselves comfortable – roast chestnuts on my little coal shovel.' William glanced from the wainscot to the empty grate, but Mrs May seemed not to see its emptiness. 'Once, when I had a *nice* governess, we roasted some over the schoolroom fire. But the next governess would never let me do anything that pleased me. "Want must be your master," she said. She had many low phrases of that kind. Yes, "want must be your master",' she said again, and sighed.

The visit was running down and her visitor simply sitting there until he could go. Courageously, when he had refused another peppermint cream and showed that he did not want to see again the photograph of her home, she released him, she even urged him to go, speeding him on his way, and watched him from the open door, her hands clasped close to her flat chest. He was like a most beloved caged bird that she had set at liberty. She felt regret and yet a sense of triumph, seeing him go.

She returned to the room and looked dully at the stuffed parrot, feeling a little like crying, but she had been brought up not to do so. 'Yes, want must be your master, Bertha,' she said, in a soft but serene voice.

'I can't see harm in it,' William's father told his wife. Jennifer had seen William leaving Mrs May's and hurried to tell her mother, who began complaining the moment her husband returned for lunch.

'She's stark, staring mad and the place is filthy, everybody says so.'

'Children sometimes see what we can't.'

'I don't know what you mean by that. I forbade him to go there and he repeatedly disobeyed me. You should speak to him.'

So his father spoke to William – rather off-handedly, over his shoulder, while hanging his coat up in the hall, as William passed through.

To be reprimanded for what he had not wanted to do, for what he looked on as a duty, did not vex William. It was the kind of thing that happened to him a great deal and he let it go, rather than tie himself up in explanations.

'You did hear what I said?' his father asked.

'Yes, I heard.'

'Your mother has her reasons. You can leave it at that.'

It happened that he obeyed his parents. His father one day passing Mrs May's garden came on her feeding her birds there. He raised his hat and saw, as she glanced up, her ruined face, bewildered eyes, and was stirred by pity as he walked on.

As the nights grew colder, Mrs May was forced to light a fire and she wandered about the building-site collecting sawn-off pieces of batten and wood-shavings. She met William there once, playing with another boy. He returned her greeting, answered her questions unwillingly, knowing that his companion had ducked his head, trying to hide a smile. When she had wandered on at last, there were more questions from his friend. 'Oh, she's only an old witch I know,' he replied.

The truth was that he could hardly remember how once he had liked to go to see her. Then he had tired of her stories about her childhood, grew bored with her photographs, became embarrassed by her and realised, in an adult way, that the little house was filthy. One afternoon, on his way home from school, he had seen her coming out of the butcher's shop ahead of him and had slackened his pace, almost walked backwards not to overtake her.

She was alone again, except for the birds in the daytime, the mice at night. The deep winter came and the birds grew fewer and the mice increased. The cold weather birds, double their summer size, hopped dottily about the crisp, rimed grass, jabbing their beaks into frozen puddles, bewildered as refugees. Out she hurried, first thing in the mornings, to break the ice and scatter crumbs. She found a dead thrush and grieved over it. 'Oh, Bertha, one of ours,' she mourned.

Deep snow came and she was quite cut off – the garden was full of strange shapes, as if heaped with pillows and bolsters, and the birds made their dagger tracks across the drifts. She could not open her door.

Seeing the untrodden path, William's father, passing by, went to borrow a spade from the nearest house and cleared the snow from the gateway to the door. He saw her watching from a window and, when at last she could, she opened the door to thank him.

'I'm afraid I don't know who you are,' she began.

'I live in the old stables up on the hill.'

'Then I know your little boy. He used to visit me. It was very kind of you to come to my rescue.'

William's father returned the spade and then walked home, feeling sad and ashamed. 'Oh, dear, that house,' he said to his wife. 'It is quite filthy – what I glimpsed of it. You were perfectly right. Someone ought to do something to help her.'

'She should help herself. She must have plenty of money – all this building land.'

'I think she misses William.'

'It was just a passing thing,' said his wife, who was a great one herself for passing things. 'He simply lost interest.'

'Lost innocence, perhaps. The truth is, I suppose, that children grow up and begin to lose their simple vision.'

'The truth is,' she said tartly, 'that if people don't wash themselves they go unloved.' Her voice was cold and disdainful. She had summed up many other lives than Mrs May's and knew the tone to use.

The thaw began, then froze in buds upon the red twigs of the dog-wood in Mrs May's untidy hedge. The hardening snow was pitted with drips from the branches.

Mrs May was afraid to venture on her frozen path beyond her doorway, and threw her remaining bits of bread from there. There was no one to run an errand for her. The cold drove her inside, but she kept going to the window to see if the ice were melting. Instead, the sky darkened. Both sky and earth were iron.

'It's my old bones,' she said to Bertha. 'I'm afraid for my old bones.'

Then she saw William running and sliding on the ice, his red scarf flying, his cheeks bright. He fell, and scrambled up, laughing.

'It's falling I'm afraid of,' Mrs May whispered to the window-pane. 'My old bones are too brittle.'

She went to the front door and opened it. Standing shivering on the step, she called to William. He seemed not to hear and she tried to raise her voice. He took a run and, with his arms flung up above his head, slithered across a patch of ice. He shouted to someone out of sight and dashed forward.

Mrs May shut the door again. 'Someone will come,' she told Bertha briskly. She straightened her father's sword suspended above the fireplace and bustled about, trying to tidy the room ready for an unknown visitor. 'There's no knowing what might happen. Anyone might call,' she murmured.

A Nice Little Actress

The outskirts of a town are nothing at all, neither town nor village. No focal point provides a starting-place nor draws back those who have gone, who, indeed, experience no nostalgia for the built-over hillsides, the corner shop or the bus-stop. For the rest, the wind blows hard, there are few trees or birds – certainly no owls at night – and on summer evenings before the nine o'clock news a continuous clatter of mowing machines is heard; cheerful or dreary according to one's mood. Always dreary to Iris.

On bad mornings, as she washed up by the kitchen window, she could see the sides and backs of other bungalows and their doors would be shut fast beyond the sheets of rain which fell and fell over the slate roofs and into the rows of cabbages. But on bright mornings, the doors would fly open like the doors of those little weather-houses, and women in coloured overalls would pop out and shake mats, go from one fence to another for a chat, clean shoes on the back doorstep, hang out washing and go down the garden with a basket for runner beans. And from all their wirelesses would come the sounds of the cinema organ.

'Oh, God!' Iris would cry, wringing out the dish-cloth and hanging it at the edge of the sink. She was fond of music and naturally the cinema organ, even without its being multiplied, was irritating to her. Her love for – say – the Archduke Trio was only to be increased by having someone to observe her loving it. Her husband had grown too familiar with this sight not to be able to marvel at it and, while she was alone with him, she had been known to sew, or even read, through a programme of chamber music, without tears coming once.

It was through – or with the aid of – the Archduke Trio that she came to know Brin. He waited at the bus-stop outside the next house every day, a slight dark young man with a music case. Every day at three o'clock. She played a little trick on him with Beethoven on the gramophone in the front room. She was always playing little tricks and this was the first which had ever come off. He edged along the privet-hedge, stood there outside, looking down at the pavement, as if listening to some music inside himself. The bus came and filled and went. He stood there frowning.

When he realised about the bus, he looked round in perplexity, and saw her standing at the window. He came to the gate and up the path to ask her about the next one.

'Not for half an hour.'

'Oh.' He looked away down the road. 'I was ... '

'I know.'

It was the end of the record. The gramophone clicked.

'Come in ... ' she said, for she was from London and did not know how to behave in a provincial suburb. 'Come and listen to the rest.'

Wherever *he* may have come from, he agreed and, before he took himself off to play – help play – 'Selections from The Geisha' and 'Bittersweet' in a café, he had heard the rest of the Archduke and begun again at the beginning, seen the tears fill her eyes to the brim, been vaguely stirred by her, seen some likeness to Emily Brontë, smoked one or two cigarettes and promised with great willingness to come again for the Brandenburg Concertos. He was half an hour late at work, and the pianist frowned at him over the music of his fourth solo.

The early afternoon is not a time for intimacies or great revelations of one soul to another. Not before four o'clock and only then in winter. Yet this was all they had. In the mornings he played for coffee-drinkers – in any case, the morning is useless – then again at tea-time and then at half-past seven for those who dined. Her husband, a vague and agreeable man, was home early in the evenings, correcting exercise books or staring at his tomato plants or smoking. But every day now, for Iris, there was something to look forward to, her boredom was cut into by another's admiration.

' ... You know, the one painted by Branwell, which is cracked all over like old pottery,' said Brin Morris, laying 'Portsmouth Point' on the turntable.

'Oh, how unkind!' she cried, for she was enormously pleased. 'I always think she looks cross – *and* crossed-eyed.'

His eyes adored her as he wound the gramophone (she was a snob about the other kind) and, for he was very young, he said: 'She looks proud and fine. Even painted by a drunkard.'

'You're doing your hair a new way,' her husband observed that night.

'Yes.' She looked into the mirror above the mantelpiece and arranged a lock of hair on either side of her face. 'Do you like it?'

'All right for a change.' He thought it looked absurd, snaky and greasy; but knew it wouldn't be for long.

It began to be autumn, a dull time with a few leaves coming down off the tress and a bonfire at the end of each strip of garden. The gramophone played less and less. It was always put out ready, but sometimes he never seemed to get beyond screwing in the new needle.

She knew he loved her, but his self-control was abominable. Once she went down into the town and walked to the restaurant where he played. This mortified him so that she promised never to go again. 'It is bad enough playing such trash, you see,' he tried to explain, 'but for you to hear it ... I can't ...'

'All right.'

His shoes needed mending and his trousers were frayed. She was touched by him and vowed to uphold his pride. He saw in her a soul in miserable captivity.

'Your husband ...' he began one day. Her eyes looked wild in the second before she covered them up with her hands.

This was another little trick that worked. He was on his side in no time, begging her pardon, and kissing her, for she had not covered her mouth.

He had uneasy thoughts playing his 'cello – a poor instrument it was – that afternoon. Her husband – though she had not actually said so – was evidently coarse-grained, a drunkard who could not even paint, a lecher, no doubt. He bent darkly over his 'cello, like a witch drawing up endless evil from a well. They were playing 'To a Wild Rose' – quite a favourite.

Meanwhile, Iris had dried her eyes and paced the room like a caged animal. When her husband came home they had boiled eggs for tea, and went to the pictures. On the way home, they stopped at the corner pub for gin and ginger ale. It was warm and cheery there. A pleasant evening, if not memorable.

On one Sunday which grew dark around eight o'clock, her husband went down to a school concert. The school was evacuated at the beginning of the war; but, even in London, she had nothing to do with it and certainly would not go to its concerts. This evening Brin came for her. On Sundays he had his holiday. He had arrived at the stage now, the neighbours noted, when he entered the back door without knocking. She was in the bedroom. 'No!' she cried tensely, barring his way. 'Not in there!' He saw her crucified upon the marriage-bed, and great vials of pity were tipped and spilled within him. 'Let's get out of this house!' he cried.

They walked to where the rough road stopped and the fields began. Once the road was to have continued across these fields, heaven knew how far, but then the war had come. The foundations of the little bungalows had been dug out, but now were overgrown by the fine uneven grass. They climbed into one of these. 'This is my dining-room,' she cried, trying to be gay, and standing on a little patch – too small to be a room, surely? They sat down. Across the allotments came thin voices and drifts of bonfire-smoke. The moon – the harvest moon, he said – rose clear of the curd-like clouds. In the darkening grass were wild snapdragon and scabious flowers like white lace.

'This is the only house we have,' he said. 'One without walls or roof or floor.'

'It cannot imprison us then,' she cried.

After a while, he said: 'Why don't you leave him?'

'Because he'd follow me – and I'm afraid.'

It was then, probably, that he decided to kill him.

'Let's not discuss him,' she begged. 'It is too lovely here.'

She always took his love fiercely and crossly as if she bore him some grudge. He mistook this for passion. In a way, she did hate him for this affair, the first in which she had been unfaithful to her husband, though not the first time she had considered the idea. She was, in any case, incapable of passion, standing too far apart, as if a witness.

'Let's not discuss him,' she had cried, her fingers tugging, snapping up grass, plucking at harebells. But from that time on, they did discuss him a great deal. From the slack-seeming conversation Brin collected many facts to be sorted over methodically when he was alone. Some details – such as what time he rose (she could not mention the cup of tea he always brought to her then), what he taught at school and thought about the war, were useless. But others – such as the times of leaving the house and his work, which way he walked, what he did in the evenings – were stored carefully.

'Which pub?' she cried in astonishment. 'Oh, we ... he ... always drinks at home.' That is always worse.

At night, Brin, wakeful with his new obsession, sorted and rejected. The only time he would ever be alone would be going to and fro between home and school, across the fields as a quick cut, and soon he would be doing it in the dark twice a week, when he stayed on for an extra class.

Iris found that she was often bored now with Brin. They talked no more of music or the spirit or Emily Brontë. She parted her hair at the side again and felt that the Archduke Trio might never have been. He still made love, however, in a tender and grateful way, and his eyes, full of admiration and pride, would travel over her face.

It occurred to her that her husband was dispirited and morose. He gloomed about the house. He compared the trek across the fields unfavourably with hopping on a bus in London. The tomatoes somehow didn't ripen. Some of them fell off while they were still green. He gathered them up and laid them along window-ledges to redden.

'Ah, I feel like a change,' he said. 'At half-term we'll go up to town, Iris, and have a bit of a binge. A nice meal in Soho and go to a play. What's on?' He became excited and rushed to look for the Sunday paper. His enthusiasm affected her, too.

'Let's stay the night,' she begged. 'Yes, let's stay the night. I love that feeling of getting up in London, with nothing to do but have breakfast and go out to look at the shops.' She saw the Marble Arch and Oxford Street in brilliant sunshine, all gay and glittering movement. It was something to look forward to.

Brin also had something to look forward to. His life had some purpose now. He felt this, as he played at the café and sat in the bus. He walked over those fields until he knew each tussock of grass by heart. Once, he met her husband there. He was going along, in no hurry to be home as Brin would have been, slashing venomously at thistles with his stick.

When he had made his plans there was still the business of getting a gun. His father had one, but that was in Leamington. He went up one Sunday and surprised them all; but he could find no opportunity of getting the revolver and came away without it. He went again the next week-end and surprised them even more and this time, since he was not such a novelty, he was allowed out of their sight a little more and was successful. Coming back on the train, his heart was singing.

The end of all his planning seemed unreal sometimes and then at other times very simple; but the task itself, and going carefully and efficiently from one step to the next, absorbed and delighted him. But by the time the dark nights came, he was suddenly exhausted. Iris was a little alarmed.

'My darling, if this is making you unhappy, you must give it up. We won't meet again.'

He stared at her stupidly. He had not been to as many plays as she. The truth was he had begun to bore her a little. Once more, the gossiping, mat-shaking neighbours oppressed her. She noted his shabby clothes, the fringed trousers, with repulsion.

Now it was quite dark when her husband reached home on Tuesdays and Fridays. Brin fixed on the exact night. Iris kissed her husband good-bye on that day and he went off to work. On his way home across the dark fields, he heard a shot. Brin, fed up with waiting and confronted too soon and for the first time by the reality and idiocy of what he was up to, had put the revolver up to his eyes and shot himself. His life had moved with some purpose towards the killing of his man. If he was not to kill him, then the purpose of his life was gone.

At the inquest, the father explained that his son was depressed at being rejected for military service. The usual verdict was returned.

When it was half-term, Iris and her husband went up to London for their treat. They dined in Soho, sat eating ravioli and looked bored and married. But Iris enjoyed the play. 'Ah!' she sighed, as they walked back through the foggy streets to their hotel. 'How I wish I could have been an actress!'

The Voices

When the voices began again, Laura decided that she had let things go too far to demonstrate the thinness of the walls by coughing. To have to speak in whispers from then on might spoil their holiday, and would take something from her own. As they talked, she could hear movements about the room, the rattling of coat-hangers in the wardrobe. The conversation was discursive, languid, and there were long, tired silences.

She had never seen them, had never come across them in the passage or waiting for the lift, and was amused to know so much about two women she had never met. For instance, she knew that Edith's little trouble had cleared up at last, and she was glad about that. It had seemed a pity to waste two days of a holiday, from fear of leaving the hotel. Amy had seemed to be kindness itself, hardly venturing out except on little errands, and having trays of plain food sent up for her friend. 'It's the oil, all that oil,' Laura often heard.

She spent the hot part of the day in her bedroom, writing letters or lying on the bed, listening, keeping quiet. When she opened the shuttered windows, the noise of Athens roared in – traffic, pneumatic drills, the chipping of steel on masonry, bells tolling – and in flowed, too, the steady heat, the glare from the sky, and greasy smells from the kitchen below. When she had failed to find any fresh air, Laura closed the windows and flopped back on the bed to listen.

'It was just a sort of mince with a batter,' Amy said.

'Really more of a custard,' said Edith.

'"Mousaká", they called it.'

'Mousaká,' Edith said. She was the less gentle one. She liked to know more, and dominated. Taller, Laura thought. She imagined Amy rather plump and soft. Her voice was high and floating, very sweet. Edith's was abrupt and deeper. It was Amy who had been so affected by the stairs when the lift was out of order. She had puffed and blown for a long time after they reached their room. It was the morning that they visited the Acropolis (a view of which Laura could have by leaning right out over the courtyard and craning her neck upwards), and both were worn-out, but exalted. To think they had really seen it, after all these years, they said over and over again.

To Laura, at first, they had sounded like school-mistresses; but the summer term could not be ended yet. They might have retired; yet she pictured them leading some kind of busy life together – 'my colleague', they might say in introductions to other people – 'a colleague of mine'. It was clear that their holiday had been planned for a long time and Laura was glad that, apart from Edith's little trouble at the beginning, it was being a success. They went off to Delphi, having what they called 'mugged it up' first, and Laura wondered anxiously if Delphi would come up to expectations. It had, and more. Sounion, in spite of a thunderstorm (perhaps because of it, Amy suggested), had greatly impressed, and even the food was what everyone – and especially a certain Colonel Benson – had warned them that it would be.

From Myconos ('just a little bit touristy') they had apparently brought back a quantity of peasant art – the prices of it were much compared and discussed – and Laura could imagine them making their excursions draped in crudely striped stoles, their hair covered with bright scarves, guide-books and sun-tan oil in fringed and tasselled shoulder-bags.

On the other side of the wall, they often mildly argued. 'We paid no credence to Colonel Benson about drinking the water,' Amy had said, when Edith had her bout of diarrhoea.

'I paid no credence then. I pay no credence now,' said Edith sharply. 'It is a long time since the Colonel was in Athens. It was the oil – "This oil's off", I remember saying to you the first evening we were here. In that place with the wine vats. It was rancid.'

Amy had murmured something in reply, but for once Laura could not hear.

Sometimes, when Laura awoke in the morning, the voices were going on as if they had not stopped all night; other days, there was silence, broken by Alexis bringing their breakfast.

'Good-morning, good-morning, ladies,' he would call out in a warning, lilting voice, and Laura imagined the scramble for bed-wraps, the sheets drawn up to their chins as they gravely replied in the other language: 'Kali méra, Alexis.' When he had gone, Laura would hear long yawns, the sounds of breakfast beginning, and the start of the day's conversation.

'How kind Madame Petropoulos was,' said Amy. 'I made a note of the restaurant she recommended. Where did she say to get the rose-petal jam from?'

Edith had made a note of that somewhere. They had acquired a habit of writing everything down, for there was a great deal they were in danger of forgetting. They had brought a letter of introduction to Madame Petropoulos and had been greatly excited about their visit to her. Amy had even been tempted to wear the stole she had bought as a present for her niece.

Madame Petropoulos had a flat high up in a building at the foot of
Mount Lycabettos (such a pull up from the hotel; they had arrived quite
winded and then had to climb the flights of marble stairs), and they had
sat out on a balcony and looked at the view – the Acropolis golden in the
evening light, the mountains violet and Salamis darkening in the glittering sea. They had described it over and over to one another as they went
to bed the previous night, rather over-excited, like children. It had been
a high spot of their holiday. This morning, they began to marvel at it again.

'We must remember to send her a Christmas card,' Amy said. 'Although
I don't think they make as much of it as we do.'

'Don't *speak* of Christmas,' Edith begged her, with the English dread of
it in her voice.

'We needn't have worried about the language. I must confess I was quite
nervous at bringing out my few sentences.'

She had been rehearsing these – compiled from the phrase book – for
days beforehand; but Edith, whom Laura suspected of fearing to make a fool
of herself, would not try. 'We know that Madame Petropoulos can speak
English. Colonel Benson told us so,' she had reminded Amy, interrupting
her rehearsal of 'Athens pleases us very much. We go to Delphi.'
(Everything in the phrase book was in the present tense, but she hoped to
be understood.) 'Delphi pleases us very much. Myconos pleases us very
much. And Sounion.'

To her girlish wonder and – it appeared to Laura – Edith's annoyance,
the phrases had seemed to be understood and had gone down well.
Madame Petropoulos had responded with warm surprise, had said, in fact:
'Now I do not know whether to speak to you in English or Greek.'

'Such a lot of gold teeth when she laughed,' Amy said afterwards, repeating what she had said. 'And clasping her hands and shaking them over her
head like that reminded me of those boxers we saw on the television.'

'*You* saw,' Edith said.

'But the *view* – the colours changing all the time and then suddenly the
lights going on out at sea.'

'I think we stayed too long. I kept trying to catch your eye.'

'I simply forgot time existed.'

Laura could hear breakfast-trays being put aside, and then creakings and
rustlings about the room, water running. She lay very still in bed, her arms
laced under her head, and wondered what to do with her day. She also had
letters of introduction and invitations, but she had done nothing about
them. The habit of inertia is a hard one to shake off, the accidie of mind
and body torments as it takes hold. After a long illness, her parents had persuaded her to go away – perhaps as a holiday for themselves as well. For her,
it was too soon; travel had not broken into her apathy; flying in, she had

gazed down at the islands with indifference, though their tawny beauty would at one time have moved her to tears. Since then, she had wasted the holiday, mooning about in the morning sunshine, lunching at the same place every day, resting in the afternoon. It was a much more real holiday – this one she enjoyed vicariously through the bedroom wall.

When Amy and Edith had gone out, she telephoned for her own breakfast and ate it sitting up in the hard bed – spreading the pieces of dry bread with melting butter, drinking coffee from a large, thick cup.

It was such a silence, now that the next room was empty. They had gone down to the travel agency in the Square to arrange a trip to Mycenae. *I* ought to do that, Laura thought. As things were turning out, she would have nothing to say for herself when she returned home. 'Did you go there? Did you see such and such?' And to those questions, she would say, 'No, no, no,' her voice rising irritably. 'I just stayed in my room and listened to two old ladies chattering.'

She dressed and went out and wandered about the busy streets. The day was well on for other people. After a time, she found herself in a cool flower market with watered pavings. She walked all round it, breathing the scented air, made her way out of it by a different narrow street, and soon was lost. Some buildings looked familiar from other similarly aimless wanderings, but she could form no pattern from them. She could not even read the letters of the street names, or those above the shops. The feeling of isolation was the worst she had suffered since her illness, and she was ready to sit down on some church steps she had arrived at and weep until someone rescued her. She was too much of a burden to be managed by herself alone.

In the end, she found a taxi and was driven back to the hotel. When she reached her room, she was a little comforted to find that Edith and Amy had also returned, were busily counting coins as they did after all their expeditions. When they had settled everything fairly down to the last drachma, they began to sort out the picture-postcards they had bought.

'There is quite an art in timing them,' Edith said in a humorous voice. 'If you send them off too soon, one's friends are apt to think one is at a loss to know how to pass the time, that there is nothing better to do, that one can only think of people back home, and are perhaps homesick. Then, too late seems like a last-minute thought and a dreadful risk that they may arrive after one arrives oneself.'

'I think *now* is just about right,' Amy said.

'And another thing is that they must all be posted together. I haven't forgotten that rumpus when we went to Rimini and some people in the village got them early and others thought they had been forgotten.'

'Don't you think we might send Colonel Benson's off a little earlier than the rest? After all, he's been so kind. It would be a small mark of appreciation.'

'Perhaps a couple of days,' Edith conceded. 'I thought this one of the Evzones for him – it was about the nearest I could find to anything of a military nature.'

'And this Archaic statue for Mrs Campion, don't you think? It is so like her daughter-in-law.'

'Funny that that smile looks so beautiful on a statue, and is simply infuriating on a real person.'

Laura, lying on her bed, nodded to herself and smiled a different smile.

'We will go after tea and get the stamps,' said Amy, making it sound quite an expedition.

So somewhere, Laura thought, they had organised tea-time, as they had organised everything else. She felt ashamed of herself, not able to imagine *them* wanting to sit down on the steps of a church and weep.

There were some silences in the next room while – Laura supposed – they wrote their postcards. She hoped all those people in whatever village it was would value the trouble that had been taken.

'The temple of Poseidon *is* later than the Parthenon, isn't it?' asked Edith.

'I am almost sure; but you could look it up. Who is that for?'

'The Vicar.'

'I am just putting personal things. "Sitting here in the sun, drinking *retzina*."'

Laura turned her face to the pillow, laughing silently.

'But you aren't,' said Edith. 'Oh, there is so little space on a postcard, and so much to say.'

When they had gone out to tea, Laura had a shower and went for a walk in the Royal Gardens. Dusky, dappled light was shed through leaves and petals, and peacocks stepped fastidiously over fallen, rotting oranges under the trees. She sat on a seat and watched the passers-by – beautifully dressed babies in perambulators pushed by English-looking nannies in uniform, young couples hand in hand, older men wearing sunglasses, swinging key-rings, treading ponderously. One of them passed several times, staring at her with curiosity, but her indifferent English air puzzled and at last defeated him.

The sun went down quickly, and when she got up at last and came out of the Gardens the temples on the Acropolis had turned from golden to a shadowy brown.

The next morning, after Alexis's high-spirited 'Good-morning, ladies', Laura heard Edith and Amy mugging up Mycenae from the guide-book. They were to set out the next day, early in the morning, and Laura decided that she, too, must go somewhere. She felt like knocking on the wall to ask them where. Delphi, she knew, they had especially enjoyed. It had been described as picturesque.

'We now enter a circular chamber shaped like a beehive,' Edith read from the guide-book in a voice unlike the one she used in conversation.

'I can't take in so much beforehand,' Amy complained. 'I like to read about it *after* I've been there.'

'And *I* don't like going round a site with a book in my hands,' said Edith. She then must have dropped the guide-book on the floor, because Amy exclaimed about the pressed flowers that had fallen out.

'And I get the royal family so muddled up,' she said, panting a little, perhaps on her knees, gathering up wafery, dry wild flowers. 'Agamemnon and so forth.'

'Perfectly straightforward,' Edith replied. 'Agamemnon returns from the war, Aegysthus and Clytemnestra murder *him*; Orestes murders Clytemnestra; Electra—'

'Your *hands*!' interrupted Amy. 'Just look at your hands. All the time you were saying that, they weren't still for a moment. You laugh at *me*; but, goodness, you are even worse.'

'I don't do it in the street,' said Edith coldly.

It was then that Laura, diverted and off-guard, suddenly sneezed. Reaching for a handkerchief to stifle it, she was too late, and knocked over a glass of water.

There was a deep, long silence in the next room. She imagined them staring at one another, hardly daring to stir. It was some time before they began to whisper and move stealthily about the room.

Sitting in the bus, on her way back from Delphi, Laura wondered how Edith and Amy had enjoyed Mycenae. Enjoy it she knew they would; their enthusiasm would reduce the ancient horrors, dispassionately they would relate old histories as if describing house parties at Balmoral.

Laura felt put to shame by their toughness. At Delphi, brooded over by towering crags, diminished, overawed, she had tried to put herself in their state of mind in the same place – happily darting from one wild flower to another, describing – as they had – the scenery as picturesquely mountainous. They had even had someone sick on the bus, as Laura had, but were led by this simply to talk of national characteristics. Greeks had poor stomachs; they had known this beforehand; hadn't Colonel Benson himself said so?

When she reached the hotel, Laura found flowers in her room and an invitation to a party. She wondered if she might not accept it after all. The journey to Delphi, however shattering, had been a beginning. It might now be pleasant to talk again to someone in her own language. Yet she had not been so very lonely. Edith and Amy had been just the undemanding company she would have wished for, and she hoped that they were not still talking in whispers on her account.

She awoke early the next morning, and there was silence in the next room. She lay and waited for the coming of breakfast and the beginnings of conversation. 'Perhaps they have finished talking about Mycenae by now, and I shall never find out about it,' she thought.

When Alexis came along the passage and opened the door of the next room, his voice was less warning than usual, Laura thought, and less genial. 'Good-morning, good-morning,' he called, falsely bright.

Someone groaned and yawned. 'Good-morning to you,' a man's voice replied – an American voice.

Laura was quite shocked. As soon as Alexis had gone away down the passage, she began to cough sharply. She telephoned for her breakfast, making as much noise about it as she could when it arrived.

So they have gone, she thought. They have followed their postcards back home, and Colonel Benson will hear about Mycenae and the rest, not I.

In the Sun

'Oh, heavens!' said Deirdre Wallace, stepping out of the car with some of her Moroccan trophies – a water-carrier's hat from Marrakesh hanging on a string from her wrist, a native basket, and an ugly, stamped-leather bag.

Her husband, Bunny, snatched at a crumpled chiffon scarf as it loosened from her shoulders in the wind from the sea. He was a soldierly-looking little man, with receding hair; had gone bald very early; was now in his fifties. *So English*, the other visitors at the hotel would be bound to say – not only because of his clothes, but on account of every stalwart movement he made.

Deirdre, before stepping into the coolness of the hotel, looked about her in dismay. She preferred something more Arab – an old Sultan's palace, for instance; or some ancient house inside a medina, with broken mosaics, and wrought-iron lanterns casting fancy patterns on the walls. So far, she had had an instinct for finding such places. This hotel looked like being their first mistake.

Beyond a bougainvillaea-hedge, people were actually playing tennis in this broiling sun. Scarlet Thames-valley geraniums bordered the drive – though more brilliant than any in England, and exuberantly climbing the trunks of trees.

Driving through the town, Deirdre had remarked how very much it was in the style of the departed French, with its *boulevards*, *ronds-points*, shuttered villas named Les Mimosas, Les Rosiers, La Terrasse. There were more bicycles than in Oxford, where the Wallaces lived.

Arab women in *djellabahs* and *yashmaks* looked absurd riding them, Deirdre thought.

Despite the *palmeraie* near which it was built, the new white hotel looked very European. 'It might be anywhere in the world,' Deirdre complained, 'from Nice to the Bahamas – or Torquay.'

Beside a peacock-blue swimming-pool, sunbathers were spread out like starfish on brightly cushioned furniture. Limbs stirred occasionally, but hardly a word was spoken. One lone swimmer stood as if bemused on the diving-board, then suddenly flung himself with a deep, crashing sound into the water. The shock of this interruption subsided into peaceful blowing noises, gentle splashes, as the swimmer surfaced, shook the bright water from his face and then, as if once more bemused, began to swim slowly, aimlessly about the pool. No one opened an eye to look at him.

A porter, wearing a somewhat fancy-dress version of Moorish costume, took their suitcases to the lift. A man and woman, in beach clothes, carrying sunbathing paraphernalia stepped out of it. 'English,' Deirdre murmured to Bunny, as they stood side by side in the lift, ascending.

Bunny was secretly, guiltily, a little glad to see someone from his own country. His French was not as good as Deirdre's, and he spoke it and listened to it under a sense of strain. It would be a relief to chat in his own language – in the bar before dinner, perhaps.

'Very luxe,' Deirdre said, but not in a tone of satisfaction, as she glanced about the large, cool bedroom. Bunny wound up the shutters and stepped on to the balcony. The pool, with its coloured umbrellas, was below him. No one was swimming now, but wet footprints round the edges were drying quickly. They vanished one after the other on the hot concrete.

The English couple were arranging themselves ready for their afternoon's sunbathing. They removed their wraps and lay back in their deckchairs – a stout pair, already well on with their tanning. The sun beat down. Arabs, at this time of the day, were squatting in the shade, or safely indoors.

While she was waiting for Bunny to change into his swimming-trunks, Deirdre wandered out into the stone-paved corridor, moving slowly along from window to window, looking at the distant hills, the pink and paprika landscape. The heat seemed to move, to rise and fall, making the dusty air whirl giddily.

A commotion beneath one of the windows made her lean out. A smell of rotting fruit rose from below. This was the back of the hotel and a rough road ran close to it, leading to the cemetery. As she leant out of the window, Deirdre could see beneath her a swarm of children picking over a cart of refuse, disturbing the flies. The sight of this sickened her. 'Oh, it is quite upsetting,' she told herself. Especially was she moved by one little girl standing apart from the others, tearing pieces off a crust of bread. She was barefooted as they all were, but wore a crumpled party dress of violet-coloured velvet. This, too, had probably come off a rubbish cart, Deirdre thought. It was threadbare, like some old banner hanging in a chapel.

'It was so upsetting,' she told Bunny as they went down in the lift. 'The back of the hotel might be in a different sphere from the front.'

The company about the swimming-pool was still somnolent. The large couple they had seen in the lift had been joined now by two other people – a man and a woman – and a lazy conversation had begun.

Deirdre took Bunny's wrap and went to sit in the shade under a blue

umbrella. Very smartly, Bunny stepped on to the diving-board, sprang out-
wards and did a belly-flop into the still water. The French visitors cried out
with good-natured shouts of anguish. Most of the English pretended that
nothing had happened. Bunny came up through the water with a crimson
chest. Deirdre blushed.

The Troughtons and the Crouches had struck up a desultory holiday friendship. They chatted when they met about the hotel, and joined one another
for drinks before dinner, but did not yet go on expeditions together. The
Troughtons, for that matter, very rarely went on expeditions. They had
come here to get a tan, and seriously developed it from breakfast until the
moment when the sun suddenly dropped out of the sky at six o'clock.

'Yes, they were getting into the lift as we got out,' Mrs Troughton told
Mrs Crouch, who had turned her attention to the newcomers on the other
side of the pool. 'So English,' she murmured. 'Simply couldn't be anything
else.'

Bunny flailed about in the water – a splashy, disorganised crawl – and
Deirdre sat under the umbrella in her white blouse, her flowered dirndl
skirt, a book in her hands, which she read with so little attention that she
had not turned a page. Her fond, dreamy gaze was more often upon Bunny.
Admiringly, she watched him quietly floating on his back, the little hairy
patch on his chest exposed to the sun, his eyes closed.

When at last he came out of the water, Deirdre handed him his robe.
Something about her devoted attitude irritated Mrs Crouch. She doubted
if they were married to one another, she said; but Mrs Troughton could not
think why else they would be on holiday together.

Other people greatly engaged Mrs Crouch, and her husband shared her
interest – a rather unmannish trait, Mrs Troughton thought. Her own husband was not, on holiday, interested in anything. Separated from the Stock
Market, his mind became a vacuum. A paperbacked thriller was part of his
sunbathing equipment, but he had not so far opened it. His hands were
always covered with sun-tan oil, and for much of the time he dozed.

'Doesn't she remind you of Miss Simpson, Daddy?' Mrs Crouch suggested to her husband, gazing across the pool at Deirdre Wallace.

'He reminds me of someone,' Mrs Troughton said, thinking what awful
company one sometimes fell in with on holiday – and often, through proximity and one's tolerant holiday spirit, became quite absorbed in their lives.
'Someone I've seen somewhere or seen a photograph of,' she added.

'Miss Simpson was Janice's music mistress,' Mrs Crouch explained. No
need to explain who Janice was. The Troughtons knew all about Janice,
who was training to be a nurse. They knew about the hospital, too – the
matron, sisters, patients. Mrs Troughton thought she could find her way

blindfold about it ... poor staff nurse found crying in the sluice; old Mr Norwich's registrar kicking up a rumpus in Casualty. She would also be quite at home in the other Crouch girl's, Carol's, office, and in their house (or home – as Mrs Crouch always called it) in Guildford, with its frilled nylon curtains at seven-and-elevenpence a yard; its sun-lounge and bar – quilted plastic décor done by Mr Crouch ... Leslie ... Daddy ... himself.

Well, they were a nice homeloving pair, Mrs Troughton thought, though this Daddy business grated rather. The world would be better with more such peaceable, easily pleased creatures in it.

'Don't you think so, Daddy? The image of Miss Simpson.'

He looked at Deirdre over the top of his spectacles and agreed. Part of Brenda's unflagging interest in other people was to be constantly finding likenesses between them. She had at the very beginning – last Saturday – decided that Ralph Troughton was a younger, shorter General de Gaulle, and that his Peggy might have been an identical twin to their doctor's wife back home.

That was how Mrs Crouch had introduced herself to them, sitting at the bar before dinner. 'Oh, you must think me terribly rude,' she said. 'I just found myself staring at you. It quite took my breath away when you walked in. You're so like our doctor's wife back home – we live in Guildford – I thought for a moment ...'

Mrs Troughton was easy, benign, friendly. She smiled. 'Here we go,' she thought. It will be like those Tillotsons in Majorca and the funny couple in Corfu. She was quite prepared to be genial for a fortnight. Her placid disposition was never disturbed by other people. At home, in London, she protected Ralph from such intrusions; on holiday it was unnecessary, he was not really there.

Mr Troughton now stirred himself, slapped a fly away from his ankle, got stiffly up and stretched. 'Time for a drink,' he said. 'Last dip,' he added. He had few words to spare.

He dived in expertly from the side of the pool, swam powerfully across it, and hauled himself out. The others, feeling rather dazed and enervated by the sun, began to collect their belongings.

After dinner, the Wallaces drank coffee in the hotel courtyard. Light fell from wrought-iron lanterns and printed scrolled shadows on the white walls around them, together with the shadows of giant leaves. A fountain dribbled water back into a pool. An orange dropped from a tree.

Next to them at dinner sat a young American and his Moroccan wife – perhaps on their honeymoon, it was thought. His wife dealt deftly with every situation, speaking in Arabic, French or Spanish. She was as curt with waiters as Deirdre had earlier watched her being with rug-sellers and beggars who hung about the entrance to the hotel. Her shift was of a pale lime-green silk and clung to her, showing her beautiful, wide-apart breasts.

Now she and her husband were sitting across the courtyard, under a climbing-rose tree. She was feeding a thin grey cat with popcorn. Deirdre, who loved cats, had tried to make this one come to her, but it had edged away at her touch. The popcorn made it thirsty, and it kept pattering off to the fountain pool in the middle of the courtyard to have a drink. A boy had hosed the paving-stones. Although they had dried at once, there was still the delicious smell of wet stone.

Deirdre refilled Bunny's coffee-cup and then sat back. He was glancing too often at the young Moroccan woman, almost staring at her at the moment, and to underline his inattention, Deirdre twisted her fingers in her lap and looked fixedly down at them. The message was received. With a little start of confusion, Bunny said, 'I was just remembering when you had a dress that colour.'

'What colour?' asked Deirdre, glancing round the courtyard.

'That yellowish green.'

'When?'

'Oh, I can't remember. Probably years ago.'

'Not that colour, I'm quite sure. It wouldn't suit me in the least.'

'Oh well …' he said vaguely, taking up his coffee-cup, his eyes anywhere but on that lime-green dress under the roses.

'But,' she persisted, 'what on earth was it like?'

He regretted mentioning it. He had made a mistake, and she was beginning to think it was some other woman's dress he had remembered. It had been a difficult evening.

In the bar before dinner, she had looked huffily at the other visitors as if cross with them for being English; then had turned away to chat in French with the Arab barman. 'Until we came here, we hadn't seen a single English person since we left Ouezzane.'

When they reached home after their holidays, she liked to tell people that hardly a word of English had offended their ears from start to finish. Now she would not be able to – for she would not exaggerate, or tell a lie.

Bunny had smiled and said good-evening when Ralph Troughton had come into the bar, and Ralph had nodded back quite genially, settling himself on a high stool and helping himself to olives. It was soon plain, however, that Deirdre was annoying him, monopolising the attentions of the barman as she was, asking him what was the Arabic for peanuts, for cherries, for everything she could see around her.

'Large Scotch,' said Ralph Troughton, when he could get a word in.

Deirdre turned her eyes to him and then away.

It was always the same, Bunny thought wistfully, and without bitterness. She drove people from him, shooed them off, as if he were private ground. Sometimes he longed to have a conversation with someone else, another man – this one drinking whisky, for instance.

At dinner, they had found themselves sitting next to the Crouches. The Troughtons, earlier established in the hotel, had a table by the veranda overlooking the swimming-pool and beyond that the dark seashore.

Deirdre recognised Mrs Crouch as the one who had stared so much at them that afternoon, had been talking about them, had murmured to her companions, Deirdre thought, when poor Bunny had done his belly-flop. To punish her, when she was overheard remarking to her husband how strange it seemed that the scarecrows in the fields should be dressed as Arabs, Deirdre put her tongue in her cheek and smiled, giving a glance under her lids at Bunny.

The food was extremely boring, but Mrs Crouch was either hungry or easily pleased. That her chop should be tender was enough for her, and several times she told her husband how tender it was.

'Do you remember the *tajine de poulet aux amandes* in Fes?' Deirdre asked Bunny, leaving most of her own chop, putting her knife and fork together. He could see that she had taken a great dislike to Mrs Crouch.

Now, sitting in the courtyard, listening to nightingales, looking through leaves at the stars – for safety – they both felt tired; tired by one another. Deirdre was exhausted by trying to interest him and keep him happy, trying, in fact, to make up for all the rest of the world; to be a world in herself.

'Shall we hire a *calèche* and drive round for a bit?' Bunny suggested. The Crouches and Troughtons had come out into the courtyard and were settling down at a nearby table. He had written them off. They were not for him.

'Oh, I should love to,' said Deirdre. She seemed in ecstasies at the idea and hurried upstairs to select one of her many stoles.

The air was beautifully soft and smelt of orange blossom, as they drove in the *calèche* down the *boulevard*, across the *rond-point* and into the old part of the town. Under the walls, by one of the gates into the medina, a circle of men were sitting on the ground, wrapped round in their *djellabahs*, listening to an old man who was reading to them from a large book. Light from a paraffin flare waved over the pages, over their intent faces. They were absorbed, like children, and did not lift their eyes to Deirdre and Bunny jolting by in their *calèche*.

'It is so beautiful,' whispered Deirdre, taking Bunny's hand.

They drove round the walls, and when they came back past the gateway, the circle of Arabs had broken up; the men were dispersing in silence, going their own ways thoughtfully, through the quiet streets, still under the spell of what they had heard.

'It is what we came to see,' Deirdre said, with a sweep of her hand at the white walls, beyond them the tower of a mosque topped with a stork's nest. 'Not that boring new hotel, not all those tiresome English people. We can have plenty of them at home.'

Yet don't, thought Bunny sadly . . .

It was becoming colder and the fronds of the trees in the palmeraie clashed softly together. Moonlight was enough to read by. It blanched Deirdre's face as she lifted it to look at the stars, it glinted on some metal threads woven into her stole.

The streets were quiet. The only sound was of the horse's hoofs on the road, the creaking of the *calèche*, and then, as they drew near, dance music coming from the hotel.

The Troughtons and the Crouches were just setting out for a stroll before bed. They felt drowsy from the day's sun and non-exertion.

As they went down the steps of the hotel, they saw Bunny helping Deirdre from the *calèche* . . . her radiant smile as she took his hand.

'*Of course* they aren't married,' Mrs Crouch murmured as she and Mrs Troughton fell into step together.

'I'd like to go in one of those, Ralph,' Mrs Troughton said, over her shoulder. But she didn't suppose they'd ever bother . . .

Peggy Troughton sat up in bed and drank her coffee; croissant crumbs scattered on her sunburned chest.

'And his name is Bunny. Isn't that wonderful?' she asked her husband, who was pottering about, getting into his swimming-trunks and sandals, ready for the day's lying-out in the sun. He was rather irritable in the mornings when he was on holiday, having slept most of the day and, so, badly at night.

'What do you think he does?' Peggy Troughton went on.

'Does? What do you mean *does?*'

'I think he travels in lingerie. Or he might own a launderette. It's obvious that *she* has the money, don't you think?'

'What money?'

'Well, for this sort of holiday, for instance, and all those moonstones and seed pearls and garnets that she wears in the evening.'

'Poor sod, whatever he does,' Ralph said. He found Deirdre's airs and graces intolerable. Her pale-blue eyes, baby hair, and crushed scarves irritated him. Not that she ever talked to him, but she talked *at* him.

'Very henpecked,' Peggy agreed. 'His accent isn't quite right. A bit too much of a good thing.'

She put her breakfast-tray aside and got heavily out of bed. When she had pulled off her nightgown she stood in front of the long mirror, turned round slowly, trying to look over her fat shoulders at her sunburned back. Between the top of her thighs and the lower part of her breasts her flesh was as white as lard.

'Ralph, I'm not peeling, am I? Don't tell me I'm peeling. I am itching all down my spine.'

He came across the room and peered at her, as if he were making up his mind about a joint of meat, not looking at a woman, his wife. The red skin across her shoulders was puckered and creased from the crushed-up nightgown.

'Looks a bit angry,' he said. 'I should give your back a rest today.'

But she could not bear to waste a whole day – and what else was there to do?

Going into the bathroom, she said, 'And the way she drags him off to those mosques. And all that shopping, and going into those smelly *souks*.'

It was another world that these Europeans briefly made – nothing to do with the country they were in, and little to do with the one from which they had come. Everything was centred on the sun cult and its rituals – the oiling, the turning, the rules for exposure and non-exposure, the setbacks – particularly blisters – the whole absorbing process.

They were mostly middle-aged married people who lolled about the swimming-pool all day. The young French girls – the bikini brigade, as Leslie Crouch called them – went to the shore and lay on the sands where a group of straw umbrellas was planted above tide level.

Deirdre was rather relieved when Bunny decided to swim in the sea for a change. There he would have to wade out and she would be spared the anxiety of the dive in.

She went with him, taking her book. She would not bathe herself. The last time she had put on a swimsuit, she had felt absurd, too thin – not the kind of thinness of the young bikini girls, but a wide flatness which looked ridiculous or pathetic; her skin, which never tanned, looked almost mauve. She suffered, deprived of her floating stoles, her floppy hats.

On their way, they passed Mr and Mrs Troughton. She was oiling his back, finishing with an affectionate little pat. Then, sternly turbaned and wearing her sunglasses, she opened a book and began to read to him. She had pulled down the straps of her sunsuit and all that showed of her large bosom was reddish brown. The morning air smelt heavily of sun-tan oil.

'A very large lobster,' Deirdre whispered to Bunny when they had passed by. 'She only needs a dollop of mayonnaise.'

They made their way through some dusty oleanders, across the shore road and on to the beach. When they had taken off their sandals, their feet sank deeply into the sharp, hot sand. They plodded slowly through it down towards the water's edge.

Bunny's forehead was peeling, so he wore a little white jockey cap with a long peak. As he strutted, very upright, arms swinging, on the hard ribbed sand they had come to, he resembled some kind of bird. Deirdre thought Mrs Troughton had looked amused as they passed by, but it was difficult to be sure. Sunglasses take so much expression from the face.

'People come out here,' said Deirdre, glaring at the bodies about her, 'and bake themselves all day, only glad if they can go back home the colour that they punish other people for being.'

'So true,' said Bunny.

Without discussing where they should sit, they moved apart from the others and spread towels out on the sand. Bunny removed his hat and shirt, and went trotting down to the sea, his crooked arms jerking back and forth like a long-distance runner's.

Languid, shallow waves came in, gathering little crests of foam, spilling over and fanning out on the sands. After quite a long time, Deirdre could still see Bunny wading out, not even knee-deep in the water.

Quite close to where Deirdre sat guarding his towel and shirt, two young girls came and flopped down on the sand. They were smoothly brown, slim-waisted. One had a pale appendectomy scar showing above the little triangle of bikini. She rolled her almost bare, oiled body over to switch on her transistor-set and a French song blared out.

Not entirely because of this, Deirdre gathered up her things and moved away into the shade beneath an umbrella. She sat there primly, reading; sometimes glancing at the sea, her shiny, white legs tucked under her flowered skirt. When she saw Bunny coming out of the water, she stood up and waved to him. He altered his course and came towards the umbrella.

'Some shade,' she explained, handing him his towel. 'And that awful transistor-set. They oughtn't to be allowed.'

He patted his wet, sunburned face with the towel, glanced towards the two girls, and then quickly back at Deirdre. 'You look very pretty sitting under this umbrella,' he said. 'I wish I had brought the camera.'

On Friday it was their last evening. The Crouches and the Troughtons were leaving too, and seemed to be in an especially festive mood. Trying to make less of their jollity, Deirdre worked hard at her now. She was animated, smiling at Bunny and raising her wine-glass to her lips, as if at some deep and secret understanding between them. She gave her dazzled attention to every word he said – as if his fascination for her was endless.

'What can she see in him?' Mrs Crouch asked her husband, exasperated by curiosity.

'Or *he* in *her?*'

'No, but I mean, to keep it up like this? She must be very new to the game. Don't tell me any woman can find her husband as enthralling as that all the time. Or any man his wife, for that matter. Well, the novelty has to wear off.'

'I can't see why she has to try so hard. Don't look now. She just tapped him on the hand as if he'd said something *risqué*. Naughty, naughty.'

'Perhaps she has to try so hard because they're not married. She may be in a very insecure position. He may have a real wife somewhere.'

'We shall never know.'

'Well, they've kept themselves to themselves so much,' Mrs Crouch complained, taking her husband's arm.

'*She's* kept *him* to *herself.*'

When they had had coffee in the courtyard, Deirdre went upstairs to tidy her hair. The hotel lounge was being arranged for dancing, the chairs pushed back and the rugs rolled up.

She did her hair, put on an extra necklace, then went out on to the balcony, feeling suddenly limp, headachy. The dance band had begun to play. From below, she could hear the rhythmic beat which depressed her and made her feel nervy.

She wished that the evening was over, or that they might go away from the hotel on another drive in a *calèche* – just quiet – and she and Bunny on their own; but she had not liked to suggest it.

At last, she went downstairs, and rather self-consciously made her way to the lounge. Bunny was dancing with the American's Moroccan bride, who was again wearing the lime-green shift. He looked miserable and embarrassed when he saw Deirdre hesitating by the door, seemed to be trying to send a message to her, as if to say, with his anxious expression, 'Wait, I shall come to you as soon as ever I can'.

But she did not wait. She turned and went out into the deserted courtyard and sat down, shivering beside the fountain. Bunny found her there, nursing the little grey cat, for warmth, and consolation.

'Did you *see* her face?' Mrs Crouch asked her husband, as they reversed nattily out of the way of the large bulldozing Troughtons. 'He's obviously not allowed to dance with other women.'

'Certainly not with the second most beautiful woman in the room,' said Mr Crouch, gazing down at Brenda's faded hair . . .

'I couldn't avoid it,' said Bunny.

'Avoid what?' asked Deirdre faintly.

'He came up to me in the bar and insisted on buying me a drink. She was with him. We stood chatting. They are on their honeymoon. Then the band struck up. He said he didn't dance.'

The fountain dribbled. A nightingale was singing. She lifted the cat and kissed its fur.

'It was the least I could do,' he went on. He could not say how grateful he had been for someone else to have spoken to him at last.

'Will you come and dance with me?' he asked.

'I'd rather not.'

'To please me,' he implored.

Carefully she put the cat down, brushed her lap and went before him to the lounge.

Bunny was quite deft at all the old-fashioned dances. Deirdre was taken into his arms as if into a stranger's embrace. She had no sense of rhythm. Stiffly she shuffled, stumbled, blushed. He smiled gallantly and held her tighter, guiding her as adroitly as he could.

To make up for everything, she smiled. She smiled until her cheeks ached. Then she whispered, 'After this, can we go for a walk?'

On the next day, on Saturday, the new, pale intake from the north began to arrive. The porter kept bringing down luggage for departing guests and piling it up in the hall – suitcases, and other loot such as camel saddles, rolled-up rugs and brass trays.

The Crouches and Troughtons came in from their last sunbathe, and there were the Wallaces in the hall, ready to depart. At this moment, the American came leaping up the steps with an armful of lilies, and just as Deirdre was going through the hall door he put them into her arms and said, with the most beautiful smile, 'In homage!'

Mrs Troughton took off her sunglasses and stared at him.

He had gone down the steps and opened the car door for her, and Bunny wrote something on a piece of paper and handed it through the window.

'In *homage!*' Mrs Crouch repeated unbelievingly.

None of them had talked to the American before. His honeymoon state seemed to have insulated him; but when he came back into the hotel, Mrs Crouch could not contain herself. 'Everyone departing,' she said dramatically, throwing wide her arms. 'After lunch, we're off ourselves.'

'I hope you have a good trip,' he said politely. He was still holding the piece of paper in his hand.

'Kind regards, Gerald Wallace, Morocco '64,' Mrs Troughton, a little behind him, read.

'For my young brother,' he said, waving the paper. 'Sure he'll be thrilled. I nerved myself last night and introduced myself. Maybe he gets tired of that, but he was pleasant all right, very pleasant.'

'Gerald Wallace,' Mrs Crouch said faintly. 'But how did you know?'

'Well, there's the face in the photographs, and the name.'

'*Gerald Wallace?*' Mrs Troughton said, when the American had left them. 'Well, really! That Bunny business put us off the scent. To think that Ralph's been reading his book all the holiday – carrying it around, anyway! Where is it, my love?' She took the paperback and looked at the photograph on the cover.

'That must have been taken at least fifteen years ago. All that hair! Well, who would have thought it. How can that man have recognised him?'

'Well, he did,' said Mrs Crouch rather snappily. This was the nearest she had ever been to a celebrity, and she had let him slip through her fingers . . .

At lunch – since it could not now create a precedent – the Crouches were invited to join the Troughtons at their table.

They could talk of nothing else. 'I wish I'd asked for his autograph,' said Mrs Crouch, the most incredulous of them all. 'Oh, the girls would have been fascinated, intrigued. Of course, Janice has got Sir Malcolm Sargent, you know. I could kick myself.'

'It's awfully odd, really,' said Mrs Troughton. 'Such a mild, henpecked little man, writing all those exotic stories.'

'How does he get off the chain to find out about the underworld – all that violence?' asked Ralph Troughton.

'To think it's the last meal,' said his wife, gazing out of the window at the familiar scene, so soon to be a thing of the past.

'All those spies and loose women, Buenos Aires and those sorts of places. Casablanca, Monte Carlo.'

'We didn't get to Casablanca after all, Ralph,' said Mrs Troughton.

'International harlots,' said Mrs Crouch, flushing with excitement.

'The last dates,' said her husband, taking a few.

'Well, we have tripped up,' his wife said, in a more resigned voice. Then, as if suddenly she couldn't get home fast enough, she put down her napkin and asked, 'Have we time for coffee?'

She was back in Guildford in her mind, all the tiresome travelling suddenly over, and she was saying to the girls, and her daily help, and her friends at the bridge club, 'Now you'll never guess who we met on holiday. Staying in the hotel.' They would never guess, and when they were told, they would crowd in with questions that she would be able to answer.

'Now you've got our address,' she said to the Troughtons. 'And we shall never forgive you if you don't drop in any time you're in Guildford.'

Mrs Troughton let it go. Dreamily, she peeled an orange – knew that she was unlikely to be in Guildford, whereas everybody was in London at some time or another – especially in the part in which she and Ralph had their flat.

The Crouches went upstairs to finish packing, and Mrs Troughton smiled at her husband as if to say, 'What odd people! But it's over now.' They would certainly go out to see them off in the car, before they got ready to leave themselves; but really the Crouches had already changed into shades – like the Tillotsons in Majorca and those people whose name they had forgotten in Corfu.

Guildford was gloomy, an anticlimax. The sun-lounge was dark and the large windows streaming with rain. The girls were glad to see their parents, and they listened dutifully – even appreciatively – to the holiday stories. A most united family.

The very next morning, after their homecoming, Mrs Crouch went out to the public library to look up Gerald Wallace in *Who's Who*: WALLACE, Gerald, *author*; *b.* 3 July 1912. Looked older, thought Mrs Crouch. What a long list of books! European War – despatches three times. Who would have thought it? We were as wrong as could be, Mrs Crouch decided, peering at the rather small print, her finger underlining it. So very wrong. It was twenty-seven years ago that he had married Deirdre Imogen Burnett – his one and only wife.

Mrs Crouch left the library, put up her umbrella and picked her way through the streets to the coffee-shop.

'Goodness, how brown you are!' her friends said enviously, who were waiting for her among the horse-brasses and copper warming-pans.

'Did you have a marvellous time?' they asked.

She sat down and drew off her gloves, smiling as if to herself; then she raised her head and looked round the table at her friends' pale faces and, 'Guess,' she began, 'guess who ... '

Vron and Willie

Here was London – Willie, Vron and Aunt in the station hotel restaurant. Aunt had brought them from the country, to settle them in their new homes; but before taking them – Vron to the hostel, Willie to lodgings – she had stopped at one or two discreet-looking bars and, finally, at a shabby corner public house – discretion, by then, having ceased to count for anything.

Vron and Willie loved her in a vague way, rather as they had after a fashion still loved their animal pets when the novelty of them had worn off: but it was from a sense of responsibility that they had come back to the station with her, to see her safely on to the train. It was, after all, because of them that she had taken to drink, although they had always suspected that she must in the first place have been a little that way inclined.

It was early evening and the restaurant, luckily, was almost empty. A pale light fell on the white table-cloth and the silvery dish-covers the waitress lifted off their in-between-meals food – poached eggs on toast, with baked beans under the eggs for Willie and sardines (the waitress had looked aghast) for Vron.

They watched Aunt put her knife uncertainly into her egg; and, as the yolk ran out, she seemed to recoil. Nevertheless, they intended her to eat something. Having stowed her in the train, with food in her, they could feel at peace, and forget her. At the other end, the village taxi-driver would meet her, and he knew her habits. They might call at the Bell on their way home. Safely there – the Bell *or* home – she was in her own country. There were people to lift a finger.

'But will you ever find your way back?' she now asked *them*, and for the fifth or sixth time. 'Keep seeing one another to and fro could go on all night.'

'I *dote* on sardines,' said Vron. 'I feel I could never have enough of them. Even when they make me sick, the minute after, I'm ready for them again. What could *you* never have enough of, Willie? Aunt?'

Well, the latter of course she knew, and Willie never answered such questions, which seemed to him like talking for the sake of talking.

'I do hope you'll both be all right,' Aunt said. She carefully lifted her fork to her mouth, and runny yolk dropped through the prongs on to her blouse. Vron inexpertly dabbed at her.

'I shall miss them,' Aunt thought. (In fits and starts, but such very terrible fits and starts.) The angelic siblings, who had never quarrelled, whose rare gravity, even, was amiable. They had the charmed relationship she and their mother had had until the hour of her death. That was a grief, a lack, which did not come and go in fits and starts; but remained, like a long, tired yawn, in the depth of her heart.

She glanced mistily at the two – Vron and Willie – the fluorescent light falling on their silky, beige hair, their pale, composed faces. Vron ate her disgusting mixture with style – as she did everything – appreciatively, but without absorption. Then Aunt put her knife and fork together, defeated. She longed to be home. She sat quite still, with bent head, attempting to assemble facts; but it was like trying to catch goldfish with her hand – the facts slithered from her grasp. She was at the end of her tether, not daring to ask questions, lest she had asked them before, and before that, and had perhaps all day done nothing else but ask. However, no clue from her muddled mind coming to aid her, she said suddenly, in an off-hand voice, barely saying it, looking at the same time into her handbag, 'Let me see, I *did* give you your money, didn't I? You're all *right?*'

'Yes, Aunt,' they said, not glancing at one another – their manners towards her too good for that.

Willie paid the waitress, and Vron put Aunt's arms back into her coat-sleeves; then, one on each side of her, they made their way to the platform. The train was in, and they found an empty, first-class compartment.

'Don't wait, darlings,' she said, leaning out of the window. They looked so pale and slight, standing there together, looking up at her. Could she be doing the right thing, she wondered; leaving them in London, so young, only just left school? Today, London had seemed like a jungle to her, with noisy, discordant public houses, terrifying traffic, jostling throngs. Other hazards of London, not being in her experience, she did not envisage for them.

But of course her decision was right, she told herself firmly. To go to London had been just what she and her sister had so badly wanted to do – and had not been allowed.

She closed her eyes for a moment, feeling exhausted. She had done her best. She had brought them up, almost from babyhood, the poor little orphans; and *she* had done so, who was quite out of her depth in such a situation, with such responsibilities. Now she could be proud of them – of their goodness and charm.

But there was one more thing to be settled – surely? At the back of her mind, a certain question shifted about. Matters were getting worse; now that she could not even remember what the question was. She leant forward out of the window.

'Darlings, I forget ... did I ... ?'

'Yes, Aunt, you did,' they said together.

'"Darling Aunt,

The hostel was so frightful, that I have moved to a room at Miss Bassage's, next to Willie's. I know that you will think this the best thing to do; for you could not have borne it yourself where I was. I was so homesick; it was a thousand times worse than school. Those awful girls drink hot chocolate all the time, and I got spots on my face, trying to join in. They wash one another's hair, and talk about sex until I was sick at heart."'

'That's good,' Willie said, interrupting Vron's reading of the letter. 'We know our aunt.'

She had never married; but she rather resented sex than feared it. It was what had stolen her sister from her.

'Very good about the chocolate, too,' Willie added. Neither he nor Vron had ever had spots. For their transparent and unblemished skin, they were, Aunt said, indebted to their mother. Their father, it seemed, had been rubicund.

'It was true, all that,' Vron said rapidly, then read on. '"Simply, it wasn't what I have been brought up to. Don't for a moment blame yourself, Aunt dear. No one could have guessed, unless there, what went on behind the façade." I shall leave about leaving the other place until next week,' she said, looking across at Willie.

The other place was the secretarial school where – so soon, Aunt would learn – the girls did not only *talk* about sex.

'Give it a fair chance,' Willie said slyly, agreeing.

None of their schools had been good enough for these angels, as Aunt had so very often said, when trouble after trouble had mounted up. *She* knew what they were like, and who could know better? She was misunderstood herself. They formed a little misunderstood family, and had been almost entirely happy.

Willie, applauding his sister's way of cutting loose from her tedious commitments, could find, for the present, no way of severing himself from his own. Daily – almost daily – he went on the Underground to work in a land agent's office in Knightsbridge. One of the partners of the firm was related to Aunt. Willie was vague as to the exact relationship; had not listened when it was explained to him. He hoped it was not too close as to cause unpleasantness when at last, as he must, he found he could bear no more.

'He's like an old bull,' he told Vron. 'His face the colour of this.' They were drinking *cappuccinos* in a coffee-bar, and he stared into his cup with disgust, as if at Mr Waterhouse's creased old face. 'Straggly moustache; hunched-up shoulders,' he went on.

Luckily, Mr Waterhouse did not come often to the office. It was the only thing in his favour.

On the day of this conversation, Willie had been so tempted by the prospect of the sort of day Vron was going to have – doing hardly anything, that is, and nothing she did not want to do – that he could not bring himself to set out for the office. He felt snuffles coming in his head. It was not that he ever found it necessary to lie to himself; but he had been interested to discover that, by a steady concentration, almost self-hypnotism, he could produce symptoms, could make himself sneeze, even raise his temperature, certainly increase his pulse.

Miss Bassage – to whom he first rehearsed – had said it would be folly to go out at all on such a drizzly morning; but at twelve o'clock he and Vron set forth.

London enchanted them – even on such a dreary day as this, with the windows of the Scherzo coffee-bar steamed over, and umbrellas going by in the street. They sat at a corner table, backed by a blown-up print of the Grand Canal at Venice. The ceiling was hung with strings of onions, Chianti bottles, and bunches of plastic grapes. Every now and then, the coffee-machine gave out a dreadful gasp, like a giant's death-rattle.

Although rather impeded by financial worries, Vron and Willie were very happy this noon-day. Aunt's money was harder to come by at their new distance from it. No letters from them to her had yet been answered. Their allowances arrived – the sum judged suitable by Aunt's old solicitor – but the past, of having what they wanted, had not fitted them for cheese-paring, or putting sums aside. In London, surrounded by so many new needs that they had hardly before pictured (such as coffee-bars, cinemas, record-shops), their condition could have been vexatious but for their sunny dispositions.

'This is the life,' said Willie, and put his lips to the creamy froth of his coffee.

Beautiful, glossy Danish buns were put on the next table, and he turned his head away quickly from the sight. He could too well imagine biting into the flaky, soft texture of them, tasting the thin sugary icing, smelling the spice. His imagination was like some extra, unfair pain he had to bear – one of the few things that separated him from Vron, who seemed free of it. 'Very nice,' she had said, as they had stood looking into a shop window earlier that morning. When she turned away, he had turned away, too; but reluctantly, and with pictures still in his head – they would remain – of what he would look like in the striped *matelot*'s sweater – bands of dark blue and white – cut high and straight across at the neck. It would make a different person of him for two pounds ten.

Used only to school tuck-shops and the village post office, London was too much for them. Some sort of saliva of the spirit flowed continually, excruciatingly. At every turn was something saying mutely, Behold! There were beckoning fingers, luring suggestions, and no Aunt, any longer, to provide.

Vron, more philosophical, less sensitive, was able to watch – though with detestation – the woman at the next table helping herself to another bun, biting daintily at it, dabbing her lips with her paper napkin, into which she then screwed her sticky fingers.

'I might go and work there,' Vron said presently. While Willie's eyes had been fixed on the *matelot* sweater, hers had strayed to the notice in the corner of the window, advertising for what was termed a 'saleslady'.

There was something from her childhood which gave glamour to the idea of serving in a shop. She remembered the satisfaction of turning a garden seat into a counter and standing behind it to count acorns and put them in a paper bag, to hand them across the seat to Willie, taking leaves from him, and giving back smaller ones for change. The shopkeeper had a more positive role than the customer. To work in a big store must be the game on an exotic scale.

Willie had not noticed the advertisement and, as soon as she told him, his heart eased. Pounds, several pounds, perhaps many pounds (he really had no idea), would be added to their pittance.

'Let's go straight away,' he said. He pushed aside his empty cup, edged round the table and went to the cash desk. Vron tilted her head back, sucking the last of the froth from her cup, and wiping her hand across her mouth, followed him out into the street.

'I simply took it. It was perfectly easy,' said Vron. 'It was there. *You* wanted it. I took it.' Impatience, posing as patience, gave precision to her words.

'But it was hanging up in the window.'

'It was *displayed* in the window,' she corrected him. 'Not this one, though. Inside there were dozens. Different colours, too. But I thought you would prefer the blue.'

'Oh, yes,' he said quickly, blinking his eyes at the thought of anything but this colour. 'I only like the blue.' Having said this, he had accepted the situation, accepted the sweater. He began to tear off his shirt excitedly.

They were in his room, where the gas-ring was, and Vron emptied a tin of baked beans into a saucepan and began to heat them.

The two rooms they had on the second floor were at the end of a dark

passage. (Also use of bathroom, one flight down; and, by special arrangement, kitchen on ground floor.) They had never made any especial
arrangements, preferring to keep out of Miss Bassage's way. ('Pack', they
had nicknamed her, between themselves.) They saw her only by chance,
as they went through the hall, on their way in or out. They kept their
own rooms tidy – or otherwise, according to their whim – and ate in
hamburger bars, or else, as on this evening, opened a tin of something at
home.

Once upon a time they had been more ambitious about food, and Miss
Bassage, meeting them as they came home from the market – Vron with
an armful of leeks to make soup – had cried out in horror, 'Do my eyes
deceive me? You surely aren't going to *cook* those? You'll smell the whole
house out.'

They had watched with fascination the bead of mucus wavering on the
end of her nose, trembling more and more, as her indignation rose.

'Isn't she scrawny?' Willie said, as they reached their own landing. He
had to hold his stomach for a while, so pained was he by kept-back
laughter.

It was true that they had certainly stunk the house out with the leeks,
which boiled and boiled in the only saucepan, but never turned themselves
into soup.

Thinking of this failure, Vron stirred the safe and easy beans, her smooth
hair hanging down round her pale face. She yawned, as she crouched there
by the gas-ring, so tired, most awfully tired. All day long, she was at everybody's beck and call, running errands, taking messages. Not once had she
been allowed to sell anything and, as soon as one o'clock on Saturday came,
she was going to take her wages, and a pair of doe-skin gloves she had her
eye on for a present to Aunt, and then Price & Trounsell would never see
her again.

'It's so quiet,' Willie complained, pacing about the room as she heated
the beans. It was indeed quiet in this faded cul-de-sac, much quieter than
the country. There were no animal noises, for a start. This was a respectable
district. Aunt's solicitor's friend's nephew had once lodged here as a student
of something or other, and Miss Bassage had been like a guardian angel to
him, had even taken him to the Chapel social, and to an amateur performance of The Pirates of Penzance.

Willie looked out of the window at all the railings and steps, the high,
narrow houses, some with old, dusty ivy on the walls, and all of yellowish-
grey bricks. It was not the kind of London in whose glittering swirl they
were elsewhere caught up.

'We ought to have one of those little transistor-sets,' he said, turning
to Vron. She looked up from the saucepan, shaking her hair away from her

face. Their eyes rested on one another's for a moment; but not a word was said.

Aunt was delighted with the doe-skin gloves – in fact, so gladdened that she wept. Although they were several sizes too small, she carried them to the pub and showed them to people; and continued to, one evening after another, always forgetting she had done so before. She passed them round to be admired. Sometimes, she left them behind, and had them back next day. Although winks were exchanged, her gloves were treated with reverence, with murmurs tinged with simulated envy. And they grew soiled from constant handling.

'Such an unerring instinct,' Aunt would say. 'That comes from *our* side. We have always had this feeling for quality. Their mother was just like the Princess with a pea in her bed.'

Her cronies had never known her to be coarse before, and they always waited for this pronouncement with an especial, wicked glee.

Aunt's life was now a contented one. She believed that she had faced her duties fairly and squarely, and at last was justly freed from them. She had reared her sister's paragons, and brought them to perfection. She took credit for their grace, their good manners, their clear complexions. (Hadn't there been something quite lately about Vron drinking hot chocolate – so ruinous to the skin? But she, her aunt, had very properly put a stop to it.)

Puzzling letters had recently come about Vron, from the hostel and the secretarial school, written on a note of uncalled-for tartness, and almost as if in reply to letters from herself to them.

But the catspaw they occasioned soon was smoothed. The young ones' footwork had been put in. That remedy they had made habitual Aunt turned to as a matter of course. She had thrown the letters on the fire and made for the sideboard. Standing there, she poured out brandy into a large glass and drank quickly, her hand still on the uncorked bottle, and very soon it seemed that the letters were a long-ago matter, which she had dealt with and settled satisfactorily.

It was like an illumination to Vron – the idea that having left Price & Trounsell's did not cut her off entirely from the pleasures of shop-lifting. Obviously, there were other shops. She realised that all of London lay at hand, glittering with treasures. Her grace and deftness, her small alert body, her way of weaving herself unerringly through a crowd, made the pursuit seem almost pre-ordained. She had a vocation for it, she felt; and it was not long before Willie heard his own call.

At first, they took only what seemed to them necessities – a tin of baked beans from the back of the display, because they were hungry; or the little transistor-set (under the folded raincoat on Willie's arm), because number seven Enniskillen Grove was too quiet for their liking. But soon, these children of the Princess who had the pea under the mattresses developed an exquisite taste in shop-lifting. They chose the softest cashmere sweaters in beautiful shades of slate blue and apricot; silk shirts; little pots of Beluga caviare. They had not eaten caviare before, but a nice instinct led Vron's hand to the Beluga. 'It opens up a new kingdom,' said Willie, spooning it from the jar.

'Shall we try *pâté de foie gras* tomorrow?' Vron suggested.

'No, it's frightfully cruel,' he said, looking shocked.

They sampled a very small bottle of cherry brandy, taking it from a tablespoon like medicine; pulling faces. They were rather prim and disapproving where alcohol was concerned. It seemed to them that it was the clever ones who did not drink, and it was quite clear to them that those who did so were exploited. In the old days, they had only to pour more and more brandy into Aunt's glass, topping it up constantly, to get practically anything they wanted. She usually gave in. If she did not, they pretended that she had, and she would easily be convinced. 'But, Aunt, don't you remember promising last night?' In shame, she would quickly agree that it had been so; had for a moment slipped her memory.

Muzzy, and just where they wanted her, she deteriorated. They flourished. And the lessons they most needed and respected were those they had taught themselves.

'I shall speak to Charlie Garter,' Miss Bassage said, in her angry, wobbly voice, standing with her fists on her hips, blocking their way to the stairs.

'Who he?' asked Willie insolently, bending to tie his shoe-lace just to his liking, as if the last thing in the world he wanted to do was to go upstairs.

'Police Constable Garter to you,' Miss Bassage said.

Vron noted tears of anger in her eyes. Of *anger!* she thought. Such an unusual manifestation. *She* knew who PC Garter was. She took more interest in people than did Willie. She had seen the constable going up Enniskillen Grove, padding along with his slow pace. She had recognised him at once when she met him coming out of Miss Bassage's kitchen to the hall where she, Vron, stood with a little tray of *petits fours* she had just pinched scattered on the floor.

'Allow me,' said PC Garter stopping. He looked quite different, she thought, holding his helmet in one hand, snatching up thieved *petits fours* with the other; really looked so unfamiliar, bare-headed. She felt quite shy of him in this informal situation, as if she had caught him off his guard.

He had just been having a cup of tea with Miss Bassage, she guessed.

They went to the same Wesleyan Chapel. Miss Bassage had stood watching him, with the look which should be accompanied by purring.

She was not purring now.

'I shall write to your aunt,' she went on.

Willie was still arranging his shoe-laces. ('Oh, they *rile* me,' she would tell PC Garter later on. 'They just *rile* me.')

'Do my ears deceive me?' Vron asked, unwinding a marabou stole from her neck. 'Oh, dear! That dewdrop!' she thought.

'A little common consideration. You're not the only people in the world, nor in this house, either.'

Someone in a room below had complained of the noise; for Vron and Willie would come back from their forays in the early evening, dump the loot, turn up the wireless very loud, and dance. They danced non-stop, as gay as birds in April.

Really, Vron thought, her feet were itching already, while she stood there whirling the marabou stole in circles.

'Or go – *you* – *will*,' Miss Bassage ended, stepping across the hall at last, slamming the kitchen door. She had threatened PC Garter, their aunt, and expulsion. She could think of nothing else, and what she *had* thought of would surely be enough.

With hands over their mouths, Vron and Willie bolted upstairs, flung themselves into the room, laughing convulsively.

'It's "akimbo", isn't it, like this?' Willie asked, imitating Miss Bassage.

They collapsed into chairs, writhing with laughter, and Vron stuffed her stole into her mouth, then wiped her eyes with it.

But they were too hungry to go on laughing for long. Vron fetched the bread-knife, and cut a couple of lobsters in half. While they ate them, they felt at peace; they enjoyed the contentment of those who have discovered their real way of life; the deepest satisfaction.

'What *else* do we want?' Vron asked, looking round the crowded room.

'Those portable record-players are rather neat,' said Willie, putting a lobster claw on the floor, and stamping on it. 'Not too big, either.'

'And to think of all the records we could get,' said Vron. 'And dead easy, too.'

After supper, they switched on the transistor-set and danced, obliged to make up a kind of very slow twist to the last movement of Brahms' Symphony Number One.

'You see what I mean about the record-player?' said Vron. 'This is hopeless.'

They danced on, however, and with vigour, not hearing someone banging furiously on the ceiling below.

*

'So light, you could eat it with your teeth out,' said PC Garter, praising Miss Bassage's Victoria sponge.

'Oh, I fancied it wasn't quite up to the usual,' she said, flushing with pleasure.

At this moment, Vron and Willie were going upstairs, with the record-player in a large rush basket, hidden under packets of popcorn. Soon all hell was let loose. The tenant in the room below banged at his ceiling until he was breathless with exertion and anger. Then he descended the stairs and knocked on Miss Bassage's kitchen door.

'Well, *this* is final,' she said grimly. 'This has done it. They'll have to go. I wrote to their aunt, but not a word from her. I've *warned* them enough.'

Her eyes strayed to PC Garter, sitting there so happily, drinking tea, his helmet on the horsehair sofa behind him. She hesitated. 'A word from you,' she suggested. 'With the authority of the law behind it.' For, indeed, how *could* she turn them out into the street, at their age, having had Willie, at least, practically put into her care?

'Quite unofficial, of course,' she added.

PC Garter rose and took up his helmet. As he and Miss Bassage climbed the two flights of stairs, the clamour from above grew louder, beat down on them. Miss Bassage put her hands over her ears.

The dancing stopped as he flung open the door. Vron and Willie froze like statues. Their faces were pink, making their green eyes look greener; their hair was tangled.

The record came to an end; and in the sudden silence, PC Garter said, '*Well*, now,' and took a slow stride or two forward, crunching on popcorn which was scattered over the floor. Neither Vron nor Willie moved. Miss Bassage's eyes, astonished, flew about the room. PC Garter's, more calculating and interested, travelled slowly, at loot piled on loot; chairs, bed, cupboard and chest tops heaped with plunder.

'Well, well, *well*,' he said, taking a turn about the room, picking up a large pot of caviare and reading the label aloud. 'Well, well, well,' he said again. All the time, he was watched by the statues, followed by the thoughtful-looking bright green eyes, in the now pale faces.

When Aunt was asked questions about the children – often by malicious, winking people who already knew the answer – she would think for a little, trying to gather what was left of her ravelled wits, and say at last, 'They are continuing their education.' And this was true.

The Devastating Boys

Laura was always too early; and this was as bad as being late, her husband, who was always late himself, told her. She sat in her car in the empty railway station approach, feeling very sick, from dread.

It was half-past eleven on a summer morning. The country station was almost spellbound in silence, and there was, to Laura, a dreadful sense of self-absorption – in herself – in the stillness of the only porter standing on the platform, staring down the line: even – perhaps especially – in inanimate things; all were menacingly intent on being themselves, and separately themselves – the slanting shadow of railings across the platform, the glossiness of leaves, and the closed door of the office looking more closed, she thought, than any door she had ever seen.

She got out of the car and went into the station walking up and down the platform in a panic. It was a beautiful morning. If only the children weren't coming then she could have enjoyed it.

The children were coming from London. It was Harold's idea to have them, some time back, in March, when he read of a scheme to give London children a summer holiday in the country. This he might have read without interest, but the words 'Some of the children will be coloured' caught his eye. He seemed to find a slight tinge of warning in the phrase; the more he thought it over, the more he was convinced. He had made a long speech to Laura about children being the great equalisers, and that we should learn from them, that to insinuate the stale prejudices of their elders into their fresh, fair minds was such a sin that he could not think of a worse one.

He knew very little about children. His students had passed beyond the blessed age, and shades of the prison-house had closed about them. His own children were even older, grown-up and gone away; but, while they were young, they had done nothing to destroy his faith in them, or blur the idea of them he had in his mind, and his feeling of humility in their presence. They had been good children carefully dealt with and easy to handle. There had scarcely been a cloud over their growing-up. Any little bothers Laura had hidden from him.

In March, the end of July was a long way away. Laura, who was lonely

in middle-age, seemed to herself to be frittering away her days, just waiting for her grandchildren to be born: she had agreed with Harold's
suggestion. She would have agreed anyway, whatever it was, as it was her
nature – and his – for her to do so. It would be rather exciting to have two
children to stay – to have the beds in Imogen's and Lalage's room slept in
again. 'We could have two boys, or two girls,' Harold said. 'No stipulation,
but that they must be coloured.'

Now *he* was making differences, but Laura did not remark upon it. All
she said was, 'What will they do all the time?'

'What our own children used to do – play in the garden, go for
picnics ... '

'On wet days?'

'Dress up,' he said at once.

She remembered Imogen and Lalage in her old hats and dresses, slopping about in her big shoes, see-sawing on high heels, and she had to turn
her head away, and there were tears in her eyes.

Her children had been her life, and her grandchildren one day would be;
but here was an empty space. Life had fallen away from her. She had never
been clever like the other professors' wives, or managed to have what they
called 'outside interests'. Committees frightened her, and good works made
her feel embarrassed and clumsy.

She *was* a clumsy person – gentle, but clumsy. Pacing up and down the
platform, she had an ungainly walk – legs stiffly apart, head a little poked
forward because she had poor sight. She was short and squarely-built and
her clothes were never right; often she looked dishevelled, sometimes even
battered.

This morning, she wore a label pinned to her breast, so that the children's escort would recognise her when the train drew in; but she felt
self-conscious about it and covered it with her hand, though there was no
one but the porter to see.

The signal dropped, as if a guillotine had come crashing down, and her
heart seemed to crash down with it. 'Two boys!' she thought. Somehow, she
had imagined girls. She was used to girls, and shy of boys.

The printed form had come a day or two ago and had increased the
panic which had gradually been gathering. Six-year-old boys, and she had
pictured perhaps eight- or ten-year-old girls, whom she could teach to sew
and make cakes for tea, and press wild flowers as she had taught Imogen
and Lalage to do.

Flurried and anxious entertaining at home; interviewing headmistresses;
once – shied away from failure – opening a sale-of-work in the village –
these agonies to her diffident nature seemed nothing to the nervousness
she felt now, as the train appeared round the bend. She simply wasn't good

with children – only with her own. *Their* friends had frightened her, had
been mouse-quiet and glum, or had got out of hand, and she herself had
been too shy either to intrude or clamp down. When she met children –
perhaps the small grandchildren of her acquaintances, she would only
smile, perhaps awkwardly touch a cheek with her finger. If she were asked
to hold a baby, she was fearful lest it should cry, and often it would, sensing lack of assurance in her clasp.

The train came in and slowed up. 'Suppose that I can't find them,' she
thought, and she went anxiously from window to window, her label uncov-
ered now. 'And suppose they cry for their mothers and want to go home.'

A tall, authoritative woman, also wearing a label, leant out of a window,
saw her and signalled curtly. She had a compartment full of little children
in her charge to be delivered about Oxfordshire. Only two got out on to
this platform, Laura's two, Septimus Smith and Benny Reece. They wore
tickets, too, with their names printed on them.

Benny was much lighter in complexion than Septimus. He was obviously a half-caste and Laura hoped that this would count in Harold's eyes.
It might even be one point up. They stood on the platform, looking about
them, holding their little cardboard cases.

'My name is Laura,' she said. She stooped and clasped them to her in
terror, and kissed their cheeks. Sep's in particular was extraordinarily soft,
like the petal of a poppy. His big eyes stared up at her, without expression.
He wore a dark, long-trousered suit, so that he was all over sombre and
unchildlike. Benny had a mock-suède coat with a nylon-fur collar and a
trilby hat with a feather. They did not speak. Not only was she, Laura,
strange to them, but they were strange to one another. There had only
been a short train-journey in which to sum up their chances of becoming
friends.

She put them both into the back of the car, so that there should be no
favouritism, and drove off, pointing out – to utter silence – places on the
way. 'That's a café where we'll go for tea one day.' The silence was dreadful. 'A caff,' she amended. 'And there's the little cinema. Not very grand,
I'm afraid. Not like London ones.'

They did not even glance about them.

'Are you going to be good friends to one another?' she asked.

After a pause, Sep said in a slow grave voice, 'Yeah, I'm going to be a
good friend.'

'Is this the country?' Benny asked. He had a chirpy, perky Cockney voice
and accent.

'Yeah, this is the countryside,' said Sep, in his rolling drawl, glancing
indifferently at some trees.

Then he began to talk. It was in an aggrieved sing-song. 'I don't go on that train no more. I don't like that train, and I don't go on that again over my dead body. Some boy he say to me, "You don't sit in that corner seat. I sit there." I say, "You don't sit here. I sit here." "Yeah," I say, "you don't own this train, so I don't budge from here." Then he dash my comic down and tore it.'

'Yep, he tore his comic,' Benny said.

'"You tear my comic, you buy me another comic," I said. "Or else. Or *else*," I said.' He suddenly broke off and looked at a wood they were passing. 'I don't go near those tall bushes. They full of snakes what sting you.'

'No, they ain't,' said Benny.

'My mam said so. I don't go.'

'There aren't any snakes,' said Laura, in a light voice. She, too, had a terror of them, and was afraid to walk through bracken. 'Or only little harmless ones,' she added.

'I don't go,' Sep murmured to himself. Then, in a louder voice, he went on. 'He said, "I don't buy no comic for you, you nigger," he said.'

'He never said that,' Benny protested.

'Yes, "You dirty nigger," he said.'

'He never.'

There was something so puzzled in Benny's voice that Laura immediately believed him. The expression on his little monkey-face was open and impartial.

'I don't go on that train no more.'

'You've got to. When you go home,' Benny said.

'Maybe I don't go home.'

'We'll think about that later. You've only just arrived,' said Laura, smiling.

'No, I think about that right now.'

Along the narrow lane to the house, they were held up by the cows from the farm. A boy drove them along, whacking their messed rumps with a stick. Cow-pats plopped on to the road and steamed there, zizzing with flies. Benny held his nose and Sep, glancing at him, at once did the same. 'I don't care for this smell of the countryside,' he complained in a pinched tone.

'No, the countryside stinks,' said Benny.

'Cows frighten me.'

'They don't frighten me.'

Sep cringed against the back of the seat, whimpering; but Benny wound his window right down, put his head a little out of it, and shouted, 'Get on, you dirty old sods, or else I'll show you.'

'Hush,' said Laura gently.

'He swore,' Sep pointed out.

They turned into Laura's gateway, up the short drive. In front of the house was a lawn and a cedar tree. From one of its lower branches hung the old swing, on chains, waiting for Laura's grandchildren.

The boys clambered out of the car and followed her into the hall, where they stood looking about them critically; then Benny dropped his case and shot like an arrow towards Harold's golf-bag and pulled out a club. His face was suddenly bright with excitement and Laura, darting forward to him, felt a stab of misery at having to begin the 'No's so soon. 'I'm afraid Harold wouldn't like you to touch them,' she said. Benny stared her out, but after a moment or two gave up the club with all the unwillingness in the world. Meanwhile, Sep had taken an antique coaching-horn and was blowing a bubbly, uneven blast on it, his eyes stretched wide and his cheeks blown out. 'Nor that,' said Laura faintly, taking it away. 'Let's go upstairs and unpack.'

They appeared not at all overawed by the size of this fairly large house; in fact, rather unimpressed by it.

In the room where once, as little girls, Imogen and Lalage had slept together, they opened their cases. Sep put his clothes neatly and carefully into his drawer; and Benny tipped the case into his – comics, clothes and shoes, and a scattering of peanuts. 'I'll tidy it later,' Laura thought.

'Shall we toss up for who sleeps by the window?' she suggested.

'I don't sleep by no window,' said Sep. 'I sleep in *this* bed; with *him*.'

'I want to sleep by myself,' said Benny.

Sep began a babyish whimpering, which increased into an anguished keening. 'I don't like to sleep in the bed by myself. I'm scared to. I'm real scared to. I'm scared.'

This was entirely theatrical, Laura decided, and Benny seemed to think so, too; for he took no notice.

'A fortnight!' Laura thought. This day alone stretched endlessly before her, and she dared not think of any following ones. Already she felt ineffectual and had an inkling that they were going to despise her. And her brightness was false and not infectious. She longed for Harold to come home, as she had never longed before.

'I reckon I go and clean my teeth,' said Sep, who had broken off his dirge.

'Lunch is ready. Afterwards would be more sensible, surely?' Laura suggested.

But they paid no heed to her. Both took their toothbrushes, their new tubes of paste, and rushed to find the bathroom. 'I'm going to bathe myself,' said Sep. 'I'm going to bathe all my skin, and wash my head.'

'Not *before* lunch,' Laura called out, hastening after them; but they did not hear her. Taps were running and steam clouding the window, and Sep was tearing off his clothes.

'He's bathed three times already,' Laura told Harold.

She had just come downstairs, and had done so as soon as she heard him slamming the front door.

Upstairs, Sep was sitting in the bath. She had made him a lacy vest of soap-froth, as once she had made them for Imogen and Lalage. It showed up much better on his grape-dark skin. He sat there, like a tribal warrior done up in war-paint.

Benny would not go near the bath. He washed at the basin, his sleeves rolled up: and he turned the cake of soap over and over uncertainly in his hands.

'It's probably a novelty,' Harold said, referring to Sep's bathing. 'Would you like a drink?'

'Later perhaps. I daren't sit down, for I'd never get up again.'

'I'll finish them off. I'll go and see to them. You just sit there and drink this.'

'Oh, Harold, how wonderfully good of you.'

She sank down on the arm of a chair, and sipped her drink, feeling stunned. From the echoing bathroom came shouts of laughter, and it was very good to hear them, especially from a distance. Harold was being a great success, and relief and gratitude filled her.

After a little rest, she got up and went weakly about the room, putting things back in their places. When this was done, the room still looked wrong. An unfamiliar dust seemed to have settled all over it, yet, running a finger over the piano, she found none. All the same, it was not the usual scene she set for Harold's home-coming in the evenings. It had taken a shaking-up.

Scampering footsteps now thundered along the landing. She waited a moment or two, then went upstairs. They were in bed, in separate beds; Benny by the window. Harold was pacing about the room, telling them a story: his hands flapped like huge ears at either side of his face; then he made an elephant's trunk with his arm. From the beds, the children's eyes stared unblinkingly at him. As Laura came into the room, only Benny's flickered in her direction, then back at once to the magic of Harold's performance. She blew a vague, unheeded kiss, and crept away.

'It's like seeing snow begin to fall,' Harold said at dinner. 'You know it's going to be a damned nuisance, but it makes a change.'

He sounded exhilarated; clashed the knife against the steel with vigour, and started to carve. He kept popping little titbits into his mouth. Carver's perks, he called them.

'Not much for me,' Laura said.

'What did they have for lunch?'

'Fish-cakes.'

'Enjoy them?'

'Sep said, "I don't like that." He's very suspicious, and that makes Benny all the braver. Then he eats too much, showing off.'

'They'll settle down,' Harold said, settling down himself to his dinner. After a while, he said, 'The little Cockney one asked me just now if this were a private house. When I said "Yes", he said, "I thought it was, because you've got the sleeping upstairs and the talking downstairs." Didn't quite get the drift.'

'Pathetic,' Laura murmured.

'I suppose where they come from, it's all done in the same room.'

'Yes, it is.'

'Pathetic,' Harold said in his turn.

'It makes me feel ashamed.'

'Oh, come now.'

'And wonder if we're doing the right thing – perhaps unsettling them for what they have to go back to.'

'My dear girl,' he said. 'Damn it, those people who organise these things know what they're doing.'

'I suppose so.'

'They've been doing it for years.'

'Yes, I know.'

'Well, then . . . '

Suddenly she put down her knife and fork and rested her forehead in her hands.

'What's up, old thing?' Harold asked, with his mouth full.

'Only tired.'

'Well, they've dropped off all right. You can have a quiet evening.'

'I'm too tired to sit up straight any longer.' After a silence, lifting her face from her hands, she said, 'Thirteen more days! What shall I do with them all that time?'

'Take them for scrambles in the woods,' he began, sure that he had end-less ideas.

'I tried. They won't walk a step. They both groaned and moaned so much that we turned back.'

'Well, they can play on the swing.'

'For how long, how *long*? They soon got tired of that. Anyhow, they quarrel about one having a longer turn than the other. In the end, I gave them the egg-timer.'

'That was a good idea.'

'They broke it.'

'Oh.'

'Please God, don't let it rain,' she said earnestly, staring out of the window. 'Not for the next fortnight, anyway.'

The next day, it rained from early morning. After breakfast, when Harold had gone off, Laura settled the boys at the dining-room table with a snakes-and-ladders board. As they had never played it, she had to draw up a chair herself, and join in. By some freakish chance, Benny threw one six after another, would, it seemed, never stop; and Sep's frustration and fury rose. He kept snatching the dice-cup away from Benny, peering into it, convinced of trickery. The game went badly for him and Laura, counting rapidly ahead, saw that he was due for the longest snake of all. His face was agonised, his dark hand, with its pale scars and scratches, hovered above the board; but he could not bring himself to draw the counter down the snake's horrid speckled length.

'I'll do it for you,' Laura said. He shuddered, and turned aside. Then he pushed his chair back from the table and lay, face-down on the floor, silent with grief.

'And it's not yet ten o'clock,' thought Laura, and was relieved to see Mrs Milner, the help, coming up the path under her umbrella. It was a mercy that it was her morning.

She finished off the game with Benny, and he won; but the true glory of victory had been taken from him by the vanquished, lying still and wounded on the hearth-rug. Laura was bright and cheerful about being beaten, trying to set an example; but she made no impression.

Presently, in exasperation, she asked, 'Don't you play games at school?'

There was no answer for a time, then Benny, knowing the question wasn't addressed to him, said, 'Yep, sometimes.'

'And what do you do if you lose?' Laura asked, glancing down at the hearth-rug. 'You can't win all the time.'

In a muffled voice, Sep at last said, 'I don't win any time. They won't let me win any time.'

'It's only luck.'

'No, they don't *let* me win. I just go and lie down and shut my eyes.'

'And are these our young visitors?' asked Mrs Milner, coming in with the vacuum-cleaner. Benny stared at her; Sep lifted his head from his sleeve for a brief look, and then returned to his sulking.

'What a nasty morning I've brought with me,' Mrs Milner said, after Laura had introduced them.

'You brought a nasty old morning all right,' Sep agreed, mumbling into his jersey.

'But,' she went on brightly, putting her hands into her overall pockets, 'I've also brought some lollies.'

Benny straightened his back in anticipation. Sep, peeping with one eye, stretched out an arm.

'That's if Madam says you may.'

'They call me "Laura".' It had been Harold's idea and Laura had foreseen this very difficulty.

Mrs Milner could not bring herself to say the name and she, too, could foresee awkwardnesses.

'No, Sep,' said Laura firmly. 'Either you get up properly and take it politely, or you go without.'

She wished that Benny hadn't at once scrambled to his feet and stood there at attention. Sep buried his head again and moaned. All the sufferings of his race were upon him at this moment.

Benny took his sweet and made a great appreciative fuss about it.

All the china had gone up a shelf or two, out of reach, Mrs Milner noted. It was like the old days, when Imogen's and Lalage's friends had come to tea.

'Now, there's a good lad,' she said, stepping over Sep, and plugging in the vacuum-cleaner.

'Is that your sister?' Benny asked Laura, when Mrs Milner had brought in the pudding, gone out again, and closed the door.

'No, Mrs Milner comes to help me with the housework – every Tuesday and Friday.'

'She must be a very kind old lady,' Benny said.

'Do you like that?' Laura asked Sep, who was pushing jelly into his spoon with his fingers.

'Yeah, I like this fine.'

He had suddenly cheered up. He did not mention the lolly, which Mrs Milner had put back in her pocket. All the rest of the morning, they had played excitedly with the telephone – one upstairs, in Laura's bedroom; the other downstairs, in the hall – chattering and shouting to one another, and running to Laura to come to listen.

That evening, Harold was home earlier than usual and could not wait to complain that he had tried all day to telephone.

'I know, dear,' Laura said. 'I should have stopped them, but it gave me a rest.'

'You'll be making a rod for everybody's back, if you let them do just what they like all the time.'

'It's for such a short while – well, relatively speaking – and they haven't got telephones at home, so the question doesn't arise.'

'But other people might want to ring you up.'

'So few ever do, it's not worth considering.'

'Well, someone did today. Helena Western.'

'What on earth for?'

'There's no need to look frightened. She wants you to take the boys to tea.' Saying this, his voice was full of satisfaction, for he admired Helena's husband. Helena herself wrote what he referred to as 'clever-clever little novels'. He went on sarcastically, 'She saw you with them from the top of a bus, and asked me when I met her later in Blackwell's. She says she has absolutely *no* feelings about coloured people, as some of her friends apparently have.' He was speaking in Helena's way of stresses and breathings. 'In fact,' he ended, 'she rather goes out of her way to be extra pleasant to them.'

'So she does have feelings,' Laura said.

She was terrified at the idea of taking the children to tea with Helena. She always felt dull and overawed in her company, and was afraid that the boys would misbehave and get out of her control, and then Helena would put it all into a novel. Already she had put Harold in one; but, luckily, he had not recognised his own transformation from professor of archaeology to barrister. Her simple trick worked, as far as he was concerned. To Harold, that character, with his vaguely left-wing opinions and opinionated turns of phrase, his quelling manner to his wife, his very appearance, could have nothing to do with him, since he had never taken silk. Everyone else had recognised and known, and Laura, among them, knew they had.

'I'll ring her up,' she said; but she didn't stir from her chair, sat staring wearily in front of her, her hands on her knees – a very resigned old woman's attitude; Whistler's mother. 'I'm *too* old,' she thought. 'I'd be too old for my own grandchildren.' But she had never imagined *them* like the ones upstairs in bed. She had pictured biddable little children, like Lalage and Imogen.

'They're good at *night*,' she said to Harold, continuing her thoughts aloud. 'They lie there and talk quietly, once they're in bed. I wonder what they talk about. Us, perhaps.' It was an alarming idea.

In the night she woke and remembered that she had not telephoned Helena. 'I'll do it after breakfast,' she thought.

But she was still making toast when the telephone rang, and the boys left the table and raced to the hall ahead of her. Benny was first and, as he grabbed the receiver, Sep stood close by him, ready to shout some messages into the magical instrument. Laura hovered anxiously by, but Benny warned her off with staring eyes. 'Be polite,' she whispered imploringly.

'Yep, my name's Benny,' he was saying.

Then he listened, with a look of rapture. It was his first real telephone conversation, and Sep was standing by, shivering with impatience and envy.

'Yep, that'll be OK,' said Benny, grinning. 'What day?'

Laura put out her hand, but he shrank back, clutching the receiver. 'I got the message,' he hissed at her. 'Yep, he's here,' he said, into the telephone. Sep smiled self-consciously and drew himself up as he took the receiver. 'Yeah, I am Septimus Alexander Smith.' He gave his high, bubbly chuckle. 'Sure I'll come there.' To prolong the conversation, he went on, 'Can my friend Benny Reece come, too? Can Laura come?' Then he frowned, looking up at the ceiling, as if for inspiration. 'Can my father Alexander Leroy Smith come?'

Laura made another darting movement.

'Well, no, he can't then,' Sep said, 'because he's dead.'

This doubled him up with mirth, and it was a long time before he could bring himself to say good-bye. When he had done so, he quickly put the receiver down.

'Someone asked me to tea,' he told Laura. 'I said, "Yeah, sure I come."'

'And me,' said Benny.

'Who was it?' Laura asked, although she knew.

'I don't know,' said Sep. 'I don't know *who* that was.'

When later and secretly, Laura telephoned Helena, Helena said, 'Aren't they simply *devastating* boys?'

'How did the tea party go?' Harold asked.

They had all arrived back home together – he, from a meeting; Laura and the boys from Helena's.

'They were good,' Laura said, which was all that mattered. She drew them to her, one on either side. It was her movement of gratitude towards them. They had not let her down. They had played quietly at a fishing game with real water and magnetised tin fish, had eaten unfamiliar things, such as anchovy toast and brandy-snaps, without any expression of alarm or revulsion: they had helped carry the tea-things indoors from the lawn. Helena had been surprisingly clever with them. She made them laugh, as seldom Laura could. She struck the right note from the beginning. When Benny picked up sixpence from the gravelled path, she thanked him casually and put it in her pocket. Laura was grateful to her for that and proud that Benny ran away at once so unconcernedly. When Helena had praised them for their good behaviour, Laura had blushed with pleasure, just as if they were her own children.

'She is really very nice,' Laura said later, thinking still of her successful afternoon with Helena.

'Yes, she talks too much, that's all.'

Harold was pleased with Laura for having got on well with his colleague's wife. It was so long since he had tried to urge Laura into academic circles, and for years he had given up trying. Now, sensing his pleasure, her own was enhanced.

'When we were coming away,' Laura said, 'Helena whispered to me, "Aren't they simply *devastating?*"'

'You've exactly caught her tone.'

At that moment, they heard from the garden, Benny also exactly catching her tone.

'Let's have the bat, there's a little pet,' he mimicked, trying to snatch the old tennis-racquet from Sep.

'You sod off,' drawled Sep.

'Oh, my dear, you shake me rigid.'

Sep began his doubling-up-with-laughter routine; first, in silence, bowed over, lifting one leg then another up to his chest, stamping the ground. It was like the start of a tribal dance, Laura thought, watching him from the window; then the pace quickened, he skipped about, and laughed, with his head thrown back, and tears rolled down his face. Benny looked on, smirking a little, obviously proud that his wit should have had such an effect. Round and round went Sep, his loose limbs moving like pistons. 'Yeah, you shake me rigid,' he shouted. 'You shake me entirely rigid.' Benny, after hesitating, joined in. They circled the lawn, and disappeared into the shrubbery.

'She *did* say that. Helena,' Laura said, turning to Harold. 'When Benny was going on about something he'd done she said, "My dear, you shake me entirely rigid."' Then Laura added thoughtfully, 'I wonder if they are as good at imitating *us*, when they're lying up there in bed, talking.'

'A sobering thought,' said Harold, who could not believe he had any particular idiosyncrasies to be copied. 'Oh, God, someone's broken one of my sherds,' he suddenly cried, stooping to pick up two pieces of pottery from the floor. His agonised shout brought Sep to the French windows, and he stood there, bewildered.

As the pottery had been broken before, he hadn't bothered to pick it up, or confess. The day before, he had broken a whole cup and nothing had happened. Now this grown man was bowed over as if in pain, staring at the fragments in his hand. Sep crept back into the shrubbery.

The fortnight, miraculously, was passing. Laura could now say, 'This time next week.' She would do gardening, get her hair done, clean all the paint. Often, she wondered about the kind of homes the other children had gone to – those children she had glimpsed on the train; and she imagined them staying on farms, helping with the animals, looked after by buxom farmers' wives – pale London children, growing gratifyingly brown, filling out, going home at last with roses in their cheeks. She could see no difference in Sep and Benny.

What they had really got from the holiday was one another. It touched her to see them going off into the shrubbery with arms about one another's shoulders, and to listen to their peaceful murmuring as they lay in bed, to hear their shared jokes. They quarrelled a great deal, over the tennis-racquet or Harold's old cricket-bat, and Sep was constantly casting himself down on the grass and weeping, if he were out at cricket, or could not get Benny out.

It was he who would sit for hours with his eyes fixed on Laura's face while she read to him. Benny would wander restlessly about, waiting for the story to be finished. If he interrupted, Sep would put his hand imploringly on Laura's arm, silently willing her to continue.

Benny liked her to play the piano. It was the only time she was admired. They would dance gravely about the room, with their bottles of Coca-Cola, sucking through straws, choking, heads bobbing up and down. Once, at the end of a concert of nursery-rhymes, Laura played 'God Save the Queen', and Sep rushed at her, trying to shut the lid down on her hands. 'I don't like that,' he keened. 'My mam don't like "God Save the Queen" neither. She say "God save *me*".'

'Get out,' said Benny, kicking him on the shin. 'You're shaking me entirely rigid.'

On the second Sunday, they decided that they must go to church. They had a sudden curiosity about it, and a yearning to sing hymns.

'Well, take them,' said liberal-minded and agnostic Harold to Laura.

But it was almost time to put the sirloin into the oven. 'We did sign that form,' she said in a low voice. 'To say we'd take them if they wanted to go.'

'Do you *really* want to go?' Harold asked, turning to the boys, who were wanting to go more and more as the discussion went on. 'Oh, God!' he groaned – inappropriately, Laura thought.

'What religion are you, anyway?' he asked them.

'I am a Christian,' Sep said with great dignity.

'Me, too,' said Benny.

'What time does it begin?' Harold asked, turning back to Laura.

'At eleven o'clock.'

'Isn't there some kids' service they can go to on their own?'

'Not in August, I'm afraid.'

'Oh, God!' he said again.

Laura watched them setting out; rather overawed, the two boys; it was the first time they had been out alone with him.

She had a quiet morning in the kitchen. Not long after twelve o'clock they returned. The boys at once raced for the cricket-bat, and fought over it, while Harold poured himself out a glass of beer.

'How did it go?' asked Laura.

'Awful! Lord, I felt such a fool.'

'Did they misbehave, then?'

'Oh, no, they were perfectly good – except that for some reason Benny kept holding his nose. But I knew so many people there. And the Vicar shook hands with me afterwards and said, "We are especially glad to see *you*." The embarrassment!'

'It must have shaken you entirely rigid,' Laura said, smiling as she basted the beef. Harold looked at her as if for the first time in years. She so seldom tried to be amusing.

At lunch, she asked the boys if they had enjoyed their morning.

'Church smelt nasty,' Benny said, making a face.

'Yeah,' agreed Sep. 'I prefer my own country. I prefer Christians.'

'Me, too,' Benny said. 'Give me Christians any day.'

'Has it been a success?' Laura asked Harold. 'For them, I mean.'

It was their last night – Sep's and Benny's – and she wondered if her feeling of being on the verge of tears was entirely from tiredness. For the past fortnight, she had reeled into bed, and slept without moving.

A success for *them*? She could not be quite sure; but it had been a success for her, and for Harold. In the evenings, they had so much to talk about, and Harold, basking in his popularity, had been genial and considerate.

Laura, the boys had treated as a piece of furniture, or a slave, and humbly she accepted her place in their minds. She was a woman who had never had any high opinions of herself.

'No more cricket,' she said. She had been made to play for hours – always wicket-keeper, running into the shrubs for lost balls while Sep and Benny rested full-length on the grass.

'He has a lovely action,' she had said to Harold one evening, watching Sep taking his long run up to bowl. 'He might be a great athlete one day.'

'It couldn't happen,' Harold said. 'Don't you see, he has rickets?'

One of her children with rickets, she had thought, stricken.

Now, on this last evening, the children were in bed. She and Harold were sitting by the drawing-room window, talking about them. There was a sudden scampering along the landing and Laura said, 'It's only one of them going to the toilet.'

'The *what?*'

'They ticked me off for saying "lavatory",' she said placidly. 'Benny said it was a bad word.'

She loved to make Harold laugh, and several times lately she had managed to amuse him, with stories she had to recount.

'I shan't like saying good-bye,' she said awkwardly.

'No,' said Harold. He got up and walked about the room, examined his shelves of pottery fragments. 'It's been a lot of work for you, Laura.'

She looked away shyly. There had been almost a note of praise in his voice. 'Tomorrow,' she thought. 'I hope I don't cry.'

At the station, it was Benny who cried. All the morning he had talked about his mother, how she would be waiting for him at Paddington station. Laura kept their thoughts fixed on the near future.

Now they sat on a bench on the sunny platform, wearing their name-labels, holding bunches of wilting flowers, and Laura looked at her watch and wished the minutes away. As usual, she was too early. Then she saw Benny shut his eyes quickly, but not in time to stop two tears falling. She was surprised and dismayed. She began to talk brightly, but neither replied. Benny kept his head down, and Sep stared ahead. At last, to her relief, the signal fell, and soon the train came in. She handed them over to the escort, and they sat down in the compartment without a word. Benny gazed out of the further window, away from her, rebukingly; and Sep's face was expressionless.

As the train began to pull out, she stood waving and smiling; but they would not glance in her direction, though the escort was urging them to do so, and setting an example. When at last Laura moved away, her head and throat were aching, and she had such a sense of failure and fatigue that she hardly knew how to walk back to the car.

It was not Mrs Milner's morning, and the house was deadly quiet. Life, noise, laughter, bitter quarrelling had gone out of it. She picked up the cricket-bat from the lawn and went inside. She walked about, listlessly tidying things, putting them back in their places. Then fetched a damp cloth and sat down at the piano and wiped the sticky, dirty keys.

She was sitting there, staring in front of her, clasping the cloth in her lap, when Harold came in.

'I'm taking the afternoon off,' he said. 'Let's drive out to Minster Lovell for lunch.'

She looked at him in astonishment. On his way across the room to fetch his tobacco pouch, he let his hand rest on her shoulder for a moment.

'Don't fret,' he said. 'I think we've got them for life now.'

'Benny cried.'

'Extraordinary thing. Shall we make tracks?'

She stood up and closed the lid of the keyboard. 'It was awfully nice of you to come back, Harold.' She paused, thinking she might say more; but he was puffing away, lighting his pipe with a great fuss, as if he were not listening. 'Well, I'll go and get ready,' she said.

The Excursion to the Source

'England was like this when I was a child,' Gwenda said. She was fifteen years older than Polly, and had had a brief, baby's glimpse of the gay twenties – though, as an infant, could hardly have been really conscious of their charms.

It was France – the middle of France – which so much resembled that unspoilt England. In the hedgerows grew all the wild flowers that urbanisation, ribbon-development and sprayed insecticides had turned into rarities, delights of the past, in the South of England where Gwenda and Polly lived.

Polly had insisted on Gwenda's stopping the car so that she could get out and add to her bunch some new blue flower she was puzzling over. She climbed the bank to get a good specimen and stung her bare legs on nettles. Gwenda sat in the car with her eyes closed.

Polly, having spat into her palm and rubbed it on her smarting legs, began to search for the blue flower in *Fleurs de Prés et des Bois*, instead of looking at the map. Crossroads were on them suddenly and she had no directions to give. Gwenda pulled to the side of the road, having taken the wrong turning, and reached for the map, screwing in her monocle. As she was studying it, frowning, or looking up at the sun for her bearings, Polly said, 'I suppose it's a sort of campanula. What on earth does "*lancéolées*" mean? Oh, I *wish* I'd brought my proper flower book from home.'

'It's *this* road we want,' Gwenda said, following it on the map with her nicotined finger. 'If you could remember, we turn off *here*, and about eight kilometres further on bear right.' She handed back the map. Polly had scarcely glanced at it, but she took it obediently, although she could never read it unless they were travelling north, which at present they were not.

'And when we've surmounted *that* little problem, you'd better look in the Michelin for somewhere for tonight,' Gwenda added, and began to wrench the car round grimly, as if it were a five-ton lorry.

It was ten years since she had been in this part of France; with her husband then. They had travelled along the Dordogne valley, from the mouth to the source, crossing from bank to bank. It was in the year that he died, and she remembered with a turn of her heart, how, as she was driving, she would give secret glances at him, knowing him so well that he could never hide the signs of pain coming on – the difference in breathing, the slight shifting in his seat, the hand going involuntarily to his chest, and then at once returning to his lap to grip hold of the map. He could read maps in whichever direction they were heading.

Polly had put the flower book into the dashboard pocket and had her head in the Michelin guide. She was dreadfully short-sighted, but would not wear spectacles, however much Gwenda nagged her. She would not even use the subterfuge of lenses in sunglasses, which had been suggested.

'There's one with two pairs of those scissors at a place called – I think it's Sebonac.'

'Selonac,' Gwenda said. 'How much?'

'I can't see.'

'I'll have a look later. Can you find it on the map?'

'I already have,' Polly said with pride.

Gwenda was always fussing about money – heading Polly off the *menu gastronomique* on to the eleven-franc one. Although it was Polly's money, Polly sometimes thought.

Gwenda's husband had left her poorly provided for, and she had taken a job managing an hotel until Polly's mother, her own godmother, had begged her to look after Polly, *poor* Polly she always called her, and administer her affairs. This was before the operation from which she did not recover (as the doctor put it, but Gwenda did not), 'if anything should happen', as she put *that*. Polly was left very comfortable indeed. Long ago, people had thought Gwenda's parents clever to have chosen so rich a slight acquaintance to be Gwenda's godmother.

As soon as Mrs Hervey had died, Gwenda moved into her place; into the house in Surrey – red brick with a green dome, monkey-puzzle trees and dark banks of rhododendrons, everywhere smelling of pine trees. Polly was acquiescent. She could not have managed on her own. This was clear to everyone. And at twenty-seven it was thought unlikely that she would marry. In spite of the solid worth of her position, men seemed uncertain with her, found her scatter-brained and childish conversation maddening, wondered among themselves if she were really all there. She was like a lanky child with her pale, freckled face, soft, untidy hair, her awkwardness. She was forever tripping over carpets or walking into doors. She got on people's nerves.

The responsibility of having quite a little heiress on her hands was one Gwenda felt she could shoulder. She was ready to deal with impoverished widowers or ambitious younger men; but few came their way in Surrey. Fork luncheons for women was their manner of entertaining, or an evening's bridge which Polly did not join in. She would sit apart, sticking foreign stamps crookedly into an album. Besides stamps, she collected Victorian bun pennies, lustre jugs, fans, sea-shells, match-boxes and pressed wild flowers. There was a pile of albums full of pressed flowers, and what she seemed to love best about being in France was the chance of collecting different varieties. She hoped that Selonac, when they arrived there, would have more surprises. In a foreign country there was always the delight of not knowing what she might discover next – some rare strange orchid, perhaps, that she had never found before.

But Selonac was, at first sight, a disappointment – a few straggling houses on either side of the road. They were nearly through it when they saw a sign – '*Auberge*' – pointing down a lane to the right. 'There!' shouted Polly, trying to be efficient, but Gwenda was already turning the corner. They came to a little cobbled *place*, with a church and a baker's shop and a garage and the *auberge* – with one or two umbrellaed tables and some box trees in tubs on the pavement before it.

'I'll go and ask,' Gwenda said. She always did all the fixing-up, while Polly sat mooning in the car over her wild flowers, or squinting short-sightedly at the *guide Michelin*, looking up for the twentieth time the difference between a black bath-tub and a white.

When Gwenda came back, she was followed by a young man, who dragged their suitcases out of the boot and lurched back into the darkness of the hotel with them.

It was a very dark and silent hotel. Polly felt depressed, as she went upstairs after Gwenda. She was never asked for her opinions about where they should stay. They never shared a room, and Gwenda always told her which was hers – and it was never the one nearest the bathroom or with the best view. She was glad that sharing a room was not one of Gwenda's economies. Gwenda snored like a man. She had heard her through many a thin wall.

This time they had the same view from their windows – across an orchard to a row of silvery trees which looked as if they bordered a stream. There was very little difference between the two rooms. Madame Peloux, the proprietress, showed Polly and Gwenda both, as if there were any chance of Polly making a choice; and then she began to chivvy her son, Jean, about the luggage. He was a clumsy, silent young man, and seemed to be sulking. His mother nagged him monotonously, as if from an old habit.

Like some wine, Polly did not travel well. She became more and more creased and greasy-faced. And the clothes in her suitcase, among the layers of tattered tissue-paper, all were creased, too, and all a little grubby, yet not *quite* grubby enough, she decided, to warrant all the fuss of getting them washed.

'Aren't you ready *yet?*' asked Gwenda at the door. 'After all that driving, what I need is some *violent* exercise.'

She usually said something like this, and once upon a time Polly had had amusing visions of her running across-country or playing a few chukkas of polo. Now she knew that all that would happen would be that Gwenda would drape her cardigan over her shoulders and go for a stroll round the garden, or amble round the village, stopping to look in shop-windows – longest at the *charcuteries* to marvel at terrines. She examined them with a professional eye; for her own pâté was quite the talk of their part of Surrey. When she was asked for the recipe, she became carefully vague and said she had none; that she just chucked in anything that came to hand.

This evening there was a pâté on the ten-franc menu, so she was happy. She had had her stroll through the orchard, and Polly, still unpacking, had watched her from the bedroom window. Gwenda pushed her way through the long grass, lifting her neat ankles over briars. She had a top-heavy look, especially when viewed from above. Her large bosom was out of character, Polly thought. It was altogether too motherly-looking. And to think of Gwenda with children was impossible.

In the end, the unpacking was done, and the little walk was over, and they went into the almost empty dining-room. There were red and pink table-cloths, and large damp napkins to match, and Jean, Madame Peloux's son, had combed his frizzy hair, and was waiting inexpertly at table.

'Mosquitoes,' Gwenda was saying. 'I'm afraid there might be. I went up and closed the shutters.'

There *was* a stream at the bottom of the orchard, across a narrow lane. She had come to it on her wanderings, and had been bitten a little by midges.

'The pâté's not bad,' she said, dipping into the jar of gherkins.

Polly thought it a bit 'off' – well, sour anyway; but she said nothing. She was too often told that the taste she objected to was the very one that had been aimed at, the absolute perfection of flavour.

Jean annoyed Gwenda by saying the name of everything he put on the table – as if she and Polly were children. '*Truites,*' he announced, setting the dish down. They looked delicious – sprinkled with parsley and shredded almonds.

Gwenda, whose French – like everything else – was so much better than Polly's, asked if they were from the stream below the orchard, and Jean looked evasive, as if he could not understand her. '*Truites,*' he said again, and turned away, knocking over a glass as he did so.

The only other guests sat across the room. They were obviously not newcomers. They were favoured by the best table at the garden window, whereas Gwenda and Polly looked out on to the square. They had a bottle of wine with their name scribbled on the label, and the man poured it out himself, looking very serious as he did so. The woman drank water, holding the glass in a shaking hand, tinkling it against her false teeth. She was ancient. He was in his sixties, and she was his mother.

As they were French, Gwenda had to listen with a little extra concentration to what they said – although they said little, and that in muted voices, as they stared before them, waiting for Jean to bring the next dish.

The old woman was thin and ashen and wore a sort of half-mourning of grey and mauve, and a hat – a floppy, linen garden hat. The only real colour about her was her crimson shiny lips, crookedly done, which she kept pressed together, and smudged, after every sip of water, with a purple handkerchief. Large diamond rings kept slipping on her old fingers.

'Mother and son,' Gwenda said in a low explanatory voice to Polly.

Jean had brought a tart to be cut from. Glazed slices of apple were slightly burnt. He made a great business of cutting their slices, frowning and pursing his lips as if it were a very tricky job.

Monsieur and Madame Devancourt, as he then addressed them, waved the tart away. Gwenda fastened on the name; repeated it once or twice in her mind, and had it secure.

'How *good* not to have anything frozen,' she said, as she said at nearly every meal-time.

'The tart is lovely,' Polly said. She loved sweet things, and longed for them through the other courses.

Madame Devancourt played with her rings and stared about her, while her tall, bald son was peeling an orange for her. They really were a very silent pair; but sometimes he made a little joke, and she gave a smothered snigger behind her handkerchief. It was surprising – sounded like a naughty little girl laughing in church.

Through the window, Polly watched one or two people sitting at the tables outside the inn, looking rather bored as they sipped their evening drink. A middle-aged woman, with a bitter, closed expression on her face, sat beside an older woman who was bowed-over, so hunch-backed that she kept losing balance and slipping sideways. Then the younger woman – she was obviously her daughter – would put her right, and turn her head away again, without a word. After a while, she suddenly stood up, got her mother to her feet and began a slow progress back across the *place*.

Jean brought coffee to Gwenda and Polly and slopped it into the saucers pouring it out. Gwenda asked for another saucer and when he brought it, he looked so sulky that Polly smiled up at him, and thanked him in her atrocious accent. She knew so well herself what it was like to be clumsy and inadequate.

'Such a moron,' Gwenda said. 'Never mind, it's only for one night.' Although it turned out to be for six.

Gwenda always got up for breakfast. She found French beds uncomfortable, and 'liked to be about', as she put it.

The Devancourts were also up. Madame was wearing her floppy hat, and a pair of grubby tennis-shoes. Her son peeled another orange for her, and made a few more jokes. She seemed to be his life, and accepted his attentions placidly. But she was, in her own way, protective to him. When he half stood up, with his napkin in one hand and the orange in the other, and bowed to Gwenda and Polly as they came in, she stared hard at him, as if willing him back into his seat, and Polly could imagine her having guarded him from women since he was a young man, just as Gwenda had warded off young men from herself. When he had sat down again and resumed his careful orange-peeling, the old woman turned a cold and steady gaze on Gwenda, as if to say, 'Don't waste any time on *this* one. He is mine.' At Polly she did not so much as glance. Few people did. It was surprising that Jean darted forward and drew out her chair before he attended to Gwenda, although he shot it out so fast and so far that she almost fell on the floor.

'I really don't think he's all there,' Gwenda said.

She had brought the maps down to breakfast, and said that she thought that they could get to the source of the river that day. It was so beautiful up there in the Auvergne, she said. The air so clear. The flowers so beautiful. At the thought of the flowers, Polly brightened; but there was also the thought of the day ahead, with all the difficulties of the map-reading and Gwenda's making a martyrdom of the driving – though it was she who forced the pace, who was determined to retrace every footstep of that last holiday with her husband. Why she wanted to do this, Polly found a puzzle – especially as that holiday must have been permeated with tragedy. Gwenda had always talked of it a great deal, and she talked of her husband more than Polly could endure. Such trivial repetitions – such as, every morning, '*How* Humphrey loved French bread!' and reminiscences all the way along the road. And there were implications that Polly knew none of the secret joys of matrimony, and would be unlikely ever to learn them. So Polly felt excluded, as well as bored.

Sometimes, alone in her bedroom, she lay for a little while face-down on the bed, upset by vague desires. If the desires were to be loved, she had no face to match her longing; simply nothing to define her day-dreams. 'I want! I just *want*!' she sometimes moaned softly into the pillows.

'Oh, *lazy*-bones!' Gwenda would say, opening the door as she knocked on it. 'Even at *my* age, I wouldn't dream of lying down in the day-time.' As like as not, she would be on her way downstairs for some of her *violent* exercise. This morning, having mused once more on Humphrey's love of French bread, Gwenda put in her monocle and unfolded a map.

They were breakfasting in the bar, with a view through the open door across the *place*. It was early in the morning, and children were gathered at the tables outside, waiting for the school bus. The boys smoked, and some of the older girls were playing a game of cards. They were very orderly, though gay, and made a sound like starlings. Gwenda kept glancing up in annoyance, and glaring through her monocle. Polly felt envious of the children.

Madame Devancourt padded past them in her tennis-shoes, followed by her son. He bowed again, but she kept her eyes ahead. Presently, Jean appeared outside with a stiff broom and began to sweep between the tables; then he leant on the broom and talked to some of the children; almost seeming to be one of them, without, for once, his shy or sullen look. Perhaps he too was envious of them, Polly thought.

'Jean, Jean!' Madame Peloux came in in her black overall and called her son's attention to his work, and he shrugged and glowered and began to sweep again.

The school bus came, was filled, and drove off, and there was silence except for the rasping of the broom on the pavement. When he had finished the sweeping, Jean watered the box-shrubs and a sharp, cold smell cut off the heat of the morning for a while.

'Have you packed?' Gwenda asked Polly, knowing that she had not.

As Polly got up, she bumped against the table, and Gwenda looked up sharply and clicked her tongue. Polly, catching Jean's eyes, blushed, ashamed to be rebuked in front of him. He was standing in the doorway, flicking the last drops from the watering-can about the pavement.

As she went upstairs, Polly thought, 'I'll bet old Humphrey never bumped into things,' and she hoped for his sake that he hadn't.

Gwenda paid the bill, then she walked about the courtyard, smoking to soothe herself. The exasperation she felt at having to wait always for Polly was a trembling pain. She hated to wait, and now spent hours of her life doing so. She herself was quick and decisive, always thinking one step ahead. Routine things, like packing, for instance, were so boring that she would get them done with great speed, only to waste time she had saved pacing up and down while Polly dithered.

Jean brought down her case and put it in the boot of the car.

Monsieur Devancourt came out to the garage with his fishing-rods. He stopped to wish Gwenda a pleasant journey, then drove off in his old and dusty Citroën. As Gwenda looked back to the inn for any sign of Polly, she saw old Madame Devancourt, still wearing her hat, staring down at her from a window.

Already the sun was strong. Smells of baking came through the kitchen window, and Gwenda began to long for the cool air of the Auvergne.

At last Jean brought down Polly's suitcase, and Polly followed soon after. Madame Peloux came out from the kitchen, wiping her floury hands on her apron.

As they drove out of the courtyard, Polly thought, 'As soon as I get to like a place, we have to move on,' and she turned back and waved to Jean, who was staring after them in his vacant way.

But Gwenda was insistent on moving on, on retracing every mile of her holiday with Humphrey. They had to get up to the source and back through Northern France, and there were only ten days left. Then Gwenda had to go home to open a garden fête.

'I love this feeling of starting out fresh in the mornings,' she said, as they drove out of the square. 'Humphrey used to say ...' She slowed down, reaching the main road; the engine stalled, and stopped, and would not start again.

'Oh, drat it,' said Gwenda.

Now the heat poured into the car. While Gwenda tugged at the starter and made her mild, but furious-sounding imprecations, Polly placidly looked at her wild-flower book, as if the hitch did not involve her, and would soon be put right.

Jean, who had watched the car and seen it stop, came running towards them. He opened the bonnet and seemed to take a very grave view. After a while he fetched his friend from the garage. The car was towed away, and Gwenda and Polly decided to return temporarily to the *auberge* and drink a *citron pressé*.

'Now, we shall have a job to get to the mountains by this evening,' Gwenda said.

Polly was playing with a cat.

As the day went on, the idea of the mountains receded. Jean carried their suitcases back upstairs, and they unpacked.

'A week at *least*,' Gwenda moaned. 'And if they say that, goodness only knows what it might really mean. Stuck in this place.'

'It's quite a *nice* place,' said Polly.

'Yes, but it's not what we planned.'

The car was in the village garage, and a spare part had been telephoned for, and for once there seemed nothing that Gwenda could do. So she went to lie down, in the heat of the afternoon – the thing she said she never did. Polly, at a loose end, wandered in the orchard, looking for flowers. It was like the afternoons of her childhood, when her mother rested, and she was left to her own devices. In those days, she had felt under a spell. Through an open window she could hear the solid ticking of a grandfather-clock and on the terrace, the peacocks squawked with a sound of rusty shears being forced open. Here there was only the busy noise of the cicadas in the grass.

At the bottom of the orchard, she saw Jean. He was beckoning to her eagerly, and she hurried forward, with a wading motion, through the long grass. He had few words to say – from habit, from *gaucherie*, from fear of her foreignness. To make up for his dumbness, his gestures were all exaggerated, like Harpo Marx's. They came out of the orchard and crossed the narrow, gritty lane, which was lanced by sunlight striking through birch trees.

With a complete disregard for Polly's bare legs, he took her hand and drew her through looped and tangled brambles, disturbing dozens of small blue butterflies. Polly could hear the stream, but not see it for all the undergrowth. She wondered where they were going, and what all the secrecy and haste and excitement were about. Jean parted some reeds and she could see the stream again. It looked less deep than it was, for it was very clear, and the fat brown stones on its bed seemed near the surface. Jean turned and lifted Polly with his hands round her waist. He swung her down over the bank on to a boulder. It had seemed a sudden, reckless thing to do and her breath was taken away; but she landed quite safely on the boulder, with his large rough hands steadying her.

He became more secretive than ever, carefully drawing aside branches to show to her a part of the stream, caged off by wire netting. The water flowed through the trap, which was full of trout, turning back and forth, and swimming as best they could. So this was his secret? Polly smiled, and he watched her face intently, and when she turned to him and nodded – she knew not why – he put a finger to his lips and narrowed his eyes. To an onlooker they would have seemed like people in a silent movie.

For a moment or two, they stood in contemplation, hypnotised by the slowly moving fish; then, suddenly, with more frantic gestures, Jean dashed off again. He took a spade from a hiding-place under a bush and began to try to thrust it into the earth. Polly turned to watch him with amazement. The earth was hard. He lifted a piece of rough turf and bent to examine the soil, clicking his tongue in disapproval. In spite of the dryness of the earth, he managed, as he dug deeper, to find a few worms. He brought them eagerly to Polly and put them into the palm of her hand, as if they were a handful of precious stones. She recoiled, but he did not notice and, to show her how, he took one of the worms from her and tore it into pieces and threw them to the fish. With a feeling of revulsion, Polly flung her handful suddenly into the trap. Some fell through, others lay on the wire-netting, writhing. She bent down and dipped her hand into the cool water, while Jean poked at the worms with a stick, clicking his tongue in vexation.

'Jean! Jean!' They could hear his mother calling him across the orchard.

He frowned. He watched the trout a little longer, then he seemed to gather himself from a trance, braced himself, and gave his hands to Polly, dragging her clumsily up the bank. 'Jean! Jean!' the voice went on calling, getting shriller. He looped briars carefully over the trap and he and Polly set off.

Madame Peloux was standing in the orchard. She waved a basket at them, for there was some errand for Jean to run – he had to go to the farm to fetch a chicken for dinner. An old boiler, she explained rapidly, aside from Polly.

Polly stood, hesitating, unsure whether to walk on or not. Then, feeling very bold and having composed the sentence in French before she spoke it, she asked if she might go with him to the farm. His face at once lost its sulkiness, and the errand seemed to take on a bright aspect. Madame Peloux stood looking suspiciously after them as they set off.

'What *has* come over you?' Gwenda asked Polly, fearing that she knew. She had found the girl sitting by her bedroom window, studying a phrase-book. It was opened at *Le Marché*.

'You always said I should improve my French,' Polly replied defensively.

'But you never cared to try, did you? Before?'

It was a brilliant early evening, and Gwenda had looked in on her way downstairs. In the garden the acacias were full of sunlight against the pale blue sky. Martins and swallows darted about the terra-cotta, crenellated outhouse roof, catching, Gwenda hoped, the mosquitoes which otherwise might have plagued her later. There was a smell of lime-blossom and honeysuckle and, down below, in the vegetable-garden lilies grew like weeds.

'I could stay here for ever, I think,' Polly said, glancing across the orchard.

'This was hardly the object of our holiday,' Gwenda said. She was fretful to complete their journey. She talked continually of getting to the source, to the mountains, so infuriatingly near, where she and Humphrey had been so happy. As they were arrested on their travels, there were no fresh sights to discuss, so she talked about Humphrey, and Polly wished that she would not. Gwenda spoke of marriage as if it were something exclusive to herself and her late husband. She referred to past experiences, implying that Polly would never know similar ones.

'Humphrey and I climbed right to the summit,' she said. 'There was an enormous view, and gentians – great patches of gentians.'

'I should love to see gentians,' Polly said.

'Well, I doubt if we shall now,' Gwenda said briskly. 'It's so infuriating. You really ought not to read that small print. Your nose almost touches the page. So ridiculous. We shall have to see about getting you some spectacles when we get back.'

'I shan't wear them,' Polly said, in a mild but firm voice. Sometimes, quietly, she put her foot down, and then Gwenda let the matter go. It was such a rare occurrence that it did not constitute a threat. All the same, only that morning Polly had insisted on going to the market with Jean, and had left Gwenda at the garage and gone on with him alone. Gwenda was always at the garage, making the same complaints, asking the same questions.

'You'll find you'll come to them in the end,' she said, referring to the spectacles. 'Now do take your head out of that book, there's a dear girl. Let's go down and have a drink. I promised the Devancourts we'd join them.'

Madame Devancourt now seemed warmly disposed to them. She had decided that they were lesbians, and so of no danger to her son. Passing their table at breakfast, the day after the breakdown, the old lady had commiserated with them. She was formal and condescending. By dinner-time, she had warmed a little more; and the following morning had come to them, with her son hovering behind her, to invite them to a drive out in the afternoon. 'Having no car you will see nothing of our country,' she said.

So they had driven out along rutted, dusty lanes to see a small *château*. It stood high on a slope over the river, bone-white, with black candle-snuffer turrets. Madame Devancourt had the name of a friend to mention, and the housekeeper admitted them. The family was away, and she went ahead from room to room, opening shutters, drawing dust-covers from furniture, lifting drugget from needle-work carpets. There were some portraits, some pieces of tapestry, deer's heads and antlers growing from almost every wall, and a chilly smell from the stone floors. Madame Devancourt and Gwenda exclaimed over everything, drew one another to view this and that treasure or curiosity. Each was impressed by the other's knowledge. Monsieur Devancourt looked out of the windows, and Polly trailed behind, immeasurably bored.

She regretted this new friendship. Gwenda's fluency with French debarred Polly from any part in the conversation – not that she had anything to say. She was frightened of the old lady, and thought her son a pitiful creature. Now they must spend an hour with them sitting under the umbrellas outside the *auberge*. She took her wild-flower book with her, and looked for a picture of a gentian. '*Gentiane*,' said Jean, pointing at the illustration, when he had set down her drink before her.

'*Oui*,' she said, smiling and blushing.

'*Oui, gentiane*,' he repeated, turning to take an order from another table.

'He will drive me *mad*,' said Gwenda.

Then there was the little commotion of having to get up as Madame Devancourt shuffled out to join them, her son following, carrying her handbag and her cardigan.

At another table came the other sorry pair, the habituées, the crippled mother and the bitter-faced daughter. Every evening, they sat for twenty minutes in the *place*. The daughter sipped a drink, and kept propping up her mother. Not a word was spoken. When it was time to go, the daughter stood up in silence and helped her mother to her feet, and then to go slowly across the square. Homewards. Polly tried not to imagine any more – the dreadful ritual of getting Mother to bed. All old, she thought, looking round her. Whenever Jean passed by, he nodded his head at her, as if he were saying, 'Ah, yes, you're still there.'

Gwenda, missing nothing, frowned.

He continued to madden her through dinner. When he brought the trout, he winked at Polly, collusively.

'One can grow tired even of trout,' Gwenda complained. 'Every evening. I do wish, Polly, you would try to ignore that terrible young man. He is quite oafish. I would have said he winked at you just now, if I could believe it possible.'

She had ordered a bottle of wine to be put on the Devancourts' table – a token of gratitude for their kindness – and now Monsieur Devancourt across the room raised his glass in a courtly gesture, and Madame her glass of water, with a shaking hand.

'Very affy,' said Polly in a low voice.

After dinner, the four of them sat in the stuffy little salon, and Gwenda told them stories about her husband.

'Excuse me,' Polly murmured, slipping away suddenly – the very thing Gwenda had been determined she should not do.

In the courtyard, Jean was watering the tubs of geraniums. The air had a delicious smell.

At once, before Gwenda could find an excuse to come after them, he put down the watering-can and they set off across the orchard. Every evening he went to the stream to clean the trout-trap of drifting weeds and sticks and to dig up worms. They said very little – although Polly persevered with a few short sentences, and sometimes Jean pointed at plants and trees and said their name clearly in French, which she obediently repeated.

Although he was clumsy and unpredictable and could not speak a word of her language, Polly felt safe and at home with him. There was never anyone young in her life – neither here nor at home. She liked to go shopping with him in the market. It was the simplest, poorest of markets. Old women sat patiently beside whatever they had for sale – a few broad beans tied in a bundle, a live duck in a basket, lime-flowers for tisane, a bucketful of arum lilies or Canterbury bells. She and Jean went from one to the other, comparing cheeses, and pressing the bean-pods, and she felt a sense of intimacy, as if they were playing a game of being husband and wife. Nothing Gwenda could say would prevent her from going to the market.

This evening, she helped him to clean the trap, she fed worms to the fish, having lost her squeamishness. They were as busy and absorbed as children.

Throwing the last worm, she lost her balance on the boulder, and one foot went into the water; but he was there at once to steady her. She was annoyed with herself, wondering how to explain to Gwenda her soaking wet sandal, without revealing the secret of this place.

Jean lifted her up and sat her on the bank.

'I shall stay here for a while,' she said. Perhaps Gwenda would go up to bed early, although more likely not.

He understood her, and sat down beside her, feeling worried, because soon his mother would be calling 'Jean! Jean!' all round the garden – there would be some job to be done.

When they had been together before, there had always been something to be busy about – the marketing, the fish. Now each had only the other one in mind. He sat there staring in front of him, as if he were wondering what on earth to do next, for he had scarcely been allowed five minutes' idleness in his life. Then he suddenly had an inspiration. He turned and kissed her suddenly on the side of her face, then, less awkwardly, on her forehead. Polly had been kissed only by her mother and elderly relations; but she felt that she knew more about it than Jean. She put her hands behind his head and kissed him very strongly on the mouth. She felt quite faint with delight. But hardly had they had any time to enjoy their kissing, when that far-off, coming and going, mosquito-plaint began – 'Jean! Jean!' – across the orchard.

Until they were in sight of the house, they went hand in hand, saying nothing. Although the kissing was over, something remained – an excitement, a gladness. Something Gwenda, surely, could never have experienced.

That Gwenda guessed something of what had happened was shown by her coldness and huffiness. She had felt awkward, sitting in the salon with the Devancourts. Polly had excused herself so abruptly, and Madame Devancourt kept looking towards the door. Gwenda was glad when, at their usual time, Monsieur Devancourt fetched the draught-board and set out the counters. She watched for a little while, and realised that the son was making stupid mistakes so that his mother could win. Then, hearing Madame Peloux outside, calling for Jean, Gwenda got up uneasily, and said that she was going to have an early night. She went upstairs and threw open the window, regardless of mosquitoes.

Polly and Jean were coming back across the orchard. Gwenda began to shake violently, and moved back a few steps from the window. Jean answered his mother, but did not say a word to Polly, not even when she turned away from him to enter the house.

Gwenda was so unpleasantly disturbed that she felt unable to face Polly, and dreaded her coming to say good-night. But she did not come. The footsteps stopped at the next room, and Gwenda heard the door open, and then shut. This was something that had never happened before. There were too many things happening for the first time. Gwenda lay in bed worrying about them, and she slept badly.

At breakfast, nothing was right. She snapped at Jean for slopping the coffee, she complained that the butter was rancid, and she found every word that Polly said in French excruciating. 'Your command of the language grows as fast as your accent deteriorates.' She preferred the days when Polly did not try, and had no reason for doing so. 'Whatever must the Devancourts think? They must wonder where on earth you picked up such an accent.'

'It's not *for* them to wonder,' Polly said calmly. 'They can't speak a *word* of English.'

She *was* calm. She was *too* calm, Gwenda decided. And Jean did not look at her this morning, nor she at him. It seemed to Gwenda that they no longer felt they needed to.

'Oh, *damn* the car,' she suddenly said.

Polly looked a little surprised, but said nothing.

'I think I'll have a look round the market this morning,' Gwenda said casually.

The three of them later set off, and there was only a brief chance to make an assignation, when Gwenda almost instinctively paused to look at a terrine on a stall.

The friendship with the Devancourts played into Polly's hands. Just at the right moment of the afternoon, Madame Devancourt came downstairs with a photograph-album to show to Gwenda – her collection of photographs of great houses, all to be gone over and explained in detail, trapping Gwenda who thought that she would scream. Monsieur Devancourt was attending to his fishing-tackle, so the two women were left alone, sitting in the stuffy salon. It was too hot to go out-of-doors, Madame Devancourt said.

Polly, who had gone into the lavatory, to try to plan her escape, saw the delightful sight of Gwenda with the album on her knees and Madame Devancourt leaning over, pointing at a photograph with a shaking finger. She slipped away without being seen. Jean, whose slack time it was, was waiting for her by the trout-trap. He pulled briars and bracken round them, like a nest, and, without much being said, made love to her.

The old lady smelled of camphor and lavender. She leant so close that Gwenda almost choked. Sometimes little flecks of spit fell on the pages of the album, and were quickly wiped away with the purple handkerchief. Gwenda tried to turn the pages quickly, but this would not do; for every coign and battlement and drawbridge had to be explained.

At last Monsieur Devancourt interrupted them. He had finished with his fishing-tackle and had come to take them for a little drive. Where was Mademoiselle Polly, he wondered. Gwenda flushed, and said that she must be writing letters in her room; and she excused herself from the outing, having a headache, she explained.

When they had gone, Gwenda walked up and down the garden-path. She strutted, with rather apart legs, like a starling. She listened and she looked about her. But there were no voices. It was a hot, humming afternoon. The Devancourts' car went off, and then there was nothing but the sound of insects, and hardly a leaf moved.

'Her mother!' Gwenda kept saying to herself. 'What would her mother think?'

It was a real headache she had, and the sun was making it much worse. It drove her inside – up to the vantage-point of her bedroom window.

It was a long time before she saw Polly coming back across the orchard. She walked slowly, and was alone. But that was only a ruse, a piece of trickery, Gwenda was sure.

She leant out of the window and called to her.

Polly seemed to come unwillingly, and stood hesitating at Gwenda's door.

'Where have you been?'

'For a walk.'

'With that dreadful loutish youth.'

Polly pressed her lips together.

'He's not even . . . ' Gwenda shrugged and turned aside; and after a few moments in which nothing else was said, Polly went quietly to her own room. Although she foresaw all the agonising awkwardness of the rest of the holiday – even, vaguely, of the rest of her life (Gwenda going on being huffy in Surrey) – she dismissed its importance. She stood before the looking-glass, combing her hair dreamily, staring at her freckled face with its band of sunburn across the forehead. It was she now, she decided, who had something exclusively her own, and it seemed to her that Gwenda had nothing – for even her memories were threadbare.

*

In the night, just before dawn, Gwenda woke up. Something had disturbed her, and she lay listening. There was silence, save for far-away cow-bells occasionally heard, then a floor-board creaked on the landing, and another. There was a gentle tapping on a bedroom door, and whispering.

She felt very cold, and sick, and deceived. She groped for her watch and peered at its luminous dial. It was nearly five o'clock. There was no real light in the sky, but perhaps a lessening of darkness.

Boards now creaked quite heavily along the passage, down the stairs. Gwenda got out of bed and went to the window, gently easing the shutters apart. As she did so, she heard an outside door open, and then a man's voice, speaking in low tones just below her. As her eyes grew used to the dark, she could make out two figures. After a moment, they moved off towards the courtyard, and she could see then that they were Jean and Monsieur Devancourt, both carrying fishing-rods. After a while, she heard the car starting up. It drove away, and she listened to it fading into the distance. Then the church clock struck five.

She left the shutters opened, and got back into bed. The sky slowly lightened, and she turned about heavily on the rough, darned sheets, longing for day to come so that she could get on with it, hasten through it. She searched her mind for plans for escaping from this hated place and, faced with all the complications, found none.

At breakfast, Gwenda was tired and silent. She seemed to brood over her coffee, staring before her, the drooping lines of her face deeper than ever. Monsieur Devancourt and Jean returned, having caught a large pike. Jean quickly slipped on a white jacket and brought fresh coffee. Monsieur Devancourt joined his mother, and peeled her orange for her, was full of simple triumph at his successful expedition, and now wanted nothing but to devote the rest of the day to her. They discussed their plans with great pleasure.

As usual, Madame Devancourt stopped on her way past Gwenda's and Polly's table.

'How early a riser would it be possible for you to be?' she asked. She seemed playful, like a child with a secret. She hardly waited for Gwenda's reply. 'Then,' she went on, 'we have a little plan, Louis and I. We know your disappointment at not reaching the source of the river, and we think that if we can start early tomorrow we can make the journey and spend the following night en route. It would give us great pleasure. How does it strike you?'

It struck Gwenda very well, and she said so. She brightened at once. Polly, who never understood what Madame Devancourt said, had not tried to listen. When it was explained to her, she was appalled, and too artless to hide the fact. Gwenda touched her foot under the table to bring her to her senses; but she could only stammer her thanks, while looking quite dismayed.

'But it's dreadful for *me*,' she complained to Gwenda afterwards. 'I can't understand a single word they say. To have a long drive like that with them!'

She knew that she would have to go. She was not strong enough to resist Gwenda over this. After a while she forgot what was hanging over her. She was living in the present, and it was time to go to market with Jean. Gwenda, more relaxed now, let them go alone, while she visited the garage and made another fuss.

The next day, they left very early. Jean was up before them and brought them coffee and bread. It was a strange, cold dawn, and they moved about quietly, with lowered voices, putting things into the boot of the car. At the last moment, Polly found she had forgotten her wild-flower book and had to get out of the car and go and find it. It was her only solace – and such a small one to her in her altered life – that she might see gentians growing in the mountains. Jean stood ready to open the car door for her when she returned. His eyes rested mournfully upon her. As they drove off, she could see him standing there, staring after her, look-ing sulky.

Madame Devancourt was quite talkative this morning. She sat in front beside her son, and half turned her wedge-shaped face back towards Gwenda. Polly she completely ignored. She thought her an imbecile and wondered that Gwenda had not found a more intelligent and presentable partner. It seemed to her that they were not so very much in love, though in such cases, she found it difficult to tell.

They stopped for lunch at an inn full of memories for Gwenda. She was delighted. Her spirits had been rising all morning, as they climbed higher into the colder air. She became animated, and infected Madame Devancourt with her liveliness. Both had such recollections – and all along the route the two widows exchanged them. La Bourboule! Le mont-Dore! There were changes to be noted. Yet so much had remained the same. Monsieur Devancourt listened to them as he drove, smiling to see his mother so gay. It was unusual for her to have feminine compan-ionship, and it seemed to do her good. Polly stared at the wild flowers along the way. She was obviously not allowed to stop to gather them. Monsieur Devancourt sometimes addressed a remark to her and then she started out of her dreams and became confused, and Gwenda had to rescue her.

After lunch, they went on to the source. The river they had driven beside became, at last, a thin fast trickle down the mountain-side. The road ended. They got out of the car and felt the air cold on their faces, and Polly looked about for flowers. The gentians were higher up, Gwenda told her, and she said that she for one was determined to climb to the summit, as she and Humphrey had done. They could be taken nearly there in the funicular.

Madame Devancourt declined. She would sit in the car and wait for them, and be quite happy reading her novel, she explained.

'Your mother is charming,' Gwenda told Monsieur Devancourt as they waited for the lift to come down.

'It is altogether a charming day,' he said.

As they were hauled up by the cable-car, Polly, although dizzy, peered down at the rocks for flowers. She saw miniature daffodils, drifts of white anemones, and then, in a crevice, a patch of gentians. The funicular swung high above them and came to a stop.

This much higher up, it was windy. Strands of hair kept lashing her cheeks. She hated the wind, and she hated being so high. Above them, at the top of a zigzagging path, she could see two tiny figures waving from the highest rock.

'I shouldn't like to go up there,' she said to Gwenda.

'But that's why we've come,' Gwenda said with a tone of scorn. 'Humphrey . . .' Then she changed her mind about what she was going to say. She would climb to the summit alone with Monsieur Devancourt and say not a word about her husband all the way.

Polly, on this lower slope, was quite content to scramble about and pick flowers. The tiny daffodils were exquisite, and there were varieties she could not classify until she got back to the car and found them in her book. But she could find no gentians. They seemed to grow in rockier parts. Here, there was only shabby, wind-bitten grass and patches of dirty snow. Barbed-wire ran along the edge of the ridge. Beyond it rocks went sheer down to the valley.

From the summit, Gwenda and Monsieur Devancourt, rather out-of-breath, paused triumphantly and looked about them at the wide view. They could see Polly below, darting like a child or a bee, from one flower to another, and they called to her, but their voices were snatched out of their throats by the wind. Then Gwenda began to shout in earnest, for she could see that Polly was trying to crawl under the barbed wire. She was lying on her stomach, reaching for something. Gwenda and Monsieur Devancourt called out in warning and began to scramble down the slippery path as quickly as they could. Before they could come within Polly's hearing, there was a dreadful rushing noise of bouncing and cascading scree, of rocks dropping with an echo upon other rocks. The noise continued long after Polly had disappeared and Gwenda and Monsieur Devancourt had come to the newly-opened fissure. Beside it was a handful of flowers, and a piece of gentian-blue chocolate-paper which Polly must have been reaching for.

Monsieur Devancourt had been a tower of strength. He had interviewed police officials and undertakers, intercepted newspaper-men, booked the flight home, arranged about the coffin, sent telegrams, and brought Gwenda back to Selonac to pack the cases. And every now and then he bewailed the fact that the tragic excursion had been his idea.

Gwenda was stunned, rather than grief-stricken. She leant on his kindness. She let him do everything for her.

Madame Devancourt now seemed to have withdrawn. Her son's solicitude was irksome and disturbing, and looks of suspicion were cast on him and Gwenda. The episode had been distasteful, encroaching – and she had had enough of her, this Englishwoman, with her demanding ways. Instead of taking command, as one of her kind should have done, she had clung to a man like any silly girl.

'I can never say "thank you" enough,' Gwenda said. She had come to them in the salon to bid them good-bye. 'When you visit England, I hope you will stay with me, in my house in Surrey.'

Madame Devancourt nodded forbiddingly; but Gwenda hardly noticed. In her mind, she was introducing Monsieur Devancourt – he had asked her to call him 'Louis' – to her friends. 'Do you play bridge?' she very nearly asked him; but she stopped herself in time. She shook hands. Once more Louis blamed himself for Polly's death, and his mother clicked her tongue impatiently.

Out in the courtyard, the car was waiting – ready at last; ready too late – and Jean was packing the cases into the boot. Gwenda had forgotten all about him. Madame Peloux stood by to wish her 'Bon voyage'.

She looked into her bag for a tip, and advanced with it folded in her hand, ready to slip it into Jean's. He slammed down the lid of the boot and, as Gwenda came up to him, he turned sulkily aside, and walked away.

His face was swollen; he made a blubbering noise, like a miserable child, and, going faster and faster, made off across the orchard.

'Ah, Jean! Jean!' his mother said, with a sigh and a shake of her head, looking after him.

Gwenda got into the car. It started perfectly. She waved to Madame Peloux and to Louis Devancourt, who had come out of the inn to watch her go, and drove away, towards the airport.

Mothers

Outside the hospital entrance the gravel was bright and unrelenting. She stood with the other mothers and waited for the doors to open. Each had a basket; the clean clothes and picture books, barley-sugar, the bunch of pansies from the garden.

'What will he do?' she wondered. She was prepared for tears and pleading and an appalling scene at the end. Some of the mothers chatted as they waited. These had been before, knew the ropes, knew the way in and the nurses by sight. She stood a little apart, with her back against the warm roughness of the brick wall, feeling immature – she could never overcome the sense that she was too young to have a child and she was uncertain of her voice and of her eyes, always too readily filled with tears.

In the hot sunlight the weathervane over the clock tower flashed brightly; the smell of the hot gravel mingled with the other dry mid-summer scents, of crumbling grey earth and geraniums, tar and the brick wall; but little wafts of coolness came occasionally from the hospital windows, little cool dreadful smells which froze her bowels, hollowed her inside.

The rounded, solid notes of the clock stuck two. The women sauntered closer and then the doors were opened. As they passed into the vestibule, she was conscious of another smell, the damp sharp sweat of the other mothers in their summer frocks. Then the cold neutral air of the hospital engulfed them as they went forward. She felt like Alice going down the rabbit hole. They kept passing room with half-open doors, but there was never time to look into the rooms; just a glimpse of a nurse writing at a desk, a place filled with strange shining apparatus, flowers in the centre – of a large ward, a white kitchen.

She followed the others into the children's ward.

'Hello, Mummy.'

She came straight to him, was at once confronted by the brightness of his little face, made strange by the bandage over his brow. He was facing the door – in a draught, she thought immediately.

Their greeting was casual in contrast to the embraces of all the others. Again she felt her immaturity. She felt that she would never look motherly.

In her sandals and blue cotton frock she seemed too young for the part. She did not even have the womanly smell of the others.

'How are you, darling?'

'All right. Better.'

'And what's it like, being here?'

'All right. They think you're really babyish. They give you a plate with Bo-Peep on it.'

'How amusing.'

'And cut up your meat.'

'Perhaps they are afraid you'll spill your gravy.'

'One girl has her legs burnt. They paint them blue and she screams like mad. Her mother upset a saucepan over her.'

'How frightful for her mother.'

'Frightful for her, you mean.' He laughed excitedly.

She looked round quickly and turned over his temperature chart. It jagged halfway across the paper.

'They don't tell you what your temperature is.'

'No. They never do. It *is* nice to see you.' She sat on the bed and took one of his rough warm little paws in her hand. His wrists were impossibly thin, had always been. He kept shoving up the bandage which had slipped over one eye. Cotton-wool with bits of lint stuck out in all directions. Tufts of hair stood up from the top of his head like feathers. His bed was like a battlefield. She tried to straighten the sheets, looking round at the neat children sitting up in tidy cots and beds, while their mothers displayed one thing after another from their baskets.

'I brought you a present,' she said, suddenly remembering, and conscious that he waited. 'But I want you to keep it till I go.'

'Why?'

'It will be something to think about after I've gone.'

'Oh.'

'What did you have for dinner?'

'Mince and rice.'

'Are you good?'

'Yes. One of the nurses said I'd wet my bed. "Oh, you dirty little boy," she said to me. And I hadn't done any such thing.'

'Oh, darling. So what did you say?'

'I said, "Go on! You! Liar! Rat!" To myself.'

She bit her lip. 'What are the others like? The other nurses.'

'Sister's very nice. She's not a bit cruel. She lets me mind that little baby in the corner. If it falls on its back, I ring the bell. Now can I read to you?'

She sat and watched the clock and listened to him reading, stumbling and monotonous. He sat bolt upright in his untidy bed, with the book held high before him. One or two of the other women looked across and smiled at him, then at her. A boy at the end seemed very ill. He stared before him, his face grey and small; his eyes and the way of holding his head, like an old man. His mother sat beside him and watched him. They did not speak.

'The fox then hid behind the door ... ' he read on.

'Children's stories are always full of foxes, and they are forever wicked,' she mused. 'How odd, coming to hospital to be read to.'

And then the clock outside in the sunlight struck the hour. Three o'clock. A young nurse came in and stood there smiling in the doorway, waiting for them to go.

'Darling, I have to go now.'

'Oh, I haven't finished the book.'

'Practise it and read the rest next time.'

'I've been practising it since half past five this morning.'

'I'm sorry, pet.' She bent and kissed him and cords twisted up tightly in her throat as she felt his warm, dry lips on her face. He was sitting up straight on the high, narrow bed, his eyes steady and bright beneath the bandage.

'Good-bye, my darling. The minute I am gone you shall open your parcel.' He looked excited at that. Other children were setting up a wild howling. The look he exchanged with her showed contempt for this. He waved his thin hand as she turned away. The other was on the string of the parcel.

'Good-bye.'

She walked proudly down the corridor with the other mothers. All their eyes were over-brilliant with anxiety; hers with pride and anxiety.

'He's not spoilt,' she thought. 'When it comes to it, he isn't. He's independent and he adapts himself.'

She stepped out on the bright gravel.

He laid the parcel unopened on his pillow and lay down and closed his eyes. Tears were red-hot and hard like bullets beneath his lids. 'My darling Mummy,' he said to himself. 'My darling Mummy. My darling ... '

'Tea, Harry,' said the nurse. 'Tired already?'

He sat up and smiled.

'You haven't opened your parcel.'

'I couldn't – undo it.'

'Oh, it's only a bow, you lazy-bones. And look at your bed. Let me tidy you up again. Now Sheila, that's quite enough of that. You try to be sensible like Harry.'

Harry looked neither to left nor right, neither at Sheila nor the nurse. He picked up a piece of bread and butter from his plate and took a bite. It hurt his throat going down, but he went on eating. He sat there with his eyelids lowered, looking rather prim and self-satisfied as he ate.

Tall Boy

This Sunday had begun well, by not having begun too early. Jasper Jones overslept – or, rather, slept later than usual, for there was nothing to get up for – and so had got for himself an hour's remission from the Sunday sentence. It was after half-past ten and he had escaped, for one thing, the clatter of the milk-van, a noise which for some reason depressed him. But church bells now began to toll – to him an even more dispiriting sound, though much worse in the evening.

The curtains drawn across the window did not meet. At night, they let a steamy chink of light out on to the darkness, and this morning let a grey strip of daylight in.

Jasper got out of bed and went to this window. It was high up in the house, and a good way down below, in the street, he could see some children playing on the crumbling front steps, and two women, wearing pale, tinselly saris and dark overcoats, hurrying along on the other side of the road.

In this part of London, nationalities clung together – Poles in one street, African negroes in the next. This road – St Luke's – was mostly Pakistani. Jasper thought he was the only West Indian all the way along it. *His* people were quite distant – in the streets near the railway-bridge, where the markets were, where he had been unable to find a room.

This bed-sitter was his world. There was distinction in having it all to himself. In such a neighbourhood, few did. He had never in his life known such isolation. Back in his own country, home had bulged with people – breadwinners or unemployed, children, the elderly helpless – there was never an empty corner or time of real silence.

White people and coloured people now walked in twos and threes along St Luke's Road to the church on the corner. The peal of bells jangled together, faltered, then faded. Church-goers stepped up their pace. The one slow bell began and, when that stopped, the road was almost empty. For a time, there were only the children below playing some hopping game up and down the steps.

It was a very wide road. Fifty years ago, all those four-storeyed houses had been lived in by single families – with perhaps a little servant girl sleeping in an attic – in a room on the same floor as Jasper's. The flights of broken front steps led up to the porches with scabby pillars and – always – groups of dirty milk bottles. The sky was no-colour above the slate roofs and chimney-pots and television aerials, and the street looked no-colour, too – the no-colour of most of Jasper's Sunday mornings in London. Either the sky pressed down on him, laden with smog or rain or dark, lumbering clouds, or it vanished, it simply wasn't there, was washed away by rain, or driven somewhere else by the wind.

He was bored with the street, and began to get dressed. He went down several times to the lavatory on the half-landing, but each time the door was bolted. He set about shaving – trimming his moustache neatly in a straight line well above his full, up-tilted lip. He washed a pair of socks and some handkerchiefs. When he had dusted the window, he spread the wet handkerchiefs, stretched and smoothed, against the pane to dry, having no iron. Then – in between times he was trying the lavatory door without luck – he fried a slice of bread in a little black pan over the gas-ring and, when it was done, walked about the room eating it, sometimes rubbing the tips of his greasy fingers in his frizzy hair, which was as harsh as steel wool.

He was a tall, slender young man, and his eyes had always looked mournful, even when he was happier, though hungry, at home in his own country. Tomorrow, he would be twenty-six. He remained, so far, solitary, worked hard, and grieved hard over his mistakes. He saved, and sent money back home to Mam. Poverty from the earliest days – which makes some spry and crafty – had left him diffident and child-like.

At last – having found the lavatory door open – he set out for his usual Sunday morning walk. People were coming out of St Luke's, standing in knots by the porch, taking it in turns to shake hands with the Vicar. Their clothes – especially the women's – were dauntingly respectable. One Sunday, Jasper had rather fearfully gone to the service, but the smell of damp stone, the mumbled, hurried prayers, the unrhythmical rush and gabble of psalms dismayed him. He had decided that this sense of alien-ation was one he could avoid.

Pubs had just opened, and he went into one – the Victoria and Albert – and ordered a glass of beer. This he did for passing time and not for enjoyment. Sweet, thick drinks were too expensive, and this warmish, wry-tasting one, for which he tried to acquire a liking, was all he could afford. It made him wonder about Londoners, though, as that church service had. There seemed to be inherent in them a wish for self-punishment he could not understand – a greyness of soul and taste, to match the climate. Perhaps in total depression there was safety. His own depression – of fits and starts – held danger in it, he guessed.

The barman went round the tables collecting glasses, carrying away five in each hand, fingers hooked into them. The pub was filling up. As soon as the door swung to, it was pushed open again. After a time, people coming in had rain on their shoulders, and wiped it from their faces. The sight of this was a small calamity to Jasper, who had planned to spend at least half an hour queasily sipping his beer. Now he would have to drain his glass quickly and go, because of his shoes and the need to have them dry for the morning – and his suit.

The rain brushed the streets, swept along by the wind. He changed into a run, shoulders high and his head held back to stop the rain running down his spine, so that it spurted instead from his eyelids and his moustache. His arms going like pistons, his knees lifted high, he loped slowly, easily. In one way, he loved and welcomed the rain, for giving him the chance to run. He always wanted to run, but people stared when he did so, unless he were running for a bus. Running for running's sake was an oddity. He was worried only about his suit and shoes, and the shoes were already soaked, and there was a soapy squelch in his socks.

He reached home, panting and elated, and sprang lightly up the three flights of stairs. When he had hung up his damp suit and put on his working overalls, stuffed his wet shoes with newspaper and set them to dry, soles facing the gas-ring, steaming faintly, he began to mix up his dinner. Two rashers of bacon went into the frying-pan, then he took a handful or two of flour and rubbed in some dripping. He shaped the dough carefully into balls with his long, pale-palmed hands, and put them into the bacon fat. They were as near as he could get to his mother's fried dumplings. Perhaps, just at this moment, she would be making them at home, dumplings and sweet potato pudding. He imagined home having the same time as England. He would have felt quite lost to his loved ones if, when he woke in the night, he could not be sure that they were lying in darkness, too; and, when his own London morning came, theirs also came, the sun streamed through the cracks of their hut in shanty-town, and the little girls began to chirp and skip about. He could see them clearly now, as he knelt by the gas-ring – their large, rolling eyes, their close-cropped, frizzy hair. Most of the time, they had bare patches on their scalps from sores they would not leave alone, those busy fingers scratching, slapped down by Mam. They all had names of jewels, or semi-precious stones – Opal, Crystal and Sapphyra, his little sisters. He smiled, and gently shook his head, as he turned the dumplings with a fork.

All the afternoon, the rain flew in gusts against the window. If he could not go out and walk about the streets, there was nothing to do. He took the chair to the window, and looked through the blurred pane at the street below; but there was no life down there – only an occasional umbrella bobbing along, or a car swishing by slowly, throwing up puddle-water with a melancholy sound.

The launderette round the corner was open on Sunday afternoons and evenings, and sometimes he took his dirty shirts and overalls and sat there before the washing-machine, waiting, his hands hanging loose between his knees, and the greenish, fluorescent light raining down on him. He might make a dash towards it, if the rain eased up a little. His heart began to ache for the bright launderette, as if for a dear dream.

Half-way through the afternoon, he quite suddenly experienced utter desolation. He knew the signs of it coming, and he closed his eyes and sat warily still, feeling silence freezing in his ear-drums. Then he got up quietly and began to pad up and down the room; stopping at the far wall from the window, he leant against the wall and rhythmically banged his forehead against it, his eyes shut tight again, his lips parted. Very soon, a sharp rapping came back from the other side – his only human recognition of the day. He reeled away from the wall, and sat on the edge of the bed, sighing dramatically, for something to do.

What light there had been during the day seemed to be diminishing. Time was going. Sunday was going. He lay on his back on the bed, while the room darkened, and he counted his blessings – all off by heart, he knew them well. There was nothing wrong. He was employed. He had a room, and a good suit, and his shoes would soon be dry. There was money going back home to Mam. No one here, in England, called him 'Nigger', or put up their fists to him. That morning, he had sat there in the pub without trouble. There *was* no trouble. Once, at work, they had all laughed at him when he was singing 'I'm Dreaming of a White Christmas' as he loaded a van; but it was good-humoured laughter. *Tall Boy* they called him; but they had nick-names for some of the others, too – Dusty and Tiny and Buster.

Jasper thought about each of them in turn, trying to picture their Sundays from Monday morning chat that he always listened to carefully. The single ones tinkered with their motor-bikes, then went out on them, dressed in black mock leather, with a white-helmeted girl on the pillion. The married ones mended things, and put up shelves, they 'went over to Mother's to tea', and looked at the telly as soon as the religious programmes were over. Dusty had even built a greenhouse in his back garden, and grew chrysanthemums. But, whatever they did, all were sorry when Monday morning came. They had not longed for it since Friday night, as Jasper had.

The rain fell into the dark street. Whether it eased up or not, he had to catch the last post. He fetched pen and ink and the birthday-card for himself that he had chosen with great care, gravely conscious of the rightness of receiving one. He dipped the pen in the ink, then sat back, wondering what to write. He would have liked to sign it 'From a well-wisher', as if it were to come out of the blue; but this seemed insincere, and he prized sincerity. After a while, he simply wrote, 'With greetings from Mr Jasper

Jones', stamped the envelope, and went again to the window to look at his Sunday enemy, the rain.

In the end, he had to make a dash for it, splashing up rain from the wet pavements as he ran with long, loose strides through the almost deserted streets.

He thought Monday morning tea-break talk the best of the week. He could not sincerely grouse with the others about beginning work again, so he listened happily to all they had to say. This had a comforting familiarity, like his dreams of home – the game of darts, the fish-and-chips, Saturday night at White City, and *Sunday Night at the Palladium* on telly while the children slap-dashed through the last of their homework; beef was roasted, a kitchen chair repainted and a fuse mended, mother-in-law was visited; someone had touched a hundred on the motorway, and was ticked off by his elders and betters; there had been a punch-up outside the Odeon, but few sexual escapades this week – as far as the young ones were concerned – because of the weather.

'What about you, Tall Boy?' Buster asked.

Jasper smiled and shrugged. 'Well, I just had a quiet time,' he said.

The birthday-card had not arrived that morning. At first, he had been disappointed, for the lack of it made his birthday seem not to have happened, but now he had begun to look forward to finding it there when he got home from work. He kept fingering the knot of his tie, and opening the collar of his overalls more.

'Hey, Tall Boy, what the devil you got there?' Dusty came over, stared at Jasper's tie, then appeared to be blinded by it, reeling away theatrically, saying 'Strewth!', his hands over his eyes.

Some of the others joined in in a wonderful, warm sort of abuse – just how they talked to one another, and which made Jasper so happy, grinning, putting up his fists at them, dancing up and down on his toes like a boxer.

'No, come off it, mate,' Dusty said, recovering a little. 'You can't wear that.'

'It's hand-painted,' said Jasper. 'I got it for my birthday.'

'So it's his birthday,' Dusty said, turning to the others. He advanced slowly, menacingly towards Jasper, stuck out his finger and prodded his tie. 'You know what that means, don't you?'

To prolong the delight of being in the middle of it all, Jasper pretended that he did not.

'It means,' said Dusty slowly, knocking his fist against Jasper's chest. 'It means, Tall Boy, you got to buy the cakes for tea.'

'Yeah, that's right,' said Buster. 'You buy the cakes.'

'I know, I know,' said Jasper in his sing-song voice. He threw back his head and gave his high bubbling laugh, and jingled coins in both his pockets.

The weather had brightened and, as Jasper walked home from work, groups of women were sitting out on the steps of houses, waiting for their husbands to come home, shouting warnings to their children playing on the pavements.

Traffic at this hour was heavy and the streets were crowded, as London was emptying out its workers – thousands of arteries drawing them away, farther and farther from the heart of the city, out to the edges of the countryside.

At home, his birthday-card was waiting for him, and there was a miracle there, too; something he hardly dared to pick up – one of the rare letters from home, come on the right day. He sat down on the edge of the bed and opened it. Mam could never write much. It was a great labour and impatience to her to put pen to paper, and here was only a line or two to say the money had arrived safely and all were well. She did not mention his birthday. When she was writing, it must have been far ahead, and out of mind.

The letter was folded round a photograph. Who had taken it, he could not imagine; but there were the three little girls, his sisters, sitting on the steps of the wooden house – Opal, Crystal and Sapphyra. They were grinning straight at him, and Sapphyra's middle top teeth were missing. She looked quite different, he thought for a moment; then decided no, she was the same – the lovely same. He stared at the photograph for a long time, then got up with a jerk, and put it on the shelf by his bed, propped against the alarm clock, and his birthday-card beside it.

He went to the window and pushed down the sash and leant out, his elbows resting on the frame. The noise of children playing came up. He had a peaceful feeling, listening to the street sounds, looking at a golden, dying light on the rooftops across the road.

He stayed there until the gold went out of the light, and he felt suddenly hungry. Then he shut the window, unhooked the frying-pan and took an opener to a tin of beans. He smiled as he edged the opener round the rim. 'They liked the cakes,' he kept on thinking. The cakes he'd bought for tea.

He squatted by the gas-ring, turning the beans about in the pan, humming to himself. He was glad he'd bought the tie – otherwise they'd never have known, and he could never have treated them. The tie had been a good idea. He might give it another airing, this nice, dry evening – stroll among the crowds outside the Odeon and the bowling alley.

He ate the beans out of the pan, spooning them up contentedly as he sat on the bed, staring at Opal and Crystal and Sapphyra, who grinned cheekily back at him, sitting in a neat row, their bare feet stuck out in front of them, out of focus, and sharp black shadows falling on their white dresses.

Praises

The sunlight came through dusty windows into Miss Smythe's Gown Department on the first floor of the building. Across the glass were red and white notices announcing the clearance sale. It was an early summer's early evening, and the London rush hour at its worst. Rush hours were now over for Miss Smythe, and she listened to the hum of this one, feeling strange not to be stepping along the crowded pavement towards the Underground.

In a corner of the department some of the juniors had begun to blow up balloons. The last customers had gone, and several of the office staff came in with trays of glasses. With remarkable deftness as soon as the shop was closed – for the last time – they had draped and decorated Miss Smythe's display counter, and they set the trays down on this.

The great store, built in the 1860s, was due for demolition. As business had slowly failed, like a tide on its way out, the value of the site had gone on growing. The building had lately seemed to be demolishing itself, or at least not hindering its happening. Its green dome still stood with acid clarity against the summer sky; but the stone walls had not been washed for many years and were black with grime and dashed by pigeons' droppings.

The red and white SALE notices added to the look of dereliction. In the past, sales had been discreetly managed, really not more than a passing round of the word. The clientele – the ex-clientele – was miserable about the notices. Going by in Bentleys and taxis, they glanced away, hurt, as if catching an old friend out in some vulgarity.

Miss Smythe trod softly across the carpeted way to the ladies' cloakroom – the customers' cloakroom. Here she took off her rings – her mother's engagement ring and her father's signet – and carefully washed her hands. She went over and over with the lather, as if she were about to perform an operation. Then she took a long time drying her hands, easing back cuticles, from habit, and looking thoughtfully about her.

She passed a hand over grey, tightly permed hair, and studied herself in the full-length glass. She knew that a presentation was to be made, and she wished to look her best. It was rumoured that Mr Wakelin himself was to give a little speech.

Her figure was more imposing by being top-heavy. Although her hips were quite trim and her legs slender – she prided herself on her legs – her bosom was full, and there was a softness about her sloping shoulders. Her hands were plump, too, and white. She also prided herself on her hands.

Back in the salon things were livening up, and assistants from other departments crowding in. She saw her friend, Miss Fortescue, from Hats. (Millinery was not a word one used: clients who did were subtly put right.) Miss Fortescue, a younger woman than Miss Smythe, now had to find another position. It would not be easy for her, in her forties. However, she had a gentleman friend and could marry tomorrow if she cared to, as she had often told her juniors.

Miss Smythe did not discuss her private life with her assistants. Some mornings she had arrived with a bunch of flowers, and let the girls conjecture. There was really nothing to conjecture. She had lived alone since her parents died and knew that she always would, being now too fastidious, she thought, for marriage.

She was glad that it was time for her to retire. She could not have brought herself to work elsewhere, or to lower her standards. She had grown old along with her customers. Some she had known as young women, brought by their mothers to the salon for the first time. In those days she had been an assistant, handing pins and running errands. In these last years, or perhaps it was since the war, young women had not come with their mothers. Miss Smythe always enquired after them, but never met them.

'Well, you'll be glad to see the back of it all,' Miss Fortescue said to her. 'These last few weeks!'

'It has had its sordid side,' Miss Smythe agreed. 'But, no, I shan't be glad to see the back of it.'

Some of the last marked-down, soiled, leftover garments lay crumpled on countertops, as if at a jumble sale, and, really, Miss Fortescue complained, some of the goods she had been expected to dispose of had come from a bygone age. 'We now know what "old hat" means,' she had told her assistants, spinning round on her hand a confection of satin and osprey feathers. She *was* too familiar with the girls, and they led her on with a kind of sycophantic raillery, even daring.

The evening sun slanted across the room at its last angle, showing up shabbiness. Where fixtures and showcases had already been removed the surrounding walls had dirty, yellowing paint, and there were cobwebs clinging to nails. For days the cleaners – those who remained – had done nothing but shift stock. In this showroom the trodden carpet, once so deep, so rich, had been left, and the dusty chandelier with its grubby drops of glass, its rosettes and flutings. Someone, giggling, climbed on to a stool and tied a bunch of balloons to it.

One of Miss Smythe's own girls came to her with a tray of drinks and she put out her plump white hand and selected a glass of sherry. She also accepted from someone else two prawns on a little biscuit. Soon there would be crumbs and cigarette ash all over her carpet; but it was gritty already, with days of people traipsing through. She remembered it when it was new, replacing the faded moss-green one of her early days, and how proud she was of it, for it was her own, she alone had been responsible for it. Now she watched ash being flicked on it – regardless, as she told herself.

Because her showroom had been chosen for the party, Miss Smythe was regarded as their hostess by the older members of the staff. They came to greet her as soon as they entered – old Mr Messenger from Accounts, the restaurant manageress, and Miss Chivers from Hairdressing.

She received them graciously, standing beneath the decorated chandelier; but was not too much taken up with them to ignore one of her own girls who, drinking her third gin-and-French, was laughing noisily. She gave her one of her little glances and, for the first time, the girl looked at her defiantly, as if to imply that the old reign was over; habit won, however, and she fell silent.

'My dear Miss Smythe,' said Mr Wakelin, coming in almost unnoticed, taking her hand. He was an unknown figure to most of those present, who were ruled by his underlings and hardly wondered if there were anyone in higher authority.

Miss Smythe received him with her usual poise. She had served royalty in her time, and knew how to behave – with calm deference, but her own kind of dignity.

Ineffectually Mr Wakelin tapped with a gold pencil on the side of his glass; then someone helpfully – but without taste, Miss Smythe thought – banged on a tray. 'Uncalled for,' was always one of her sternest terms of condemnation.

'This poignant party,' Mr Wakelin began, standing beside her. She moved back a little, discreetly. 'For it is farewell for all of us,' he went on, 'for some after many, many years.'

Miss Smythe looked down at the carpet, saw a match-stick, but forbore to pick it up.

With great authority, Mr Wakelin handed his glass to someone standing nearby; unhurriedly took out his bifocal spectacles, polished them, put them on, took from his pocket a piece of paper. He glanced at this and touched the knot of his Old Etonian tie. No one moved. 'Ah! the *savoir faire!*' Miss Smythe thought admiringly.

'Our dear old friend, Mr Messenger, from Accounts,' Mr Wakelin said. He smiled across at him and made a little joke about his resistance to the computer being installed, and a ruffle of laughter came from his staff, and then clapping as he came forward to accept an envelope and a gold watch, handed first to Mr Wakelin by his secretary. Besides their envelopes Miss Fortescue received a tooled leather writing case, the restaurant manager-ess a fountain pen. It was obvious that Mr Wakelin's secretary had known how to grade the presents.

'And to all of you – some of you for too short a time our friends – I say thank you for your loyalty and support, and not least in these last difficult weeks; and may God go with you in all your days, and bring you into your desired haven.'

A deeply religious man, Miss Smythe had always heard, and his beau-tiful, unhurried voice and the last cadence brought tears into her eyes. All the same, she was a little shocked, a little embarrassed, thinking he had fin-ished speaking. Someone even began to clap. However, raising his hand and turning towards her he went on: 'I have left mention of Miss Smythe until the very end.' For a moment she had been afraid that his secretary had at last been found wanting, but there she was at his side, with the last parcel and envelope.

Because of her momentary confusion, Mr Wakelin's words came as a shock to Miss Smythe, sweeping away her emotion, making her feel apprehen-sive.

'How long Miss Smythe has been with us is her own secret,' Mr Wakelin said. 'I will only say that she is our oldest friend, and one who has never fal-tered, never failed us. Never spared herself, or lowered the standards which so many young people under her have learnt to accept and live by. This is no mean thing to look back upon, at the end of a successful career, and I hope that she will do so with pleasure and satisfaction in many years of happy retirement.

'Much of the good that has been done in this ... well, I almost said *hal-lowed* building ... can be traced to her influence. And nothing that was wrong *can* be. The building will go, alas! as you all know; but that spirit will be scattered more broadly because of it. So out of disaster comes good; out of sorrow, inspiration. Miss Smythe, this present which I give you on behalf of the company and your colleagues cannot be in any measure what you deserve, but simply a token of our respect and, may I say, our love? Under this roof, where you have served so long, I should like to think that the last words said were yours.'

Miss Smythe stepped forward and took the little gift-wrapped, oblong box. She stood under the chandelier again, holding her present in both hands before her, and thanked them all, after half-turning to Mr Wakelin to thank him personally.

His rhythm was infectious, and she fell easily into it.

'I shall not say very much to you,' she continued, 'for there is so little to be said. Our hearts have their own knowledge, and there we must strive to keep alive all that went on here – even when we see another building standing where this one stood, and others working in it.

'It has been a great thing to all of us, I know; but may I for a moment be personal? For this place has been my life.' (One of her juniors thought it strange that the word 'shop' had not been mentioned all evening.) 'And I have never wanted another. I remember the great days. It has been my privilege to serve – and to have for friends – the highest in the land. It has been a – a very glamorous life.'

She stepped back, and the clapping began again. Mr Wakelin thanked her quietly, obviously much moved, conversation broke out and the trays were being carried round.

Five minutes after Mr Wakelin left, Miss Smythe decided, was her time to go. She did her rounds, put on her Persian lamb coat and her paisley turban and went down in the lift for the last time.

The street had a golden, dusty look; there were flowers on barrows, and the smell of them in the air. The rush hour was over.

She repeated in her mind, as she went towards the Underground, the words of Mr Wakelin's speech. So many had flown away for ever, but a few phrases she captured and imprisoned. All the way to Marylebone station she was in a strange state, as if the two glasses of sherry had gone to her head.

It was an unfamiliar train she got into, and none of her regular friends was on it – all gone homewards long ago. Strangers got in and sat in silence. In one day her friends had vanished. And those years of coming on the train from Denham had made many friends for her – even gentlemen friends, the only ones of that kind she had ever had. 'Good-morning, Miss Smythe, and how are we this morning? Now, can you help me with nine across? Animal wrongly chained. Seven letters, h the third.'

After a while of looking at her own *Daily Telegraph*, she could say, 'Echidna,' and blush at her erudition.

'Miss Smythe, you are a genius.' Perhaps, she thought, she had had too much praise all her life, and nothing else. Or might have been praised so much, *because* she had nothing else.

And her train friends, even if not – all of them – gentlemen, had been so gentlemanly. Mr Parkinson, so gallant; Mr Taylor, so serious-minded; Mr Westropp, that great rose-grower, a little flirtatious, but nothing objectionable – leaning out of the carriage window, lifting his folded *Times* to signal to her as she came on to the platform. 'We can't take off without Miss Smythe.'

And sometimes he brought those bouquets of roses from his garden in Gerrards Cross over which the juniors – Miss Smythe's girls – had conjectured; or, much earlier in the year, bunches of what he called 'daffs'. He was well-intentioned and Miss Smythe, deploring 'daffs', forgave him although none of her clients, from whom she took her standards, would have allowed the word (or non-word) to pass their lips.

Now she opened her large handbag and looked at the beautifully wrapped package. She knew what it was and had one already, but would treasure it none the less. She would have liked to have shown it to Mr Parkinson and the others, but would probably never see them again.

'Too much praise?' she wondered again. But it would have to last her for the rest of her life, and she had to remember it. She wished that she had refused the second glass of sherry, for her head ached and she kept recalling a jarring note among the praises.

When she had told them of her glamorous life, one of the women from the alterations room had smothered a laugh – or pretended to try to smother it. For Miss Smythe had had her battles. It had not been, all of it, a bed of roses without thorns. *That* woman had been a thorn. 'A *thorn*,' Miss Smythe repeated to herself, glancing muzzily out at fleeting houses and gardens.

There had been, lately, enemies up there in the alterations room. That one especially. The chief thorn, kneeling in the fitting room, going round a hemline, flicking pins out of the black velvet pad on her wrist, spitting out measurements. For she resented criticism. And workmanship was a thing of the past, of the days of shoulder-paddings and moulded bustlines. Now they had nothing to do but take up a straight skirt an inch.

The Persian lamb was too warm for this evening; but she wore it because she had it. And it was the slowest journey she had ever made along that line – stopping at every station. Coming out of London in this sunset, on this last day, everything looked new to her – she noted men working in blossoming gardens, stretches of water with sea-gulls on them, and silver birches, her favourite tree.

The stations at which they stopped were like sets in an old Western film, ramshackle with wooden buildings, and pointed slat fences and platform shelters. And no one about. No streams of dark-suited men hastening, with their evening papers, towards the ticket barriers.

She sat back idly, her hands clasped over the bag on her lap, and looked out of the window at the evening scene as if for the first time, not the last.

In and Out the Houses

Kitty Miller, wearing a new red hair-ribbon, bounced along the vicarage drive, skipping across ruts and jumping over puddles.

Visiting took up all of her mornings in the school holidays. From kitchen to kitchen, round the village, she made her progress, and, this morning, felt drawn towards the vicarage. Quite sure of her welcome, she tapped on the back door.

'Why, Kitty Miller!' said the Vicar, opening it. He looked quite different from in church, Kitty thought. He was wearing an open-necked shirt and an old, darned cardigan. He held a tea-towel to the door-handle, because his fingers were sticky. He and his wife were cutting up Seville oranges for marmalade and there was a delicious, tangy smell about the kitchen.

Kitty took off her coat, and hung it on the usual peg, and fetched a knife from the dresser drawer.

'You are on your rounds again,' Mr Edwards said. 'Spreading light and succour about the parish.'

Kitty glanced at him rather warily. She preferred him not to be there, disliking men about her kitchens. She reached for an orange, and watching Mrs Edwards for a moment out of the corners of her eyes, began to slice it up.

'What's new?' asked the Vicar.

'Mrs Saddler's bad,' she said accusingly. He should be at that bedside, she meant to imply, instead of making marmalade. 'They were saying at the Horse and Groom that she won't last the day.'

'So we are not your first call of the morning?'

She had, on her way here, slipped round the back of the pub and into the still-room, where Miss Betty Benford, eight months pregnant, was washing the floor, puffing and blowing as she splashed grey soapy water over the flags with a gritty rag. When this job was done – to Miss Betty's mind, not Kitty's – they drank a cup of tea together and chatted about the baby, woman to woman. The village was short of babies, and Kitty visualised pushing this one out in its pram, taking it round with her on her visits.

In his office, the landlord had been typing the luncheon menus. The keys went down heavily, his finger hovered, and stabbed. He often made mistakes, and this morning had typed 'Jam Fart and Custard'. Kitty considered – and then decided against – telling the Vicar this.

'They have steak-and-kidney pie on the set menu today,' she said instead.

'My favourite!' groaned the Vicar. 'I *never* get it.'

'You had it less than a fortnight ago,' his wife reminded him.

'And what pudding? If it's treacle tart I shall cry bitterly.'

'Jam tart,' Kitty said gravely. 'And custard.'

'I quite like custard, too,' he said simply.

'Or choice of cheese and biscuits.'

'I should have cheese and biscuits,' Mrs Edwards said.

It was just the kind of conversation Kitty loved.

'Eight-and-sixpence,' she said. 'Coffee extra.'

'To be rich! To be rich!' the Vicar said. 'And what are *we* having, my dear? Kitty has caused the juices to run.'

'Cold, of course, as it's Monday.'

He shuddered theatrically, and picked up another orange. 'My day off, too!'

Kitty pressed her lips together primly, thinking it wrong for clergymen to have days off, especially with Mrs Saddler lying there, dying.

The three of them kept glancing at one another's work as they cut the oranges. Who was doing it finely enough? Only Mrs Edwards, they all knew.

'I like it fairly chunky,' the Vicar said.

When it was all done, Kitty rinsed her hands at the sink, and then put on her coat. She had given the vicarage what time she could spare, and the morning was getting on, and all the rest of the village waiting. She was very orderly in her habits and never visited in the afternoons, for then she had her novel to write. The novel was known about in the village, and some people felt concerned, wondering if she might be another little Daisy Ashford.

With the Vicar's phrases of gratitude giving her momentum, Kitty tacked down the drive between the shabby laurels, and out into the lane.

'The Vicar's having cold,' she told Mrs De Vries, who was preparing a *tajine* of chicken in a curious earthenware pot she had brought back from Morocco.

'Poor old Vicar,' Mrs De Vries said absent-mindedly, as she cut almonds into slivers. She had a glass of something on the draining-board and often took a sip from it. 'Do run and find a drink for yourself, dear child,' she said. She was one of the people who wondered about Daisy Ashford.

'I'll have a bitter lemon, if I may,' Kitty said.

'Well, do, my dear. You know where to find it.'

As Kitty knew everything about nearly every house in the village, she did not reply; but went with assurance to the bar in the hall. She stuck a plastic straw in her drink, and returned to the kitchen sucking peacefully.

'Is there anything I can do?' she enquired.

'No, just tell me the news. What's going on?'

'Mr Mumford typed "Jam Fart and Custard" on the menu card.'

'Oh, he didn't! You've made me do the nose-trick with my gin. The *pain* of it!' Mrs De Vries snatched a handkerchief from her apron pocket and held it to her face. When she had recovered, she said, 'I simply can't wait for Tom to come home, to tell him that.'

Kitty looked modestly gratified. 'I called at the vicarage, too, on my way.'

'And what were *they* up to?'

'They are up to making marmalade.'

'Poor darlings! They *do* have to scrimp and scratch. Church mice, indeed!'

'But isn't home-made marmalade nicer than shop?'

'Not all *that* much.'

After a pause, Kitty said, 'Mrs Saddler's on her way out.'

'Who the hell's Mrs Saddler?'

'At the almshouse. She's dying.'

'Poor old thing.'

Kitty sat down on a stool and swung her fat legs.

'Betty Benford is eight months gone,' she said, shrugging her shoulders.

'I wish you'd tell me something about people I *know*,' Mrs De Vries complained, taking another sip of gin.

'Her mother plans to look after the baby while Betty goes on going out to work. Mrs Benford, you know.'

'Not next door's daily?'

'She won't be after this month.'

'Does Mrs Glazier know?' Mrs De Vries asked, inclining her head towards next door.

'Not yet,' Kitty said, glancing at the clock.

'My God, she'll go up the wall,' Mrs De Vries said with relish. 'She's had that old Benford for years and years.'

'What do you call that you're cooking?'

'It's a *tajine* of chicken.'

'Mrs De Vries is having *tajine* of chicken,' Kitty said next door five minutes later.

'And what might that be when it's at home?'

Kitty described it as best she could, and Mrs Glazier looked huffy. 'Derek wouldn't touch it,' she said. 'He likes good, plain, English food, and no messing about.'

She was rolling out pastry for that evening's steak-and-kidney pie.

'They're having that at the Horse and Groom,' Kitty said.

'*And* we'll have sprouts. *And* braised celery,' Mrs Glazier added, not letting Mrs De Vries get away with her airs and graces.

'Shall I make a pastry rose to go on the top of the pie?' Kitty offered. 'Mrs Prout showed me how to.'

'No, I think we'll leave well alone.'

'Do you like cooking?' Kitty asked in a conversational tone.

'I don't mind it. Why?'

'I was only thinking that then it wouldn't be so hard on you when Mrs Benford leaves.'

Mrs Benford was upstairs. There was a bumping, droning noise of a vacuum-cleaner above, in what Kitty knew to be Mrs Glazier's bedroom.

Mrs Glazier, with an awful fear in her heart, stared, frowning, at Kitty, who went on, 'I was just telling Mrs De Vries that after Mrs Benford's grandchild's born she's going to stay at home to mind it.'

The fact that next door had heard this stunning news first made the blow worse, and Mrs Glazier put a flour-covered hand to her forehead. She closed her eyes for a moment. 'But why can't the girl look after the little – baby herself?'

Kitty took the lid off a jar marked 'Cloves' and looked inside, sniffing. 'Her daughter earns more money at the Horse and Groom than her mother earns here,' she explained.

'I suppose you told Mrs De Vries that too.'

Kitty went to the door with dignity. 'Oh, no! I never talk from house to house. My mother says I'll have to stop my visiting, if I do. Oh, by the way,' she called back, 'you'd better keep your dog in. The De Vrieses' bitch is on heat.'

She went home and sat down to lamb and bubble-and-squeak.

'The Vicar's having cold, too,' she said.

'And that's *his* business,' her mother said warningly.

A few days later, Kitty called on Mrs Prout.

Mrs Prout's cottage was one of Kitty's favourite visits. Many years ago, before she was married, Mrs Prout had been a school-teacher, and she enjoyed using her old skills to deal with Kitty. Keeping her patience pliant, she taught her visitor new card games (and they were all educational), and got her on to collecting and pressing wild flowers. She would give her pastry-trimmings to cut into shapes, and showed her how to pop corn and make fudge. She was extremely kind, though firm, and Kitty respected the rules – about taking off her Wellingtons and washing her hands and never calling on Mondays or Thursdays, because these were turning-out days when Mrs Prout was far too busy to have company.

They were very serious together. Mrs Prout enjoyed being authoritative to a child again, and Kitty had a sense of orderliness which obliged her to comply.

'They sent this from the vicarage,' she said, coming into the kitchen with a small pot of marmalade.

'How jolly nice!' Mrs Prout said. She took the marmalade, and tilted it slightly, and it moved. Rather sloppy. But she thought no worse of the Vicar's wife for that. 'That's really *jolly* nice of them,' she said, going into the larder. 'And they shall have some of my apple jelly, in fair return. *Quid pro quo*, eh? And one good turn deserves another.'

She came out of the larder with a different little pot and held it to the light; but the clear and golden content did not move when she tipped it sideways.

'What's the news?' she asked.

'Mrs Saddler still lingers on,' Kitty said. She had called at the almshouse to enquire, but the district nurse had told her to run off and mind her own business. 'I looked in at the Wilsons' on my way here. Mrs Wilson was making a cheese-and-onion pie. Of course, they're vegetarians; but I have known him to sneak a little chicken into his mouth. I was helping to hand round at the De Vrieses' cocktail party, and he put out his hand towards a patty. "It's chicken," I said to him in a low voice. "Nary a word," he said, and he winked at me and ate it.'

'And now you *have* said a word,' Mrs Prout said briskly.

'Why, so I have,' Kitty agreed, looking astonished.

Mrs Prout cleared the kitchen table in the same brisk way, and said, 'If you like, now, I'll show you how to make ravioli. We shall have it for our television supper.'

'Make ravioli,' cried Kitty. 'You can't *make* ravioli. Mrs Glazier buys it in a tin.'

'So Mrs Glazier may. But I find time to make my own.'

'I shall be fascinated,' Kitty said, taking off her coat.

'Then wash your hands, and don't forget to dry them properly. Isn't it about time you cut your nails?' Mrs Prout asked, in her schoolmistressy voice, and Kitty, who would take anything from her, agreed. ('We all know Mrs Prout is God,' her mother sometimes said resentfully.)

'Roll up those sleeves, now. And we'll go through your tables while we work.'

Mrs Prout set out the flour-bin and a dredger and a pastry-cutter and the mincer. Going back and forth to the cupboard, she thought how petty she was to be pleased at knowing that by this time tomorrow, most of the village would be aware that she made her own ravioli. But perhaps it was only human, she decided.

'Now this is what chefs call the *mise en place*,' she explained to Kitty, when she had finished arranging the table. 'Can you remember that? *Mise en place*.'

'*Mise en place*,' Kitty repeated obediently.

'Shall I help you prepare the *mise en place*?' Kitty enquired of Mrs Glazier.

'Mr Glazier wouldn't touch it. I've told you he will only eat English food.'

'But you have ravioli. That's Italian.'

'I just keep it as a stand-by,' Mrs Glazier said scornfully. She was very huffy and put out these days, especially with Mrs De Vries next door and her getting the better of her every time. Annette De Vries was French, and didn't they all know it. Mrs Glazier, as a result, had become violently insular.

'I can make ravioli,' Kitty said, letting the *mise en place* go, for she was not absolutely certain about it. 'Mrs Prout has just been teaching me. She and Mr Prout have television trays by the fire, and then they sit and crack walnuts and play cards, and then they have hot milk and whisky and go to bed. I think it is very nice and cosy, don't you?'

'Mr Glazier likes a proper sit-down meal when *he* gets back. Did you happen to see Tiger anywhere down the lane?'

'No, but I expect he's next door. I told you their bitch is on heat. You ought to shut him up.'

'It's their affair to shut *theirs* up.'

'Well, I'm just calling there, so I'll shoo him off.'

She had decided to cut short this visit. Mrs Glazier was so bad-tempered these days, and hardly put herself out at all to give a welcome, and every interesting thing Kitty told her served merely to annoy.

'And I must get on with my jugged hare,' Mrs Glazier said, making no attempt to delay the departure. 'It should be marinating in the port wine by now,' she added grandly. 'And I must make the soup and the croutons.'

'Well, then, I'll be going,' Kitty said, edging towards the door.

'And apricot mousse,' Mrs Glazier called out after her, as if she were in a frenzy.

'Shall I prepare your *mise en place*?' Kitty enquired of Mrs De Vries, trying her luck again.

'My! We *are* getting professional,' said Mrs De Vries, but her mind was really on what Kitty had just been telling her. 'Soup and jugged hare!' she was thinking. 'What a dreadful meal!'

She was glazing a terrine of chicken livers and wished that all the village might see her work of art, but having Kitty there was the next best thing.

'What's that?' she asked, as Kitty put the jar of apple jelly on the table.

'I have to take it to the vicarage on my way home. It's some of Mrs Prout's apple jelly.'

Mrs De Vries gave it a keen look, and notched up one point to Mrs Prout. She notched up another when she heard about the ravioli, and wondered if she had underestimated the woman.

'I shooed that Tiger away,' Kitty said.

'The wretched cur. He is driving Topaze insane.'

Kitty mooched round the kitchen, peeking and prying. Mrs De Vries was the only one in the village to possess a *mandoline* for cutting vegetables. There was a giant pestle and mortar, a wicker bread-basket, ropes of Spanish onions, and a marble cheese-tray.

'You can pound the fish for me, if you have the energy,' said Mrs De Vries.

As this was not a house where she was made to wash her hands first, Kitty immediately set to work.

'I was just going to have pears,' Mrs De Vries said, in a half-humorous voice. 'But if the Glaziers are going in for apricot mousse I had better pull my socks up. That remark, of course, is strictly *entre nous*.'

'Then Mrs De Vries pulled her socks up, and made a big apple tart,' Kitty told her mother.

'I have warned you before, Kitty. What you see going on in people's houses, you keep to yourself. Or you stay out of them. Is that finally and completely understood?'

'Yes, Mother,' Kitty said meekly.

'My dear girl, I couldn't eat it. I couldn't eat another thing,' said Mr Glazier, confronted by the apricot mousse. 'A three-course meal. Why, I shouldn't sleep all night if I had any more. The hare alone was ample.'

'I think Mr De Vries would do better justice to his dinner,' said Mrs Glazier bitterly. She had spent all day cooking and was exhausted. 'It's not much fun slaving away and not being appreciated. And what on earth can I do with all the left-overs?'

'Finish them up tomorrow and save yourself a lot of trouble.'

Glumly, Mrs Glazier washed the dishes, and suddenly thought of the

Prouts sitting peacefully beside their fire, cracking walnuts, playing cards. She felt ill-done-by, as she stacked the remains of dinner in the fridge, but was perfectly certain that lie as she might have to to Kitty in the morning, the whole village should not know that for the second day running the Glaziers were having soup, and jugged hare, and apricot mousse.

Next day, eating a slice of apple tart, Kitty saw Mrs De Vries test the soup and then put the ladle back into the saucepan. 'What the eye doesn't see, the heart cannot grieve over,' Mrs De Vries said cheerfully. She added salt, and a turn or two of pepper. Then she took more than a sip from the glass on the draining-board, seeming to find it more to her liking than the soup.

'The vicarage can't afford drinks,' Kitty said.

'They *do* confide in you.'

'I said to the Vicar, Mrs De Vries drinks gin while she is cooking, and he said, "Lucky old her."'

'There will be a lot of red faces about this village if you go on like this,' said Mrs De Vries, making her part of the prophecy come true at once. Kitty looked at her in surprise. Then she said – Mrs De Vries's flushed face reminding her – 'I think next door must be having the change of life. She is awfully grumpy these days. Nothing pleases her.'

'You are too knowing for your years,' Mrs De Vries said, and she suddenly wished she had not been so unhygienic about the soup. Too late now. 'How is your novel coming along?' she enquired.

'Oh, very nicely, thank you. I expect I shall finish it before I go back to school, and then it can be published for Christmas.'

'We shall all look forward to that,' said Mrs De Vries, in what Kitty considered an unusual tone of voice.

'Mrs De Vries cuts up her vegetables with a *mandoline*,' Kitty told Mrs Glazier some days later.

'I always knew she must be nuts,' said Mrs Glazier, thinking of the musical instrument.

Seeing Kitty dancing up the drive, she had quickly hidden the remains of a shepherd's pie at the back of a cupboard. She was more than ever ruffled this morning, because Mrs Benford had not arrived or sent a message. She had also been getting into a frenzy with her ravioli and, in the end, had thrown the whole lot into the dustbin. She hated waste, especially now that her house-keeping allowance always seemed to have disappeared by Wednesday, and her husband was, in his dyspeptic way, continually accusing her of extravagance.

Kitty had been hanging about outside the almshouses for a great part of the morning, and had watched Mrs Saddler's coffin being carried across the road to the church.

'Only one wreath and two relations,' she now told Mrs Glazier. 'That's what comes of being poor. What are you having for dinner tonight? I could give you a hand.'

'Mr Glazier will probably be taking me to the Horse and Groom for a change,' Mrs Glazier lied.

'They are all at sixes and sevens there. Betty Benford started her pains in the night. A fortnight early. Though Mr Mumford thinks she may have made a mistake with her dates.'

Then Mrs Benford would never come again, Mrs Glazier thought despondently. She had given a month's notice the week before, and Mrs Glazier had received it coldly, saying, 'I think I should have been informed of this before it became common gossip in the village.' Mrs Benford had seemed quite taken aback at that.

'Well, I mustn't hang around talking,' Mrs Glazier told Kitty. 'There's a lot to do this morning, and will be from now on. When do you go back to school?'

'On Thursday.'

Mrs Glazier nodded, and Kitty felt herself dismissed. She sometimes wondered why she bothered to pay this call, when everyone else made her so welcome; but coming away from the funeral she had seen Mrs De Vries driving into town, and it was one of Mrs Prout's turning-out days. She had hardly liked to call at the vicarage under the circumstances of the funeral, and the Horse and Groom being at sixes and sevens had made everyone there very boring and busy.

'I hope you will enjoy your dinner,' she said politely to Mrs Glazier. 'They have roast Surrey fowl and all the trimmings.'

When she had gone, Mrs Glazier took the shepherd's pie from its hiding place, and began to scrape some shabby old carrots.

'Kitty, will you stop chattering and get on with your pudding,' her mother said in an exasperated voice.

Kitty had been describing how skilfully the undertaker's men had lowered Mrs Saddler's coffin into the grave, Kitty herself peering from behind the tombstone of Maria Britannia Marlowe – her favourite dead person on account of her name.

It was painful to stop talking. A pain came in her chest, severe enough to slow her breathing, and gobbling the rice pudding made it worse. As soon as her plate was cleared she began again. 'Mrs Glazier has the change of life,' she said.

'How on earth do you know about such things?' her mother asked on a faint note.

'As *you* didn't tell me, I had to find out the hard way,' Kitty said sternly.

Her mother pursed her lips together to stop laughing, and began to stack up the dishes.

'How Mrs De Vries will miss me!' Kitty said dreamily, rising to help her mother. 'I shall be stuck there at school doing boring things, and she'll be having a nice time drinking gin.'

'Now *that* is enough. You are to go to your room immediately,' her mother said sharply, and Kitty looked at her red face reflectively, comparing it with Mrs Glazier's. 'You will have to find some friends of your own age. You are becoming a little menace to everyone with your visiting, and we have got to live in this village. Now upstairs you go, and think over what I have said.'

'Very well, Mother,' Kitty said meekly. If she did not have to help Mother with the washing-up, she could get on with her novel all the sooner.

She went upstairs to her bedroom and spread her writing things out on the table and soon, having at once forgotten her mother's words, was lost in the joy of authorship.

Her book was all about little furry animals, and their small adventures, and there was not a human being in it, except the girl, Katherine, who befriended them all.

She managed a few more visits that holiday; but on Thursday she went back to school again, and then no one in the village knew what was happening any more.

It Makes a Change

Oh, the peace of the street! he always thought, stepping out of the office at six-five. It fell against him, this peace, coolly and beautifully, with the scent of flowers and sky in it, with the soft sounds of tyres upon the road and a thrush or two singing in the churchyard. He forgot the dusty office (the clack-clack of the typewriter, the air filled with chalk-motes, the corner of blotting-paper idly drinking the spreading ink), and he would be dazed a little by the clear beauty of the street, he would take his first breath of the day.

This evening, he breathed and then breathed quickly again, until his surprised lungs exploded almost. The air smelled mysteriously, unaccountably of the country. It was the first evening of spring. Going down the street it seemed to him that flowers unfolded their petals in his breast. It was half-painful, half-pleasurable, he thought, his eyes lifted to the beauty of bomb-wreckage, of the torn side of a house, the pastel colouring of wallpapers and plaster, peach and lavender, grey and duck's-egg-blue, broken brickwork gilded in the evening light. A pigeon flew out of a bedroom grate, high, perched at the top of a ruin. On barrows at the corner, daffodils and rhubarb were banked against blue paper and bright imitation grass. How happy! he thought. Happy! And he stopped to look at a picture set back a little in the window of an art gallery. You never do see women like that. The long narrow eyes, velvet black, in the creamy face. The pink and dove-grey. Marie Laurencin. Nice to have a real picture of your own. Something someone had painted – in your own home – look at it every day.

He moved on down the street towards the Underground. In your own home. In your own home the torn linoleum in the passage and the dusty untidiness on the mantelpiece. At the front door, the key fidgeting reluctantly in the keyhole, you take your last breath of the day. Enter the darkness. Smell of parsnips, from dinner. Up in the steamy bathroom taps rushing, cistern refilling, child being slapped; through the steam the voice. The Voice. 'What did I tell you ... Always the same ... When I say a thing ... Now here's your father ...' and so on. The Voice accompanied him now, down the street. 'I've only one pair of hands ... because I said so ... and that's for answering back!' Answering back! he mused. That's the trouble. When you are older no one answers back. You speak and no one listens. You send the dove out on its journey, you send it forth, but it never returns with a leaf in its beak. It does not return at all.

He raised his eyes to the pearly sky, the high, leaden balloons, turning idly, veering, nosing clouds. Soon the Underground, the soft, hot rush of air. When he emerged again the evening would be dead. He walked resolutely past the smell of the Underground and continued down the street.

First editions pressed their brown-spotted title pages to a shop window. Coloured plates of fruit and birds. To have something beautiful of your own. 'You're late tonight ... It's always the same ... Food's like a cinder ... Spoilt for me too ... Backache ... Gave her a good hiding ... What's the use ...' This is the first time I ever *meant* to be late. Nine years. Hard to believe. Better be, though, with Veronica eight the other day. Veronica – once loved that name. 'Veronica! How many more times. Did you *hear* me?' Christ! how can you help hearing? The Voice. Peace one needs. Peace like this evening. And gentle sounds.

Here were the steps of a church – small London church between shops – and the rambling, elephantine sounds of an organ – 'I *mean* to be late,' he said again to himself. And went up the steps. Inside, the impersonal smell of stone and wood and old books. Pale pillars rose to the black and indigo shadows.

He sat down at the back, so that he might easily escape should anyone ... What? What harm was he doing? 'I should kneel down and begin to pray,' he decided. But gradually he relaxed. The sounds from the organ trailed away and presently recommenced. Nice to come in here alone and play. Peace. Even the Voice could not pursue him here. Nine years. Sin they had committed before that. He thought of it with tranquillity now in church. Nice to look back upon. Might not have been the same person. Now, always to ready to condemn all the young ones. That type often turns to the other extreme. 'I'm broad-minded but ...' Now it finished with 'but'. The 'but' at the end means the first part was a lie.

A woman came in and sat against a pillar. With her hand on the end of a pew, she had bent her knee towards the altar. The grace and gravity of this gesture caught his interest. He watched her drop down on to a hassock, bow her head, watched the pale profile net in prayer. Creamy face, the eyes a sloe-dark smudge. Black clothes against the pillar. Something *in* religion. Beautiful. Catches your throat. Now with black-gloved hand she crossed herself. Couldn't bring myself to do that. Feel daft. Think people laughing at me. Quiet she is. Violets pinned on her ... no ... the smell of them is cool and fresh ... breast ... no ... cool and fresh ... something beautiful ... of your own ... my own. A nice picture, wild-flower book, marsh-marigolds, hand-painted lilies, fritillaries, violets. Would like to hear her speak. Voice. 'If you men aren't the bloody limit!' Hate women to swear. 'Good-evening!' I would say, holding that level with face. Respect. 'Oh!' Her eyes lifted, startled, velvet sloes. Can't go home. After nine years, can't go home at last.

He slid to his knees – no one watching – and rested the bridge of his nose against the back of the next pew. Not praying. Don't believe in it, only want the peace, want something beautiful of my own. 'Good-evening!' She wouldn't answer. Draw back away from me. Wouldn't like that. 'Lovely evening.' She wouldn't answer. That one's for answering back. Please God. The heart is encircled by silence. Nothing enters there, nor breaks the ice of it. Nothing. As we die, we know that, if we don't know before. When we are lonely we dwell there. Life shouldn't be that, sitting alone with our own silence. We should speak to one another. 'Good-evening!' And stretch out our hands to one another. Violets. Black and black fur and a little veil. Widow. I would comfort her. Put my arm across her shoulder while she weeps.

As the image of that drew clear from the mists of his mind, he was stirred and shaken. He raised his head. She was standing now by the pillar, smoothing her gloves. For a second, her face turned in his direction. Pale, closed, remote, like a nun. The church darkened as she left. He picked up his hat. For nine years the first time he would be late deliberately. Down the steps. She walked not like a nun, like a queen, one foot before the other. At the corner, by the chemist's shop, she paused, began to saunter. From the swirl of people on the pavement a man detached himself and joined her. They spoke and moved on together.

'Remember me?'

'Course.'

'Your legs I noticed first, coming down those steps. Nice stockings. I like nice stockings. I thought it was a church at first . . . ' He sounded disconcerted.

'It was.'

He seemed to await her explanation.

'Sometimes want to look nice to myself,' she was thinking as she walked carefully down a meaner street. 'Want to act nicely just for myself alone. Do something beautiful and not for other people to see.'

'Oh, it made a change,' she said impatiently, shifting her fur on her shoulder, fingering the linen violets. 'Used to go every Sunday once, when I was a girl. Sometimes week-nights. Reverend forget his name – High Church. People used to complain.' What had she expected? What experience was it which she dimly perceived, but which always evaded her? 'It is the same thing for ever,' she told herself. She trailed her fur behind her now, as they went up some stairs at the side of a tailor's shop. It comes to the same thing in the end. Yet does it?

He followed her upstairs, his eyes on the seams of her stockings. He felt gloomy, dubious, put out.

'Yes,' she thought, glancing out of the window on the half-landing. 'I feel as if I had missed something. Yet I know that there is nothing to miss.' She looked back and grinned, puffed, panted from the stairs and blew out her lips comically.

'That's the girl,' he said.

Flesh

Phyl was always one of the first to come into the hotel bar in the evenings, for what she called her *aperitif*, and which, in reality, amounted to two hours' steady drinking. After that, she had little appetite for dinner, a meal to which she was not used.

On this evening, she had put on one of her beaded tops, of the kind she wore behind the bar on Saturday evenings in London, and patted back her tortoiseshell hair. She was massive and glittering and sunburned – a wonderful sight, Stanley Archard thought, as she came across the bar towards him.

He had been sitting waiting for her. They had found their own level in one another on about the third day of the holiday. Both being heavy drinkers drew them together. Before that had happened, they had looked one another over warily as, in fact, they had all their fellow-guests.

Travelling on their own, speculating, both had watched and wondered. Even at the airport, she had stood out from the others, he remembered, as she had paced up and down in her emerald-green coat. Then their flight number had been called, and they had gathered with others at the same channel, with the same pink labels tied to their hand luggage, all going to the same place; a polite, but distant little band of people, no one knowing with whom friendships were to be made – as like would no doubt drift to like. In the days that followed, Stanley had wished he had taken more notice of Phyl from the beginning, so that at the end of the holiday he would have that much more to remember. Only the emerald-green coat had stayed in his mind. She had not worn it since – it was too warm – and he dreaded the day when she would put it on again to make the return journey.

Arriving in the bar this evening, she hoisted herself up on a stool beside him. 'Well, here we are,' she said, glowing, taking one peanut; adding, as she nibbled, 'Evening, George,' to the barman. 'How's tricks?'

'My God, you've caught it today,' Stanley said, and he put his hands up near her plump red shoulders as if to warm them at a fire. 'Don't overdo it,' he warned her.

'Oh, I never peel,' she said airily.

He always put in a word against the sunbathing when he could. It separated them. She stayed all day by the hotel swimming-pool, basting herself
with oil. He, bored with basking – which made him feel dizzy – had hired
a car and spent his time driving about the island, and was full of alienating information about the locality, which the other guests – resenting the
hired car, too – did their best to avoid. Only Phyl did not mind listening
to him. For nearly every evening of her married life she had stood behind
the bar and listened to other people's boring chat: she had a technique for
dealing with it and a fund of vague phrases. 'Go on!' she said now, listening – hardly listening – to Stanley, and taking another nut. He had gone
off by himself and found a place for lunch: *hors d'œuvre*, nice-sized slice of
veal, two veg, *crème caramel*, half bottle of rosé, coffee – twenty-two
shillings the lot. 'Well, I'm blowed,' said Phyl, and she took a pound note
from her handbag and waved it at the barman. When she snapped up the
clasp of the bag it had a heavy, expensive sound.

One or two other guests came in and sat at the bar. At this stage of the
holiday they were forming into little groups, and this was the jokey set who
had come first after Stanley and Phyl. According to them all sorts of funny
things had happened during the day, and little screams of laughter ran
round the bar.

'Shows how wrong you can be,' Phyl said in a low voice. 'I thought they
were ever so starchy on the plane. I was wrong about you, too. At the start,
I thought you were ... you know ... one of *those*. Going about with that
young boy all the time.'

Stanley patted her knee. 'On the contrary,' he said, with a meaning
glance at her. 'No, I was just at a bit of a loose end, and he seemed to
cotton-on. Never been abroad before, he hadn't, and didn't know the routine. I liked it for the first day or two. It was like taking a nice kiddie out
on a treat. Then it seemed to me he was sponging. I'm not mean, I don't
think; but I don't like that – sponging. It was quite a relief when he suddenly took up with the Lisper.'

By now, he and Phyl had nicknames for most of the other people in the
hotel. They did not know that the same applied to them, and that to the
jokey set he was known as Paws and she as the Shape. It would have put
them out and perhaps ruined their holiday if they had known. He thought
his little knee-pattings were of the utmost discretion, and she felt confidence from knowing her figure was expensively controlled under her
beaded dresses when she became herself again in the evenings. During the
day, while sun-bathing, she considered that anything went – that, as her
mind was a blank, her body became one also.

The funny man of the party – the awaited climax – came into the bar,
crabwise, face covered slyly with his hand, as if ashamed of some earlier

misdemeanour. 'Oh, my God, don't look round. Here comes trouble!' someone said loudly, and George was called for from all sides. 'What's the poison, Harry? No, my shout, old boy. George, if you *please*.'

Phyl smiled indulgently. It was just like Saturday night with the regulars at home. She watched George with a professional eye, and nodded approvingly. He was good. They could have used him at the Nelson. A good quick boy.

'Heard from your old man?' Stanley asked her.

She cast him a tragic, calculating look. 'You must be joking. He can't *write*. No, honest, I've never had a letter from him in the whole of my life. Well, we always saw each other every day until I had my hysterectomy.'

Until now, in conversations with Stanley, she had always referred to 'a little operation'. But he had guessed what it was – well, it always was, wasn't it? – and knew that it was the reason for her being on holiday. Charlie, her husband, had sent her off to recuperate. She had sworn there was no need, that she had never felt so well in her life – was only a bit weepy sometimes late on a Saturday night. 'I'm not really the crying sort,' she had explained to Stanley. 'So he got worried, and sent me packing.'

'You clear off to the sun,' he had said, 'and see what that will do.'

What the sun had done for her was to burn her brick-red, and offer her this nice holiday friend. Stanley Archard, retired widower from Hove.

She enjoyed herself, as she usually did. The sun shone every day, and the drinks were so reasonable – they had many a long discussion about that. They also talked about his little flat in Hove; his strolls along the front; his few cronies at the Club; his sad, orderly and lonely life.

This evening, he wished he had not brought up the subject of Charlie's writing to her, for it seemed to have fixed her thoughts on him and, as she went chatting on about him, Stanley felt an indefinable distaste, an aloofness.

She brought out from her note-case a much-creased cutting from the *Morning Advertiser*. 'Phyl and Charlie Parsons welcome old friends and new at the Nelson, Southwood. In licensed hours only!' 'That was when we changed Houses,' she explained. There was a photograph of them both standing behind the bar. He was wearing a dark blazer with a large badge on the pocket. Sequins gave off a smudged sparkle from her breast, her hair was newly, elaborately done, and her large, ringed hand rested on an ornamental beer-handle. Charlie had his hands in the blazer pockets, as if he were there to do the welcoming, and his wife to do the work: and this, in fact, was how things were. Stanley guessed it, and felt a twist of annoyance in his chest. He did not like the look of Charlie, or anything he had heard about him – how, for instance, he had seemed like a fish out of water visiting his wife in hospital. 'He used to sit on the edge of the chair and stare at the clock, like a boy in school,' Phyl had said, laughing. Stanley could not bring himself to laugh, too. He had leant forward and taken her knee in his hand and wobbled it sympathetically to and fro.

No, she wasn't the crying sort, he agreed. She had a wonderful buoyancy and gallantry, and she seemed to knock years off his age by just *being* with him, talking to him.

In spite of their growing friendship, they kept to their original, separate tables in the hotel restaurant. It seemed too suddenly decisive and public a move for him to join her now, and he was too shy to carry it off at this stage of the holiday, before such an alarming audience. But after dinner, they would go for a walk along the sea-front, or out in the car for a drink at another hotel.

Always, for the first minute or two in a bar, he seemed to lose her. As if she had forgotten him, she would look about her critically, judging the set-up, sternly drawing attention to a sticky ring on the counter where she wanted to rest her elbow, keeping a professional eye on the prices.

When they were what she called 'nicely grinned-up', they liked to drive out to a small headland and park the car, watching the swinging beam from a lighthouse. Then, after the usual knee-pattings and neck-strokings, they would heave and flop about in the confines of the Triumph Herald, trying to make love. Warmed by their drinks, and the still evening and the romantic sound of the sea idly turning over down below them, they became frustrated, both large, solid people, she much corseted and, anyhow, beginning to be painfully sunburned across the shoulders, he with the confounded steering-wheel to contend with.

He would grumble about the car and suggest getting out on to a patch of dry barley grass; but she imagined it full of insects; the chirping of the cicadas was almost deafening.

She also had a few scruples about Charlie, but they were not so insistent as the cicadas. After all, she thought, she had never had a holiday-romance – not even a honeymoon with Charlie – and she felt that life owed her just one.

After a time, during the day, her sunburn forced her into the shade, or out in the car with Stanley. Across her shoulders she began to peel, and could not bear – though desiring his caress – him to touch her. Rather glumly, he waited for her flesh to heal, told her 'I told you so'; after all, they had not for ever on this island, had started their second, their last week already.

'I'd like to have a look at the other island,' she said, watching the ferry leaving, as they sat drinking nearby.

'It's not worth just going there for the inside of a day,' he said meaningfully, although it was only a short distance.

Wasn't this, both suddenly wondered, the answer to the too-small car, and the watchful eyes back at the hotel. She had refused to allow him into her room there. 'If anyone saw you going in or out? Why, they know where I live. What's to stop one of them coming into the Nelson any time, and chatting Charlie up?'

'Would you?' he now asked, watching the ferry starting off across the water. He hardly dared to hear her answer.

After a pause, she laughed. 'Why not?' she said, and took his hand. 'We wouldn't really be doing any harm to anyone.' (Meaning Charlie.) 'Because no one could find out, could they?'

'Not over there,' he said, nodding towards the island. 'We can start fresh over there. Different people.'

'They'll notice we're both not at dinner at the hotel.'

'That doesn't prove anything.'

She imagined the unknown island, the warm and starlit night and, somewhere, under some roof or other, a large bed in which they could pursue their daring, more than middle-aged adventure, unconfined in every way.

'As soon as my sunburn's better,' she promised. 'We've got five more days yet, and I'll keep in the shade till then.'

A chambermaid advised yoghourt, and she spread it over her back and shoulders as best she could, and felt its coolness absorbing the heat from her skin.

Damp and cheesy-smelling in the hot night, she lay awake, cross with herself. For the sake of a tan, she was wasting her holiday – just to be a five minutes' wonder in the bar on her return, the deepest brown any of them had had that year. The darker she was, the more *abroad* she would seem to have been, the more prestige she could command. All summer, pallid herself, she had had to admire others.

Childish, really, she decided, lying rigid under the sheet, afraid to move, burning and throbbing. The skin was taut behind her knees, so that she could not stretch her legs; her flesh was on fire.

Five more days, she kept thinking. Meanwhile, even this sheet upon her was unendurable.

On the next evening, to establish the fact that they would not always be in to dinner at the hotel, they complained in the bar about the dullness of the menu, and went elsewhere.

It was a drab little restaurant, but they scarcely noticed their surroundings. They sat opposite one another at a corner table and ate shell-fish briskly, busily – he, from his enjoyment of the food; she, with a wish to be rid of it. They rinsed their fingers, quickly dried them and leant forward and twined them together – their large placid hands, with heavy rings, clasped on the table-cloth. Phyl, glancing aside for a moment, saw a young girl, at the next table with a boy, draw in her cheekbones to suppress laughter then, failing, turn her head to hide it.

'At *our* age,' Phyl said gently, drawing away her hands from his. 'In public, too.'

She could not be defiant; but Stanley said jauntily, 'I'm damned if I care.'

At that moment, their chicken was placed before them, and he sat back, looking at it, waiting for vegetables

As well as the sunburn, the heat seemed to have affected Phyl's stomach. She felt queasy and nervy. It was now their last day but one before they went over to the other island. The yoghourt – or time – had taken the pain from her back and shoulders, though leaving her with a dappled, flaky look, which would hardly bring forth cries of admiration or advance her prestige in the bar when she returned. But, no doubt, she thought, by then England would be too cold for her to go sleeveless. Perhaps the trees would have changed colour. She imagined – already – dark Sunday afternoons, their three o'clock lunch done with, and she and Charlie sitting by the electric log fire in a lovely hot room smelling of oranges and the so-called hearth littered with peel. Charlie – bless him – always dropped off among a confusion of newspapers, worn out with banter and light ale, switched off, too, as he always was with her, knowing that he could relax – be nothing, rather – until seven o'clock, because it was Sunday. Again, for Phyl, imagining home, a little pang, soon swept aside or, rather, swept aside *from*.

She was in a way relieved that they would have only one night on the little island. That would make it seem more like a chance escapade than an affair, something less serious and deliberate in her mind. Thinking about it during the day-time, she even felt a little apprehensive; but told herself sensibly that there was really nothing to worry about: knowing herself well, she could remind herself that an evening's drinking would blur all the nervous edges.

'I can't get over that less than a fortnight ago I never knew you existed,' she said, as they drove to the afternoon ferry. 'And after this week,' she added, 'I don't suppose I'll ever see you again.'

'I wish you wouldn't talk like that – spoiling things,' he said heavily, and he tried not to think of Hove, and the winter walks along the promenade, and going back to the flat, boiling himself a couple of eggs, perhaps; so desperately lost without Ethel.

He had told Phyl about his wife and their quiet happiness together for many years, and then her long, long illness, during which she seemed to be going away from him gradually; but it was dreadful all the same when she finally did.

'We could meet in London on your day off,' he suggested.

'Well, maybe.' She patted his hand, leaving that disappointment aside for him.

There were only a few people on the ferry. It was the end of summer, and the tourists were dwindling, as the English community was reassembling, after trips 'back home'.

The sea was intensely blue all the way across to the island. They stood by the rail looking down at it, marvelling, and feeling like two people in a film. They thought they saw a dolphin, which added to their delight.

'Ethel and I went to Jersey for our honeymoon,' Stanley said. 'It poured with rain nearly all the time, and Ethel had one of her migraines.'

'I never had a honeymoon,' Phyl said. 'Just the one night at the Regent Palace. In our business, you can't both go away together. This is the first time I've ever been abroad.'

'The places I could take you to,' he said.

They drove the car off the ferry and began to cross the island. It was hot and dusty, hillsides terraced and tilled; green lemons hung on the trees.

'I wouldn't half like to actually *pick* a lemon,' she said.

'You shall,' he said, 'somehow or other.'

'And take it home with me,' she added. She would save it for a while, showing people, then cut it up for gin and tonic in the bar one evening, saying casually, 'I picked this lemon with my own fair hands.'

Stanley had booked their hotel from a restaurant, on the recommendation of a barman. When they found it, he was openly disappointed; but she managed to be gallant and optimistic. It was not by the sea, with a balcony where they might look out at the moonlit waters or rediscover brightness in the morning; but down a dull side street, and opposite a garage.

'We don't *have* to,' Stanley said doubtfully.

'Oh, come on! We might not get in anywhere else. It's only for sleeping in,' she said.

'It *isn't* only for sleeping in,' he reminded her.

An enormous man in white shirt and shorts came out to greet them. 'My name is Radam. Welcome,' he said, with confidence. 'I have a lovely room for you, Mr and Mrs Archard. You will be happy here, I can assure you. My wife will carry up your cases. Do not protest, Mr Archard. She is quite able to. Our staff has slackened off at the end of the season, and I have some trouble with the old ticker, as you say in England. I know England well. I am a Bachelor of Science of England University. Once had digs in Swindon.'

A pregnant woman shot out of the hotel porch and seized their suit-cases, and there was a tussle as Stanley wrenched them from her hands. Still serenely boasting, Mr Radam led them upstairs, all of them panting but himself.

The bedroom was large and dusty and overlooked a garage.

'Oh, God, I'm sorry,' Stanley said, when they were left alone. 'It's still not too late, if you could stand a row.'

'No. I think it's rather sweet,' Phyl said, looking round the room. 'And, after all, don't blame yourself. You couldn't know any more than me.'

The furniture was extraordinarily fret-worked, as if to make more crevices for the dust to settle in; the bedside-lamp base was an old gin bottle filled with gravel to weight it down, and when Phyl pulled off the bed cover to feel the bed she collapsed with laughter, for the pillow-cases were embroidered 'Hers' and 'Hers'.

Her laughter eased him, as it always did. For a moment, he thought dis-loyally of the dead – of how Ethel would have started to be depressed by it all, and he would have hard work jollying her out of her dark mood. At the same time, Phyl was wryly imagining Charlie's wrath, how he would have carried on – for only the best was good enough for him, as he never tired of saying.

'He's quite right – that awful fat man,' she said gaily. 'We shall be very happy here. I dread to think who he keeps "His" and "His" for, don't you?'

'I don't suppose the maid understands English,' he said, but warming only slightly. 'You don't expect to have to read off pillow-cases.'

'I'm sure there *isn't* a maid.'

'The bed is very small,' he said.

'It'll be better than the car.'

He thought, 'She is such a woman as I have never met. She's like a mar-vellous Tommy in the trenches – keeping everyone's pecker up.' He hated Charlie for his luck.

'I shan't ever be able to tell anybody about "Hers" and "Hers",' Phyl thought regretfully – for she dearly loved to amuse their regulars back home. Given other circumstances, she might have worked up quite a story about it.

A tap on the door, and in came Mr Radam with two cups of tea on a tray. 'I know you English,' he said, rolling his eyes roguishly. 'You can't be happy without your tea.'

As neither of them ever drank it, they emptied the cups down the hand basin when he had gone.

Phyl opened the window and the sour, damp smell of new cement came up to her. All round about, building was going on; there was also the whine of a saw-mill, and a lot of clanking from the garage opposite. She leant

farther out, and then came back smiling into the room, and shut the
window on the dust and noise. 'He was quite right – that barman. You can
see the sea from here. It's down the bottom of the street. Let's go and have
a look as soon as we've unpacked.'

On their way out of the hotel, they came upon Mr Radam, who was sitting in a broken old wicker chair, fanning himself with a folded newspaper.

'I shall prepare your dinner myself,' he called after them. 'And shall go
now to make soup. I am a specialist of soup.'

They strolled in the last of the sun by the glittering sea, looked at the
painted boats, watched a man beating an octopus on a rock. Stanley
bought her some lace-edged handkerchiefs, and even gave the lace-maker
an extra five shillings, so that Phyl could pick a lemon off one of the trees
in her garden. Each bought for the other a picture-postcard of the place,
to keep.

'Well, it's been just about the best holiday I ever had,' he said. 'And
there I was in half a mind not to come at all.' He had for many years
dreaded the holiday season, and only went away because everyone he knew
did so.

'I just can't remember when I last had one,' she said. There was not –
never would be, he knew – the sound of self-pity in her voice.

This was only a small fishing-village; but on one of the headlands
enclosing it and the harbour was a big new hotel, with balconies overlooking the sea, Phyl noted. They picked their way across a rubbly car-park
and went in. Here, too, was the damp smell of cement; but there was a
brightly lighted empty bar with a small dance floor, and music playing.

'We could easily have got in here,' Stanley said. 'I'd like to wring that
bloody barman's neck.'

'He's probably some relation, trying to do his best.'

'I'll best him.'

They seemed to have spent a great deal of their time together hoisting
themselves up on bar stools.

'Make them nice ones,' Stanley added, ordering their drinks. 'Perhaps
he feels a bit shy and awkward, too,' Phyl thought.

'Not very busy,' he remarked to the barman.

'In one week we close.'

'Looks as if you've hardly opened,' Stanley said, glancing round.

'It's not *his* business to get huffy,' Phyl thought indignantly, when the
young man, not replying, shrugged and turned aside to polish some glasses.
'Customer's always right. He should know that. Politics, religion, colour-
bar – however they argue together, they're all of them always right, and if
you know your job you can joke them out of it and on to something safer.'

The times she had done that, making a fool of herself, no doubt, anything for peace and quiet. By the time the elections were over, she was usually worn out.

Stanley had hated her buying him a drink back in the hotel; but she had insisted. 'What all that crowd would think of me!' she had said; but here, although it went much against her nature, she put aside her principles, and let him pay; let him set the pace, too. They became elated, and she was sure it would be all right – even having to go back to the soup-specialist's dinner. They might have avoided that; but too late now.

The barman, perhaps with a contemptuous underlining of their age, shuffled through some records and now put on 'Night and Day'. For them both, it filled the bar with nostalgia.

'Come *on*!' said Stanley. 'I've never danced with you. This always makes me feel . . . I don't know.'

'Oh, I'm a terrible dancer,' she protested. The Licensed Victuallers' Association annual dance was the only one she ever went to, and even there stayed in the bar most of the time. Laughing, however, she let herself be helped down off her stool.

He had once fancied himself a good dancer; but, in later years, got no practice, with Ethel being ill, and then dead. Phyl was surprised how light he was on his feet; he bounced her round, holding her firmly against his stomach, his hand pressed to her back, but gently, because of the sunburn. He had perfect rhythm and expertise, side-stepping, reversing, taking masterly control of her.

'Well, I never!' she cried. 'You're making me quite breathless.'

He rested his cheek against her hair, and closed his eyes, in the old, old way, and seemed to waft her away into a different dimension. It was then that he felt the first twinge, in his left toe. It was doom to him. He kept up the pace, but fell silent. When the record ended, he hoped that she would not want to stay on longer. To return to the hotel and take his gout pills was all he could think about. Some intuition made her refuse another drink. 'We've got to go back to the soup-specialist some time,' she said. 'He might even be a good cook.'

'Surprise, surprise!' Stanley managed to say, walking with pain towards the door.

Mr Radam was the most abominable cook. They had – in a large cold room with many tables – thin greasy chicken soup, and after that the chicken that had gone through the soup. Then peaches; he brought the tin and opened it before them, as if it were a precious wine, and no hanky-panky going on. He then stood over them, because he had much to say. 'I was offered a post in Basingstoke. Two thousand pounds a year, and a car and a house thrown in. But what use is that to a man like me? Besides, Basingstoke has a most detestable climate.'

Stanley sat, tight-lipped, trying not to lose his temper; but this man, and the pain, were driving him mad. He did not – dared not – drink any of the wine he had ordered.

'Yes, the Basingstoke employment I regarded as not *on*,' Mr Radam said slangily.

Phyl secretly put out a foot and touched one of Stan's – the wrong one – and then thought he was about to have a heart attack. He screwed up his eyes and tried to breathe steadily, a slice of peach slithering about in his spoon. It was then she realised what was wrong with him.

'Oh, sod the peaches,' she said cheerfully, when Mr Radam had gone off to make coffee, which would be the best they had ever tasted, he had promised. Phyl knew they would not complain about the horrible coffee that was coming. The more monstrous the egoist, she had observed from long practice, the more normal people hope to uphold the fabrication – either for ease, or from a terror of any kind of collapse. She did not know. She was sure, though, as she praised the stringy chicken, hoisting the unlovable man's self-infatuation a notch higher, that she did so because she feared him falling to pieces. Perhaps it was only fair, she decided, that weakness should get preferential treatment. Whether it would continue to do so, with Stanley's present change of mood, she was uncertain.

She tried to explain her thoughts to him when, he leaving his coffee, she having gulped hers down, they went to their bedroom. He nodded. He sat on the side of the bed, and put his face into his hands.

'Don't let's go out again,' she said. 'We can have a drink in here. I love a bedroom gin, and I brought a bottle in my case.' She went busily to the wash-basin, and held up a dusty tooth-glass to the light.

'You have one,' he said.

He was determined to keep unruffled, but every step she took across the uneven floorboards broke momentarily the steady pain into burning splinters. 'I've got gout,' he said sullenly. 'Bloody hell, I've got my gout.'

'I thought so,' she said. She put down the glass very quietly and came to him. 'Where?'

He pointed down.

'Can you manage to get into bed by yourself?'

He nodded.

'Well, then!' She smiled. 'Once you're in, I know what to do.'

He looked up apprehensively, but she went almost on tiptoe out of the door and closed it softly.

He undressed, put on his pyjamas, and hauled himself on to the bed. When she came back, she was carrying two pillows. 'Don't laugh, but they're "His" and "His",' she said. 'Now, this is what I do for Charlie. I make a little pillow house for his foot, and it keeps the bedclothes off. Don't worry, I won't touch.'

'On this one night,' he said.

'You want to drink a lot of water.' She put a glass beside him. '"My husband's got a touch of gout," I told them down there. And I really felt quite married to you when I said it.'

She turned her back to him as she undressed. Her body, set free at last, was creased with red marks, and across her shoulders the bright new skin from peeling had ragged, dirty edges of the old. She stretched her spine, put on a transparent nightgown and began to scratch her arms.

'Come here,' he said, unmoving. 'I'll do that.'

So gently she pulled back the sheet and lay down beside him that he felt they had been happily married for years. The pang was that this was their only married night and his foot burned so that he thought that it would burst. 'And it will be a damn sight worse in the morning,' he thought, knowing the pattern of his affliction. He began with one hand to stroke her itching arm.

Almost as soon as she had put the light off, an ominous sound zigzagged about the room. Switching on again, she said, 'I'll get that devil, if it's the last thing I do. You lie still.'

She got out of bed again and ran round the room, slapping at the walls with her *Reader's Digest*, until at last she caught the mosquito, and Stanley's (as was apparent in the morning) blood squirted out.

After that, once more in the dark, they lay quietly. He endured his pain, and she without disturbing him rubbed her flaking skin.

'So this is our wicked adventure,' he said bitterly to the moonlit ceiling.

'Would you rather be on your own?'

'No, no!' He groped with his hand towards her.

'Well, then ...'

'How can you forgive me?'

'Let's worry about you, eh? Not me. That sort of thing doesn't matter much to me nowadays. I only really do it to be matey. I don't know ... by the time Charlie and I have locked up, washed up, done the till, had a bit of something to eat ...'

Once, she had been as insatiable as a flame. She lay and remembered the days of her youth; but with interest, not wistfully.

Only once did she wake. It was the best night's sleep she'd had for a week. Moonlight now fell over the bed, and on one chalky white-washed wall. The sheet draped over them rose in a peak above his feet, so that he looked like a figure on a tomb. 'If Charlie could see me now,' she suddenly thought.

She tried not to have a fit of giggles for fear of shaking the bed. Stanley shifted, groaned in his sleep, then went on snoring, just as Charlie did.

He woke often during that night. The sheets were as abrasive as sand-paper. 'I knew this damn bed was too small,' he thought. He shifted warily on to his side to look at Phyl who, in her sleep, made funny little whim-pering sounds like a puppy. One arm flung above her head looked, in the moonlight, quite black against the pillow. Like going to bed with a coloured woman, he thought. He dutifully took a sip or two of water and then settled back again to endure his wakefulness.

'Well, I was happy,' she said, wearing her emerald-green coat again, sitting next to him in the plane, fastening her safety-belt.

His face looked worn and grey.

'Don't mind me asking,' she went on, 'but did he charge for that tea we didn't order?'

'Five shillings.'

'I *knew* it. I wish you'd let me pay my share of everything. After all, it was me as well wanted to go.'

He shook his head, smiling at her. In spite of his prediction, he felt better this departure afternoon, though tired and wary about himself.

'If only we were taking off on holiday now,' he said, 'not coming back. Why can't we meet up in Torquay or somewhere? Something for me to look forward to,' he begged her, dabbing his mosquito-bitten forehead with his handkerchief.

'It was only my hysterectomy got me away this time,' she said.

They ate, they drank, they held hands under a newspaper, and presently crossed the twilit coast of England, where farther along grey Hove was waiting for him. The trees had not changed colour much and only some – she noticed, as she looked down on them, coming in to land – were yellower.

She knew that it was worse for him. He had to return to his empty flat; she, to a full bar, and on a Saturday, too. She wished there was something she could do to send him off cheerful.

'To me,' she said, having refastened her safety-belt, taking his hand again. 'To me, it was lovely. To me it was just as good as if we had.'

Sisters

On a Thursday morning, soon after Mrs Mason returned from shopping – in fact she had not yet taken off her hat – a neat young man wearing a dark suit and spectacles, half-gold, half-mock tortoiseshell, and carrying a rolled umbrella, called at the house, and brought her to the edge of ruin. He gave a name, which meant nothing to her, and she invited him in, thinking he was about insurance, or someone from her solicitor. He stood in the sitting-room, looking keenly about him, until she asked him to sit down and tell her his business.

'Your sister,' he began. 'Your sister Marion,' and Mrs Mason's hand flew up to her cheek. She gazed at him in alarmed astonishment, then closed her eyes.

In this town, where she had lived all her married life, Mrs Mason was respected, even mildly loved. No one had a word to say against her, so it followed there were no strong feelings either way. She seemed to have been made for widowhood, and had her own little set, for bridge and coffee mornings, and her committee-meetings for the better known charities – such as the National Society for the Prevention of Cruelty to Children, and the Royal Society for the Prevention of Cruelty to Animals.

Her husband had been a successful dentist, and when he died she moved from the house where he had had his practice, into a smaller one in a quiet road nearby. She had no money worries, no worries of any kind. Childless and serene, she lived from day to day. They were almost able to set their clocks by her, her neighbours said, seeing her leaving the house in the mornings, for shopping and coffee at the Oak Beams Tea Room, pushing a basket on wheels, stalking rather on high-heeled shoes, blue-rinsed, rouged. Her front went down in a straight line from her heavy bust, giving her a stately look, the weight throwing her back a little. She took all of life at the same pace – a sign of ageing. She had settled to it a long time ago, and all of her years seemed the same now, although days had slightly varying patterns. Hers was mostly a day-time life, for it was chiefly a woman's world she had her place in. After tea, her friends' husbands came home, and then Mrs Mason pottered in her garden, played patience in the winter, or read historical romances from the library. 'Something light,' she would tell the assistant, as if seeking suggestions from a waiter. She could never remember the names of authors or their works, and it was quite a little disappointment when she discovered that she had read a novel before. She had few other disappointments – nothing much more than an unexpected shower of rain, or a tough cutlet, or the girl at the hairdresser's getting her rinse wrong.

Mrs Mason had always done, and still did, everything expected of women in her position – which was a phrase she often used. She baked beautiful Victoria sponges for bring-and-buy sales, arranged flowers, made *gros-point* covers for her chairs, gave tea parties, even sometimes, daringly, sherry parties with one or two husbands there, much against their will – but this was kept from her. She was occasionally included in other women's evening gatherings for she made no difference when there was a crowd, and it was an easy kindness. She mingled, and chatted about other people's holidays and families and jobs. She never drank more than two glasses of sherry, and was a good guest, always exclaiming appreciatively at the sight of canapés, 'My goodness, *someone's* been busy!'

Easefully the time had gone by.

This Thursday morning, the young man, having mentioned her sister, and seen her distress, glanced at one of the needlework cushions, and rose for a moment to examine it. Having ascertained that it was her work (a brief, distracted nod), he praised it, and sat down again. Then, thinking the pause long enough, he said, 'I am writing a book about your sister, and I did so hope for some help from you.'

'How did you know?' she managed to ask with her numbed lips. 'That she was, I mean.'

He smiled modestly. 'It was a matter of literary detection – my great hobby. My life's work, I might say.'

He had small, even teeth, she noticed, glancing at him quickly. They glinted, like his spectacles, the buttons on his jacket and the signet ring on his hand. He was a hideously glinty young man, she decided, looking away again.

'I have nothing to say of any interest.'

'But anything you say will interest us.'

'Us?'

'Her admirers. The reading public. Well, the world at large.' He shrugged.

'The world at large' was menacing, for it included this town where Mrs Mason lived. It included the Oak Beams Tea Room, and the Societies of Prevention.

'I have nothing to say.' She moved, as if she would rise.

'Come! You had your childhoods together. We know about those only from the stories. The beautiful stories. That wonderful house by the sea.'

He looked at a few shelves of books beside him, and seemed disappointed. They were her late husband's books about military history.

'It wasn't so wonderful,' she said, for she disliked all exaggeration. 'It was a quite ordinary, shabby house.'

'Yes?' he said softly, settling back in his chair and clasping his ladylike hands.

The shabby, ordinary house – the rectory – had a path between cornfields to the sea. On either side of it now were caravan sites. Her husband, Gerald, had taken her back there once when they were on holiday in Cornwall. He, of course, had been in the know. She had been upset about the caravans, and he had comforted her. She wished that he were here this morning to deal with this terrifying young man.

Of her childhood, she remembered – as one does – mostly the still hot afternoons, the cornflowers and thistles and scarlet pimpernels, the scratchy grass against her bare legs as they went down to the beach. Less clearly, she recalled evenings with shadows growing longer, and far-off sounding voices calling across the garden. She could see the picture of the house with windows open, and towels and bathing-costumes drying on upstairs sills and canvas shoes, newly whitened, drying too, in readiness for the next day's tennis. It had all been so familiar and comforting; but her sister, Marion, had complained of dullness, had ungratefully chafed and rowed and rebelled – although using it all (twisting it) in later years to make a name for herself. It had never, never been as she had written of it. And she, Mrs Mason, the little Cassie of those books, had never been at all that kind of child. These more than forty years after, she still shied away from that description of her squatting and peeing into a rock-pool, in front of some little boys Marion had made up. 'Cassie! Cassie!' her sisters had cried, apparently, in consternation. But it was Marion herself who had done that, more like. There were a few stories she could have told about Marion, if she had been the one to expose them all to shame, she thought grimly. The rock-pool episode was nothing, really, compared with some of the other inventions – 'experiments with sex', as reviewers had described them at the time. It was as if her sister had been compelled to set her sick fancies against a background that she knew.

Watching Mrs Mason's face slowly flushing all over to blend with her rouged cheekbones, the young man, leaning back easily, felt he had bided his time long enough. Something was obviously being stirred up. He said

gently – so that his words seemed to come to her like her own thoughts –
'A few stories now, please. Was it a happy childhood?'

'Yes. No. It was just an ordinary childhood.'

'With such a genius among you? How *awfully* interesting!'

'She was no different from any of the rest of us.' But she *had* been, and
so unpleasantly, as it turned out.

'Really *extraordinarily* interesting.' He allowed himself to lean forward a
little, then, wondering if the slightest show of eagerness might silence her,
he glanced about the room again. There were only two photographs – one
of a long-ago bride and bridegroom, the other of a pompous-looking man
with some sort of chain of office hanging on his breast.

It was proving very hard-going, this visit; but all the more of a challenge
for that.

Mrs Mason, in her silvery-grey wool dress, suddenly seemed to him to
resemble an enormous salmon. She even had a salmon shape – thick from
the shoulders down and tapering away to surprisingly tiny, out-turned feet.
He imagined trying to land her. She was demanding all the skill and ten-
acity he had. This was very pleasurable. Having let him in, and sat down,
her good manners could find no way of getting rid of him. He was sure of
that. Her good manners were the only encouraging thing, so far.

'You know, you are really not at all what I expected,' he said boldly,
admiringly. 'Not in the very least like your sister, are you?'

What he had expected was an older version of the famous photograph
in the Collected Edition – that waif-like creature with the fly-away fringe
and great dark eyes.

Mrs Mason now carefully lifted off her hat, as if it were a coronet. Then
she touched her hair, pushing it up a little. 'I was the pretty one,' she did
not say; but, feeling some explanation was asked for, told him what all the
world knew. 'My sister had poor health,' she said. 'Asthma and migraines,
and so on. Lots of what we now call allergies. I never had more than a
couple of days' illness in my life.' She remembered Marion always being
fussed over – wheezing and puking and whining, or stamping her feet up
and down in temper and frustration, causing scenes, a general rumpus at
any given moment.

He longed to get inside her mind; for interesting things were going on
there he guessed. Patience, he thought, regarding her. She was wearing
opaque grey stockings; to hide varicose veins, he thought. He knew everything about women, and mentally unclothed her. In a leisurely fashion –
since he would not hurry anything – he stripped off her peach-coloured slip
and matching knickers, tugged her out of her sturdy corselette, whose straps
had bitten deep into her plump shoulders, leaving a permanent indenta-
tion. He did not even jib at the massive, mottled flesh beneath, creased, as

it must be, from its rigid confinement, or the suspender imprints at the top of her tapering legs. Her navel would be full of talcum powder.

'It was all so long ago. I don't want to be reminded,' she said simply.

'Have you any photographs – holiday snapshots, for instance? I adore looking at old photographs.'

There was a boxful upstairs, faded sepia scenes of them all paddling – dresses tucked into bloomers – or picnicking, with sandwiches in hand, and feet out of focus. Her father, the Rector, had developed and printed the photographs himself, and they had not lasted well. 'I don't care to live in the past,' was all she said in reply.

'Were you and Marion close to one another?'

'We were sisters,' she said primly.

'And you kept in touch? I should think that you enjoyed basking in the reflected glory.' He knew that she had not kept in touch, and was sure by now that she had done no basking.

'She went to live in Paris, as no doubt you know.'

Thank heavens, Mrs Mason had always thought, that she *had* gone to live in Paris, and that she herself had married and been able to change her name. Still quite young, and before the war, Marion had died. It was during Mr Mason's year as Mayor. They had told no one.

'Did you ever meet Godwin? Or any of that set?'

'Of course not. My husband wouldn't have had them in the house.'

The young man nodded.

Oh, that dreadful clique. She was ashamed to have it mentioned to her by someone of the opposite sex, a complete stranger. She had been embarrassed to speak of it to her own husband, who had been so extraordinarily kind and forgiving about everything connected with Marion. But that raffish life in Paris in the thirties! Her sister living with the man Godwin, or turn and turn about with others of her set. They all had switched from one partner to the other; sometimes – she clasped her hands together so tightly that her rings hurt her fingers – to others of the same sex. She knew about it; the world knew; no doubt her friends knew, although it was not the sort of thing they would have discussed. Books had been written about that Paris lot, as Mrs Mason thought of them, and their correspondence published. Godwin, and Miranda Braun, the painter, and Grant Opie, the American, who wrote obscene books; and many of the others. They were all notorious: that was Mrs Mason's word for them.

'I think she killed my father,' she said in a low voice, almost as if she were talking to herself. 'He fell ill, and did not seem to want to go on living. He would never have her name mentioned, or any of her books in the house. She sent him a copy of the first one – she had left home by then, and was living in London. He read some of it, then took it out to the incinerator in the garden and burned it. I remember it now, his face was as white as a sheet.'

'But *you* have read the books surely?' he asked, playing her in gently.

She nodded, looking ashamed. 'Yes, later, I did.' A terrified curiosity had proved too strong to resist. And, reading, she had discovered a childhood she could hardly recognise, although it was all there: all the pieces were there, but shifted round as in a kaleidoscope. Worse came after the first book, the stories of their girlhood and growing up and falling in love. She, the Cassie of the books, had become a well-known character, with all her secrets laid bare; though they were really the secrets of Marion herself and not those of the youngest sister. The candour had caused a stir in those far-off days. During all the years of public interest, Mrs Mason had kept her silence, and lately had been able to bask indeed – in the neglect which had fallen upon her sister, as it falls upon most great writers at some period after their death. It was done with and laid to rest, she had thought – until this morning.

'And you didn't think much of them, I infer,' the young man said.

She started, and looked confused. 'Of what?' she asked, drawing back, tightening his line.

'Your sister's stories.'

'They weren't true. We were well-brought-up girls.'

'Your other sister died, too.'

He *had* been rooting about, she thought in dismay. 'She died before all the scandal,' Mrs Mason said grimly. 'She was spared.'

The telephone rang in the hall, and she murmured politely and got up. He heard her, in a different, chatty voice, making arrangements and kind enquiries, actually laughing. She rang off presently, and then stood for a moment steadying herself. She peered into a glass and touched her hair again. Full of strength and resolution, she went back to the sitting-room and just caught him clipping a pen back into the inside of his jacket.

'I'm afraid I shall have to get on with some jobs now,' she said clearly, and remained standing.

He rose – had to – cursing the telephone for ringing, just when he was bringing her in so beautifully. 'And you are sure you haven't even one little photograph to lend me,' he asked. 'I would take enormous care of it.'

'Yes, I am quite sure.' She was like another woman now. She had been in touch with her own world, and had gained strength from it.

'Then may I come to see you again when you are not so busy?'

'Oh, no, I don't think so.' She put out an arm and held the door-handle. 'I really don't think there would be any point.'

He really felt himself that there would not be. Still looking greedily about him, he went into the hall towards the front door. He had the idea of leaving his umbrella behind, so that he would have to return for it; but she firmly handed it to him. Even going down the path to the gate, he seemed to be glancing from side to side, as if memorising the names of flowers.

'I said nothing, I said nothing,' Mrs Mason kept telling herself, on her way that afternoon to play bridge. 'I merely conveyed my disapproval.' But she had a flustered feeling that her husband would not have agreed that she had done only that. And she guessed that the young man would easily make something of nothing. 'She killed my father.' She had said that. It would be in print, with her name attached to it. He had been clever to ferret her out, the menacing young man and now he had something new to offer to the world – herself. What else had she said, for heaven's sake? She was walking uphill, and panted a little. She could not for the life of her remember if she had said any more. But, ah yes! How her father had put that book into the incinerator. Just like Hitler, some people would think. And her name and Marion's would be linked together. Ex-Mayoress, and that rackety and lustful set. Some of her friends would be openly cool, others too kind, all of them shocked. They would discuss the matter behind her back. There were even those who would say they were 'intrigued' and ask questions.

Mrs Oldfellow, Mrs Fitch and Miss Christy all thought she played badly that afternoon, especially Mrs Oldfellow who was her partner. She did not stay for sherry when the bridge was over but excused herself, saying that she felt a cold coming on. Mrs Fitch's offer to run her back in the car she refused, hoping that the fresh air might clear her head.

She walked home in her usual sedate way; but she could not rid herself of the horrible idea they were talking about her already.

Hôtel du Commerce

The hallway, with its reception desk and hat-stand, was gloomy. Madame Bertail reached up to the board where the keys hung, took the one for room eight, and led the way upstairs. Her daughter picked up the heavier suit-case, and began to lurch lopsidedly across the hall with it until Leonard, blushing as he always (and understandably) did when he was obliged to speak French, insisted on taking it from her.

Looking offended, she grabbed instead Melanie's spanking-new wedding present suitcase, and followed them grimly, as *they* followed Madame Bertail's stiffly corseted back. Level with her shoulder-blades, the corsets stopped and the massive flesh moved gently with each step she took, as if it had a life of its own.

In Room Eight was a small double bed and wallpaper with a paisley pat-tern, on which what looked like curled-up blood-red embryos were repeated every two inches upon a sage-green background. There were other patterns for curtains and chair covers and the thin eiderdown. It was a depressing room, and a smell of some previous occupier's Ambre Solaire still hung about it.

'I'm so sorry, darling,' Leonard apologised, as soon as they were alone.

Melanie smiled. For a time, they managed to keep up their spirits. 'I'm so tired, I'll sleep anywhere,' she said, not knowing about the mosquito hidden in the curtains, or the lumpiness of the bed, and other horrors to follow.

They were both tired. A day of driving in an open car had made them feel, now they had stopped, quite dull and drowsy. Conversation was an effort.

Melanie opened her case. There was still confetti about. A crescent-shaped white piece fluttered on to the carpet, and she bent quickly and picked it up. So much about honeymoons was absurd – even little reminders like this one. And there had been awkwardnesses they could never have foreseen – especially that of having to make their way in a for-eign language. (*Lune de miel* seemed utterly improbable to her.) She did not know how to ask a maid to wash a blouse, although she had pages of irregu-lar verbs somewhere in her head, and odd words, from lists she had learnt as a child – the Parts of the Body, the Trees of the Forest, the Days of the Week – would often spring gratifyingly to her rescue.

When she had unpacked, she went to the window and leant out, over a narrow street with lumpy cobbles all ready for an early-morning din of rattling carts and slipping hooves.

Leonard kept glancing nervously at her as he unpacked. He did everything methodically, and at one slow pace. She was quick and untidy, and spent much time hanging about waiting for him, growing depressed, then exasperated, leaning out of windows, as now, strolling impatiently in gardens.

He smoked in the bedroom: she did not, and often thought it would have been better the other way about, so that she could have had something to do while she waited.

He hung up his dressing-gown, paused, then trod heavily across to his suitcase and took out washing things, which he arranged neatly on a shelf. He looked at her again. Seen from the back, hunched over the window-sill, she seemed to be visibly drooping, diminishing, like melting wax; and he knew that her mood was because of him. But a lifetime's habit – more than that, something inborn – made him feel helpless. He also had a moment of irritation himself, seeing her slippers thrown anyhow under a chair.

'Ready, then,' he said, in a tone of anticipation and decision.

She turned eagerly from the window, and saw him take up his comb. He stood before the glass, combing, combing his thin hair, lapsing once more into dreaminess, intent on what he was doing. She sighed quietly and turned back to look out of the window.

'I can see a spire of the Cathedral,' she said presently; but her head was so far out of the window – and a lorry was going by – that he did not hear her.

'Well, we've *had* the Cathedral,' she thought crossly. It was too late for the stained glass. She would never be able to make him see that every minute counted, or that there should not be some preordained method but, instead, a shifting order of priorities. Unpacking can wait; but the light will not.

By the time they got out for their walk, and saw the Cathedral, it was floodlit, bone-white against the dark sky, bleached, flat, stagey, though beautiful in this unintended and rather unsuitable way. Walking in the twisting streets, Leonard and Melanie had glimpsed the one tall spire above roof-tops, then lost it. Arm in arm, they had stopped to look in shop windows, at glazed pigs' trotters, tarts full of neatly arranged strawberries, sugared almonds on stems, in bunches, tied with ribbons. Leonard lingered, comparing prices of watches and cameras with those at home in England;

Melanie, feeling chilly, tried gently to draw him on. At last, without warning, they came to the square where the Cathedral stood, and here there were more shops, all full of little plaster statues and rosaries, and antiques for the tourists.

'Exorbitant,' Leonard kept saying. 'My God, how they're out to fleece you!'

Melanie stood staring up at the Cathedral until her neck ached. The great rose window was dark, the light glaring on the stone façade too static. The first sense of amazement and wonder faded. It was part of her impatient nature to care most for first impressions. On their way south, the sudden, and far-away sight of Chartres Cathedral across the plain, crouched on the horizon, with its lop-sided spires, like a giant hare, had meant much more to her than the close-up details of it. Again, for *that*, they had been too late. Before they reached the town, storm-clouds had gathered. It might as well have been dusk inside the Cathedral. She, for her part, would not have stopped to fill up with petrol on the road. She would have risked it, parked the car anywhere, and run.

Staring up at *this* Cathedral, she felt dizzy from leaning backwards, and swayed suddenly, and laughed. He caught her close to him and so, walking rather unevenly, with arms about the other's waist, moved on, out of the square, and back to the hotel.

Such moments, of more-than-usual love, gave them both great confidence. This time, their mood of elation lasted much longer than a moment.

Although the hotel dining-room was dark, and they were quite alone in it, speaking in subdued voices, their humour held; and held, as they took their key from impassive Madame Bertail, who still sat at the desk, doing her accounts; it even held as they undressed in their depressing room, and had no need to hold longer than that. Once in bed, they had always been safe.

'Don't tell me! Don't tell me!'

They woke at the same instant and stared at the darkness, shocked, wondering where they were.

'Don't tell me! I'll spend my money how I bloody well please.'

The man's voice, high and hysterical, came through the wall, just behind their heads.

A woman was heard laughing softly, with obviously affected amusement.

Something was thrown, and broke.

'I've had enough of your nagging.'

'I've had enough of *you*,' the woman answered coolly.

Melanie buried her head against Leonard's shoulder and he put an arm round her.

'I had enough of *you*, a very long time ago,' the woman's voice went on. 'I can't honestly remember a time when I *hadn't* had enough of you.'

'What I've gone through!'

'What *you've* gone through?'

'Yes, that's what I said. What *I've* gone through.'

'Don't shout. It's so common.' She had consciously lowered her own voice, then said, forgetting, in almost a shout, 'It's a pity for both our sakes, you were so greedy. For Daddy's money, I mean. That's all you ever cared about – my father's money.'

'All *you* cared about was getting into bed with me.'

'You great braggart. I've always loathed going to bed with you. Who wouldn't?'

Leonard heaved himself up in bed, and knocked on the damp wallpaper.

'I always felt sick,' the woman's voice went on, taking no notice. She was as strident now as the man; had begun to lose her grip on the situation, as he had done. 'And God knows,' she said, 'how many other women you've made feel sick.'

Leonard knocked louder, with his fist this time. The wall seemed as soft as if it were made from cardboard.

'I'm scared,' said Melanie. She sat up and switched on the light. 'Surely he'll kill her, if she goes on like that.'

'You little strumpet!' The man slurred this word, tried to repeat it and dried up, helplessly, goaded into incoherence.

'Be careful! Just be careful!' A dangerous, deliberate voice hers was now.

'Archie Durrant? Do you think I didn't know about Archie Durrant? Don't take me for a fool.'

'I'll warn you; don't put ideas into my head, my precious husband. At least Archie Durrant wouldn't bring me to a lousy place like this.'

She then began to cry. They reversed their rôles and he in his turn became the cool one.

'He won't take you anywhere, my pet. Like me, he's had enough. *Unlike* me, *he* can skedaddle.'

'Why doesn't someone *do* something!' asked Melanie, meaning, of course, that Leonard should. 'Everyone must be able to hear. And they're English, too. It's so shaming, and horrible.'

'Go on, then, skedaddle, skedaddle!' The absurd word went on and on, blurred, broken by sobs. Something more was thrown – something with a sharp, hard sound; perhaps a shoe or book.

Leonard sprang out of bed and put on his dressing-gown and slippers.

'Slippers!' thought Melanie, sitting up in bed, shivering.

As Leonard stepped out into the passage, he saw Madame Bertail coming along it, from the other direction. She, too, wore a dressing-gown, corded round her stout stomach: her grey hair was thinly braided. She looked steadily at Leonard, as if dismissing him, classing him with his loose compatriots, then knocked quickly on the door and at once tried the door-handle. The key had been turned in the lock. She knocked again, and there was silence inside the room. She knocked once more, very loudly, as if to make sure of this silence, and then, without a word to Leonard, seem-ing to feel satisfied that she had dealt successfully with the situation, she went off down the corridor.

Leonard went back to the bedroom and slowly took off his dressing-gown and slippers.

'I think that will be that,' he said, and got back into bed and tried to warm poor Melanie.

'You talk about your father's money,' the man's voice went on, almost at once. 'But I wouldn't want any truck with that kind of money.'

'You just want it.'

Their tone was more controlled, as if they were temporarily calmed. However, although the wind had dropped they still quietly angled for it, keeping things going for the time being.

'I'll never forget the first time I realised how you got on my nerves,' he said, in the equable voice of an old friend reminiscing about happier days. 'That way you walk upstairs with your bottom waggling from side to side. My God, I've got to walk upstairs and downstairs behind that bottom for the rest of my life, I used to think.'

'Such triviality!' Melanie thought fearfully, pressing her hands against her face. To begin with such a thing – for the hate to grow from it – not nearly as bad as being slow and keeping people waiting.

'I wasn't seriously loathing you then,' the man said in a conversational tone. 'Even after that fuss about Archie Durrant. I didn't seriously *hate* you.'

'Thank you very much, you ... cuckold.'

If Leonard did not snore at that moment, he certainly breathed sonorously.

During that comparative lull in the next room, he had dropped off to sleep, leaving Melanie wakeful and afraid.

'She called him a cuckold,' she hissed into Leonard's ear.

'No, the time, I think,' said the man behind the wall, in the same deadly flat voice, 'the time I first really hated you, was when you threw the pota-toes at me.'

'Oh, yes, that was a *great* evening,' she said, in tones chiming with affected pleasure.

'In front of my own mother.'

'She seemed to enjoy it as much as I did. Probably longed for years to do it herself.'

'That was when I first realised.'

'Why did you stay?' There was silence. Then, 'Why stay now? Go on! Go now! I'll help you to pack. There's your bloody hairbrush for a start. My God, you look ridiculous when you duck down like that. You sickening little coward.'

'I'll kill you.'

'Oh God, he'll kill her,' said Melanie, shaking Leonard roughly.

'You won't, you know,' shouted the other woman.

The telephone rang in the next room.

'Hello?' The man's voice was cautious, ruffled. The receiver was quietly replaced. 'You see what you've done?' he said. 'Someone ringing up to complain about the noise you're making.'

'You don't think I give a damn for anyone in a crumby little hotel like this, do you?'

'Oh, my nerves, my nerves, my nerves,' the man suddenly groaned. Bedsprings creaked, and Melanie imagined him sinking down on the edge of the bed, his face buried in his hands.

Silence lasted only a minute or two. Leonard was fast asleep now. Melanie lay very still, listening to a mosquito coming and going above her head.

Then the crying began, at first a little sniffing, then a quiet sobbing.

'Leonard, you must wake up. I can't lie here alone listening to it. Or *do* something, for heaven's sake.'

He put out a hand, as if to stave her off, or calm her, without really disturbing his sleep, and this gesture infuriated her. She slapped his hand away roughly.

'There's nothing I can do,' he said, still clinging to the idea of sleep; then, as she flounced over in the bed, turning her back to him, he resignedly sat up and turned on the light. Blinking and tousled, he stared before him, and then leaned over and knocked on the wall once more.

'*That* won't do any good,' said Melanie.

'Well, their door's locked, so what else can I do?'

'Ring up the police.'

'I can't do that. Anyhow, I don't know how to in French.'

'Well, try. If the hotel was on fire, you'd do something, wouldn't you?'

Her sharp tone was new to him, and alarming.

'It's not really our business.'

'If he kills her? While you were asleep, she called him a cuckold. I thought he was going to kill her then. And even if he doesn't, we can't hope to get any sleep. It's perfectly horrible. It sounds like a child crying.'

'Yes, with temper. Your feet are frozen.'

'Of course, they're frozen.' Her voice blamed him for this.

'My dear, don't let *us* quarrel.'

'I'm so tired. Oh, that – damned mosquito.' She sat up, and tried to smack it against the wall, but it had gone. 'It's been such an awful day.'

'I thought it was a perfectly beautiful day.'

She pressed her lips together and closed her eyes, drawing herself away from him, as if determined now, somehow or other, to go to sleep.

'Didn't you like your day?' he asked.

'Well, you must have known I was disappointed about the Cathedral. Getting there when it was too dark.'

'I didn't know. You didn't give me an inkling. We can go first thing in the morning.'

'It wouldn't be the same. Oh, you're so hopeless. You hang about, and hang about, and drive me mad with impatience.'

She lay on her side, well away from him on the very edge of the bed, facing the horribly patterned curtains, her mouth so stiff, her eyes full of tears. He made an attempt to draw her close, but she became rigid, her limbs were iron.

'You see, she's quietening down,' he said. The weeping had gone through every stage – from piteous sobbing, gasping, angry moans, to – now – a lulled whimpering, dying off, hardly heard. And the man was silent. Had he dropped senseless across the bed, Melanie wondered, or was he still sitting there, staring at the picture of his own despair.

'I'm so sorry about the Cathedral. I had no idea ...' said Leonard, switching off the light, and sliding down in bed. Melanie kept her cold feet to herself.

'We'll say no more about it,' she said, in a grim little voice.

They slept late. When he awoke, Leonard saw that Melanie was almost falling out of bed in her attempt to keep away from him. Disquieting memories made him frown. He tried to lay his thoughts out in order. The voices in the next room, the nightmare of weeping and abuse; but worse, Melanie's cold voice, her revelation of that harboured disappointment; then, worse again, even worse, her impatience with him. He drove her nearly mad, she had said. Always? Since they were married? When?

At last Melanie awoke, and seemed uncertain of how to behave. Unable to make up her mind, she assumed a sort of non-behaviour to be going on with, which he found most mystifying.

'Shall we go to the Cathedral?' he asked.

'Oh, I don't think so,' she said carelessly. She even turned her back to him while she dressed.

There was silence from the next room, but neither of them referred to it. It was as if some shame of their own were shut up in there. The rest of the hotel was full of noises – kitchen clatterings and sharp voices. A vacuum-cleaner bumped and whined along the passage outside, and countrified traffic went by in the cobbled street.

Melanie's cheeks and forehead were swollen with mosquito bites, which gave her an angry look. She scratched one on her wrist and made it water. They seemed the stigmata of her irritation.

They packed their cases.

'Ready?' he asked.

'When you are,' she said sullenly.

'Might as well hit the trail as soon as we've had breakfast,' he said, trying to sound optimistic, as if nothing were wrong. He had no idea of how they would get through the day. They had no plans, and she seemed disinclined to discuss any.

They breakfasted in silence in the empty dining-room. Some of the tables had chairs stacked on them.

'You've no idea where you want to go, then?' he asked.

She was spreading apricot jam on a piece of bread and he leant over and gently touched her hand. She laid down the knife, and put her hand in her lap. Then picked up the bread with her left hand and began to eat.

They went upstairs, to fetch their cases and, going along the passage, could see that the door of the room next to theirs now stood wide open. Before they reached it, a woman came out and hesitated in the doorway, looking back into the room. There was an appearance of brightness about her – her glowing face, shining hair, starched dress. Full of gay anticipation as it was, her voice, as she called back into the room, was familiar to Melanie and Leonard.

'Ready, darling?'

The other familiar voice replied. The man came to the doorway, carrying the case. He put his arm round the woman's waist and they went off down the passage. Such a well turned-out couple, Melanie thought, staring after them, as she paused at her own doorway, scratching her mosquito bites.

'Let's go to that marvellous place for lunch,' she heard the man suggesting. They turned a corner to the landing, but as they went on downstairs, their laughter floated up after them.

Miss A and Miss M

A new motorway had made a different landscape of that part of England I loved as a child, cutting through meadows, spanning valleys, shaving off old gardens and leaving houses perched on islands of confusion. Nothing is recognisable now: the guest-house has gone, with its croquet-lawn; the cherry orchard; and Miss Alliot's and Miss Martin's week-end cottage. I should think that little is left anywhere, except in *my* mind.

I was a town child, and the holidays in the country had a sharp delight which made the waiting time of school term, of traffic, of leaflessness, the unreal part of my life. At Easter, and for weeks in the summer, sometimes even for a few snatched days in winter, we drove out there to stay – it wasn't far – for my mother loved the country, too, and in that place we had put down roots.

St Margaret's was the name of the guest-house, which was run by two elderly ladies who had come down in the world, bringing with them quantities of heavily riveted Crown Derby, and silver plate. Miss Louie and Miss Beatrice.

My mother and I shared a bedroom with a sloping floor and threadbare carpet. The wallpaper had faint roses, and a powdery look from damp. Oil-lamps or candles lit the rooms, and, even now, the smell of paraffin brings it back, that time of my life. We were in the nineteen twenties.

Miss Beatrice, with the help of a maid called Mabel, cooked deliciously. Beautiful creamy porridge, I remember, and summer puddings, suckling pigs and maids-of-honour and marrow jam. The guests sat at one long table with Miss Louie one end and Miss Beatrice the other, and Mabel scuttling in and out with silver domed dishes. There was no wine. No one drank anything alcoholic, that I remember. Sherry was kept for trifle, and that was it, and the new world of cocktail parties was elsewhere.

The guests were for the most part mild, bookish people who liked a cheap and quiet holiday – schoolmasters, elderly spinsters, sometimes people to do with broadcasting who, in those days, were held in awe. The guests returned, so that we had constant friends among them, and looked forward to our reunions. Sometimes there were other children. If there were not, I did not care. I had Miss Alliot and Miss Martin.

These two were always spoken of in that order, and not because it was easier to say like that, or more euphonious. They appeared at luncheon and supper, but were not guests. At the far end of the orchard they had a cottage for week-ends and holidays. They were schoolmistresses in London.

'Cottage' is not quite the word for what was little more than a wooden shack with two rooms and a veranda. It was called Breezy Lodge, and draughts did blow between its ramshackle clap-boarding.

Inside, it was gay, for Miss Alliot was much inclined to orange and yellow and grass-green, and the cane chairs had cushions patterned with nasturtiums and marigolds and ferns. The curtains and her clothes reflected the same taste.

Miss Martin liked misty blues and greys, though it barely mattered that she did. She had a small smudged-looking face with untidy eyebrows, a gentle, even submerged nature. She was a great – but quiet – reader and never seemed to wish to talk of what she had read. Miss Alliot, on the other hand, would occasionally skim through a book and find enough in it for long discourses and an endless supply of allusions. She wrung the most out of everything she did or saw and was a great talker.

That was a time when one fell in love with who ever was *there*. In my adolescence the only males available to me for adoration were such as Shelley or Rupert Brooke or Owen Nares. A rather more real passion could be lavished on prefects at school or the younger mistresses.

Miss Alliot was heaven-sent, it seemed to me. She was a holiday goddess. Miss Martin was just a friend. She tried to guide my reading, as an elder sister might. This was a new relationship to me. I had no elder sister, and I had sometimes thought that to have had one would have altered my life entirely, and whether for better or worse I had never been able to decide.

How I stood with Miss Alliot was a reason for more pondering. Why did she take trouble over me, as she did? I considered myself sharp for my age: now I see that I was sharp only for the age I *lived* in. Miss Alliot cultivated me to punish Miss Martin – as if she needed another weapon. I condoned the punishing. I basked in the doing of it. I turned my own eyes from the troubled ones under the fuzzy brows, and I pretended not to know precisely what was being done. Flattery nudged me on. Not physically fondled, I was fondled all the same.

In those days before – more than forty years before – the motorway, that piece of countryside was beautiful, and the word 'countryside' still means there to me. The Chiltern Hills. Down one of those slopes below St Margaret's streamed the Cherry Orchard, a vast delight in summer of marjoram and thyme. An unfrequented footpath led through it, and every step was aromatic. We called this walk the Echo Walk – down through the trees and up from the valley on its other side to larch woods.

Perched on a stile at the edge of the wood, one called out messages to be rung back across the flinty valley. Once, alone, I called out, 'I love you,' loud and strong, and 'I love you' came back faint, and mocking. 'Miss Alliot,' I added. But that response was blurred. Perhaps I feared to shout too loudly, or it was not a good echo name. I tried no others.

On Sunday mornings I walked across the fields to church with Miss Martin. Miss Alliot would not join us. It was scarcely an intellectual feast, she said, or spiritually uplifting, with the poor old Vicar mumbling on and the organ asthmatic. In London, she attended St Ethelburga's in the Strand, and spoke a great deal of a Doctor Cobb. But, still more, she spoke of the Townsends.

For she punished Miss Martin with the Townsends too.

The Townsends lived in Northumberland. Their country house was grand, as was to be seen in photographs. Miss Alliot appeared in some of these shading her eyes as she lay back in a deckchair in a sepia world or – with Suzanne Lenglen bandeau and accordion-pleated dress – simply standing, to be photographed. By whom? I wondered. Miss Martin wondered, too, I thought.

Once a year, towards the end of the summer holiday (mine: theirs) Miss Alliot was invited to take the train north. We knew that she would have taken that train at an hour's notice, and, if necessary, have dropped everything for the Townsends.

What they consisted of – the Townsends – I was never really sure. It was a group name, both in my mind and in our conversations. 'Do the Townsends play croquet?' I enquired, or 'Do the Townsends change for dinner?' I was avid for information. It was readily given.

'I know what the Townsends would think of *her*,' Miss Alliot said, of the only common woman, as she put it, who had ever stayed at St Margaret's. Mrs Price came with her daughter, Muriel, who was seven years old and had long, burnished plaits, which she would toss – one, then the other – over her shoulders. Under Miss Alliot's guidance, I scorned both Mrs Price and child, and many a laugh we had in Breezy Lodge at their expense. Scarcely able to speak for laughter, Miss Alliot would recount her 'gems', as she called them. 'Oh, she *said* ... one can't believe it, little Muriel ... Mrs Price *insists* on it ... changes her socks and knickers twice a day. She likes her to be nice and fresh. And ... ' Miss Alliot was a good mimic, '"she always takes an apple for recess". What in God's name is recess?'

This was rather strong language for those days, and I admired it.

'It's "break" or ... ' Miss Martin began reasonably. This was her mistake. She slowed things up with her reasonableness, when what Miss Alliot wanted, and I wanted, was a flight of fancy.

I tried, when those two were not there, to gather foolish or despicable phrases from Mrs Price, but I did not get far. (I suspect now Miss Alliot's inventive mind at work – rehearsing for the Townsends.)

All these years later, I have attempted, while writing this, to be fair to Mrs Price, almost forgotten for forty years; but even without Miss Alliot's direction I think I should have found her tiresome. She boasted to my mother (and no adult was safe from my eavesdropping) about her hysterectomy, and the gynaecologist who doted on her. 'I always have my operations at the Harbeck Clinic.' I was praised for that titbit, and could not run fast enough to Breezy Lodge with it.

I knew what the medical words meant, for I had begun to learn Greek at school – Ladies' Greek, as Elizabeth Barrett Browning called it, 'without any accents'. My growing knowledge served me well with regard to words spoken in lowered tones. 'My operations! How Ralph Townsend will adore that one!' Miss Alliot said.

A Townsend now stepped forward from the general family group. Miss Martin stopped laughing. I was so sharp for my years that I thought she gave herself away by doing so, that she should have let her laughter die away gradually. In that slice of a moment she had made clear her sudden worry about Ralph Townsend. Knowing as I did then so much about human beings, I was sure she had been meant to.

Poor Miss Martin, my friend, mentor, church-going companion, mild, kind and sincere – I simply used her as a stepping-stone to Miss Alliot.

I never called them by their first names, and have had to pause a little to remember them. Dorothea Alliot and Edith Martin. 'Dorothea' had a fine ring of authority about it. Of course, I had the Greek meaning of that, too, but I knew that Miss Alliot was the giver herself – of the presents and the punishments.

My mother liked playing croquet and cards, and did both a great deal at St Margaret's. I liked going across the orchard to Breezy Lodge. There, both cards and croquet were despised. We sat on the veranda (or, in winter, round an oil-stove which threw up petal patterns on the ceiling) and we talked – a game particularly suited to three people. Miss Alliot always won.

Where to find such drowsy peace in England now is hard to discover. Summer after summer through my early teens, the sun shone, bringing up the smell of thyme and marjoram from the earth – the melting tar along the lane and, later, of rotting apples. The croquet balls clicked against one another on the lawn, and voices sounded lazy and far-away. There were droughts, when we were on our honour to be careful with the water. No water was laid on at Breezy Lodge, and it had to be carried from the house. I took this duty from Miss Martin, and several times a day stumbled through the long grass and buttercups, the water swinging in a pail, or slopping out of a jug. As I went, I disturbed clouds of tiny blue butterflies, once a grass snake.

Any excuse to get to Breezy Lodge. My mother told me not to intrude, and I was offended by the word. She was even a little frosty about my two friends. If for some reason they were not there when we ourselves arrived on holiday I was in despair, and she knew it and lost patience.

In the school term I wrote to them and Miss Martin was the one who replied. They shared a flat in London, and a visit to it was spoken of, but did not come about. I used my imagination instead, building it up from little scraps as a bird builds a nest. I was able to furnish it in unstained oak and hand-woven rugs and curtains. All about would be jars of the beech-leaves and grasses and berries they took back with them from the country. From their windows could be seen, through the branches of a monkey-puzzle tree, the roofs of the school – Queen's – from which they returned each evening.

That was their life on their own where I could not intrude, as my mother would have put it. They had another life of their own in which I felt aggrieved at not participating: but I was not invited to. After supper at St Margaret's, they returned to Breezy Lodge, and did not ask me to go with them. Games of solo whist were begun in the drawing-room, and I sat and read listlessly, hearing the clock tick and the maddening mystifying card-words – 'Misère' 'Abundance' – or 'going a bundle', 'prop and cop', and 'Misère Ouverte' (which seemed to cause a little stir). I pitied them and their boring games, and I pitied myself and my boring book – imposed holiday reading, usually Sir Walter Scott, whom I loathed. I pecked at it dispiritedly and looked about the room for distraction.

Miss Louie and Miss Beatrice enjoyed their whist, as they enjoyed their croquet. They really were hostesses. We paid a little – astonishingly little – but it did not alter the fact that we were truly guests, and they entertained us believing so.

'Ho ... ho ... hum ... hum,' murmured a voice, fanning out a newly-dealt hand, someone playing for time. 'H'm, h'm, now let me see.' There were relaxed intervals when cards were being shuffled and cut, and the players leant back and had a little desultory conversation, though nothing amounting to much. On warm nights, as it grew later, through the open windows moths came to plunge and lurch about the lamps.

Becoming more and more restless, I might go out and wander about the garden, looking for glow-worms and glancing at the light from Breezy Lodge shining through the orchard boughs.

On other evenings, after Miss Beatrice had lit the lamps, Mrs Mayes, one of the regular guests, might give a Shakespeare recital. She had once had some connection with the stage and had known Sir Henry Ainley. She had often heard his words for him, she told us, and perhaps, in consequence of that, had whole scenes by heart. She was ageing wonderfully – that is, hardly at all. Some of the blonde was fading from her silvery-blonde hair, but her skin was still wild-rose, and her voice held its great range. But most of all, we marvelled at how she remembered her lines. I recall most vividly the Balcony Scene from *Romeo and Juliet*. Mrs Mayes sat at one end of a velvet-covered *chaise-longue*. When she looped her pearls over her fingers, then clasped them to her bosom, she was Juliet, and Romeo when she held out her arms, imploringly (the rope of pearls swinging free). Always she changed into what, in some circles, was then called semi-evening dress, and rather old-fashioned dresses they were, with bead embroidery and loose panels hanging from the waist. Once, I imagined, she would have worn such dresses *before* tea, and have changed again later into something even more splendid. She had lived through grander days: now, was serenely widowed.

Only Mrs Price did not marvel at her. I overheard her say to my mother, 'She must be forever in the limelight, and I for one am sick and tired, *sick and tired*, of Henry Ainley. I'm afraid I don't call actors "sir". I'm like that.' And my mother blushed, but said nothing.

Miss Alliot and Miss Martin were often invited to stay for these recitals; but Miss Alliot always declined.

'One is embarrassed, being recited *at*,' she explained to me. 'One doesn't know where to look.'

I always looked at Mrs Mayes and admired the way she did her hair, and wondered if the pearls were real. There may have been a little animosity between the two women. I remember Mrs Mayes joining in praise of Miss Alliot one day, saying, 'Yes, she is like a well-bred race-horse,' and I felt that she said this only because she could not say that she was like a horse.

Mrs Price, rather out of it after supper, because of Mrs Mayes, and not being able to get the hang of solo whist, would sulkily turn the pages of the *Illustrated London News*, and try to start conversations between scenes or games.

'*Do* look at *this*.' She would pass round her magazine, pointing out something or other. Or she would tiptoe upstairs to see if Muriel slept, and come back to report. Once she said, *à propos* nothing, as cards were being re-dealt, 'Now who can clasp their ankles with their fingers? Like *that* – with no gaps.' Some of the ladies dutifully tried, but only Mrs Price could do it. She shrugged and laughed. 'Only a bit of fun,' she said, 'but they do say that's the right proportion. Wrists, too, that's easier, though.' But they were all at cards again.

One morning, we were sitting on the lawn and my mother was stringing redcurrants through the tines of a silver fork into a pudding-basin. Guests often helped in these ways. Mrs Price came out from the house carrying a framed photograph of a bride and bridegroom – her son, Derek, and daughter-in-law, Gloria. We had heard of them.

'You don't look old enough,' my mother said, 'to have a son that age.' She had said it before. She always liked to make people happy. Mrs Price kept hold of the photograph, because of my mother's stained fingers, and she pointed out details such as Gloria's veil and Derek's smile and the tuberoses in the bouquet. 'Derek gave her a gold locket, but it hasn't come out very clearly. Old enough! You are trying to flatter me. Why my husband and I had our silver wedding last October. Muriel was our little after-thought.'

I popped a string of currants into my mouth and sauntered off. As soon as I was out of sight, I sped. All across the orchard, I murmured the words with smiling lips.

The door of Breezy Lodge stood open to the veranda. I called through it, 'Muriel was their little after-thought.'

Miss Martin was crying. From the bedroom came a muffled sobbing. At once, I knew that it was she, never could be Miss Alliot. Miss Alliot, in fact, walked out of the bedroom and shut the door.

'What is wrong?' I asked stupidly.

Miss Alliot gave a vexed shake of her head and took her walking-stick from its corner. She was wearing a dress with a pattern of large poppies, and cut-out poppies from the same material were appliquéd to her straw hat. She was going for a walk, and I went with her, and she told me that Miss Martin had fits of nervous hysteria. For no reason. The only thing to be done about them was to leave her alone until she recovered.

We went down through the Cherry Orchard and the scents and the butterflies were part of an enchanted world. I thought that I was completely happy. I so rarely had Miss Alliot's undivided attention. She talked of the Townsends, and I listened as if to the holy intimations of a saint.

'I thought you were lost,' my mother said when I returned.

Miss Alliot always wore a hat at luncheon (that annoyed Mrs Price). She sat opposite me and seemed in a very good humour, taking trouble to amuse us all, but with an occasional allusion and smile for me alone. 'Miss Martin has one of her headaches,' she explained. By this time I was sure that this was true.

The holidays were going by, and I had got nowhere with *Quentin Durward*. Miss Martin recovered from her nervous hysteria, but was subdued.

Miss Alliot departed for Northumberland, wearing autumn tweeds. Miss Martin stayed on alone at Breezy Lodge, and distempered the walls primrose, and I helped her. Mrs Price and Muriel left at last, and a German governess with her two little London pupils arrived for a breath of fresh air. My mother and Mrs Mayes strolled about the garden. Together they did the flowers, to help Miss Louie, or sat together in the sunshine with their *petit point*.

Miss Martin and I painted away, and we talked of Miss Alliot and how wonderful she was. It was like a little separate holiday for me, a rest. I did not try to adjust myself to Miss Martin, or strive, or rehearse. In a way, I think she was having a well-earned rest herself; but then I believed that she was jealous of Northumberland and would have liked some Townsends of her own to retaliate with. Now I know she only wanted Miss Alliot.

Miss Martin was conscientious; she even tried to take me through *Quentin Durward.*

She seemed to be concerned about my butterfly mind, its skimming over things, not stopping to understand. I felt that knowing things ought to 'come' to me, and if it did not, it was too bad. I believed in instinct and intuition and inspiration – all labour-saving things.

Miss Martin, who taught English (my subject, I felt), approached the matter coldly. She tried to teach me the logic of it – grammar. But I thought 'ear' would somehow teach me that. Painless learning I wanted, or none at all. She would not give up. She was the one who was fond of me.

We returned from our holiday, and I went back to school. I was moved up – by the skin of my teeth, I am sure – to a higher form. I remained with my friends. Some of those had been abroad for the holidays, but I did not envy them.

Miss Martin wrote to enquire how I had got on in the *Quentin Durward* test, and I replied that as I could not answer one question, I had written a general description of Scottish scenery. She said that it would avail me nothing, and it did not. I had never been to Scotland, anyway. Of Miss Alliot I only heard. She was busy producing the school play – A *Tale of Two Cities*. Someone called Rosella Byng-Williams was very good as Sidney Carton, and I took against her at once. 'I think Dorothea has made quite a discovery,' Miss Martin wrote – but I fancied that her pen was pushed along with difficulty, and that she was due for one of her headaches.

Those three 'i's' – instinct, intuition, inspiration – in which I pinned my faith were more useful in learning about people than logic could be. Capricious approach to capricious subject.

Looking back, I see that my mother was far more attractive, lovable, than any of the ladies I describe; but there it was – she was my mother.

Towards the end of that term, I learnt of a new thing, that Miss Alliot was to spend Christmas with the Townsends. This had never been done before:

there had been simply the early autumn visit – it seemed that it had been for the sake of an old family friendship, a one-sided one, I sharply guessed. Now, what had seemed to be a yearly courtesy became something rather more for conjecture.

Miss Martin wrote that she would go to Breezy Lodge alone, and pretend that Christmas wasn't happening – as lonely people strive to. I imagined her carrying pails of cold water through the wet, long grasses of the orchard, rubbing her chilblains before the oil-stove. I began to love her as if she were a child.

My mother was a little flustered by my idea of having Miss Martin to stay with us for Christmas. I desired it intensely, having reached a point where the two of us, my mother and I alone, a Christmas done just for me, was agonising. What my mother thought of Miss Martin I shall never know now, but I have a feeling that schoolmistresses rather put her off. She expected them all to be what many of them in those days were – opinionated, narrow-minded, set in their ways. She had never tried to get to know Miss Martin. No one ever did.

She came. At the last moment before her arrival I panicked. It was not Miss Alliot coming, but Miss Alliot would hear all about the visit. Our house was in a terrace (crumbling). There was nothing, I now saw, to commend it to Miss Martin except, perhaps, water from the main and a coal fire.

After the first nervousness, though, we had a cosy time. We sat round the fire and ate Chinese figs and sipped ginger wine and played paper games which Miss Martin could not manage to lose. We sometimes wondered about the Townsends and I imagined a sort of Royal-Family-at-Sandringham Christmas with a giant tree and a servants' ball, and Miss Alliot taking the floor in the arms of Ralph Townsend – but then my imagination failed, the picture faded: I could not imagine Miss Alliot in the arms of any man.

After Christmas, Miss Martin left and then I went back to school. I was too single-minded in my devotion to Miss Alliot to do much work there, or bother about anybody else. My infatuation was fed by her absence, and everything beautiful was wasted if it was not seen in her company.

The Christmas invitation bore glorious fruit. As a return, Miss Martin wrote to ask me to stay at Breezy Lodge for my half-term holiday. Perfect happiness invaded me, remembered clearly to this day. Then, after a while of walking on air, the bliss dissolved. Nothing in the invitation, I now realised, had been said of Miss Alliot. Perhaps she was off to Northumberland again, and I was to keep Miss Martin company in her stead. I tried to reason with myself that even that would be better than nothing, but I stayed sick with apprehension.

At the end of the bus-ride there on a Saturday morning, I was almost too afraid to cross the orchard. I feared my own disappointment as if it were something I must protect myself – and incidentally Miss Martin – from. I seemed to become two people – the one who tapped jauntily on the door, and the other who stood ready to ward off the worst. Which did not happen. Miss Alliot herself opened the door.

She was wearing one of her bandeaux and several ropes of beads and had a rather gypsy air about her. 'The child has arrived,' she called back into the room. Miss Martin sat by the stove mending stockings – an occupation of those days. They were Miss Alliot's stockings – rather thick and biscuit-coloured.

We went over to St Margaret's for lunch and walked to the Echo afterwards, returning with branches of catkins and budding twigs. Miss Alliot had a long, loping stride. She hit about at nettles with her stick, the fringed tongues of her brogues flapped – she had long, narrow feet, and trouble with high insteps, she complained. The bandeau was replaced by a stitched felt hat in which was stuck the eye-part of a peacock's feather. Bad luck, said Miss M. Bosh, said Miss A.

We had supper at Breezy Lodge, for Miss Alliot's latest craze was for making goulash, and a great pot of it was to be consumed during the weekend. Afterwards, Miss Martin knitted – a jersey of complicated Fair Isle pattern for Miss Alliot. She sat in a little perplexed world of her own, entangled by coloured wools, her head bent over the instructions.

Miss Alliot turned her attention to me. What was my favourite line of poetry, what would I do if I were suddenly given a thousand pounds, would I rather visit Rome or Athens or New York, which should I hate most – being deaf or blind; hanged or drowned; are cats not better than dogs, and wild flowers more beautiful than garden ones, and Emily Brontë streets ahead of Charlotte? And so on. It was heady stuff to me. No one before had been interested in my opinions. Miss Martin knitted on. Occasionally, she was included in the questions, and always appeared to give the wrong answer.

I slept in their bedroom, on a camp-bed borrowed from St Margaret's. (And how was I ever going to be satisfied with staying *there* again? I wondered.)

Miss Alliot bagged (as she put it) the bathroom first, and was already in bed by the time I returned from what was really only a ewer of water and an Elsan. She was wearing black silk pyjamas with DDA embroidered on a pocket. I bitterly regretted my pink nightgown, of which I had until then been proud. I had hastily brushed my teeth and passed a wet flannel over my face in eagerness to get back to her company and, I hoped, carry on with the entrancing subject of my likes and dislikes.

I began to undress. 'People are kind to the blind, and impatient with the deaf,' I began, as if there had been no break in the conversation. 'You are so right,' Miss Alliot said. 'And people matter most.'

'But if you couldn't see . . . well, this orchard in spring,' Miss Martin put in. It was foolish of her to do so. 'You've already seen it,' Miss Alliot pointed out. 'Why this desire to go on repeating your experiences?'

Miss Martin threw in the Parthenon, which she had *not* seen, and hoped to.

'Still people matter most,' Miss Alliot insisted. 'To be cut off from them is worse than to be cut off from the Acropolis.'

She propped herself up in bed and with open curiosity watched me undress. For the first time in my life I realised what dreadful things I wore beneath my dress – lock-knit petticoat, baggy school bloomers, vest with Cash's name tape, garters of stringy elastic tied in knots, not sewn. My mother had been right . . . I should have sewn them. Then, for some reason, I turned my back to Miss Alliot and put on my nightgown. I need not have bothered, for Miss Martin was there between us in a flash, standing before Miss Alliot with Ovaltine.

On the next day – Sunday – I renounced my religion. My doubts made it impossible for me to go to church, so Miss Martin went alone. She went rather miserably, I was forced to notice. I can scarcely believe that any deity could have been interested in my lack of devotion, but it was as if, somewhere, there was one who was. Freak weather had set in and, although spring had not yet begun, the sun was so warm that Miss Alliot took a deckchair and a blanket and sat on the veranda and went fast asleep until long after Miss Martin had returned. (She *needed* a great deal of sleep, she always said.) I pottered about and fretted at this waste of time. I almost desired my faith again. I waited for Miss Martin to come back, and, seeing her, ran out and held a finger to my lips, as if Miss Alliot were royalty, or a baby. Miss Martin nodded and came on stealthily.

It was before the end of the summer term that I had the dreadful letter from Miss Martin. Miss Alliot – hadn't we both feared it? – was engaged to be married to Ralph Townsend. Of course, that put paid to my examinations. In the event of more serious matters, I scrawled off anything that came into my head. As for questions, I wanted to answer them only if they were asked by Miss Alliot, and they must be personal, not factual. As usual, if I didn't know what I was asked in the examination paper, I did a piece about something else. I imagined some *rapport* being made, and that was what I wanted from life.

Miss Martin's letter was taut and unrevealing. She stated the facts – the date, the place. An early autumn wedding it was to be, in Northumberland, as Miss Alliot had now no family of her own. I had never supposed that she had. At the beginning of a voyage, a liner needs some small tugs to help it on its way, but they are soon dispensed with.

Before the wedding, there were the summer holidays, and the removal of their things from Breezy Lodge, for Miss Martin had no heart, she said, to keep it on alone.

During that last holiday, Miss Martin's face was terrible. It seemed to be fading, like an old, old photograph. Miss Alliot, who was not inclined to jewellery ('Would you prefer diamonds to Rembrandts?' she had once asked me), had taken off her father's signet ring and put in its place a half hoop of diamonds. Quite incongruous, I thought.

I was weeks older. Time was racing ahead for me. A boy called Jamie was staying at St Margaret's with his parents. After supper, while Mrs Mayes's recitals were going on, or the solo whist, he and I sat outside the drawing-room on the stairs, and he told me blood-chilling stories, which I have since read in Edgar Allan Poe.

Whenever Jamie saw Miss Alliot, he began to hum a song of those days – 'Horsy, keep your tail up.' My mother thought he was a bad influence, and so another frost set in.

Sometimes – not often, though – I went to Breezy Lodge. The Fair Isle sweater was put aside. Miss Martin's having diminished, diminished everything, including Miss Alliot. Nothing was going on there, no goulash, no darning, no gathering of branches.

'Yes, she's got a face like a horse,' Jamie said again and again.

And I said nothing.

'But he's *old*.' Miss Martin moved her hands about in her lap, regretted her words, fell silent.

'Old? How old?' I asked.

'He's seventy.'

I had known that Miss Alliot was doing something dreadfully, danger-ously wrong. She could not be in love with Ralph Townsend; but with the Townsends entire.

On the day they left, I went to Breezy Lodge to say good-bye. It looked squalid, with the packing done – something horribly shabby, ramshackle about it.

Later, I went with Jamie to the Echo and we shouted one another's names across the valley. His name came back very clearly. When we returned, Miss Alliot and Miss Martin had gone for ever.

Miss Alliot was married in September. Miss Martin tried sharing her London flat with someone else, another schoolmistress. I wrote to her once, and she replied.

Towards Christmas my mother had a letter from Miss Louie to say that she had heard Miss Martin was dead – 'by her own hand,' she wrote, in her shaky handwriting.

'I am HORRIFIED,' I informed my diary that night – the five-year diary that was full of old sayings of Miss Alliot, and descriptions of her clothes.

I have quite forgotten what Jamie looked like – but I can still see Miss Alliot clearly, her head back, looking down her nose, her mouth contemptuous, and poor Miss Martin's sad, scribbly face.

Ever So Banal

'But not Mozart,' he cried. 'Mozart tinkles and irritates. Darling,' he added.
'Haydn, then.'

'No, not Haydn. Look, pet, if you could clasp both your hands round the
pipe like this, and I held mine over yours ... That's better. How long is
Grace going to be? No, not Haydn. Bach is precise, don't you feel? And
geometrical.'

'How could you!' cried Grace, stepping towards them across floods of
water. 'Here is the house slowly filling, and you stand there talking about
Bach. I can't get a plumber. It's too late. Oh, dear. You're hopeless. Any
other man would do something. You're not a man. You're ...' her voice
rose and broke ... 'a sissy.'

'But dear, if I let go of this pipe the water will be all over the ceiling. You
have a go. But truly my hands are stronger than yours, sissy though I may
be. The pressure's terrific ...'

'It *is* all over the ceiling, anyhow,' she wailed, and stooped and began to
bail out with Baby's pot. 'Oh, my darling house. And you don't even mind
being called a sissy. Any other man would be furious. Oh, I know, I'll try
the waterworks. Why on earth didn't I think of it before?' She was gone
again.

'Poor Grace. Oh, your darling fingers are icy cold. I'm so sorry. Things
like this are always happening in this house. How dark it's getting.'

'Look, Bernard. If you put the lid of the WC down, we could sit on that.
We might as well be comfortable.'

He kicked it down with his foot and they edged on to it. Downstairs
they could Grace's irritated voice rising and rising.

'Well, when you've turned the supply tap off what *else* can you do?' they
heard her shriek. 'It's coming through the kitchen now. No, I tried the
main, but it's just a dark hole about two yards deep and no sign of a tap.
You'll have to come. No, I've never seen or heard of any key ... I don't
know in the least what you mean ...'

Veronica giggled. 'This is fun,' she said. 'But I'm glad it's not my house.
Oh, how frightful of me to say that.'

'Your honesty, darling, is one of the things about you I most love.'

'I'm sopping wet, aren't you? Oh, look at your flannels.' She bent down, so that he could see her breasts hanging like little pears inside her summer frock. 'How funny sitting here like this ... most improper really.'

'I've no vice, Veronica, but your proximity is definitely disturbing. I've no right to say such a thing. I know that. I wouldn't hurt Grace for worlds.'

'Oh, but you embarrass me,' she cried. 'You mustn't.' She glanced down at her damp thighs. 'It is getting dark. We'd better call to Grace to put on the lights.'

'Oh no,' he was going to say when Grace approached again. 'Lights!' she exclaimed. 'Have you no sense? The ceilings are soaked. It creates an earth or something.'

'Creates an earth,' Veronica murmured incredulously. She and Bernard began to titter.

'They're coming immediately,' Grace said. 'I must pot Baby.'

'If she's wet the bed, it will be the last straw,' Bernard called after her. He suddenly removed a hand to push back a lock of hair. The water shot all over the walls and Veronica. 'Oh sod.' He clasped the torn pipe again hastily.

'It's like that little boy in Holland,' Veronica began, with her flair for the inevitable.

'Indeed yes.'

They heard Grace going downstairs. She found the kitchen floor littered with pieces of floating apple-green plaster. Tears came hotly up into her eyes. 'I've always borne all the responsibility,' she thought, as she began to drop towels on to the flood and wring them out into a pail. 'Heavy with their drink,' she said aloud. 'There ought to be some word like "despision".' It was getting very dark now, yet her eyes, accustomed to the gradual decline of light, could make out all the familiar objects looking unfamiliar in the wreckage. Laths became visible where once the ceiling had been.

'As if there's any need for them to both be sitting up there. Do they think I was born yesterday? But they can scarcely make love,' she thought. 'Not that he would. He wants nothing more than to hear the sound of his own voice.'

She left her mopping-up and went down the path to wait for the man from the waterworks. A greenish darkness hung over the landscape and there was the scent of fading elder-blossom, of clover and drying hay. She could hear the car coming up the hill and soon the pale light of its head-lamps moved towards her along the road.

A young man jumped out. He collected bags of tools and wore, appropriately enough, long sea boots.

'Here's the main,' she said, leading him inside a little tunnel behind the hedge. He said nothing, but kicked a toad aside contemptuously. Bernard would have been angry. They pulled up the cover and leant down.

'Torch? Thanks. OK. No good. Got a key for it?'

'No.'

'Can't do it without.'

He began to curse some other man's work. They went into the house. She showed him the kitchen first, ashamed rather of her husband and Veronica discussing Mozart in the lavatory. The sounds of trickling water unnerved her. Fire would be better to deal with, she thought.

He tried all the taps. He opened the larder and peered inside. She resented this. She had a middle-class attitude to the privacy of meals and food, Bernard had often told her. He opened the broom cupboard.

'Hey, what's this?' He seized upon a tap she had often dusted, scrubbed around, but never noticed. He wrenched at it.

Upstairs the flow faltered, dropped, dribbled, failed. Bernard and Veronica laughed at one another. 'Darling,' he whispered, as they unlocked their frozen hands. 'Angel.' Forgetting what they were sitting on, they relaxed damply against one another.

'I feel ashamed,' Grace was saying. 'I didn't remember that being there.'

'Stupid plumbing,' the young man said graciously. He had taken off his sea boots and paddled on the wet kitchen tiles. His feet in the near-darkness looked pallid and beautiful. I expect in the day-time they look horrid, Grace thought. Most men's do. Covered with barnacles and things.

She went into the dining-room and fished in the sideboard cupboard for the whisky bottle.

'Would you like a drink?' she asked him, coming back into the kitchen.

'I don't mind if I do,' he said inevitably and expectantly.

Standing at the sink, she flopped whisky out into a tumbler.

'Water?'

'A little,' he said reluctantly.

But when she held it to the tap, she found that in the darkness she had filled the glass higher than was necessary. There was very little room for any water. She moved towards him across the dark kitchen, the glass extended carefully before her.

'I can't thank you enough,' she cried fervently. She thought she'd have a good neat one herself but the bottle gave out the merest dribble and stopped. He could not have noticed this in the dark.

'I do feel ashamed of myself, not knowing my own house.'

'Oh, you couldn't be expected to think of that. Never saw the likes of such plumbing,' he said in a satisfied way. He stood up and pulled on his boots. 'Thank you,' he said.

'Finished already,' she thought in dismay.

He grabbed up his tool bag. She followed him to the front door.

'Many thanks.'

'Many thanks to *you*,' she cried with some asperity.

'Not at all. Good night, miss.'

'Miss' pleased her, even though it was so dark.

Off he went.

She turned back to her house, which seemed a wet and echoing shell now, rather than a home.

Bernard and Veronica had come downstairs.

'Ah, darling, having a little booze-up with the waterworks?' he cried, in guilty gaiety. 'Veronica will have to stay the night now, I'm afraid. The least we can do. I'm hell of a sorry, my sweet. It's been heavenly of you to stay and help. Well, we are so sopping wet, we do deserve a sip ourselves. This will lace thee with warmth,' he cried, taking up the bottle from the kitchen table. 'Here's to the waterworks.'

'There's none left,' Grace said happily. 'We finished it while you and Veronica were up in the lavatory.' Said like that it sounded frightful. 'Now, we must clear up.'

She stuck a candle in the top of the whisky bottle and lit it. The flame, climbing higher, flickered on their pale and exhausted faces. As she wrung out towels into the bucket, Grace's face in the candlelight seemed to the other two impervious and stern, and there came from her the faintest smell of whisky, which only those who had had none and desired some could have noticed.

The Fly-paper

On Wednesdays, after school, Sylvia took the bus to the outskirts of the nearest town for her music lesson. Because of her docile manner, she did not complain of the misery she suffered in Miss Harrison's darkened parlour, sitting at the old-fashioned upright piano with its brass candlesticks and loose, yellowed keys. In the highest register there was not the faintest tinkle of a note, only the hollow sound of the key being banged down. Although that distant octave was out of her range, Sylvia sometimes pressed down one of its notes, listening mutely to Miss Harrison's exasperated railings about her – Sylvia's – lack of aptitude, or even concentration. The room was darkened in winter by a large fir tree pressing against – in windy weather tapping against – the window, and in summer even more so by holland blinds, half-drawn to preserve the threadbare carpet. To add to all the other miseries, Sylvia had to peer short-sightedly at the music-book, her glance going up and down between it and the keyboard, losing her place, looking hunted, her lips pursed.

It was now the season of the drawn blinds, and she waited in the lane at the bus-stop, feeling hot in her winter coat, which her grandmother insisted on her wearing, just as she insisted on the music lessons. The lane buzzed in the heat of the late afternoon – with bees in the clover, and flies going crazy over some cow-pats on the road.

Since her mother's death, Sylvia had grown glum and sullen. She was a plain child, plump, mature for her eleven years. Her greasy hair was fastened back by a pink plastic slide; her tweed coat, of which, last winter, she had been rather proud, had cuffs and collar of mock ocelot. She carried, beside her music case, a shabby handbag, once her mother's.

The bus seemed to tremble and jingle as it came slowly down the road. She climbed on, and sat down on the long seat inside the door, where a little air might reach her.

On the other long seat opposite her, was a very tall man; quite old, she supposed, for his hair was carefully arranged over his bald skull. He stared at her. She puffed with the heat and then, to avoid his glance, she slewed round a little to look over her shoulder at the dusty hedges – the leaves all in late summer darkness. She was sure that he was wondering why she wore a winter's coat on such a day, and she unbuttoned it and flapped it a little to air her armpits. The weather had a threat of change in it, her grandmother had said, and her cotton dress was too short. It had already been let down and had a false hem, which she now tried to draw down over her thighs.

'Yes, it is very warm,' the man opposite her suddenly said, as if agreeing with someone else's remark.

She turned in surprise, and her face reddened, but she said nothing.

After a while, she began to wonder if it would be worth getting off at the fare-stage before the end of her journey and walk the rest of the way. Then she could spend the money on a lolly. She had to waste half-an-hour before her lesson, and must wander about somewhere to pass the time. It would be better to be wandering about with a lolly to suck. Her grandmother did not allow her to eat sweets – bathing the teeth in acid, she said it was.

'I believe I have seen you before,' the man opposite said. 'Either wending your way to or from a music lesson, I imagine.' He looked knowingly at her music case.

'To,' she said sullenly.

'A budding Myra Hess,' he went on. 'I take it that you play the piano, as you seem to have no instrument secreted about your person.'

She did not know what he meant, and stared out of the window, frowning, feeling so hot and anguished.

'And what is your name?' he asked. 'We shall have to keep it in mind for the future when you are famous.'

'Sylvia Wilkinson,' she said under her breath.

'Not bad. Not bad, Sylvia. No doubt one day I shall boast that I met the great Sylvia Wilkinson on a bus one summer's afternoon. Name-dropping, you know. A harmless foible of the humble.'

He was very neat and natty, but his reedy voice had a nervous tremor. All this time, he had held an unlighted cigarette in his hand, and gestured with it, but made no attempt to find matches.

'I expect at school you sing the beautiful song, "Who is Sylvia?" Do you?'

She shook her head without looking at him and, to her horror, he began to sing, quaveringly, 'Who is Sylvia? What is she-he?'

A woman sitting a little farther down the bus turned and looked at him sharply.

He's mad, Sylvia decided. She was embarrassed, but not nervous, not nervous at all, here in the bus with other people, in spite of all her grandmother had said about not getting into conversations with strangers.

He went on singing, wagging his cigarette in time.

The woman turned again and gave him a longer stare. She was homely-looking, Sylvia decided – in spite of fair hair going very dark at the roots.

She had a comfortable, protective manner, as if she were keeping an eye on the situation for Sylvia's sake.

Suddenly, he broke off his singing and returned her stare. 'I take it, madam,' he said, 'that you do not appreciate my singing.'

'I should think it's hardly the place,' she said shortly. 'That's all,' and turned her head away.

'Hardly the place!' he said, in a low voice, as if to himself, and with feigned amazement. 'On a fair summer's afternoon, while we bowl merrily along the lanes. Hardly the place – to express one's joy of living! I am sorry,' he said to Sylvia, in a louder voice. 'I had not realised we were going to a funeral.'

Thankfully, she saw that they were coming nearer to the outskirts of the town. It was not a large town, and its outskirts were quiet.

'I hope you don't mind me chatting to you,' the man said to Sylvia. 'I am fond of children. I am known as being *good* with them. Well known for that. I treat them on my own level, as one should.'

Sylvia stared – almost glared – out of the window, twisted round in her seat, her head aching with the stillness of her eyes.

It was flat country, intersected by canals. On the skyline were the clustered chimneys of a brick-works. The only movement out there was the faintest shimmering of heat.

She was filled by misery; for there seemed nothing in her life now but acquiescence to hated things, and her grandmother's old ways setting her apart from other children. Nothing she did was what she wanted to do – school-going, church-going, now this terrible music lesson ahead of her. Since her mother's death, her life had taken a sharp turn for the worse, and she could not see how it would ever be any better. She had no faith in freeing herself from it, even when she was grown-up.

A wasp zigzagged across her and settled on the front of her coat. She was obliged to turn. She sat rigid, her head held back, her chin tucked in, afraid to make a movement.

'Allow me!' The awful man opposite had reached across the bus, and flapped a crumpled handkerchief at her. The wasp began to fuss furiously, darting about her face.

'We'll soon settle you, you little pest,' the man said, making matters worse.

The bus-conductor came between them. He stood carefully still for a moment, and then decisively clapped his hands together, and the wasp fell dead to the ground.

'Thank you,' Sylvia said to him, but not to the other.

They were passing bungalows now, newly built, and with unmade gardens. Looking directly ahead of her, Sylvia got up, and went to the platform of the bus, standing there in a slight breeze, ready for the stopping-place.

Beyond the bus-shelter, she knew that there was a little general shop. She would comfort herself with a bright red lolly on a stick. She crossed the road and stood looking in the window, at jars of boiled sweets, and packets of detergents and breakfast cereals. There was a notice about ice-creams, but she had not enough money.

She turned to go into the empty, silent shop when the now familiar and dreaded voice came from beside her. 'Would you care to partake of an ice, this hot afternoon?'

He stood between her and the shop, and the embarrassment she had suffered on the bus gave way to terror.

'An ice?' he repeated, holding his head on one side, looking at her imploringly.

She thought that if she said 'yes', she could at least get inside the shop. Someone must be there to serve, someone whose protection she might depend upon. Those words of warning from her grandmother came into her head, cautionary tales, dark with unpleasant hints.

Before she could move, or reply, she felt a hand lightly but firmly touch her shoulder. It was the glaring woman from the bus, she was relieved to see.

'Haven't you ever been told not to talk to strangers?' she asked Sylvia, quite sharply, but with calm common sense in her brusqueness. 'You'd better be careful,' she said to the man menacingly. 'Now come along, child, and let this be a lesson to you. Which way were you going?'

Sylvia nodded ahead.

'Well, best foot forward, and keep going. And *you*, my man, can kindly step in a different direction, or I'll find a policeman.'

At this last word, Sylvia turned to go, feeling flustered, but important.

'You should *never*,' the woman began, going along beside her. 'There's some funny people about these days. Doesn't your mother warn you?'

'She's dead.'

'Oh, well, I'm sorry about that. My God, it's warm.' She pulled her dress away from her bosom, fanning it. She had a shopping-basket full of comforting, homely groceries, and Sylvia looked into it, as she walked beside her.

'Wednesday's always my day,' the woman said. 'Early closing here, so I take the bus up to Horseley. I have a relative who has the little general store there. It makes a change, but not in this heat.'

She rambled on about her uninteresting affairs. Once, Sylvia glanced back, and could see the man still standing there, gazing after them.

'I shouldn't turn round,' the woman said. 'Which road did you say?'

Sylvia hadn't, but now did so.

'Well, you can come my way. That would be better, and there's nothing much in it. Along by the gravel-pits. I'll have a quick look round before we turn the corner.'

When she did so, she said that she thought they were being followed, at a distance. 'Oh, it's disgraceful,' she said. 'And with all the things you read in the papers. You can't be too careful, and you'll have to remember that in the future. I'm not sure I ought not to inform the police.'

Along this road, there were disused gravel-pits, and chicory and con-volvulus. Rusty sorrel and rustier tin-cans gave the place a derelict air. On the other side, there were allotments, and ramshackle tool-sheds among dark nettles.

'It runs into Hamilton Road,' the woman explained.

'But I don't have to be there for another half-hour,' Sylvia said ner-vously. She could imagine Miss Harrison's face if she turned up on the doorstep all that much too soon, in the middle of a lesson with the bright-looking girl she had often met leaving.

'I'm going to give you a nice cup of tea, and make sure you're all right. Don't you worry.'

Thankfully, she turned in at the gate of a little red-brick house at the edge of the waste land. It was ugly, but very neat, and surrounded by holly-hocks. The beautifully shining windows were draped with frilly, looped-up curtains, with plastic flowers arranged between them.

Sylvia followed the woman down a side path to the back door, trying to push her worries from her mind. She was all right this time, but what of all the future Wednesdays, she wondered – with their perilous journeys to be made alone.

She stood in the kitchen and looked about her. It was clean and cool there. A budgerigar hopped in a cage. Rather listlessly, but not knowing what else to do, she went to it and ran her finger-nail along the wires.

'There's my baby boy, my little Joey,' the woman said in a sing-song, automatic way, as she held the kettle under the tap. 'You'll feel better when you've had a cup of tea,' she added, now supposedly addressing Sylvia.

'It's very kind of you.'

'Any woman would do the same. There's a packet of Oval Marie in my basket, if you'd like to open it and put them on this plate.'

Sylvia was glad to do something. She arranged the biscuits carefully on the rose-patterned plate. 'It's very nice here,' she said. Her grandmother's house was so dark and cluttered; Miss Harrison's even more so. Both smelt stuffy, of thick curtains and old furniture. She did not go into many houses, for she was so seldom invited anywhere. She was a dull girl, whom nobody liked very much, and she knew it.

'I must have everything sweet and fresh,' the woman said complacently. The kettle began to sing.

'I've still got to get home,' Sylvia thought in a panic. She stared up at a fly-paper hanging in the window – the only disconcerting thing in the room. Some of the flies were still half alive, and striving hopelessly to free themselves. But they were caught for ever.

She heard footsteps on the path, and listened in surprise; but the woman did not seem to hear, or lift her head. She was spooning tea from the caddy into the tea-pot.

'Just in time, Herbert,' she called out.

Sylvia turned round as the door opened. With astonished horror, she saw the man from the bus step confidently into the kitchen.

'Well done, Mabel!' he said, closing the door behind him. 'Don't forget one for the pot.' He smiled, smoothing his hands together, surveying the room.

Sylvia spun round questioningly to the woman, who was now bringing the tea-pot to the table, and she noticed for the first time that there were three cups and saucers laid there.

'Well, sit down, do,' the woman said, a little impatiently. 'It's all ready.'

Crêpes Flambées

Harry and Rose, returning to Mahmoud Souk, found it a great deal changed. Along the sea-road there were neat beds of mesembrianthemum. There were lamp-standards, too; branches of globes, in the Parisian manner. Four years before, there had been only a stretch of stony sand, a low sea-wall, an unmade road. Now new buildings were glittering along the shore – a hospital, a cinema, a second hotel.

Until they had reached the town, nothing in this country seemed to have changed – not in the last four years, nor in the last four thousand. Veiled women walked beside donkeys that were laden with water-pots or the trimmings of olive trees; old men, hooded against the wind, stood among grazing sheep. They were all like extras in some vast film of Bible times.

Rose remembered the Arab habit of stillness – how what had seemed to be a large boulder among the scrub would, after a quarter of an hour, stir slightly. Rather sinister, she found it – especially when the figures leant, stiff as corpses, against a wall, perhaps begging, or just *being*.

Rose and Harry had rattled along the roads in their car hired from Tunis, driving south, as they had done four years before on their honeymoon. On the other side of the bay, they could see, for a long time before they reached it, the whiteness of Mahmoud Souk. Both were excited and apprehensive. To return some might think a mistake, but they had always intended to; indeed, had promised Habib and the others that they would – those friends they had made in Habib's café: Mustapha, the thin and the fat Mohameds, Le Nègre – and other habitués whose names they had forgotten.

They drew up at the hotel right by the sandy shore, and the porter ran out to fetch their cases – a different porter, but this small disappointment could be brushed aside in the excitement of arriving.

The hotel, at least, was familiar. It had its own especial echo and smell – an echo from so much polished stone and tiles, and the smell of Tunisian cooking striving to be European.

'We'll go later, don't you think?' Harry asked Rose. He crossed the bedroom to the window, unwound the shutters and squinted down in the direction of Habib's café, though knowing that it was just out of sight.

Rose knew what he meant. They were so much alike that it was quite extraordinary. Their friends back home in London had discovered that they could confide in them both at the same time, without embarrassment. It was like confiding in one person.

They unpacked happily, looking forward to the drink later, and the welcome they would have in the little garden in front of Habib's café, facing the sea and the mimosa trees.

'You remember your birthday?' Rose said to Harry, as she had said so many times.

It stood apart from all the other birthdays in England. After dinner, there had been a party in the café. One or two English people from the hotel had looked in, had come and gone; but Harry had gone on for ever, drinking beer and bouka, anything that came to hand. And then, suddenly, Habib had stood up on a chair and declared it midnight and not Harry's birthday any more, but his own. They made more speeches to one another; they were comrades, brothers, born almost on the same day.

They always spoke in French, and Rose found it easier to understand than the French that French people speak.

She and Harry were still remembering that beautiful birthday, when they walked along the sea-road towards the café. *La Sirène* it was called. On the edge of the pavement, there had stood a sign cut out of thin wood – a blue-and-green mermaid carrying a faded list of prices.

'Perhaps they won't remember us,' Rose said. She felt rather shy and nervous.

'They will,' said Harry.

He had sent a photograph to them – of Rose and the others standing by the painted mermaid – and he could imagine this pinned up in the bar: rather curled and discoloured it may be by now, but there it would be; for photographs were hard to come by, and prized.

'It isn't there,' Rose said, as they turned the curve of the sea-road. She meant the mermaid.

'Perhaps it fell to pieces, or got blown away,' Harry said; but their pace had quickened from anxiety.

La Sirène was deserted. In fact, it no longer was *La Sirène*, but a dark shell, sliding into decay. The benches and tables were gone from the garden, and old pieces of paper had been blown against the front door.

Rose and Harry pushed open the gate, and walked up the short path. Grit and sand and fluff from the mimosa trees swirled round the garden. They peered through the window-grilles into the dim, depressing interior. There was nothing left but marks upon the bare walls and dusty floor. Marks where the bar had stood, and on the walls where shelves and notices had hung, and the big coloured picture of President Bourguiba.

They walked quite sadly away, and went back to the hotel for their drink, sitting in silence for once, feeling let down.

'I wonder what happened . . . ' Rose said. 'I wish I knew.'

'We need not stay here,' Harry said; for he knew the magic of Mahmoud Souk was gone. 'We could drive south – that would be new ground to us.'

'It's such a pity. So different from what I'd imagined.'

'After all, just because one or two Arabs in a café . . . '

'You know it isn't only that . . . although they made us seem less like strangers.'

'It was really our stake in the country as a whole.'

'I suppose . . . yes, let's go. This bar is saddening.'

There was no one else there. Outside, on the terrace, a party of Germans lay spread out on *chaises-longues* exposed to the last of the day's sun.

Next morning, their gaiety was revived by the trembling brightness of the air, and orange-juice and coffee on the terrace. The Germans were already sunbathing, stirring only to shift another part of their bodies into the sun, as if they were revolving methodically upon spits. At seven o'clock, Rose had been wakened by the voices outside – ' 'Morgen!' ' 'Morgen!' they had shouted to one another – two men – as they spread about their towels and books and lotions, bagging the best places for the day. They had taken over the hotel and this, at dinner the evening before, had made Rose and Harry feel waifish and ignored, and missing Habib and the rest more than ever.

This morning, after breakfast, stepping off the sheltered terrace, they felt the edge of a strong wind. A veil of sand was racing along the shore. Grit swirled about the building-sites, the big rubble-covered spaces where once crumbling hovels had stood, and soon hotels and blocks of flats and other cafés than Habib's would rise.

'The Germans have the best of it,' Harry grumbled. 'Organised as ever.'

The wind made them both feel inharmonious, irritable.

When they came to the high walls of the medina, they went inside with relief. Here it was sheltered, and the air smelt spicy and of burning charcoal. They wandered in the souk, Rose either feasting, or averting, her eyes – exclaiming about the heaps of young vegetables, or flinching at the sight of a furry, bloody sheep's head hanging over a butcher's stall.

The narrow alleys buzzed with children. Little girls in blue overalls wearing ear-rings were inclined to be cheeky. '*Bonjour, madame!*' they called to Rose, over their shoulders, just after they had passed by.

It became a bore. The children grew bolder.

'Don't take any notice,' Harry implored.

She always made the mistake of encouraging them, of smiling and waving and replying; so that they were usually followed by a band of youngsters, even toddlers, with hands outstretched for money, or with wilting flowers for sale. Boys were only too ready with guide-like information about souks and mosques. They jostled with one another for the job, and by the time Rose and Harry had reached the street of the carpet-makers, one slim, curious boy by some means had outwitted the others, and also, by the beauty of his manners, had forced Rose and Harry to succumb.

Courteously, he ushered them into one of the interiors, where they really did not want to go. It was dim and muffled inside and smelled of wool. Just beyond the entrance sat the Bedouin women, with kohl-rimmed eyes and rouged faces and gaudy rags and tatters, winding the wool, squatting on the floor before revolving frames, babies and little children lying beside them.

'Passez, passez,' indicated the young boy, with a graceful movement of his thin and grubby hand. His friends had disappeared, having seen that there was now nothing in it for them.

In the inner rooms, Arab women were working at the looms, knotting and snipping at a great speed, ramming down the tufted wool. Their eyes flew from the looms to the design cards pinned up beside them, but never towards Rose and Harry, whereas the Bedouins, when they passed them again, going out, stared at them mockingly, with their sharp eyes.

Having tipped the guide and refused other delights, Rose and Harry, ignoring his entreaties, strolled on. The alley was hung with skeins of dyed wool. All of the little streets had their own character. They went through the clattering metal-workers' lane into the more leisurely, gossipy street where the barbers' shops were, and the stalls of sickly-looking cakes.

Down two steps from one of the barbers' shops, only half-shaved, ran Habib, wiping soapy foam from his chin with the back of his hand, his old brown coat slung over, slipping from, one shoulder. Hitching up the coat, he shook hands, as if it were yesterday that he had seen them last, not four years ago.

It was Harry he loved; Harry upon whom the true warmth of his welcome fell. Rose knew this. She had always sat meekly by, the one whose French rarely rose to the occasion. A foreign woman was, in any case, an oddity. They broke the rules of Habib's womenfolk. Rose sat unconcernedly in cafés, smoking, drinking hard liquor, with her bare face, bare arms, bare legs. All the same, Habib and his friends had been friendly and respectful to her – live and let live – even if they could not quite admire and love her. She had set a little restraint, which perhaps only Harry's exuberance could have dispelled. If she had not been Harry's wife, none of them would have glanced at her – or only once, in passing. She was, for one thing, for their tastes, too thin.

'She has not changed,' Habib said, smiling at her, talking to Harry. 'Still so thin.'

She could understand his French, if he could not understand hers. She laughed. All her life she had had little intermittent and half-hearted struggles with her weight, always hoping to whittle away (as the fashion magazines put it) a couple of inches from her waist.

Habib had apparently forgotten about the rest of his shave. He led them triumphantly down to a café by the medina gate.

'We looked for *La Sirène* and it was not there,' Rose said, having formed the sentence in French before she spoke.

Habib agreed that this was possible; but he looked troubled and guarded. He pursed his lips in a girlish pout and shrugged his shoulders.

Coffee was brought, and he sipped it daintily. He had a round, expressive face and mournful eyes. He looked shabbier than before – but had a touch of flamboyance in the fluorescent lime-green socks, which had 'gone to sleep', as nannies say, above his grey plimsolls.

'I had a good situation offered to me,' he said at last with dignity, dropping his eyelids.

La Sirène, it was obvious, had collapsed. To say there had been no capital behind it, was a grand way of saying that it was scarcely solvent. Only when one bottle of Ricard had been sold could Habib afford to slip out to buy another. Until half-way through March the place was closed.

Harry, who seemed unlikely to give offence, enquired about his new job.

'I am chef at the new hotel,' Habib replied. He seemed not yet to have decided whether to be proud or ashamed of this. From having been his own master ... *le patron* ... He shrugged again.

'And what about all our comrades?' asked Harry. 'The two Mohameds, Le Nègre, and Mustapha?'

They had all departed – to work in the larger towns. Le Nègre had even gone as far as France.

'And you ... you are married?' Harry asked.

Habib smiled shyly, and nodded.

'To Fatma?'

They had heard of Fatma before.

Habib nodded again. 'Two little children,' he said, turning to Rose. That was her province, he felt, although, as it emerged in a minute or two, she had none of her own. He was sorry for Harry about that.

'Boys, or girls, or both?'

'Two girls,' he said, smiling bravely.

Harry got up and called for more coffee. As soon as it was served, Habib darted inside the café and came out with a few roasted almonds in a screw of sad old brown paper. He pushed them towards Rose, tapping the table, insisting that she should eat.

'It is like old times,' she said.

'The photograph,' he said eagerly, turning from one to the other and at last to Rose. 'You, me, Mustapha . . . ' He waved his hand. 'It is hanging on the wall of my new house.'

'Where is your house?'

'It is a very fine house, very large. In the country,' he added vaguely. He thought about it for a while, then said, 'I shall take you there. For a certainty. I shall introduce you to Fatma and the children. I shall cook for you. *La haute cuisine. Crêpes flambées*, you know.'

'That will be very nice,' Rose said. 'Thank you.'

'You have a car?' he asked Harry, who nodded.

'Then we shall make many journeys.'

'What about your work?'

'On my free day. In the mornings before I go to the hotel. Perhaps in the afternoons. All the time you are here, I shall not take my *siesta*.'

He knew *they* never did, had, from the upper window of *La Sirène*, while yawning, and scratching his chest, and preparing for his sleep, seen them going off, with bathing things, or scrambling on the rocks.

'Now I am afraid I must go to the hotel, to *la haute cuisine*.'

'We must dine there one evening, and sample your cooking,' Harry said.

'It is superb.'

He stood up and shook hands. 'This evening at nine o'clock, I shall be in the café next to the new cinema,' he said carelessly. He did not invite them to join him and, before they could reply, he had gone, moving swiftly as always, through the medina gateway, still only half-shaved.

After dinner at their own hotel, Rose and Harry strolled under the eucalyptus trees, through which a few street-lamps filtered their light, towards the cinema. The wind had, for the time being, dropped, and the air held a romantic stillness.

The barbers' shops, which were everywhere, were still open, and there was a leisurely coming-and-going in the rubble-strewn streets. Mahmoud Souk was beginning to be as they had remembered it.

At the café by the cinema, men in their brown *djellabahs* sat at the tables smoking, playing cards and dominoes. There were no Europeans, no women. The Germans had stayed in the hotel lounge, writing their picture-postcards of cobalt skies and camels and palm trees, and comparing the prices of rugs and copper-work. Dinner had been rather geared to them, with liver dumplings and *sauerkraut*. The old French influence was fading.

'Perhaps Habib's hotel would be better,' Rose said, sitting outside the café, her fluffy coat wrapped round her. 'To think of *him* becoming a chef! When one remembers the deplorable *couscous*.

They laughed, and then looked round cautiously.

The *couscous* had been a calamity. Habib had invited them as his guests to *La Sirène*. They had sat in a small room at the back, mercifully alone, and the big dish of greasy semolina and hunks of fat mutton and enormous carrots had been set before them. It was cold and daunting. Every time Habib popped his head round the door from serving a customer, they had nodded appreciatively, their mouths full. He went back to report on the pleasure they were having, and sometimes a customer looked in to see for himself. They had plodded on – Rose, especially, in much distress – but had seemed to make no impression upon the great heap on the dish. Then Rose had her clever idea. In her handbag was a folded plastic rain-hood. Furtively, she opened it and – whenever the coast seemed clear – dropped a handful of *couscous* into it.

'All gone,' Habib went back at last, triumphantly, to declare.

After that, those hoods were always known to Rose and Harry as *couscous* bags. The idea had been good; but the sequel to it was bad. She had tipped the contents, later, down the lavatory in the hotel, and blocked the drains.

The semolina must have swollen there, as some of it had already swollen inside her.

'The meal in his house,' she said, looking round again, and speaking in a low voice, although in English. 'This time we shan't be alone ...'

'He has promised us *la haute cuisine*.'

'I *know*,' she said doubtfully.

'We'll go to his hotel and try it first,' he said.

'Isn't he awfully late?' she suggested.

Harry looked at his watch. 'Only half an hour,' he said, and ordered another drink.

'It's getting chilly.'

'Well, let's go inside.'

But she hardly liked to. It seemed very much a man's place in there. Habib might be embarrassed.

When the time came for the next drink, however, she was driven there, shivering. No one took any notice.

It was much later – when they were talking of going back to the hotel – when Habib arrived, coming swiftly on his plimsolled feet. He was smoothly shaven now.

Rather aloof with his acquaintances, he hardly paused to speak to them as he passed their table. He came and shook hands and sat down, leaning forward to talk to them in a both confident and confiding manner.

'So many people asking for *crêpes flambées* at the last moment,' he explained importantly.

'You do French cooking always?' Rose asked.

'Every kind; any kind,' he replied.

He handed round cigarettes and leant back, crossing one leg over the other, displaying the fluorescent socks.

'Tomorrow morning, you shall take some photographs, I think,' he said. Photographs had always been of extreme importance to him. 'You will take me and Monsieur Harry, if you please,' he told Rose, who was not hurt, knowing her place. 'If you are able,' he added. Then, looking at Harry, he said, 'In exchange, I will give you a picture of Madame Bourguiba. In colour.'

'Well, that would be splendid. I will also take photographs of Fatma and your children,' he promised.

Habib nodded vaguely, as if his family were a thing he had made up, and then forgotten.

'And of your house.'

He brightened. 'It is a very big house. Quite new. There are beds, cupboards, chairs, everything.' He did not know the French for grass-matting, so pointed to some at their feet. 'A goat,' he went on, 'hens, donkey, vines. All you could wish.'

'You earn good money then,' asked Harry, who could ask anything.

'Excellent. Forty *dinars* a month.'

Harry, who was quick, worked it out at six pounds, ten shillings a week. Rose, trying to do the sum, failed (without pencil and paper) and lapsed from the conversation.

Surely, he must be only a kitchen boy for that wage, Harry thought.

'In England, would a good chef have as much?' asked Habib complacently.

Harry was torn between loyalty to his country's system, and the wish not to hurt.

'Perhaps even a little more,' he said with a vague air. 'I know very little about that business.'

'It is a good business,' Habib said simply. 'Not as good as yours, I think,' he added, glancing at Harry's gold watch, as he had often glanced at it before. Yet, he thought, Rose had nothing grand about *her* – no ear-rings or bracelets, simply a thin plain wedding ring. Fatma had more. Even his little girls had ear-rings. But wealth – great wealth – seemed indicated all the same. For instance, the Leica camera, the hired car, the hotel. Rose had perhaps been the lucky one, coming to Harry with a small dowry, no paraphernalia, and so thin, too, and with little brown spots – *rousseurs* – all over her face and arms. Beautiful eyes, though, that would look fine *just* seen above the fold of a *haïk*: in the bare face, they looked meaningless.

He toyed with the idea of westernising Fatma, even of bringing her to the café, dressed *à la* Madame Bourguiba, modern, the new Tunisian woman. But it would not do. Who would look after the little girls? It would be expensive. What would his mother say? Reputations would be lost, and difficulties would arise, and Fatma might get ideas into her head.

'Shall we drive you home to the country?' Harry asked, feeling tired – from the wind, and then the sun, and then the beer.

Habib made his pouting, secretive face, and explained in his soft voice that he had to meet a friend later. 'I will walk back to the hotel with you while I wait,' he said.

They set off down the dark street, stepping carefully over the uneven ground. Trenches being dug for drains were a trap.

Near the hotel was another open, rubbly place.

'Wasn't this, when we came before, a cemetery?' Rose asked.

Habib shivered. 'They moved the graves because of the new road,' he explained. 'But I am still afraid when I walk this way alone at night. One lady,' he said, edging closer, more confidentially, towards Harry, 'one lady in the town died in child-birth. The next day they went to bury her, and as they were putting her in the ground, she sat up.'

'Oh, dear,' Rose said. 'I don't like that.' It was an old horror with her. 'Do you have . . . ' She sought the word – '*les cercueils?*'

'No.' He hesitated, then he stroked his hands over his clothes – the old brown coat – and shuddered.

'Tomorrow,' he said, with a change of voice. 'I shall be at the café at nine-thirty.'

He disappeared, racing back past the place where the cemetery had been, alone, without Harry to protect him from the dead.

The hotel lounge was empty. The Germans had gone to bed early to be in readiness for the sunbathing arrangements of the morrow.

'What a funny holiday,' Rose said, when they were in bed. 'All alone, except for an Arab chef.'

'If he is,' Harry said.

'Will he become a bore, a tie?'

'Can't hurt feelings. He's a sensitive fellow. Does no harm to us to spend an hour or two with him.'

This was so much what Rose thought that she did not answer. Habib seemed different, away from his café and his comrades. Unshared, she could see him becoming a burden.

'I am longing to see inside an Arab house,' she said, 'and to meet Fatma and the two little girls.'

Now, they were not thinking along the same lines, for Harry had doubts he did not, for her sake, like to voice.

The pattern of their days was pleasant. The weather, though fitful, improved a little, and they drove out to bathing places and stayed the day there, alone, with a picnic lunch of bread and cheese and dates and wine. But the sun was never as hot or the sea as warm to swim in as it had been four years ago and always the wind blew steadily.

In the evenings, after dinner, they met Habib briefly at the café. Apart from him, they rarely spoke to anyone. They were running through the books they had brought.

The wind both chopped and changed, and if there were any shelter to be found, the Germans were there first, with their possessions spread about the terrace. Every morning at about seven, Rose and Harry were wakened by the two men talking outside the window, as they made sure of the *chaises-longues* for the day. There were just enough for their party, and just enough sheltering wall to the terrace. To sit on the sand was impossible. The top layer of it was always shifting in the wind.

One morning, Harry woke up at half-past six to see Rose, in her swimming suit, climbing over the balcony and jumping on to the terrace a foot or two below. She lay down on one *chaise-longue*, and put a book and a towel on the other, and waited for the consternation on the Germans' faces.

The wind had veered round in the night, and the sea beyond the shore road had white caps far out. It looked most un-Mediterranean. More like the North Sea, Rose thought. The sun shone, but every minute or so was obscured by huge, fast-scudding clouds. 'It will get warmer later on,' Rose thought; but a drop of rain fell on her bare ankle, then another on her forehead. Just before the storm broke, she scrambled back over the balcony and into the bedroom where Harry was warm in bed, and laughing.

That morning the Germans did not arrive on the terrace. And once more, Rose had to postpone taking Habib's photograph.

The rain stopped, and puddles reflected a cold, blue sky. Rose and Harry, each hiding depression from the other, went for a walk round the town. The contents of the shop windows they now knew by heart.

Habib was in the café, sitting just inside the doorway. For something to do, they joined him and ordered coffee they did not want. They listened – without any more amusement – to his tales of grandeur; his fine house and his fine cooking.

'*Steak au poivre*,' he said at random. 'What about that?'

'Not my favourite thing,' Harry said, in a grumpy voice.

Outside the door, on the pavement, the metal chairs dripped steadily.

'*Soufflé* Grand Marnier,' suggested Habib, as if he were tempting Harry to eat, and Harry said, 'I'm not really hungry.'

'As you do not like French cooking, when you come to my house, we shall eat Tunisian.'

'We *do* like French food,' Rose said hastily.

He put his lips together in a funny little smile, like a self-conscious child's. Seeing a beggar approaching, he began to rummage in his old purse, and Harry was surprised to see him drop a coin into the outstretched hand. Rather shamefacedly, he did the same. He had thought that only foreigners on their first day out gave alms, and also believed in the English principle that begging should be discouraged.

Habib was in the middle of describing his bedroom at home. Fatma had a dressing-table, he said, with pleated pink silk under a plate-glass top, and bulrushes painted on the mirror. He went into every detail.

'There is one just like that in the carpenter's shop, down the road,' Rose said.

He shrugged his shoulders.

'Isn't tomorrow your day off?' she asked, thinking of the excursion into the country to meet Fatma and the children.

'It has been postponed,' he said, in an offhand way. 'Important guests are arriving at the hotel. I have a special dinner to create. *Asperges, coq au vin ...*'

'*Crêpes flambées*,' thought Harry

'*Crêpes flambées*,' said Habib.

'When's this weather going to improve?' Harry asked sternly. 'When shall we have the sun we came for?'

'This afternoon, perhaps: tomorrow, certainly.'

'Well, I hope so, I'm sure.' Harry was unfairly sharp. It was not Habib's fault that it was cold.

However, he seemed to take the blame for it. He looked put out, then he said, 'In England, it is always raining. Here such weather is exceptional. Such a March has never been known.'

When he had left them to go off to his work, they went for a stroll along the shore, walking with their heads bent against the wind. If they could not swim and lie in the sun, there was very little else for them to do.

'Give it another day, and then go home,' Harry suggested glumly.

At the edge of the sea, women were doing their washing. There was a rhythmical, slapping sound, as they beat sad old garments into the sandy water.

'We might try Hammamet,' Rose said. 'It should be more sheltered there.' She hated the idea of giving in, of declaring defeat. It was always she who held on longest, hoping to turn their luck, or salvage something. She found it tiring, trying to jolly Harry along at the same time, deluding herself and him, seizing what brightness there was. He was all for cutting losses and clearing out.

It was nearly Independence Day, and some men were putting up triangular red flags in the square. The little flags whipped back and forth against the watery, blue sky.

Harry remembered that Habib had great plans for them for Independence Day. There was to be a procession, and a festival of Tunisian folk music in the cinema. His plans Harry found rather daunting.

A large picture of the President was being hoisted up in the square.

'Let's go to Habib's hotel for lunch,' Harry said, 'and sample *la haute cuisine.*'

This hotel was also full of people writing postcards. Rose wondered what they put on them – hopeful messages or lying ones, or cries of despair? On her own cards, she left out mention of the weather. Her friends could assume that it was good – or not, as they chose. The truth would be seen when they arrived home early, pale as all their neighbours, defeated.

They sat on stools at the hotel bar, and Rose stared in front of her, counting bottles, and reading their labels. Her bright conversational openings had at last dried up. She had said all she had to to Harry.

'We have come to try some of Habib's good cooking,' Harry said to the barman, who carefully polished a glass, and put it back on a shelf. He appeared not to have understood what was said, and was far too languid to enquire further.

In the dining-room, Rose and Harry looked about them, wondering in what region Habib was practising his new art.

There was an *hors d'œuvre* of tunny fish and raw onion; then some veal, rather tough.

'*Crème caramel,*' suggested the waiter, when the veal was finished. *Crème caramel* pursued them – or rather was waiting for them – on all their travels.

'*Crêpes flambées,*' suggested Harry.

The waiter shook his head sadly, but the sadness seemed to arise less from the lack of *crêpes* than from Harry's fanciful idea.

'Oh, God, I've let you down again,' Harry said, while Rose was eating some dates. 'I'm not speaking to God. No! I'm speaking to you. The whole damn holiday's been a fiasco.'

'You take too much upon you,' she said reprovingly. 'You think you can organise everything.'

'Well, so I do,' he said sullenly. 'And in England, so I can.'

'Right!' she said decisively. 'We'll go to Tunis in the morning, and get a flight home as soon as we can.'

She felt some relief at not having to hold on any longer.

'We'll tell Habib tonight.'

'No visiting Fatma. No Independence Day procession. No photograph of Habib.'

'No picture of Madame Bourguiba, either.'

'We won't bother with Hammamet.'

'All those dripping orange trees.'

'All the same,' she said. 'This country I love. I was so happy here.'

That evening, in the ice-cold café, they told Habib, and he stared down at the table, deeply offended.

'I am sorry we shan't be able to go out to your house in the country,' Harry said.

'It is very fine,' Habib murmured.

'Today we had lunch at your hotel,' Harry said. 'Most enjoyable.'

'Very nice,' Rose said eagerly.

His lips curved upwards very slightly.

'You did not ask for *crêpes flambées*,' he said, after a pause.

'They were not on the menu,' Harry said cautiously. 'Unless we made a mistake.'

'You should have commanded. I can arrange anything. If I had known you were coming . . .'

'May we drive you home to the country tonight?' Harry asked.

Habib had never allowed this. He always had some mysterious friend to meet later.

'Tonight, I shall not go to my home. I must be very early at the hotel tomorrow to arrange a banquet for important foreign visitors. In fact, I think I shall now say "*au revoir*" and go to bed early in readiness.'

He had tears in his eyes.

'Then where will you stay,' asked Harry, and Rose thought that she would not have asked this.

'I have many friends. I shall stay in the medina – a very poor little place, but for one night, what does it matter?'

'Well, let us drive you there, at least.'

He blinked away his tears and put his head on one side. 'As you wish,' he said.

In the car, he was silent. Once, he sighed and said what a *dommage* it all was.

'Won't Fatma miss you – out in the country, all on her own?' Harry asked.

'She is accustomed . . . it is one of the hazards of my profession.'

They drove into the medina, down the widest street, and the only one a car could manage, and Habib leant over to shake hands with Rose, who was sitting in the back. Then, more emotionally, he put his hand on Harry's shoulder.

'Until our next meeting,' he said. 'If you would slow down here. My friend's house is nearby.'

Rose thought, we shall never meet again.

Harry stopped the car, but not the engine, and with silent dignity Habib clambered out.

The street was empty, and there were stretches of darkness between wall lamps and open doorways.

Habib stood by the car for a second, with his hand lifted. Then he turned away. He was a brief shadow, and then had vanished, as if into the walls of the medina.

Husbands and Wives

That pity may be felt quite genuinely at a distance is well known; and, when Eric joined up, Alison was pitied enormously by all sorts of people, who could not bear to think of her alone in her house so far beyond the village. She was quiet and solitary there. Woods – great woods, which stretched away over the hills and ran into other woods – came up to the fence on two sides, stretched branches down over the roof and in autumn shed their leaves, which came down steadily and relentlessly as snow, across paths and lawns and cabbage patch.

This first autumn he was away, the leaves fell suddenly. It was disappointing. For a day or two, sunlight struck the great tan-coloured woods, wavered as if falling through water. Then the winds brought destruction. The ash-leaves came down in bunches, still softly green, but the beech-leaves swirled in the air, flat, like coins, or curled and convoluted like sea shells.

It was like a painting by Monet, Alison thought, standing at the sitting-room window and watching. Leaves. They dripped, cascaded; they mounted up in columns like something from the Old Testament or fell like a fountain. Inside, they would lisp drily along the passage or sail in and float in the soup. In the morning she would find them in bed with her.

It was the sort of house which seemed always conscious of the outside world, which doors could not shut out, nor drawn curtains quite conceal. There was the feeling that, left on its own for a year or so, the woods would reclaim their territory; grass would grow, leaves pile up, owls fly in and out of the windows. Then Eric's house, his effort to impose civilisation where it was despised, would be ruined, mocked at, even by the beetle crossing his hearth.

He was an architect. 'I want to live in the country,' he had explained to his wife, 'but I will not have lavatories down the garden path and hot water carried in cans.' He wanted it to be a healthy and pleasant house in which to bring up their children.

When war broke out, they had the house, but were still without the children. It had cost too much, felling trees, digging and levelling. It was, however, as comfortable as could be, Eric would think, turning the hot shower to cool, then to cold, reaching for warm towels. Now – as Trooper Watson – he must accustom himself to something less. Naturally, children were no longer a possibility.

Alison was not really to be pitied, for down there in the wood she was neither happy nor unhappy. She was never nervous, as other women thought she must be and men considered that she should be. No one came to see her. They liked to sympathise by telephone or, at all events, without the walk home afterwards.

She was busy, though, in the house and working in the garden until dark. There were all the leaves to be swept, the wrecked lurching rows of runner beans to be cleared away, logs to be sawn. She was keeping the house beautiful for Eric's first leave, looking towards that and no further.

By tea-time now, the garden grew muffled and drips of moisture fell furtively from leaves. Through the mist and bonfire smoke the great sunflowers turned their faces at her. Day by day, their heads dropped lower. Then they were collapsed and were done for and she brought them into the shed and strung them up to dry for chickens' food.

Inside, spread on window-sills to ripen, were flat baskets of green and yellow tomatoes, waxen-looking and with high-lights which reminded her of fruit she had painted at school. Marrows of a deep saffron colour with lemon stripes lay on the dresser. In the evenings, with the curtains drawn, it seemed as if part of the garden had crept inside. She would sit knitting or writing her daily letter to Eric, her report on the garden and the house. When she had listened to the nine o'clock news, she would get ready for bed. Lying flat on her back, looking out at mist or stars, listening to the endless fidgeting of the leaves, she would feel a sense of achievement, her hard, strong body aching from the day's work. Only occasionally would a breath of defeatism ruffle her tranquillity. 'Surely,' the small voice breathed – or was it the leaf upon the floorboards? 'Surely?' But that was enough. On that word, she slept.

His leave grew nearer and now his letters ended – 'In eight days ... ' 'In five ... ' They were like children towards Christmas, throwing one pebble each night from a window. Towards the end was a little rush of excitement, polishing, baking, airing his clothes.

On the last day but one, she washed her long bright hair and stood at the window in the sun drying it. She watched Rose, the gypsy woman, coming up with her copper bucket for water, watched her crossing the little orchard from the woods, a baby on her shoulders, the bucket on her arm, a young child with its hand on her skirt. Every other day she came for one bucket of water. They never wash, then, Alison thought, fluffing her hair. They had lived for three months down in the wood, in a tent under a clump of holly trees. Once she had seen the woman pushing the pram – a deep and dirty one – without a hood – back from the village. At each end of the pram, a child, between them a stack of bread.

Now, she wrapped her head in the towel, and went out to the back door. The woman stood there smiling. The children, fat, dirty and backward for their ages, recoiled from Alison towards their mother, who held out in her rough hand a present – four clothes-pegs, newly made, the wood white and gleaming as the kernel of a nut.

Alison took them and felt them damp. For a second, she saw the hand in contrast to them – ridged with dirt, scaly, and heavy with thick gold rings – the family wealth.

As the baby was hoisted up higher on the woman's shoulders, its bare bottom was exposed, bare, blue with cold, tinted like a ripe plum, and the firm thighs.

'Oh, God, the dirt!' she thought, fascinated.

That they were truly gypsies she could not be sure. Their hair was darkly yellow, their skin fair: and the names of the children – Leonard and Kathleen – were incongruous and absurd. Only once had Alison seen the father – a short, swarthy man, a knife-grinder. He went about the countryside, sharpening scissors; his eyes, when he had lifted them from the turning wheel and the knife's edge, were dark and keen and his manner suggested a strange combination, of courtesy and contempt. At night, he returned to the holly bushes, covering the grinding machine carefully with a tarpaulin – a better one than the children had. Sometimes, drawing the curtains after tea, Alison would think of them down in the wood with their long night begun.

Now, as she lifted the copper can to the tap, she thought that the woman was all courtesy but no contempt. She was timid as a squirrel, but not so clean. Human beings need so many bits and pieces in order to keep themselves clean, that when they are living in the wild state they cannot compare with animals.

The can was heavy and she lifted it with two hands. For a moment it linked the two women together – their hands lay side by side and their eyes were on the swinging water. But it was impossible to imagine that they had anything in common, anything even as general as sex or race, that they had been born in the same way and would one day share the same death, the same earth.

'Good-bye.'

'Good-bye, miss.'

The children, with their hands, their clinging ways, seemed to influence their mother away from the house and the stranger. Across the grass, slowly, she returned with the filled bucket, the baby and the child, who stumbled in the tussocky grass and held her skirt bunched in its fist. And Alison took her four clothes-pegs and laid them on the window-sill in the sun and began to brush her hair. It fell cool and sweet-smelling before her face and in this dark and fragrant tent she was smiling to herself.

That night it was still and frosty. She opened the windows and got into bed – 'This is the last night,' she thought. It is true that seven days' leave will not last for ever, but with the end of it she had not begun to concern herself. Outside, a rimed leaf loosened itself and fell, some creatures rustled in the wood, an owl hooted. The branches stood motionless as if printed upon the sky. Half a moon with a scarred face freed itself from the curd-like cloud. Her eyes, filled with that vision of laced branches, closed and she slept.

Swung in a hammock of sleep, she rocked, warm, suspended, slipping into darkness and warmth, curved with crossed arms and knees drawn up, the first attitude of humanity.

Into this safety came something alien. At first, she accepted it and then her mind refused the sound, it became strange, unearthly, she denied it, she awoke. 'I screamed in my sleep,' she thought. But while she lay, still in bed, the screaming continued. It could not be a woman screaming, for there was no woman to scream. Yet it was. Very close to the house it sounded in the frosty air, and there was nothing else, not a rustle, nor any movement, nor another voice

If it had been tomorrow, she thought foolishly and suddenly. Then Eric would have been here. The sweat had sprung from her hands and back and was damp on the sheet beneath her. The cold struck her body sharply as she crept out of bed and went to the window.

The horrifying sound went on – a woman who tried to mouth words as she screamed. Each cry chilled the blood, was uncontrolled, instinct with horror and bestiality. There was no other sound, except that Alison suddenly and boldly, so that she amazed herself, called out: 'Is anyone in trouble?' 'Inadequate!' the cool part of her noted, the unfrightened part. At once, the scream seemed to form into words, which came from the fence on the wood side. 'It's my man. All night he's been beating me. Can't I have no peace? Can't I have no peace?'

These words came brokenly again and again, grew fainter, receded, were accompanied now by plungings, rustlings, twig-snappings. She was going away. It was as if she had gained an objective. Still she cursed, her voice clotted with hatred and fear, but growing fainter.

Alison crept back to bed, lay rigid and shivering. Her reason still seemed to refuse what her ears told it – that Rose, that quiet, timid squirrel, to whom the children clung, who spoke softly and gave presents shyly and silently, should become so transformed, so horrifying.

She was too cold now to sleep. The sea roared in her ears and the sound of a leaf moving startled her. She lay rigid and alert, but now could hear nothing.

'The police,' she thought: and then, but the police could do nothing. For a man – she remembered that much of the law – must be allowed to beat his own wife. It is not for the police to interfere. She tried to sleep, desiring desperately that dawn should come, for that pallor to creep over the furniture and lighten the curtains and restore her to common sense, to the proportions proper to the day. It did not come. The world was caught up and frozen in darkness and the moon is an illumination which does not inspire common sense. As soon as the silence had settled once more, it was broken again into fragments by a small cry, lower than the first, but more heartbroken, little agonised bleatings.

'Oh, no God, no!' she cried, sitting up in bed, covering her ears with her hands. Now that the mother had wandered away had he begun to beat his children?

'Then I can't bear it,' she sobbed. Sickened by that sound she crawled from the bed and began to look for clothes. There was nothing else for her to do. One grown-up cannot lie in bed while another is hurting little children. Over her pyjamas, she pulled slacks and a jersey. Forcing her shoes on, she became desperately frightened. 'I must go quickly,' she thought, 'before I am too afraid.' She stood in the room, thinking, 'No one will come if I scream. There is no one to hear me!' She had no weapon. Things like pokers seemed too foolish to take. She crept down the stairs thinking of Eric, not knowing what she was going to do; then she let herself out of the back door. The cold solid air filled her throat and chest.

'I won't creep,' she thought, 'I will run. I will go loudly, be aggressive.' Then, perhaps, she would not hear the beating of her heart, feel all the platitudes coming true – the blood being frozen, the limbs turned to stone. So she broke through the undergrowth, leapt the fence, tore her way through brambles and plunged knee-deep sometimes into ditches of leaves. She could hear clearly now the strangled, reedy sound of the children crying and as she went she called, 'Stop it. Stop it.' She felt, like a soldier going into battle, that it was only possible to act in hatred and with the ears filled with some noise other than the whispers of fear.

And now she saw how big the woods were, how different from the daytime and she thought – and the thought irrelevant as it was silenced her and checked her – 'It is always like this at night when I am in bed' – large, menacing, watchful. From each tree – watchful.

She stood there facing the great dark clump of holly bushes and listened, but there was no sound – until one of the trees seemed to detach itself and step forward. It did not spray up leaves on all sides as she had done, yet it was a man. He came closer to her – in the moonlight she saw the dark,

level eyes, even a faint shine on the dark suit over his thighs, a belt of
plaited leather with a bright buckle. She watched the buckle as it came
towards her, and then up went her eyes to meet his. 'I must speak first,' she
thought. Her instinct told her this. At the same time, she saw that his
hands were towards his back and thought of knives, remembering his way
of getting a living.

'You can stop this,' she cried loudly. The wood echoed, the sound was
shocking. 'If I hear one more sound from those children I shall call the
police.' He smiled, but she had a feeling that she mustn't let him speak,
that she could not endure to hear his voice. 'You see?' she cried. 'You see?
That's what I shall do. I will not be disturbed in this way and I will not
have those children hurt.'

He said nothing, but now his bare hands came forward, the thumbs
were stuck inside the plaited belt. She felt only partial relief at this, for
the difficulty was now to go. She could not. Courage to turn she had not.

'Now remember,' she challenged him, but it was ridiculous, like a child's
game. He would not answer. In his eyes, she saw what she was – hysterical, shrill, a woman; middle-class, so taking for granted comforts he knew
nothing about; trying to make temper hide fear, but he knew and she knew
through him that there was no anger, only terror.

At last – only just in time – for she was at the point of dropping to her
knees and sobbing for mercy, for permission to go – he turned slightly and
listened, having heard what she had not. It was someone coming up
through the wood. It was Rose. As she approached them she came more
slowly. A man's jacket was buttoned to her throat over her long dress, her
hair on one side had fallen to her shoulder.

'Come here,' he said softly. And then nodding sideways at Alison,
'Friend of yours,' he added and slouched off, spitting into the leaves, his
hands on his belt.

The wide timid eyes sought Alison's in the moonlight. 'I'm sorry,
miss.'

'Not you,' she said quickly. 'Are you all right?'

'Oh, yes, miss.'

'And the children?'

'Oh yes.' Shocked, the eyes looked back. 'He's ever so good really – I
think he ...' she whispered, glanced, ducked her head, buttoned and
unbuttoned, brushed back her hair.

'All right,' said Alison sternly. 'I'm going now.'

He had stopped and was standing looking back, his head on one side,
mocking her, she thought, listening. Then, 'I can't think why you're not in
the army,' she suddenly called out, and turned and went, trying not to
scramble or run, but there was no dignity in how she went. (She felt fingers

locked round her ankles, daggers between her shoulder blades.) Across her
own lawn she ran without pretence and let herself in. Now the house frightened her. She bolted and barred, and put on lights, then she went into the
living-room and sat by the clock with *The Diary of a Nobody* in her lap, and
her eyes on the door.

In the morning they were gone. Eric came home at tea-time. There was
the log fire, the home-made cakes, the little sandwiches, the book he had
brought for her, his approval, his kindness, their quiet intellectual understanding. They had a serene pleasant evening, talking, listening to the
gramophone, supper by the fire, with chops and a little omelette laced with
rum. Everything went peacefully as of old, until he said: 'Our minds are like
brother and sister, close, sympathetic. Nothing could ever part us,' and she
burst into tears.

The Blossoming

Miss Partridge came back to the house after the funeral, with her solicitor walking on one side of her and the family doctor on the other – although he could scarcely now be called a 'family' doctor as, apart from her, the family had gone.

'You should take a holiday,' Dr Jenkins said, looking round the dingy drawing-room, feeling depressed for her. 'You've had a long stretch of . . .' As his voice trailed off, he was thinking of all the old-age pensioners looking after aged parents. This was the way it was going. Soon they would be looking after grandparents.

'A holiday?' Miss Partridge looked startled, but she gave a little smile as if the doctor had made a naughty suggestion. 'I couldn't afford it.' Because it was out of her reach, she could daringly consider it. She had not had a holiday for twenty years.

Dr Jenkins looked at the solicitor, who leant back as far as he could in his frail chair, said, 'Ellie, my dear, you're a rich woman now – a comparatively rich woman. You can go wherever you wish.'

She became at once alarmed, shrugged her wealth away, shuddering. 'Too late,' she said.

Having no servants, when she asked: 'Tea, or whisky?' her voice seemed to urge whisky on them. It was less trouble, and she was quite exhausted.

Even when they agreed to drink whisky, she was obliged to go through the hall and down a passage to the kitchen to fetch water.

In the sink squatted a large spider. He seemed to own the place. 'We'll be alone together tonight,' she thought – 'the spider and I!' She suddenly contorted her face and turned on the tap with a gush, washing the poor thing – all broken legs and frantic reluctance – down the plug hole. It was as if that long-bedridden mother upstairs had protected her from such horrors until now when, untrained and unprepared, and full of a new brutality, Miss Partridge must face them on her own.

She returned, trembling, with the jug of water. The drawing-room conversation of low voices broke off as she crossed the hall.

'Quite a number in church,' Mr Mavory, the solicitor, was saying as she came through the door.

But five wreaths only! she thought. It was a disgrace really. If she died, *when* she died, there would be only four.

'So, a little holiday, then,' Dr Jenkins said robustly. 'I practically insist. You deserve it if anyone does.'

After a very short time they set down their glasses and stood up.

'Oh, don't, don't go!' she cried.

'I'll be back within a day or two about business matters,' Mr Mavory said.

She stood at the front door and watched them walk down the drive. Across the road was the church: and Mother in her new grave. The church clock struck four, although it was nearly half-past.

She turned back into the house, closed the door softly, and stood looking about her, hoping not to see spiders, for it was the time of year when they did their house-invading, as if finding their way back to a place of ancestry.

'I am a rich – a comparatively rich woman,' she said aloud. All the things she did not want and had not wanted, for many years, lay now within her grasp.

The night was no more dreadful than she had foreseen. Her little luminous bedside clock took her slowly towards morning through her snatches of sleep.

'Why not move to a more convenient place?' asked Mr Mavory. 'This must be an expensive house to keep up.'

'Oh, *no!*' she said. 'It hasn't cost us a *penny*, for years.'

He looked at a great dark patch of damp on the faded William Morris wallpaper.

Following his glance, she looked, too, and saw the stains as if for the first time. Those powdery willow leaves had been there all her life. There were familiar Morris wallpapers elsewhere in the house – of honeysuckle, or of white-and-bile-green chrysanthemums. It was true that nothing had been spent on the house for years; but not, she realised, because nothing had needed to be spent. Paint had flaked off window-frames and sills, the high ceiling was dark and shadowy – with dirt, perhaps.

Mr Mavory watched her looking about the room, and held his tongue. He wondered if the house were clean, thought probably not. Miss Partridge *knew* that it was not. Cross-patch Mrs Murphy came up from the village twice a week, and flicked about with dusters, but would never climb steps or move furniture because of dropped womb trouble. She was always in such a temper that Miss Partridge shut herself in her bedroom until she had gone.

Apart from the doctor's and Mr Mavory's occasional visits, no one else came. Mrs Partridge, before and during her illness, had not encouraged visitors.

The house was not large, but had rooms into which no one went. Sometimes, Miss Partridge's sense of isolation seemed to become a physical thing, pressing into her ears, and choking her. 'I will have a glass of Dutch courage,' she would say – for she often thought aloud. She drank the whisky in gulps, as if it were medicine; but felt better afterwards.

She was lonely, though did not know it, having been too busy for years, with the trays for upstairs, and the bell ringing, and the afternoon readings-aloud, the bothers with bowels and bedsores, the staving-off of unwanted callers. To go shopping had been an adventure; but there was little she now needed to buy, eating frugally, absent-mindedly.

She passed her time drifting about the rooms, or making little forays into the webbed-over, tangled garden.

Now, the wallpapers worried her. Mr Mavory, drinking *his* glass of whisky without shuddering, saw thoughts come and go on her anxious little face.

Rummaging in her mind, oblivious of him, she put a hand to her mouth, then touched her frizzy hair. Her home – her life-long home – was creeping into decay. She saw the signs of it about her, and remembered others in other parts of the house.

Mr Mavory had come to the conclusion that she would never move from here, would not know how to. He discarded that idea, and began to talk instead about the improvement of the property. The word 'house' he never used. He threw in suggestions, which seemed to bounce back from the walls. Money no impediment, he so constantly reaffirmed.

'But I could not have men traipsing about the house. And everything would have to be moved. I couldn't bear it.'

Mason & Toope would take over, Mr Mavory assured her.

'Oh, *they* came once when we had a burst pipe, and made such a noise, and charged us so much. Mother was quite upset.'

'Then do as Dr Jenkins advised you. Take a holiday. Have a rest. Let others do things for you for a change.'

He went on to tell her of a nice guest-house where his aunt sometimes stayed. It was in Hove, in a quiet street away from the sea. The food was excellent, he said; but food meant nothing to Miss Partridge.

'I don't think I could,' she said: he saw a flicker of doubt on her face; she was beginning to recover from shock and fatigue.

The next day he called again, with a book of wallpaper patterns he had borrowed from Mason & Toope. Turning the leaves, she murmured with pleasure and surprise, at the beauty of entwined roses, lovers' knots, satin stripes and embossed fleurs-de-lis. She was almost as enthusiastic as if any part of it were to do with her.

When he went away, he left the book. And, in the evening, having nothing better to do, she took it on her lap and began to turn the great pages. Again and again, she went back to the pink roses latticed on pearly grey. It was her favourite, she decided.

Then, at last, she looked up, and gazed for a long while at the yellowing willow leaves upon the wall.

So, after a short time, Miss Partridge took herself off to the Fernhurst Guest Home in Hove, and Mason & Toope moved in to deal with the decorating.

Fernhurst was all that Mr Mavory had described. The food was simple and light, and the service was hushed. No one spoke to Miss Partridge. At first, she sat at a table by the door but, later, as guests departed, was promoted to one by the window, overlooking a hedge of golden privet and a quiet road. The season was nearly over and she walked along an almost deserted front, or sat in an empty shelter listening to the sea on the pebbles, sometimes thinking about the rose wallpaper, and wondering how far Mason & Toope had got with it. Real roses, they looked. She had felt that they might almost be scented.

After a week of Hove she began to be restless, to wonder what on earth she was doing at the Fernhurst. After ten days, she paid her bill, packed her suitcase, got on the train and went home.

It was a warm, sunny afternoon when she arrived back. She took a cab from the station, and the driver came with her to the front door with her suitcase. The door was wide open, and the house smelled of paint: no one was about.

She went into the drawing-room. Furniture was pushed into the middle of it and covered with a dust sheet. On one wall the roses blossomed, brightened by sunshine from an uncurtained window. The other walls still showed only grey plaster.

Miss Partridge stood entranced before the rose-covered wall, and could imagine the whole room in bloom. It would be quite beautiful. Her mother would have been horrified – at the change, at the expense. She had always been careful about money.

After a time, Miss Partridge became conscious of men's voices coming from the garden at the back. She went out of the front door and round the house, and discovered two young men in white overalls sitting in the last of the sun on the old garden seat. They were drinking tea, and on the iron table before them were paper bags and thermos flasks.

'Good-afternoon, miss,' one said. He was George Toope, younger son of *the* Toope. The other she recognised as Sandy Wright, who had once delivered newspapers.

'We wasn't expecting you,' George said. He did not rise, but shifted along the seat, patting the space beside him.

Miss Partridge, with hardly any hesitation, sat down. 'I found my holiday very tiring,' she said. 'I walked about too much, for there was nothing else to pass the time.'

'You could do with this, I reckon,' George said, for he seemed to be the spokesman. He unscrewed the top of his thermos flask and poured tea into it.

'Oh, how kind! I could,' Miss Partridge said.

He offered sugar in a screw of paper, and she watched him shake some into her cup; then he took a pencil from behind his ear and stirred her tea with it.

'You needn't have brought your own sugar,' she said. 'There is plenty of it in the larder. You should have helped yourself.'

'And have that old bitch Murphy after us?' Sandy said, speaking at last. 'No *thanks*.' Miss Partridge flushed.

'It is not Mrs Murphy's sugar,' she said, with unusual firmness. Of course, she would not have said that to, or before, Mrs Murphy.

Sandy held out a meat sandwich on a crumpled paper bag.

'I can't take your ... tea,' she said, confused as to what time of day it was. He wagged the paper bag up and down in the palm of his hand, commandingly. She took a thick triangle of sandwich and began to nibble it and twist it about her mouth. Doing so, she looked at the forlorn garden.

'Fag?' asked Sandy, when she had at last finished the sandwich.

'Fag? Oh, no, no; thank you.'

She wondered about this relaxed time they were having, for in less than an hour they would knock off work. But, though wondering at it, she approved of it, and she felt peaceful sitting there with them in the sun.

When they went back to their work, she went on sitting there, listening to them treading about the bare and creaking floorboards in the drawing-room, their voices echoing excitingly. When they left at five o'clock, the house seemed very silent.

Miss Partridge sat out the days which followed in the crowded dining-room, among the sickly green-and-white chrysanthemums, which did not seem to her at all like real flowers, and were soon to be replaced by poppies, cornflowers and intersecting ears of corn. Every now and then – drawn there – she would peep in at the nearly finished room with its mass of roses, and marvel at its beauty. Twice a day she made tea for her 'boys', as she thought of them. They were no trouble – nothing like the nuisance she had imagined they would be.

'Here we are then!' Miss Partridge called out gaily, waiting for the drawing-room door to be opened, lest there should be a can of paint, or George or

Sandy on a ladder on the other side. At once there was a subdued hustle: the door was opened, and George took from her the heavy tray with the silver tea-pot, and freshly made scones.

'Quite a party!' he said, winking at Sandy.

'When I was a child, I longed for a party,' Miss Partridge said. 'Did you ever have one?'

'Oh, the various old rave-up.'

She nodded, and turned back to the door.

'Only *two* cups?' George asked. 'We can't have parties on our tod – not just me and Sandy. I'll get another one out the kitchen.' She sat down on a dust-sheeted sofa, and smiled. She had not allowed herself to expect to be asked.

George returned with the extra cup and saucer. 'Shall I do the honours?' he asked. He lifted the tarnished tea-pot questioningly, his little finger quirked. 'Shall I be Mother?'

'He is never at a loss for words,' Miss Partridge thought, as Sandy went off into a fit of laughter.

'Is this real silver?' George asked, sobered by the pale amber stream coming from the spout.

'It is hall-marked seventeen hundred something.'

'Might be worth a fortune.'

'It is rather dented, as you can see.'

'Never mind: silver's silver. It could be melted down.'

'And why not?' Miss Partridge wondered placidly.

'It *could* be an antique,' Sandy said slowly, feeling that it was time he should speak. 'It could be worth its weight in gold.'

'Bloody nit,' George said, cramming a scone into his mouth.

Miss Partridge – hardly drinking, not eating – looked at the walls, and said, 'It's just like a garden. With *real* flowers, I mean. A bee could fly in here, and feel quite confused.'

'It could feel b. well confused,' said Sandy, who rarely rose to such heights of humour.

'Well, back to work! Do a bit more,' George commanded. 'Tomorrow we begin on the second reception room.'

The second reception room was really the dining-room, where the received, during the last half-century, could be counted on the fingers of two hands. It was papered with the white-and-green chrysanthemums, gone dark now, against a darker ground.

'Have you ever seen chrysanthemums like them?' Miss Partridge asked, as George and Sandy began to scrape them away.

'I never thought of them as chrysanths. Just flowers like.'

'Some of those flowers, as you call them, have over forty petals,' Miss Partridge said. 'When I didn't feel up to what was given me for lunch, I'd be obliged to sit there all afternoon, until whatever it was was gone. Forty-something petals, I counted them through my tears.'

'My dad just used to larrup me if I didn't finish my greens,' Sandy said. Miss Partridge twisted her hands together.

'I can't bear to think about that,' she said.'

'Did me no harm. I learnt to like my greens all right in the end,' Sandy said in a loaded voice, for the benefit of George, who laughed briefly, as he worked.

'Oh, if only I *could!*' Miss Partridge said, in an imploring voice. The scraping down of those walls was so wonderful to her that she felt she must be part of it. She looked at the discoloured rubbish on the floor in excitement.

'Look,' said George sternly, 'it was your Mr Mavory got the estimate: he won't let up on it. Every second we let slide, not working up to our full capacity, Sandy and me, costs *my* dad money. Real money.'

She thought of the dreamy interludes in the garden, with thermos flasks and sandwiches, and their lack of hurry and bustle. Perhaps now the autumn had set seriously in.

Sandy made a frowning face at George, who then handed over the scraper to Miss Partridge. 'OK. But I don't want this about the village, or everyone will be wanting to have a go. Might have Union bother. So please keep it to yourself.'

But to this Miss Partridge scarcely listened. Flushed with enthusiasm – and at the honour of such responsibility – she scraped away at the background of her childhood, her life.

In the evening, she walked about the flowered drawing-room, entranced by its beauty, and, because there was no longer silence all day, she did not mind the silence of these lonely hours. She knew that the next day would bring the clanking of pail-handles, the snatches of talk, the whistling of 'Galway Bay'. Week-ends, however, were long enough to remind her of the past deprivations.

Mrs Murphy grumbled about the upheaval. She said that the white paint would show the dirt; and said it in a hopeless way, as if there would be nothing she could do about it. She detested George and Sandy, and told tales behind their backs. When it came the turn for Miss Partridge's bedroom to be decorated, she stood in front of the sprays of forget-me-nots and said that her and her sister Gladys's bedroom had been done like that when they were in service. 'It was thought good enough for kitchen-maids,' she added.

But George and Sandy were enthusiastic. It was they who chose the violets for the landing, and Sandy said he intended to have the same if he married, which George said his mother would never let him do.

Mr Mavory, feeling slightly responsible for the changes, thought them all unbearably crude; but Dr Jenkins, seeing the results in Miss Partridge herself, approved. 'If she'd had strings of upside-down baboons eating bananas, I'd have been for it,' he told Mavory. 'Her circulation has improved.'

When the cold weather came, George and Sandy were glad of their indoor work. As one room was finished, they moved on to another. It became such a long-drawn-out job that George's father, Mr Toope, was obliged to ask Miss Partridge for 'a little something down', as he embarrassedly put it. She was stretching the work far beyond the matter of the original estimate, he explained. He was glad of the business, but there were difficulties. Miss Partridge wrote a cheque for three hundred pounds and – for the days of taking cheques upstairs for her mother to sign were over – wrote 'Elinor Partridge' on it with a flourish. She had waited a long time for that much authority.

George and Sandy brought with them each day all the gossip of the village, so that she began to feel set in her surroundings and a part of them for the first time. When she went shopping she *knew* about the people she met – knew that the girl at the grocer's had won twenty pounds at Bingo, which was a good thing, Sandy said, as although she didn't show yet she had an expensive time coming up: the butcher's wife was expecting, too, forlornly awaiting her fifth daughter – 'wishing it on herself,' George said. 'She needs to talk herself into a son.' And Miss Partridge knew who was out of work, and would be glad of a little job of upholstery or window-cleaning. Such simple jobs as unblocking a sink or mending a fuse George and Sandy, those marvellous men about the house, would do for her.

It was late autumn. The beech woods had a brief glory, then frosts, followed by high winds, bared the branches. A foggy, mushroomy, pre-Christmas smell filled the air.

By Christmas, George and Sandy had finished, were promised elsewhere – up at the Hall, in fact, where Lady Leadbetter was having all the rooms done with William Morris wallpaper – an aberration which amused the three of them as they discussed it at tea-time.

Miss Partridge was of course alone for Christmas. Her four expected Christmas cards arrived and were set up on the chimneypiece. On Christmas Eve, when she was feeling at her most depressed – even wishing her mother was still upstairs to run up to with a warm mince pie – she found another card lying on the doormat. She opened the envelope excitedly.

A boozy old Santa Claus was holding up a cocktail glass and saying

'Complimentsh of the Sheashon'. Inside, signed in two different hands, was 'All the best, Sandy and George'. Smiling, she set it in a central place between those of distant relations and the printed one from Mr and Mrs C.E. Mavory, with that crossed out and 'Charles and Margery' written above it – a friendly and informal touch, Miss Partridge thought.

But in spite of the unexpected card and the fire crackling busily in her bright new room, she could not fight off her depression. Christmas is always a bad time, she reminded herself; but it will pass. And after Christmas, what? she wondered – with George and Sandy up at Lady Leadbetter's pasting on all those hideous wallpapers. She did not know Lady Leadbetter, but was positively cross with her, and positively jealous, too. 'She won't make scones for them,' she said aloud. 'Or China tea. They'll find a difference.'

Apart from the cards, there was nothing Christmassy about the house. In the meat safe were two lamb chops; one for Christmas dinner, the other for Boxing Day. No one would ever make a mince pie for herself; and she had not.

Pacing about the room, grasping at anything which might help her state, she began to wonder if Mr Mavory might drop in for a minute or two after church in the morning. In her mother's day, he sometimes had. If he did, there was plenty of sherry. It became important to her that he should call: otherwise no one would – all day, and the next. Dr Jenkins, dressed up as Father Christmas, would, she knew, be carving turkeys at the hospital.

She remembered the holly tree in the garden, and decided to go out to pick a sprig or two in case of her visitors.

It was almost dark. She took a torch, and stepped out into the damp air. It was warm, un-Christmassy. 'I'll pick the holly and arrange it nicely,' she thought: 'and then it will be time for a drink.' Tomorrow really depended on Mr Mavory coming.

Such a tangle of old, dying apple trees and high nettles. The torch beam wavered among it, as she stumbled over rank grass, determined on her holly. It was a poor winter for berries, but she tore off a few twigs. Making her way back she thought of the garden of the Sleeping Princess, the stinging leaves, the arched, branched briars. It seemed sadly out of place with her bright house. Coming round the side of the house, by softly dripping hydrangeas, she suddenly stopped, swung the torch about, over high-grown hedges and recidivist flower-beds. She was tense, like an explorer on the edge of new terrain.

The words *landscape gardeners* had come into her head – an idea which dawned wonderfully in her.

After a while, she went indoors and arranged the meagre holly in a vase. 'That's better,' she said. She read again 'All the best from George and Sandy'. She poured herself out a glass of whisky, and put a knob of coal on the fire, then, remembering her new financial position, another and another. I am a comparatively rich woman, she thought, sipping her whisky. She went to the window and drew aside the curtain, but of course, could see nothing but blackness. In her mind, though, she saw men out there – two men, probably – gum-booted, rain-coated, clumping about, measuring, digging, planting, sitting on the old seat drinking pale tea, eating hot scones. She would hear them all day, calling out to one another, joking and whistling. At night silence would fall; but in the morning they would come again.

The Wrong Order

It was the year that the white lilac came up to expectations. This evening, against a thundery sky and among tenderly green leaves, the blossom crowded up as white as paper. In a freshening wind, the sky darkened, thickened, and the lilac heads jostled together, nudging each other.

Branches of other trees swayed, as if they were strange plants at the bottom of the sea.

'It has paid for lopping,' Hilda Warfield said, pausing by the sitting-room window as she so often did. 'It has never been more beautiful.'

She had her back to the two men who watched her.

Then lightning cracked the sky, and the rain came hissing down, bouncing off the marble-topped garden table.

'I'm so glad it's been good *this* year,' Hilda went on, almost as if she were talking to herself.

'Oh, God!' her friend, Tom, thought, 'she is going to say "As it's my last".'

He got up, and went into the kitchen, so that he should not hear her saying it. She insisted on talking about her death, referred to it constantly and casually, as if it were some familiar pet of hers, running always at her heels, like Charlie, her Bedlington terrier.

'It's that damn doctor,' her husband Hector – a mild man, despite his name – had said to Tom, later on that dreadful day when she had returned from London with her news.

They had lived, the three of them, in amity and comfort until this terrible thing had settled down in their midst, always tagging along with them, now, so never to be entirely ignored. When Hector woke in the night, it was on his mind in a leap. Sometimes he crept into Hilda's room, could not rest until he had done so; but she was always sleeping peacefully. He went back to his bed and lay marvelling at that.

He could not properly settle to work in his office by day; his alarmed thoughts accompanied him up in the train in the morning and down in the evening. Looking out at villas set in gardens, golf courses and new motor roads, he saw nothing: his hands holding his newspaper up for protection sometimes suddenly trembled, and fellow commuters looked at him stealthily. It was no secret about Hilda. 'I like and respect the truth,' she had told the specialist, and he had talked to her of her inoperable condition: 'but it will be for your heart to decide how long,' he had said finally, thinking her an amazing woman. She thanked him calmly for her death sentence, shook hands firmly, and went away ... she, too, back past the villas and the golf courses and all the budding trees. On that journey a certain peace, and disbelief, had fallen over her, strangely, at the same time and, presumably, from the same source.

Because of her respect for the truth everybody knew, and everyone seemed to be waiting with her, and watching her. She had become special, and set aside.

Her husband, in spite of those middle-of-the-night peeps into her room, now hated being left alone with her. Tom was a great help to him, and this evening of the storm, Hector was cross with him for going off to the kitchen just as Hilda said those dreaded words. He had to listen to them all by himself.

He drank whisky, passed a hand over his tired face, yawned. 'Getting past all this travelling up and down,' he thought. He was to retire next year. But that was the forbidden future, and his mind swerved away from it. He drank more whisky, loosened his tie, leant back in his chair, very red across his cheeks and forehead, dark and crumpled in his London clothes, unlike the other two so comfortably dressed.

And now the lilac was full of rain, the blossom like sodden sponges too heavy to be tossed about any more. Tiny, star-like florets had been shaken down on to the grass. When the shower was over, the garden dripped steadily. A rainbow appeared against the mulberry-coloured sky and all the trees were sharply green. 'How beautiful!' said Hilda.

In the kitchen, Tom snipped chives into the soup, carried the bowls into the dining-room. Mrs Clarebut had left everything ready.

He was glad to be out here, pottering about, and, apart from his own wishes, thought that Hector should have a little time with Hilda. He, Tom, was with her all day long.

At supper, Hilda asked, 'Shall we have some music after? Or those old holiday slides?' A silence from the other two, bent over soup. Neither wanted either – harking back to the *châteaux* on the Loire and themselves there, or picnicking on the banks of the Cher, brought back what had been – which, in view of what was to be, was overwhelmingly too much. Also, those rather old, blurred Chopin and Schumann records were of a twilight sadness they could no longer abide. Hector especially hated them. Never knowing what to look at when they were going on, he always closed his eyes. 'My nerves!' he thought; then dozed. He would have liked to have been like other businessmen at the end of a day's work, slumped down uncritically before a television-set. Hilda would not have one in the house. She said that they barred conversation, became an addiction, and only coronations and royal weddings were any good on them.

Tom took up the soup plates and went to fetch the chicken pie. 'You choose, Hilda,' he said on his way. Hector looked out of the window at a rather awkward backwards angle for him, and crushed up toast melba.

'Then I choose neither,' Hilda said, with a shrug. 'Ça ne fait rien.'

While she was waiting for Tom to return, she took off some heavy Celtic-like jewellery from her breast, laid it on the table and studied it carefully, as if she were loth to waste the briefest chance of looking at something lovely. She arranged the chain on the table, and peered at the milky stones set in silver, gathering it up quickly and reclasping it to her when Tom came in and handed her a plate.

After dinner, she went into the garden and threw a ball for her dog, Charlie, who tore across the squelching lawn, but knew better than to dive into flower-beds. Breathing heavily, Hilda stooped and retrieved the ball from among dripping leaves.

'How has she been?' Hector asked Tom.

'The same. Not much lunch. She had her rest.'

They talked then of other things, not thinking of them, though. Hector spoke of his city day, Tom of sowing radish seed.

I used to ask him about his painting, Hector remembered guiltily. But we were younger then.

From a window, they caught glimpses of Hilda wandering in the garden. Charlie looked like a bedraggled sheep. Tom saw her looking up into the lilac tree, her hands clasped above, resting on her large bosom. 'Rapt' was the word which came into his mind. He remembered reading about Colette on her death-bed, her absorbed and heightened passion for the little things about her, and he wondered if he could stand much more of the same thing. On week-days, Mrs Clarebut came at nine-thirty, with her little boy, Rupert – Rupe the Terrible, as he was known to Hilda and Tom. He did not do much damage, except to nerves; nor did he tear about: but he insinuated himself, was always *there*, and talked incessantly. Tom went shopping for as long as he could, pottering about the village, collecting gossip. Hilda, who was supposed to love children, and to grieve that she had none of her own, was obliged to stay at home and endure Rupe, only occasionally lapsing into asperity – as when he addressed her as 'Auntie'.

'Why are you looking out of that window all the time, Auntie?'

'Mrs Warfield.'

'I can't say that.'

'Then "Hilda". But *not* Auntie.'

'Why?'

'To answer your other question, I was looking at the white lilac tree – because this is the very best time for it; soon the flowers will topple over and die.'

'Everybody will topple over and die one of these days,' Rupe said, watching her. 'In an emergency,' he added, because it was his newest long word.

'So true,' said Hilda coldly.

In the mornings, she wore a hessian apron with a large pocket across its front, her kangaroo pouch, she told Rupe, who gave her a sideways, scornful glance. Into this pocket, to save her journeys, went everything she might need – scissors and bast and secateurs, pencils and spectacles. She had a walking stick with a rubber tip, and leant on it heavily as she went about the garden, making mental notes of little jobs for Tom when he returned from his interminable shopping.

The garden was beautiful, and very hardly kept up – with its lawns on different levels; the iris lawn, the cedar lawn, the lower lawn, the tea lawn. There were box-hedges and bowers, grass walks and borders, and the famous lilac tree.

Beyond the lower lawn was a white-painted wooden building, which Tom had once used for a studio; still thought he did. He had become, under Hilda's expert direction, less and less of a painter, more and more a gardener.

On her slow perambulating round the paths, Rupe attended Hilda, talking usually of death, since it seemed to him to be a forbidden subject. One 'hush' from his mother was enough to commit him to it. He touched on the idea of Charlie's death quite cheerfully, and then, with his sideways glance through sandy lashes, on Hilda's.

'We all come to it,' she said.

'And go to God.'

'That's as may be.'

'Do you mind dying?'

'It looks as if we haven't much choice.'

She poked with her stick at a bit of new spring groundsel. 'Pull it up, like a good boy.'

He snapped it off and left the root.

'Oh, dear, now I shall have to ask Mr Bonchurch to do it.'

'Why can't *you* do it?' Again that steady, sideways look.

'I become giddy if I bend down.'

'You might die of being giddy.'

'I might. What a bore you are with your small talk.'

'What's that?'

She sighed and turned back towards the house. By now, she was waiting impatiently for Tom's return. Such lots of little jobs she had for him to do, now that she no longer could. When old Stack, her gardener, had died, she had really felt bereft – her great partner and ally gone. Together, they had made the garden, from nothing more promising than a piece of sloping parkland and a damaged cedar tree. She had begun to train Tom as her assistant, not knowing then that he must be her successor; for Hector did nothing in the garden beyond snoozing in a deckchair, said he would be just as happy in public gardens doing that – and much less expensive, he added. At week-ends, he played golf, and drank.

Hilda deplored the golf course, for she would have preferred real country. Beyond the lower lawn, a green could be glimpsed, and the sort of people she would wish to avoid grouped about, or trundling golf-bag trolleys. Even this morning, an acquaintance, looking for a lost ball, parted the top of the hedge and peered through. 'Hi! Hilda!' she called. 'Garden's looking great. You too.'

Hilda nodded without smiling. The hedge was one of her failures. Nothing made it put on growth.

Meanwhile, Tom had come back. He unpacked his basket on the kitchen table, and told Mrs Clarebut of news from the butcher's.

In the village, he was known as Hilda's 'fancy man'. Mrs Clarebut had often given out that the three slept in different bedrooms, that she had never seen any sign of what she called 'hanky-panky'. The village, though, could not take in the strangeness of a woman living with two men, one of them related to her in no way, yet her slave. Mrs Clarebut, knowing more than most, had a glimmering of the way in which Hilda was able to claim a man's allegiance without sexuality. She wondered if it had not been rather like training a dog – a matter of getting the whip-hand from the start.

As Tom was gossiping and unpacking the basket, Hilda came to the kitchen door. 'Mrs Clarebut won't mind doing that,' she said. 'I wondered if you could give me a hand with something in the garden.'

She was dogged by her ginger-haired familiar, who said, 'If she bent down she might die.'

Like lightning, Mrs Clarebut streaked across the kitchen, seized him in a frightful grip above his thin elbow, shook him, hissed at him, making matters a hundred times worse.

'Groundsel,' Hilda said to Tom, as if nothing else were happening. 'Will you come and see?'

They went into the garden, soon to be followed by a snivelling Rupe.

As they walked down a grass path, Hilda said, taking a pencil and pad from her apron pocket, 'I'd like those delphiniums out when they're finished: they're too much on top of the phloxes. Perhaps it's a good thing poor old Stack died. He can't be faced with all these weeds. Although, of course, if *he* were here, *they* wouldn't be. All the same, I sometimes feel that I've betrayed him. Can't seem to help doing that. No doubt he'll understand.' And, belying the doubts she had earlier implied to Rupe of the existence of an after-life, she sent a rueful smile heavenwards.

In spite of the soft earth, plantains broke off at roots, groundsel snapped, as Tom cursed them. 'All right,' Hilda said. 'If you fetch my kneeling mat, my little fork, and help me down, I'll manage. I'm sorry that I bothered you.'

The future of the garden – her realm – was threatened with incompetence and indifference.

'Do they have gardens in Heaven?' Rupe enquired.

'How the hell do *I* know?' Hilda asked.

'When Charlie goes to Heaven, Jesus might mistake him for a sheep.'

'He may well do that.'

'But *I* know a sheep when I see one.'

'So you're one up on Jesus.'

'You're not allowed to say that.'

Tom returned with a small garden fork, and a trug, but no kneeling mat, and he applied himself to the weeds.

'Because it's rude,' said Rupe.

It was not illness that imposed the pattern of Hilda's days. She had always liked to do the same things at the same time – mornings, out and about in her apron; afternoons a rest, lying on a *chaise-longue* with – still – her little possessions at hand, for there was a table drawn up with her favourite gardening books, shells and pebbles in a bowl, kaleidoscopes to divert her, pills, spectacles, a fan, large amber worry beads and alabaster hand-coolers. Tom had once brought for her from Greece a lump of Parian marble; when she was feverish she held it against her brow. All these treasures were within a hand's reach, so that she need not stir.

Rupe, tagging along as usual, sometimes sat beside her, staring at the drooping face as Hilda napped and his mum washed up. He would quietly take up a large freckled shell and hold it to his freckled ear, and try to imagine the crashing, then dragging, rattling sound of the sea on the pebbles at Brighton, where once he had been for a day, sitting a lot of the time in a dampish shelter with a comic to shut him up. Shaking the shell about, clamping it to his ear, he simply felt that something had gone muffled in his head. It was annoying like catarrh; not at all like the sea. He yawned, quickly remembered to say 'Pardon me', and then, even more polite he thought, he leant forward and whispered, 'This is very nice. Can I have it when you are dead?'

Behaving beautifully – memorably, she faintly hoped – Hilda opened her eyes, looked at the shell, and gently said, 'Yes, you may. But it is not really good manners to ask for things.' She had trained herself to pitch her voice very low, and it seemed to give her an advantage over others.

After Rupe and his mother had gone, Tom would bring her a cup of tea. At five-thirty, she went up for her bath, and he roamed about the landing, dreading a sudden splash or a long silence.

And then it was evening. As time went on, she became too tired to go into the garden again. She lay on the *chaise-longue*, arranging the shells on their dish, examining each minutely; or turning her kaleidoscopes.

'What I like about the patterns,' she once said, 'is that they don't stay. Everything should vanish. And, of course, everything does.'

Hector roused himself, got up for more whisky. 'Oh, I dunno,' he said vaguely.

'I find that a comfort.'

He refilled her glass of campari, and she fished out the lump of ice and sucked it, then held it in her hand, and studied it, as if she had never seen ice before. 'Very strange,' she said, in a puzzled voice.

The lilac was over, and cut back again for another spring.

'I hope it will be lovely for you again next year,' Hilda said in her intolerable way.

'I wouldn't notice if *you* weren't here,' her husband said glumly. 'This whole place is the last place I could put up with. If anything happened, which I'm damn sure it won't, I'd skedaddle.'

Hilda looked at him, appalled.

'The garden,' she said.

'P'raps shouldn't've said that,' Hector mumbled.

'But the *garden*!'

'Of course, whatever you say.'

Tom, followed by Charlie, came into the room, and saw her face. She was trembling.

He thought, 'At last her courage has gone.' It had been a great wonder to him that it had lasted so long. He looked at Hector, who shook his head slowly.

Hilda said to Tom, 'Would *you* leave this garden – for it to go to rack and ruin?'

'Just put me foot in it,' Hector said. He waited for Tom to take over the situation. All his life, he had been used to ordering things, and had done so with calm and mastery; but not in this house.

After dinner, Tom went to fetch the slides and the screen, because conversation was becoming impossible. They looked – and Hector sipped while looking – at the wide and shallow Loire; at men fishing, bone-white *châteaux*, themselves. Hilda smiled at last. '*En pays connus*,' she said. 'Weren't they the loveliest holidays of all?'

It was not Hector's lucky evening. 'We can't live in the past,' he said; became furious, had fallen into another trap, of which there were so many.

Tom quickly slipped in a photograph of Hilda standing in the garden of an *auberge* in front of a trellis of morning glories.

'A beautiful, simple flower. *They* do the vanishing trick, too. Though I love field daisies more. What's your favourite, Tom?'

'I think those striped camellias.'

'Oh, clever you. Hector?'

Was he forgiven? He stirred suspiciously. 'Red roses,' he said in a staunch voice. 'From a shop.'

Her ripple of laughter was a relief to the other two, whether it was sarcastic or not. She felt – though had no reason to feel – that she had won her way, and that the future of her garden was secure.

'Bedtime,' Hector said.

'Oh, no! There's a lot more left to this day,' Hilda protested.

'Well, I'll push off,' her husband said. He got up stiffly from his chair.

The time had come when Hilda went about the garden in a wheelchair. By now, Tom had forgotten that he had ever been a painter. The little he had always paid, from a private income, towards the running of the house was now inadequate, he knew; but he could not bring up the matter. He worked harder with the weeds, and the shopping, and brushing Charlie and taking him for walks, and sometimes he wondered about his life when Hilda was dead. He determined to serve her till the end.

'Hector, you look so fagged,' Hilda said on a Saturday morning. 'Why *must* you go to golf?'

'Do me good, d'you know.'

'But after a hard week . . .'

'The only exercise I get.'

'If it's exercise you want, you could push me down to the village. I should like that.'

He reddened and hesitated.

Tom knew how much Hector counted on his golf, and on his friends at the club as an escape from work and worries.

'I'm going to the village, Hilda; I'll take you,' he said quickly. 'You've always refused when I've asked you before.'

'There's been the garden to think about, but today I felt like a little holiday.'

'We can have a drink in the garden at the Red Lion.'

'It would be nice,' Hilda said coolly, 'but I begin to wonder if I shan't change my mind.'

She changed her mind, and, sitting at home waiting, it seemed to her that Tom was an absurd time buying a few things for Sunday lunch.

Tom, it was true, had lingered about the village, gazing in shop windows without seeing anything, reading all the advertisements at the post office – for daily help, and help in gardens, for babysitters and second-hand prams; so many cries for aid, none offering any. He considered buying a cracked soup tureen at the junk shop. He stopped to chat to people about dogs and babies and the weather, gave news of Hilda and received messages for her, though she had never been popular, and her protracted and much-talked-about dying seemed to have made her less so. Mitchell, the butcher, would be his last call, because a leg of lamb is heavy to carry. The butcher's was the source of all gossip, the very spring-head, from which information dribbled to the general stores, the ironmonger and the barber.

There was a little queue, and it turned at once to stare at Tom. The shop was at a standstill with incredulity, and then feet shuffled in the sawdust, glances veered away. A leader seemed needed, and Mr Mitchell came round the chopping block in his bloodied apron, steel swinging from waist, a knife in hand. He looked alarming, and said in a low voice, to be remembered and described by everybody present, 'A word with you outside, Mr Bonchurch, if I may.'

Tom meekly left the shop with him, and at once someone else came in and took his place in the queue, to be immediately informed of the morning's happenings.

'On the first green,' one said, already half into the story.

'It's Mr Warfield. He's dead,' another said, filling the gap.

'They were looking all round the village for Mr Bonchurch to tell him. Only just walked in here.'

'Heart attack, I suppose. It usually is. What about *her*? Likely she's had one by now, too.'

'No, we'd have heard.' ('Standing in this place,' they thought.)

'Mr Mitchell out there telling him.'

The newcomer stepped quickly back and looked over her shoulder out of the shop window, but Tom and Mr Mitchell were out of sight.

So that was how Tom learnt of Hector's death – incredulously, in a lean-to full of bits of carcasses and hanging birds.

'I must go,' was all that he could say, with dread in his heart.

Mr Mitchell said kindly, 'Len can drive you back in the van.'

Indeed, Tom's legs felt too weak for walking. He nodded distractedly. Mr Mitchell was too kind.

'And don't worry about tomorrow's dinner,' Mr Mitchell said. 'I'll get Len to pop a little something through the back door this afternoon. A small shoulder, I should think.'

The shop was full of concern when Mr Mitchell returned. No one complained of having been kept waiting. All felt braced – eye witnesses almost.

'He didn't get his joint,' some silly, practical woman said.

When Tom got back to the house, Mrs Clarebut was standing by Hilda with a glass of brandy. The doctor was awaited, and she wished him to know, when he came, that she had done the right thing. Rupe had been shut in the kitchen and was hollering.

Hilda stared at Tom, and he went across the room and stood by her, but could only mumble her name – no other words came to him. At last, she put out a hand and took the brandy and drank it steadily, as if it were a glass of milk. Mrs Clarebut took the empty glass to the kitchen where she gave Rupe a clout. He was too outraged to care. He, who had always been so interested in people dying, was now excluded from the excitement of it. This seemed to him to be intolerably unfair.

After a time, staring before her, Hilda whispered, 'I told him not to go.'

In the next days, having to arrange the cremation, Tom was in a state of great bewilderment. He kept thinking, absurdly, that this was the sort of thing he would have left to Hector.

Hilda rarely spoke. She ate little, and she looked afraid – not sad, or grief-stricken, but terrified. At night Tom, who could not sleep himself, knew that her light was on.

When he was forced to speak to her of things to be done, she shuddered, her lips pressed together. She wheeled herself out to the garden, but almost at once turned restlessly back.

Death, which had seemed like a fantasy to her, was at her heels now, with the reality of menace to herself. Here was the truth she had said she loved.

Hector was now a non-person, though his things still lay about. Disregarding all her suffering – she thought – Tom kept asking her for decisions, such as the time of the funeral, the fitting-in of Hector's disposal in a tight crematorium schedule. ('We could manage it at eleven-thirty, or two o'clock. Well, two o'clock would be splendid for us,' the undertakers had said.) Then, long-ignored relations Hilda must be hostess to, it seemed. And police, solicitor, doctor, vicar were all bothering her, who should not, she felt, be bothered at all. Not as a rule a tearful person, she began to cry a great deal, hopelessly, with the tears trickling between the trembling fingers she spread over her face, her mouth, when glimpsed, squared and ugly, like a furious baby's.

Tom felt like running away. 'I'm in for it now,' he kept thinking – trapped, alone with her.

Although he could never have imagined that she would be so inconsolable about the loss of Hector, he now wondered if she could recover from it, and yet sometimes he felt that it was fear, rather than bereavement, which made her start and pale and open wide her eyes.

'Then there's the question of flowers,' he said timidly.

'Yes, yes.' She spoke with impatience.

'I'll order yours for you, shall I? What do you think?'

'Red roses. I remember he said . . .'

'All right, I'll see to it. Then there's a Cousin Gertrude Stubbings. She wrote after the notice in *The Times*, if you remember. Oughtn't something to be done about *her?*'

'Ask her to luncheon if you wish.'

After all, it's *her* cousin, he thought.

Mrs Clarebut enjoyed a brief importance in the village, and what *she* said in the shops her husband repeated in the Red Lion. 'Very quiet,' he told them. 'Just the relations – an Honourable among them, so I hear. The missus will be officiating, sending Rupe to my sister for the day: no spirits, or beer. Just sherry, and sandwiches and so on. Some people have funny ideas about funerals. They're meeting the deceased at the crematorium; he'll be there before they arrive.'

No coffin carried from the house, as of yore. No lowered blinds. Many of those in the pub remembered the old days, and were sad, passingly, for their children.

Hilda was not going to the funeral. Her doctor, unnecessarily, forbade it.

'Would you like your wreath sent here first, so that you can see it?' Tom asked.

'No, no, no, no!' She shook her head, looking distraught. Those red shop roses he had said were his favourites, she remembered: her own favourites, the morning glories and the meadow daisies – what sort of funeral garland would *they* make? She began to cry hysterically.

On the funeral day, after the sherry and sandwiches, the undertaker arrived. He had a relaxed, but sympathetic manner; he kept an eye on his watch, and at last gave a nod to Tom. To be too early was distressing for the mourners, who then had to hang about until a different set of mourners had gone – though there was a waiting-room, with magazines: to be late was unprofessional, besides putting the next lot out. The undertaker's timing was appreciated at the crematorium.

Hilda was kissed by a cluster of stifling relations. Under the circumstances, they found little to say, some of them wondering how long it would be before they were summoned back again. All had come from a distance, and none was young, and they would be glad to be on the homeward road.

The house was so quiet when they had gone. Mrs Clarebut, appreciating the occasion, did a sort of muffled washing-up.

Hilda lay on the *chaise-longue*, her hands in her lap. Presently, she took up one of her kaleidoscopes, but found that she resented the shifting patterns. She touched all the dead things about her, shells, marbles, pebbles. She fanned herself, exasperatedly, with a paper fan, waiting for Tom's return.

It was not long. He came in, looking strange in his dark suit. The relations had gone on their ways – to London, Hove and Bournemouth. He felt unreal, for he had had to do things for which he was not cut out, and was likely to have to do a great many more of the same kind.

Hilda did not refer to where he had been.

In the evening, to Tom's relief, the doctor called. He talked to Hilda while Tom prepared a supper tray. The dining-room, since Hector's death, was unused. Meals had become picnics on laps.

Tom, who had never wanted marriage, now knew that he had got the worst of someone else's. He began to blame other people in his mind – a girl who long ago had refused his half-hearted proposal, his father for leaving enough money to save him from starving as a painter; but especially he blamed Hilda for turning him into a slave without his knowing it until too late. He thought about running away, but only as a daydream. To deserve his own – and universal – condemnation would make life not worth living. Between daydreams and nightmares, his comfort was Mrs Clarebut. She often stood as a buffer between him and Hilda, coaxing her with hot drinks, while allowing him to go shopping – his greatest pleasure now.

The business of Hector's estate seemed involved and endless. Tom hated money and the affairs connected with it, was utterly bored and scarcely listened. Hilda simply moaned, while the solicitor inched round the subject of her own will.

'If *you* should die,' he began lightly, as if such a thing were hardly likely to happen.

'Oh, I am sure you will sort it out.'

Everyone found her difficult, but Tom most of all.

One day, something seeming miraculous to him happened. A journalist, interested in art, wrote to him of one of his paintings he had come across. He had done it years before. The gallery had quite forgotten him, but had found his address and forwarded the letter. The painting – he remembered it – was simply of rain: a window-pane, with the different-sized drops coming down it. He had done it as a difficult exercise. Perhaps all his life he had tried to make things difficult for himself.

All day, after getting the letter, he was abstracted, did not much want to talk. Were there any more paintings? the letter asked. Could they be seen? An article might be written.

Hilda repeated something she had said, and he looked both blank and glum, hadn't heard her.

'I'm sorry, I was thinking of something else.'

'Then I'm sorry, to have interrupted you.'

He still took no notice of her, but went across the room and looked out of the window.

'I may be outstaying my welcome,' Hilda said softly, as if to herself.

But, for once, he didn't bother to listen.

The next day he went down to the studio in the garden. He hadn't been inside it for months. But he only glanced about him, moved a canvas or two, and felt a great weight upon him. Then he locked the door, and went away. He kept the letter, but did not reply to it. The writer assumed that he had gone away, or died.

That evening was terrible to Tom; but all the evenings were terrible now. He suffered claustrophobia in that room with her, made any excuse to be out of it. And they were long evenings, for she would not go to bed. He was always tired, and he thought that she might as well be in bed upstairs, as doing simply nothing downstairs. But at the suspicion of his trying to bend her will, she would cry; and it did not become her to cry.

'Why wash up at night?' she asked him, as he came back into the sitting-room one evening. 'We used always to leave it for Mrs Clarebut to do in the morning.'

'She has plenty to do.'

'No more than before. Less, in fact.' She dabbed her handkerchief to her mouth. 'These evenings on our own upset you, I know; but they upset me, too, I can tell you. They're no joke to me.' She began to smooth out her handkerchief now, turn it about in her hands as women do when they are quarrelling. She pulled out all the lace edges and examined them, pouting. But she was not – never had been – that kind of woman. He stood help-lessly by.

'The least you could do ... '

'What? What?'

'You make it clear you think I'm an unconscionable time a-dying. Oh, yes!'

'Please, Hilda ... '

'It's not my fault I don't die ... and all these dreadful nights going on and on, when I can't sleep, and you always trying to pack me off to bed, so that they can begin earlier and earlier ... ' Her voice had started to rise, but from habit she drew it down again. She was like some querulous, disappointed bride, had fallen into the behaviour as to the manner born. Tom was amazed.

'Would you like to play bézique?'

'No, I would *not* like to play bézique. It might keep you from your beloved kitchen.'

'You really are not yourself this evening,' was all he could think of saying.

So she began to cry in earnest. There was nothing he could do, but try to remember good times in the past and fondness for one another when they were younger: and to try to keep his patience. He reminded himself – as he so often did – that time would pass, and then he supposed that by this he could only mean that *she* would pass, and he had come to look on her as indestructible.

When at last she consented to go to bed, he went up first, as usual, to get her room ready, and took two sleeping-pills from her bottle for his own store, his escape route. He drew the curtains and arranged her pillows.

She could manage the stairs, leaning on him. On the small half-landing there was a chair for her to rest before the last few stairs.

She sat, breathing with effort, with her hands spread over her knees. She gasped, 'Led you a bit of a dance. Sorry.'

'Nothing to be sorry *for*,' he said breezily.

'Always seem to lead you a dance these days. Good of you to bear with me, I s'pose. Don't know what ... ' she fanned herself with her hand, her breathing coming back more steadily, 'don't know quite what I'd do without you.'

Tom wondered this all the time, woke in the night and wondered it.

'No reason why you should have to,' he said, as they began to go on upstairs.

A Responsibility

Dirty confetti and the petals of cherry blossom edged the church path. When Jessie arrived, the path and porch were deserted. The building itself, the purple bricks and leaden windows, seemed to rock and swoon in the sudden thundery heat: though she herself was probably rocking more. She walked nervously towards the porch; but, as soon as she reached its cool shadow, began to shiver.

Never having been to a christening before, not even one of her own, she was angry at having let Gwen persuade her to come. That morning, in the bar, the prospect of being a godmother had fascinated her. ('My godchild,' she would be able to say.) Gwen knew no more than Jessie of procedure and etiquette, and with the smallest idea of what lay ahead, Jessie had acquiesced; had shut up the bar promptly at two o'clock and hurried to the church without having a bite to eat.

She opened her bag a little and peered in, not liking to be seen prinking outside a church, even if it was Roman Catholic. Her face looked veined and puffy, her eyes quite bloodshot. Screened by the handbag, she patted her nose and chin with a grubby puff; but now nothing would restore her but a cup of tea and a lie down.

The smell of the church terrified her. It was chilling, like the smell of a hospital. She settled her fox-fur on her shoulders and tried to stand in a casual attitude, at the same time drawing in her stomach muscles. Posture, she thought vaguely.

Then a group of people came down the path, all in black except for a dazzling white baby. They approached the church with calm authority. The men glanced briefly at Jessie and followed the women and the baby inside. She could hear their boots clanging on some gratings, and the sound added to her terror. 'Perhaps I shall have to say things in Latin!' she suddenly thought. The glaring heat of the dead Sunday afternoon, the unmoving trees, the shop windows with drawn blinds, the Guinness she had drunk, produced a feeling of stifled fury towards Gwen.

At last, she saw them coming along the street, three heads above the brick wall; Gwen, her Polish husband Nicky, and Frederick his friend.

Jessie faced them with hostility and fear. Frederick she had not bargained for. Six weeks ago, they had argued and parted from one another, never to meet again, they had said: though obviously in a little town such as this they must continually meet, for any turn in the street was likely to bring them face to face.

Gwen looked frail. She wore her pale blue wedding suit, and the skirt was creased from having the baby on her lap. Her shoes were down-at-heel and one stocking laddered. When she had come into the bar with Nicky before they were married, she had always been neat and smart. Her marriage had changed that. She was not yet twenty, but looked already a down-trodden housewife.

'Why is Frederick here?' Jessie asked when they came near.

The two Poles looked like brothers, both blond, wide-shouldered, and wearing pale suède shoes and silvery raincoats.

'He's a godparent,' Gwen said uncertainly.

'You promised for me to be that. Otherwise, why the hell am I here?'

'There can be more than one.'

'Of course,' Nicky said. He smiled and bowed. Frederick began to whistle softly through his teeth and stare up at the church roof.

'We better get inside,' Gwen said.

'Don't say you are not Catholic,' Nicky warned Jessie. He put a hand under his wife's elbow and, looking with solemn fondness at the baby, went towards the porch.

'This is no fault of mine,' Jessie said. Even her furs seemed outraged, their white-tipped hairs bristling.

'Nor mine,' Frederick shrugged.

'You're always shrugging or bowing, like a bloody penguin.'

'I am sorry to offend.'

'Oh, you don't offend me. You can do a Highland fling or fall flat on your back for all I care,' Jessie said, now in the church porch.

'What is this – a mass christening?' Frederick asked, looking at the knot of black-clad people and their baby, who with purpling face arched its back and snatched at the air with spidery hands, letting out frail sounds as a prelude to something louder.

At one end of the church, the two groups huddled, ostensibly opposed. Our sort of people seem so flimsy, Jessie thought. For one thing, we don't have any relations. On an occasion like this anyone has to do, grab up a godmother out of the bar at the last minute. She sat very straight, holding the card with the Order of Service printed on it. Inside, she felt queasy, uneasy. The enemy baby (as she now thought of it) comforted her a little by beginning to wail. Curdled milk ran out of the side of its mouth.

Gwen's baby slept. His bare, mottled feet stuck out of the shawl, and when Gwen moved him his head bobbed weakly on his thin neck, but he did not open his eyes.

'My godson!' Jessie thought. 'It is a responsibility. I'll buy him a silver tankard with his name on and when he goes up to Oxford or Cambridge, I'll visit him and he'll take me round the colleges.' Then, looking at Gwen's laddered stocking, the skirt hanging on her ('After all, she was six months gone when she bought it, though no one would have known,' Jessie thought), this seemed all too improbable, even for daydreaming. 'Glad I came, though,' she decided. 'Can lie down any afternoon.'

Frederick sat bolt upright, too, with his arms folded across his chest, as if he were on trial. Jessie tried to give him a look of contempt, to direct waves of animosity towards him, but he gazed blandly ahead. She thought: 'Whatever we may say about Nicky, he did marry poor Gwen. She was lucky about that, and doesn't have to go to work any more.'

Gwen, watching the other family, passed the baby along to Jessie, who held it self-consciously. When the ceremony was over, she carried it from the church, anxious to be out in the air again, and believing that the others were following her. Frederick caught up with her in the porch. 'A little child has brought us together,' he said, smiling at the distance.

Vexed, she walked ahead of him into the sunshine. The warmth of the afternoon wafted towards them. The street glittered and shimmered and some yellow wallflowers in the churchyard agonised the eye.

He followed her down the path.

'What a pleasant surprise!' she said, not able to leave things as they were. 'Who'd have thought, when I woke up this morning, *this* would happen?'

'Do you still drink as much?' he asked in a polite voice.

Nicky came running out of the church and down the path towards them.

'Will you please tell me your name?' he asked Jessie. 'We are to write down the godparents.' He had always known Jessie too well to have considered her surname. Jessie was nervous of being committed in any way, and believed that the less she put her name to things the better.

'Gutteridge,' she said reluctantly. The feeling of being on alien ground, which she had cast off on leaving the church, returned.

'Please will you spell this for me?'

Sullenly, she spelt it.

Nicky ran back to the church, his lips moving busily.

A taxi was waiting at the gates and Frederick opened the door and curtly signalled Jessie to get in.

'I ordered this,' he said, and sat down beside her. All of his movements, the way he crossed one leg over the other, and flicked a speck of dust off his knee, demonstrated his contempt for her, and his own ease and relaxation.

I wonder what I did wrong, she thought. He liked me at first and I thought he enjoyed the quarrelling.

She had wondered for weeks, but reached no conclusion, afraid that because she was middle-aged men would always slip through her fingers.

'Oh, go on, say something, or I shall scream,' she said, shaking with exasperation.

'What am I to say?' he asked courteously.

'Shut up!'

She stroked the baby's cheek with the tip of her finger, feeling ridiculous sitting there beside Frederick with the baby in her arms.

Gwen and Nicky came down the path.

'I ordered the taxi,' Frederick said again, opening the door for them. They climbed in and sat on the little tip-up seats, and Gwen, her hands loose in her lap, glanced across at the baby.

'Like me to have him?' she asked.

'No, he's all right.'

She looked useless and idle now, as if she were nothing when the baby was taken from her.

'They couldn't make anything of your name,' Nicky told Jessie. 'Tomorrow I must go back with it written down.'

'I should forget it,' Jessie said.

When the taxi stopped, Frederick got out first. 'I'll see to this,' he told them. 'This is on me.'

He always knew how to behave, Jessie thought. She could not help but admire him. The first time he had come into the bar, she had noticed his manner. When he had paid for his drink, he had taken a great handful of silver from his pocket and slapped it down on the bar for her to sort out what he owed. When his friends came in – Nicky perhaps, and Gwen – he would let them order their drinks and then he would push the money across to Jessie. 'I'm taking care of that,' he would say.

Awkwardly, Jessie stepped out of the car, holding the baby, who with blue eyes now wide open placidly surveyed the sky, and turned its fist hungrily against its mouth.

Gwen and Nicky lived in two rooms above a butcher's shop. When Nicky unlocked the street door, there was a cool smell of meat and scrubbed wood. Against the window hung sheaves of clean wrapping-paper on hooks. Pots of ferns stood in the shadows, and shining knives and cleavers. Jessie held her breath, fastidiously, and followed Gwen up the narrow stairs.

The rooms were sparsely furnished and the men, throwing off their raincoats, sank down as if exhausted in the only two chairs. In the bedroom, Jessie laid the baby in his cradle, which was a large wooden box from the greengrocer's. There was none of the equipment – the lined baskets and the powder puffs and enamel bowls – that Jessie had so envied her married sister. A waste of a baby, she decided.

'He's wet his frock,' she told Gwen. 'I'll change it, if you like.' She felt rather condescending and capable with the baby now, quite used to him.

'It's the only one he's got,' Gwen said. 'He just stays in his nightgown other days.'

In the morning, Jessie thought that she would go to the draper's and buy a heap of baby linen.

'I'm glad it's over,' Gwen said, as she combed her hair. 'Nicky was all for it. He was christened himself, you see.'

When she heard her husband calling, she dropped the comb at once and ran into the other room where the men lolled in their chairs, their arms trailing over the sides as if they were drifting in a punt on the river.

They are a heartless pair, Jessie thought.

'A pity if either of you over-taxed yourself. You want to take things quiet at your age,' she said. The other three could see the reason why she had never married, and, a second or two later, she saw it herself, looking at Gwen complying for all she was worth handing them cups of tea, perching on the arm of her husband's chair in a grateful way.

'Where am I supposed to sit?' she asked.

Frederick folded his arms across his chest, as he had in church, and shut his eyes. She sat on the arm of his chair.

'Such beautiful manners,' she murmured. 'Very lucky, Gwen, us having these two polite gents.'

'*You* haven't got *me*,' Frederick said.

'Gwen, get the bottle of port out of the cupboard,' Nicky said. 'We should drink the baby's health.'

'Port on top of tea!' Jessie thought. She glanced at Frederick, as if to share with him her surprise at this idea, but his eyes seemed to her transparent, without any *look* in them. His manner was transparent, too; but nothing was behind it to be revealed. He was quite negative; just *not hers*.

'To Nicholas!' Nicky said. They stood and raised their glasses, and tears rushed to Jessie's eyes. She always cried easily – when 'God Save the King' was played, or when she saw a bride. Gwen looked tearful, too, but from fatigue. While the others were drinking, she fetched the baby and sat down, opening her blouse to feed him. Once, Jessie saw her brush her lashes with her fingers. The baby fed steadily, then less steadily, then nodded; full, blissful, his eyelids at half-mast and a line of eye showing beneath.

'He's too tired to shut his eyes even,' Jessie said.

'A very tiring day,' Frederick said.

'He's just good,' Gwen said, and she buttoned her blouse and dried her eyes finally.

Nicky said: 'What about filling our glasses?'

She hurried to do so, the baby asleep over her shoulder.

'I must go,' Frederick said, when he had emptied his glass.

'Yes,' said Jessie, standing up, too. She hoped, still, that she would not be obliged to spend the evening on her own. To walk along quarrelling with Frederick would be better.

Frederick took a pound note, smoothed it flat and put it behind the clock. 'Buy the baby something,' he said to Gwen.

Nicky saw them downstairs and through the shop. He locked the door behind them, and they were left standing in the hot deserted streets.

'Never anyone much about on Sundays,' Jessie said conversationally.

He was silent.

'Going to thunder, I think,' she went on, looking at the lowering, cloudless sky, and drawing her furs round her, trying to provoke him into some response, she said: 'It's my birthday tomorrow.'

He smiled and tightened the belt of his raincoat, buckling it neatly.

'That is no concern of mine,' he said, and walked briskly away, whistling through his teeth. One after another, enormous spots of rain began to fall upon the pavement.

Violet Hour at the Fleece

They were the first in. The landlord followed them into the little side bar with two pints of stout-and-mild on a tin tray, then rattled with a poker at the fire which had been quenched with a welter of coal. It was an empty gesture, a mere pass made in the direction of hospitality. When he had gone: 'Well!' she said, turning from a picture of Lord Kitchener, tears in her eyes.

'You haven't been in here since I went,' he said.

'How did you know?'

'Because you walked up to that picture as if you were saying: "Ah, Lord Kitchener, my old friend!" If you were here every night you wouldn't have done that.' He handed her a glass of beer and went to the window. The cobbles outside, between pub and church, were full of shadows, the sun struck only the gilt weathervane on the steeple. Now the quarter was marked with rounded leaden notes. Thrushes sang from gravestones and umbrella trees.

'The violet hour. Who said that? Sappho?'

'Sappho. I like the sound of Sappho. The last time I was in here ...'

'The day before war. A Saturday. They were all here – the man in the bowler hat and his wife ...'

'The one in the corner with the paste sandwiches, reading ...'

'One moment!' She flicked her fingers. '*Extinct Civilisations*! That was it. Over there,' she pointed, 'two girls drinking. *Good* girls! There hadn't started to be tarts about then. Not here, I mean.'

'Are there now?'

She laughed. 'And *you* said: "We'll always remember this because it is a Date. It is something children will have to learn for history."'

'Poor little sods.'

'"When I am eighty," you said, "I shall tell people I remember that day. I sat drinking at the Fleece with Sarah Fletcher ..."'

'So I shall tell my children that.'

'And they will be madly bored, and you will say, "That stout old woman who lives now, I believe, at Tunbridge Wells."'

'No. I shall say, "I was drinking with Sarah Fletcher, a beautiful lady and my very dear friend."'

'No one has talked like that to me for four years.'

She sat down at the table and he came and sat down beside her. They slipped into the old habit of drinking together, elbow against elbow, their beer going down level as it used.

'How've you been for . . . ?' he tapped the glass.

'I haven't much . . .'

'Nor me. How does it go down?'

'It seems no different, though I suppose it is.'

'How is your son?' he asked politely.

'His milk teeth are coming out. Funny and touching when he grins. I love it in him. Not in other children, though.'

'And your daughter?'

'You speak very stiffly.' She laughed.

'Say "silly sod" as you used.'

'No. I've stopped saying that.'

As he tapped the table with a half-crown, he was thinking how grimy his hand looked, and curled the nails into his palm, against the coin.

'I hated all the maleness, chaps undressing together, being hearty,' he said suddenly. 'I always felt thin and blue. Good luck!' He lifted his filled glass. 'But the worst thing was Christmas dinners. All sitting there being pleased and cheery with our nice dinners and the officers being decent, but each one of us his own private self. "Poor men and soldiers unable to rejoice." Perhaps not, though. Perhaps all enjoying themselves like hell. God, this is boring. Before I came tonight, I thought I wouldn't tell any soldier stories. You see, you don't like me to talk like it.'

She wiped a little moustache of froth from her mouth. 'I want you to tell me some time, but it separates me from you, and just now it is hard enough to get back again.'

'I thought we were doing fine.'

'I thought so too.'

'And then there always *were* things to separate us. Your posh friends and your political notions. These endureth for ever, but being a soldier soon stops.'

'I can think of the fighting and your being hungry and the hospital all right, but I can't hear about the Christmas dinner. I can't think about that.'

'I enjoyed it like mad really. Look, now the fire's going to burn for us.'

The coals shuddered and collapsed and a few flames, pale like irises, grew up between them.

'Do you still cry as much as you used?'

'No.' At once, the tears rushed up into her eyes.

The landlord came in now, and placed a log on top of the flames, which wavered and sank down. It was a damp green log, with ivy still clinging to its bark.

'Tell me more, then, about being a soldier.'

'No, it's just madly boring and stupid, living miles below the subsistence level, and the chaps being so coarse, much worse even than the way posh girls like you are coarse. And when they're not being coarse, they're bloody touching and have S.W.A.K. on the backs of their letters and make you feel ashamed. It's only all being together. Then office jobs – copy lists of numbers on to ration cards, so boring you make mistakes . . . do a pile and then say, "Oh, God! October has only thirty days," correct them all, smudges and blots and then, "Oh damn! it's November has thirty." And being in a sort of dirty post-office place, dust, broken nibs, ink bottles empty, falling over and full of fluff. And stuffy. You're not listening. Let's have some more beer. Darling, what are you looking at?'

'I was watching the ivy on that log turning bronze.'

'I hate ivy. Christ! The trouble is, I've no more money.'

She felt in her coat pockets. It was a thick white coat with a fine bloom of dirt upon it.

'Angel! I do like taking money from a nice girl.'

'Ivy. My mother's favourite. She used to like to spend two or three hours fixing it all up in a jar against a white wall.'

'Your mother did do the hell of a lot of high-class things, but don't go on about *her*. You'll only cry.'

'I remember her doing that, in a long dress and *she* was crying because her mother and father had gone away for ever. I saw the back of her. I was eight. Her hair was shiny black and soft and done up like a Japanese woman's. It would be a good thing to paint. How tired I am of the fronts of people! Particularly bosoms. The back could be most expressive. You could tell by the arms and the listless way of holding the ivy that she was weeping because her father had left her in an ugly house with a nasty husband. The Victorians would have gone round to the other side and left an opened letter lying on the table and written "Parting" on the frame – or "Solitude". But Toulouse-Lautrec and I like it best the other way round . . . and *you* don't like it at all. You've had your bellyful of it, in fact.'

'No, but I'm always afraid of you crying when you speak about your mother, and when you begin to harp on bosoms and your inferiority. It worries me when you cry. It must be a thing you do a lot in your family. It's all right now while you're young and beautiful, but very uncomfortable for everyone once you're past forty.'

A woman came in and drew red serge curtains and switched on the light. It rained cruelly down on them. He curled his fingers out of sight again.

'Mike!' he suddenly cried with false *bonhomie*.

She put up her cheek for her husband to kiss, which he would not do in a pub.

'How are you, old man?'

'Fine. Fine, thanks.'

'Quite fit again?'

'Rather! You?'

'Pretty good.'

'What to drink?'

'No. Can't stop. Coming, Sarah?'

'One for the road?'

'No, nor the ditch. Many thanks, all the same. OK, Sarah?'

She looked at them both with a feeling of contempt. Men together. Or, perhaps, just men before a woman. 'They speak symbols,' she thought. 'It isn't a language at all. They make strange, half-savage noises at one another.'

She said good-bye and the two of them went out into the last few moments of the violet hour. Her husband held open the car door. She sank back into the seat, watching sullenly the road before her, regretting the bright pub.

'OK?' He fidgeted at the dashboard and they were away. The buildings made strange shapes against the darkening sky.

'Oh, crying!' he protested. 'Oh, stop for God's sake. Oh, Christ!'